S0-ARG-117

PASSPORT

PASSPORT

SOPHIA GLOCK

Ⓛ Ⓑ

LITTLE, BROWN AND COMPANY

NEW YORK   BOSTON

ABOUT THIS BOOK

THIS BOOK WAS EDITED BY SUSAN RICH AND DESIGNED BY SASHA ILLINGWORTH. THE PRODUCTION WAS SUPERVISED BY KIMBERLY STELLA, AND THE PRODUCTION EDITOR WAS MARISA FINKELSTEIN. THE TEXT WAS SET IN TEXTURE PASSPORT REGULAR. THE DISPLAY TYPE IS HAND-LETTERED WITH CORRESPONDENCE HAND-LETTERED BY JULIA WHITEHOUSE.

Copyright © 2021 by Sophia Glock • Colors by Mike Freiheit • Cover illustration copyright © 2021 by Sophia Glock. Cover design by Sasha Illingworth. • Cover copyright © 2021 by Hachette Book Group, Inc. • Hachette Book Group supports the right to free expression and the value of copyright. The purpose of copyright is to encourage writers and artists to produce the creative works that enrich our culture. The scanning, uploading, and distribution of this book without permission is a theft of the author's intellectual property. If you would like permission to use material from the book (other than for review purposes), please contact permissions@hbgusa.com. Thank you for your support of the author's rights Little, Brown and Company • Hachette Book Group • 1290 Avenue of the Americas, New York, NY 10104 • Visit us at LBYR.com • First Edition: October 2021 • Little, Brown and Company is a division of Hachette Book Group, Inc. • The Little, Brown name and logo are trademarks of Hachette Book Group, Inc. • The publisher is not responsible for websites (or their content) that are not owned by the publisher. Photographs courtesy of Sophia Glock • Library of Congress Cataloging-in-Publication Data • Names: Glock, Sophia, author. • Title: Passport / Sophia Glock. • Description: First edition. | New York: Little, Brown and Company, 2021. | Summary: Teenage Sophia, living with her American family in Central America, discovers that her parents are living double lives, leading her to explore her own boundaries around honesty and deception. • Identifiers: LCCN 2020005069 | ISBN 9780316458986 (hardcover) | ISBN 9780316459006 (paperback) | ISBN 9780316458993 (ebook) | ISBN 9780316458979 (ebook other) • Subjects: LCSH: Graphic novels. | CYAC: Graphic novels. | Secrets—Fiction. | Families—Fiction. | Central America—Fiction. • Classification: LCC PZ7.7.G63 Pas 2021 | DDC 741.5/973—dc23 • LC record available at https://lccn.loc.gov/2020005069 • ISBNs: 978-0-316-45898-6 (hardcover), 978-0-316-45900-6 (trade paperback), 978-0-316-45899-3 (ebook), 978-0-316-49507-3 (ebook), 978-0-316-49506-6 (ebook) • PRINTED IN CHINA • APS • Hardcover: 10 9 8 7 6 5 4 3 2 1 • Paperback: 10 9 8 7 6 5 4 3 2 1

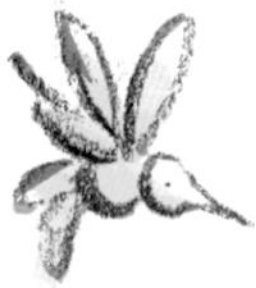

TO TATIANA & MONEIRA

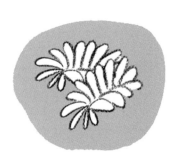

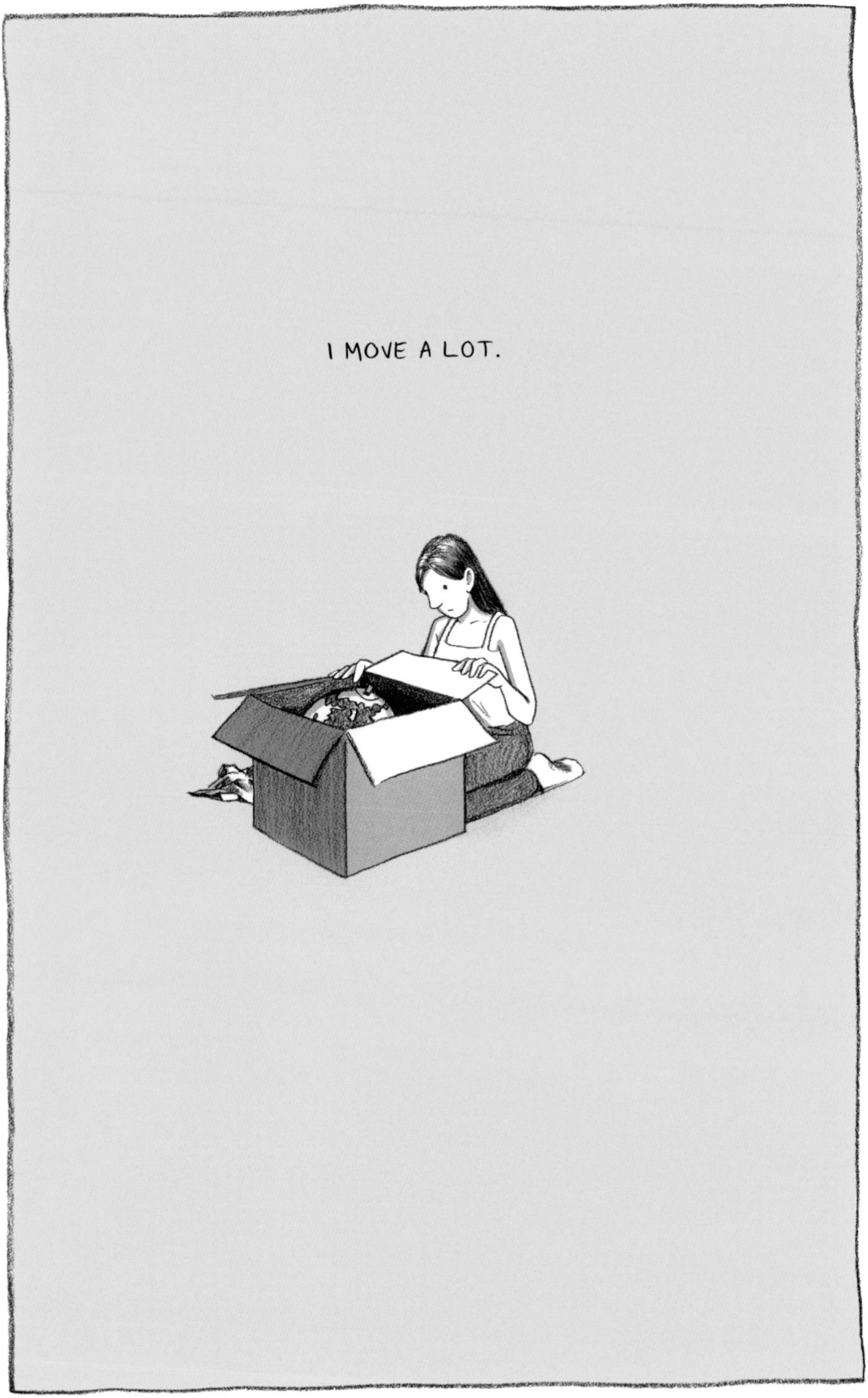
I MOVE A LOT.

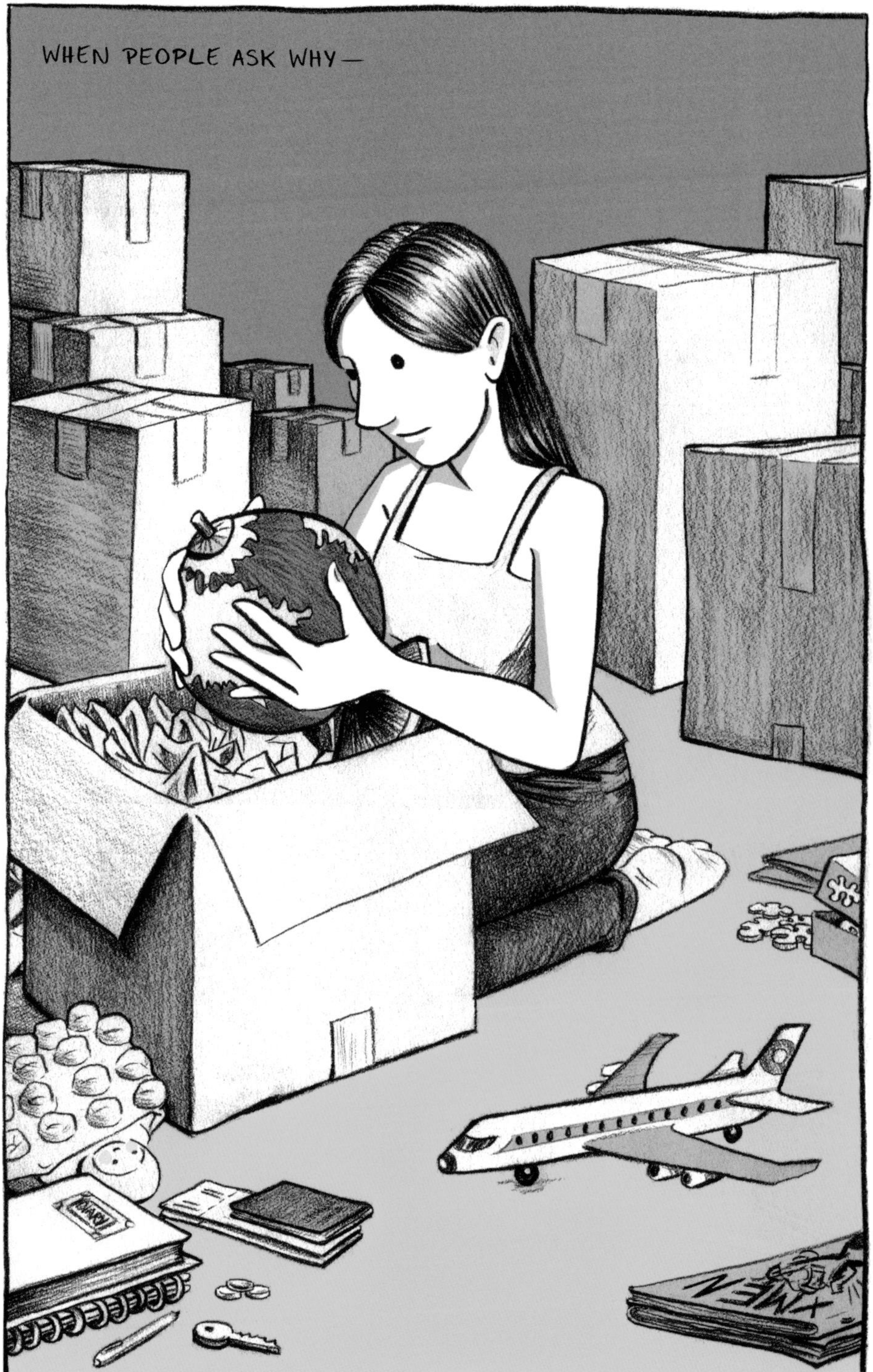
WHEN PEOPLE ASK WHY—

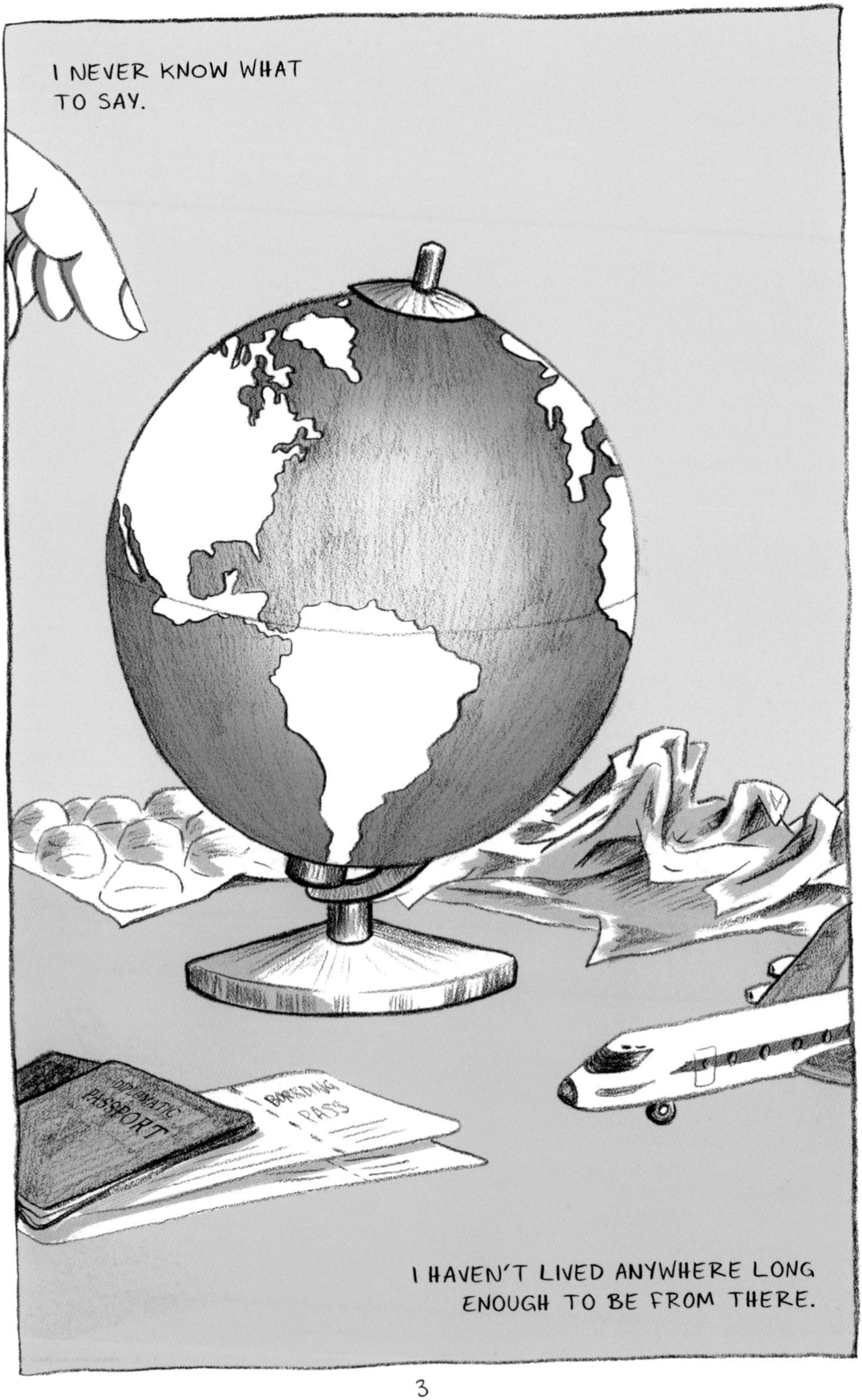
I NEVER KNOW WHAT TO SAY.
DIPLOMATIC PASSPORT
BOARDING PASS
I HAVEN'T LIVED ANYWHERE LONG ENOUGH TO BE FROM THERE.

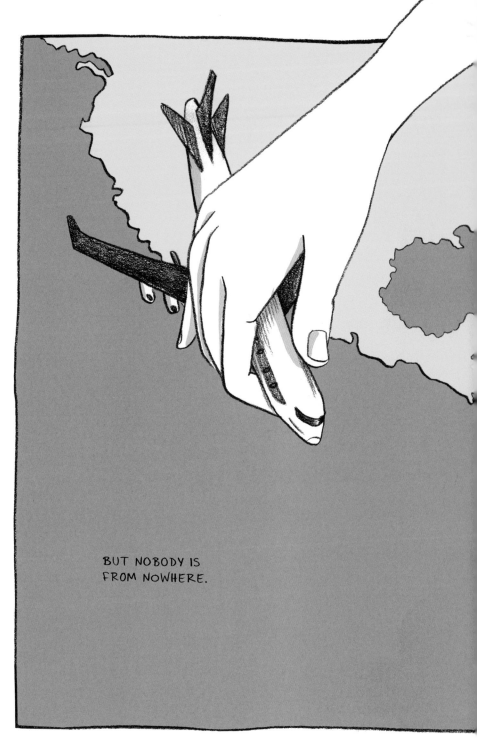

BUT NOBODY IS
FROM NOWHERE.

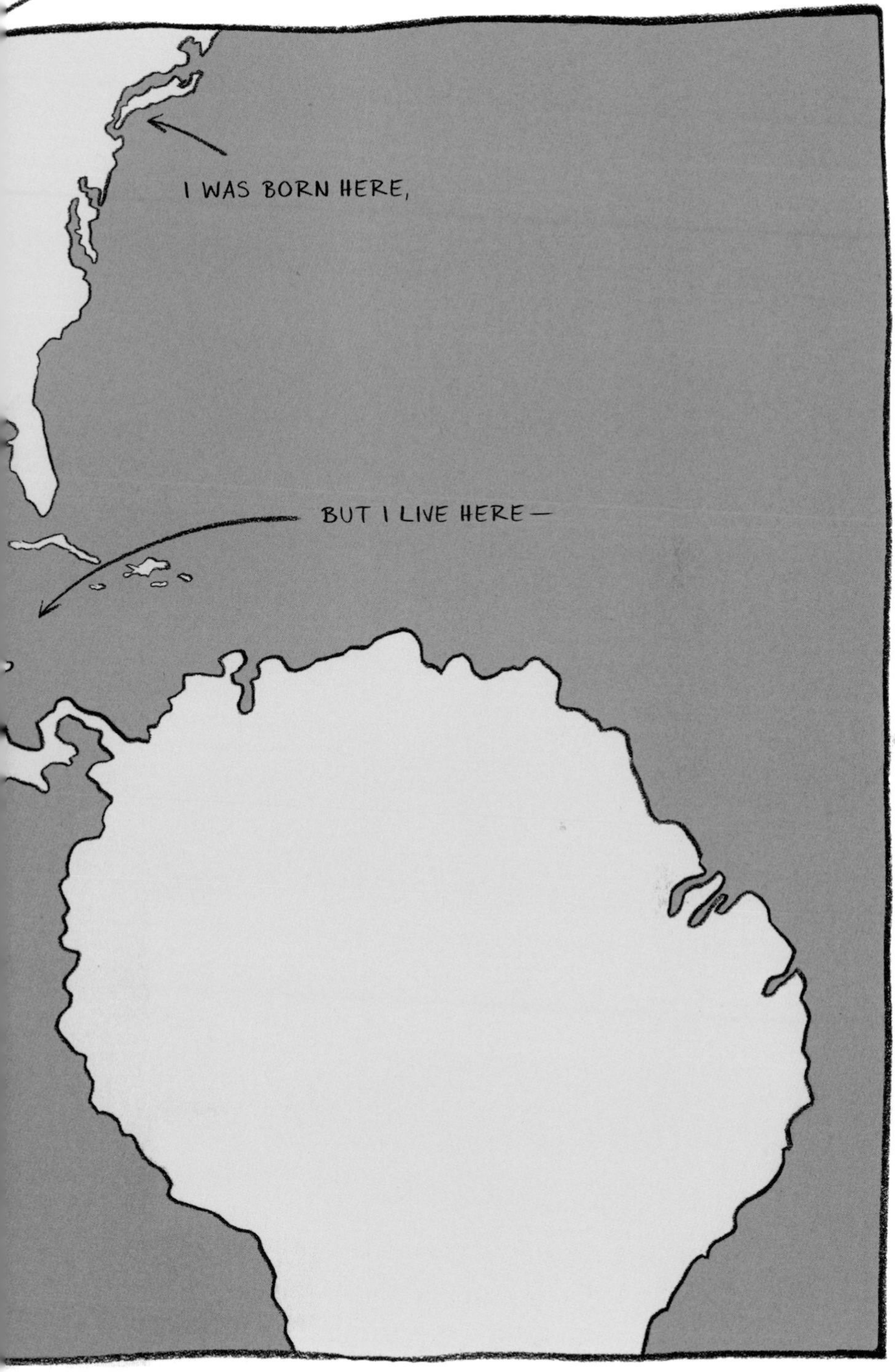
I WAS BORN HERE,
BUT I LIVE HERE—

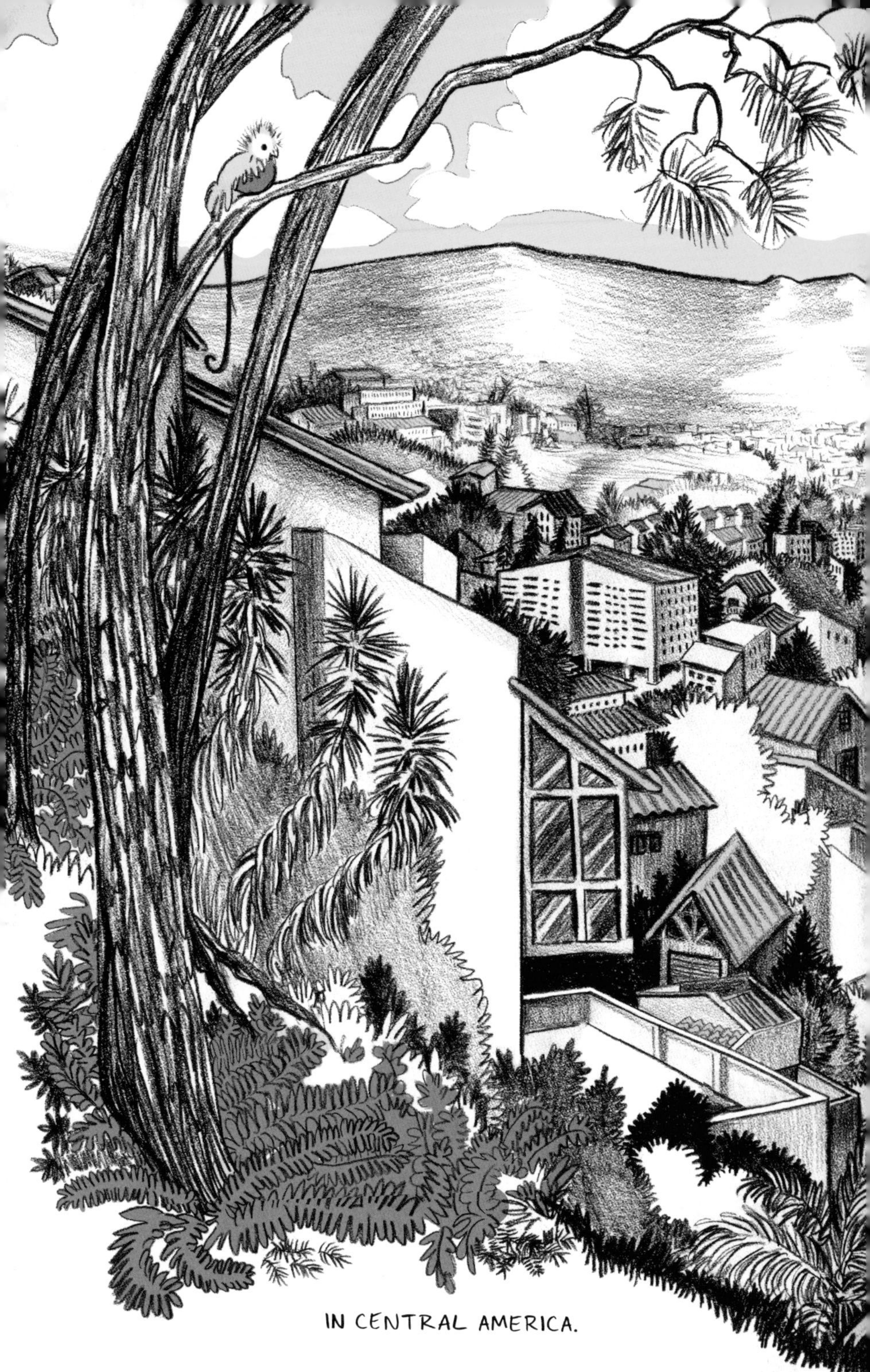

IN CENTRAL AMERICA.

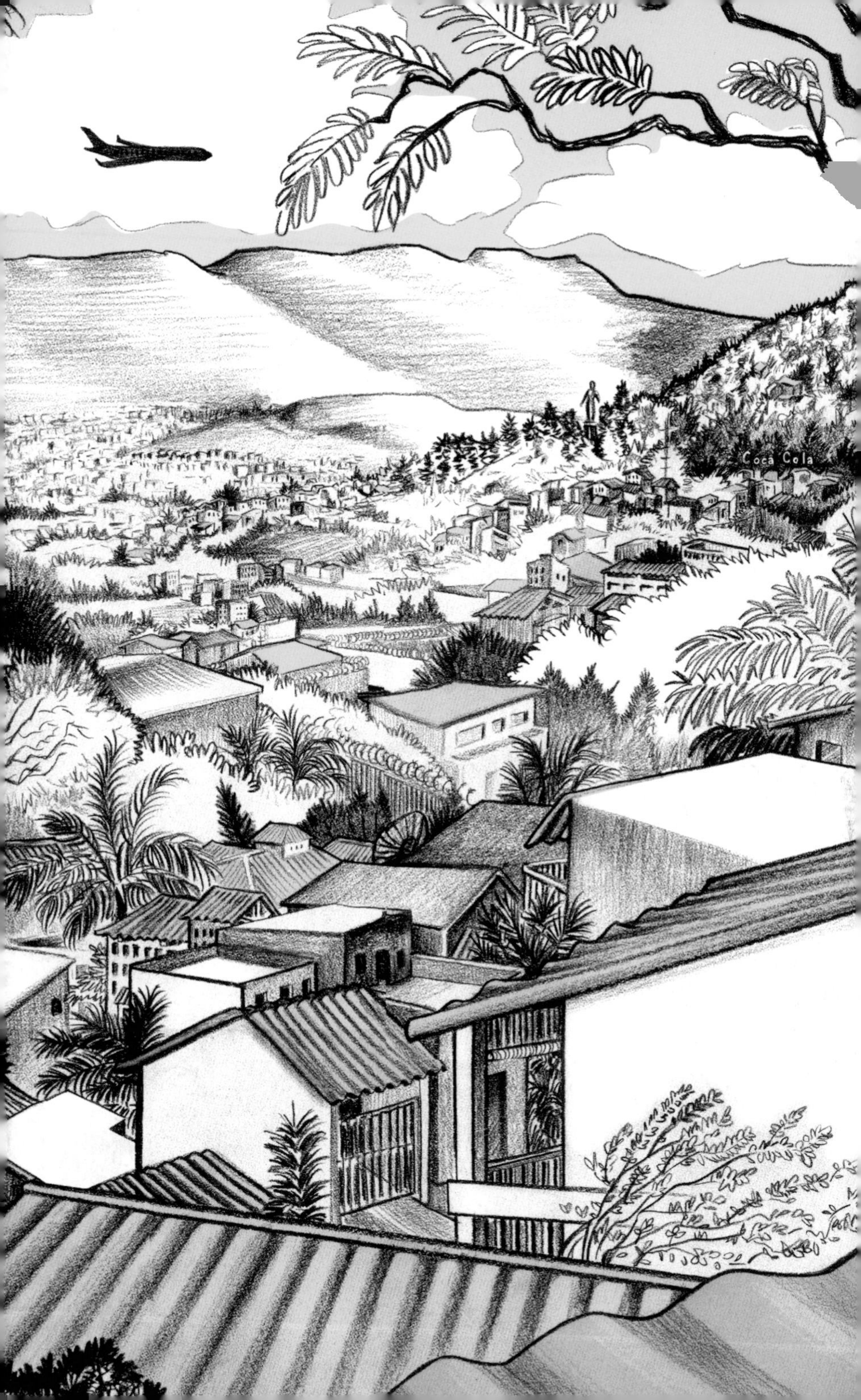
Coca Cola

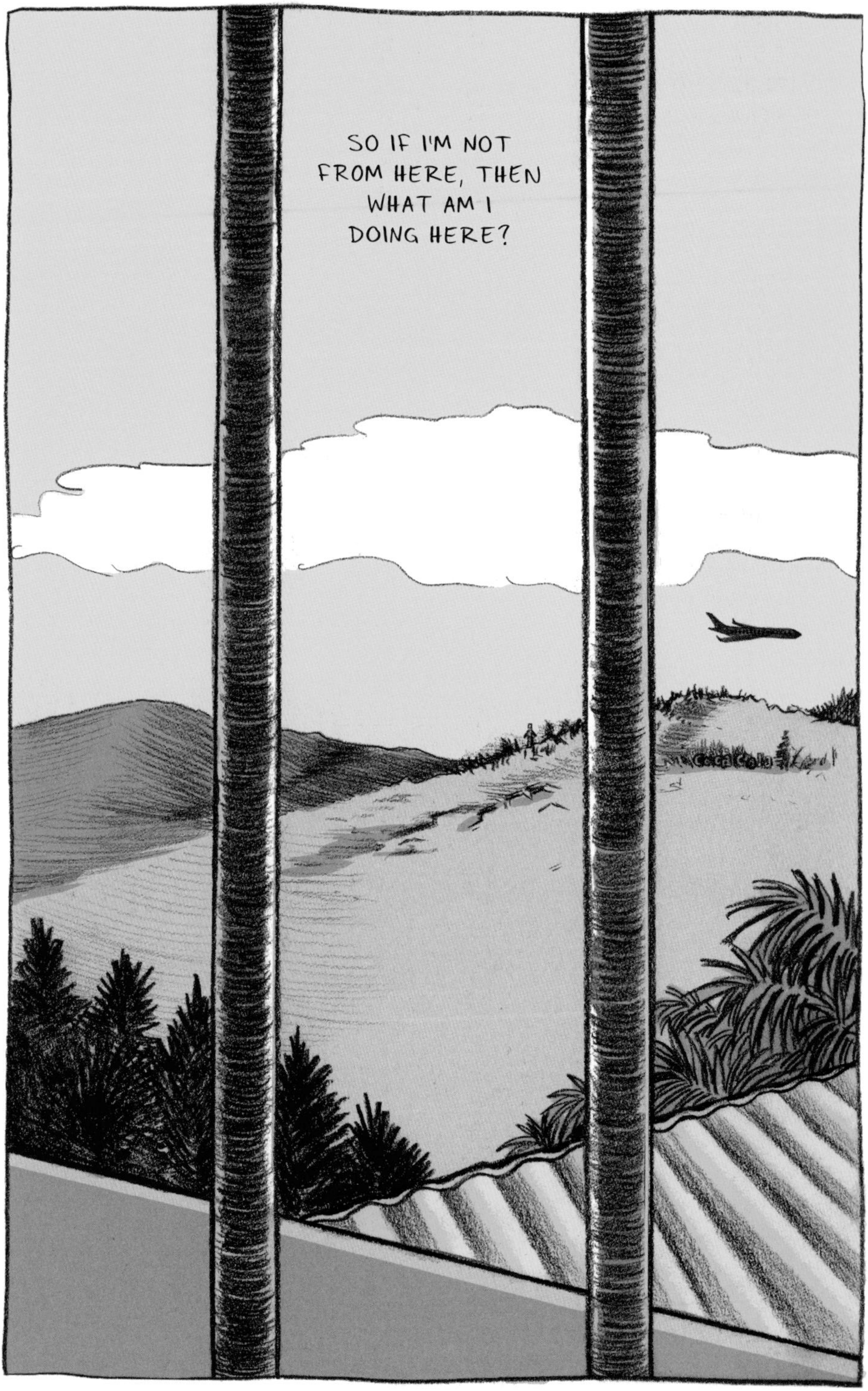
SO IF I'M NOT FROM HERE, THEN WHAT AM I DOING HERE?
CocaCola

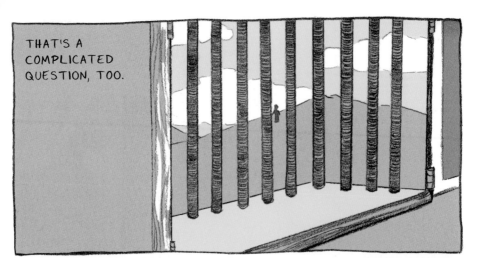

THAT'S A COMPLICATED QUESTION, TOO.

I LIVE HERE BECAUSE MY PARENTS ARE STATIONED HERE FOR WORK.

NOT THAT I ACTUALLY KNOW WHAT THAT MEANS.

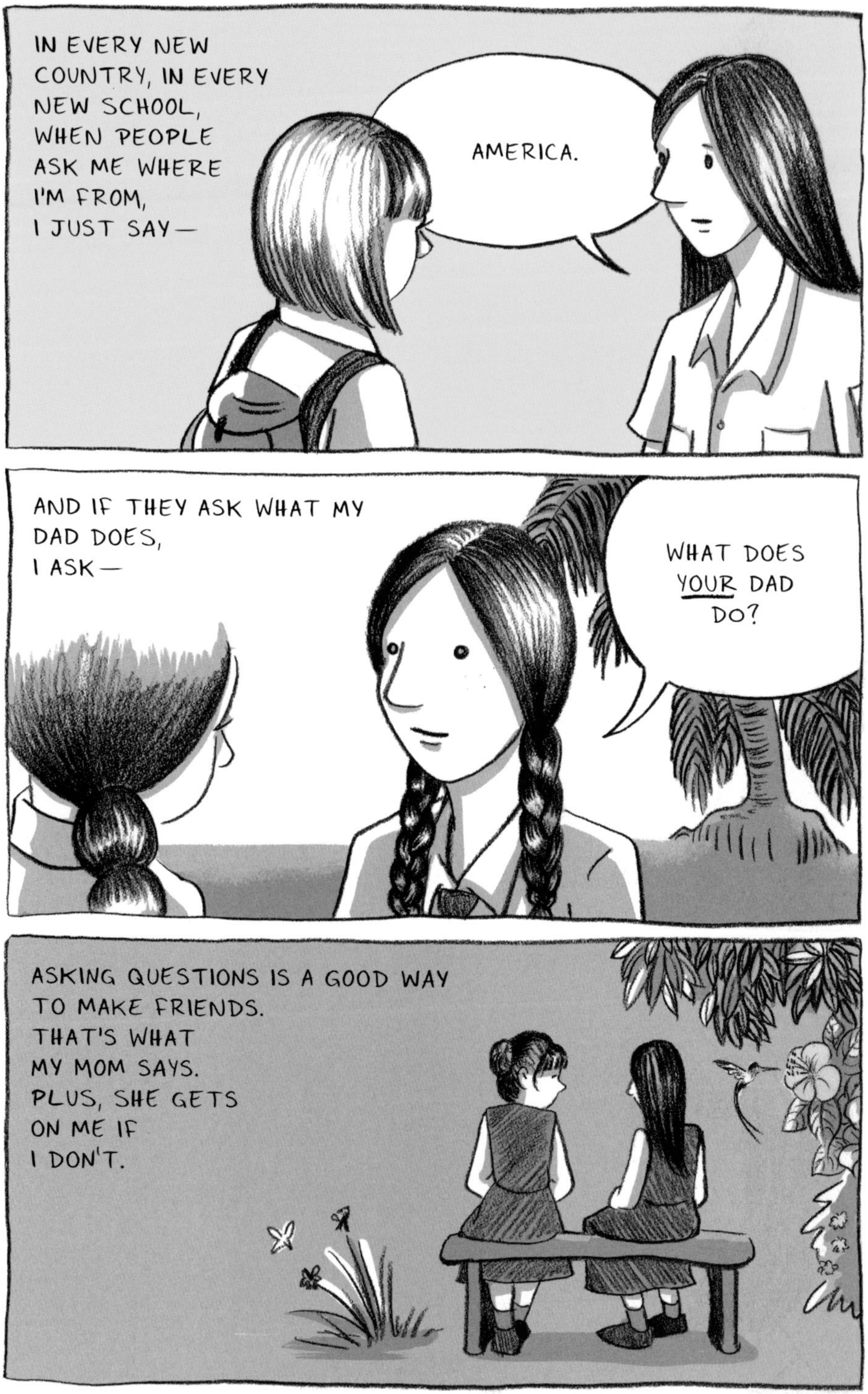
IN EVERY NEW COUNTRY, IN EVERY NEW SCHOOL, WHEN PEOPLE ASK ME WHERE I'M FROM, I JUST SAY—
AMERICA.
AND IF THEY ASK WHAT MY DAD DOES, I ASK—
WHAT DOES YOUR DAD DO?
ASKING QUESTIONS IS A GOOD WAY TO MAKE FRIENDS. THAT'S WHAT MY MOM SAYS. PLUS, SHE GETS ON ME IF I DON'T.

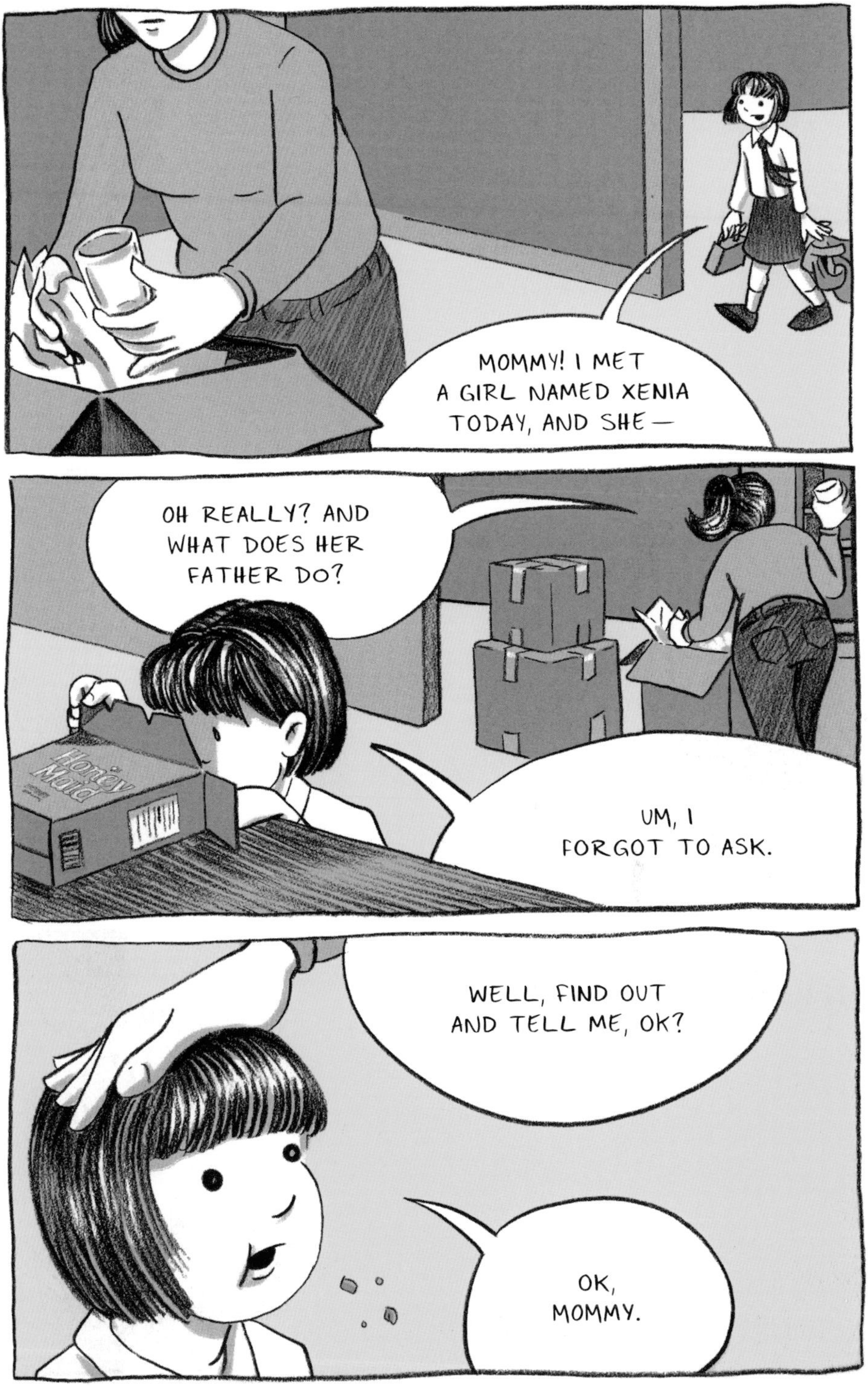
MOMMY! I MET A GIRL NAMED XENIA TODAY, AND SHE—
OH REALLY? AND WHAT DOES HER FATHER DO?
Honey Maid
UM, I FORGOT TO ASK.
WELL, FIND OUT AND TELL ME, OK?
OK, MOMMY.

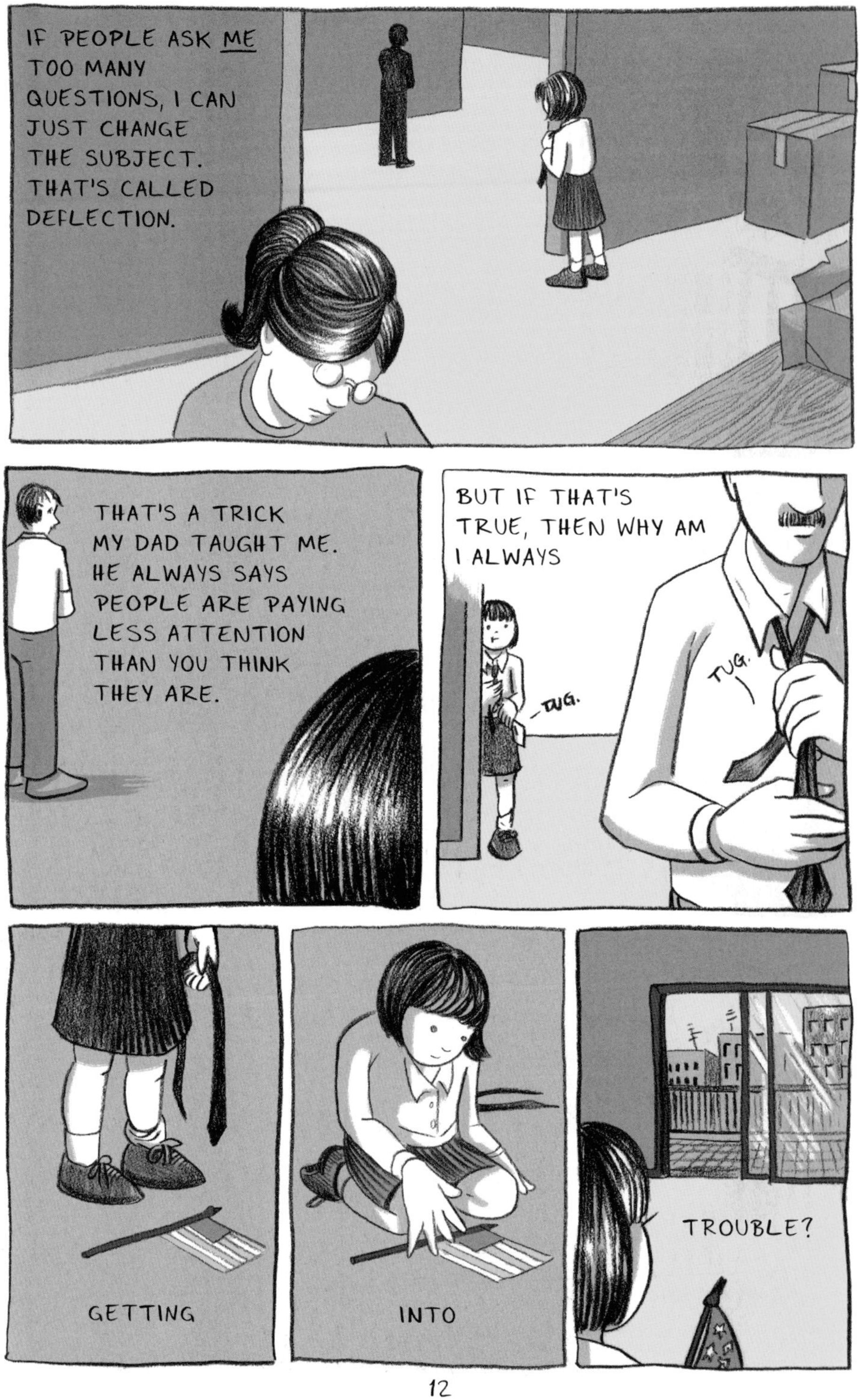
IF PEOPLE ASK ME TOO MANY QUESTIONS, I CAN JUST CHANGE THE SUBJECT. THAT'S CALLED DEFLECTION.
THAT'S A TRICK MY DAD TAUGHT ME. HE ALWAYS SAYS PEOPLE ARE PAYING LESS ATTENTION THAN YOU THINK THEY ARE.
BUT IF THAT'S TRUE, THEN WHY AM I ALWAYS
TUG.
TUG.
GETTING
INTO
TROUBLE?

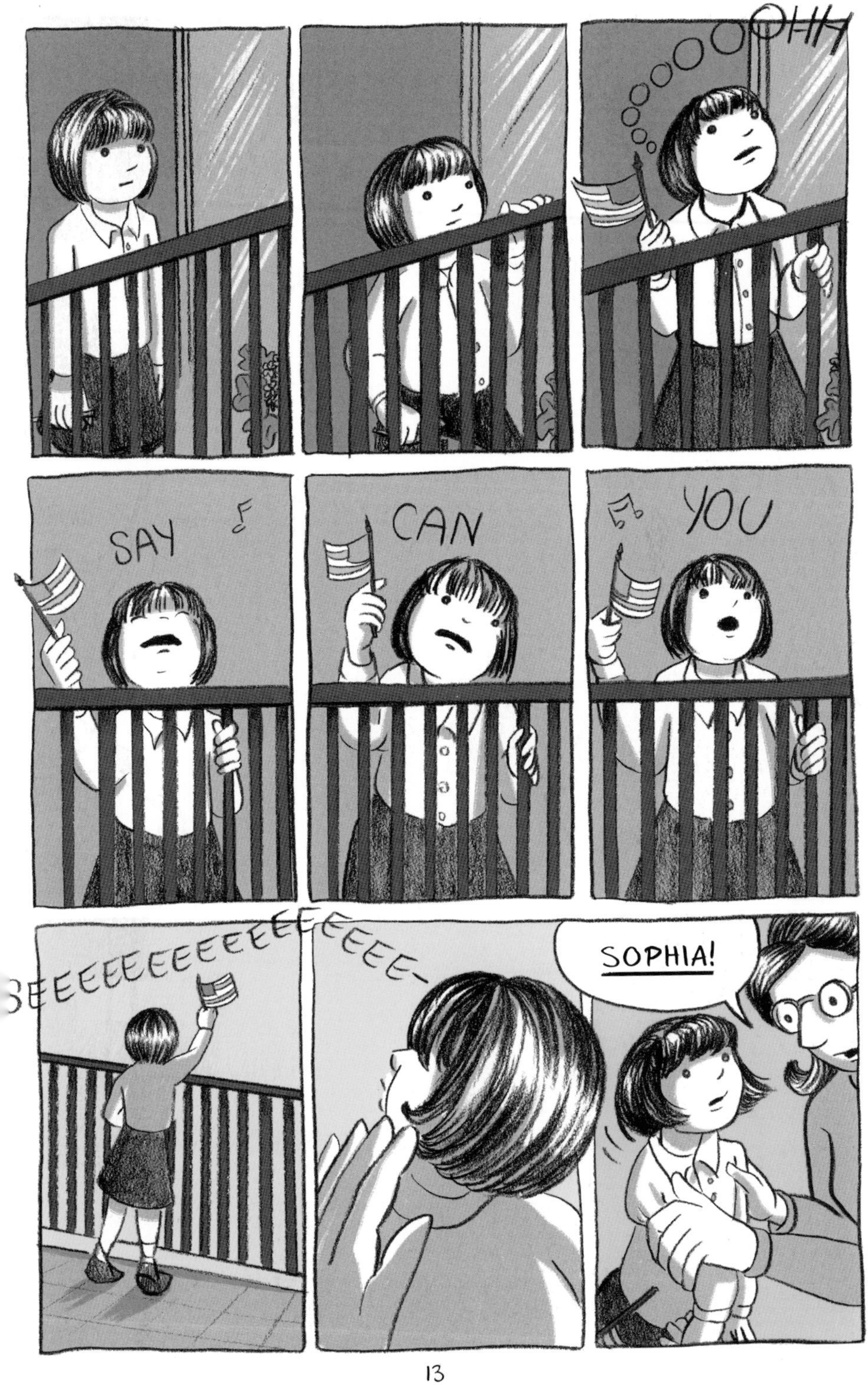

OOOOOHH
SAY
CAN
YOU
SEEEEEEEEEEEEEEEEEE-
SOPHIA!

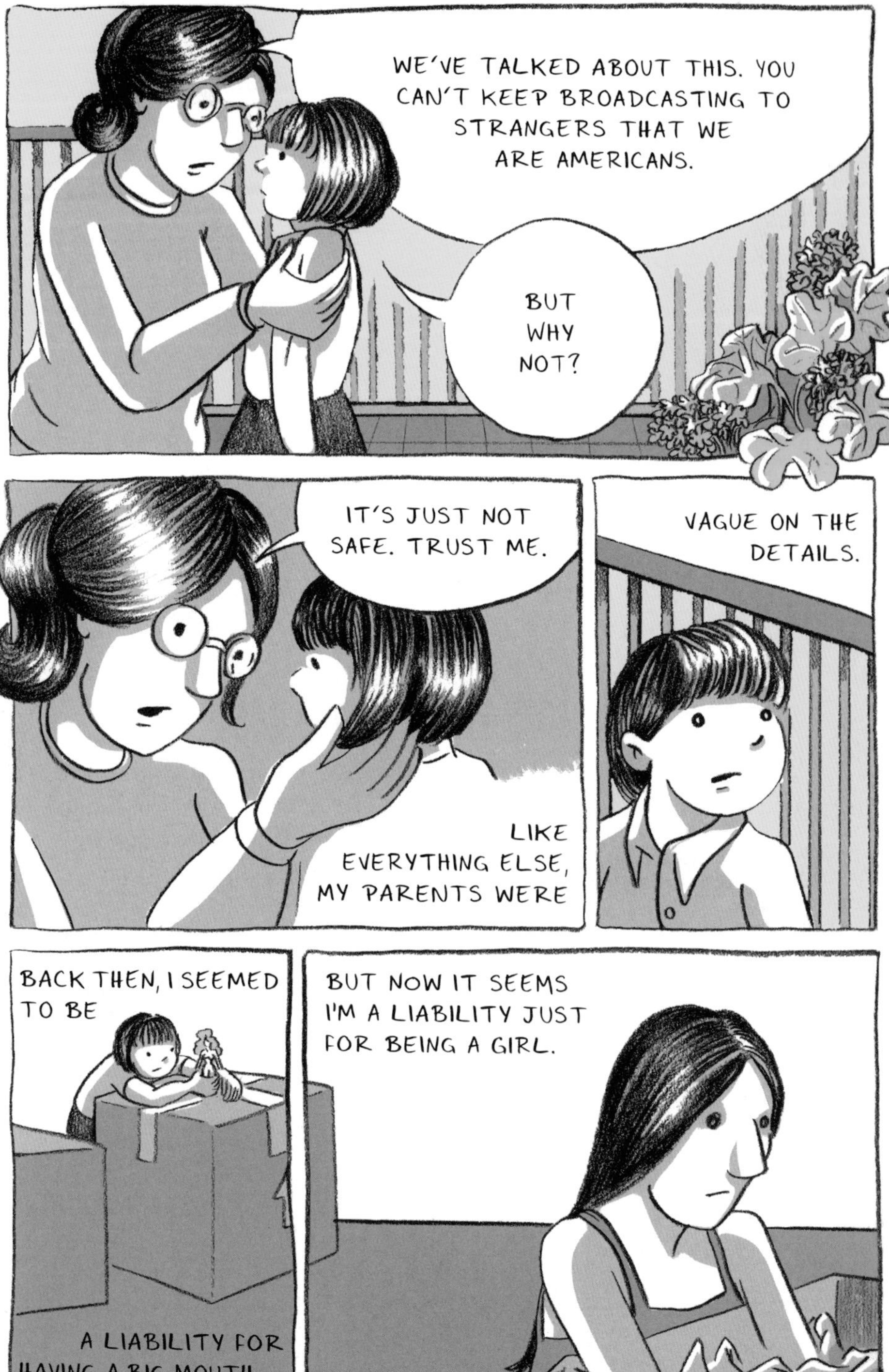
WE'VE TALKED ABOUT THIS. YOU CAN'T KEEP BROADCASTING TO STRANGERS THAT WE ARE AMERICANS.
BUT WHY NOT?
IT'S JUST NOT SAFE. TRUST ME.
LIKE EVERYTHING ELSE, MY PARENTS WERE
VAGUE ON THE DETAILS.
BACK THEN, I SEEMED TO BE
A LIABILITY FOR HAVING A BIG MOUTH—
BUT NOW IT SEEMS I'M A LIABILITY JUST FOR BEING A GIRL.

SOPHIA?

WHAT?

IS THAT WHAT YOU'RE WEARING?

YEAH ...

COVER UP.

WE'RE GOING OUT.

THEY DON'T SEEM TO GET IT.

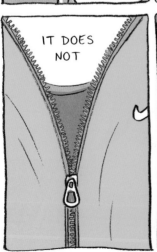

IT DOES NOT

MATTER WHAT

I WEAR.

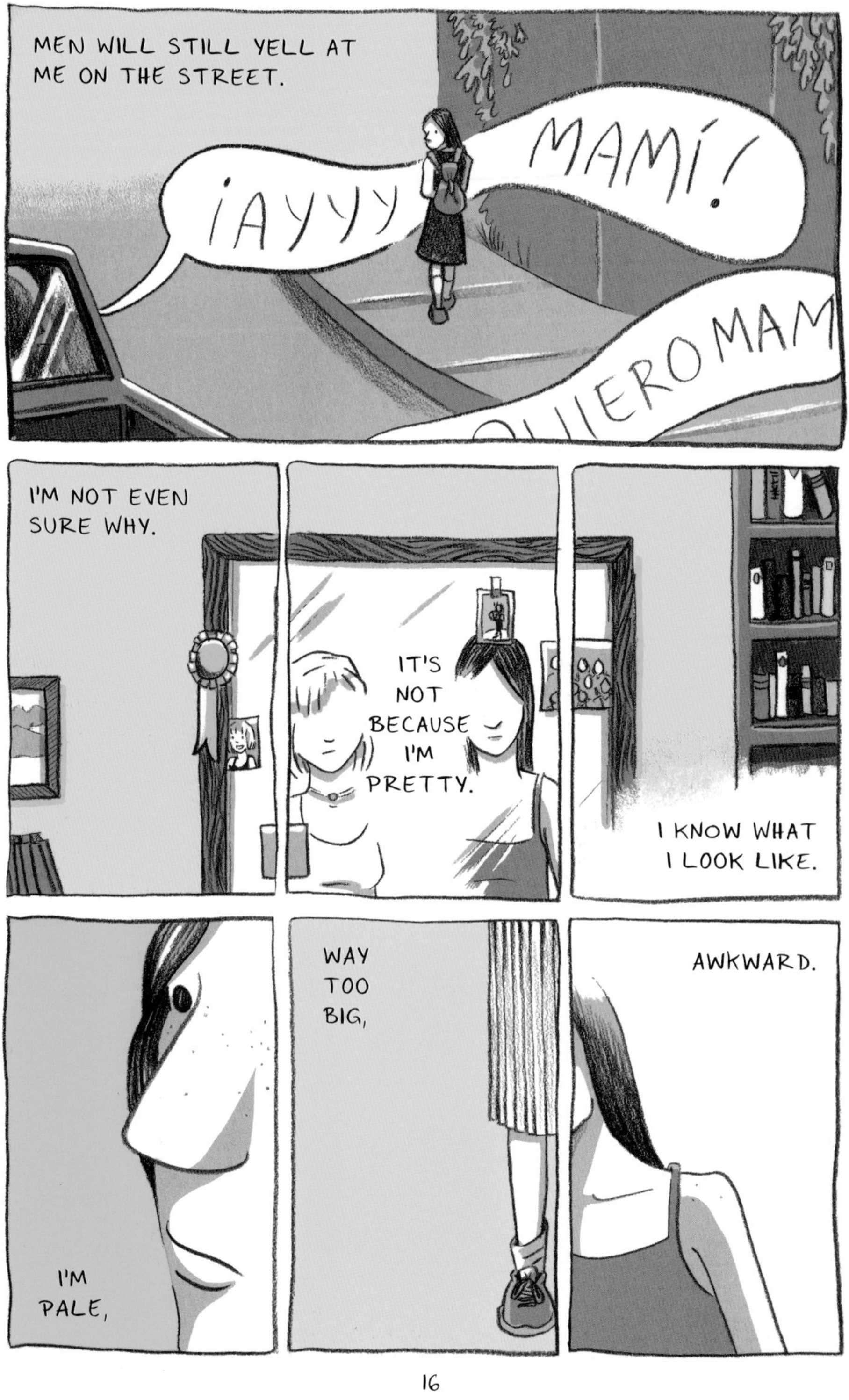
MEN WILL STILL YELL AT ME ON THE STREET.
¡AYYY MAMÍ!
QUIERO MAM
I'M NOT EVEN SURE WHY.
IT'S NOT BECAUSE I'M PRETTY.
I KNOW WHAT I LOOK LIKE.
I'M PALE,
WAY TOO BIG,
AWKWARD.

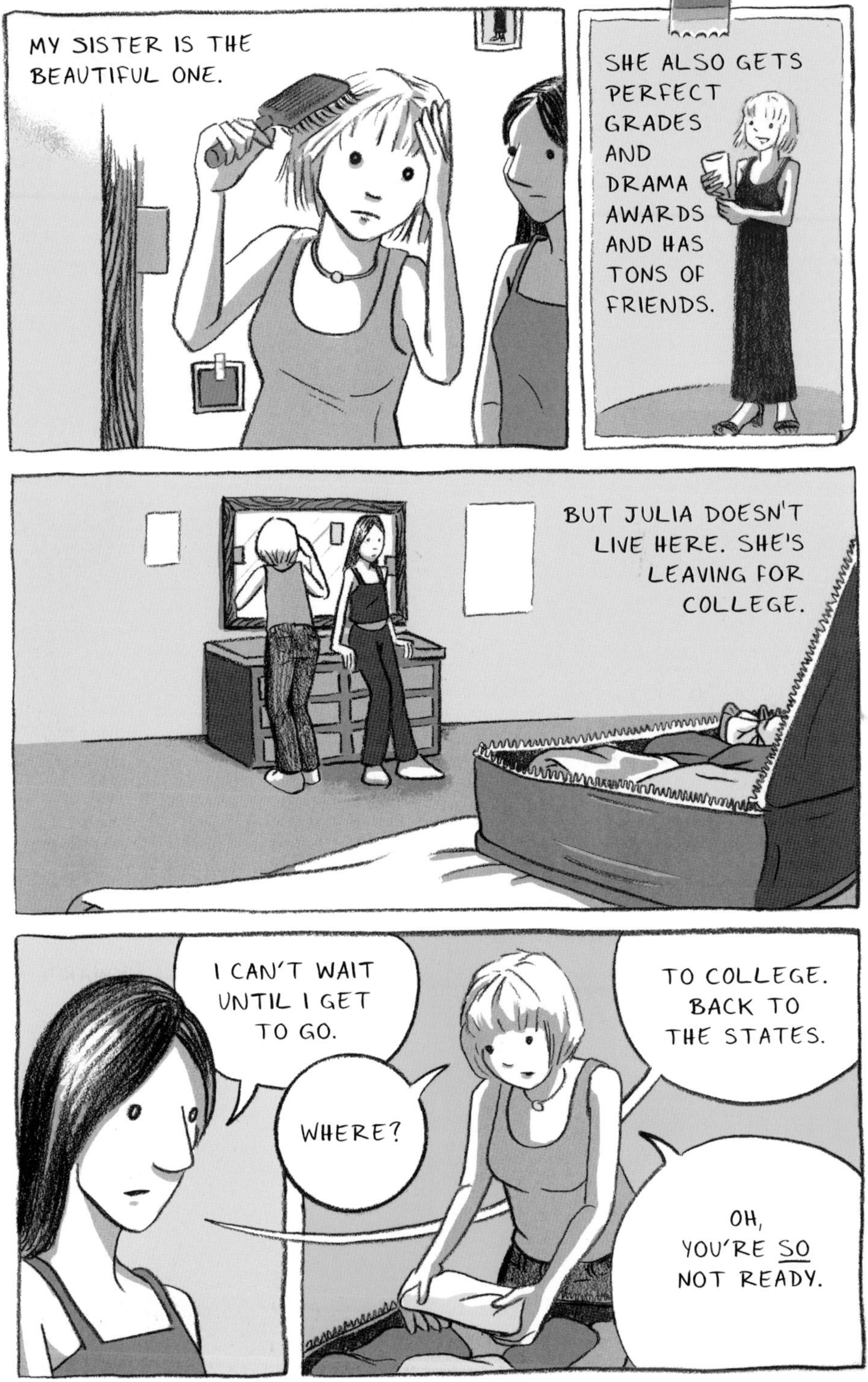
MY SISTER IS THE BEAUTIFUL ONE.
SHE ALSO GETS PERFECT GRADES AND DRAMA AWARDS AND HAS TONS OF FRIENDS.
BUT JULIA DOESN'T LIVE HERE. SHE'S LEAVING FOR COLLEGE.
I CAN'T WAIT UNTIL I GET TO GO.
WHERE?
TO COLLEGE. BACK TO THE STATES.
OH, YOU'RE SO NOT READY.

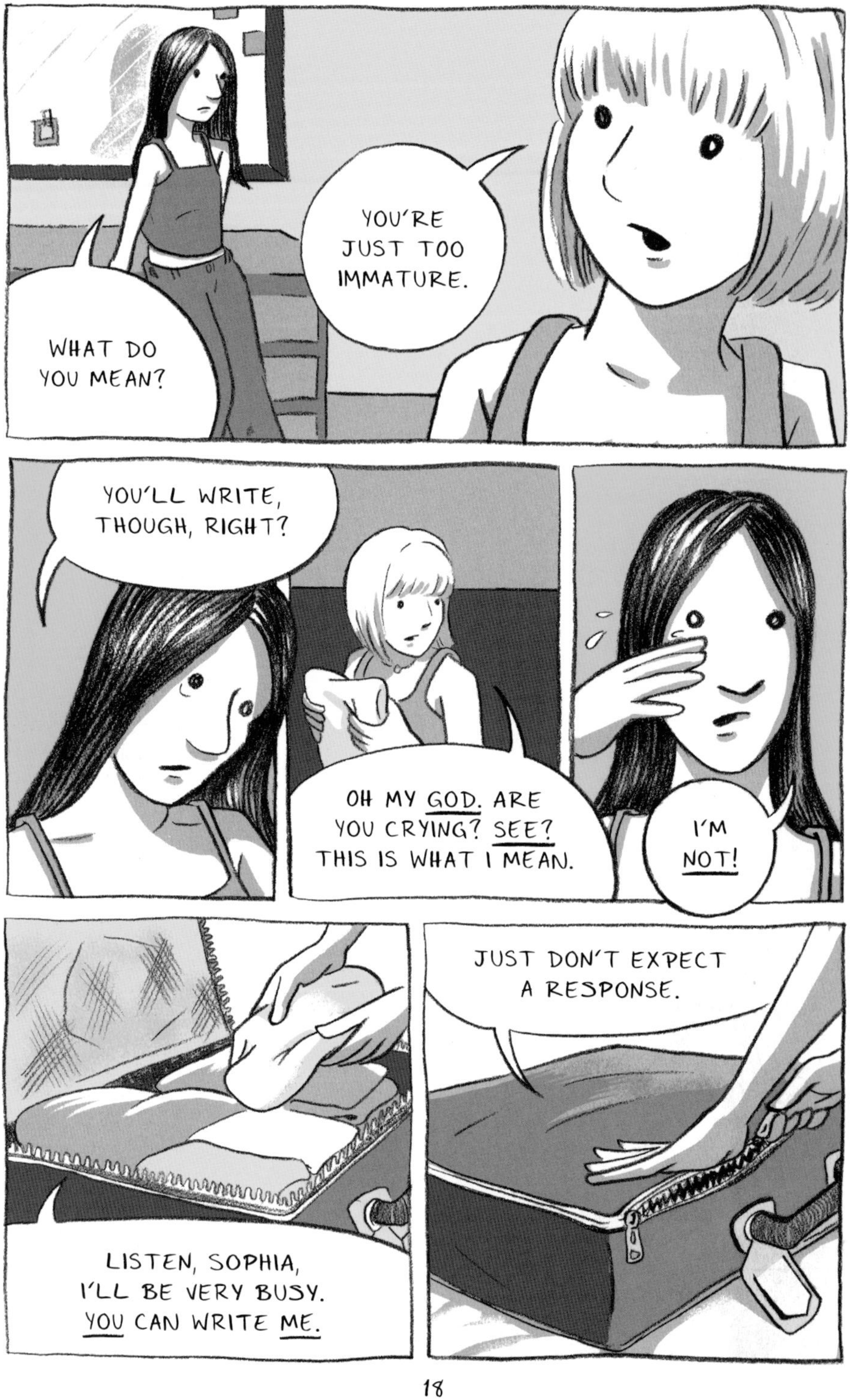
WHAT DO YOU MEAN?
YOU'RE JUST TOO IMMATURE.
YOU'LL WRITE, THOUGH, RIGHT?
OH MY GOD. ARE YOU CRYING? SEE? THIS IS WHAT I MEAN.
I'M NOT!
LISTEN, SOPHIA, I'LL BE VERY BUSY. YOU CAN WRITE ME.
JUST DON'T EXPECT A RESPONSE.

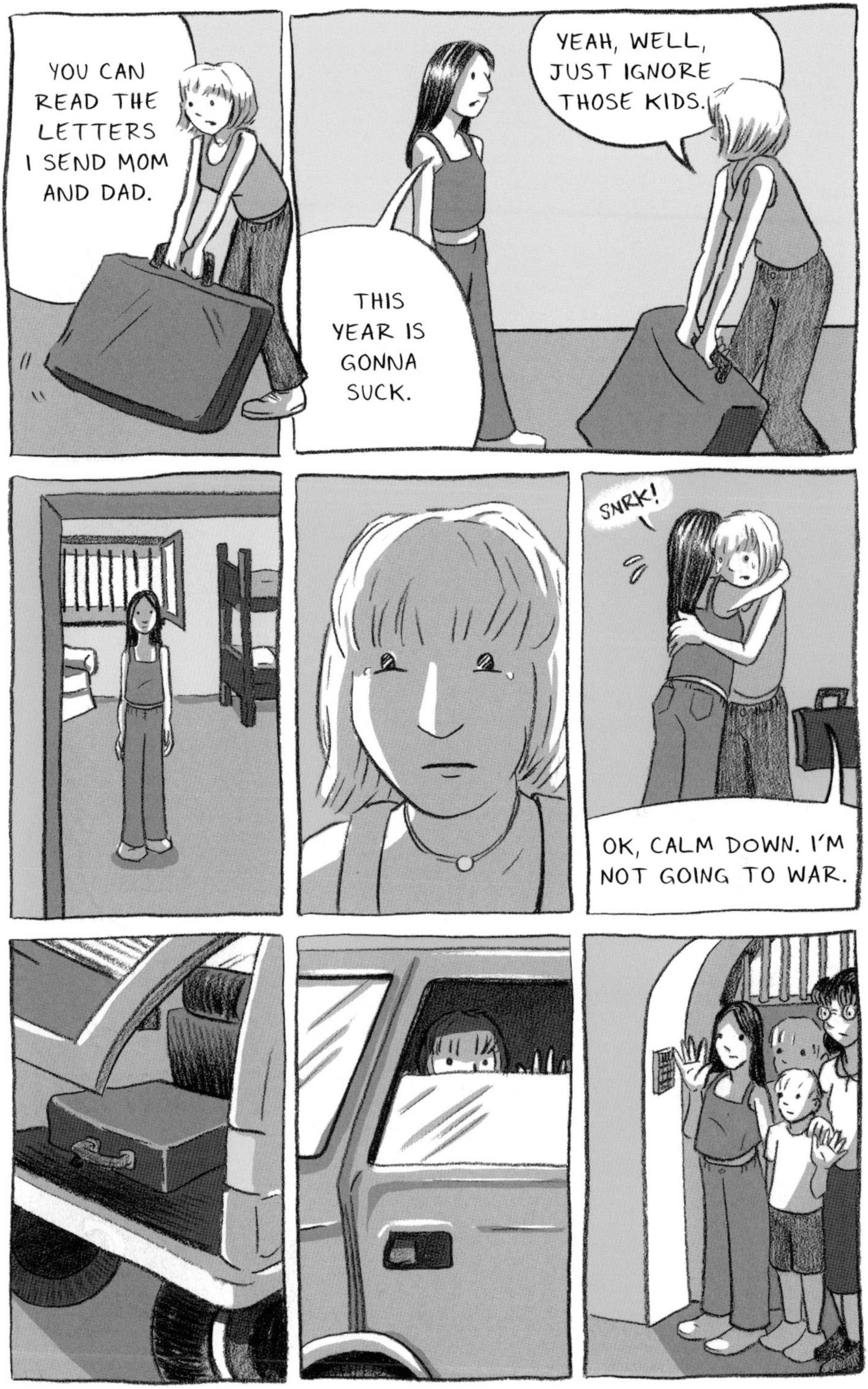
YOU CAN READ THE LETTERS I SEND MOM AND DAD.
THIS YEAR IS GONNA SUCK.
YEAH, WELL, JUST IGNORE THOSE KIDS.
SNRK!
OK, CALM DOWN. I'M NOT GOING TO WAR.

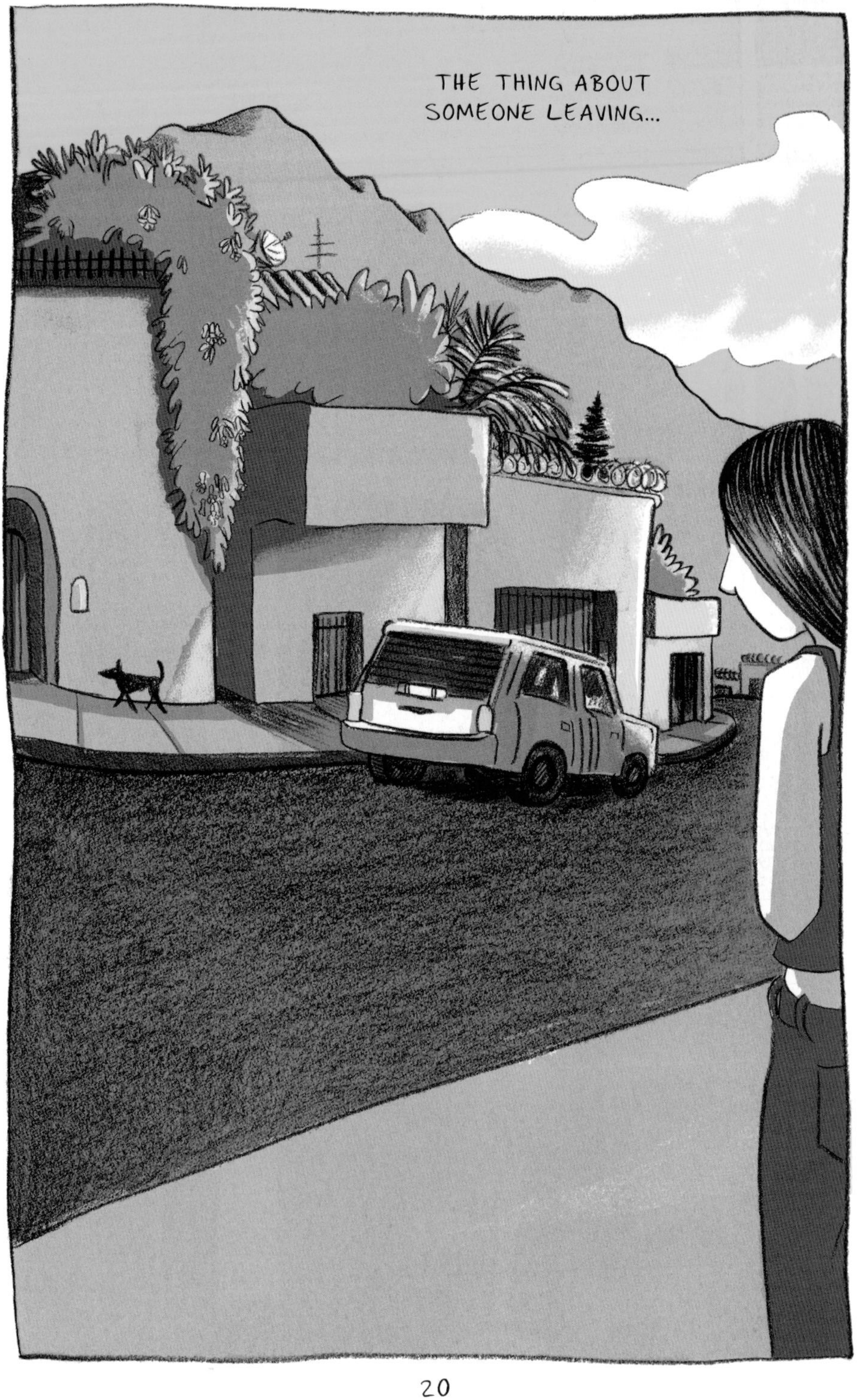
THE THING ABOUT
SOMEONE LEAVING...

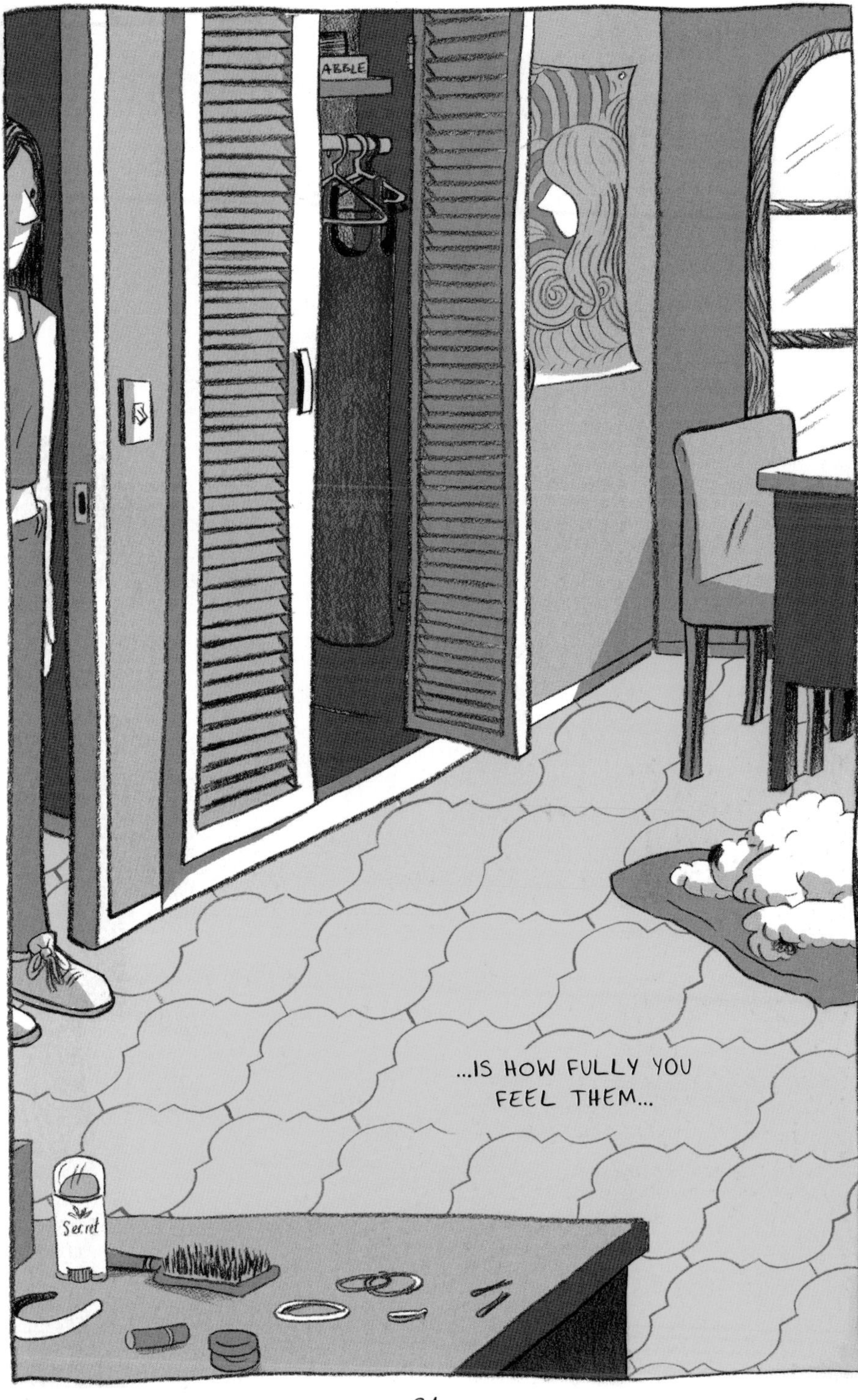
ABBLE
...IS HOW FULLY YOU
FEEL THEM...
Secret

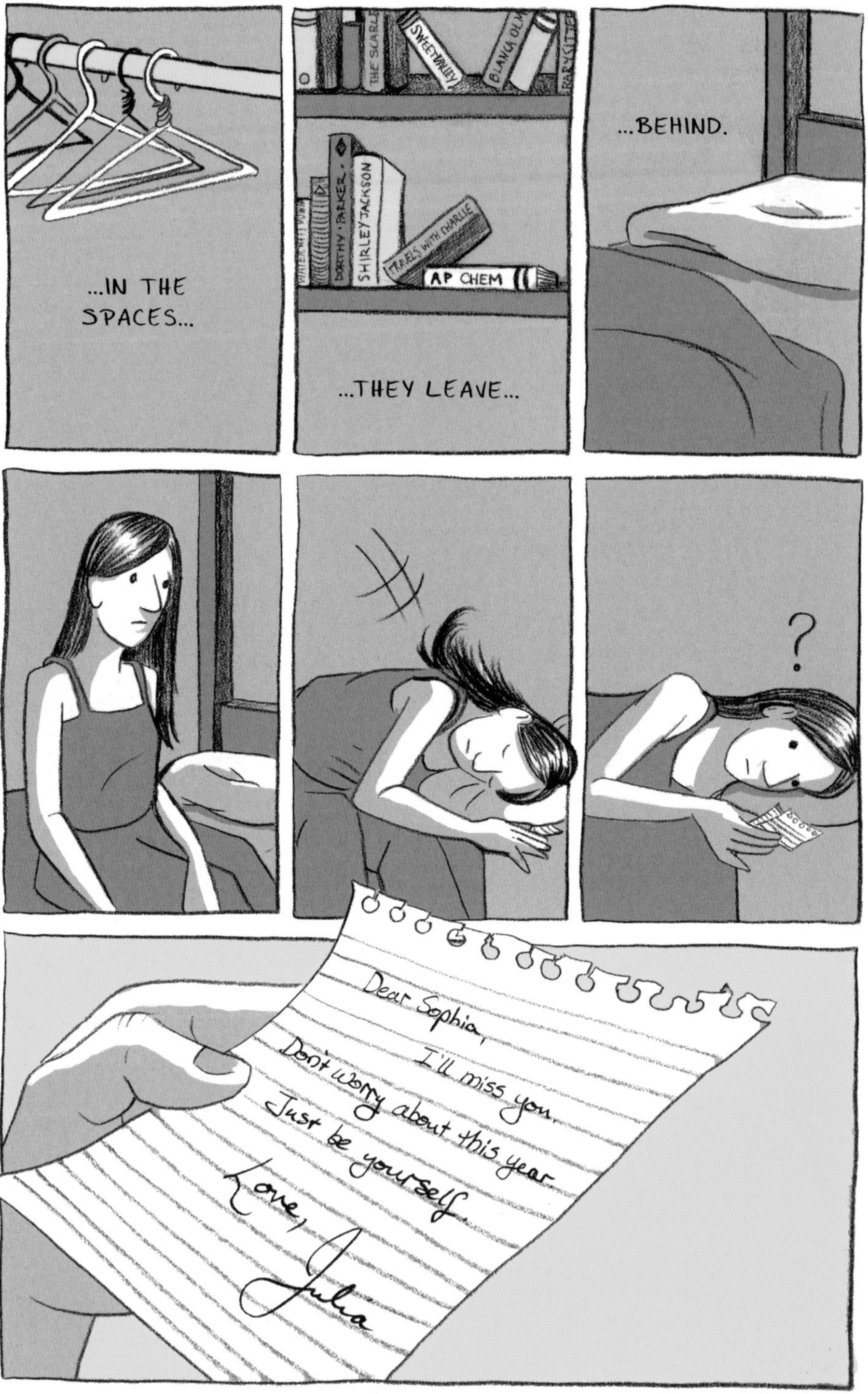
...IN THE SPACES...
SWEET VALLEY
DORTHY · PARKER
SHIRLEY JACKSON
TRAVELS WITH CHARLIE
AP CHEM
...THEY LEAVE...
...BEHIND.
?
Dear Sophia,
I'll miss you.
Don't worry about this year.
Just be yourself.
Love,
Julia

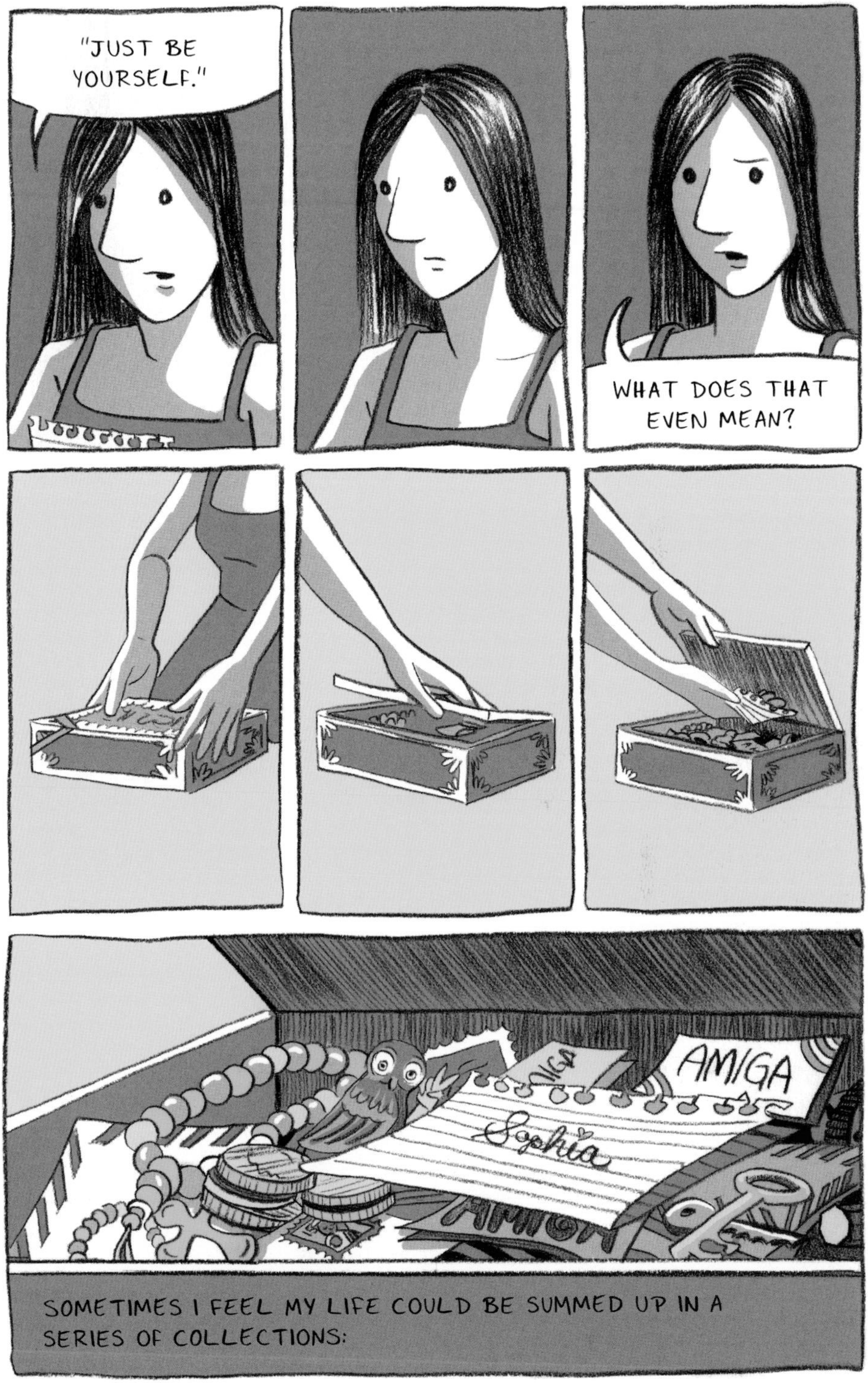
"JUST BE YOURSELF."
WHAT DOES THAT EVEN MEAN?
AMIGA
Sophia
SOMETIMES I FEEL MY LIFE COULD BE SUMMED UP IN A SERIES OF COLLECTIONS:

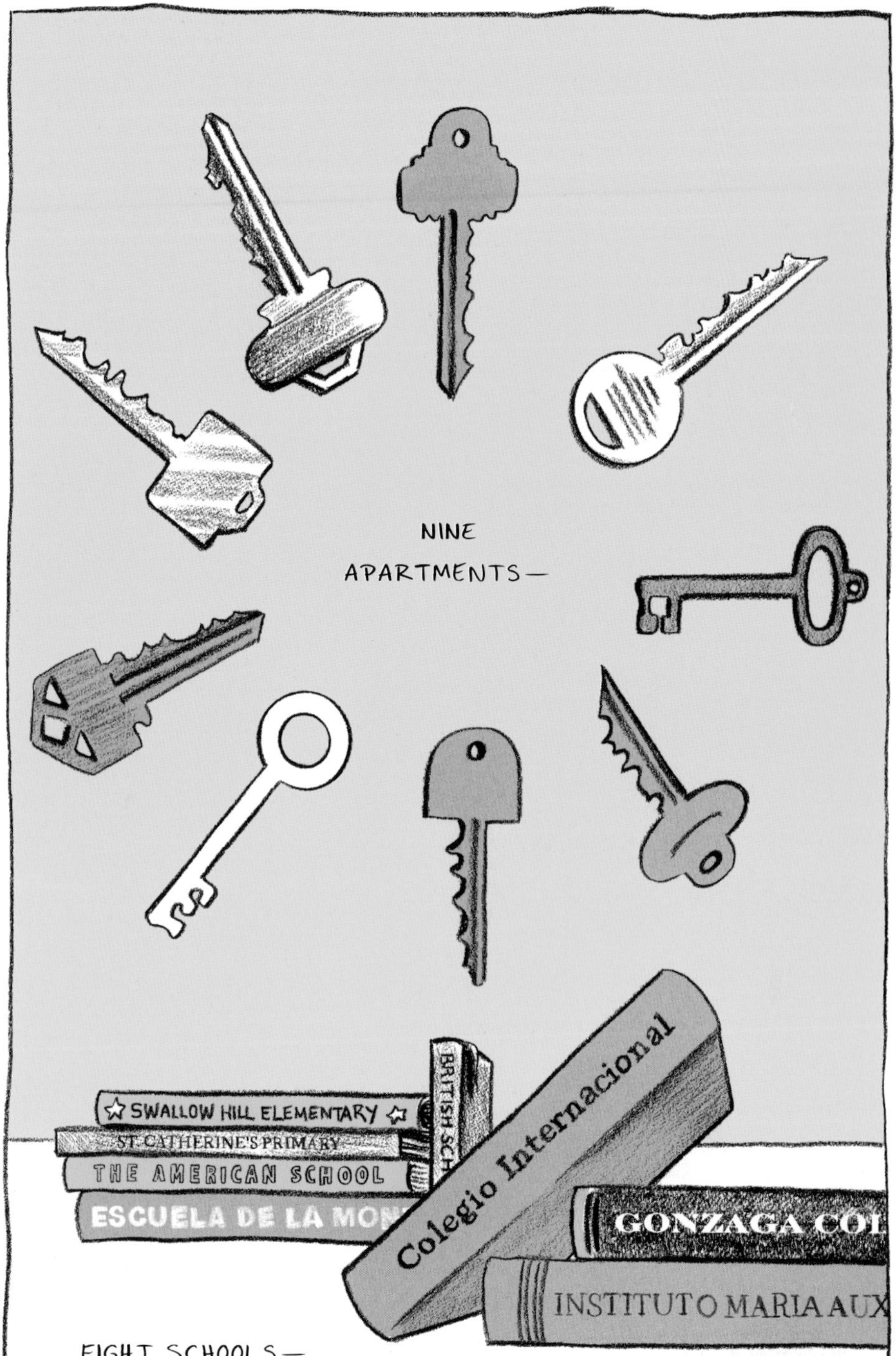
NINE
APARTMENTS—
SWALLOW HILL ELEMENTARY
ST. CATHERINE'S PRIMARY
THE AMERICAN SCHOOL
ESCUELA DE LA MON
BRITISH SCH
Colegio Internacional
GONZAGA COL
INSTITUTO MARIA AUX
EIGHT SCHOOLS—

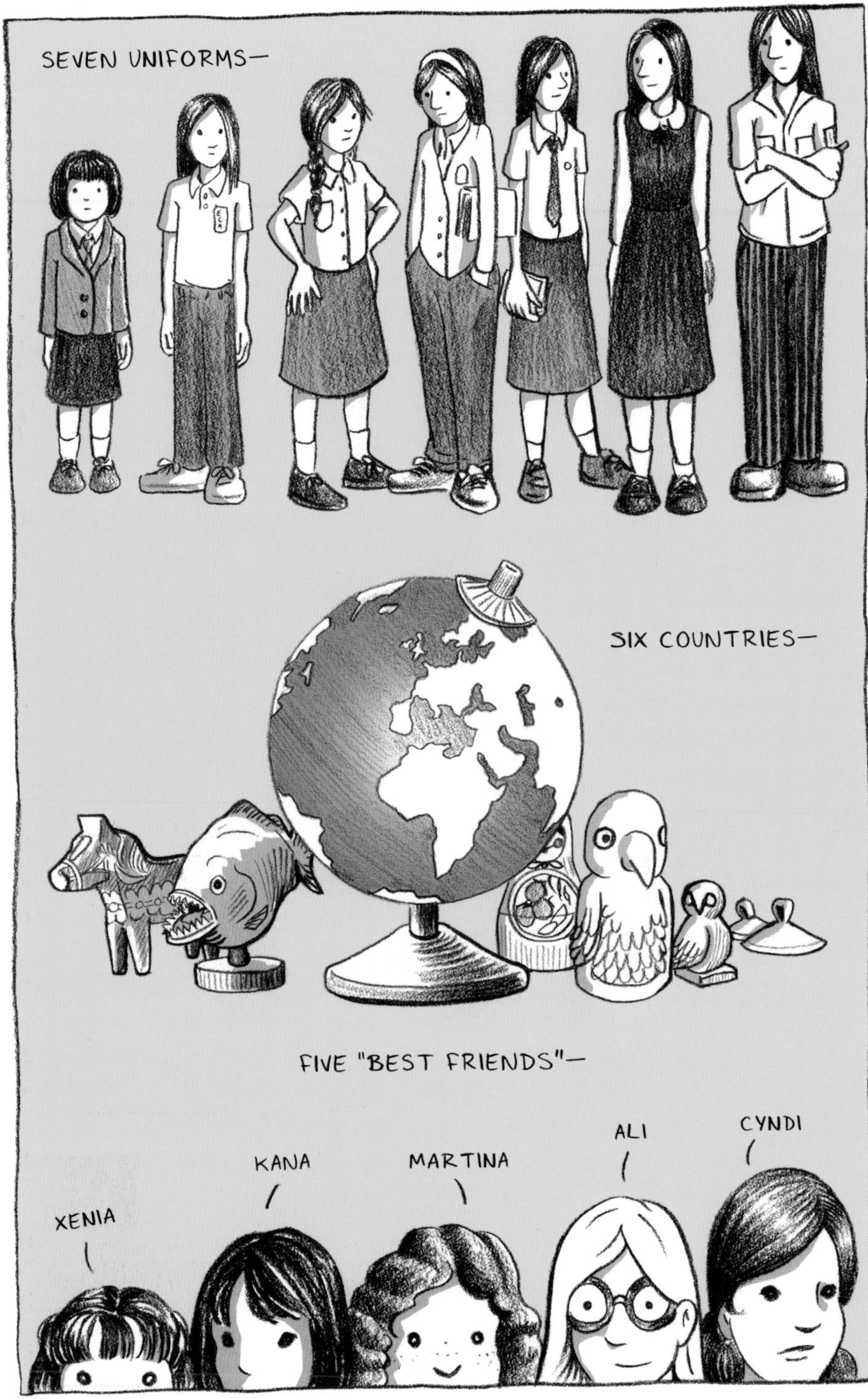
SEVEN UNIFORMS—
SIX COUNTRIES—
FIVE "BEST FRIENDS"—
XENIA
KANA
MARTINA
ALI
CYNDI

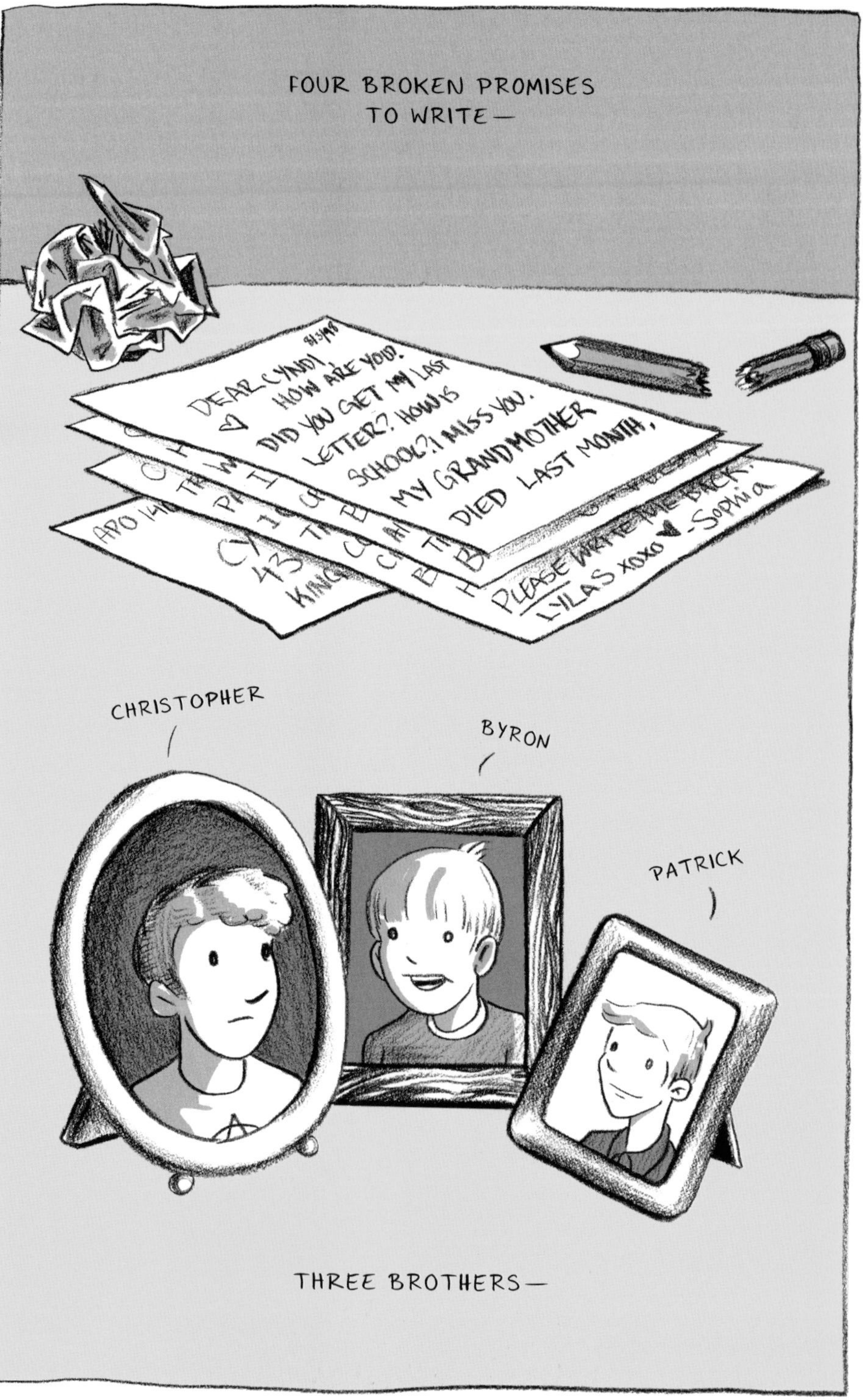
FOUR BROKEN PROMISES TO WRITE—
DEAR CYNDI,
HOW ARE YOU?
DID YOU GET MY LAST LETTER? HOW IS SCHOOL? I MISS YOU.
MY GRANDMOTHER DIED LAST MONTH,
PLEASE WRITE ME BACK.
LYLAS xoxo ♥ -Sophia
CHRISTOPHER
BYRON
PATRICK
THREE BROTHERS—

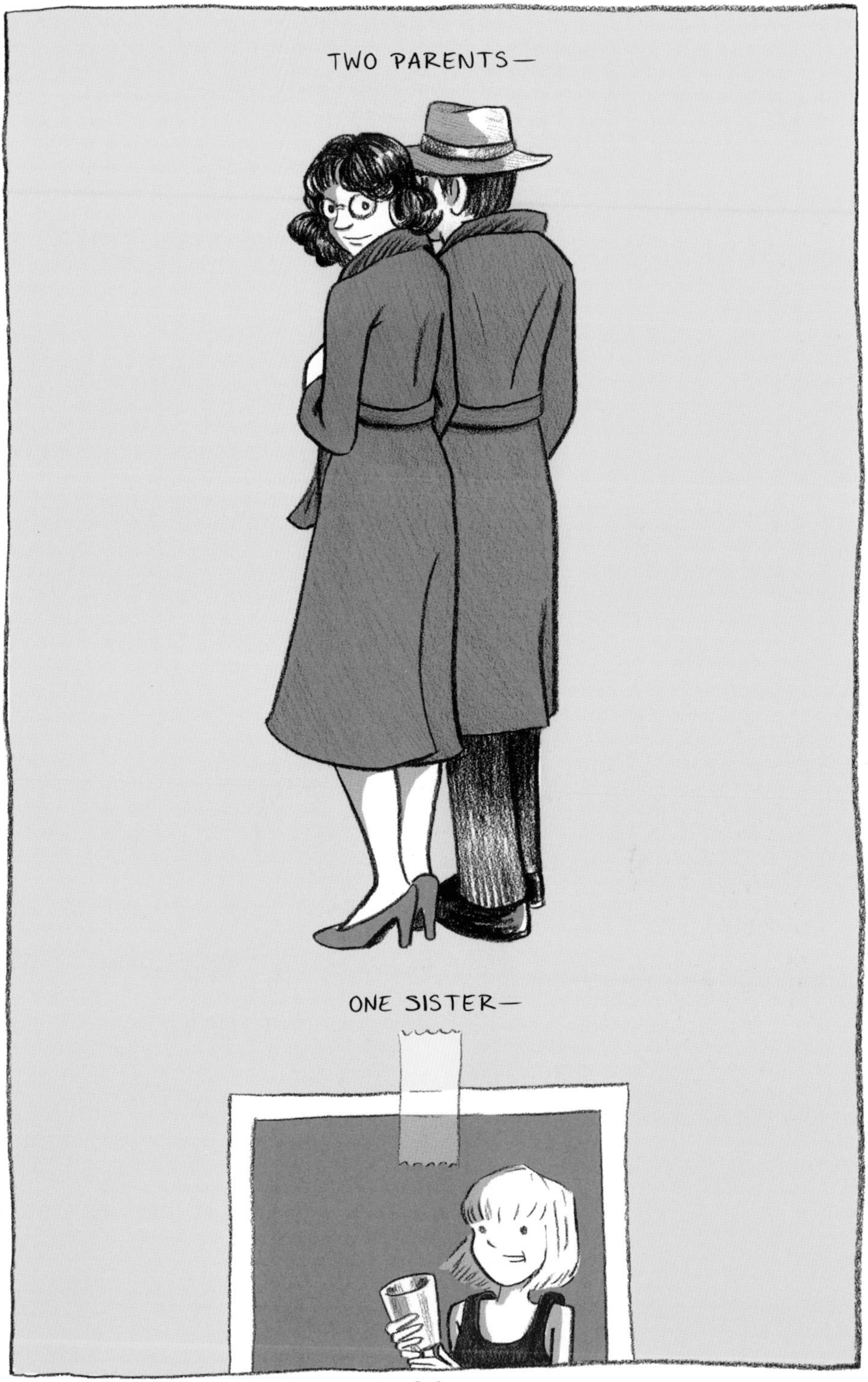

TWO PARENTS—
ONE SISTER—

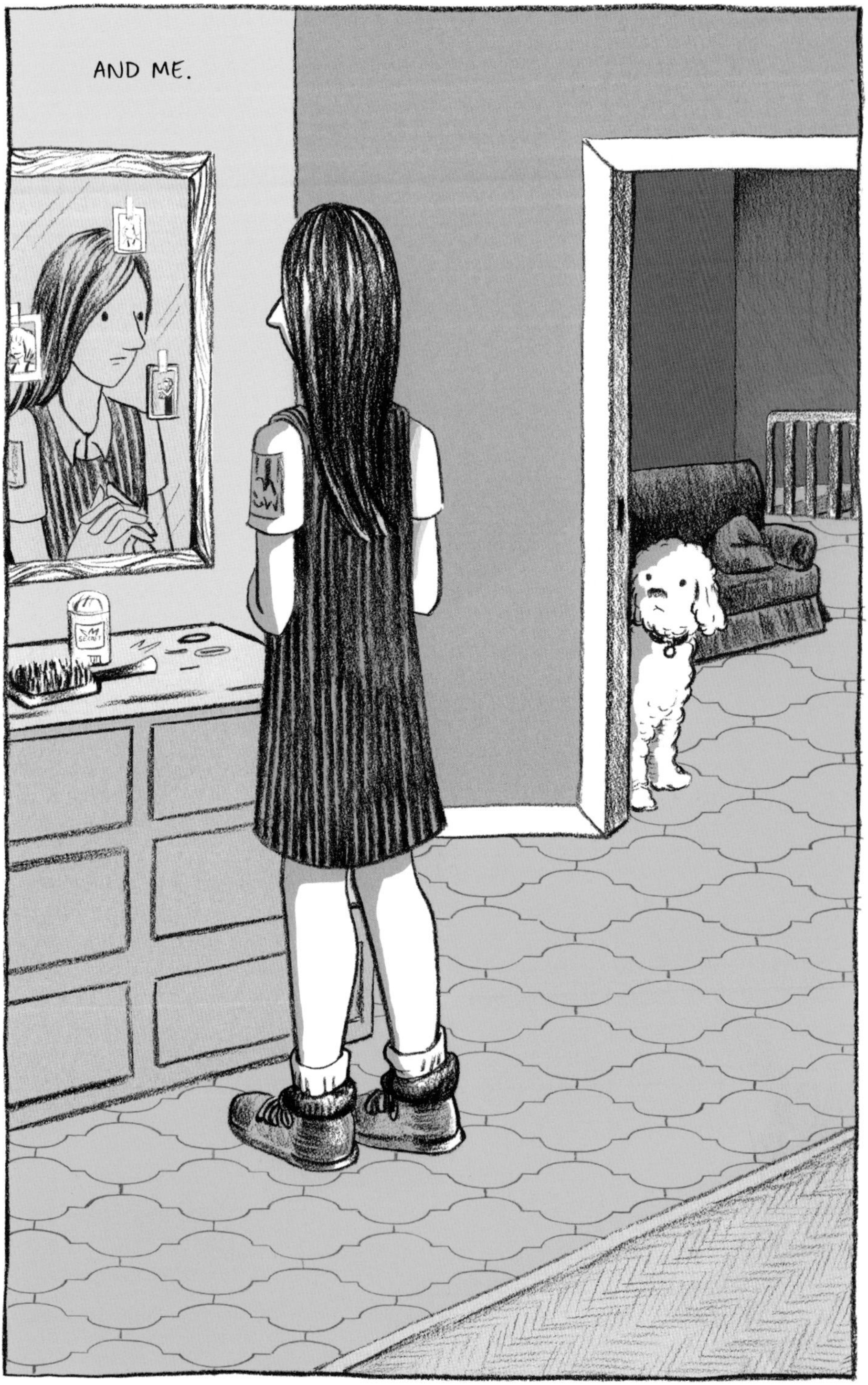
AND ME.

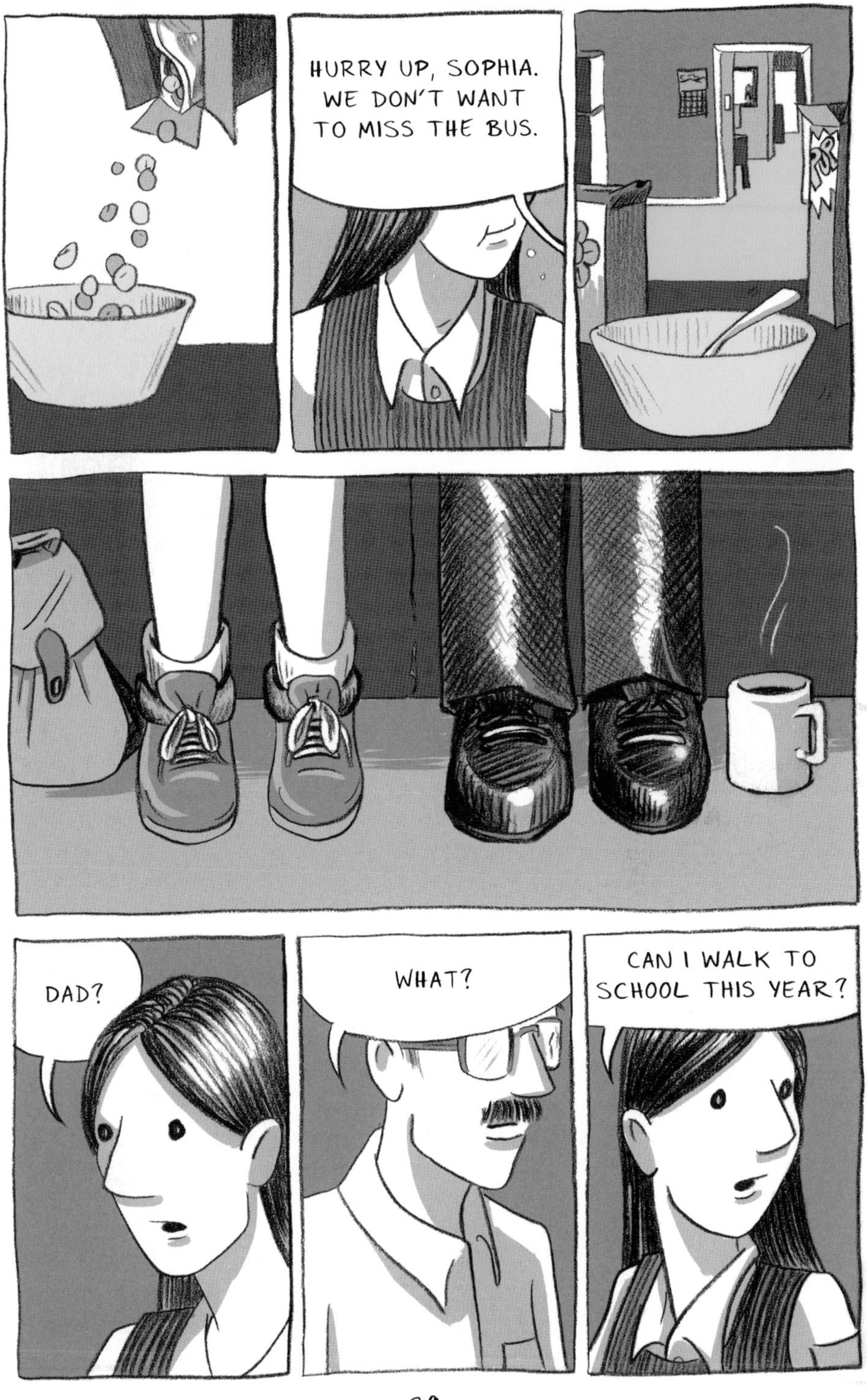
HURRY UP, SOPHIA. WE DON'T WANT TO MISS THE BUS.
POP
DAD?
WHAT?
CAN I WALK TO SCHOOL THIS YEAR?

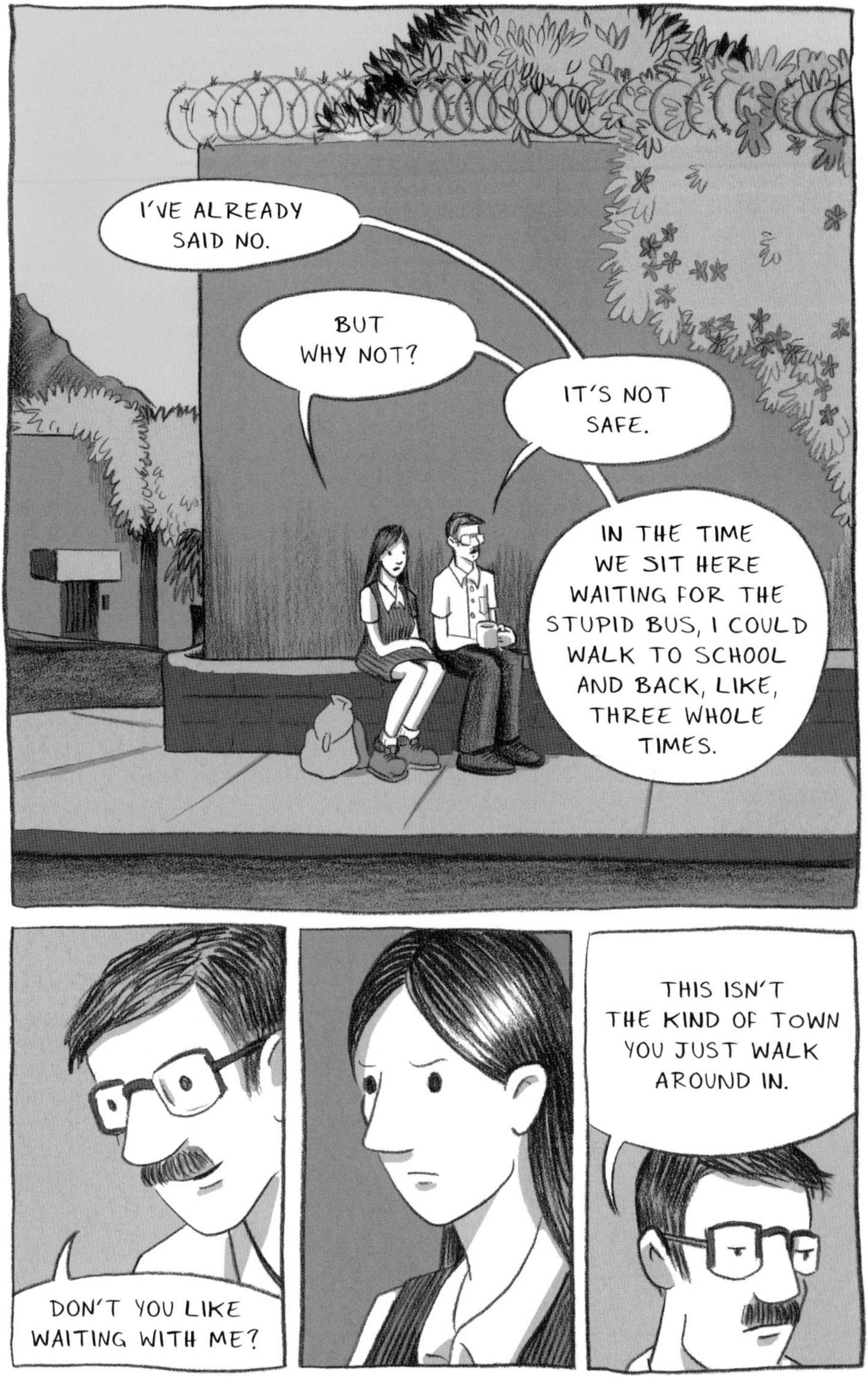
I'VE ALREADY SAID NO.
BUT WHY NOT?
IT'S NOT SAFE.
IN THE TIME WE SIT HERE WAITING FOR THE STUPID BUS, I COULD WALK TO SCHOOL AND BACK, LIKE, THREE WHOLE TIMES.
DON'T YOU LIKE WAITING WITH ME?
THIS ISN'T THE KIND OF TOWN YOU JUST WALK AROUND IN.

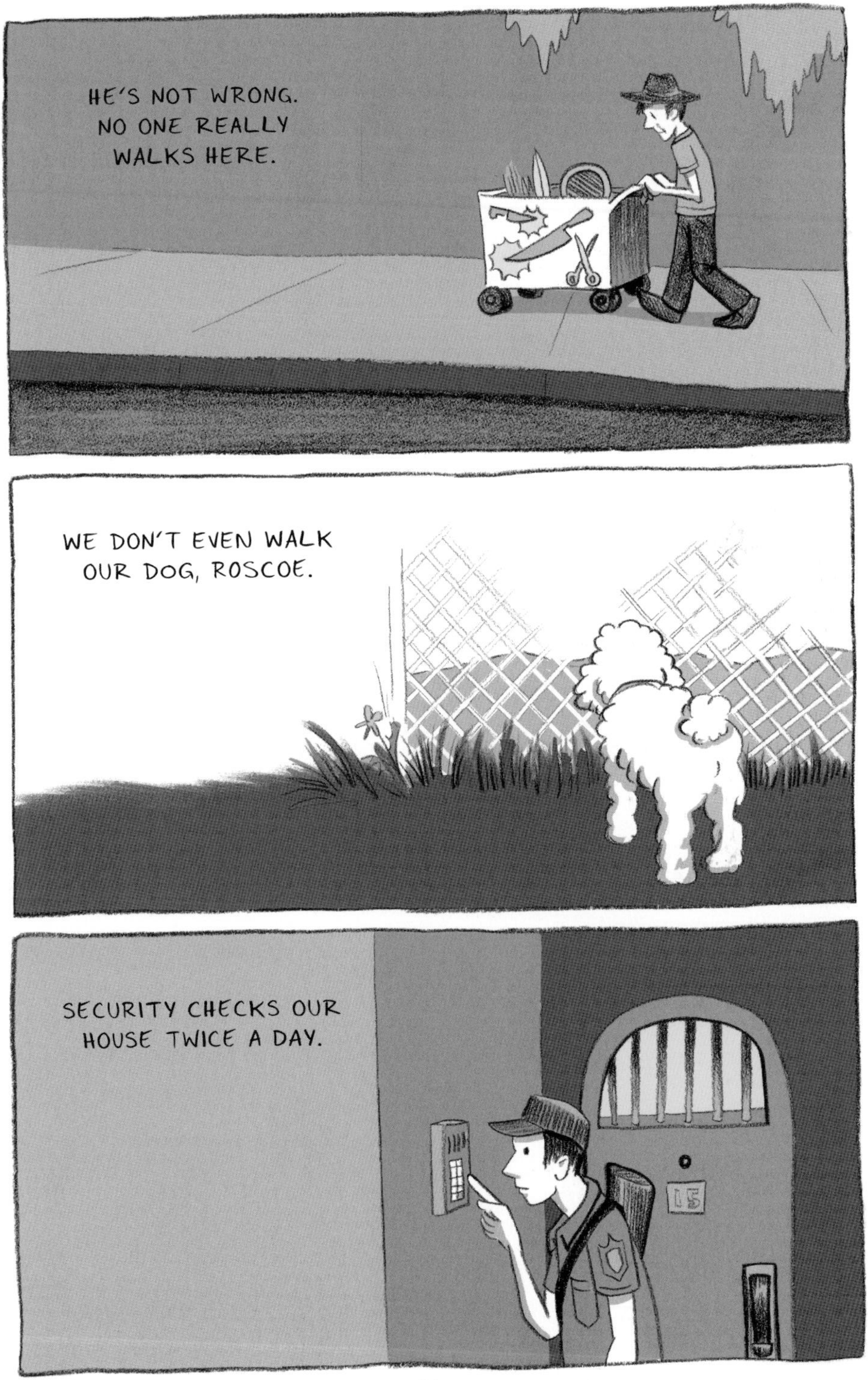
HE'S NOT WRONG. NO ONE REALLY WALKS HERE.
WE DON'T EVEN WALK OUR DOG, ROSCOE.
SECURITY CHECKS OUR HOUSE TWICE A DAY.
15

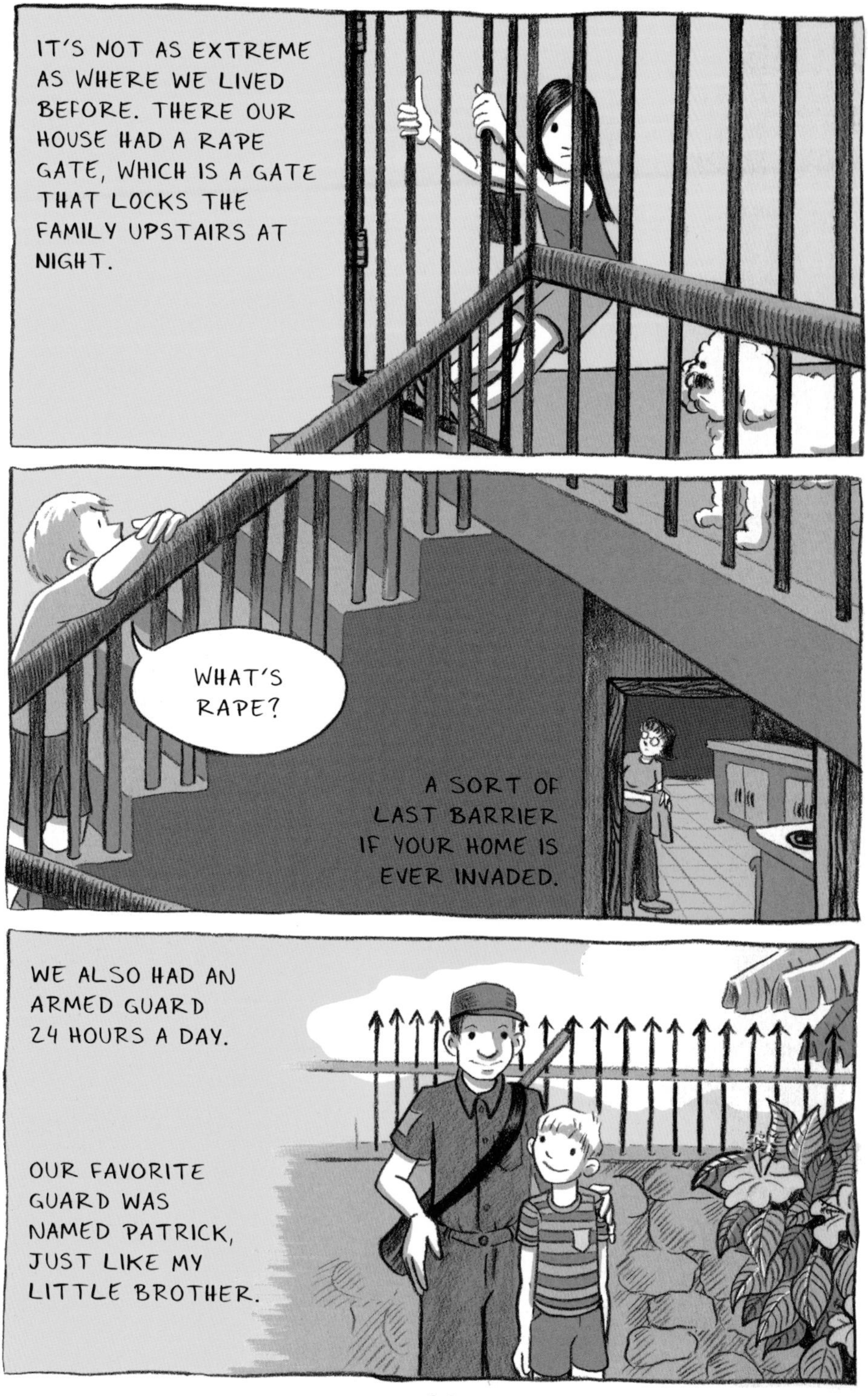
IT'S NOT AS EXTREME AS WHERE WE LIVED BEFORE. THERE OUR HOUSE HAD A RAPE GATE, WHICH IS A GATE THAT LOCKS THE FAMILY UPSTAIRS AT NIGHT.
WHAT'S RAPE?
A SORT OF LAST BARRIER IF YOUR HOME IS EVER INVADED.
WE ALSO HAD AN ARMED GUARD 24 HOURS A DAY.
OUR FAVORITE GUARD WAS NAMED PATRICK, JUST LIKE MY LITTLE BROTHER.

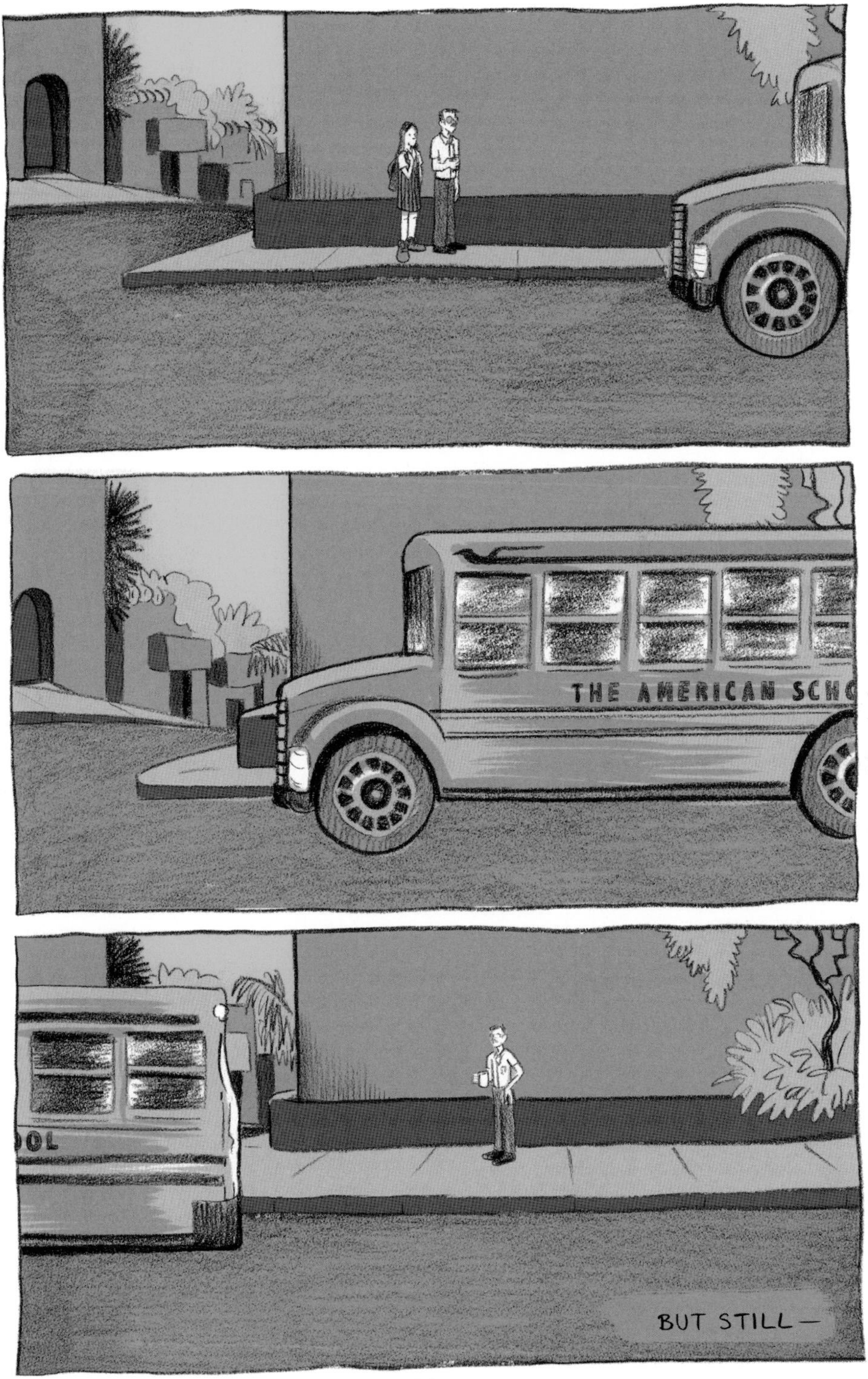
THE AMERICAN SCHO
BUT STILL—

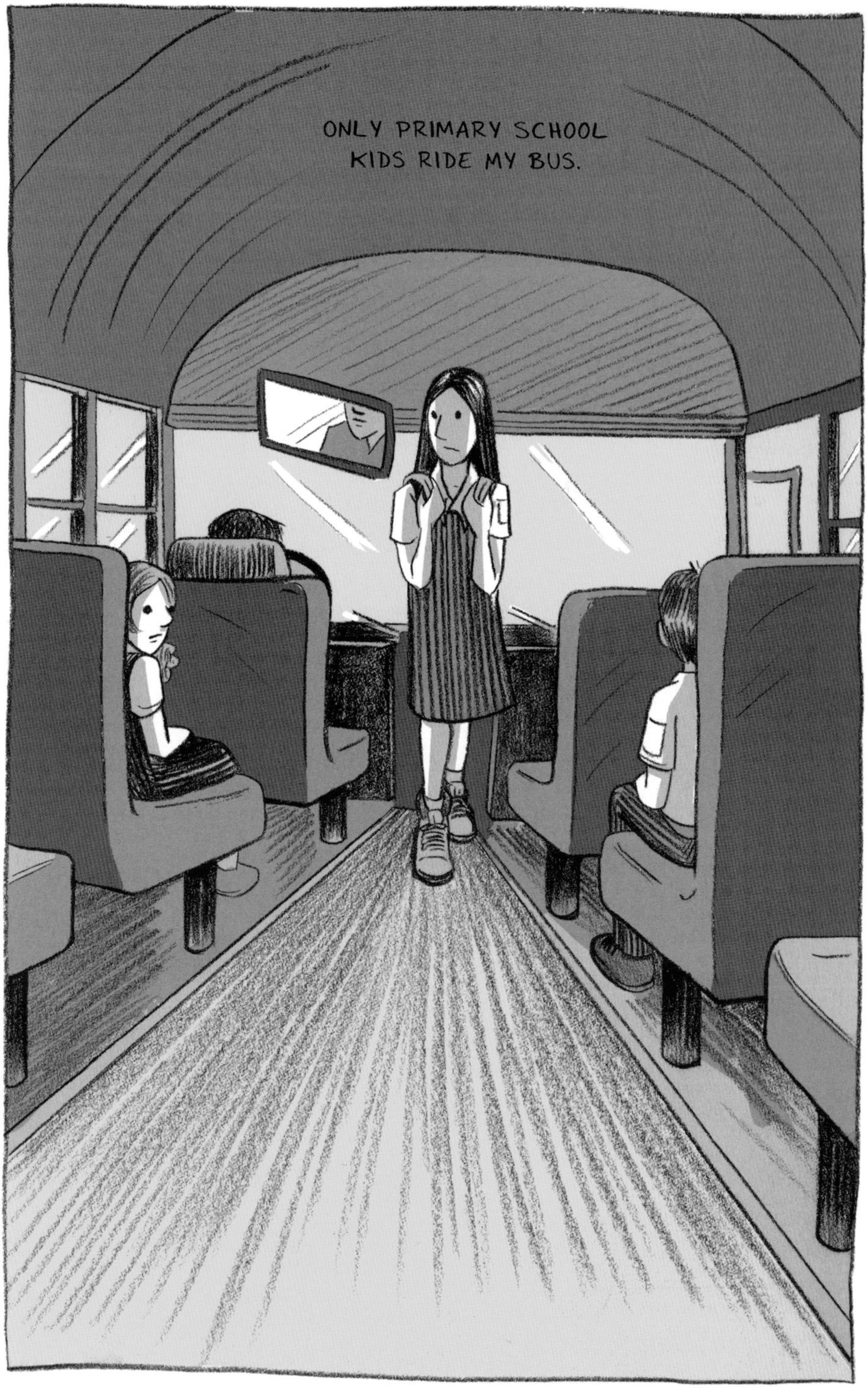
ONLY PRIMARY SCHOOL
KIDS RIDE MY BUS.

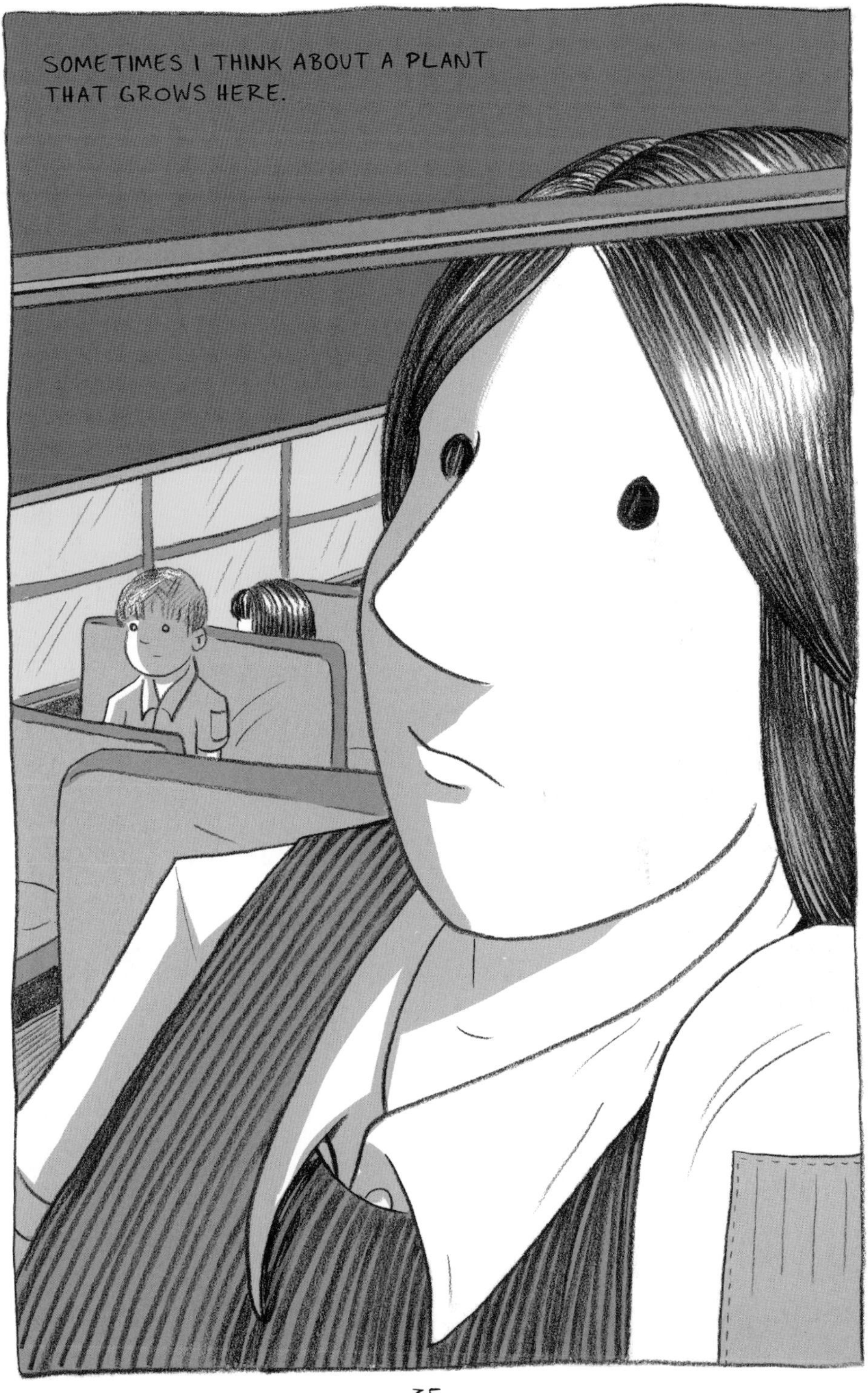
SOMETIMES I THINK ABOUT A PLANT
THAT GROWS HERE.

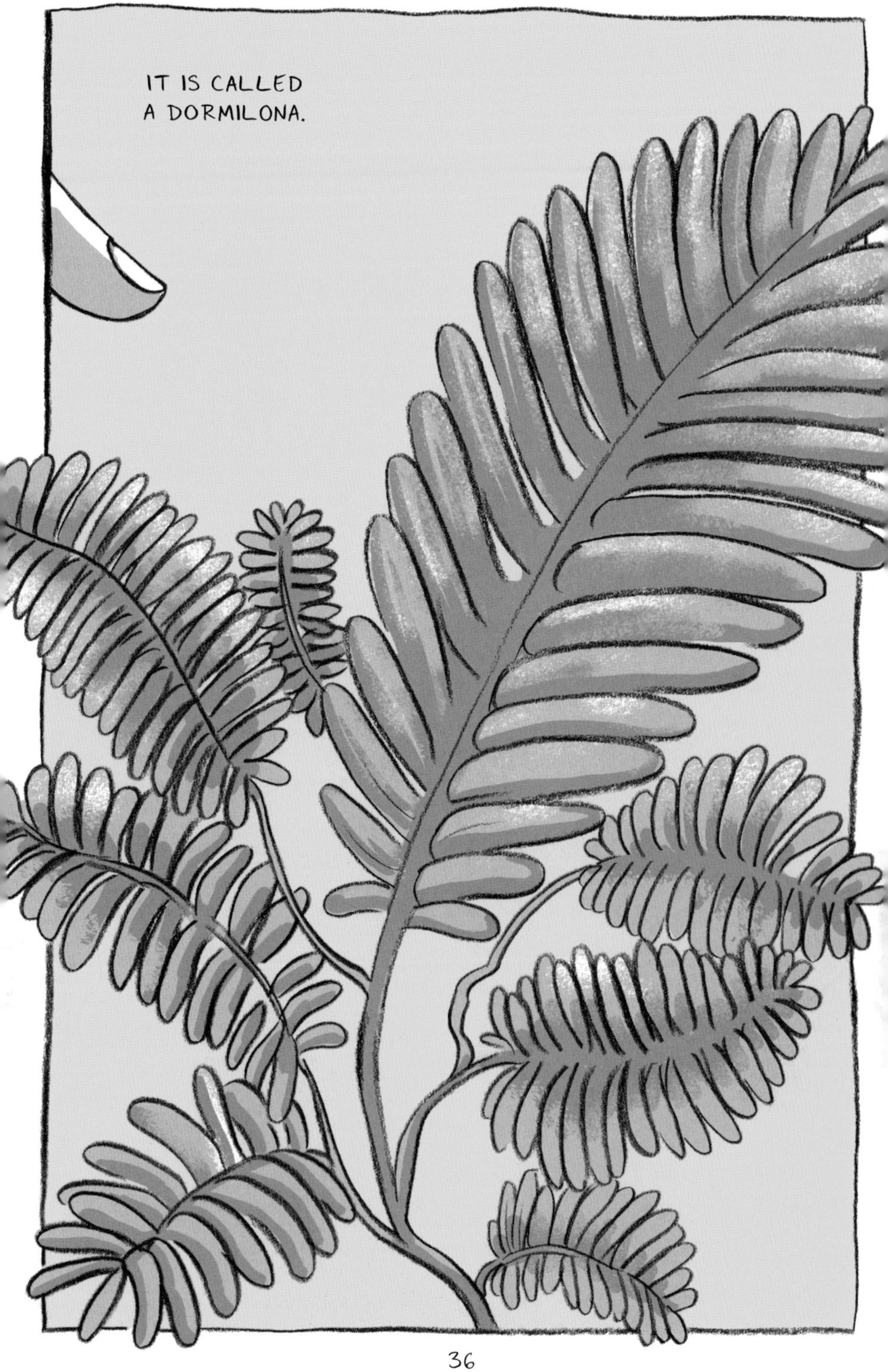
IT IS CALLED
A DORMILONA.

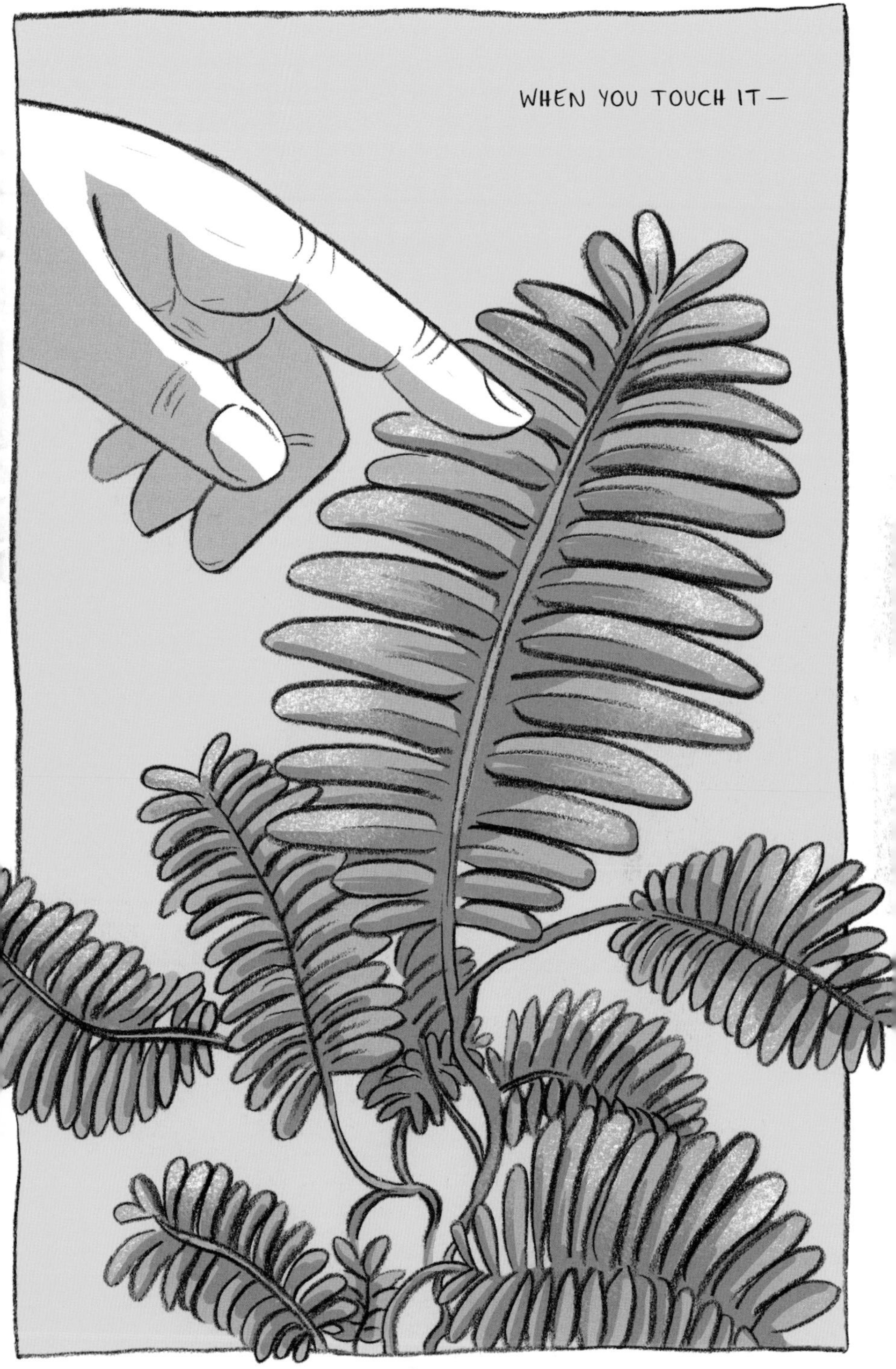
WHEN YOU TOUCH IT—

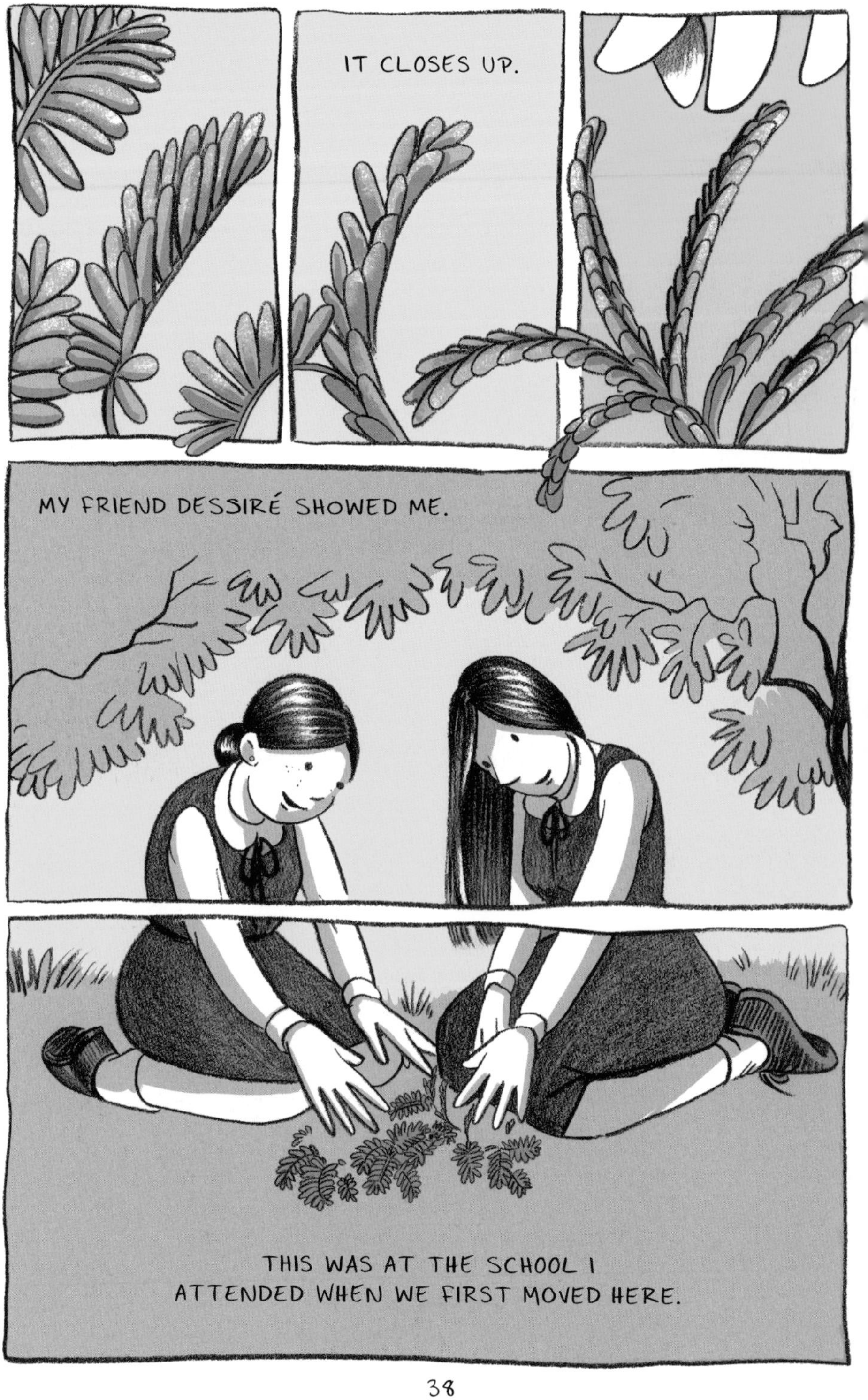
IT CLOSES UP.
MY FRIEND DESSIRÉ SHOWED ME.
THIS WAS AT THE SCHOOL I ATTENDED WHEN WE FIRST MOVED HERE.

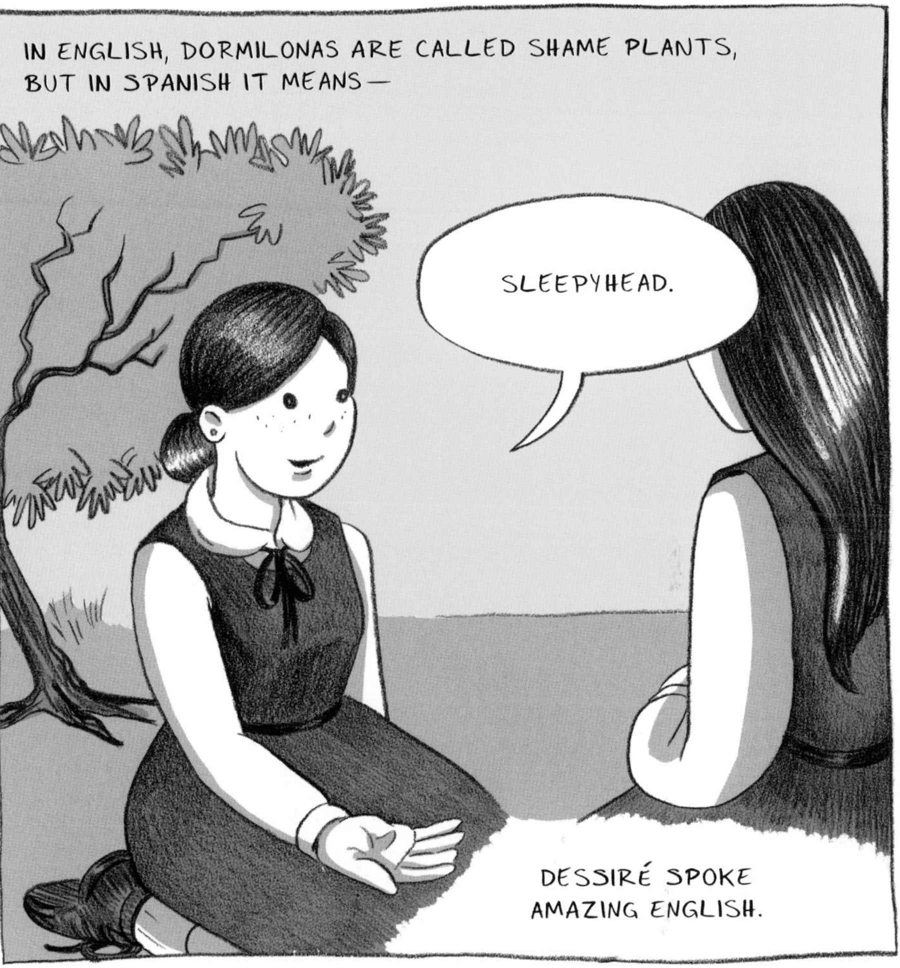
IN ENGLISH, DORMILONAS ARE CALLED SHAME PLANTS, BUT IN SPANISH IT MEANS—
SLEEPYHEAD.
DESSIRÉ SPOKE AMAZING ENGLISH.

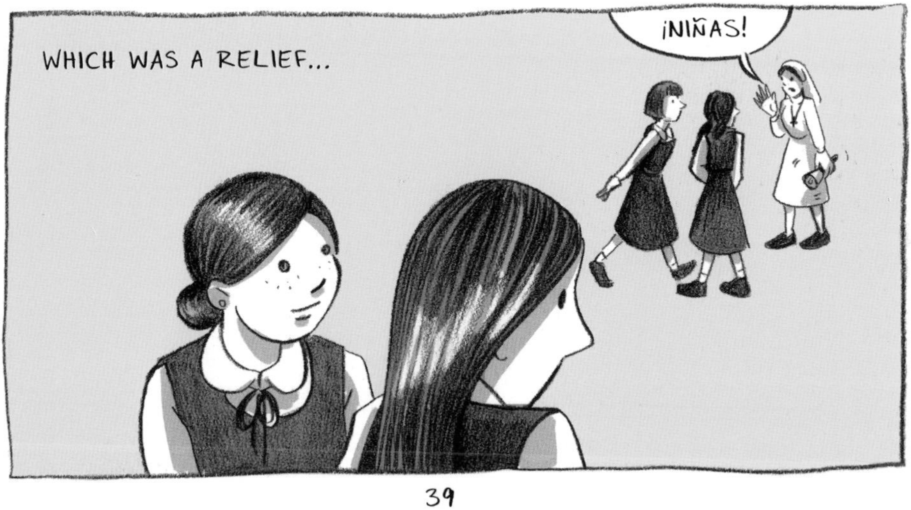
WHICH WAS A RELIEF...
¡NIÑAS!

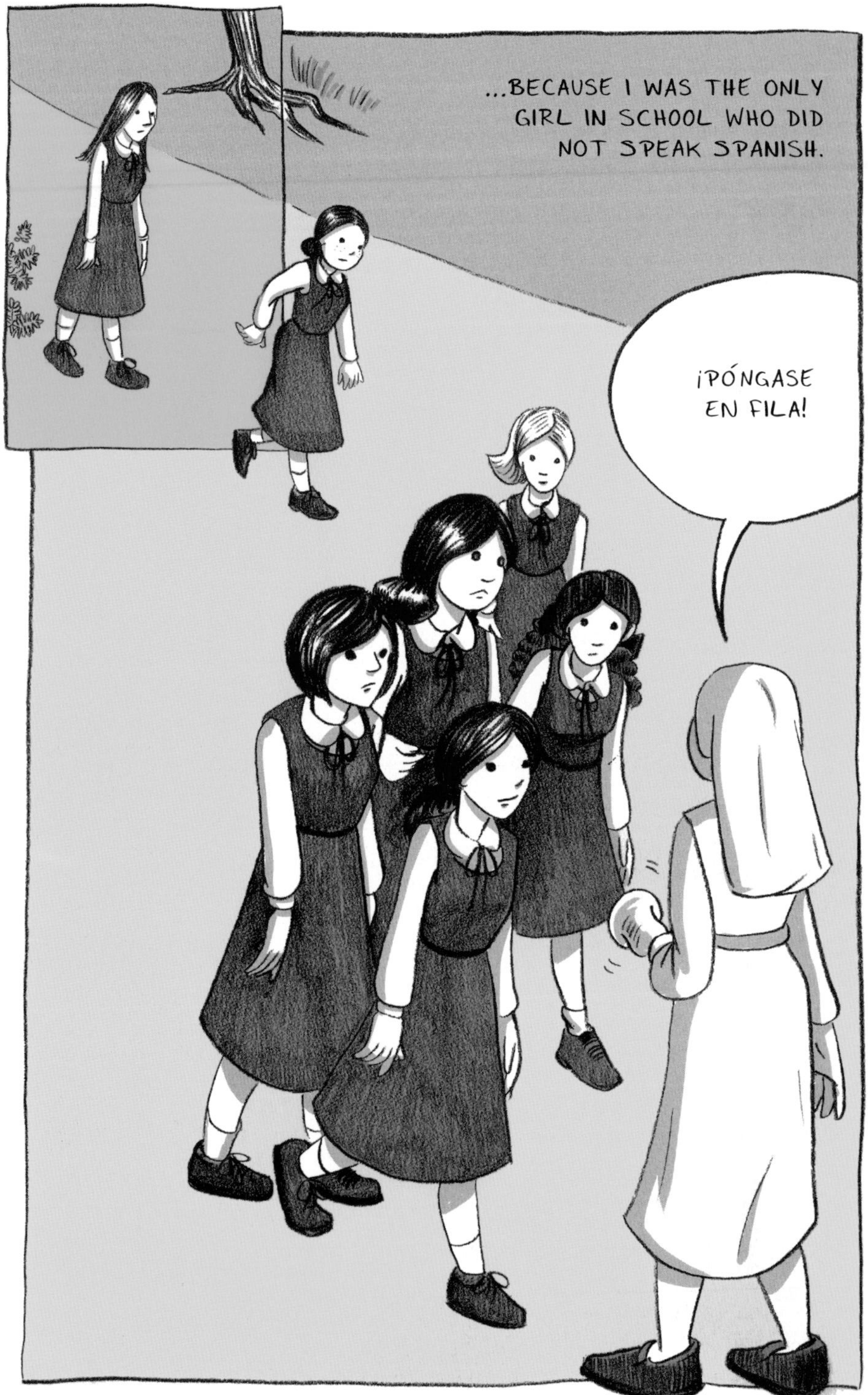
...BECAUSE I WAS THE ONLY GIRL IN SCHOOL WHO DID NOT SPEAK SPANISH.
¡PÓNGASE EN FILA!

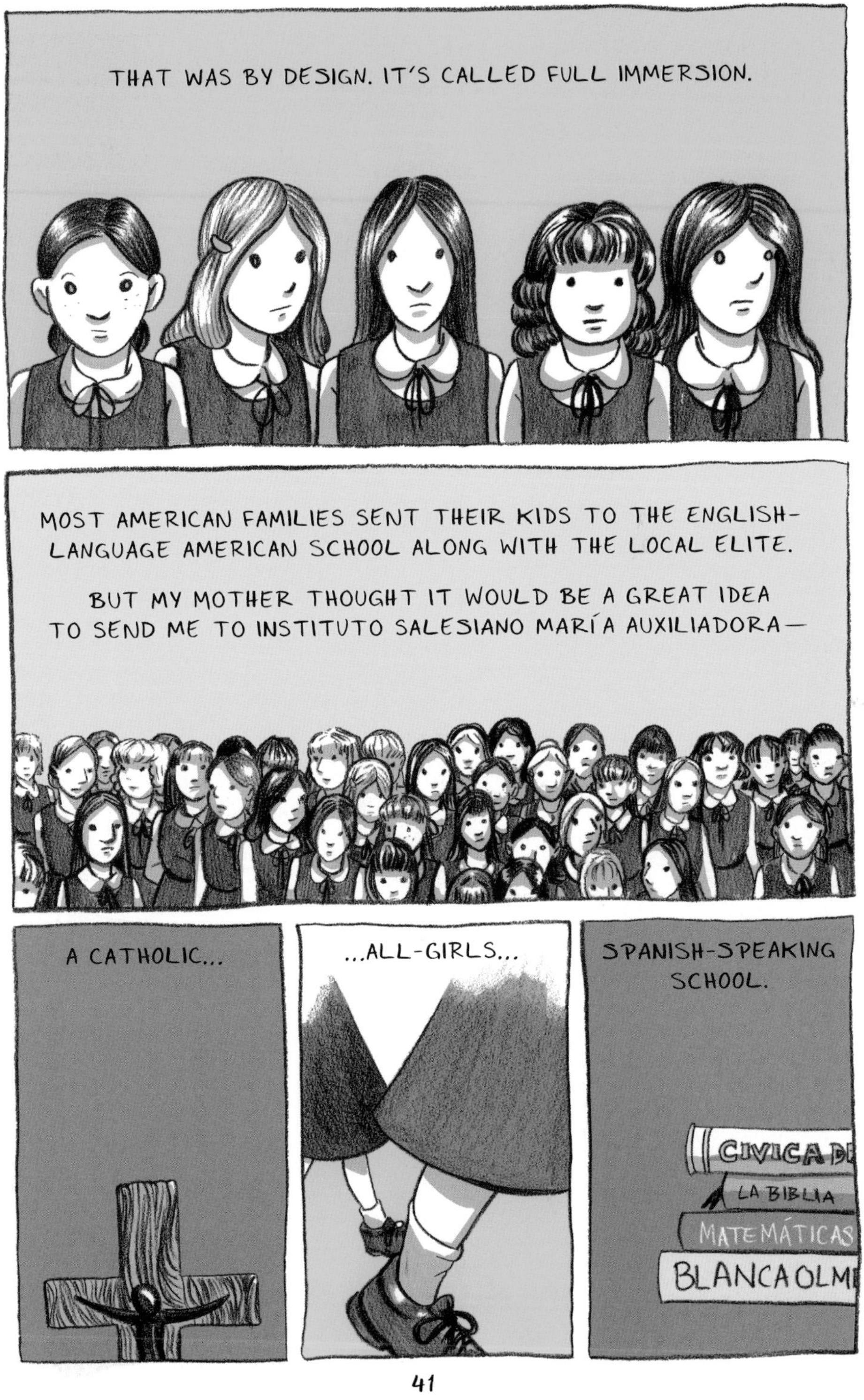
THAT WAS BY DESIGN. IT'S CALLED FULL IMMERSION.
MOST AMERICAN FAMILIES SENT THEIR KIDS TO THE ENGLISH-LANGUAGE AMERICAN SCHOOL ALONG WITH THE LOCAL ELITE.
BUT MY MOTHER THOUGHT IT WOULD BE A GREAT IDEA TO SEND ME TO INSTITUTO SALESIANO MARÍA AUXILIADORA—
A CATHOLIC...
...ALL-GIRLS...
SPANISH-SPEAKING SCHOOL.
LA BIBLIA
MATEMÁTICAS

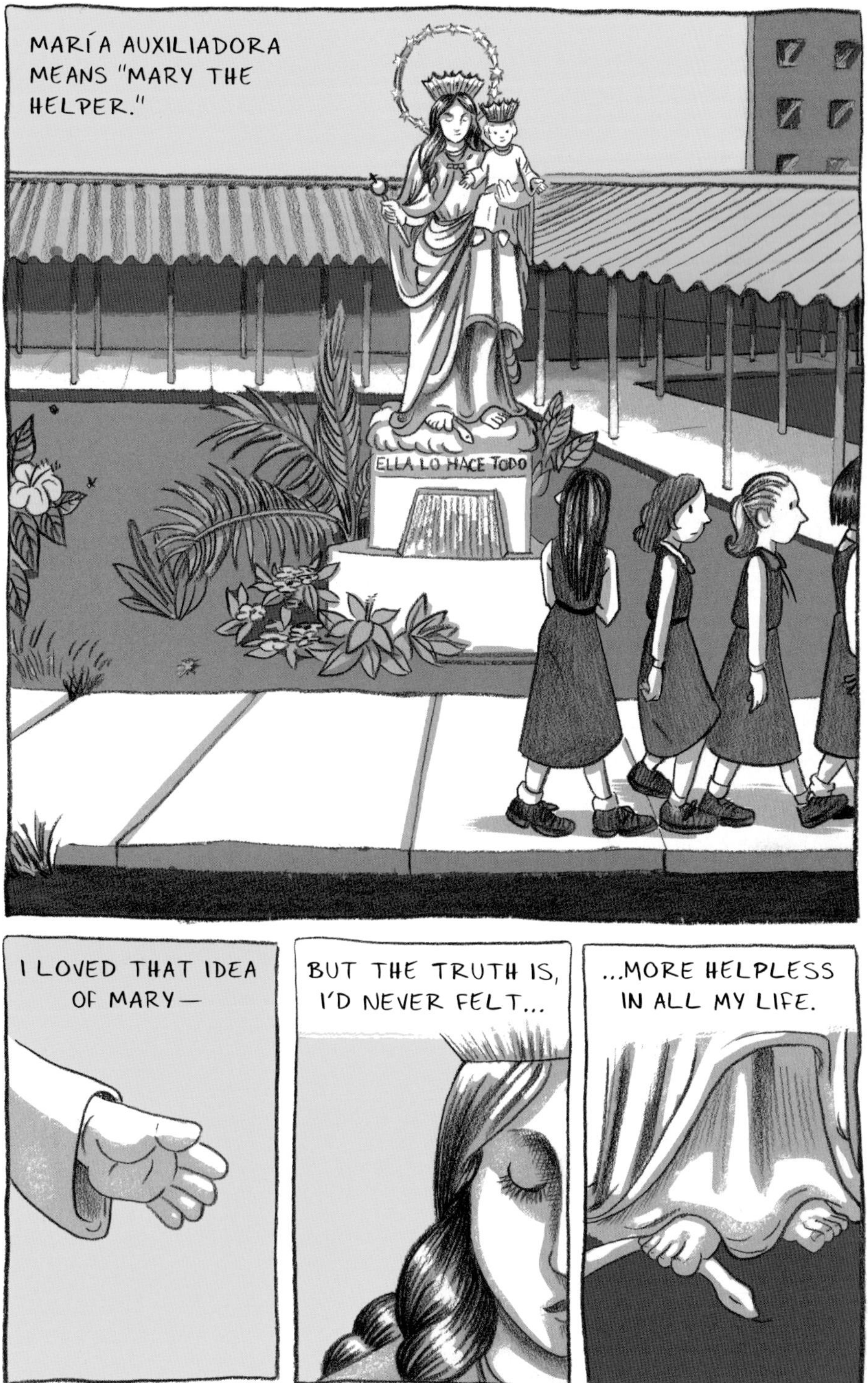
MARÍA AUXILIADORA MEANS "MARY THE HELPER."
ELLA LO HACE TODO
I LOVED THAT IDEA OF MARY—
BUT THE TRUTH IS, I'D NEVER FELT...
...MORE HELPLESS IN ALL MY LIFE.

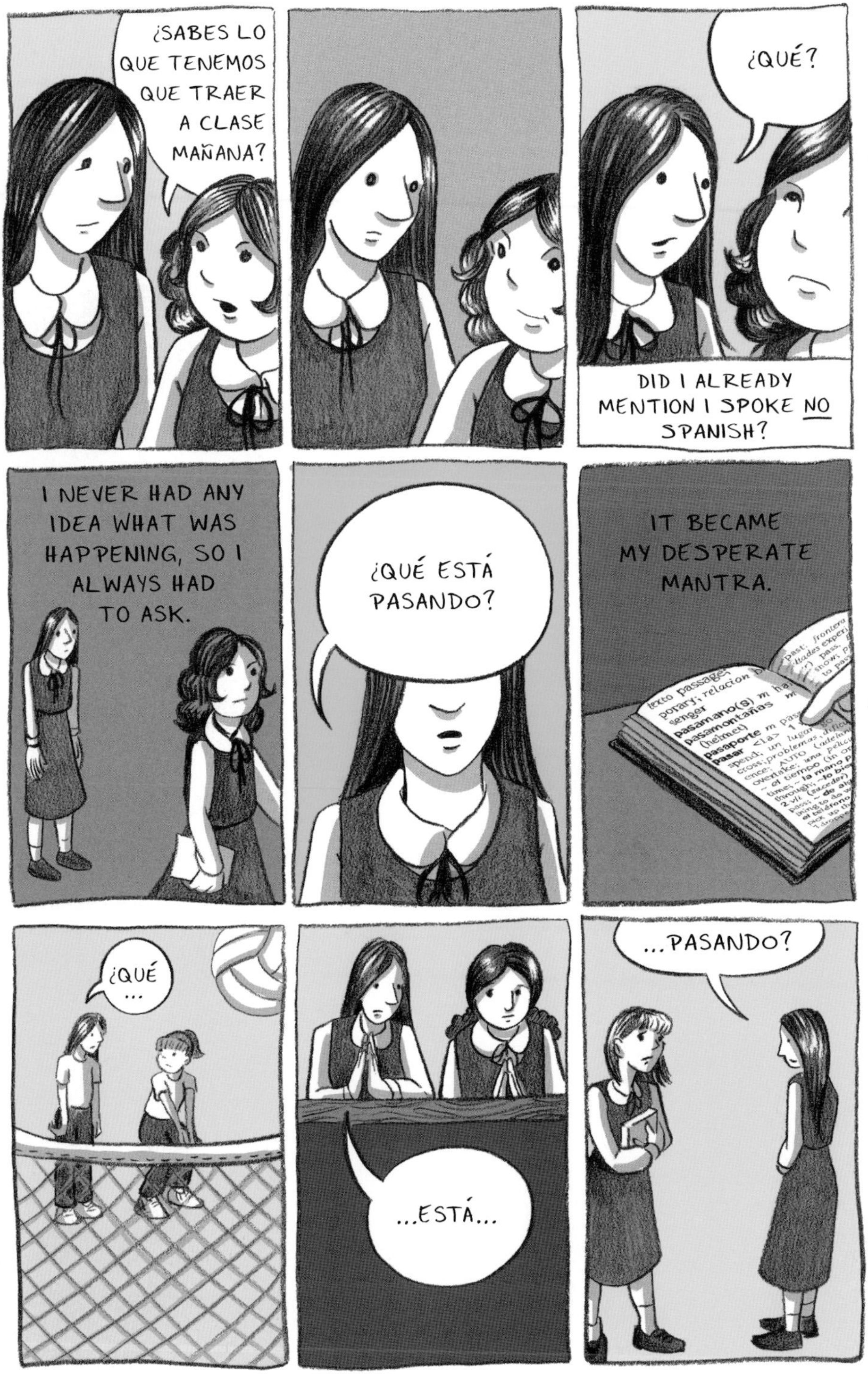
¿SABES LO QUE TENEMOS QUE TRAER A CLASE MAÑANA?
¿QUÉ?
DID I ALREADY MENTION I SPOKE NO SPANISH?
I NEVER HAD ANY IDEA WHAT WAS HAPPENING, SO I ALWAYS HAD TO ASK.
¿QUÉ ESTÁ PASANDO?
IT BECAME MY DESPERATE MANTRA.
¿QUÉ ...
...ESTÁ...
...PASANDO?

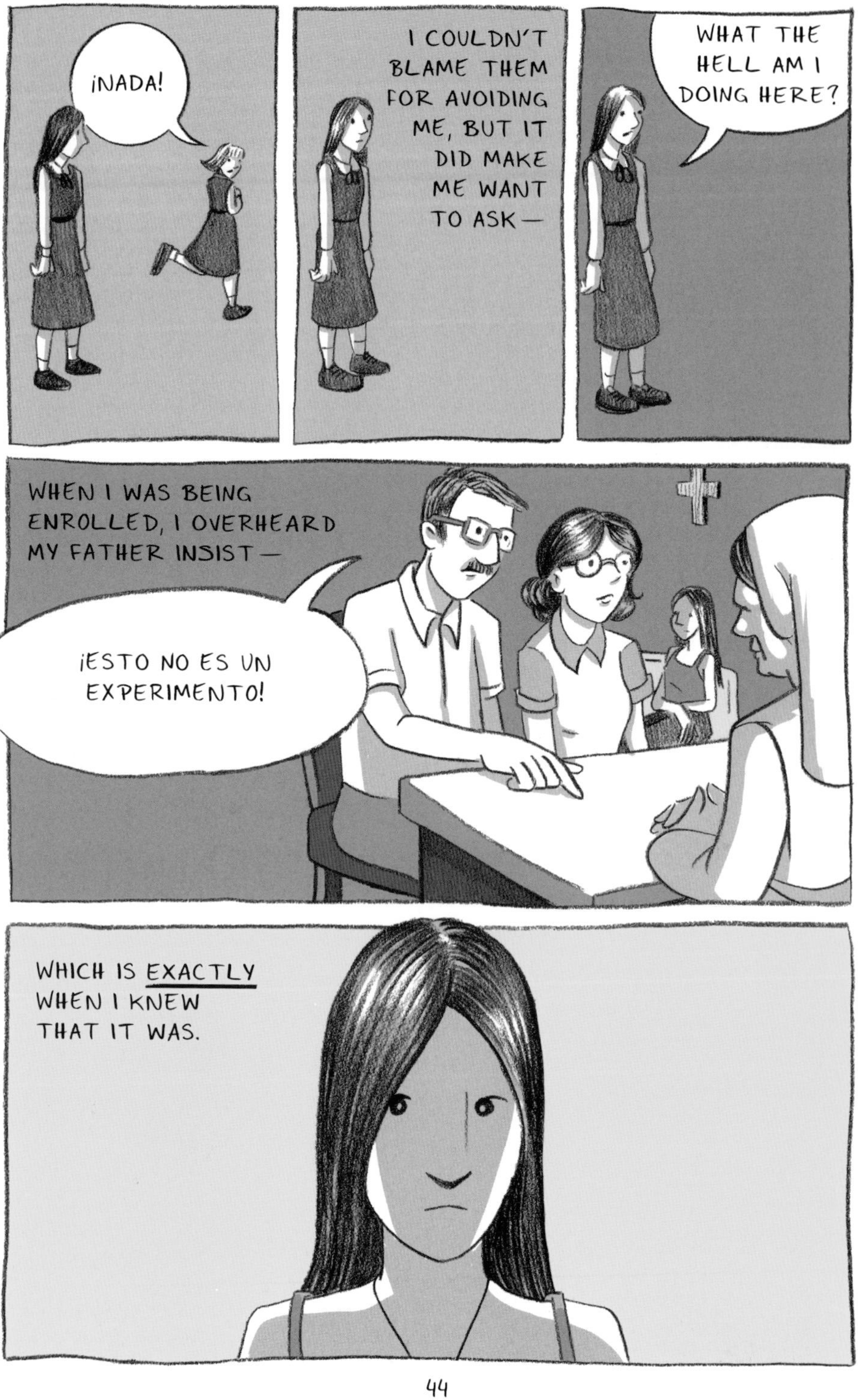
¡NADA!
I COULDN'T BLAME THEM FOR AVOIDING ME, BUT IT DID MAKE ME WANT TO ASK—
WHAT THE HELL AM I DOING HERE?
WHEN I WAS BEING ENROLLED, I OVERHEARD MY FATHER INSIST—
¡ESTO NO ES UN EXPERIMENTO!
WHICH IS EXACTLY WHEN I KNEW THAT IT WAS.

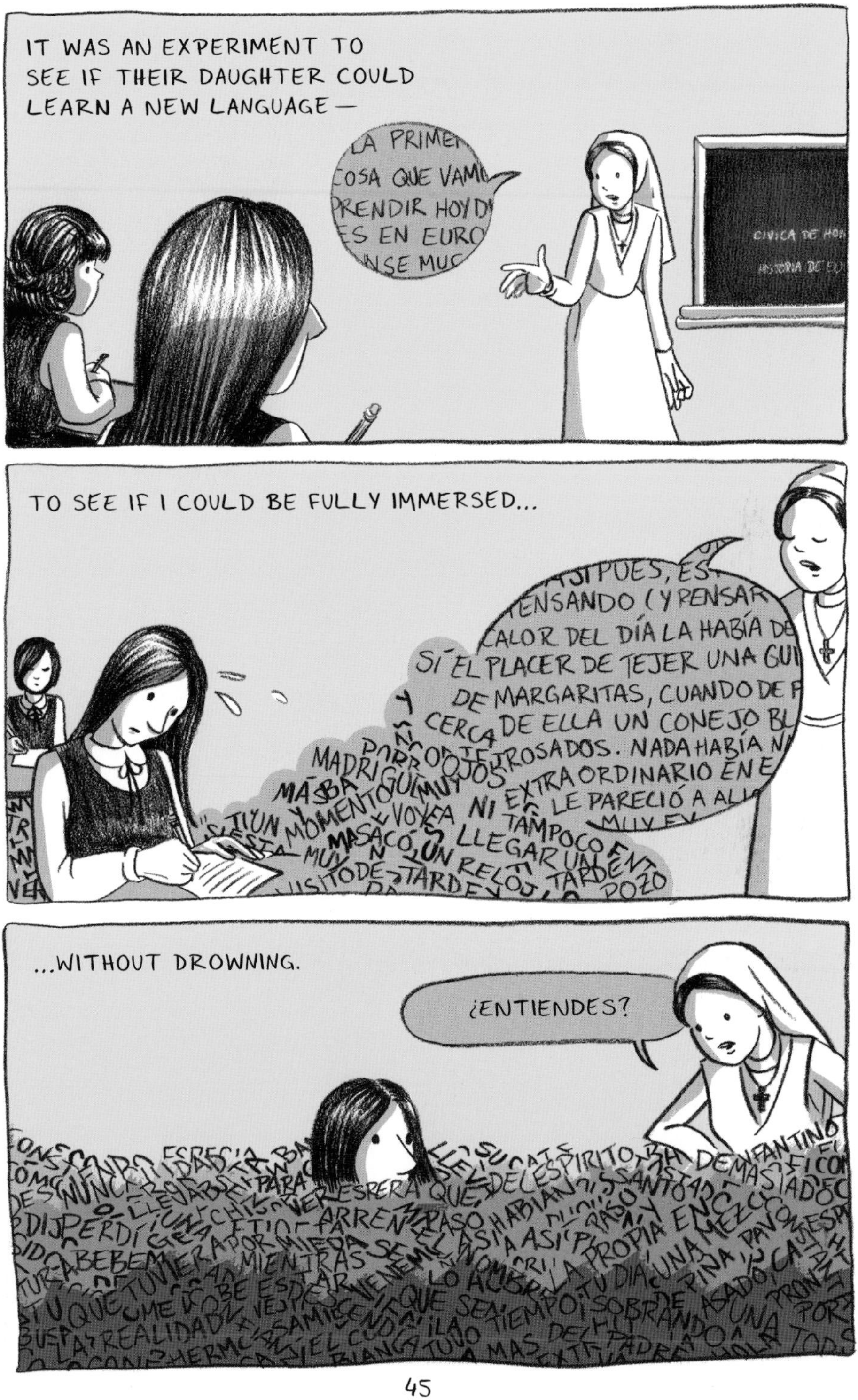
IT WAS AN EXPERIMENT TO SEE IF THEIR DAUGHTER COULD LEARN A NEW LANGUAGE—
LA PRIME
COSA QUE VAM
PRENDIR HOY D
ES EN EURO
TO SEE IF I COULD BE FULLY IMMERSED...
PENSANDO (Y PENSAR
CALOR DEL DÍA LA HABÍA DE
SÍ EL PLACER DE TEJER UNA GUI
DE MARGARITAS, CUANDO DE P
DE ELLA UN CONEJO BL
ROSADOS. NADA HABÍA N
EXTRA ORDINARIO EN E
LE PARECIÓ A ALI
...WITHOUT DROWNING.
¿ENTIENDES?

THERE WASN'T MUCH REPRIEVE AT HOME.

HI, MOM!

¡HOLA! ♪

TODAY WAS TOU—

¡EN ESPAÑOL!

WHAT?

¡NECESITAMOS PRACTICAR NUESTRO ESPAÑOL!

I'VE BEEN PRACTICING ALL DAY.

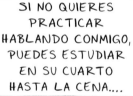

SI NO QUIERES PRACTICAR HABLANDO CONMIGO, PUEDES ESTUDIAR EN SU CUARTO HASTA LA CENA....

FINE!

SLAM!

THUNK

THUNK

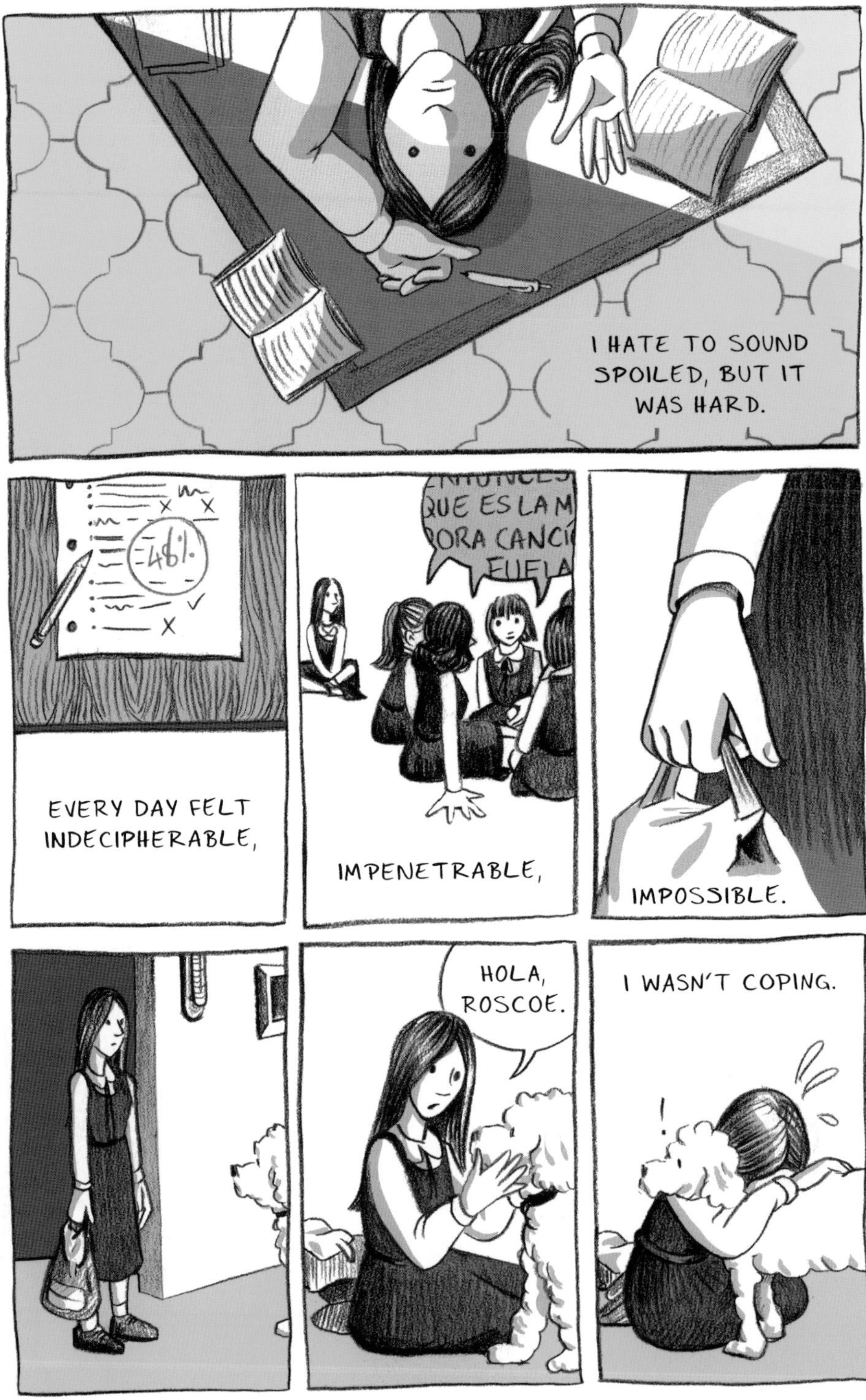

I HATE TO SOUND SPOILED, BUT IT WAS HARD.
48%
EVERY DAY FELT INDECIPHERABLE,
IMPENETRABLE,
IMPOSSIBLE.
HOLA, ROSCOE.
I WASN'T COPING.

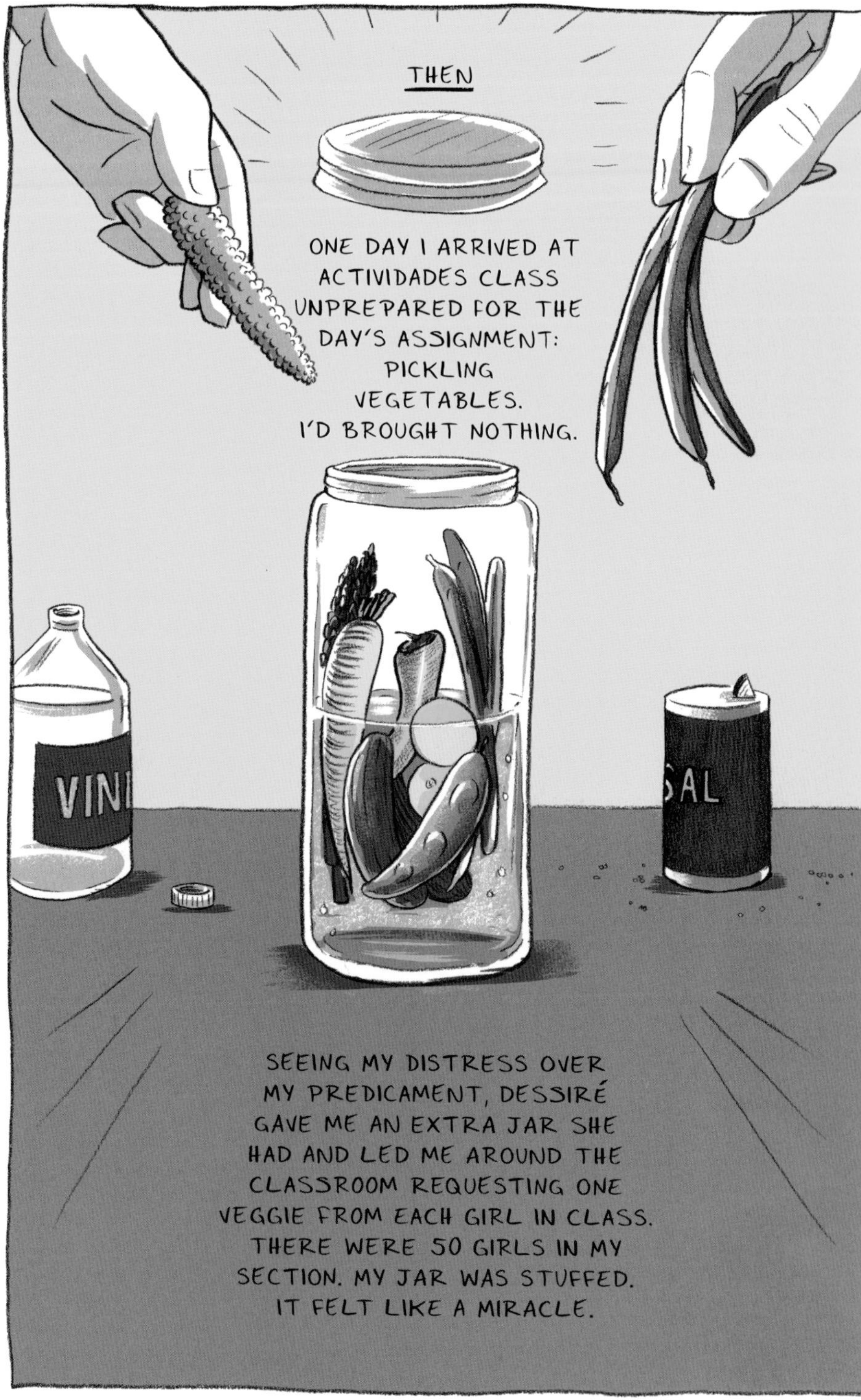
THEN
ONE DAY I ARRIVED AT ACTIVIDADES CLASS UNPREPARED FOR THE DAY'S ASSIGNMENT: PICKLING VEGETABLES. I'D BROUGHT NOTHING.
VIN
SAL
SEEING MY DISTRESS OVER MY PREDICAMENT, DESSIRÉ GAVE ME AN EXTRA JAR SHE HAD AND LED ME AROUND THE CLASSROOM REQUESTING ONE VEGGIE FROM EACH GIRL IN CLASS. THERE WERE 50 GIRLS IN MY SECTION. MY JAR WAS STUFFED. IT FELT LIKE A MIRACLE.

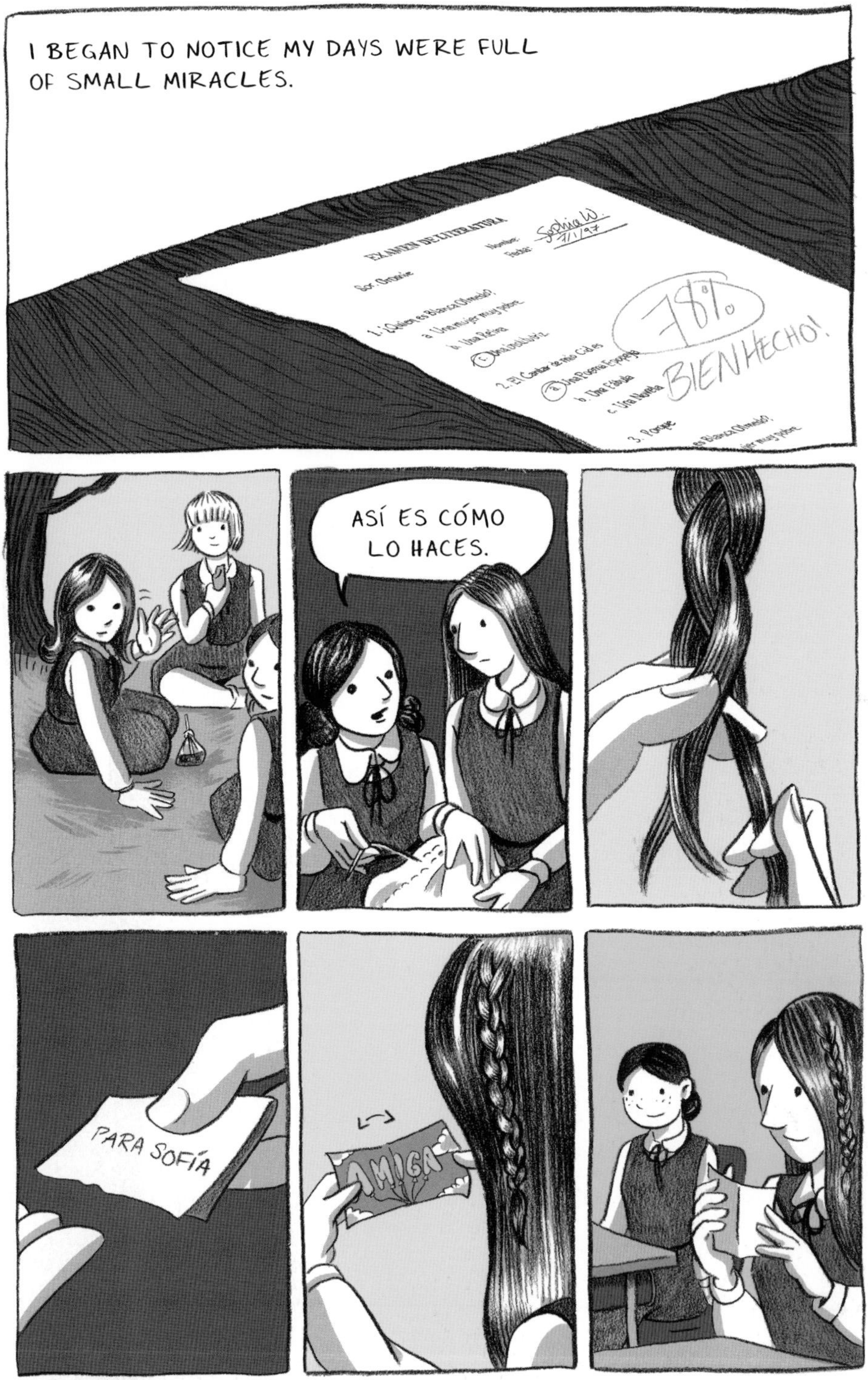

I BEGAN TO NOTICE MY DAYS WERE FULL OF SMALL MIRACLES.
EXAMEN DE LITERATURA
Nombre: Sophia W.
Fecha: 7/1/97
1. ¿Quien es Blanca Olmedo?
a. Una mujer muy pobre
b. Una Reina
2. El Cantar de mio Cid es
a. Una Poema Epopeya
b. Una Fábula
c. Una Novela
3. Porque
78%
BIEN HECHO!
ASÍ ES CÓMO LO HACES.
PARA SOFÍA
AMIGA

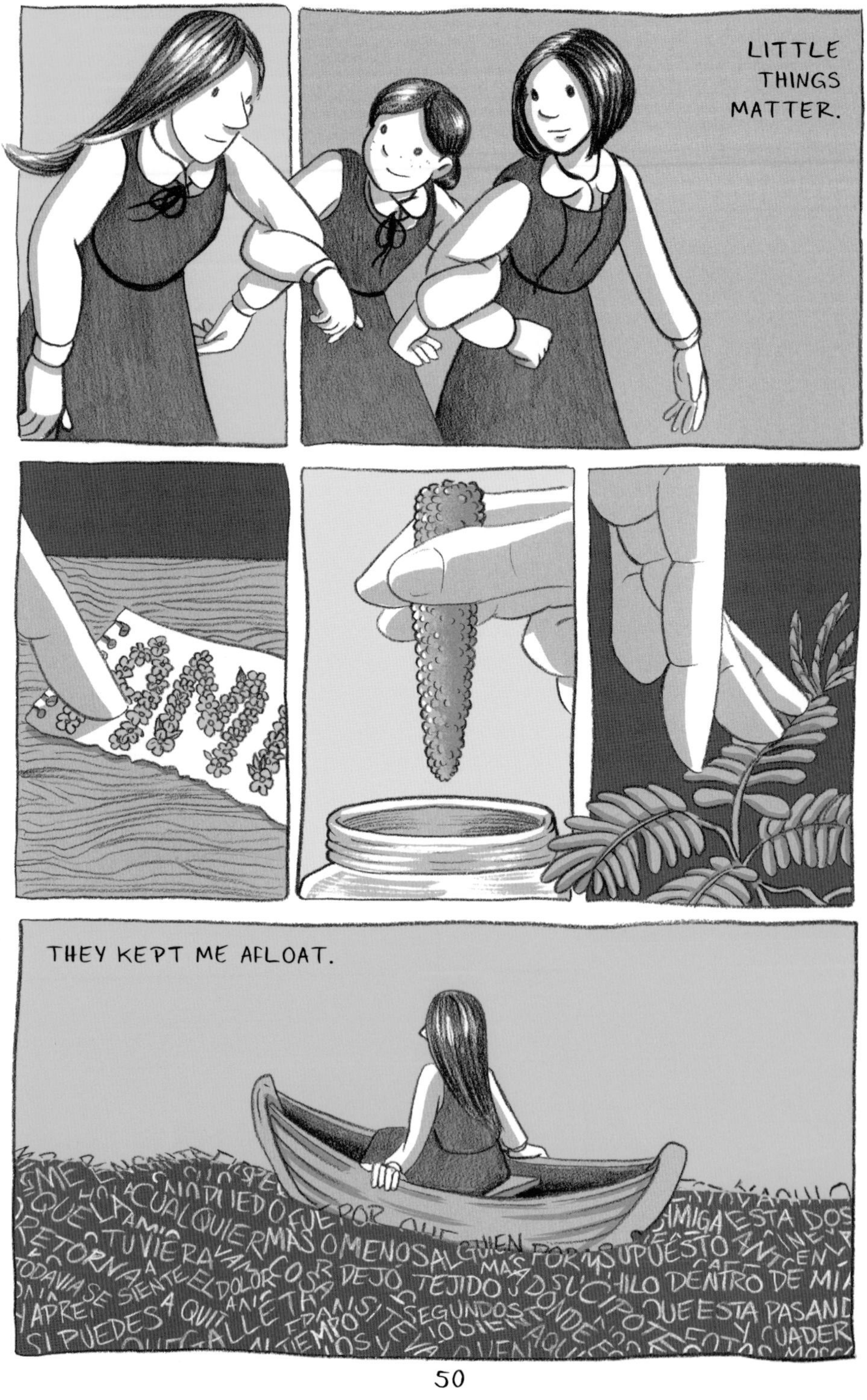
LITTLE THINGS MATTER.
THEY KEPT ME AFLOAT.

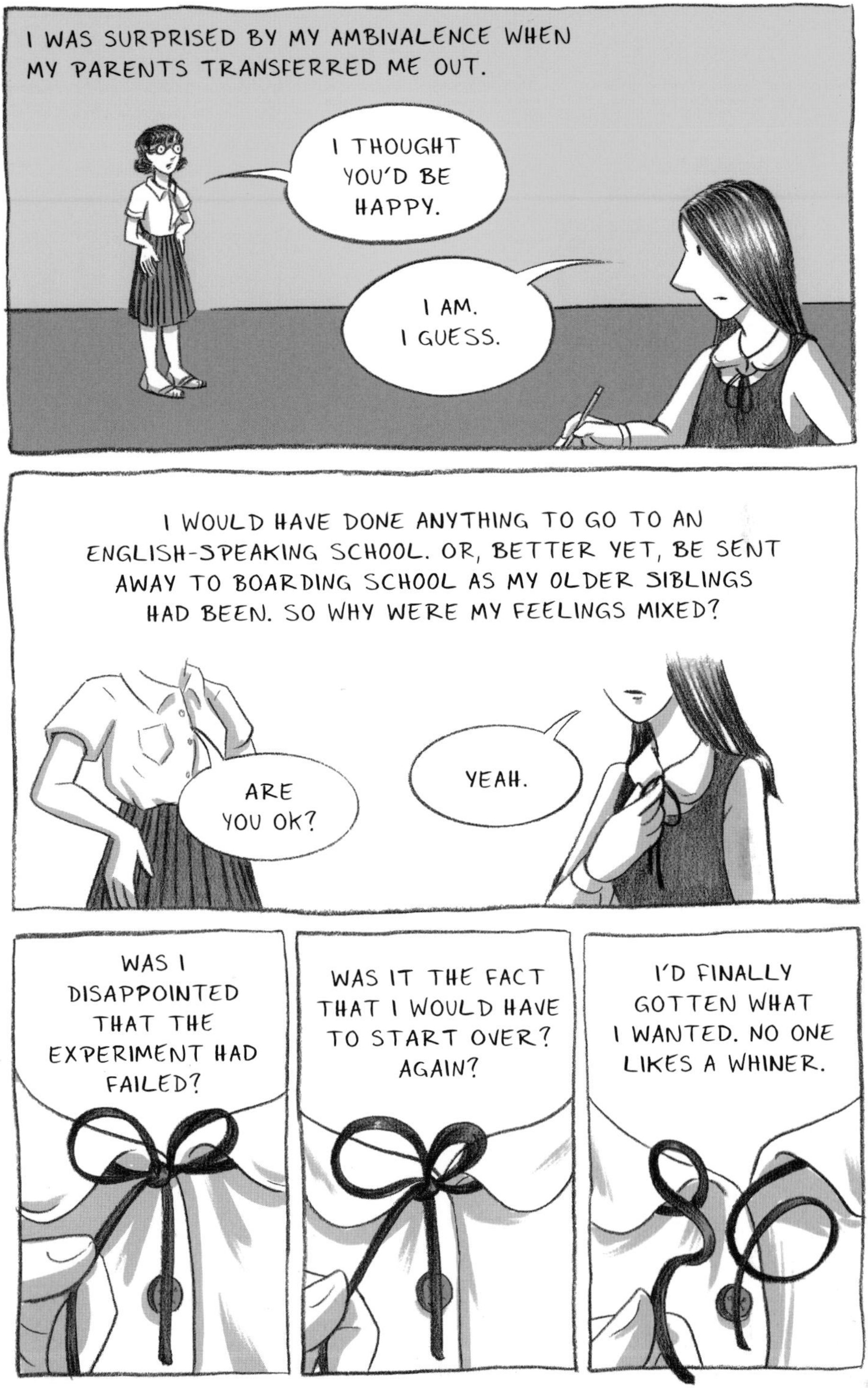

I WAS SURPRISED BY MY AMBIVALENCE WHEN MY PARENTS TRANSFERRED ME OUT.
I THOUGHT YOU'D BE HAPPY.
I AM. I GUESS.
I WOULD HAVE DONE ANYTHING TO GO TO AN ENGLISH-SPEAKING SCHOOL. OR, BETTER YET, BE SENT AWAY TO BOARDING SCHOOL AS MY OLDER SIBLINGS HAD BEEN. SO WHY WERE MY FEELINGS MIXED?
ARE YOU OK?
YEAH.
WAS I DISAPPOINTED THAT THE EXPERIMENT HAD FAILED?
WAS IT THE FACT THAT I WOULD HAVE TO START OVER? AGAIN?
I'D FINALLY GOTTEN WHAT I WANTED. NO ONE LIKES A WHINER.

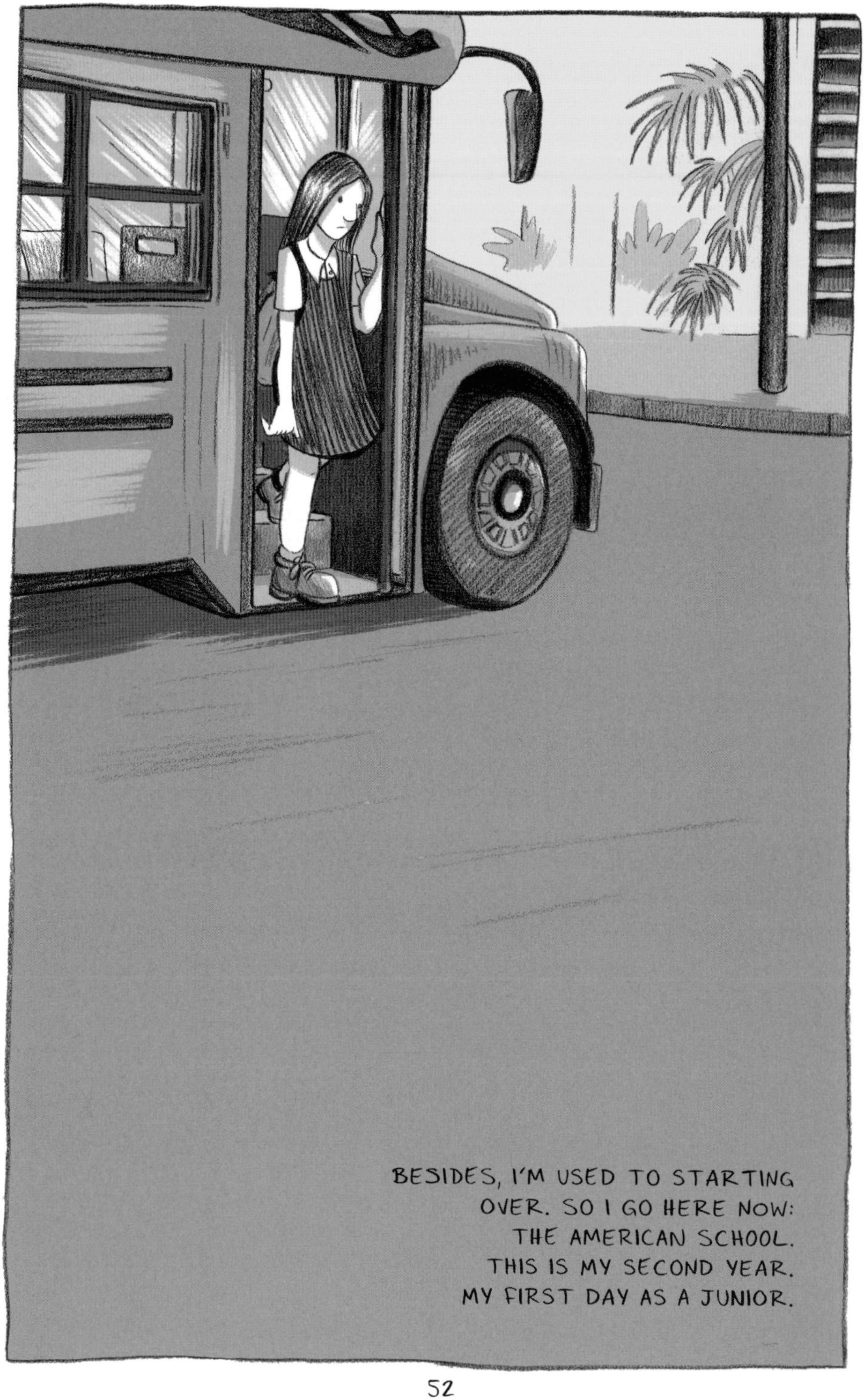
BESIDES, I'M USED TO STARTING OVER. SO I GO HERE NOW: THE AMERICAN SCHOOL. THIS IS MY SECOND YEAR. MY FIRST DAY AS A JUNIOR.

EVERYTHING IS DIFFERENT AT THIS SCHOOL.

IT'S EXCLUSIVE.

THERE ARE A LOT OF RICH KIDS.

THEY DON'T RIDE THE BUS.

THERE ARE ARMED GUARDS.

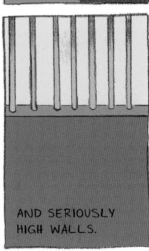

AND SERIOUSLY HIGH WALLS.

AS MY MOTHER IS CONSTANTLY REMINDING ME, KIDNAPPINGS ACTUALLY DO HAPPEN HERE.

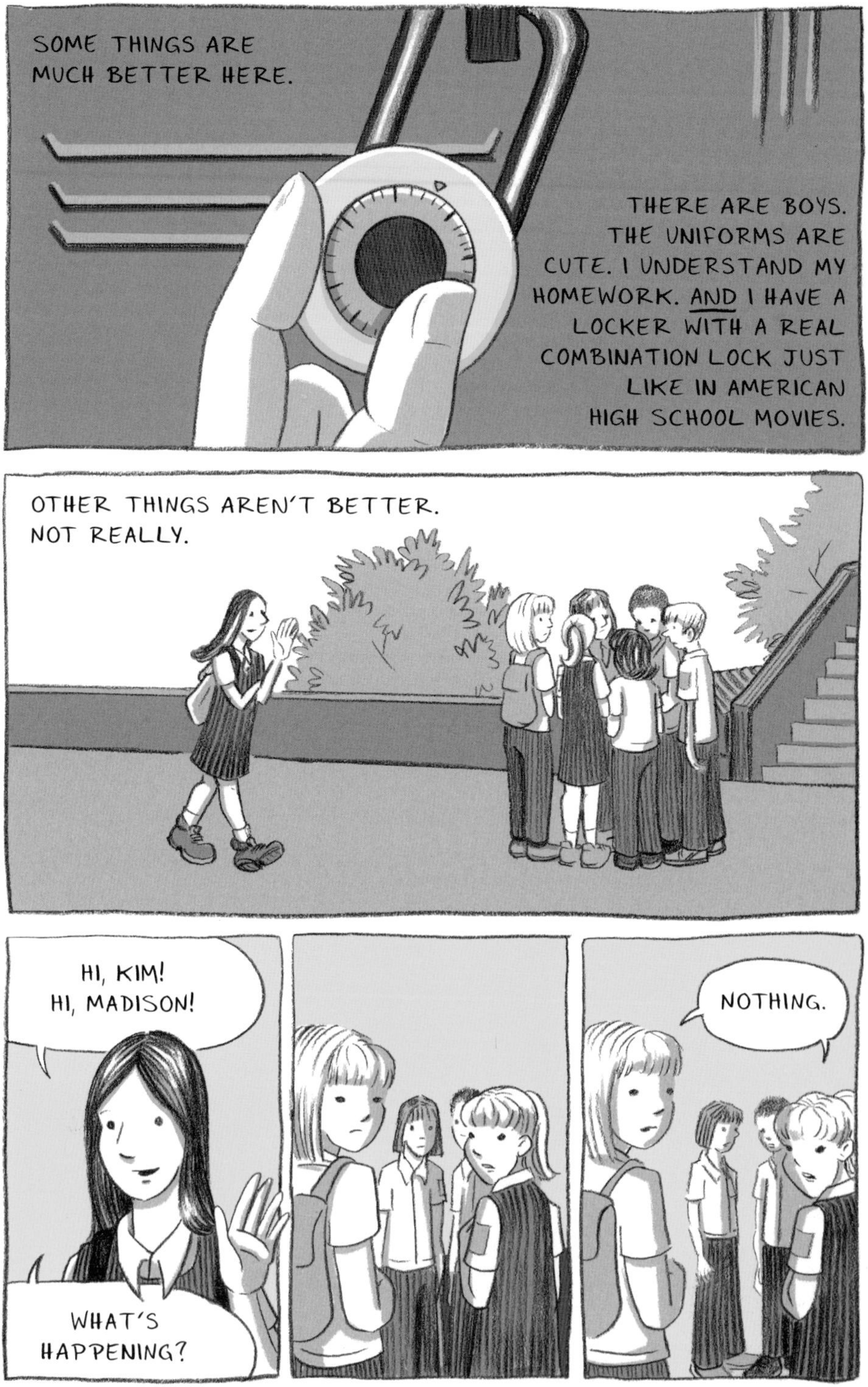
SOME THINGS ARE MUCH BETTER HERE.
THERE ARE BOYS. THE UNIFORMS ARE CUTE. I UNDERSTAND MY HOMEWORK. AND I HAVE A LOCKER WITH A REAL COMBINATION LOCK JUST LIKE IN AMERICAN HIGH SCHOOL MOVIES.
OTHER THINGS AREN'T BETTER. NOT REALLY.
HI, KIM! HI, MADISON!
WHAT'S HAPPENING?
NOTHING.

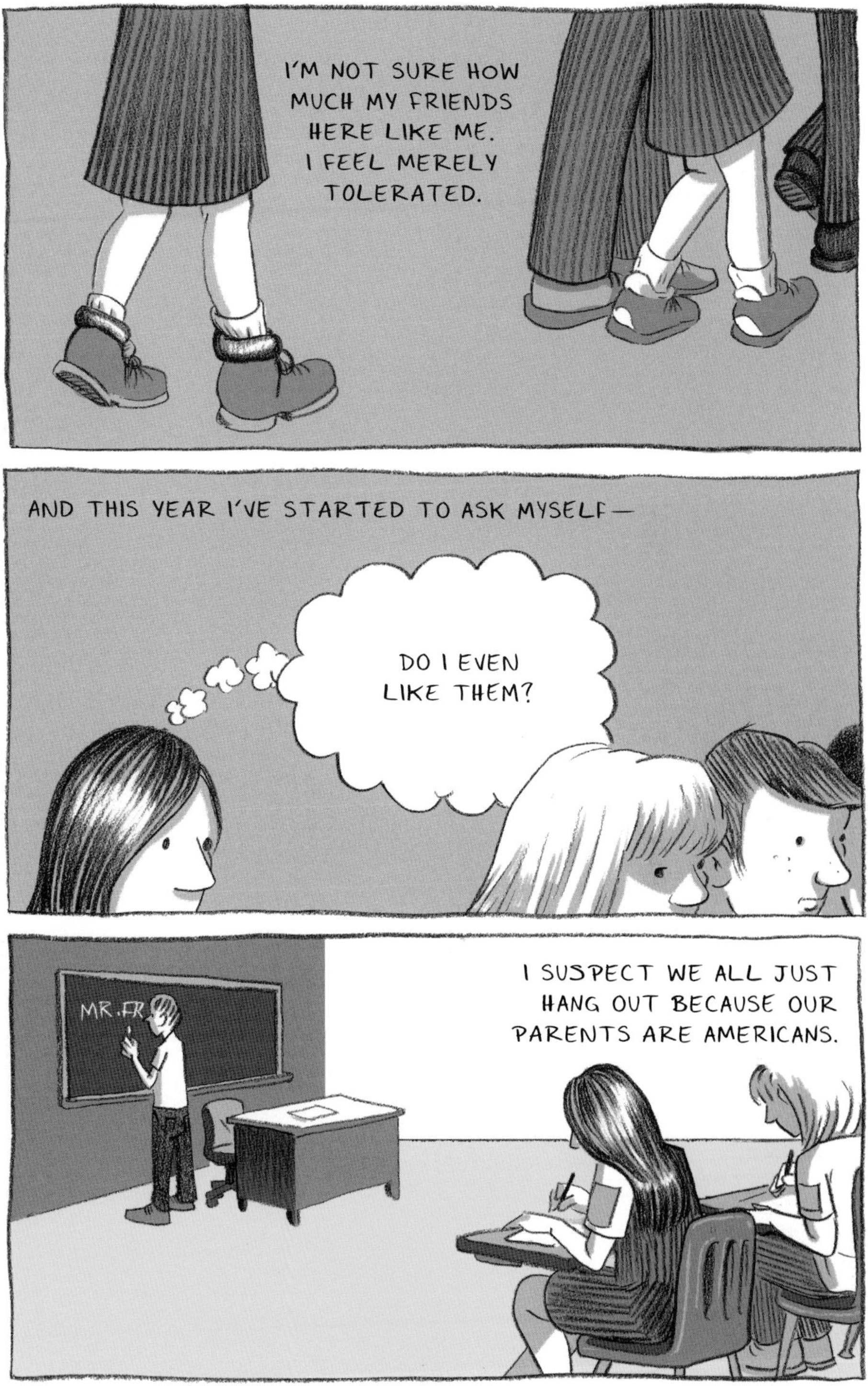
I'M NOT SURE HOW MUCH MY FRIENDS HERE LIKE ME. I FEEL MERELY TOLERATED.
AND THIS YEAR I'VE STARTED TO ASK MYSELF—
DO I EVEN LIKE THEM?
MR. FR
I SUSPECT WE ALL JUST HANG OUT BECAUSE OUR PARENTS ARE AMERICANS.

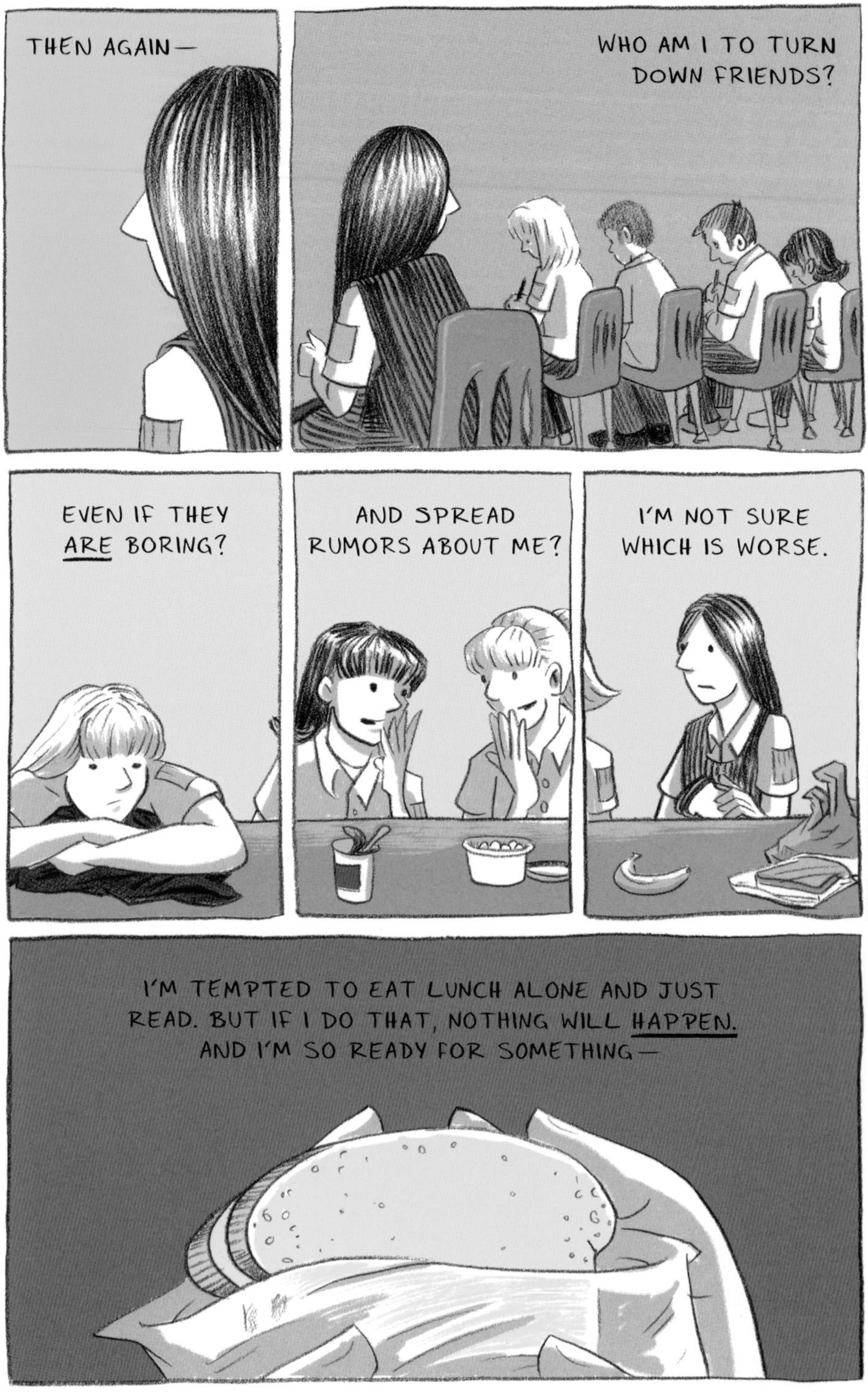
THEN AGAIN—
WHO AM I TO TURN DOWN FRIENDS?
EVEN IF THEY ARE BORING?
AND SPREAD RUMORS ABOUT ME?
I'M NOT SURE WHICH IS WORSE.
I'M TEMPTED TO EAT LUNCH ALONE AND JUST READ. BUT IF I DO THAT, NOTHING WILL HAPPEN. AND I'M SO READY FOR SOMETHING—

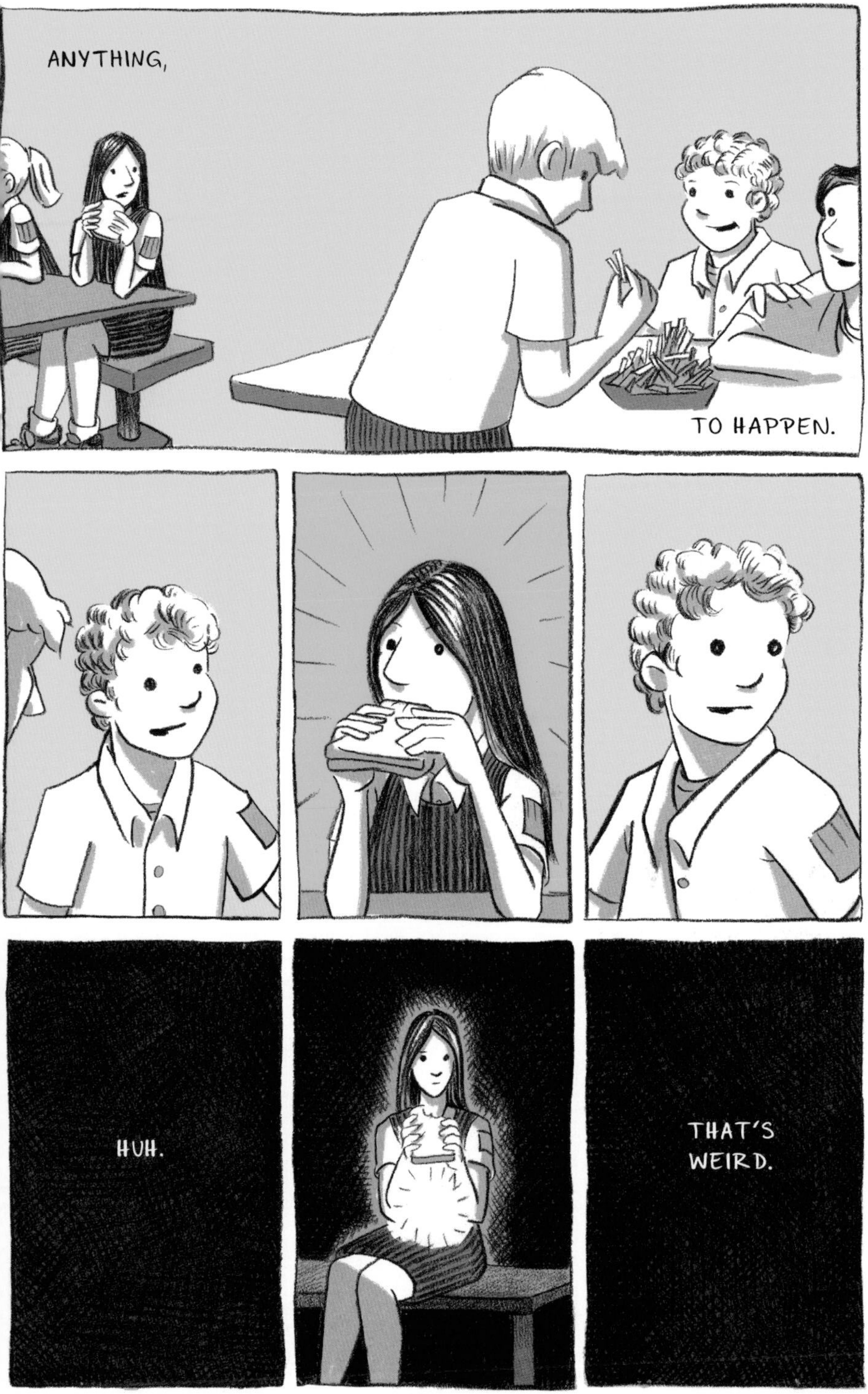
ANYTHING,
TO HAPPEN.
HUH.
THAT'S WEIRD.

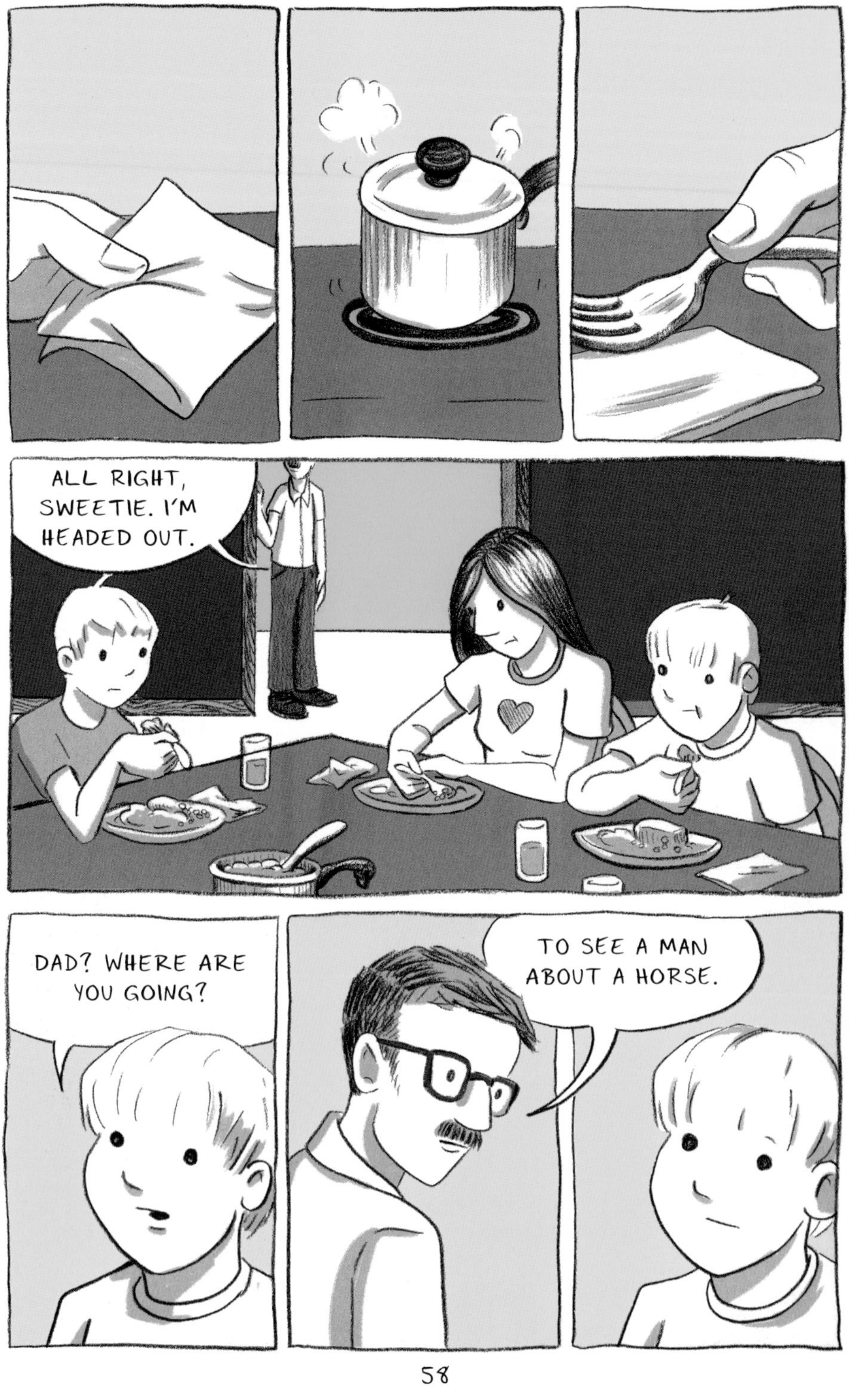
ALL RIGHT, SWEETIE. I'M HEADED OUT.
DAD? WHERE ARE YOU GOING?
TO SEE A MAN ABOUT A HORSE.

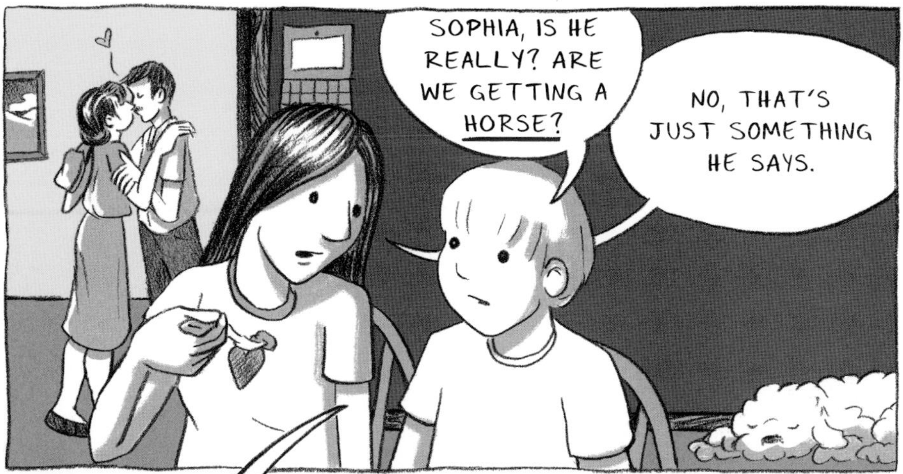
SOPHIA, IS HE REALLY? ARE WE GETTING A HORSE?
NO, THAT'S JUST SOMETHING HE SAYS.
THEN WHERE IS HE REALLY GOING?

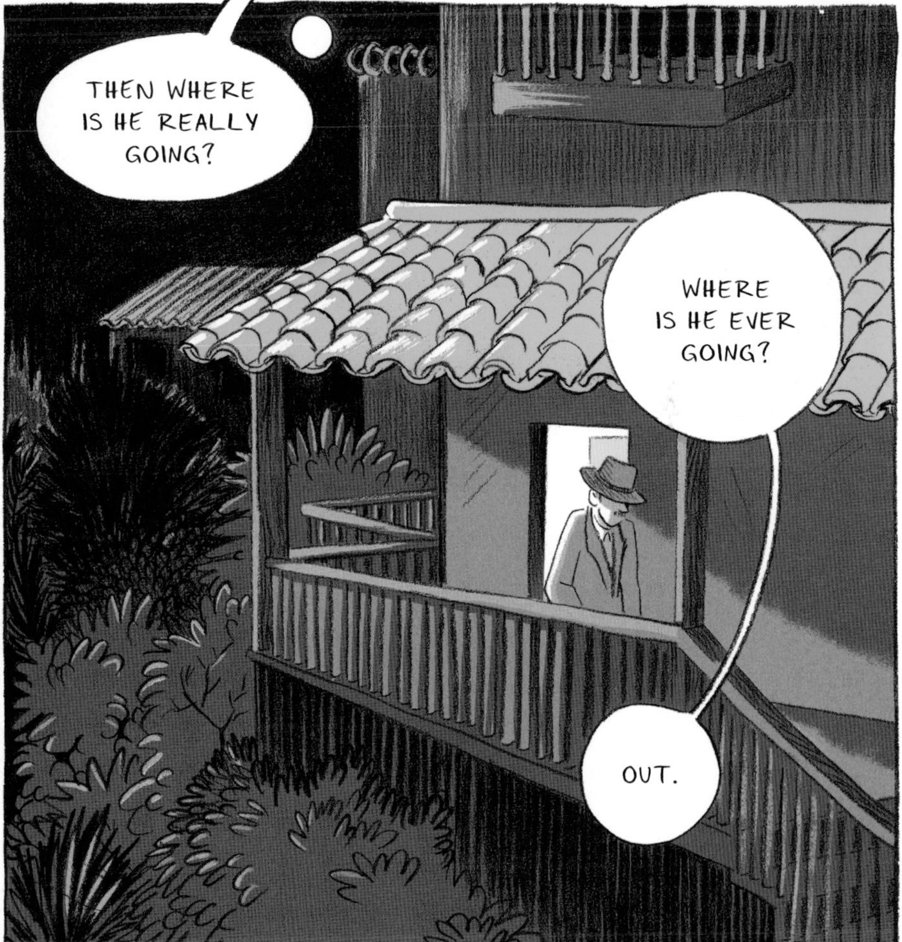
WHERE IS HE EVER GOING?
OUT.

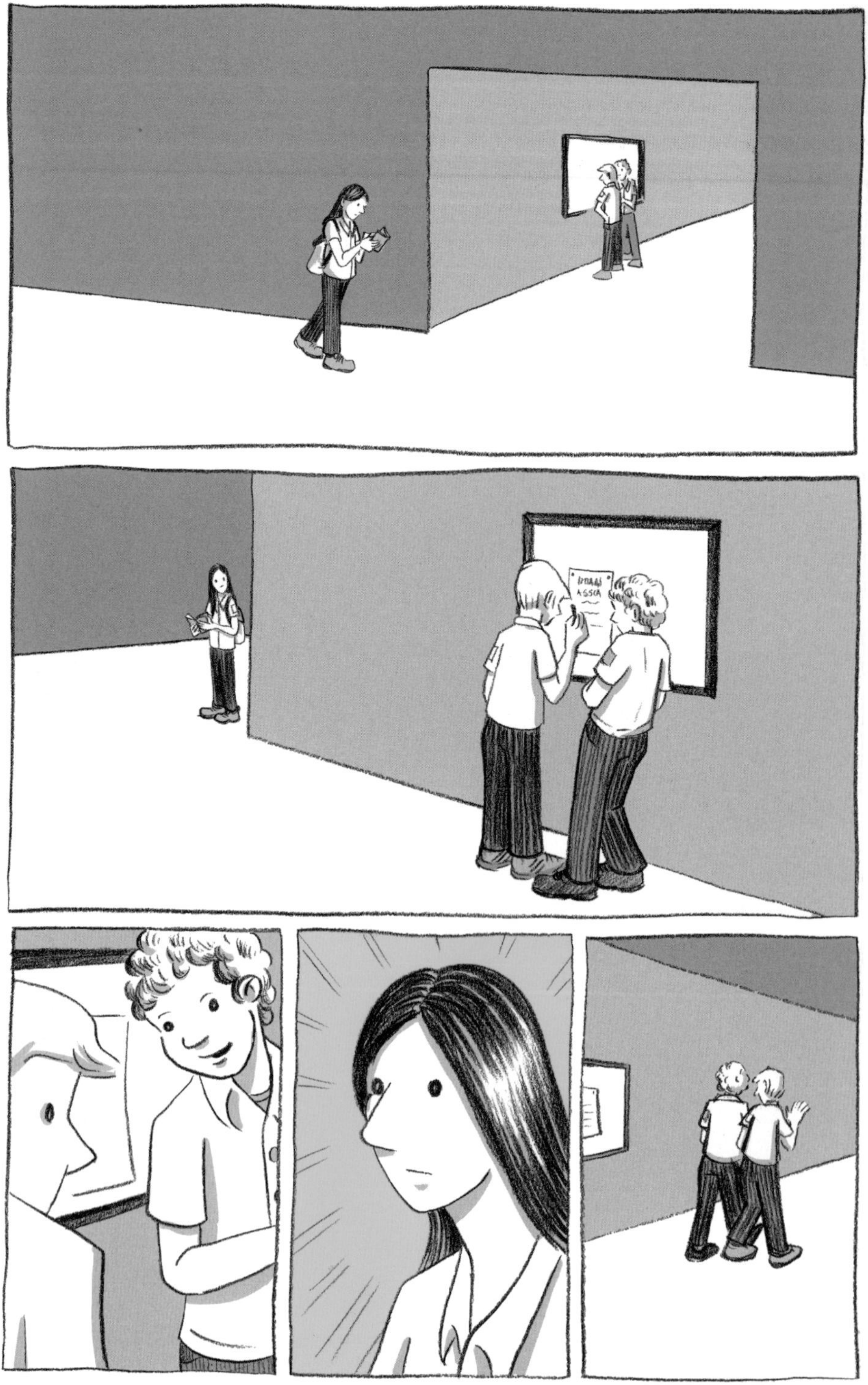

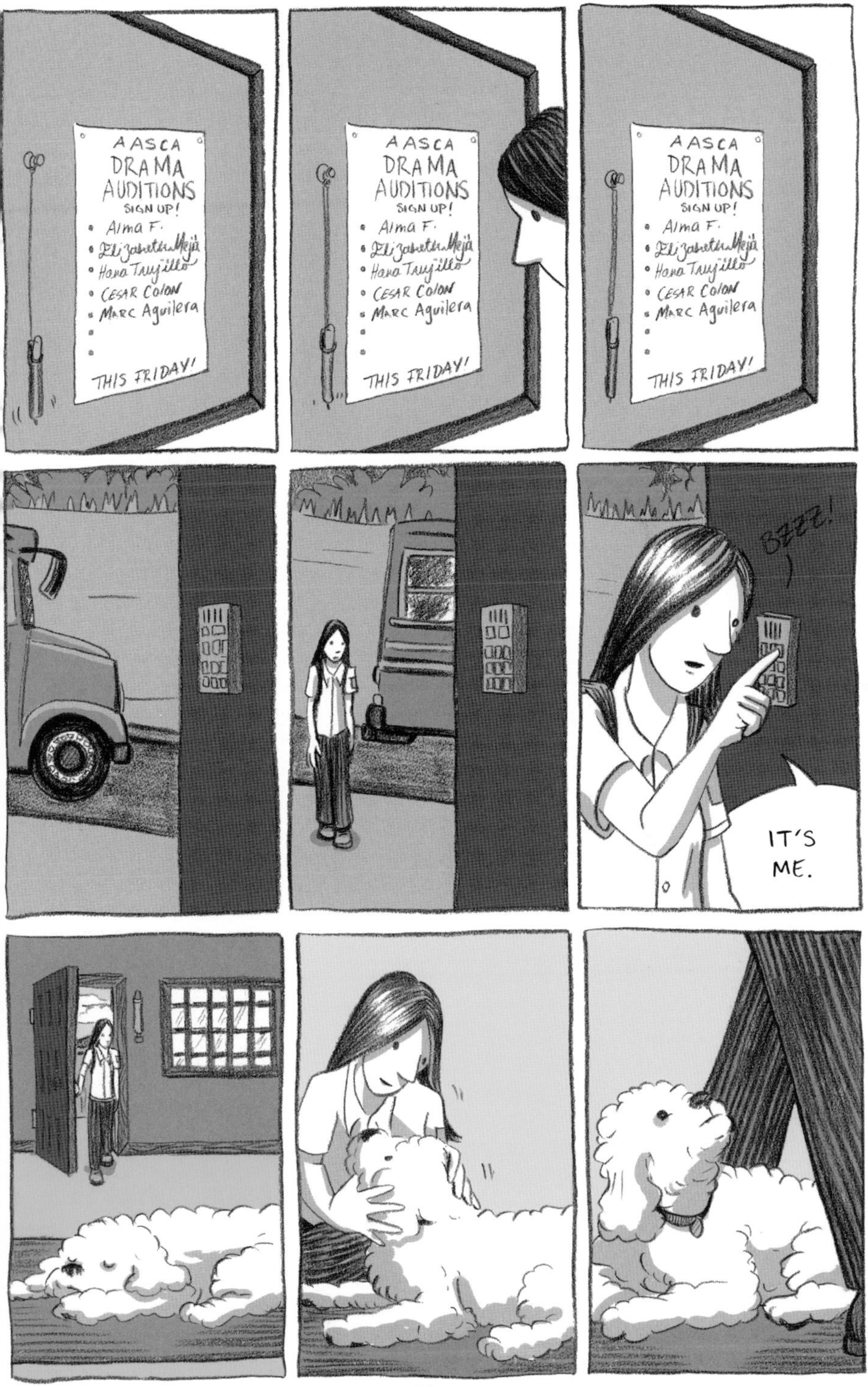
AASCA
DRAMA
AUDITIONS
SIGN UP!
Alma F.
Hana Trujillo
CESAR COLON
Marc Aguilera
THIS FRIDAY!
BZZZ!
IT'S ME.

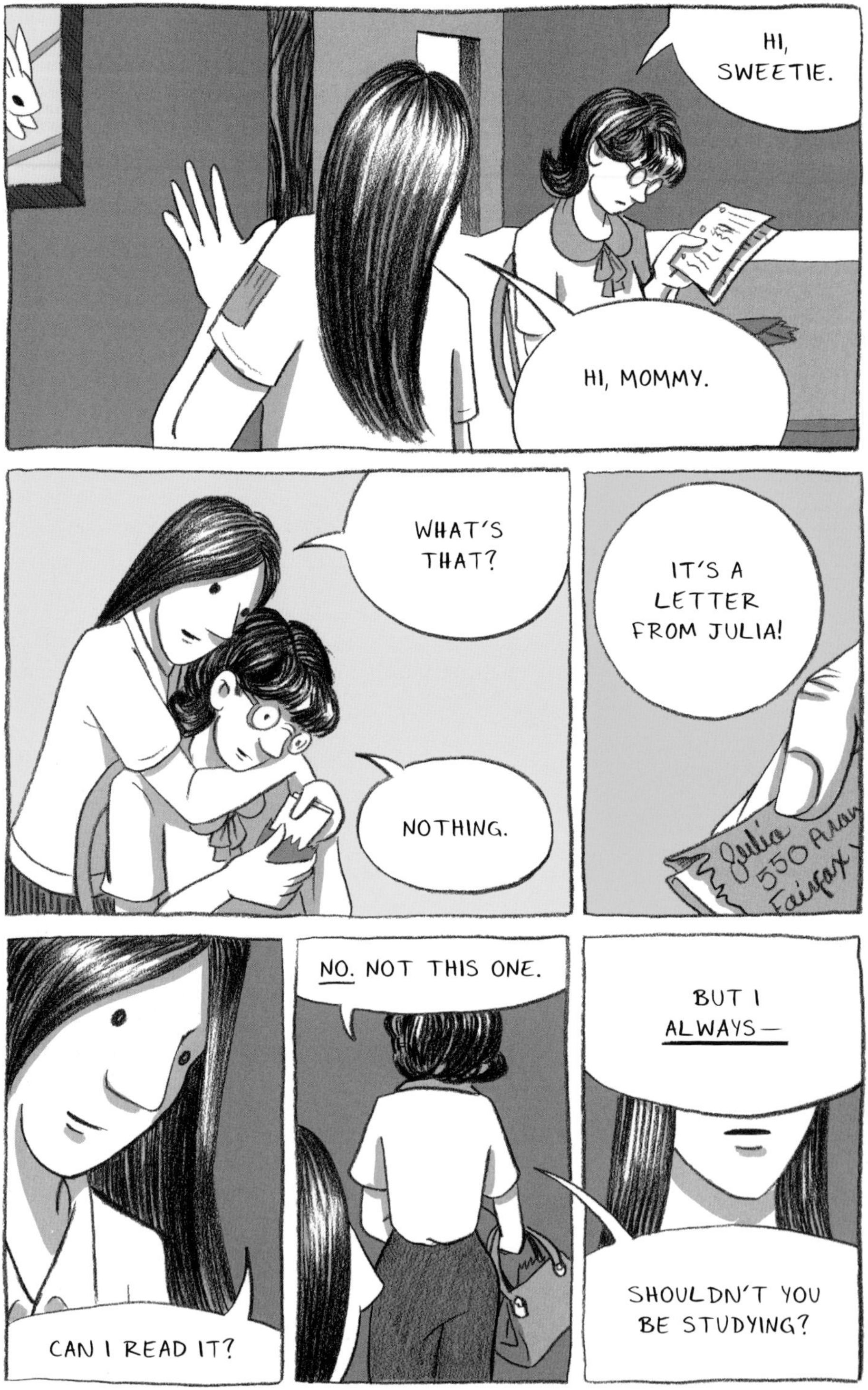
HI, SWEETIE.
HI, MOMMY.
WHAT'S THAT?
NOTHING.
IT'S A LETTER FROM JULIA!
Julia
550
Fairfax
CAN I READ IT?
NO. NOT THIS ONE.
BUT I ALWAYS—
SHOULDN'T YOU BE STUDYING?

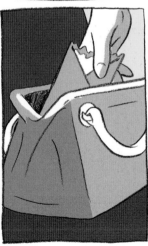

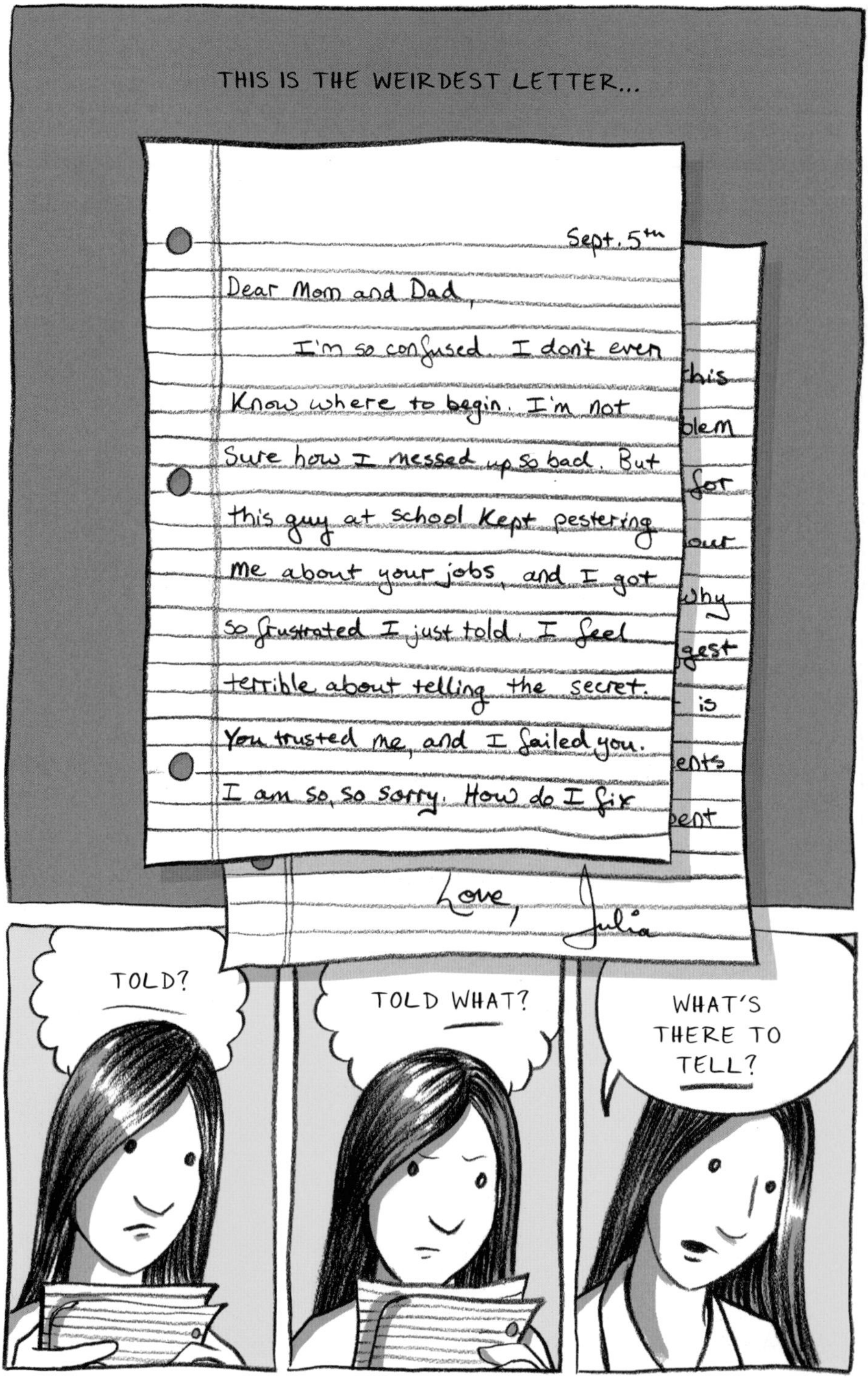
THIS IS THE WEIRDEST LETTER...
Sept. 5th
Dear Mom and Dad,
I'm so confused. I don't even know where to begin. I'm not sure how I messed up so bad. But this guy at school kept pestering me about your jobs, and I got so frustrated I just told. I feel terrible about telling the secret. You trusted me, and I failed you. I am so, so sorry. How do I fix
Love,
Julia
TOLD?
TOLD WHAT?
WHAT'S THERE TO TELL?

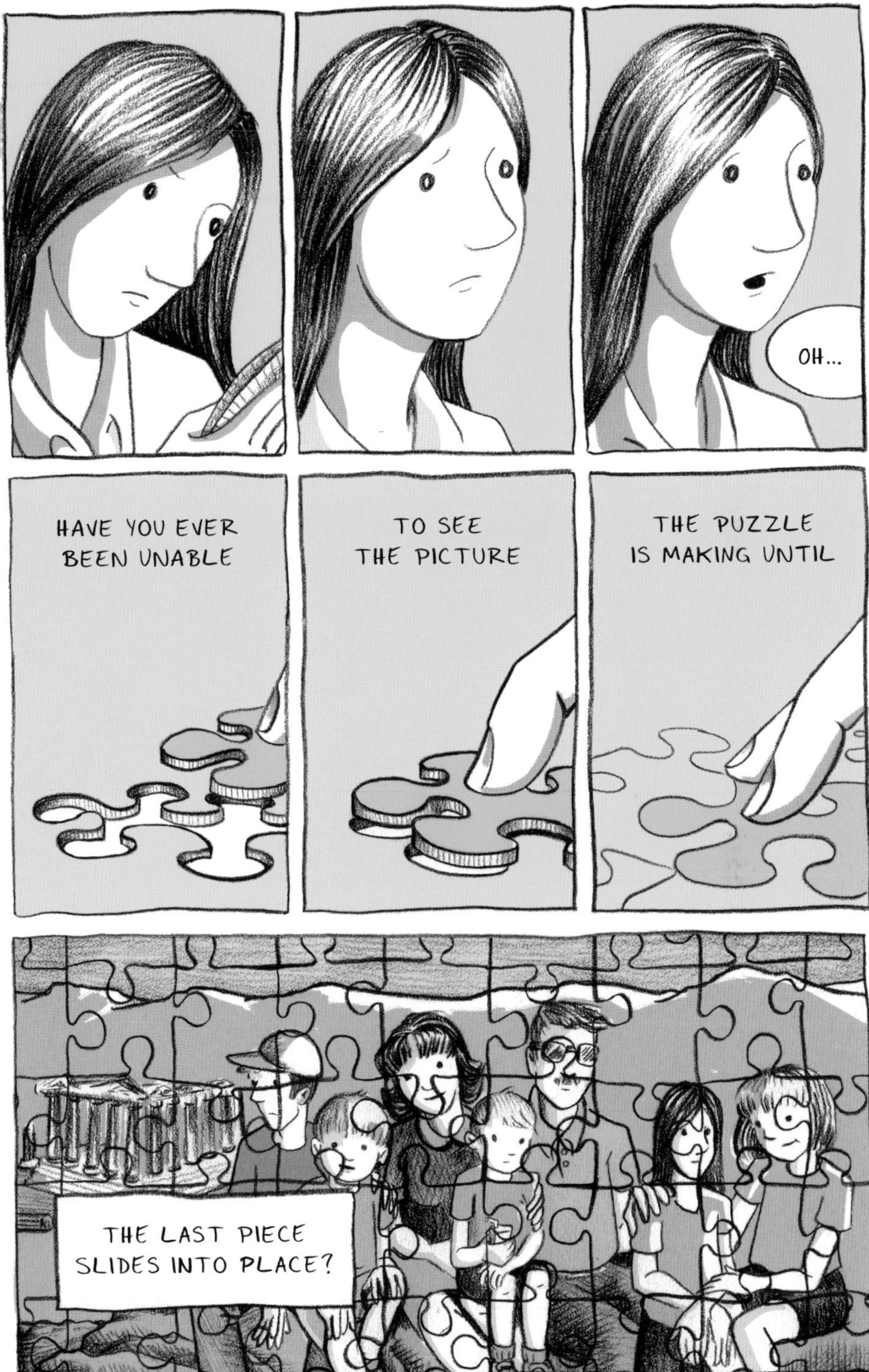
OH...
HAVE YOU EVER BEEN UNABLE
TO SEE THE PICTURE
THE PUZZLE IS MAKING UNTIL
THE LAST PIECE SLIDES INTO PLACE?

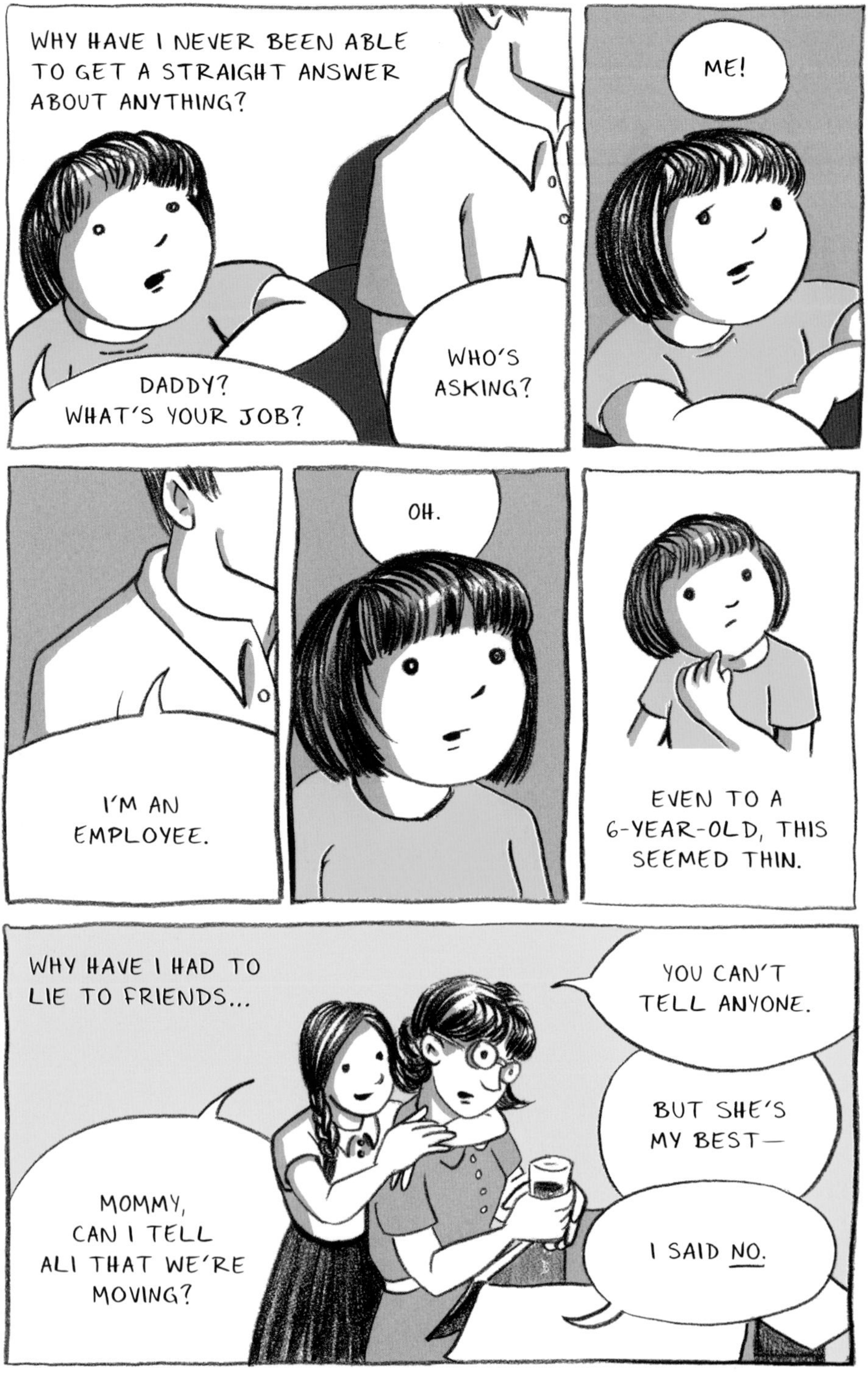
WHY HAVE I NEVER BEEN ABLE TO GET A STRAIGHT ANSWER ABOUT ANYTHING?
DADDY? WHAT'S YOUR JOB?
WHO'S ASKING?
ME!
I'M AN EMPLOYEE.
OH.
EVEN TO A 6-YEAR-OLD, THIS SEEMED THIN.
WHY HAVE I HAD TO LIE TO FRIENDS...
MOMMY, CAN I TELL ALI THAT WE'RE MOVING?
YOU CAN'T TELL ANYONE.
BUT SHE'S MY BEST—
I SAID NO.

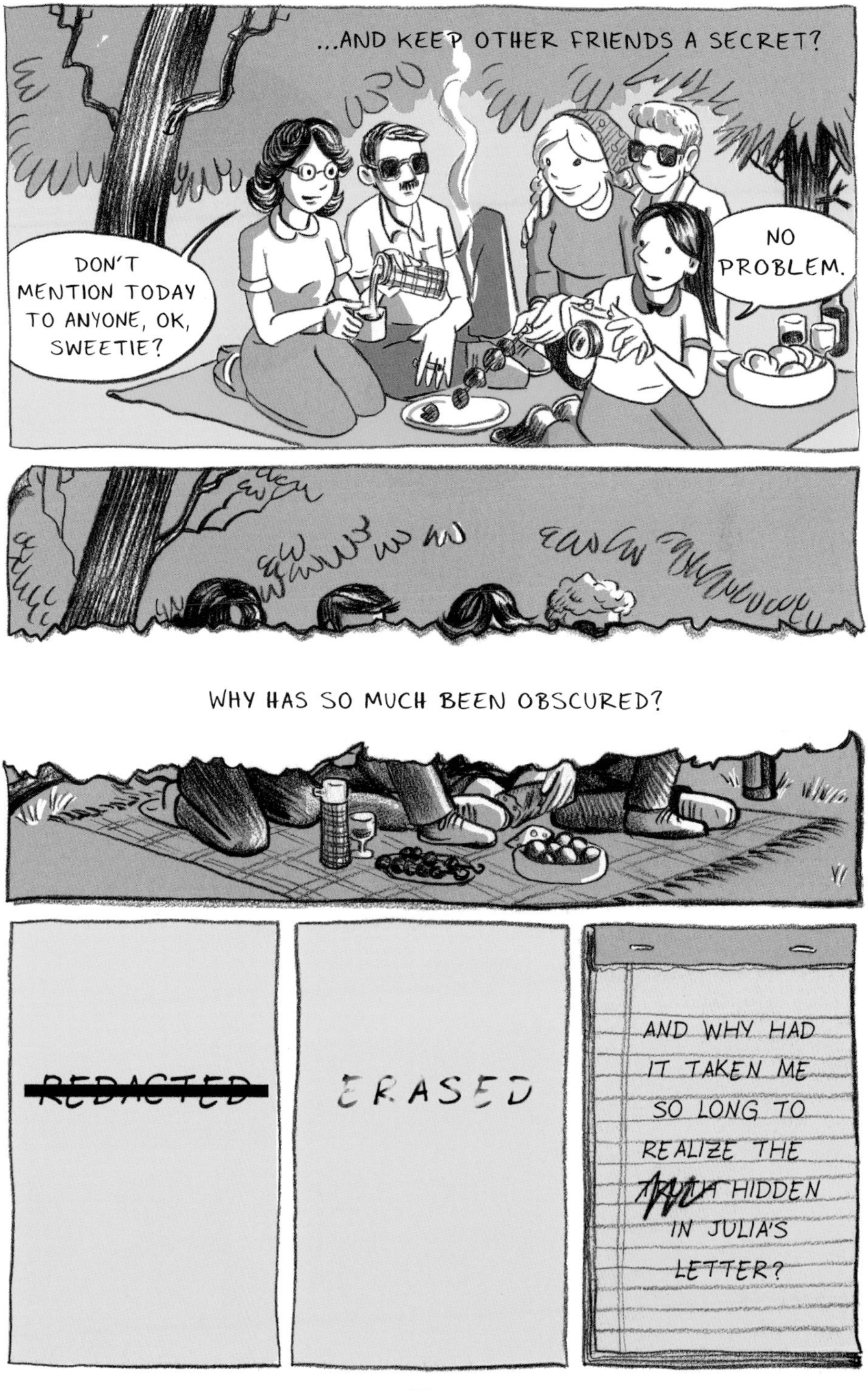
...AND KEEP OTHER FRIENDS A SECRET?
DON'T MENTION TODAY TO ANYONE, OK, SWEETIE?
NO PROBLEM.
WHY HAS SO MUCH BEEN OBSCURED?
REDACTED
ERASED
AND WHY HAD IT TAKEN ME SO LONG TO REALIZE THE TRUTH HIDDEN IN JULIA'S LETTER?

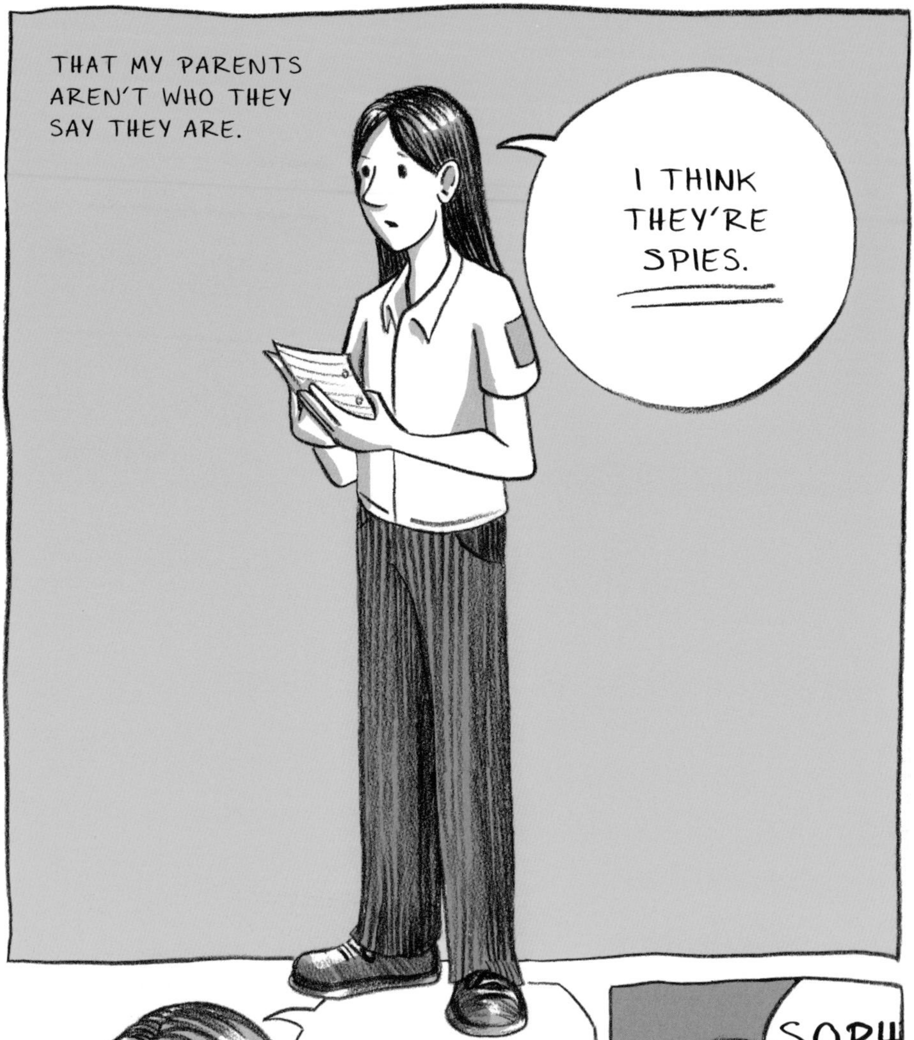
THAT MY PARENTS AREN'T WHO THEY SAY THEY ARE.
I THINK THEY'RE SPIES.

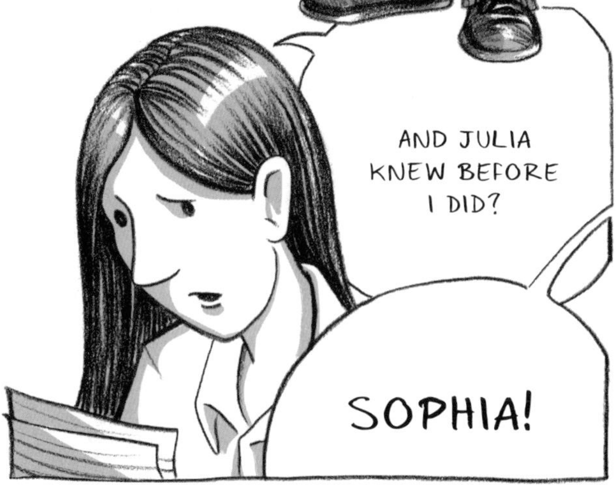
AND JULIA KNEW BEFORE I DID?
SOPHIA!

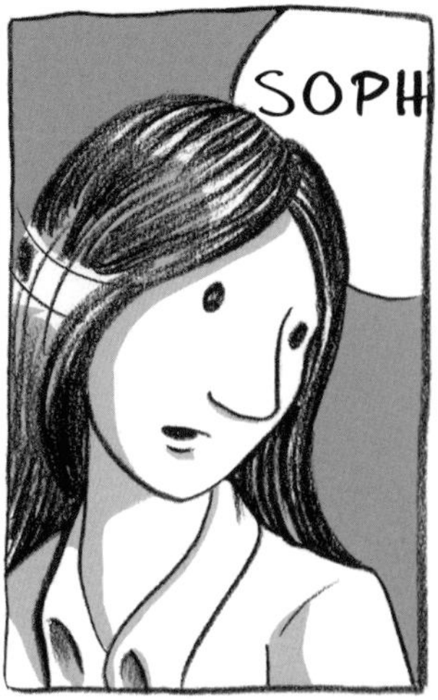
SOPH

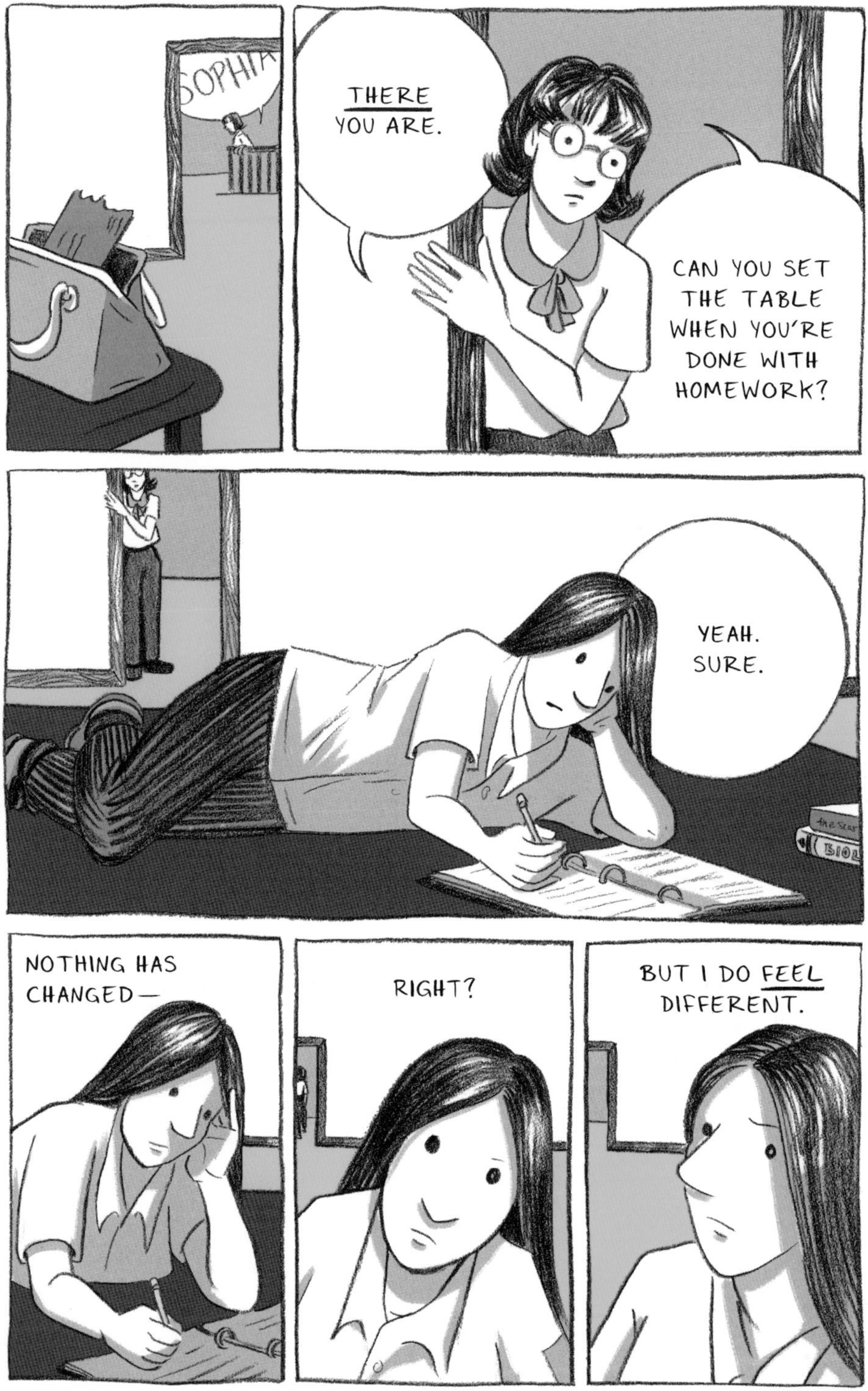
SOPHIA
THERE YOU ARE.
CAN YOU SET THE TABLE WHEN YOU'RE DONE WITH HOMEWORK?
YEAH. SURE.
NOTHING HAS CHANGED—
RIGHT?
BUT I DO FEEL DIFFERENT.

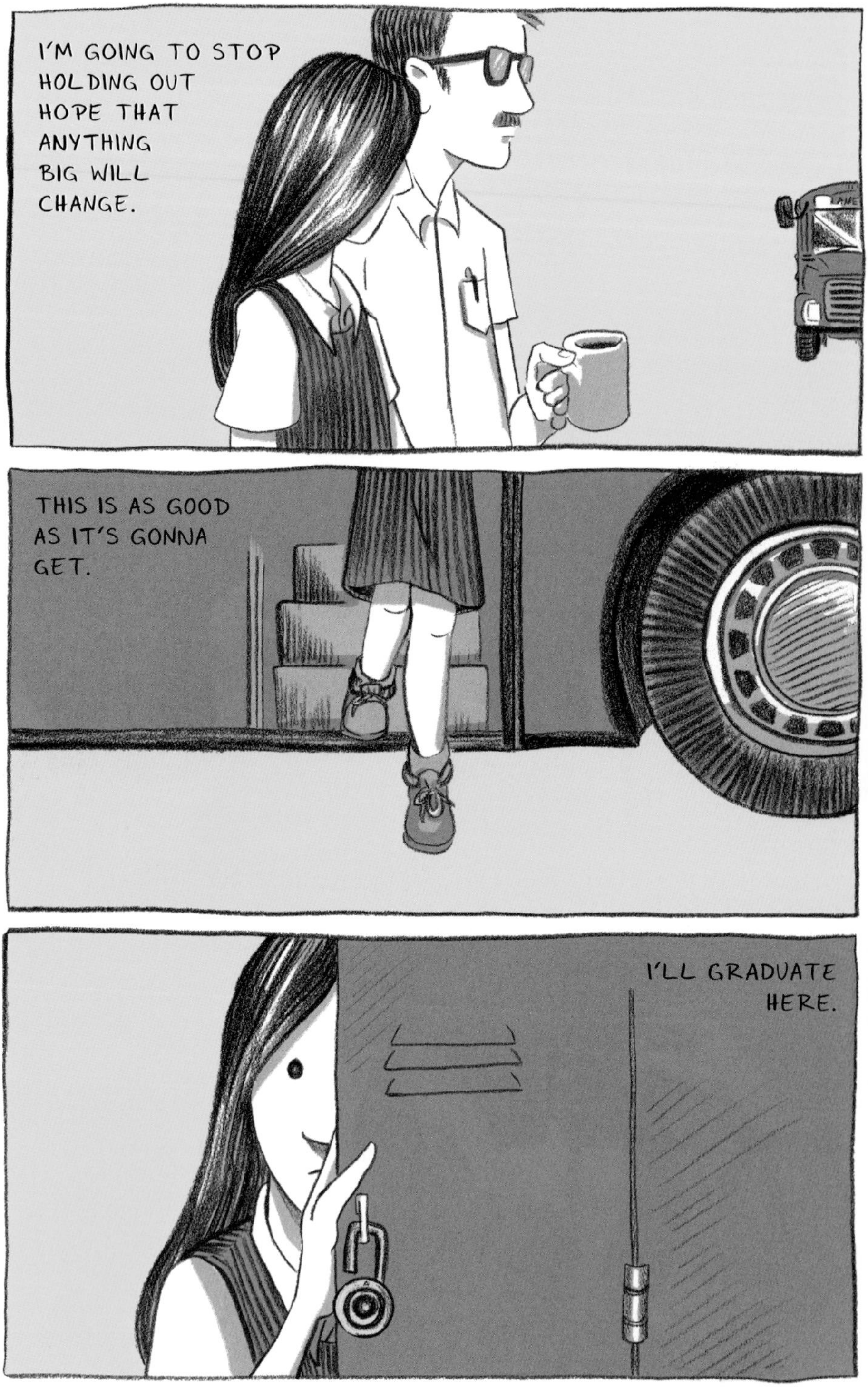
I'M GOING TO STOP HOLDING OUT HOPE THAT ANYTHING BIG WILL CHANGE.
THIS IS AS GOOD AS IT'S GONNA GET.
I'LL GRADUATE HERE.

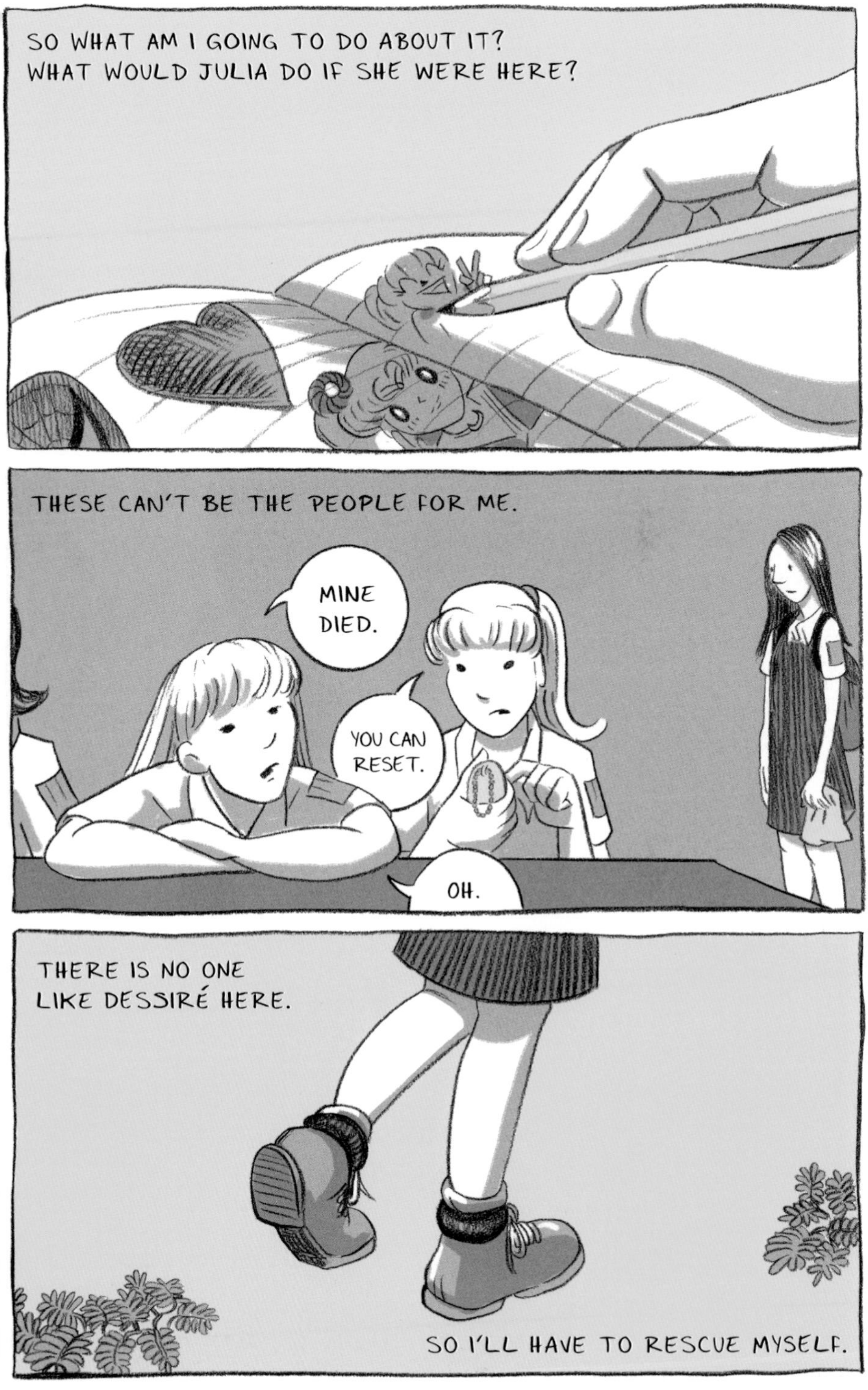
SO WHAT AM I GOING TO DO ABOUT IT?
WHAT WOULD JULIA DO IF SHE WERE HERE?
THESE CAN'T BE THE PEOPLE FOR ME.
MINE DIED.
YOU CAN RESET.
OH.
THERE IS NO ONE LIKE DESSIRÉ HERE.
SO I'LL HAVE TO RESCUE MYSELF.

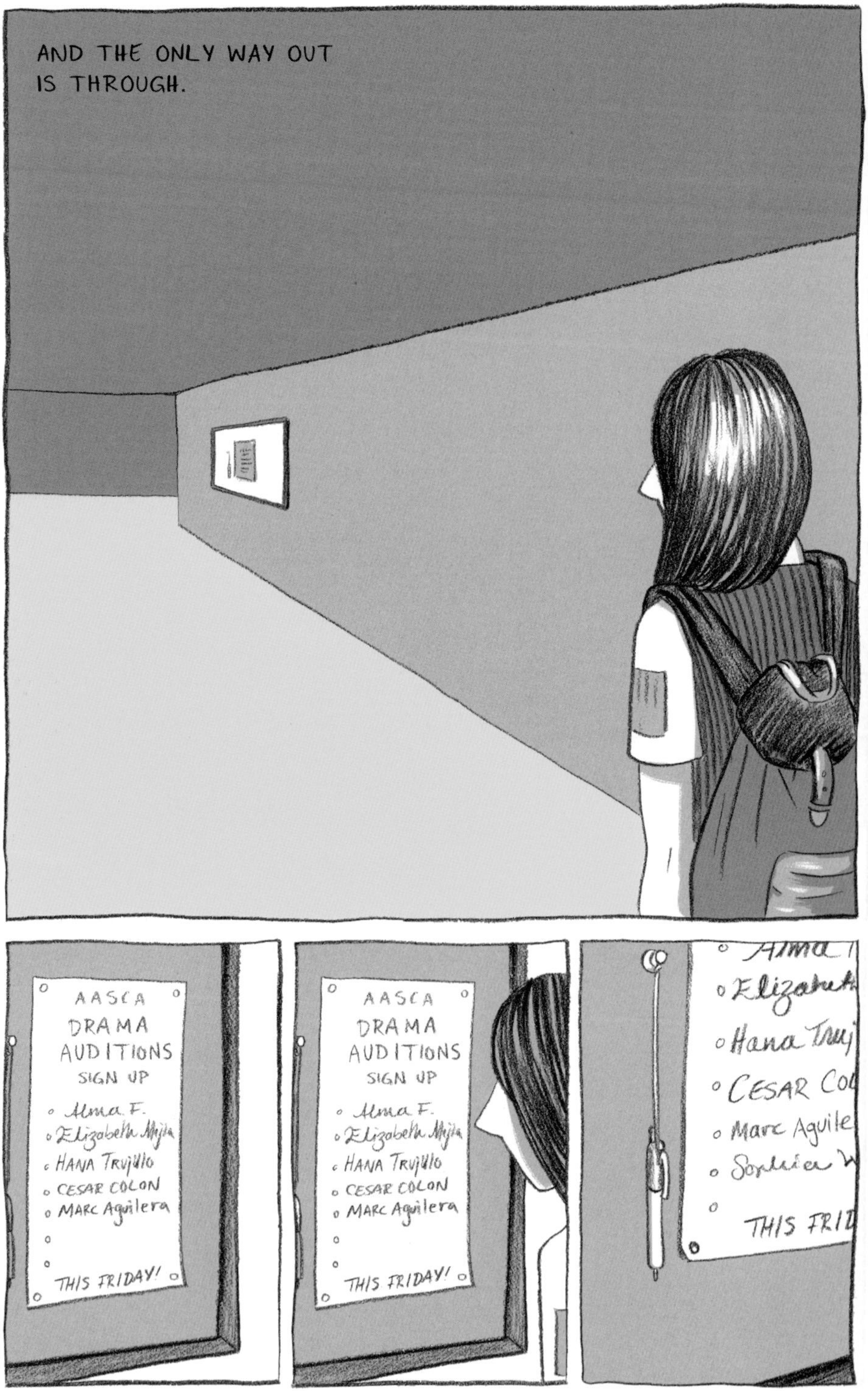
AND THE ONLY WAY OUT IS THROUGH.
AASCA
DRAMA
AUDITIONS
SIGN UP
Alma F.
Elizabeth Mejia
HANA Trujillo
CESAR COLON
MARC Aguilera
THIS FRIDAY!
AASCA
DRAMA
AUDITIONS
SIGN UP
Alma F.
Elizabeth Mejia
HANA Trujillo
CESAR COLON
MARC Aguilera
THIS FRIDAY!

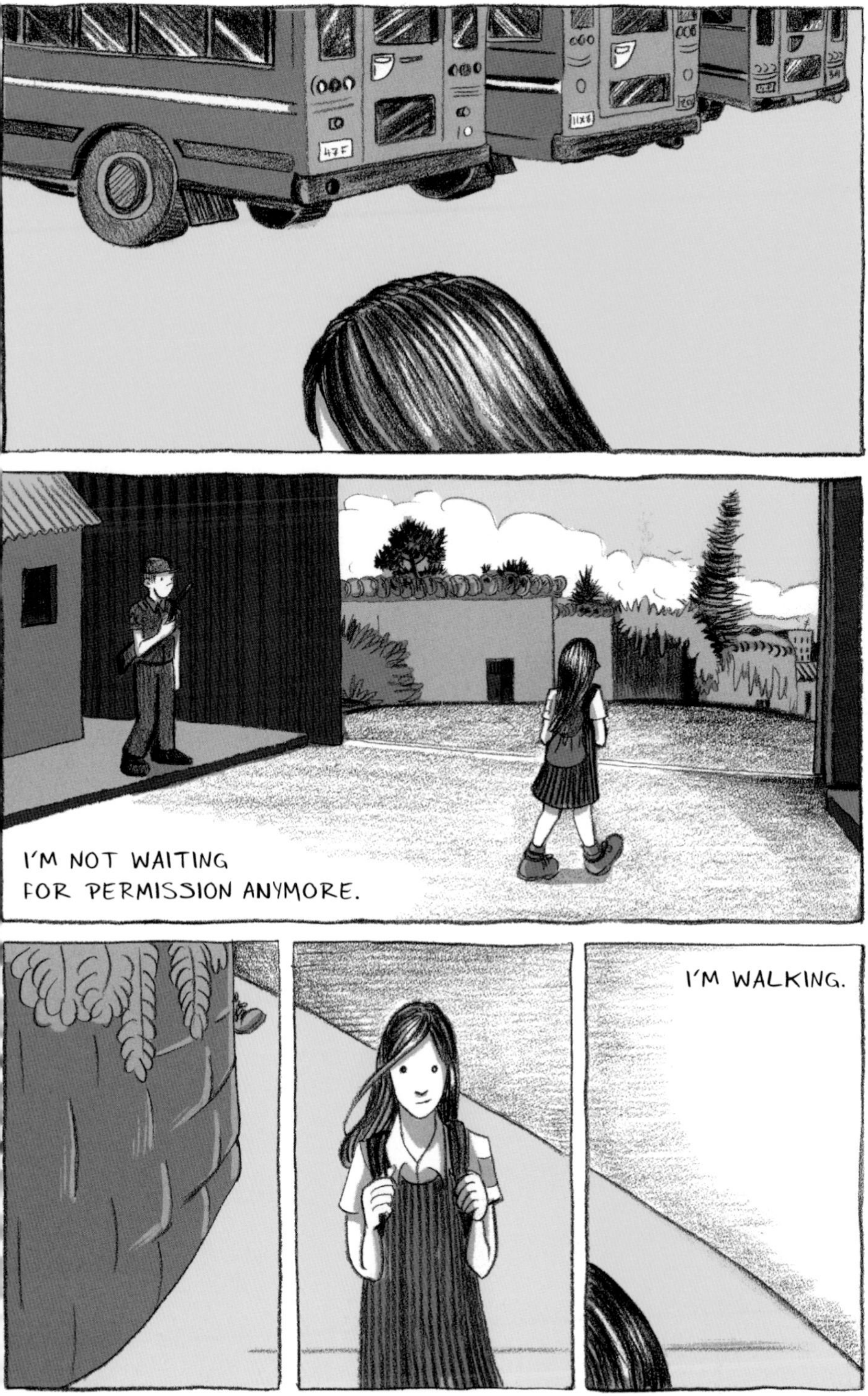
I'M NOT WAITING
FOR PERMISSION ANYMORE.
I'M WALKING.

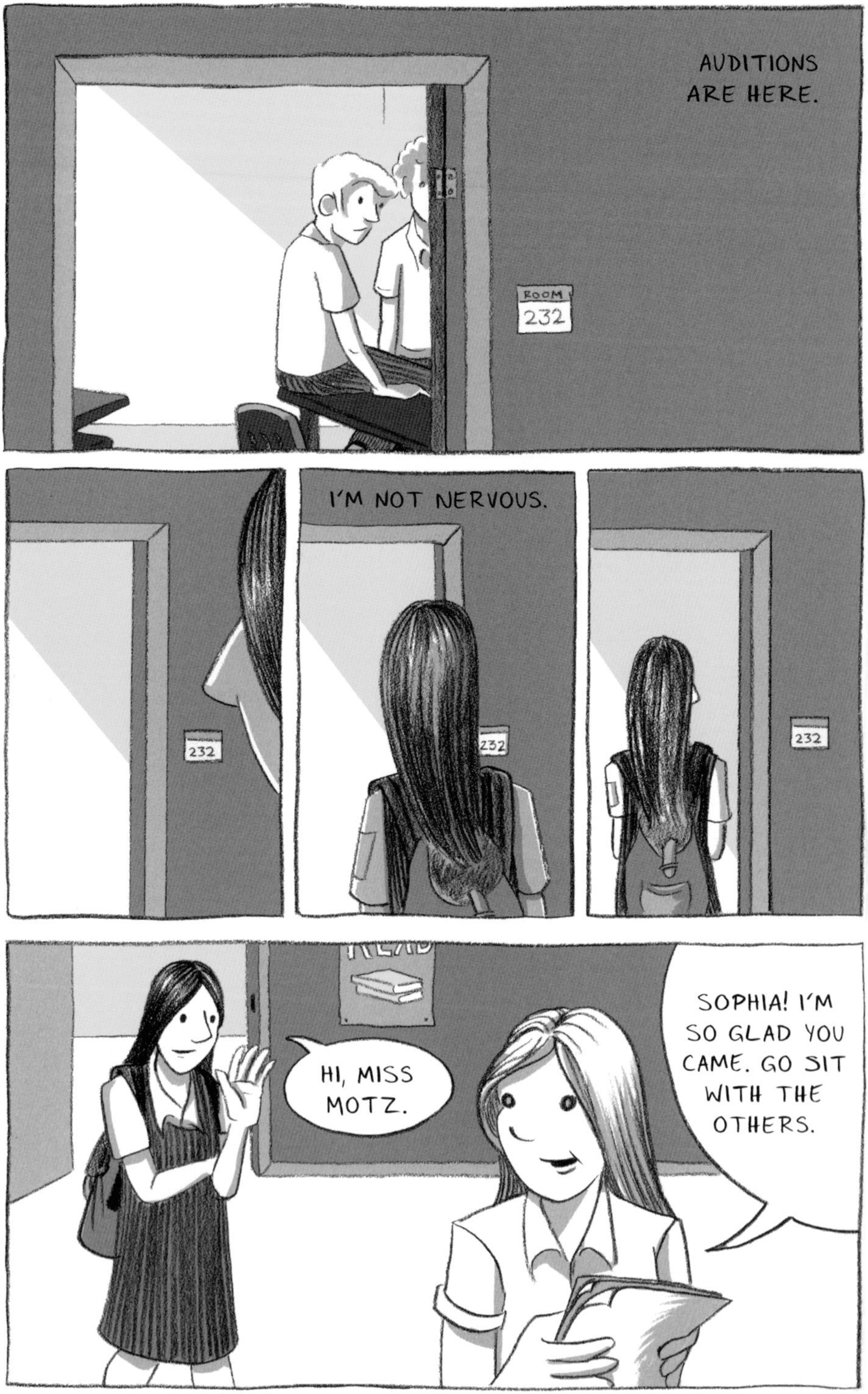
AUDITIONS ARE HERE.
ROOM 232
232
I'M NOT NERVOUS.
232
232
HI, MISS MOTZ.
SOPHIA! I'M SO GLAD YOU CAME. GO SIT WITH THE OTHERS.

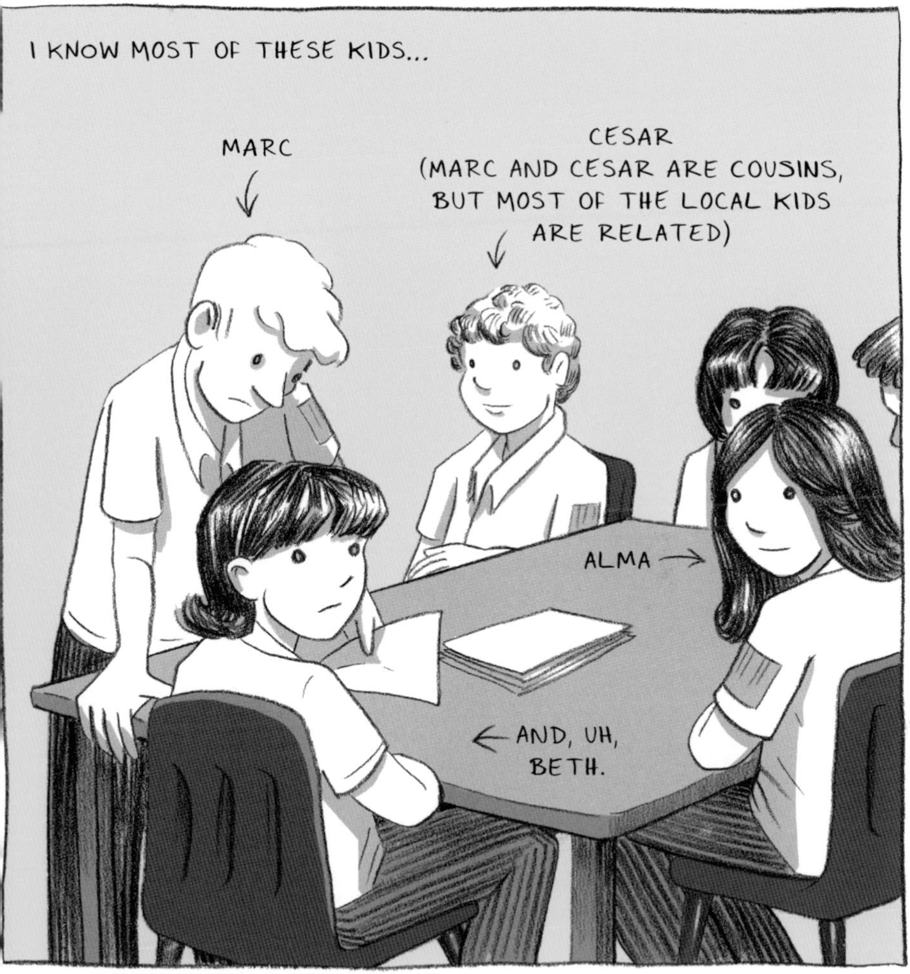
I KNOW MOST OF THESE KIDS...
MARC
CESAR
(MARC AND CESAR ARE COUSINS, BUT MOST OF THE LOCAL KIDS ARE RELATED)
ALMA
AND, UH, BETH.

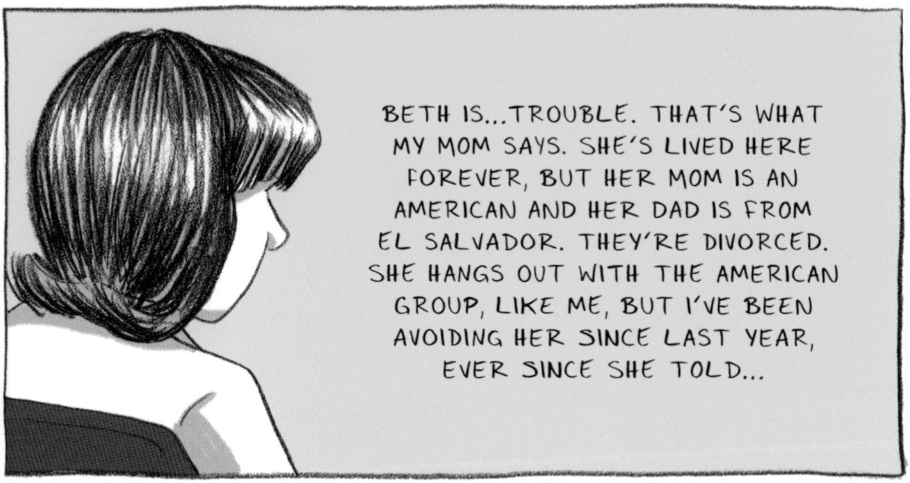
BETH IS...TROUBLE. THAT'S WHAT MY MOM SAYS. SHE'S LIVED HERE FOREVER, BUT HER MOM IS AN AMERICAN AND HER DAD IS FROM EL SALVADOR. THEY'RE DIVORCED. SHE HANGS OUT WITH THE AMERICAN GROUP, LIKE ME, BUT I'VE BEEN AVOIDING HER SINCE LAST YEAR, EVER SINCE SHE TOLD...

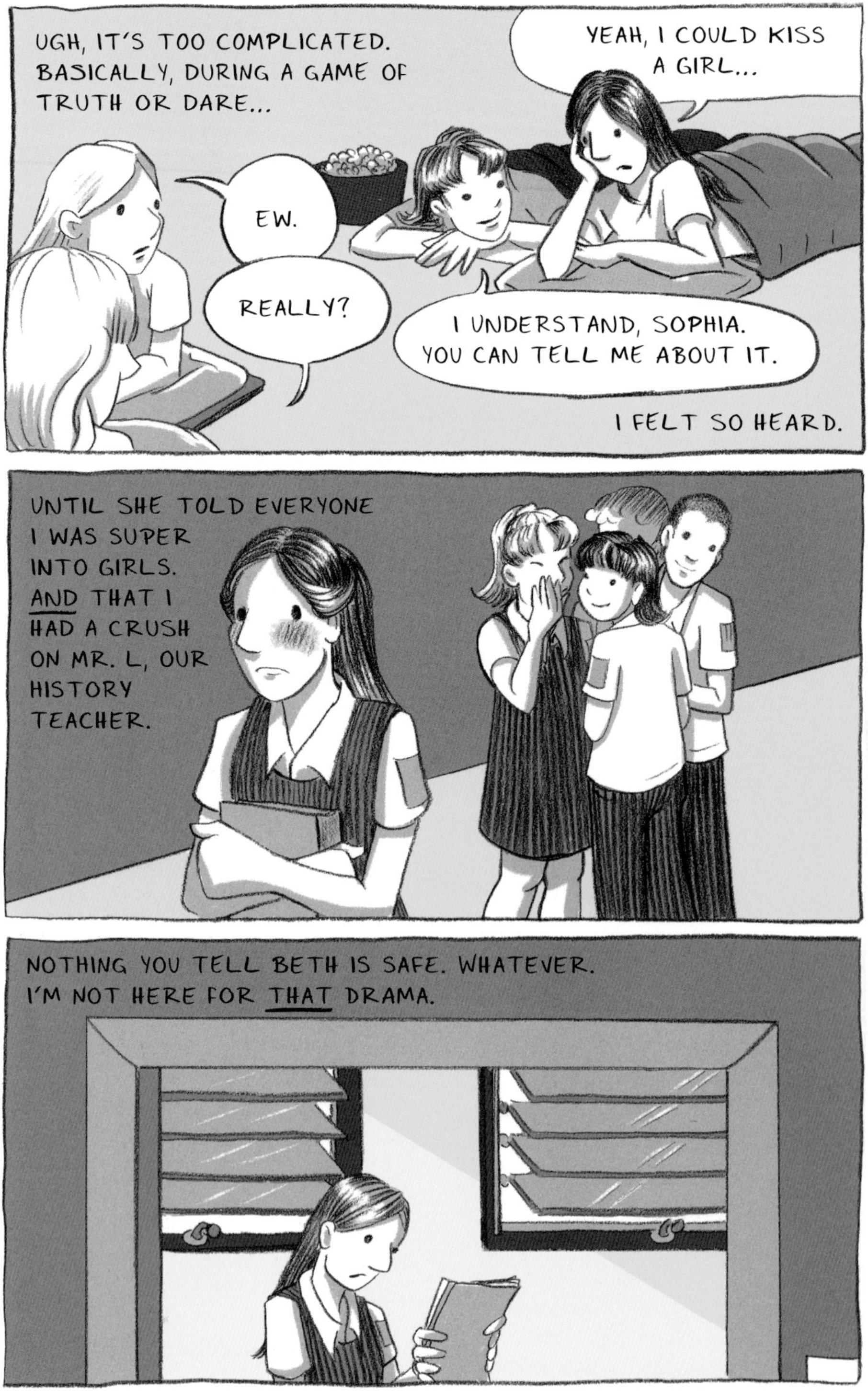

UGH, IT'S TOO COMPLICATED. BASICALLY, DURING A GAME OF TRUTH OR DARE...
YEAH, I COULD KISS A GIRL...
EW.
REALLY?
I UNDERSTAND, SOPHIA. YOU CAN TELL ME ABOUT IT.
I FELT SO HEARD.
UNTIL SHE TOLD EVERYONE I WAS SUPER INTO GIRLS. AND THAT I HAD A CRUSH ON MR. L, OUR HISTORY TEACHER.
NOTHING YOU TELL BETH IS SAFE. WHATEVER. I'M NOT HERE FOR THAT DRAMA.

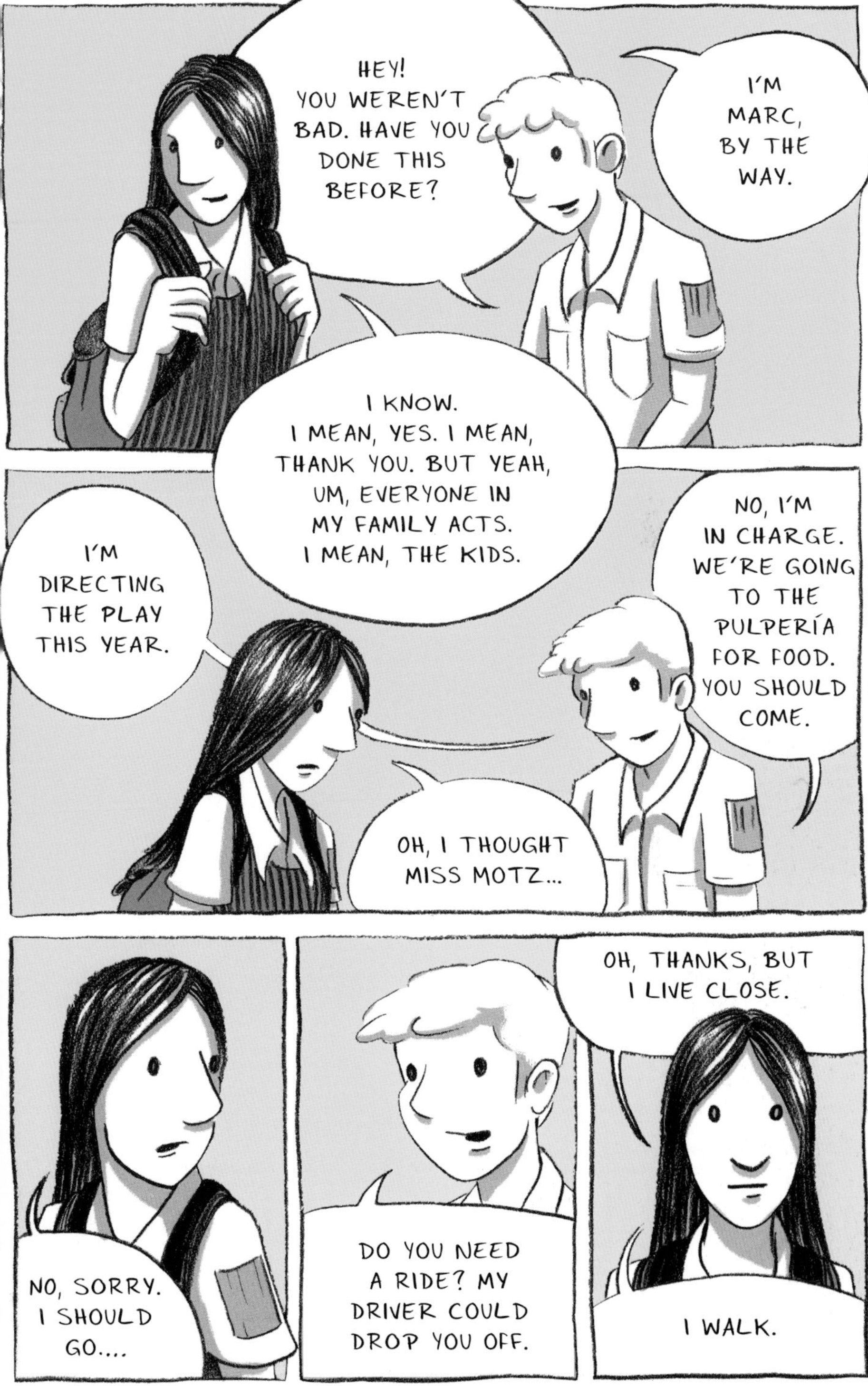
HEY! YOU WEREN'T BAD. HAVE YOU DONE THIS BEFORE?
I'M MARC, BY THE WAY.
I KNOW. I MEAN, YES. I MEAN, THANK YOU. BUT YEAH, UM, EVERYONE IN MY FAMILY ACTS. I MEAN, THE KIDS.
I'M DIRECTING THE PLAY THIS YEAR.
OH, I THOUGHT MISS MOTZ...
NO, I'M IN CHARGE. WE'RE GOING TO THE PULPERÍA FOR FOOD. YOU SHOULD COME.
NO, SORRY. I SHOULD GO....
DO YOU NEED A RIDE? MY DRIVER COULD DROP YOU OFF.
OH, THANKS, BUT I LIVE CLOSE.
I WALK.

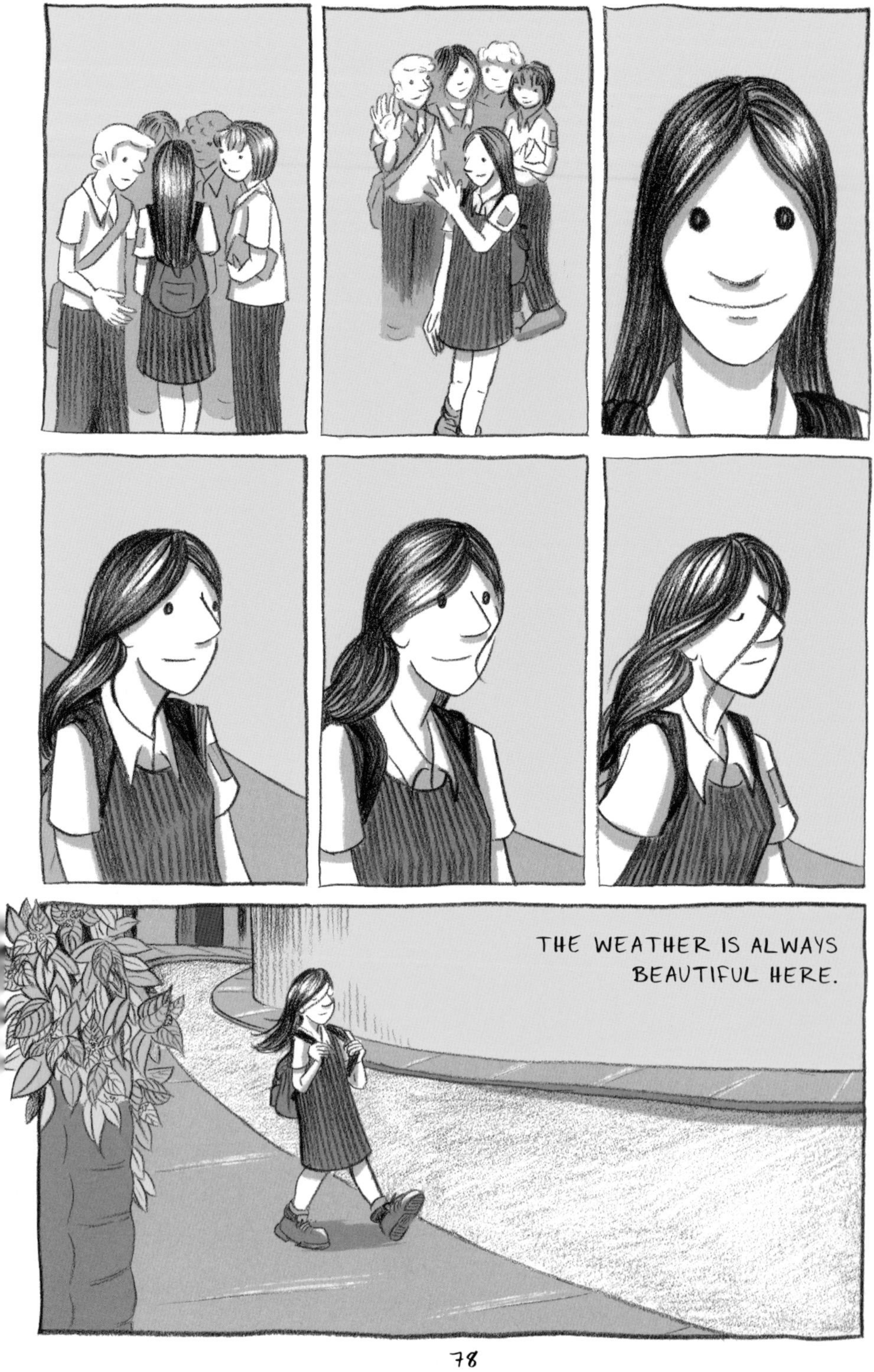
THE WEATHER IS ALWAYS BEAUTIFUL HERE.

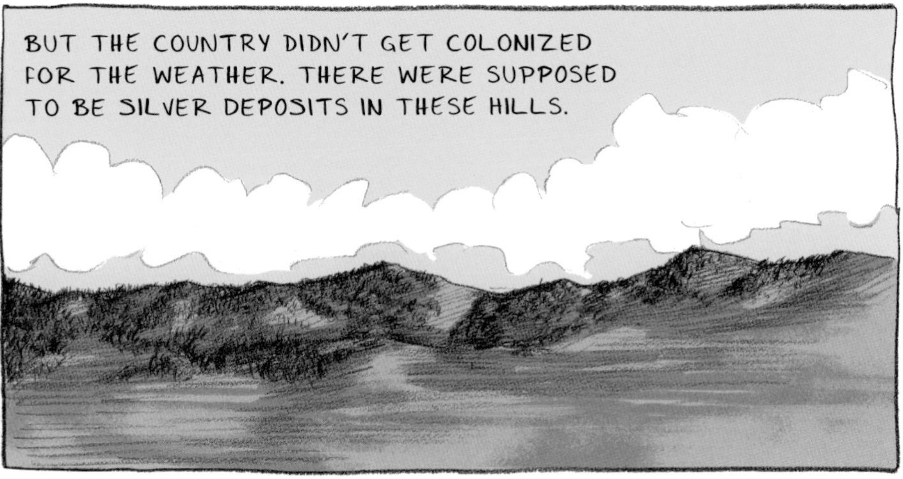
BUT THE COUNTRY DIDN'T GET COLONIZED FOR THE WEATHER. THERE WERE SUPPOSED TO BE SILVER DEPOSITS IN THESE HILLS.

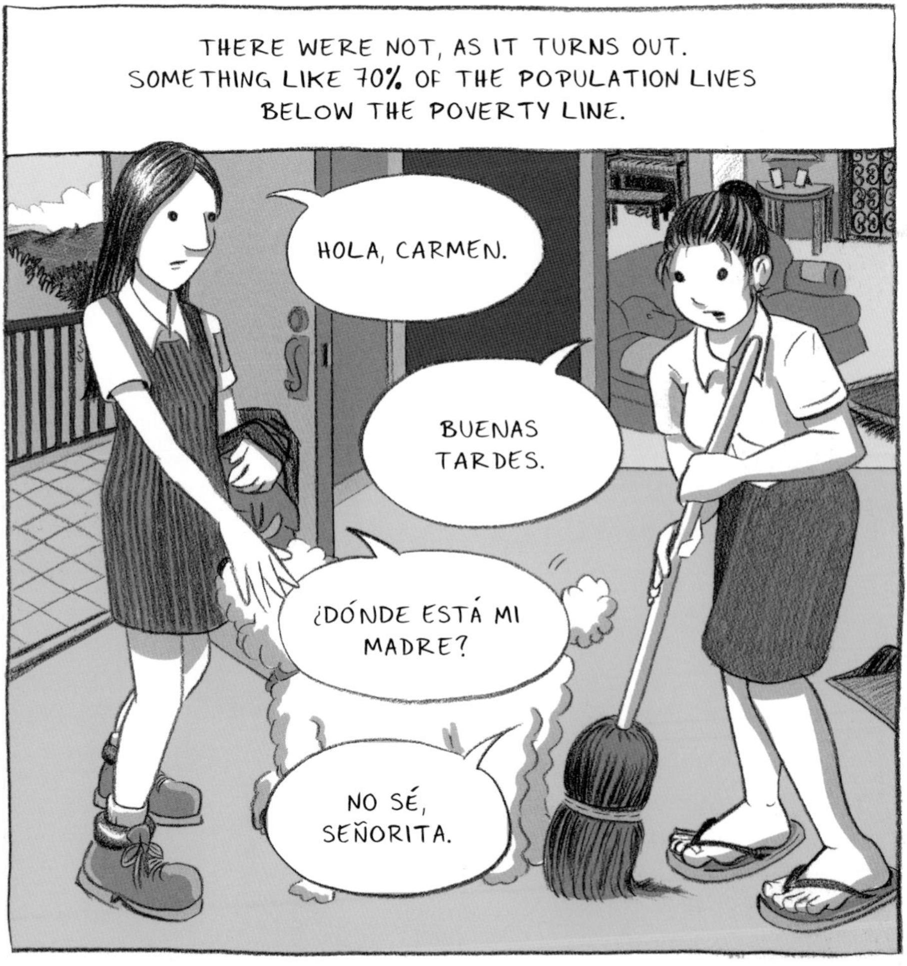
THERE WERE NOT, AS IT TURNS OUT. SOMETHING LIKE 70% OF THE POPULATION LIVES BELOW THE POVERTY LINE.
HOLA, CARMEN.
BUENAS TARDES.
¿DÓNDE ESTÁ MI MADRE?
NO SÉ, SEÑORITA.

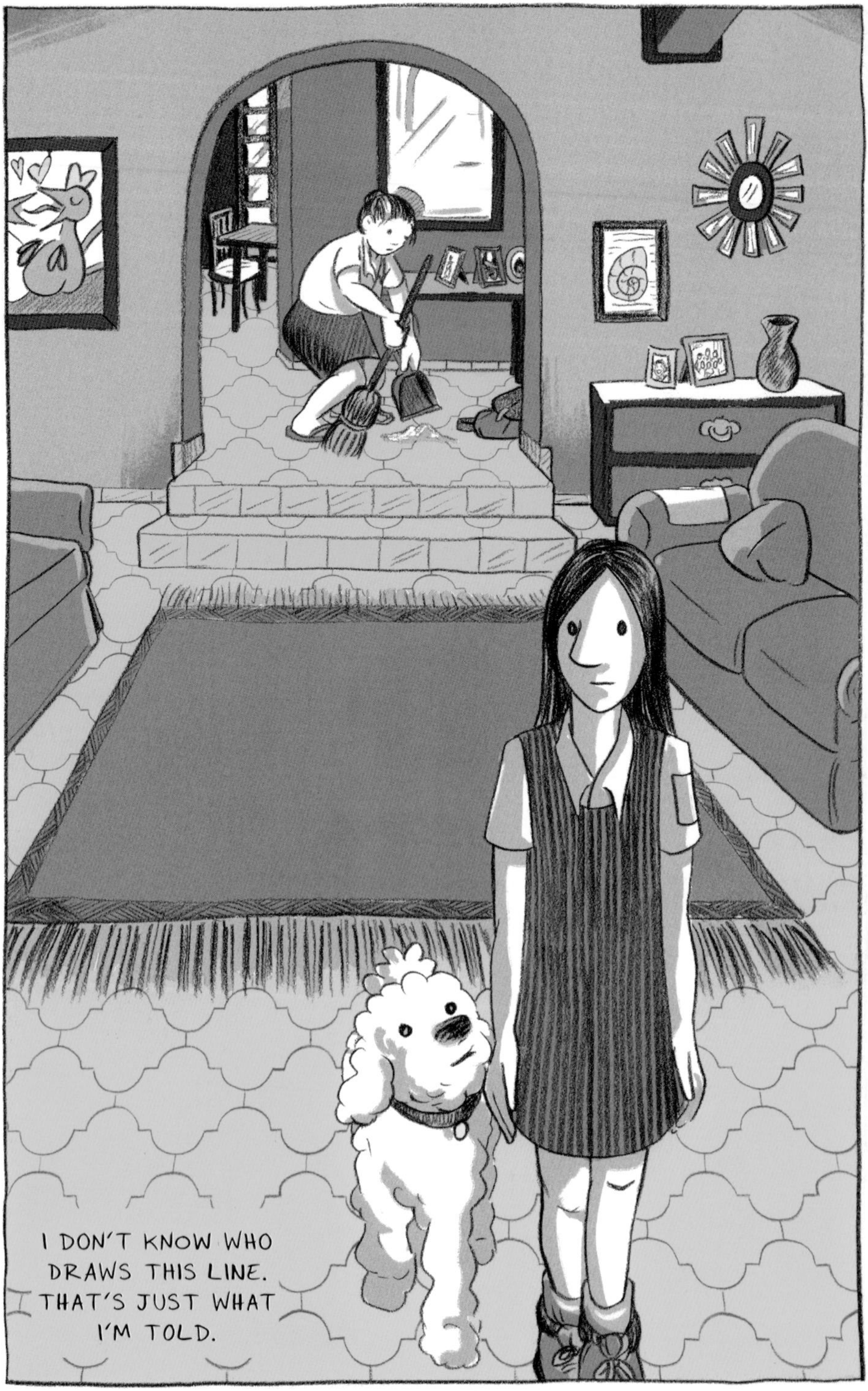
I DON'T KNOW WHO DRAWS THIS LINE. THAT'S JUST WHAT I'M TOLD.

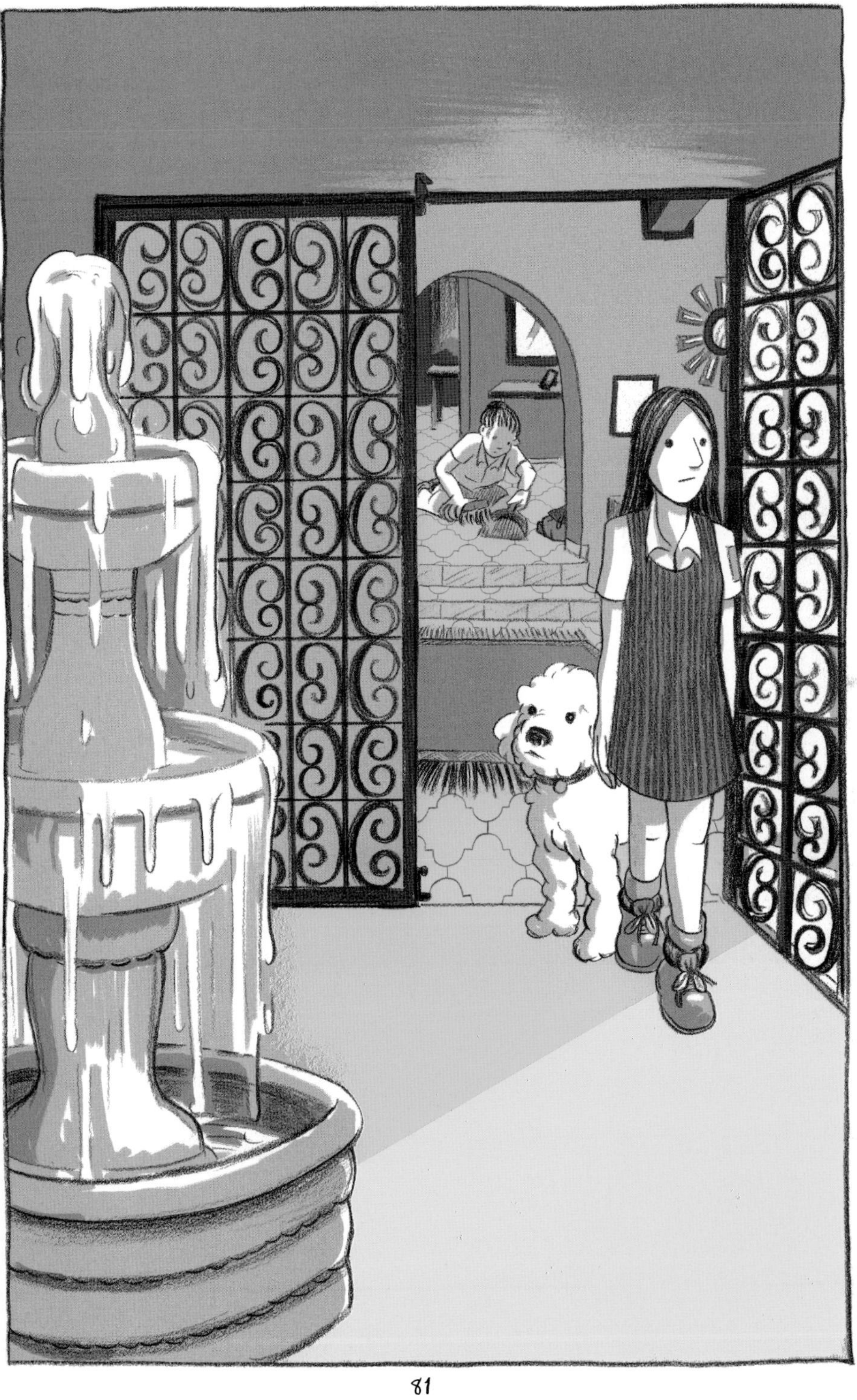

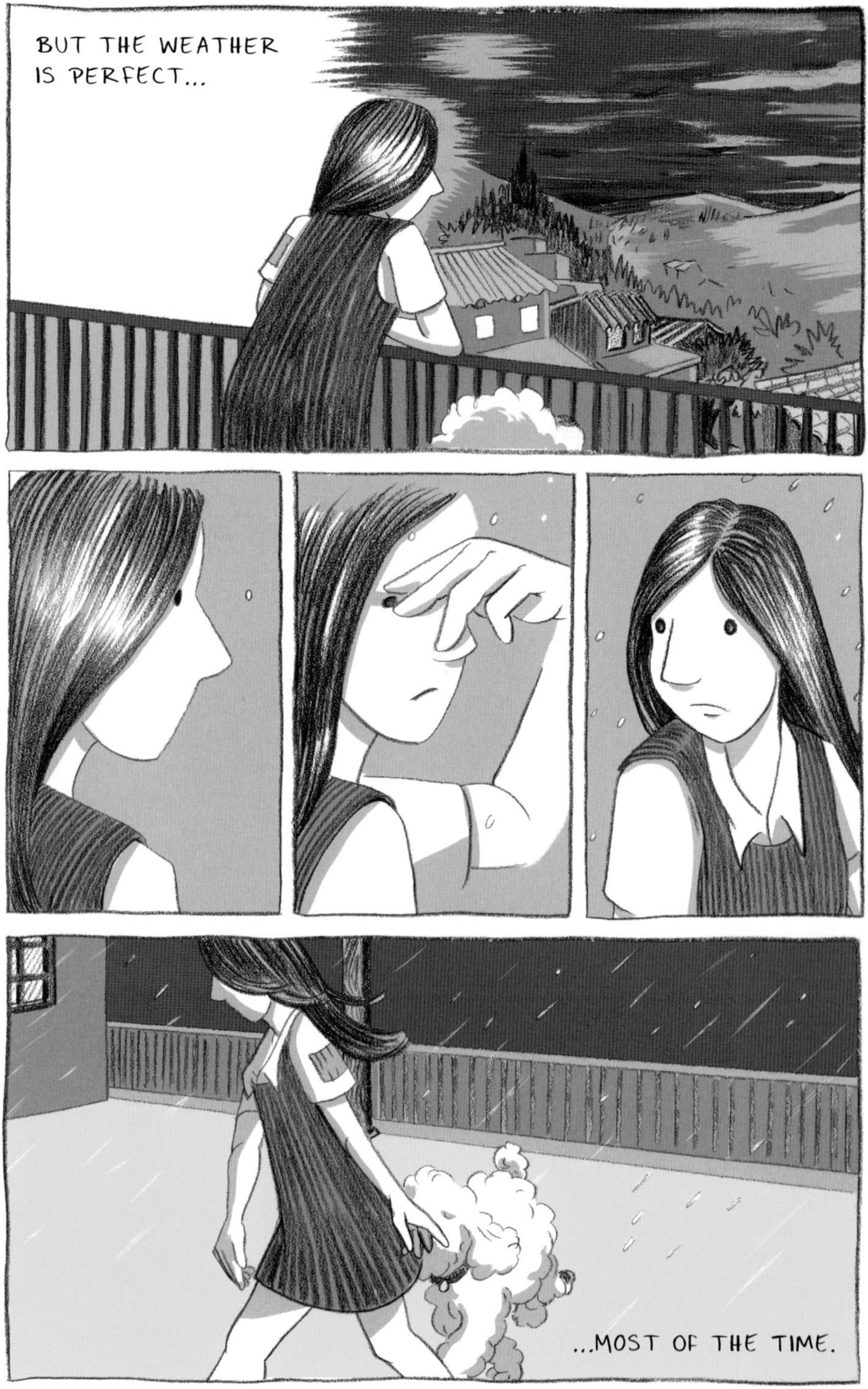
BUT THE WEATHER IS PERFECT...
...MOST OF THE TIME.

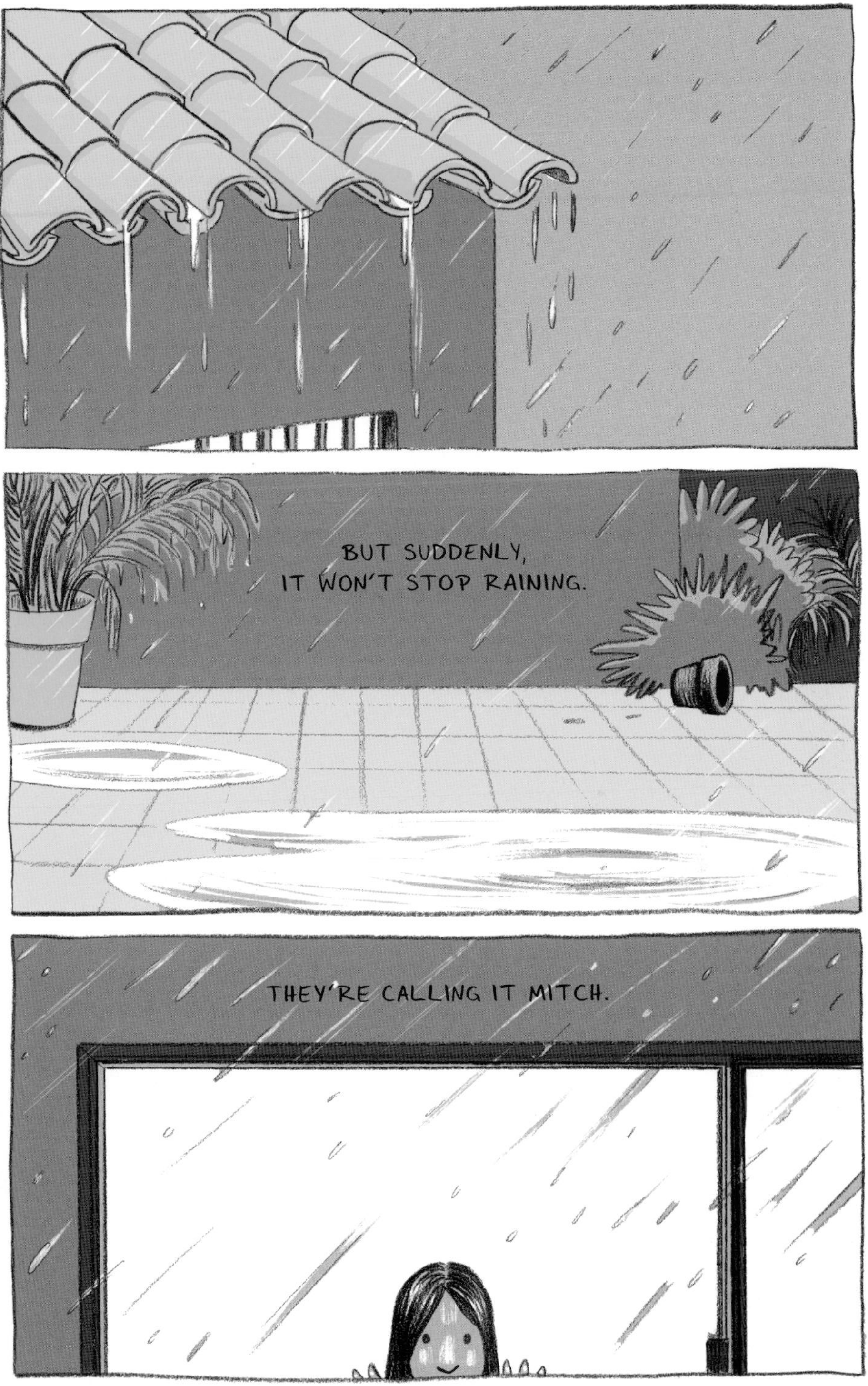
BUT SUDDENLY,
IT WON'T STOP RAINING.
THEY'RE CALLING IT MITCH.

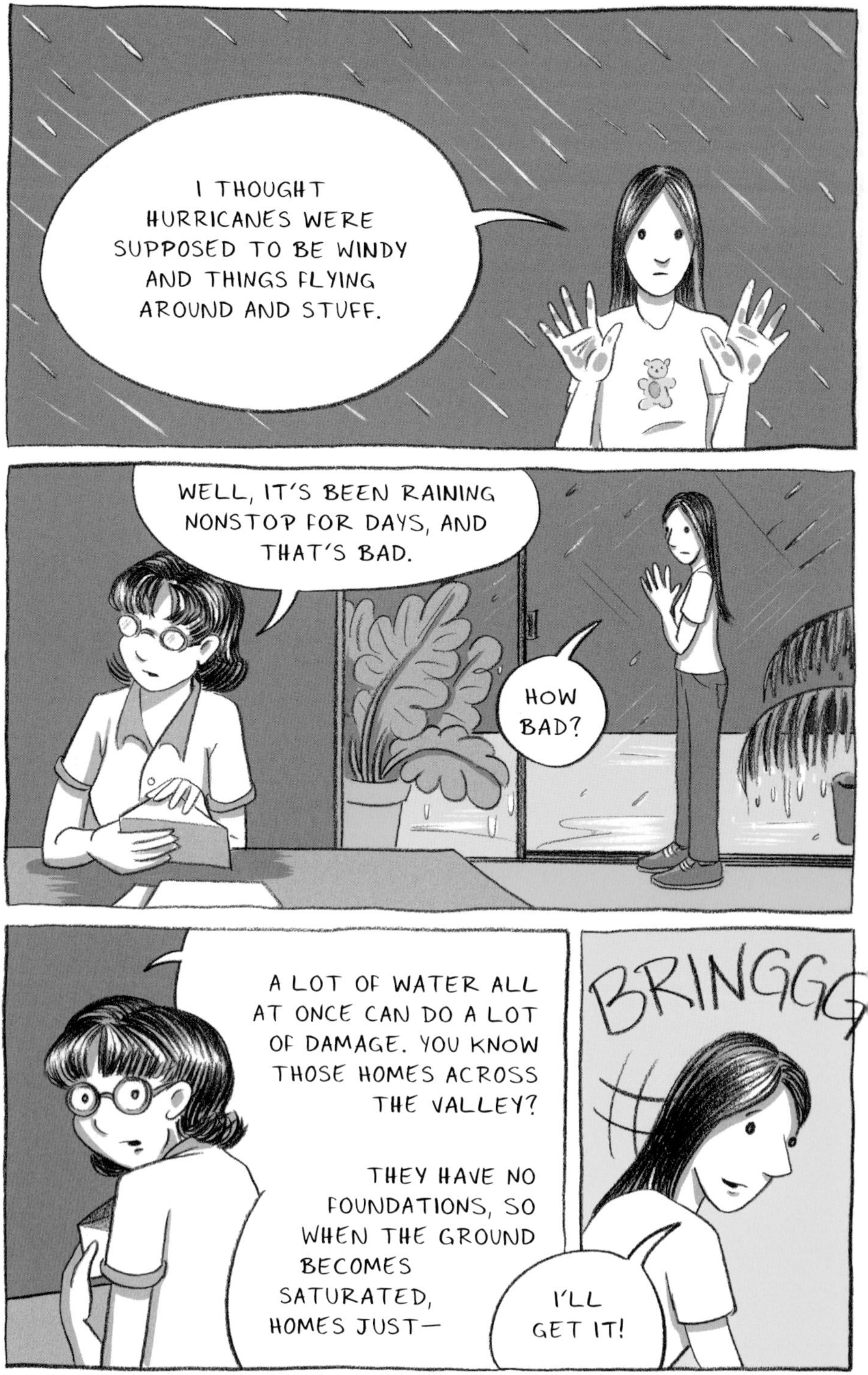
I THOUGHT HURRICANES WERE SUPPOSED TO BE WINDY AND THINGS FLYING AROUND AND STUFF.
WELL, IT'S BEEN RAINING NONSTOP FOR DAYS, AND THAT'S BAD.
HOW BAD?
A LOT OF WATER ALL AT ONCE CAN DO A LOT OF DAMAGE. YOU KNOW THOSE HOMES ACROSS THE VALLEY?
THEY HAVE NO FOUNDATIONS, SO WHEN THE GROUND BECOMES SATURATED, HOMES JUST—
BRINGGG
I'LL GET IT!

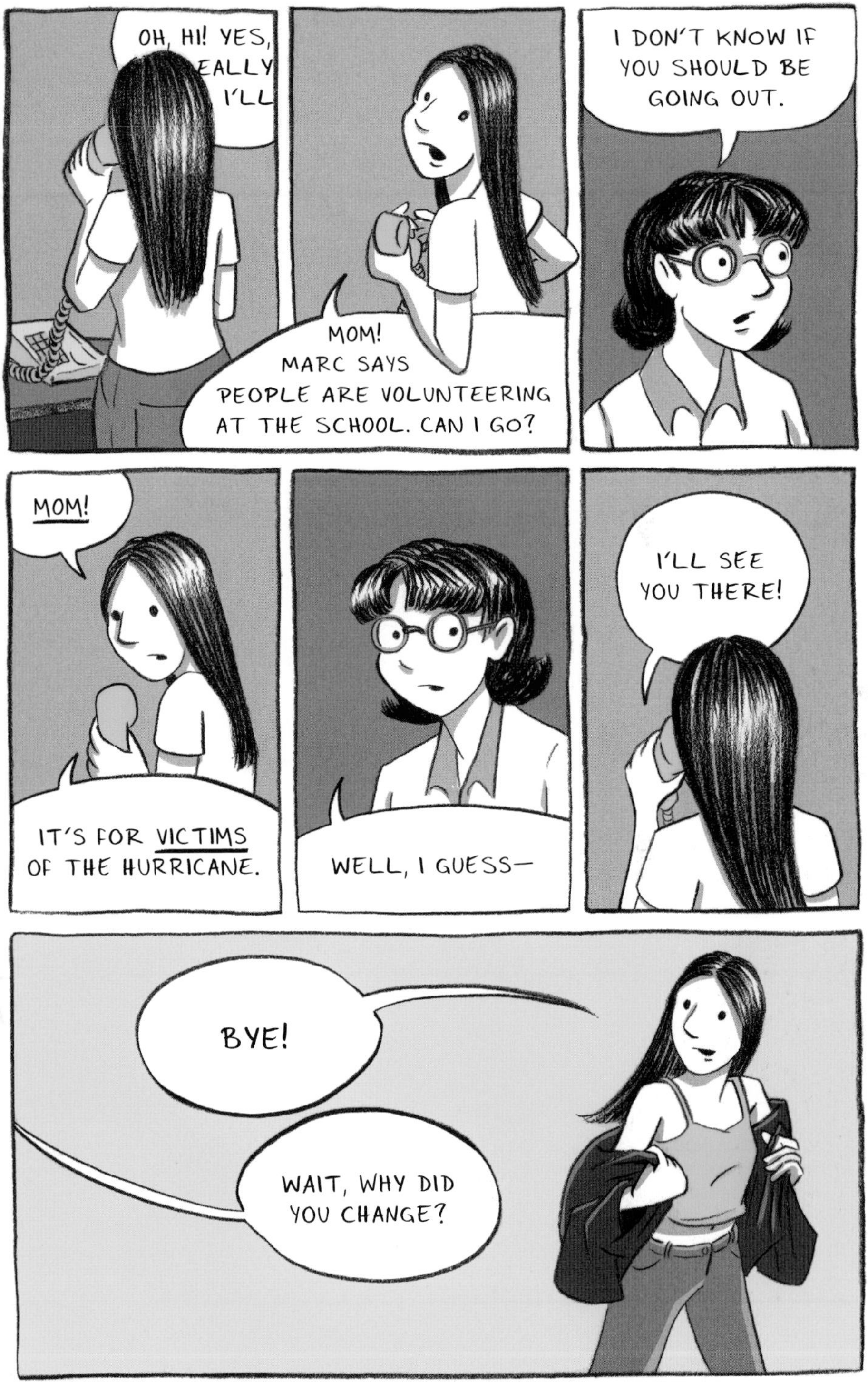
OH, HI! YES, EALLY I'LL
MOM! MARC SAYS PEOPLE ARE VOLUNTEERING AT THE SCHOOL. CAN I GO?
I DON'T KNOW IF YOU SHOULD BE GOING OUT.
MOM!
IT'S FOR VICTIMS OF THE HURRICANE.
WELL, I GUESS—
I'LL SEE YOU THERE!
BYE!
WAIT, WHY DID YOU CHANGE?

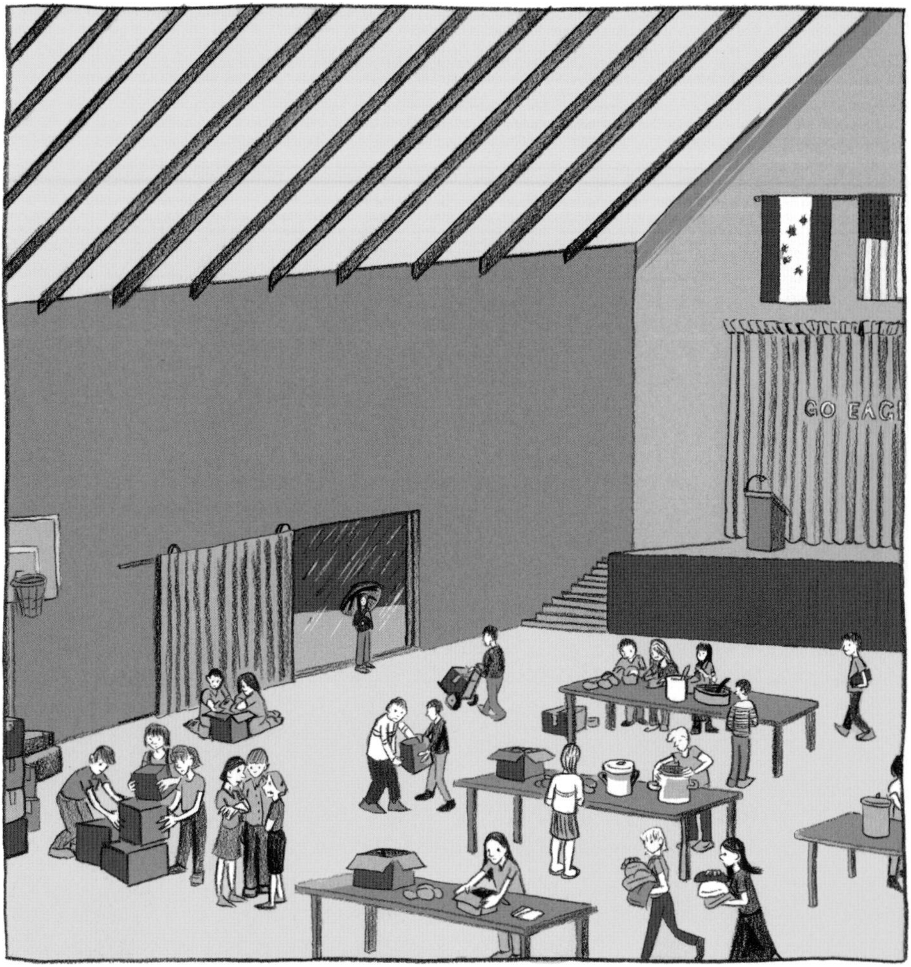
GO EAG

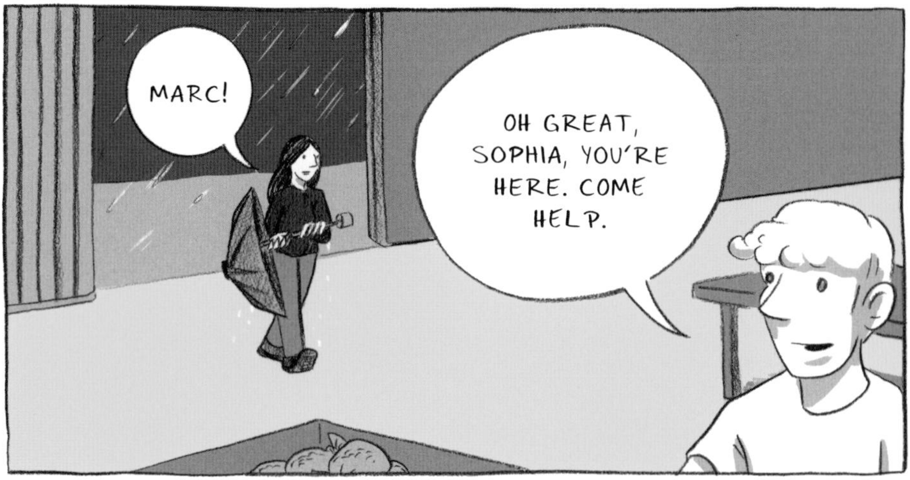
MARC!
OH GREAT, SOPHIA, YOU'RE HERE. COME HELP.

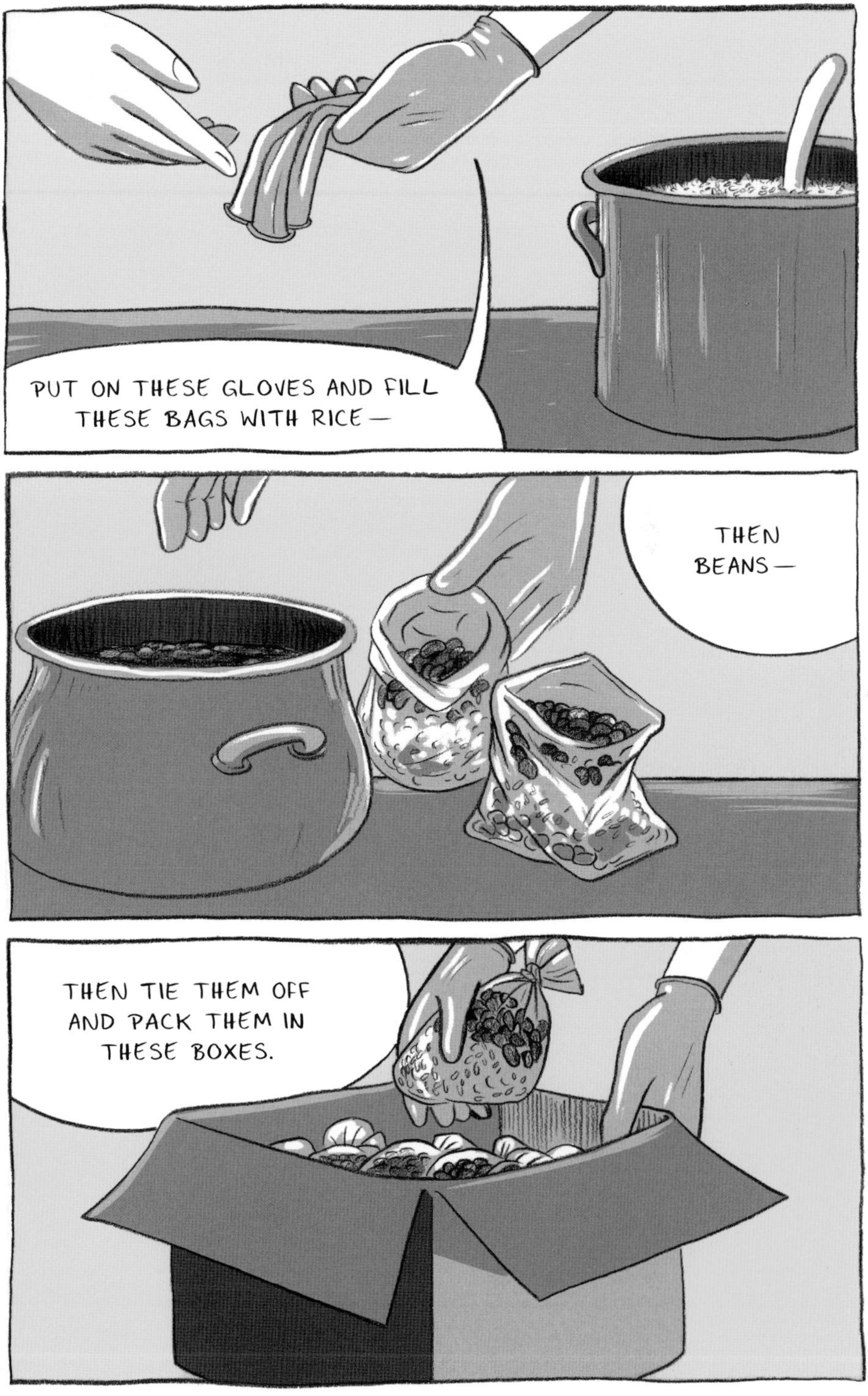
PUT ON THESE GLOVES AND FILL THESE BAGS WITH RICE—
THEN BEANS—
THEN TIE THEM OFF AND PACK THEM IN THESE BOXES.

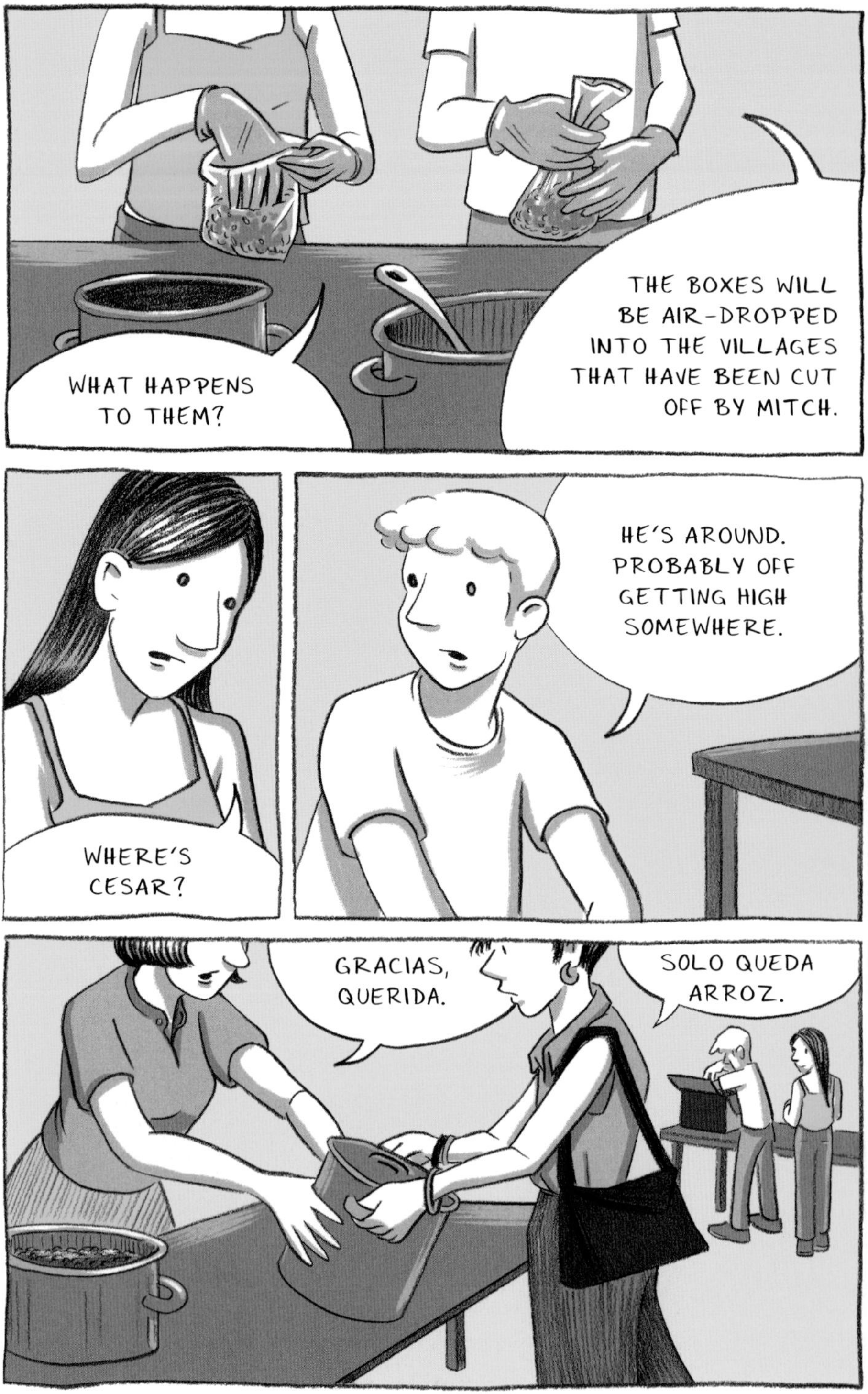
WHAT HAPPENS TO THEM?
THE BOXES WILL BE AIR-DROPPED INTO THE VILLAGES THAT HAVE BEEN CUT OFF BY MITCH.
WHERE'S CESAR?
HE'S AROUND. PROBABLY OFF GETTING HIGH SOMEWHERE.
GRACIAS, QUERIDA.
SOLO QUEDA ARROZ.

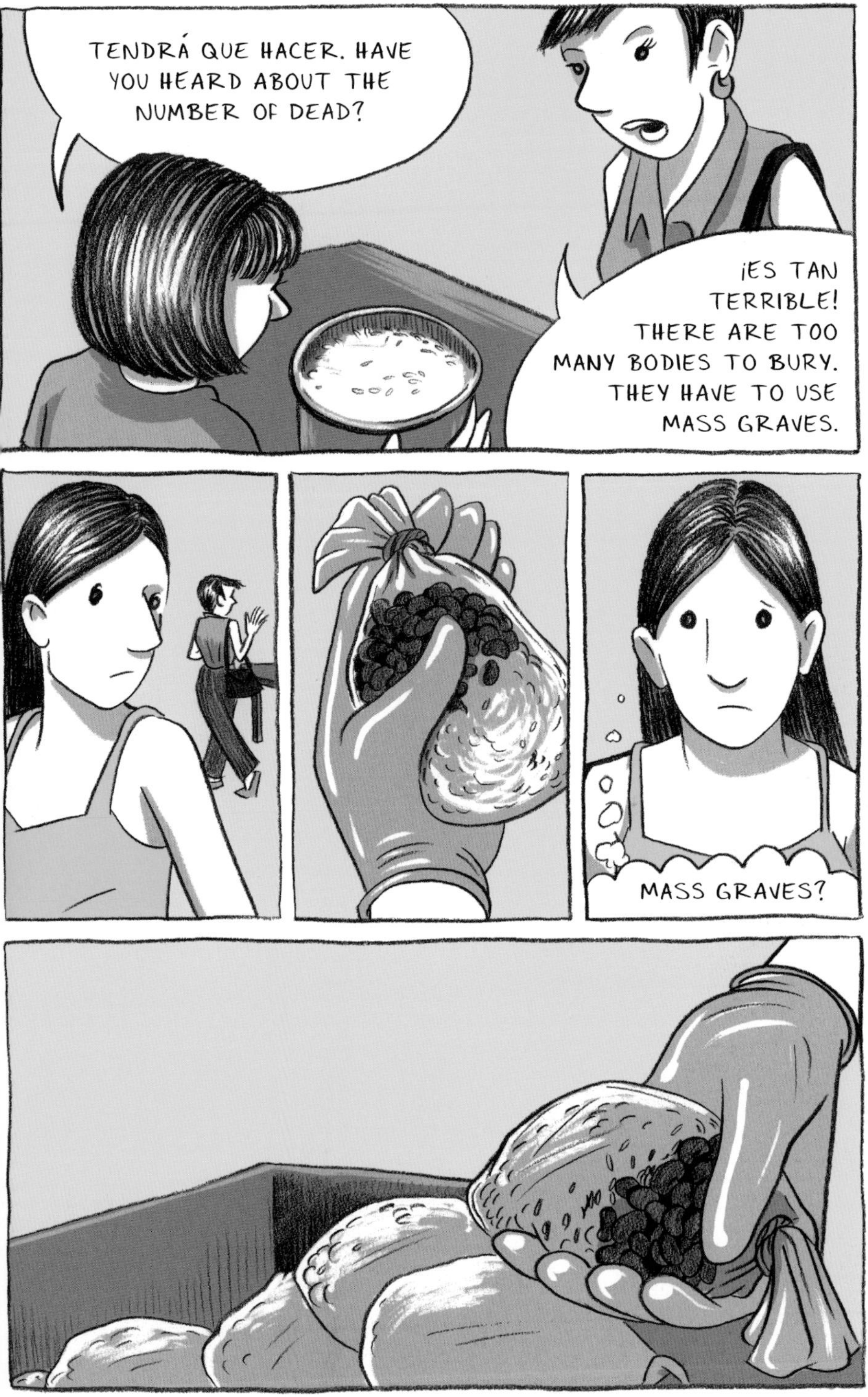
TENDRÁ QUE HACER. HAVE YOU HEARD ABOUT THE NUMBER OF DEAD?
¡ES TAN TERRIBLE! THERE ARE TOO MANY BODIES TO BURY. THEY HAVE TO USE MASS GRAVES.
MASS GRAVES?

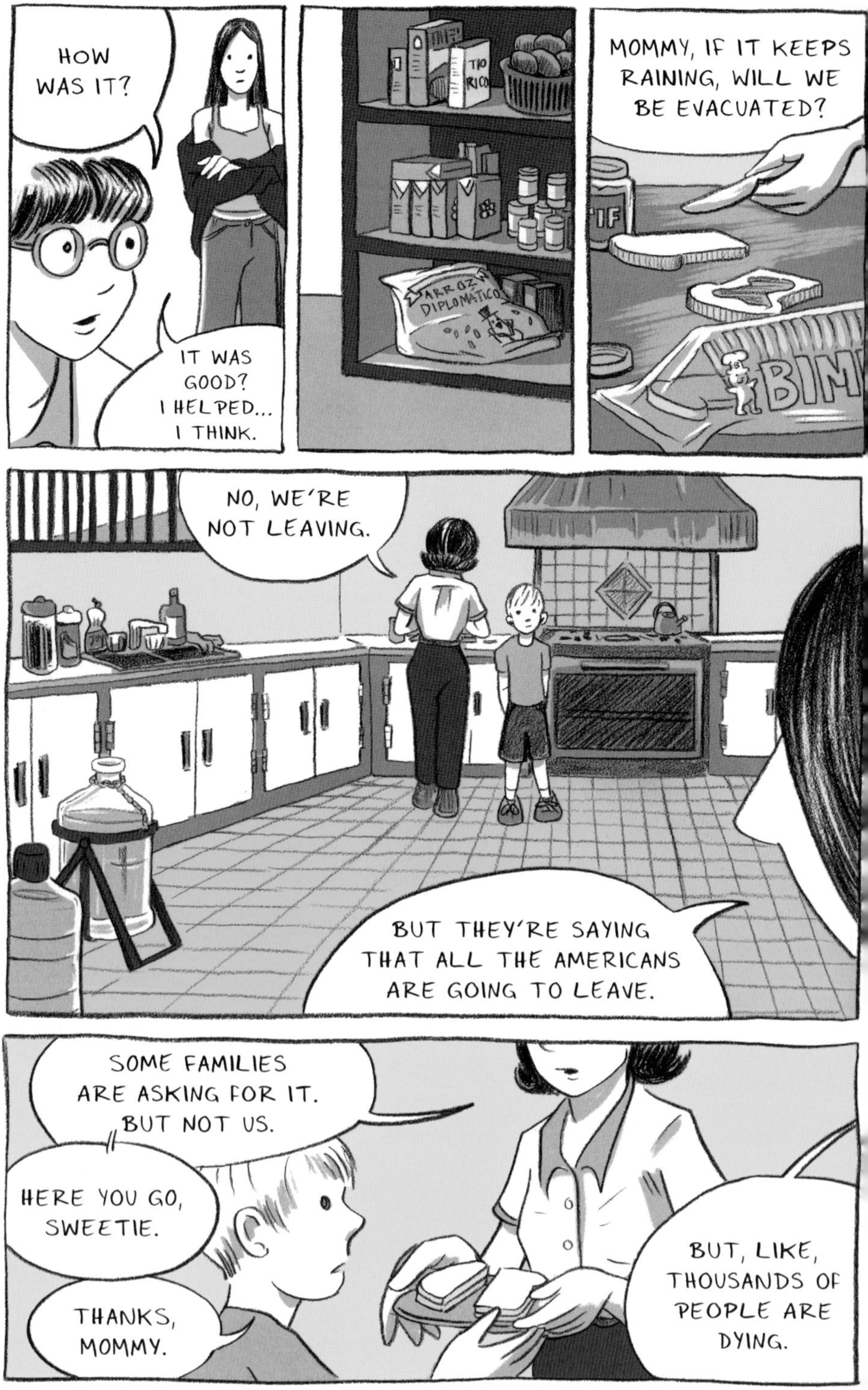
HOW WAS IT?
IT WAS GOOD? I HELPED... I THINK.
ARROZ DIPLOMATICO
MOMMY, IF IT KEEPS RAINING, WILL WE BE EVACUATED?
NO, WE'RE NOT LEAVING.
BUT THEY'RE SAYING THAT ALL THE AMERICANS ARE GOING TO LEAVE.
SOME FAMILIES ARE ASKING FOR IT. BUT NOT US.
HERE YOU GO, SWEETIE.
THANKS, MOMMY.
BUT, LIKE, THOUSANDS OF PEOPLE ARE DYING.

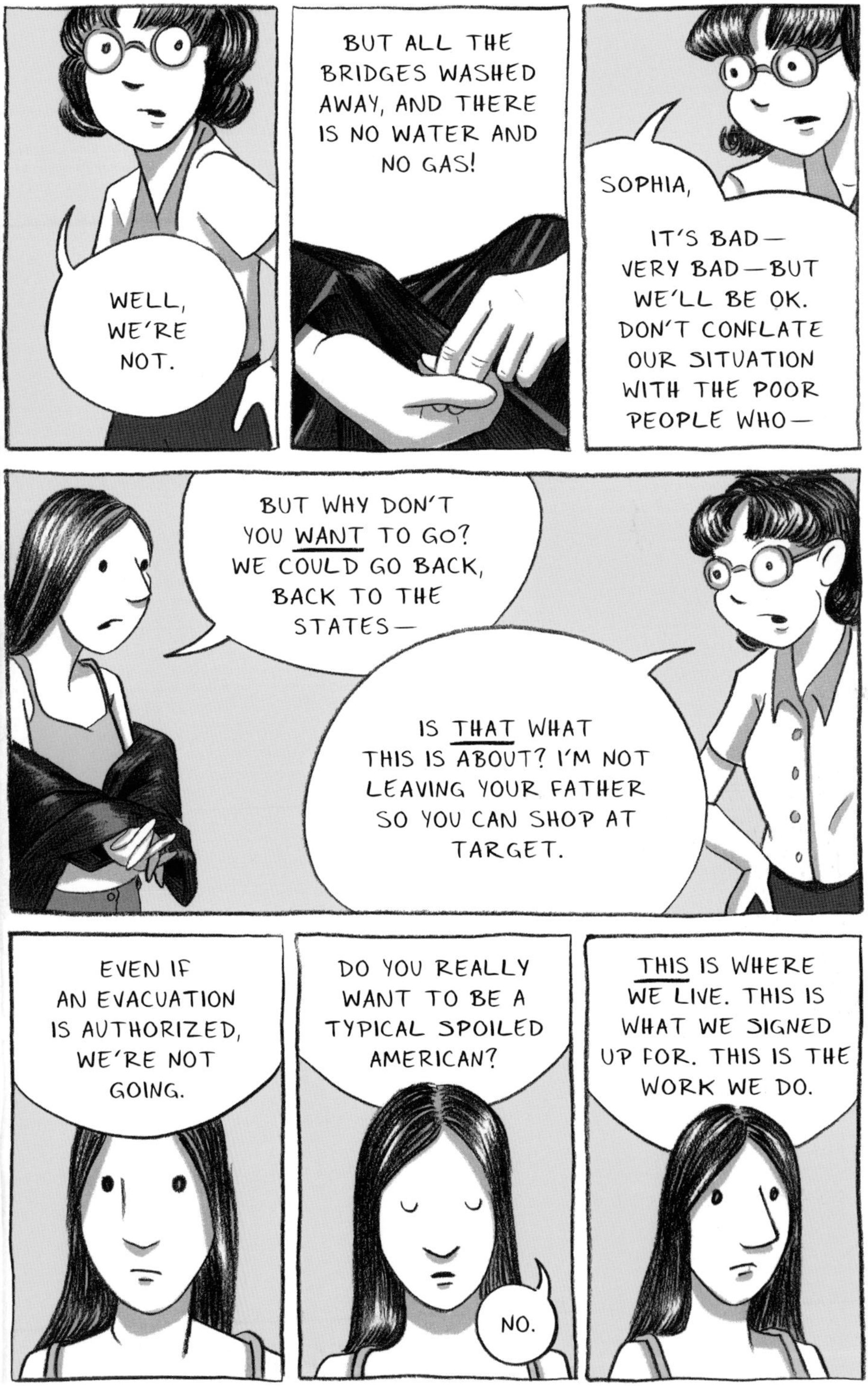
WELL, WE'RE NOT.
BUT ALL THE BRIDGES WASHED AWAY, AND THERE IS NO WATER AND NO GAS!
SOPHIA,
IT'S BAD— VERY BAD—BUT WE'LL BE OK. DON'T CONFLATE OUR SITUATION WITH THE POOR PEOPLE WHO—
BUT WHY DON'T YOU WANT TO GO? WE COULD GO BACK, BACK TO THE STATES—
IS THAT WHAT THIS IS ABOUT? I'M NOT LEAVING YOUR FATHER SO YOU CAN SHOP AT TARGET.
EVEN IF AN EVACUATION IS AUTHORIZED, WE'RE NOT GOING.
DO YOU REALLY WANT TO BE A TYPICAL SPOILED AMERICAN?
NO.
THIS IS WHERE WE LIVE. THIS IS WHAT WE SIGNED UP FOR. THIS IS THE WORK WE DO.

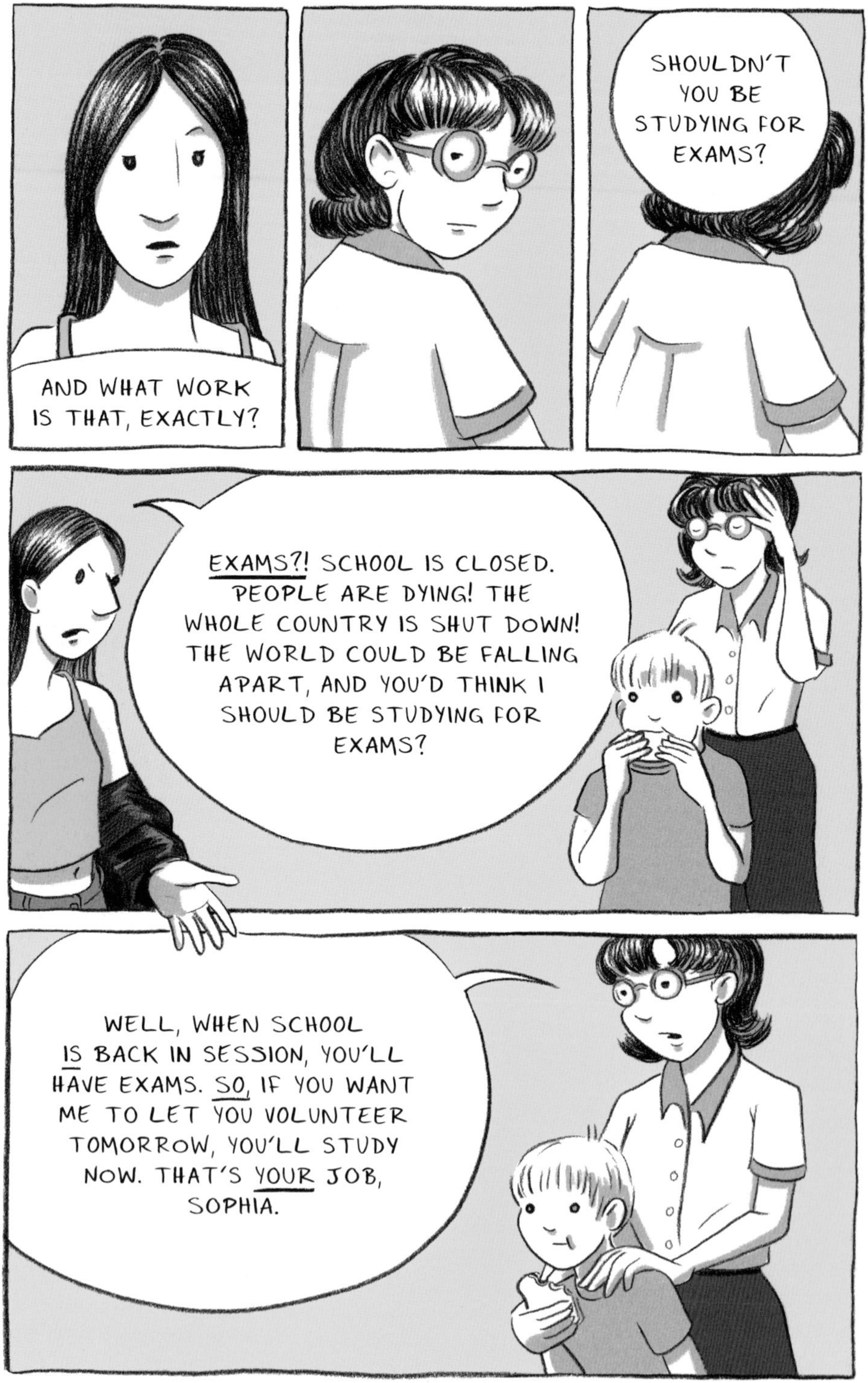
AND WHAT WORK IS THAT, EXACTLY?
SHOULDN'T YOU BE STUDYING FOR EXAMS?
EXAMS?! SCHOOL IS CLOSED. PEOPLE ARE DYING! THE WHOLE COUNTRY IS SHUT DOWN! THE WORLD COULD BE FALLING APART, AND YOU'D THINK I SHOULD BE STUDYING FOR EXAMS?
WELL, WHEN SCHOOL IS BACK IN SESSION, YOU'LL HAVE EXAMS. SO, IF YOU WANT ME TO LET YOU VOLUNTEER TOMORROW, YOU'LL STUDY NOW. THAT'S YOUR JOB, SOPHIA.

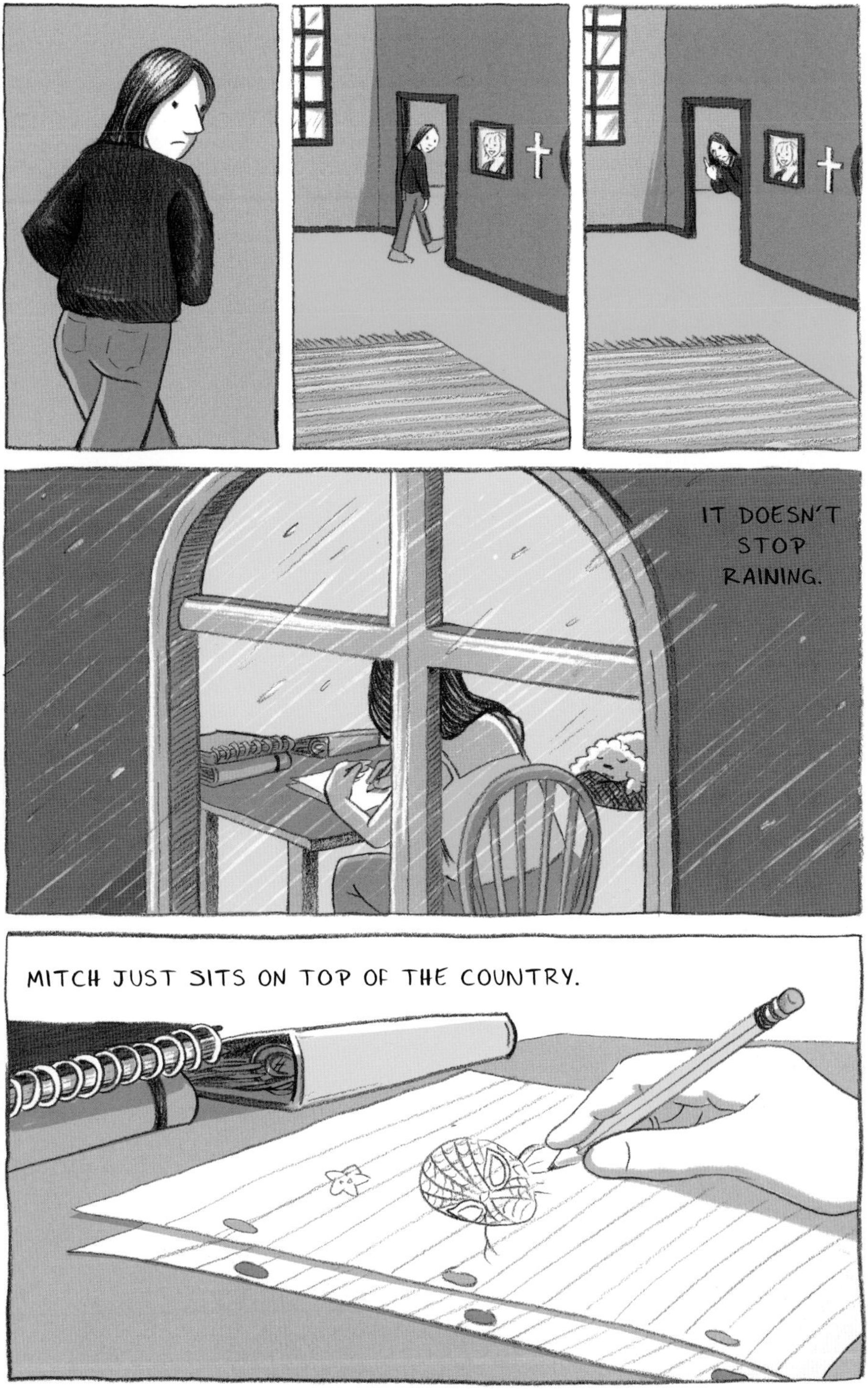
IT DOESN'T
STOP
RAINING.
MITCH JUST SITS ON TOP OF THE COUNTRY.

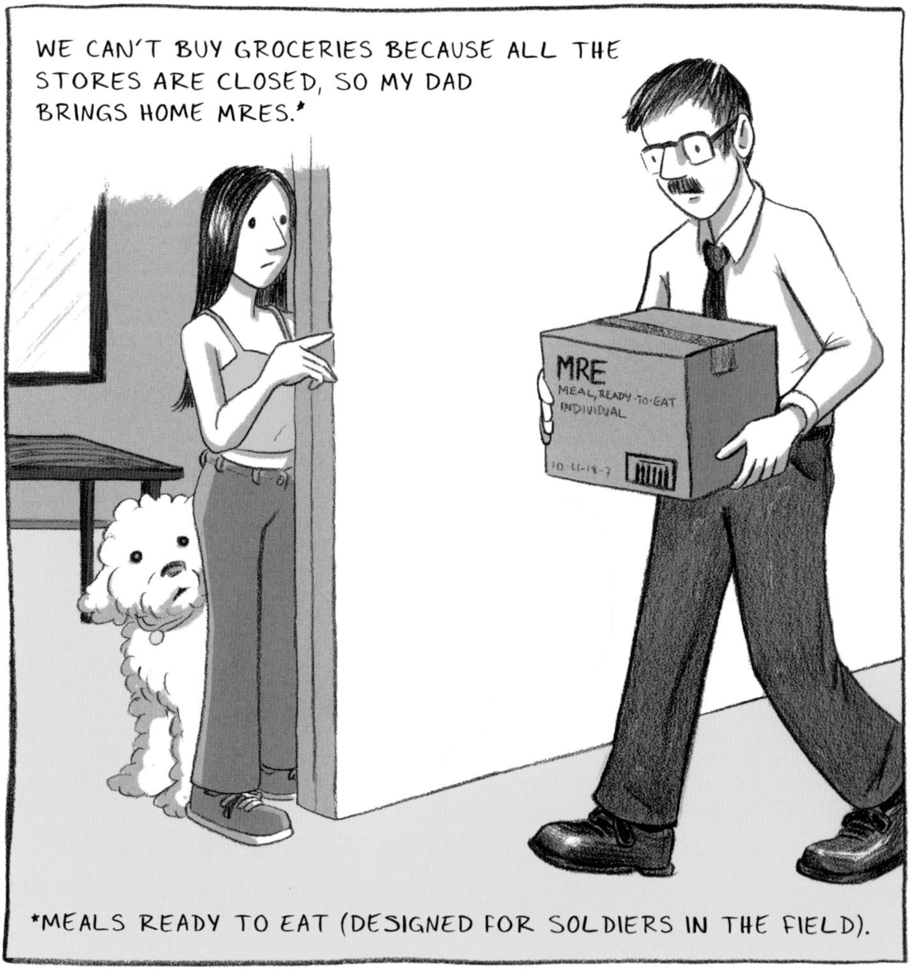
WE CAN'T BUY GROCERIES BECAUSE ALL THE STORES ARE CLOSED, SO MY DAD BRINGS HOME MRES.*
MRE
MEAL, READY-TO-EAT
INDIVIDUAL
*MEALS READY TO EAT (DESIGNED FOR SOLDIERS IN THE FIELD).

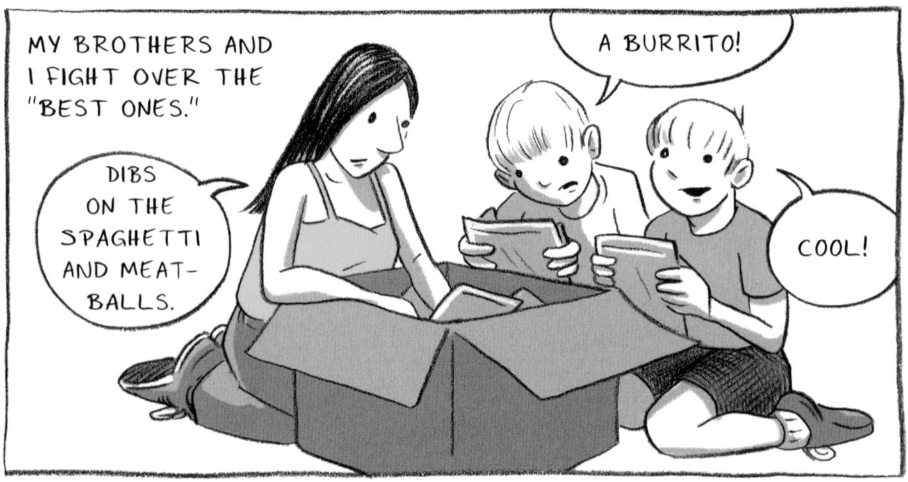
MY BROTHERS AND I FIGHT OVER THE "BEST ONES."
DIBS ON THE SPAGHETTI AND MEAT-BALLS.
A BURRITO!
COOL!

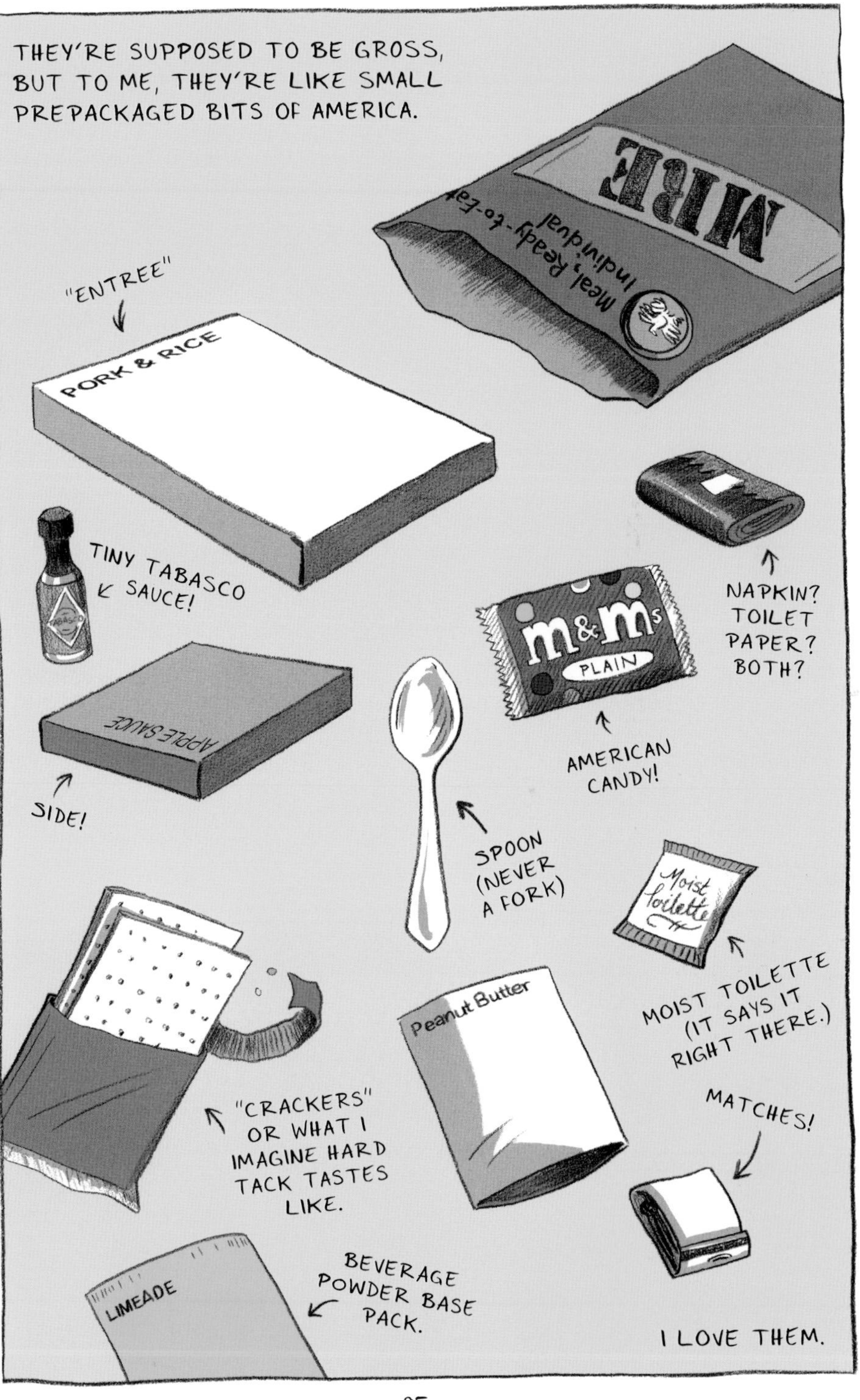
THEY'RE SUPPOSED TO BE GROSS, BUT TO ME, THEY'RE LIKE SMALL PREPACKAGED BITS OF AMERICA.
MRE
Meal, Ready-to-Eat
Individual
"ENTREE"
PORK & RICE
TINY TABASCO SAUCE!
APPLE SAUCE
SIDE!
m&m's
PLAIN
AMERICAN CANDY!
NAPKIN? TOILET PAPER? BOTH?
SPOON (NEVER A FORK)
Moist toilette
MOIST TOILETTE (IT SAYS IT RIGHT THERE.)
"CRACKERS" OR WHAT I IMAGINE HARD TACK TASTES LIKE.
Peanut Butter
MATCHES!
LIMEADE
BEVERAGE POWDER BASE PACK.
I LOVE THEM.

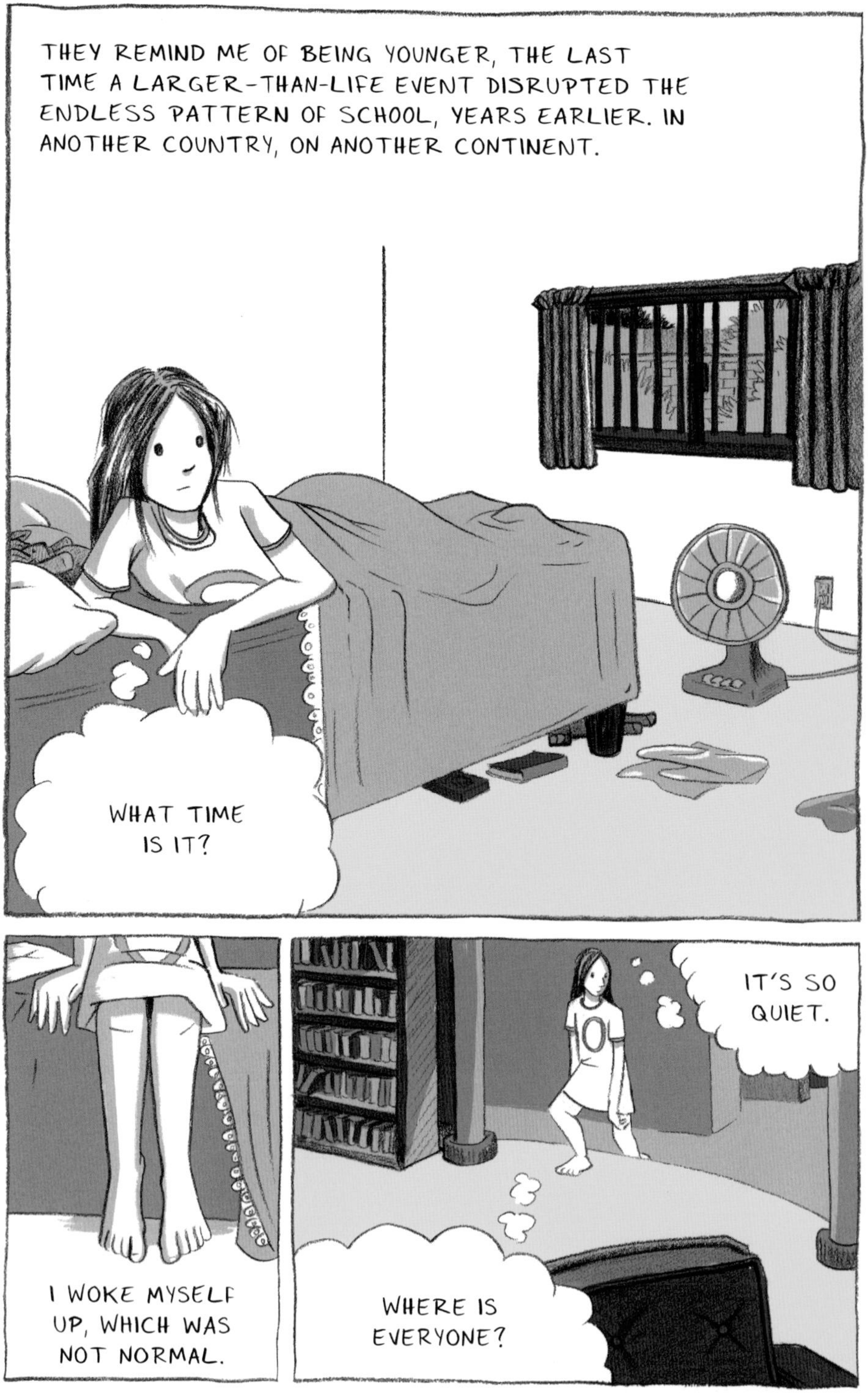
THEY REMIND ME OF BEING YOUNGER, THE LAST TIME A LARGER-THAN-LIFE EVENT DISRUPTED THE ENDLESS PATTERN OF SCHOOL, YEARS EARLIER. IN ANOTHER COUNTRY, ON ANOTHER CONTINENT.
WHAT TIME IS IT?
I WOKE MYSELF UP, WHICH WAS NOT NORMAL.
IT'S SO QUIET.
WHERE IS EVERYONE?

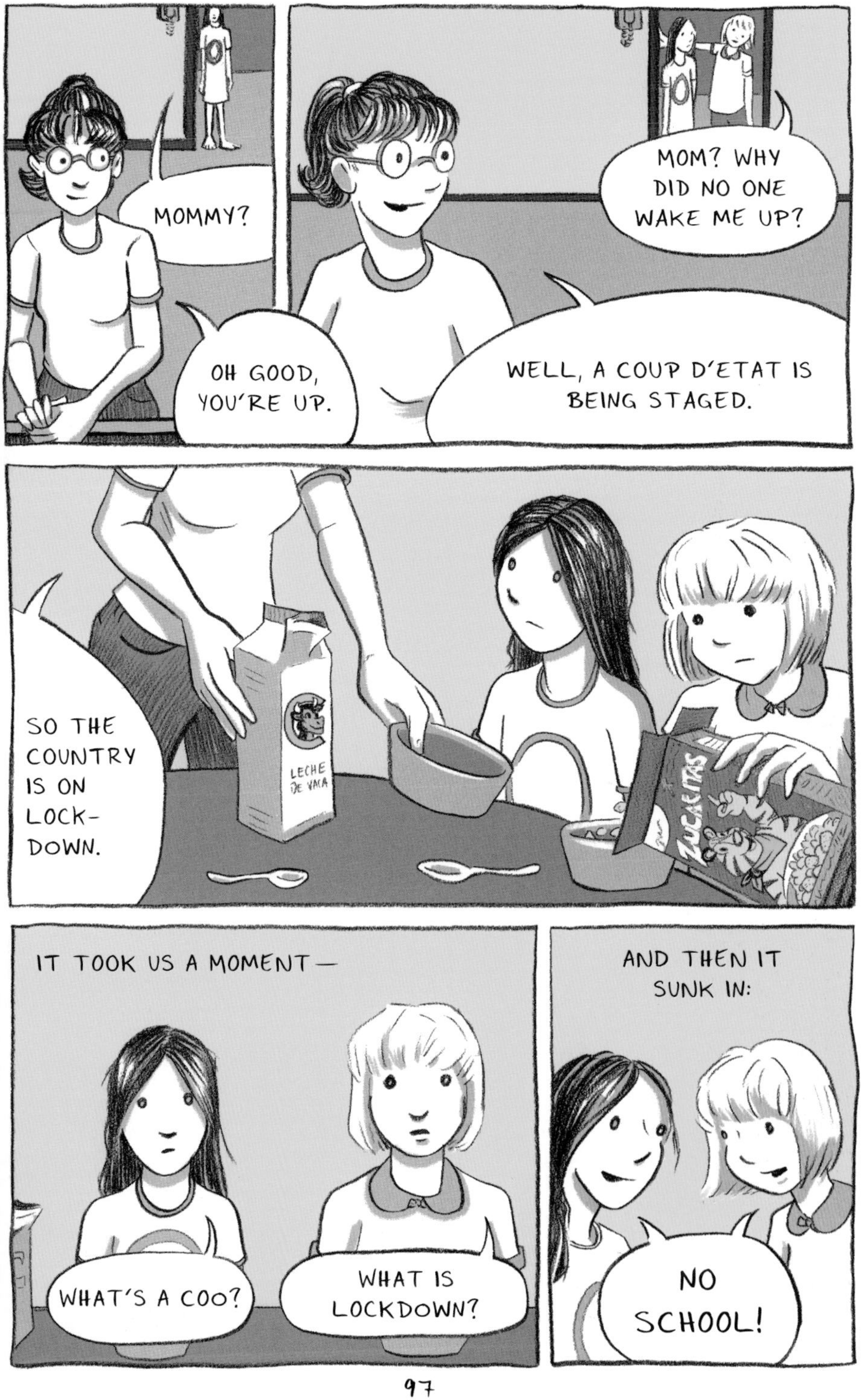
MOMMY?
MOM? WHY DID NO ONE WAKE ME UP?
OH GOOD, YOU'RE UP.
WELL, A COUP D'ETAT IS BEING STAGED.
SO THE COUNTRY IS ON LOCK-DOWN.
LECHE DE VACA
ZUCARITAS
IT TOOK US A MOMENT—
WHAT'S A COO?
WHAT IS LOCKDOWN?
AND THEN IT SUNK IN:
NO SCHOOL!

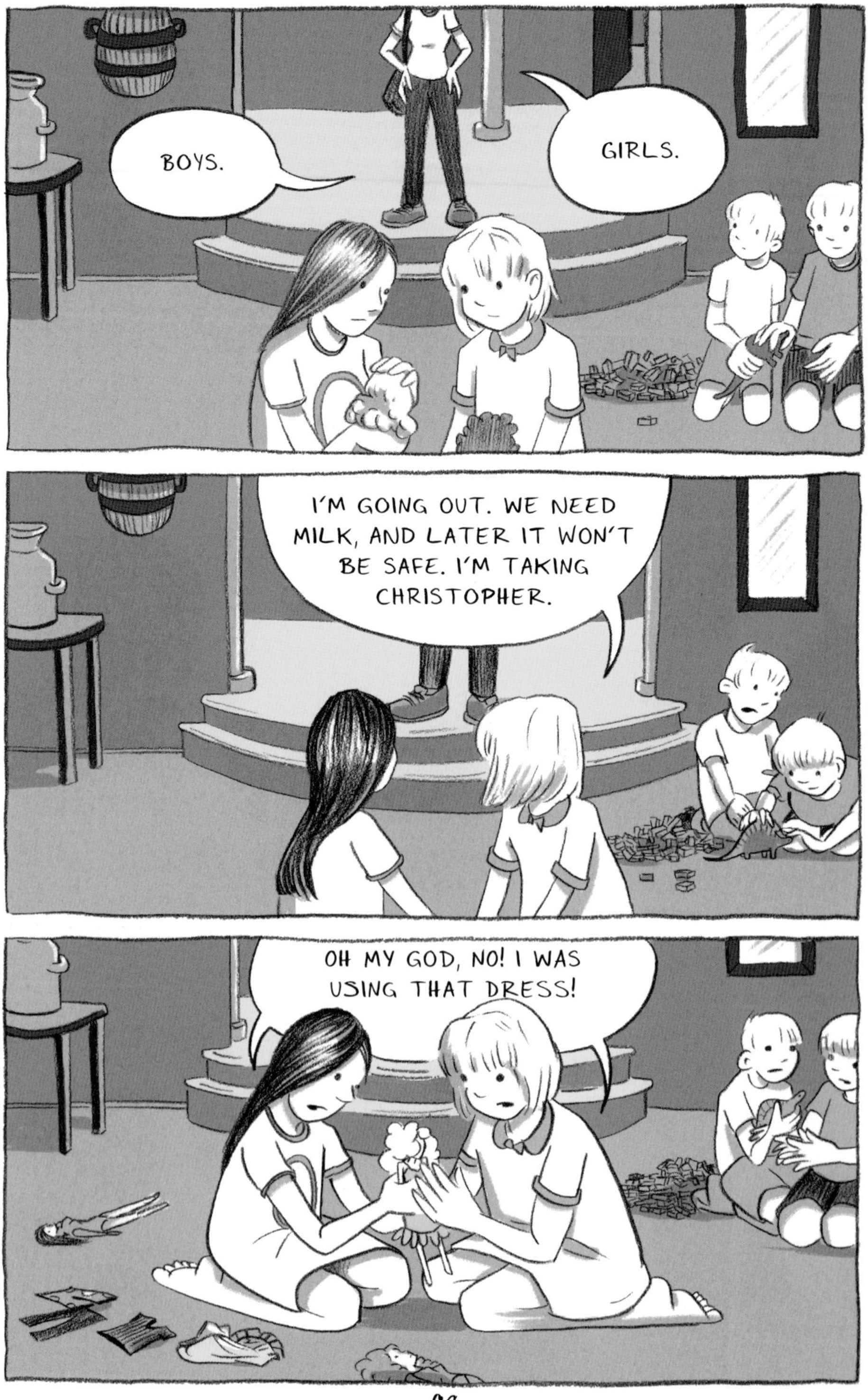
BOYS.
GIRLS.
I'M GOING OUT. WE NEED MILK, AND LATER IT WON'T BE SAFE. I'M TAKING CHRISTOPHER.
OH MY GOD, NO! I WAS USING THAT DRESS!

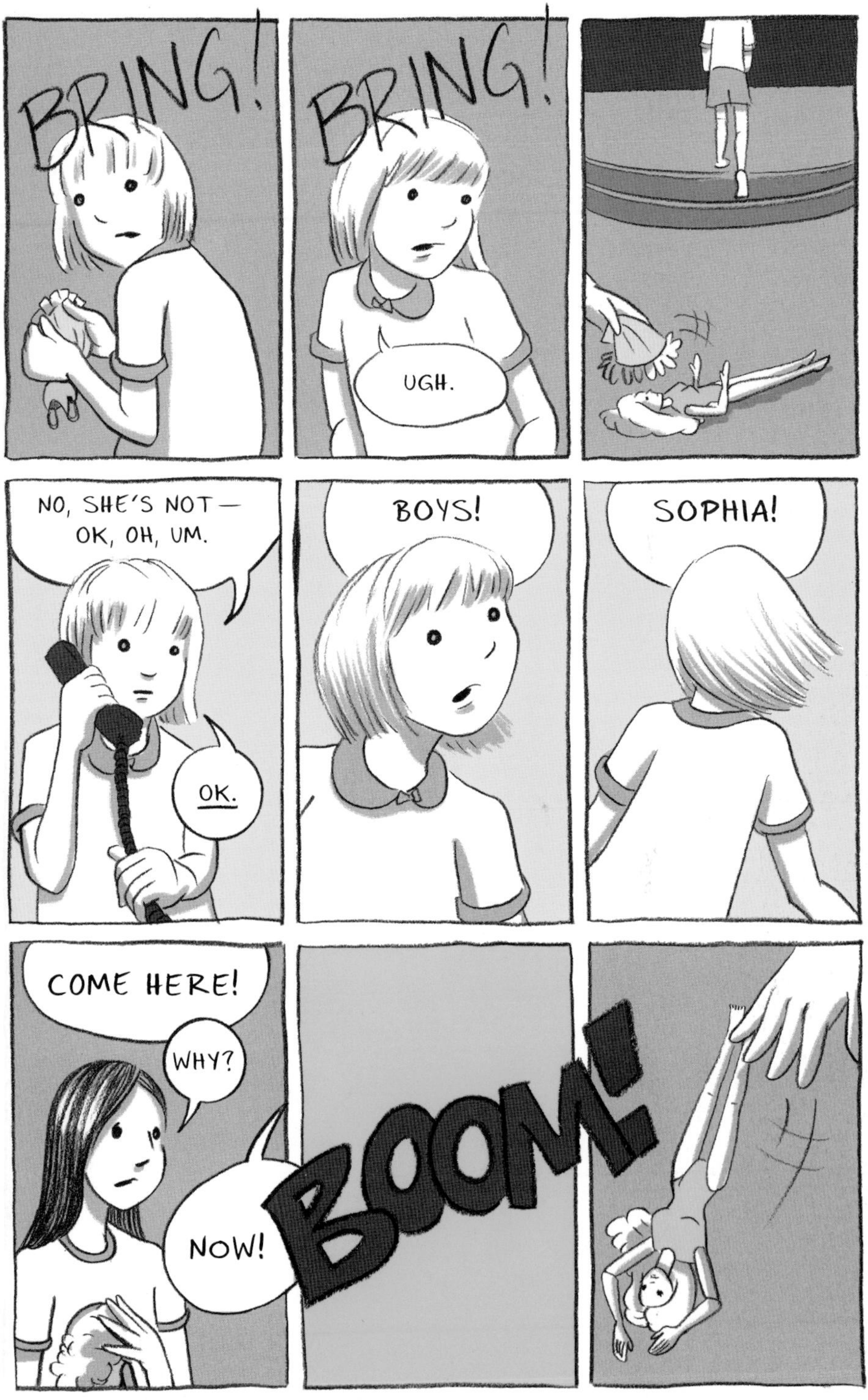
BRING!
BRING!
UGH.
NO, SHE'S NOT— OK, OH, UM.
OK.
BOYS!
SOPHIA!
COME HERE!
WHY?
NOW!
BOOM!

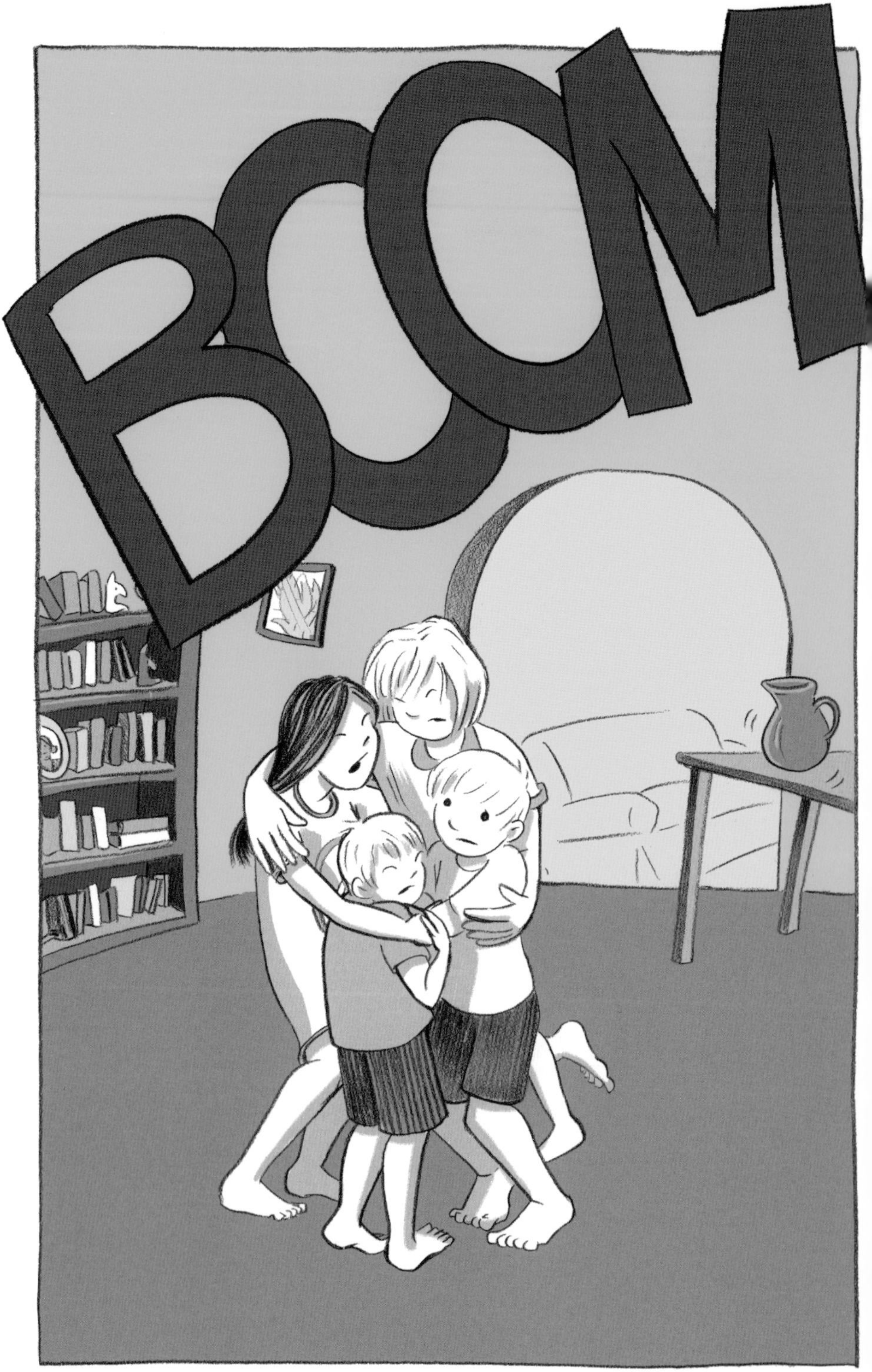
BOOM

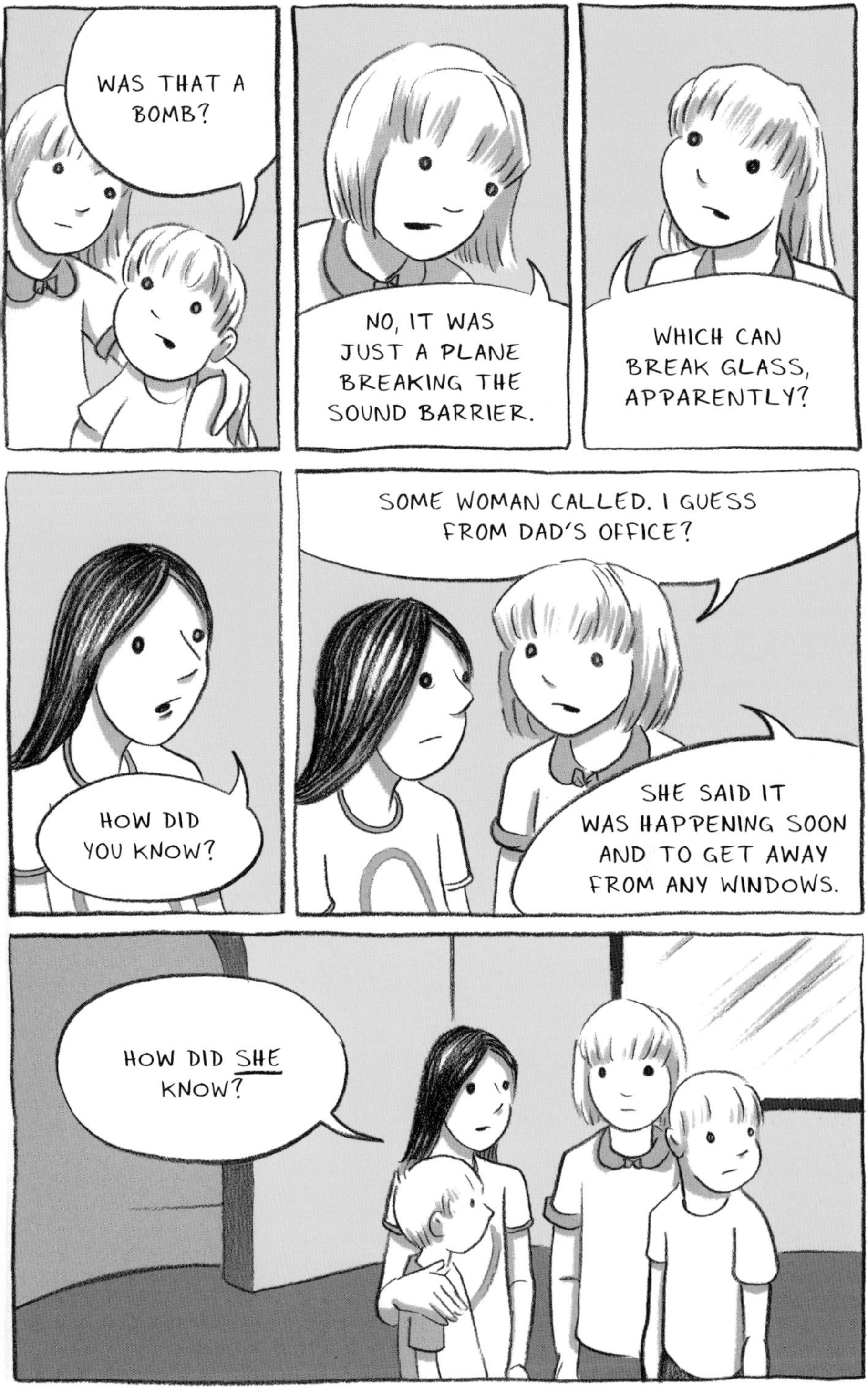
WAS THAT A BOMB?
NO, IT WAS JUST A PLANE BREAKING THE SOUND BARRIER.
WHICH CAN BREAK GLASS, APPARENTLY?
HOW DID YOU KNOW?
SOME WOMAN CALLED. I GUESS FROM DAD'S OFFICE?
SHE SAID IT WAS HAPPENING SOON AND TO GET AWAY FROM ANY WINDOWS.
HOW DID SHE KNOW?

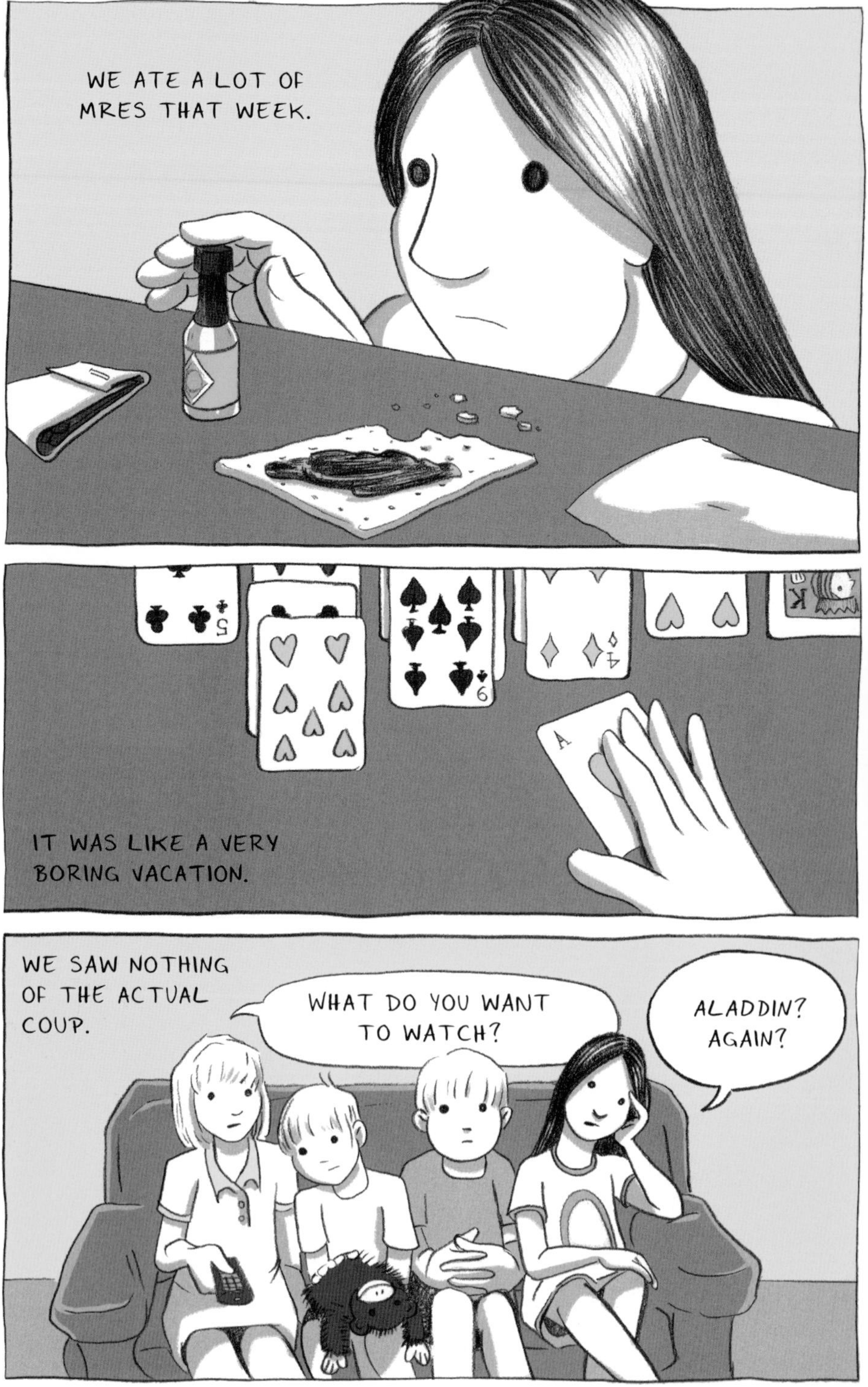
WE ATE A LOT OF MRES THAT WEEK.
IT WAS LIKE A VERY BORING VACATION.
WE SAW NOTHING OF THE ACTUAL COUP.
WHAT DO YOU WANT TO WATCH?
ALADDIN? AGAIN?

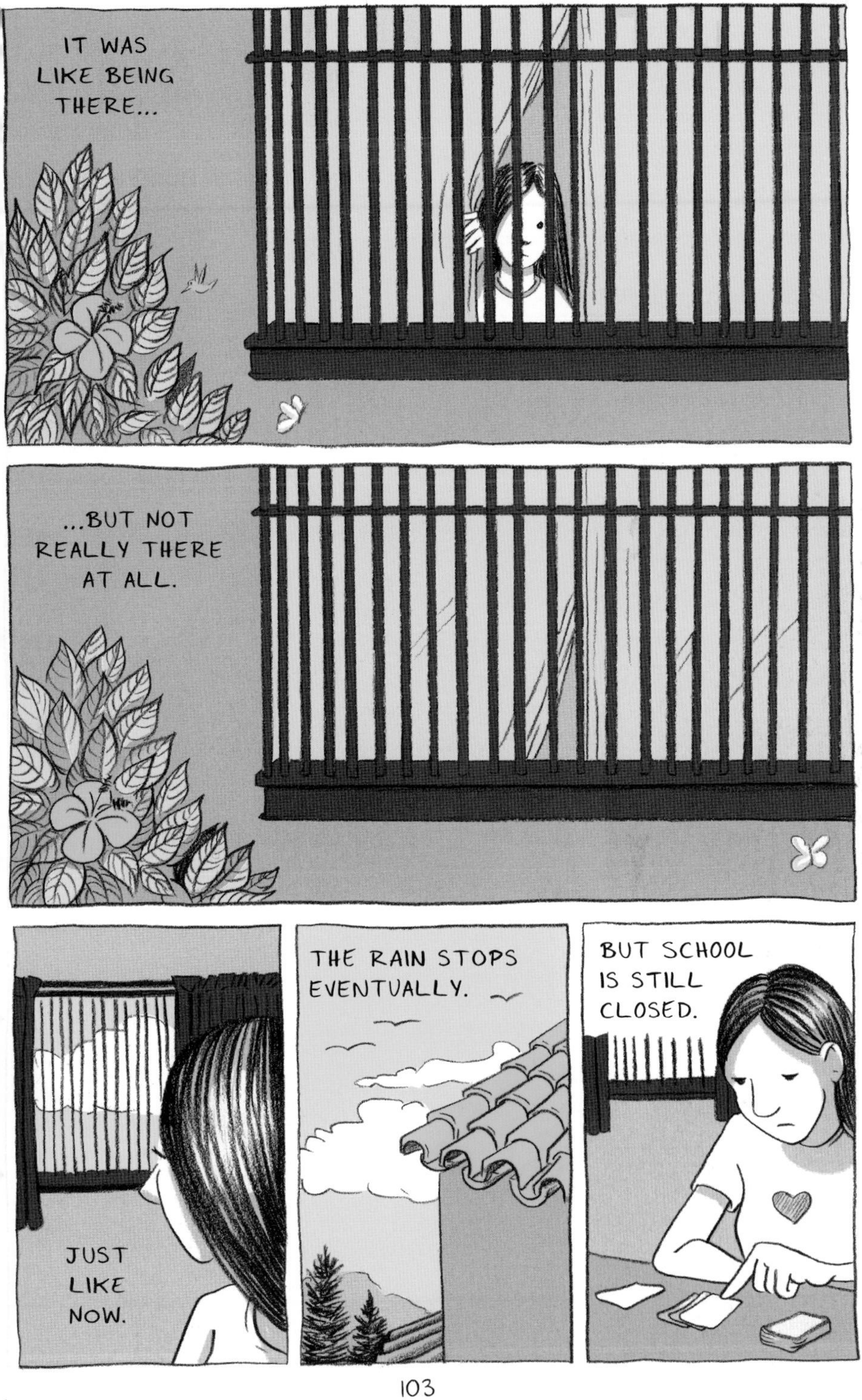
IT WAS LIKE BEING THERE...
...BUT NOT REALLY THERE AT ALL.
JUST LIKE NOW.
THE RAIN STOPS EVENTUALLY.
BUT SCHOOL IS STILL CLOSED.

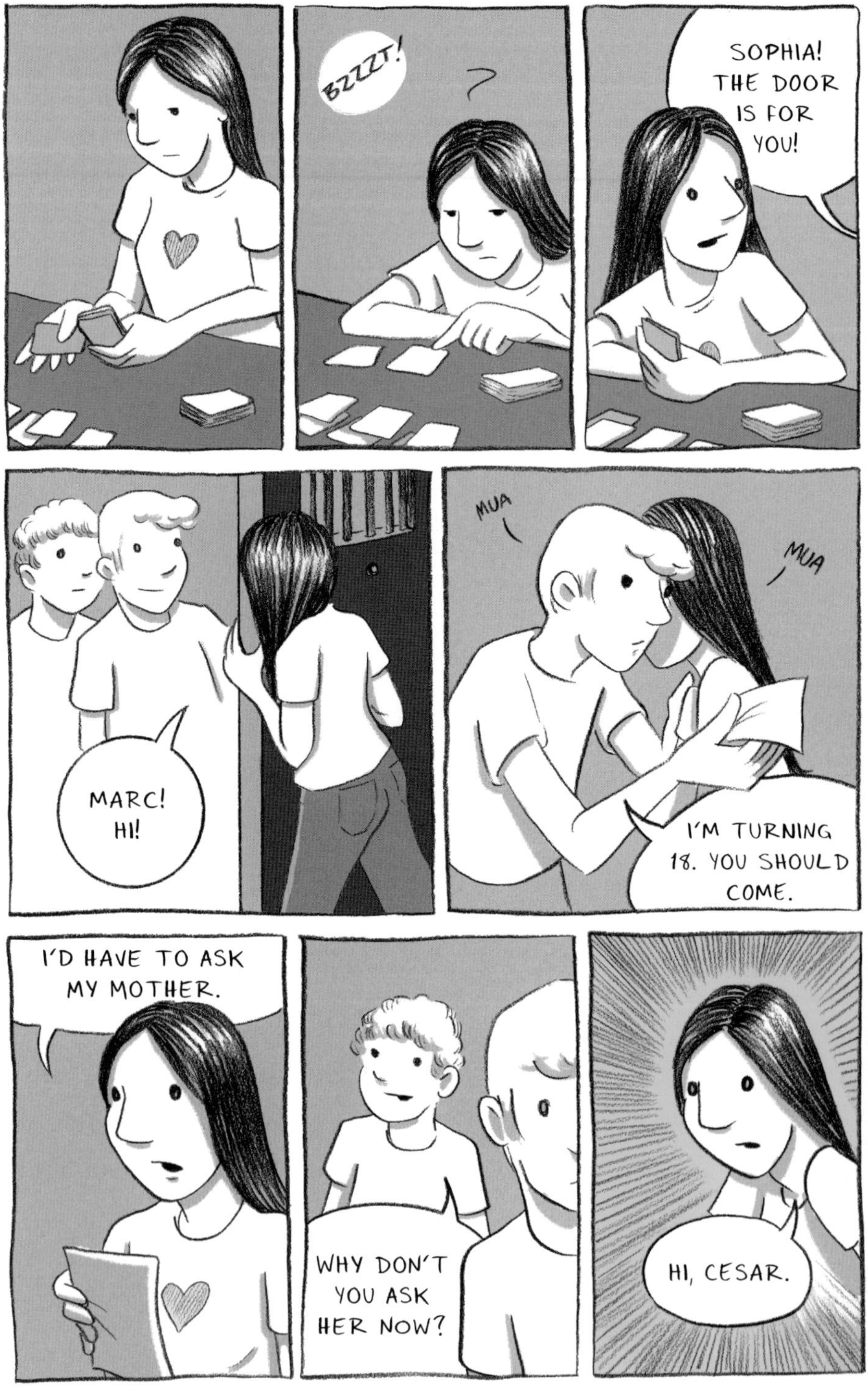
BZZZT!
?
SOPHIA! THE DOOR IS FOR YOU!
MARC! HI!
MUA
MUA
I'M TURNING 18. YOU SHOULD COME.
I'D HAVE TO ASK MY MOTHER.
WHY DON'T YOU ASK HER NOW?
HI, CESAR.

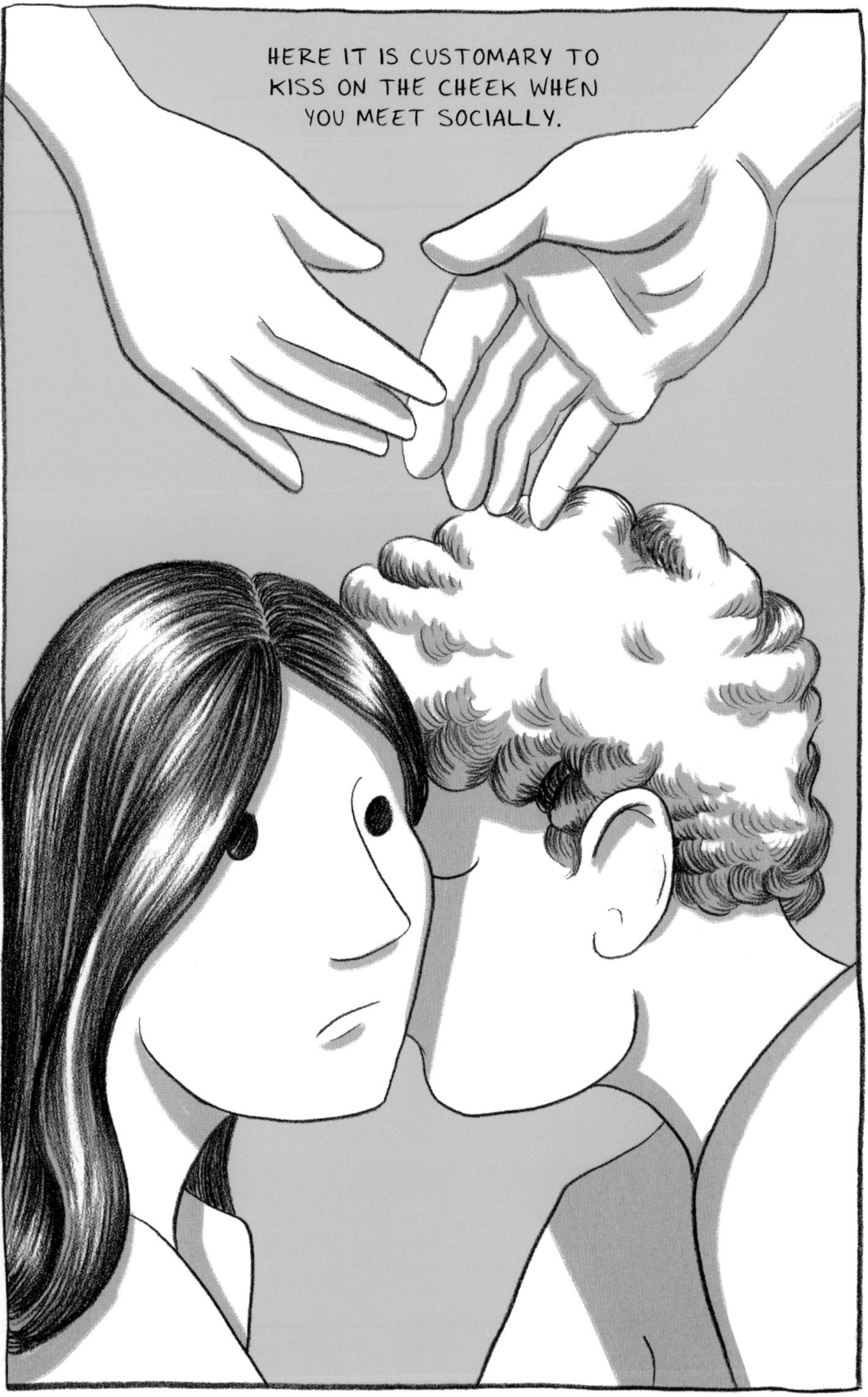
HERE IT IS CUSTOMARY TO
KISS ON THE CHEEK WHEN
YOU MEET SOCIALLY.

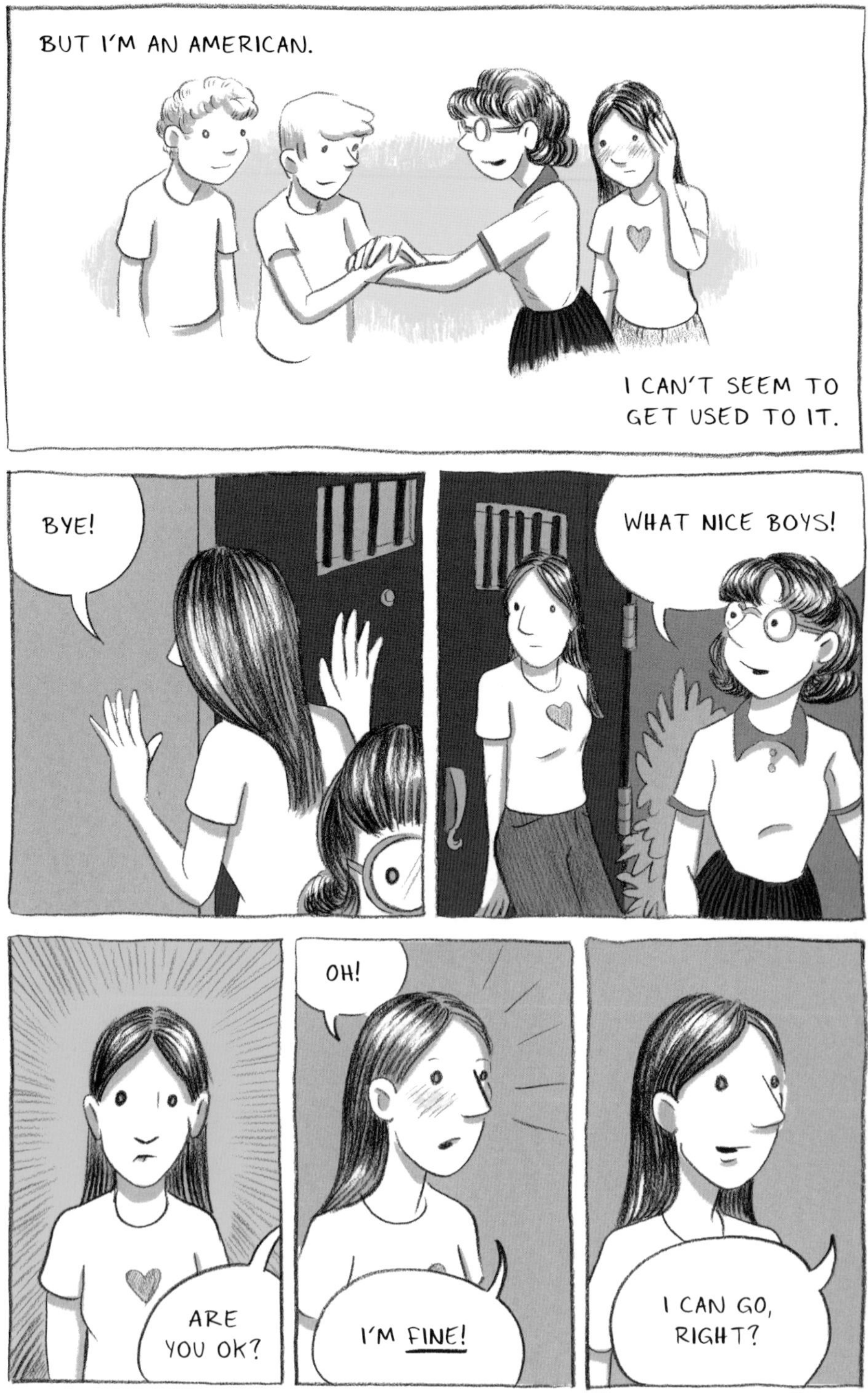
BUT I'M AN AMERICAN.
I CAN'T SEEM TO GET USED TO IT.
BYE!
WHAT NICE BOYS!
ARE YOU OK?
OH!
I'M FINE!
I CAN GO, RIGHT?

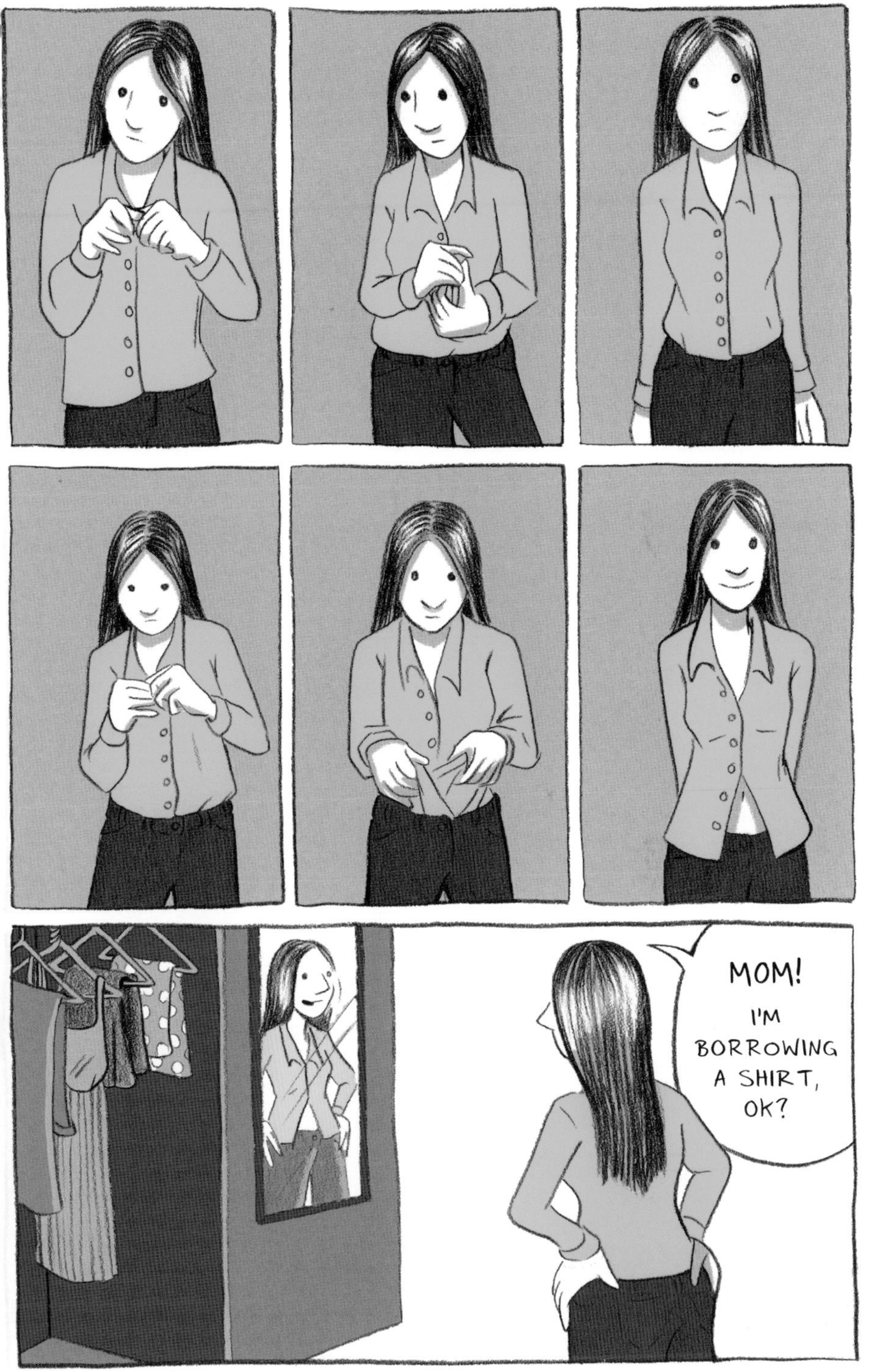
MOM!
I'M BORROWING A SHIRT, OK?

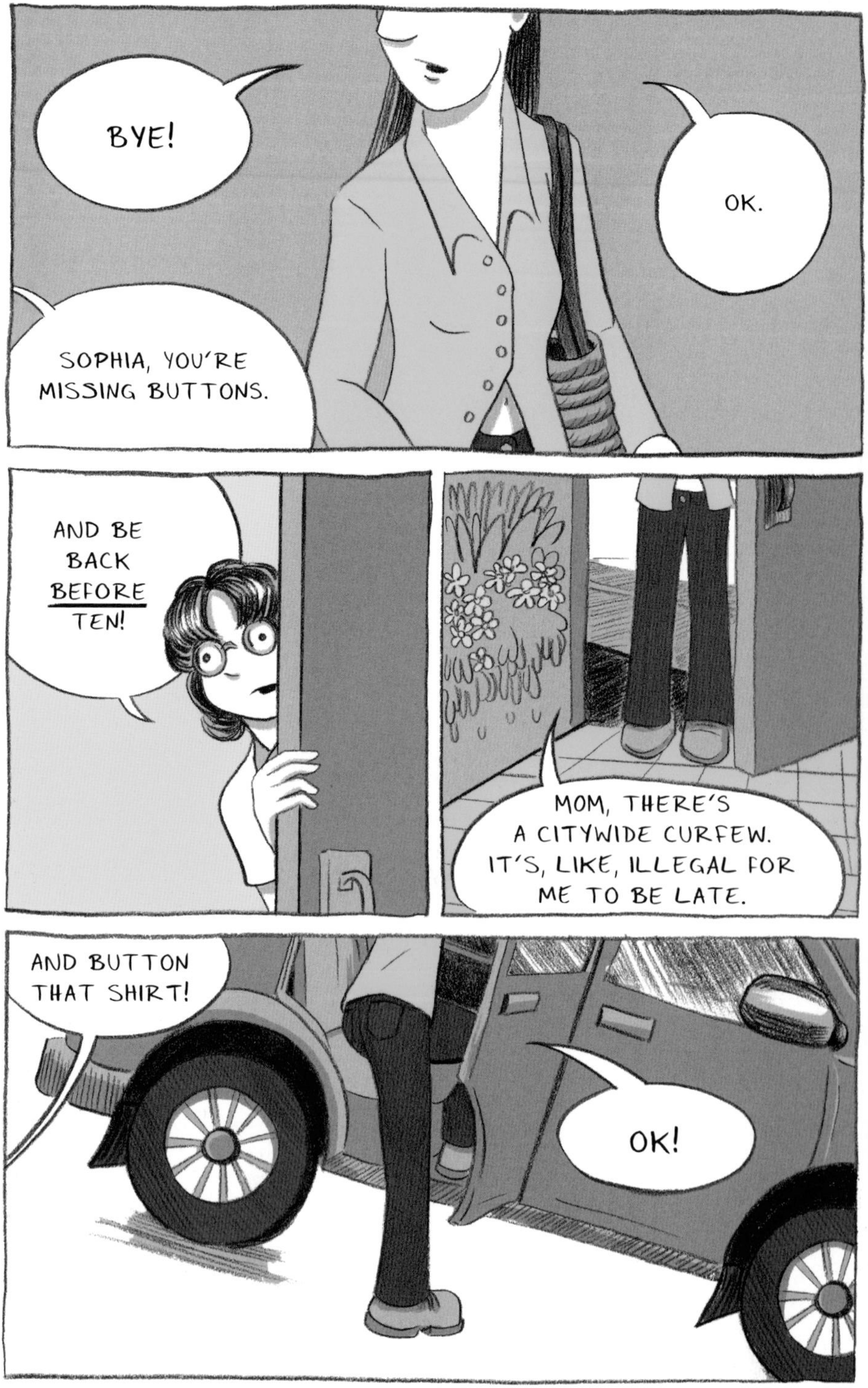
BYE!
OK.
SOPHIA, YOU'RE MISSING BUTTONS.
AND BE BACK BEFORE TEN!
MOM, THERE'S A CITYWIDE CURFEW. IT'S, LIKE, ILLEGAL FOR ME TO BE LATE.
AND BUTTON THAT SHIRT!
OK!

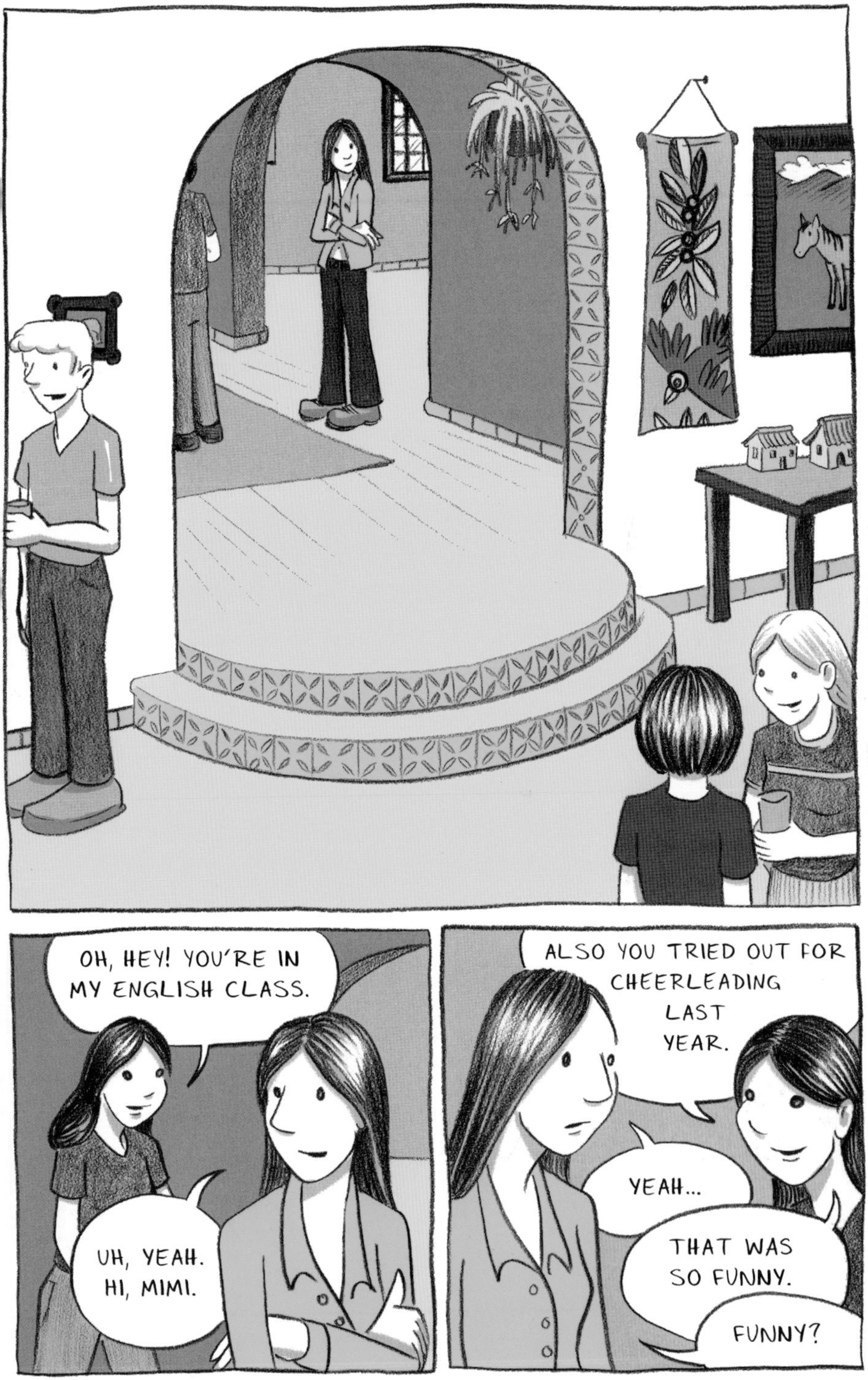
OH, HEY! YOU'RE IN MY ENGLISH CLASS.
UH, YEAH. HI, MIMI.
ALSO YOU TRIED OUT FOR CHEERLEADING LAST YEAR.
YEAH...
THAT WAS SO FUNNY.
FUNNY?

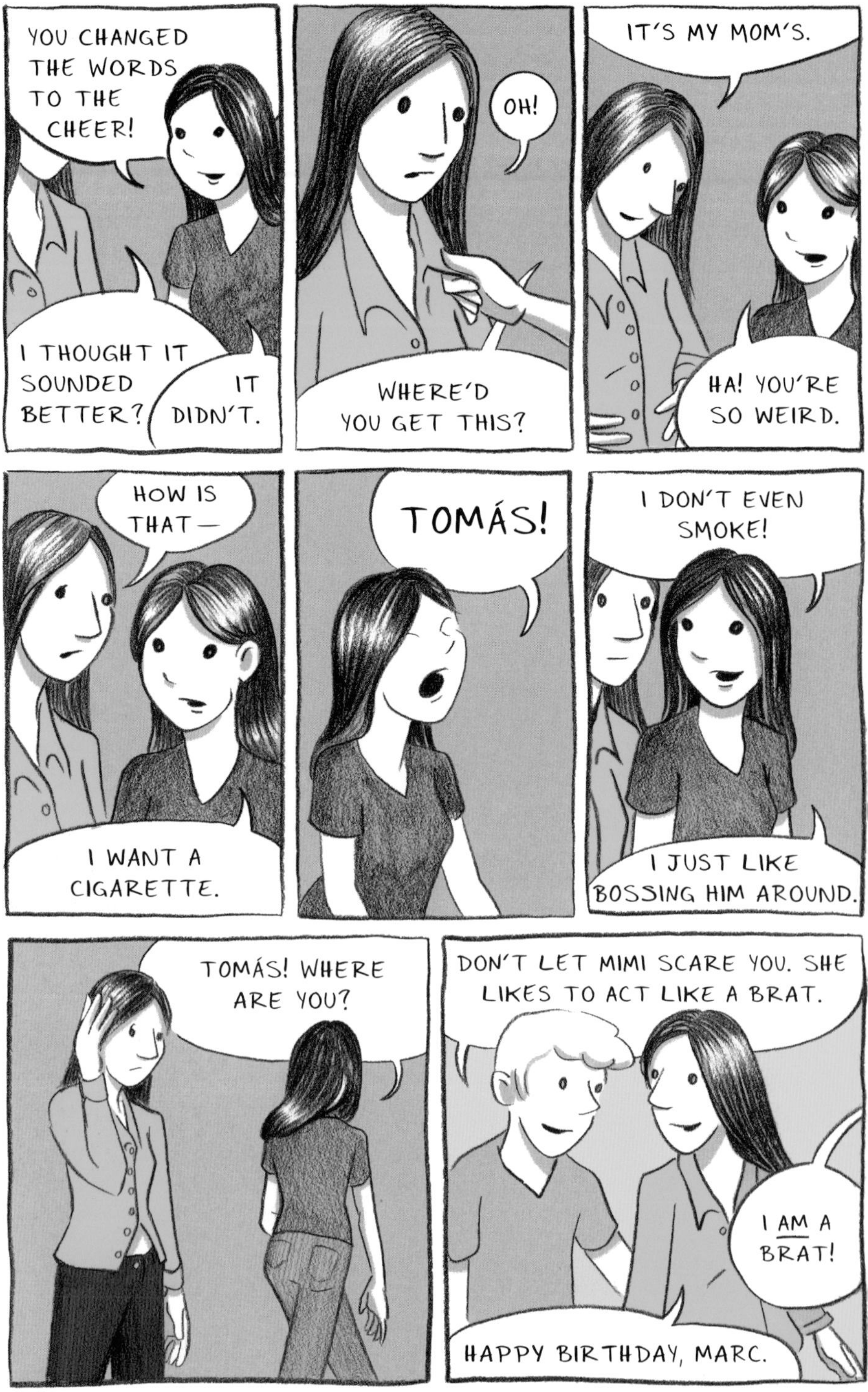
YOU CHANGED THE WORDS TO THE CHEER!
I THOUGHT IT SOUNDED BETTER?
IT DIDN'T.
OH!
WHERE'D YOU GET THIS?
IT'S MY MOM'S.
HA! YOU'RE SO WEIRD.
HOW IS THAT—
I WANT A CIGARETTE.
TOMÁS!
I DON'T EVEN SMOKE!
I JUST LIKE BOSSING HIM AROUND.
TOMÁS! WHERE ARE YOU?
DON'T LET MIMI SCARE YOU. SHE LIKES TO ACT LIKE A BRAT.
I AM A BRAT!
HAPPY BIRTHDAY, MARC.

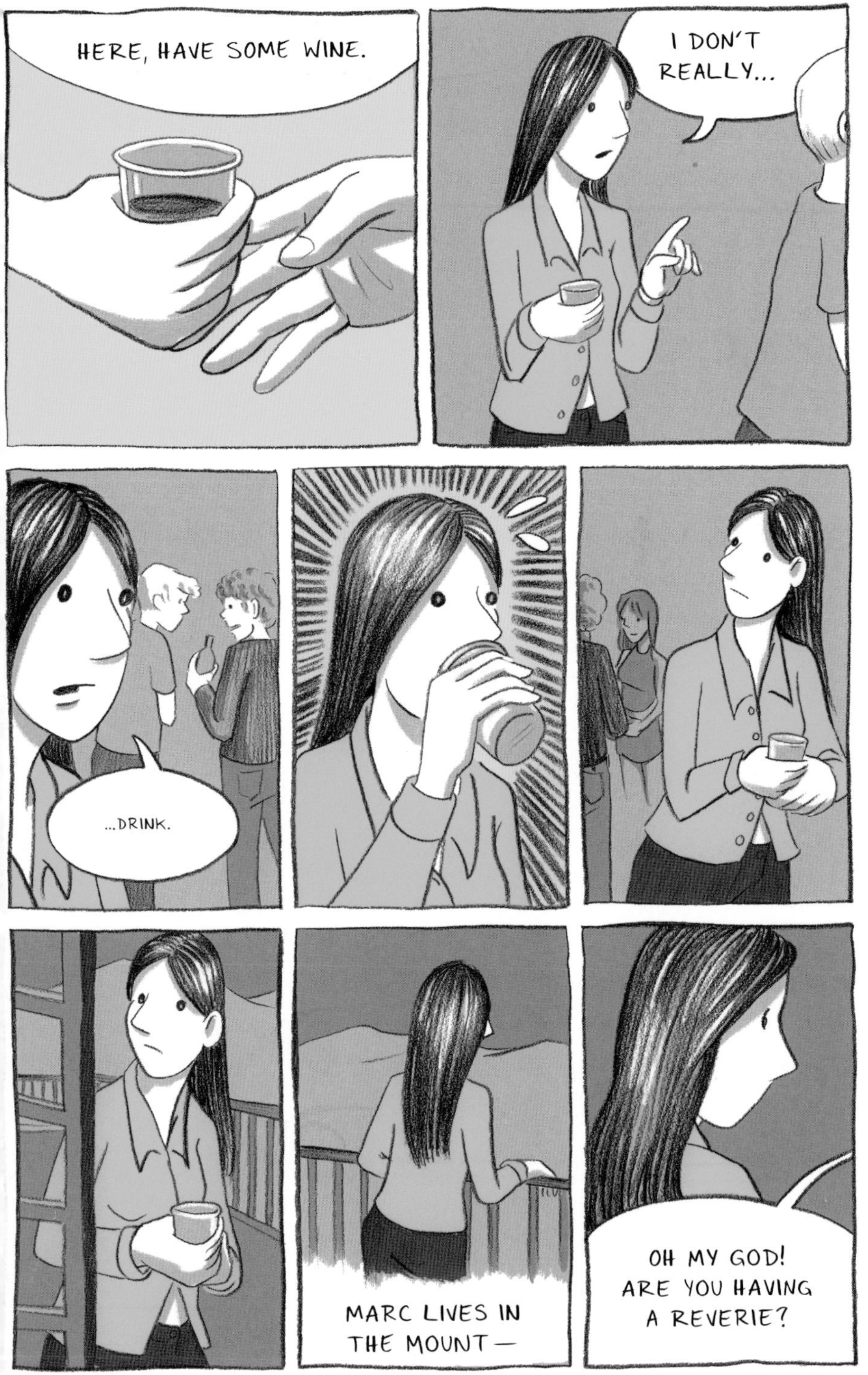
HERE, HAVE SOME WINE.
I DON'T REALLY...
...DRINK.
MARC LIVES IN THE MOUNT—
OH MY GOD! ARE YOU HAVING A REVERIE?

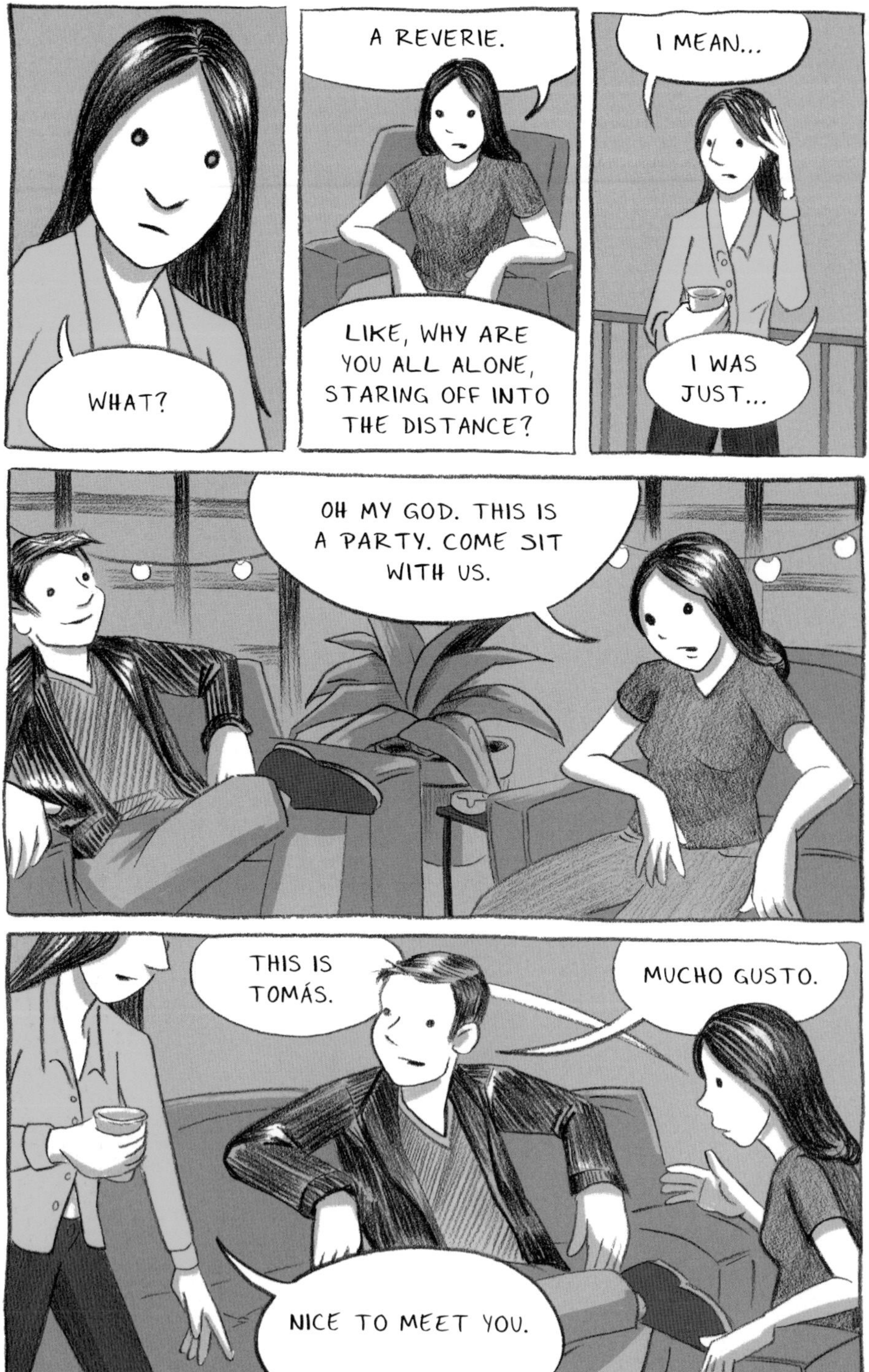
WHAT?
A REVERIE.
LIKE, WHY ARE YOU ALL ALONE, STARING OFF INTO THE DISTANCE?
I MEAN...
I WAS JUST...
OH MY GOD. THIS IS A PARTY. COME SIT WITH US.
THIS IS TOMÁS.
MUCHO GUSTO.
NICE TO MEET YOU.

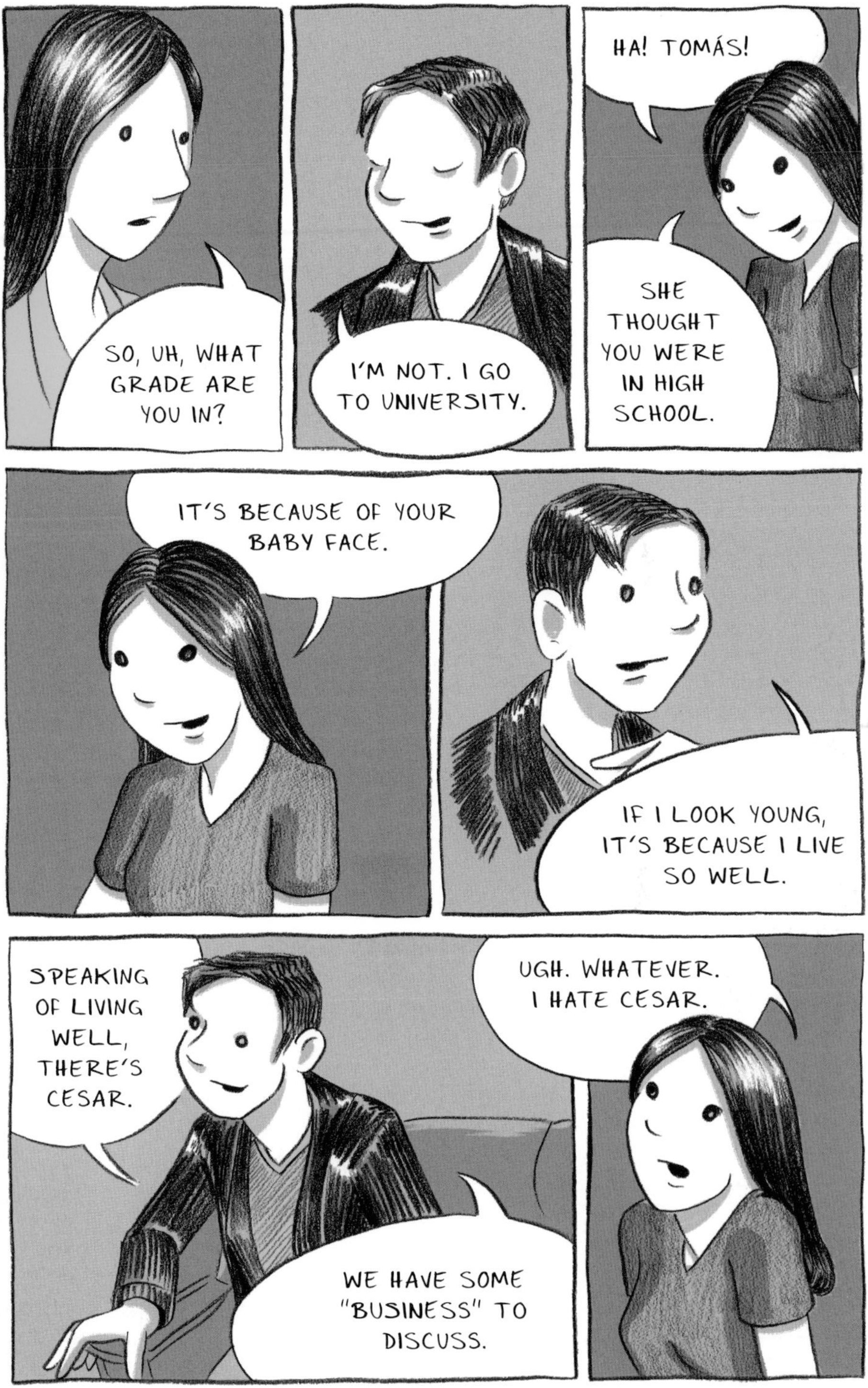
SO, UH, WHAT GRADE ARE YOU IN?
I'M NOT. I GO TO UNIVERSITY.
HA! TOMÁS!
SHE THOUGHT YOU WERE IN HIGH SCHOOL.
IT'S BECAUSE OF YOUR BABY FACE.
IF I LOOK YOUNG, IT'S BECAUSE I LIVE SO WELL.
SPEAKING OF LIVING WELL, THERE'S CESAR.
WE HAVE SOME "BUSINESS" TO DISCUSS.
UGH. WHATEVER. I HATE CESAR.

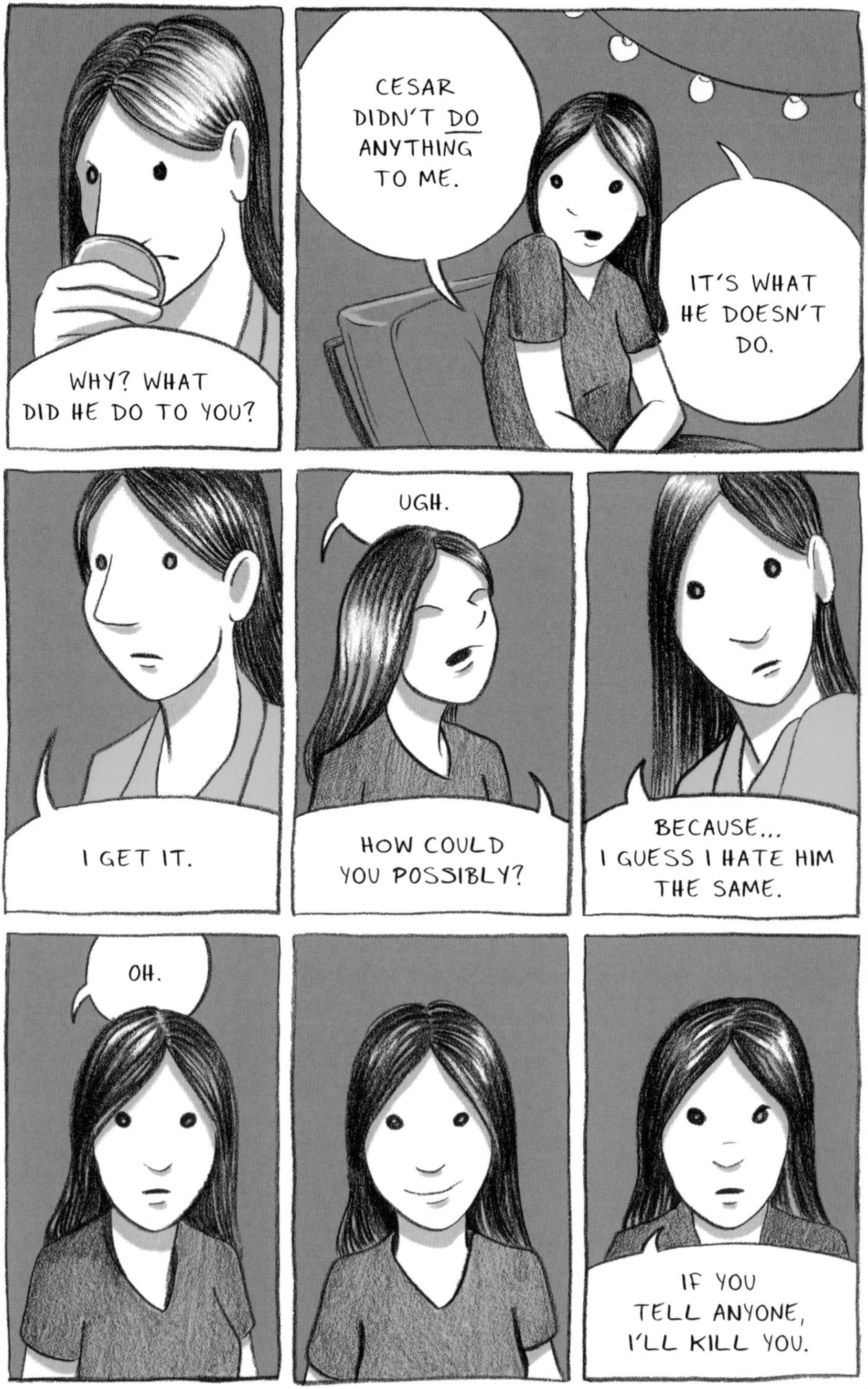
WHY? WHAT DID HE DO TO YOU?
CESAR DIDN'T DO ANYTHING TO ME.
IT'S WHAT HE DOESN'T DO.
I GET IT.
UGH.
HOW COULD YOU POSSIBLY?
BECAUSE... I GUESS I HATE HIM THE SAME.
OH.
IF YOU TELL ANYONE, I'LL KILL YOU.

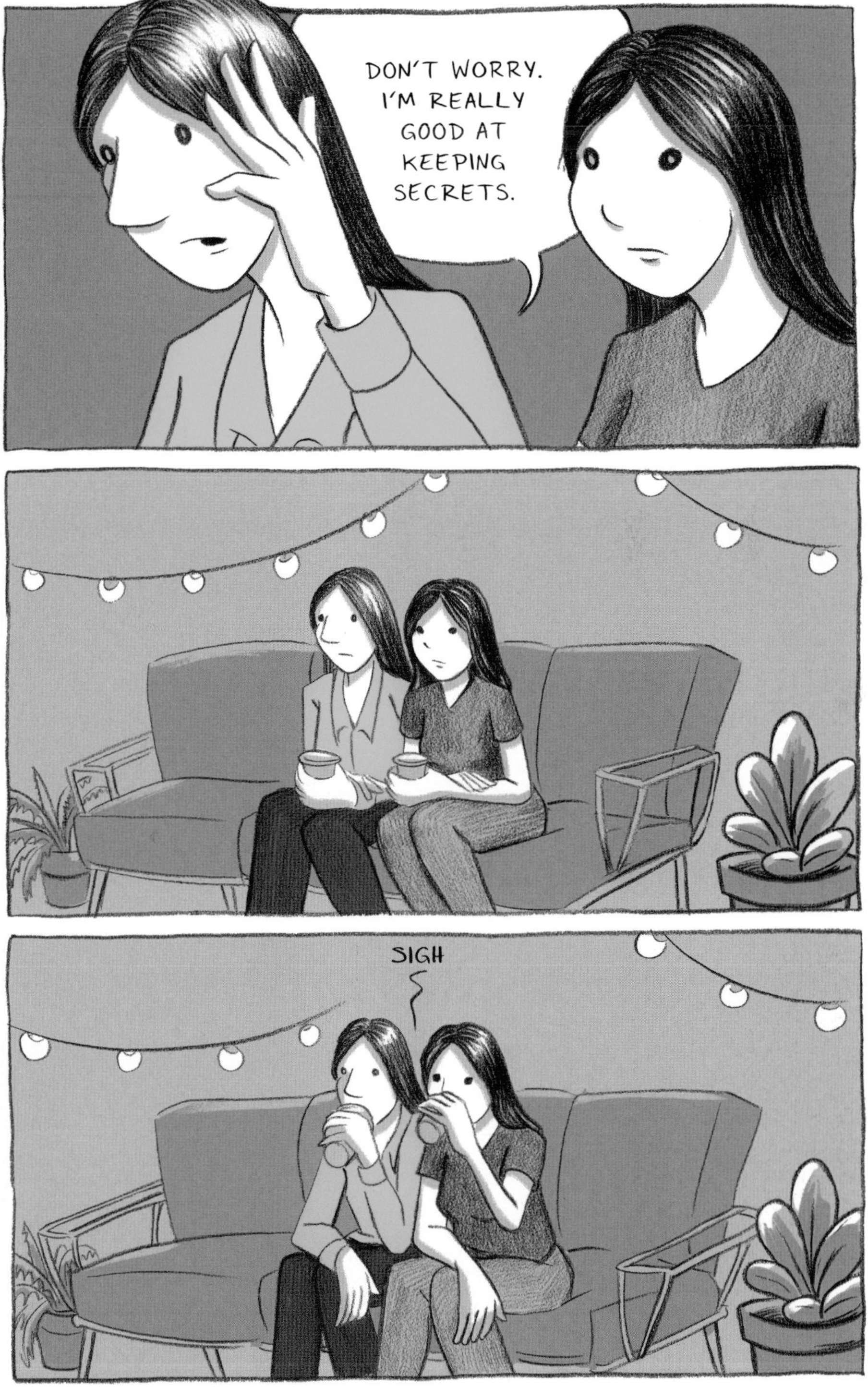
DON'T WORRY. I'M REALLY GOOD AT KEEPING SECRETS.
SIGH

ON THE WAY HOME, I SCAN THE
LANDSCAPE FOR SIGNS OF DESTRUCTION.

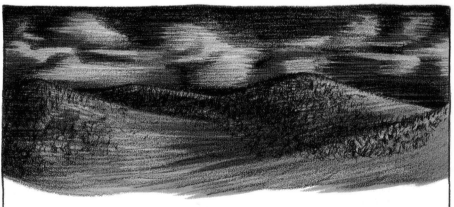

BUT IT'S SO DARK I CAN'T SEE ANYTHING.

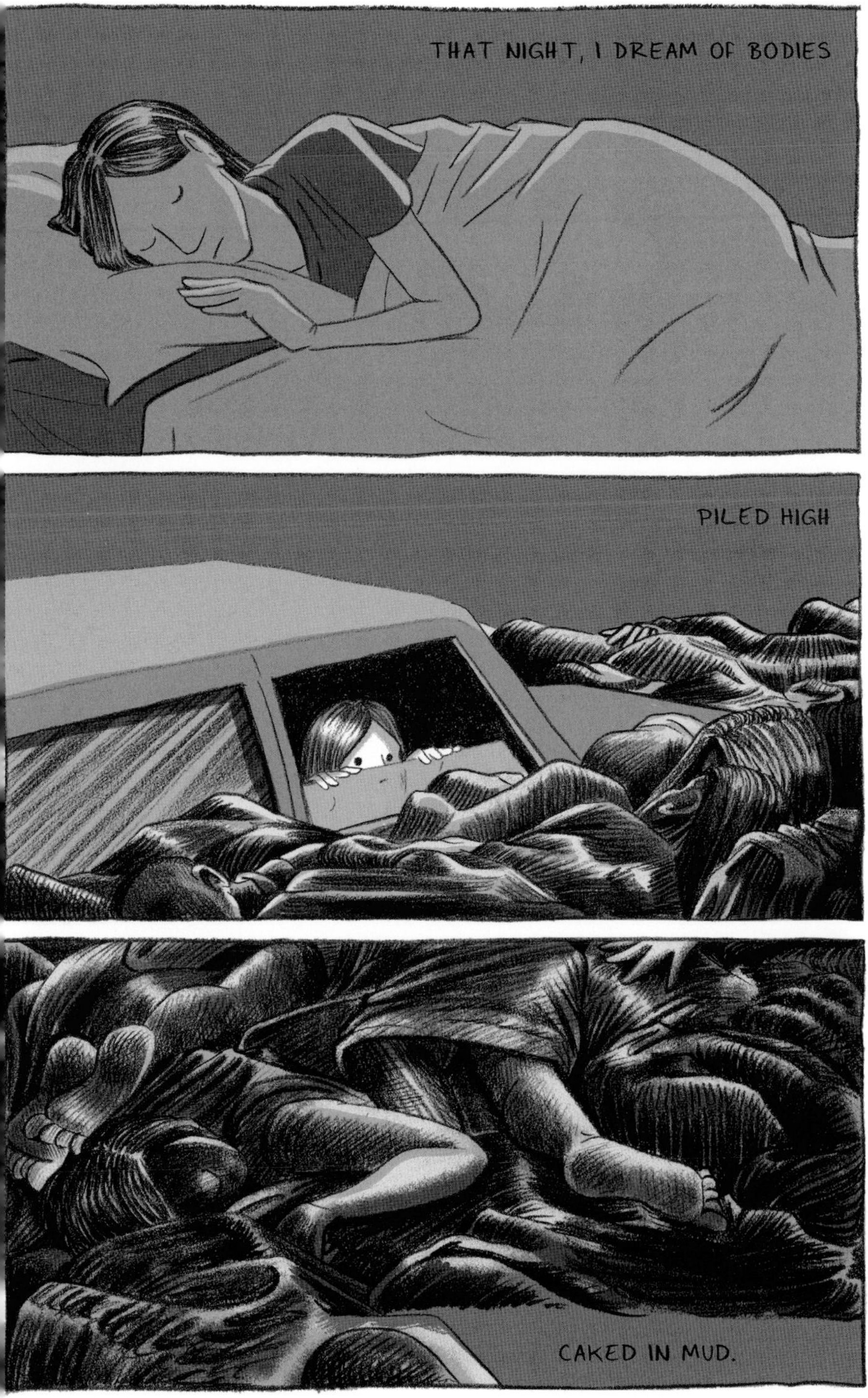
THAT NIGHT, I DREAM OF BODIES
PILED HIGH
CAKED IN MUD.

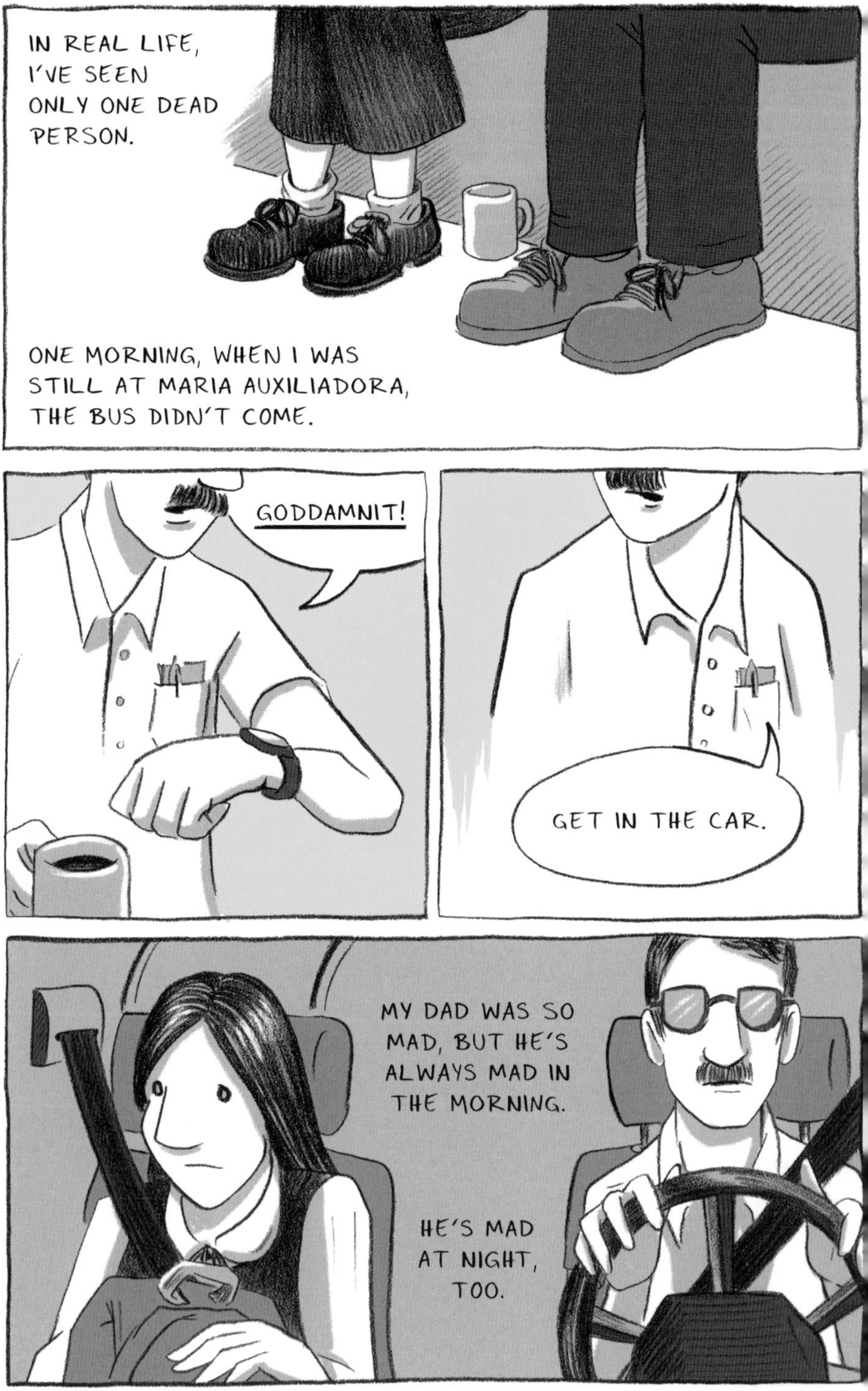
IN REAL LIFE, I'VE SEEN ONLY ONE DEAD PERSON.
ONE MORNING, WHEN I WAS STILL AT MARIA AUXILIADORA, THE BUS DIDN'T COME.
GODDAMNIT!
GET IN THE CAR.
MY DAD WAS SO MAD, BUT HE'S ALWAYS MAD IN THE MORNING.
HE'S MAD AT NIGHT, TOO.

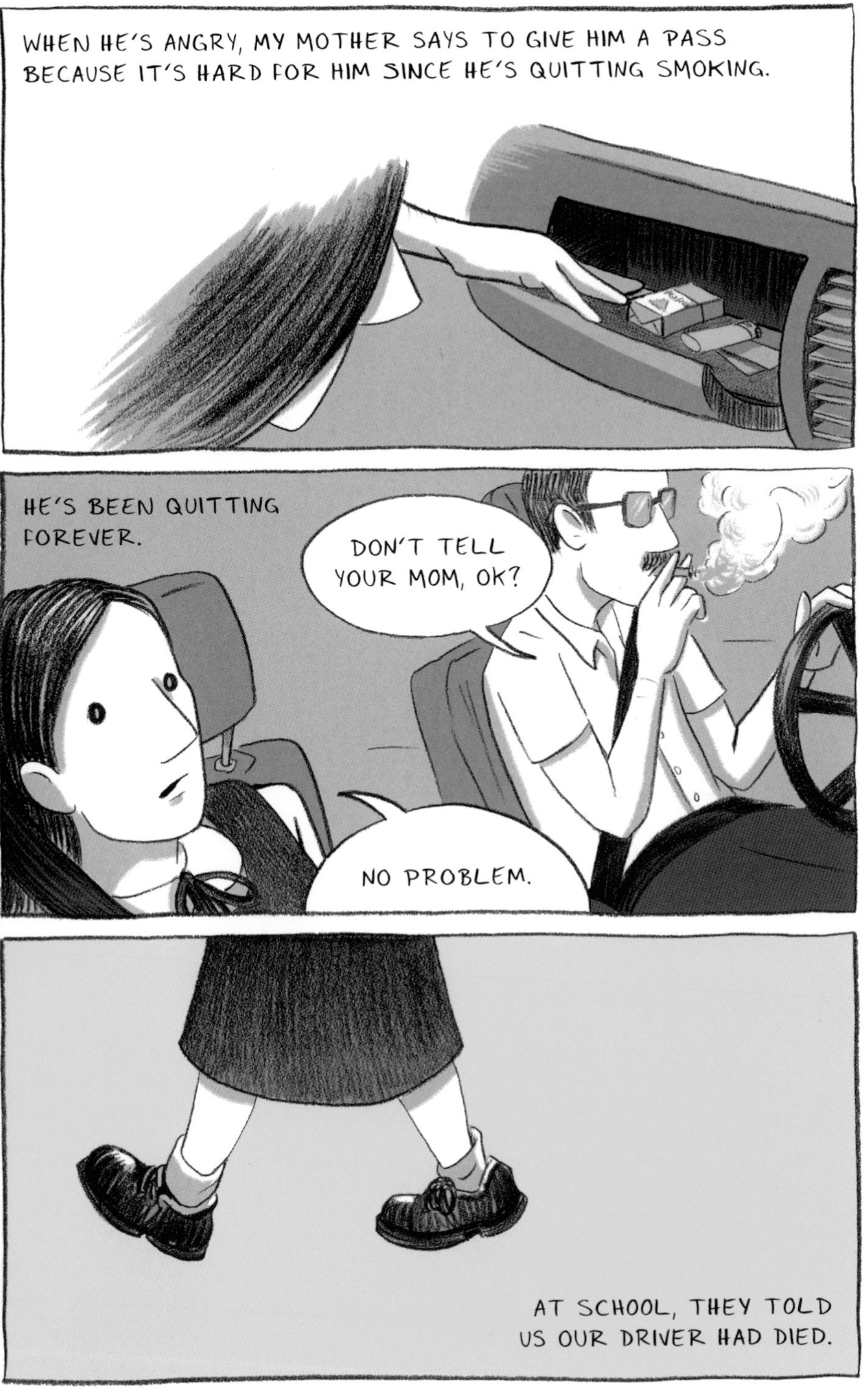
WHEN HE'S ANGRY, MY MOTHER SAYS TO GIVE HIM A PASS BECAUSE IT'S HARD FOR HIM SINCE HE'S QUITTING SMOKING.
HE'S BEEN QUITTING FOREVER.
DON'T TELL YOUR MOM, OK?
NO PROBLEM.
AT SCHOOL, THEY TOLD US OUR DRIVER HAD DIED.

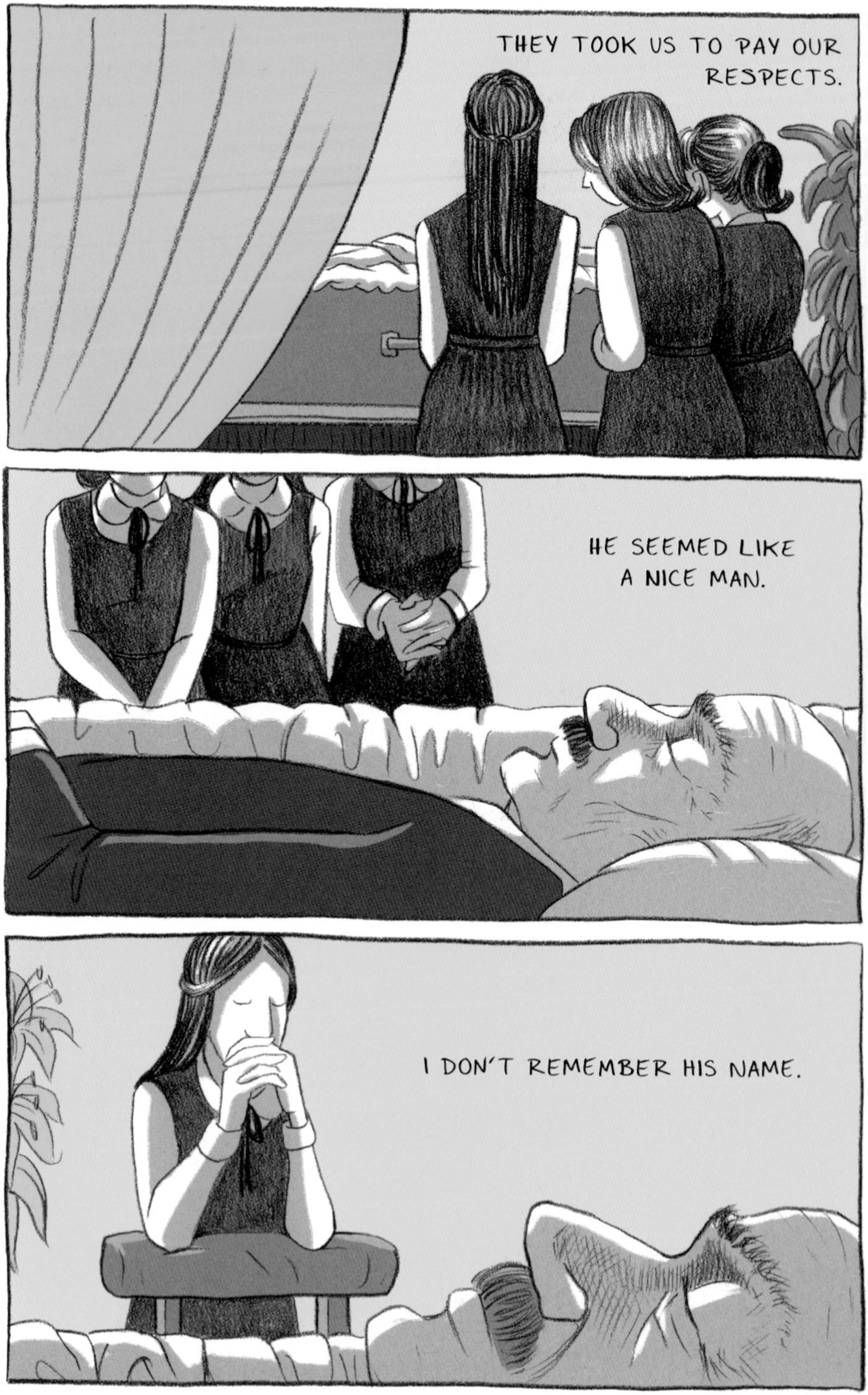
THEY TOOK US TO PAY OUR RESPECTS.
HE SEEMED LIKE A NICE MAN.
I DON'T REMEMBER HIS NAME.

LAST SUMMER, MY GRANDMOTHER DIED.

YES, YES. THANK YOU FOR CALLING.

OF COURSE, [UR DEEP]EST [C]OLENCES [...] PLEASE

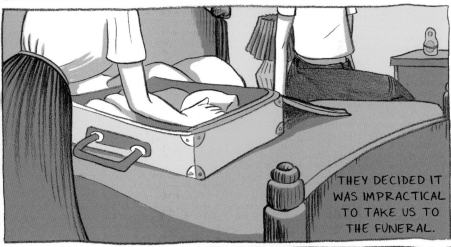

THEY DECIDED IT WAS IMPRACTICAL TO TAKE US TO THE FUNERAL.

SHE WAS THE ONLY GRANDPARENT I EVER KNEW.

MY MOTHER'S MOTHER.

HER NAME WAS MARY.

11,000 PEOPLE DIE BECAUSE OF HURRICANE MITCH.

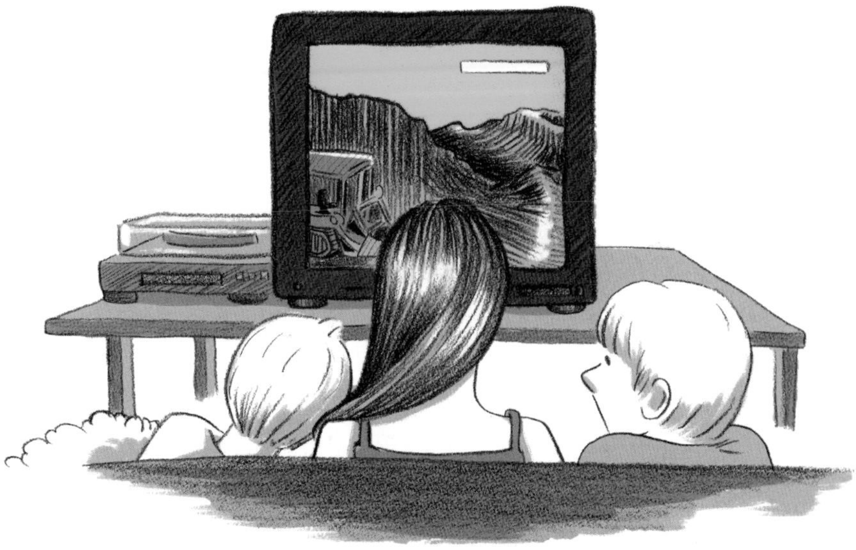

HUNDREDS OF THOUSANDS LOSE THEIR HOMES.
NO ONE I KNOW, THOUGH.

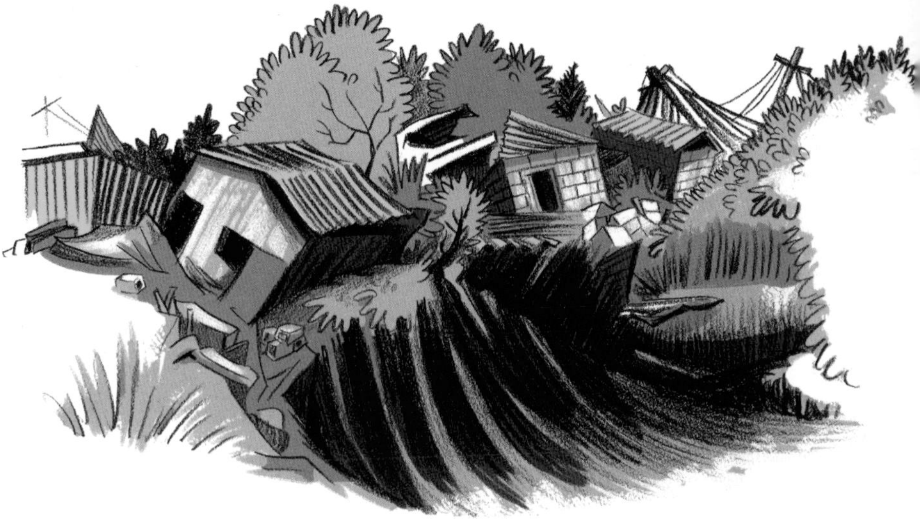

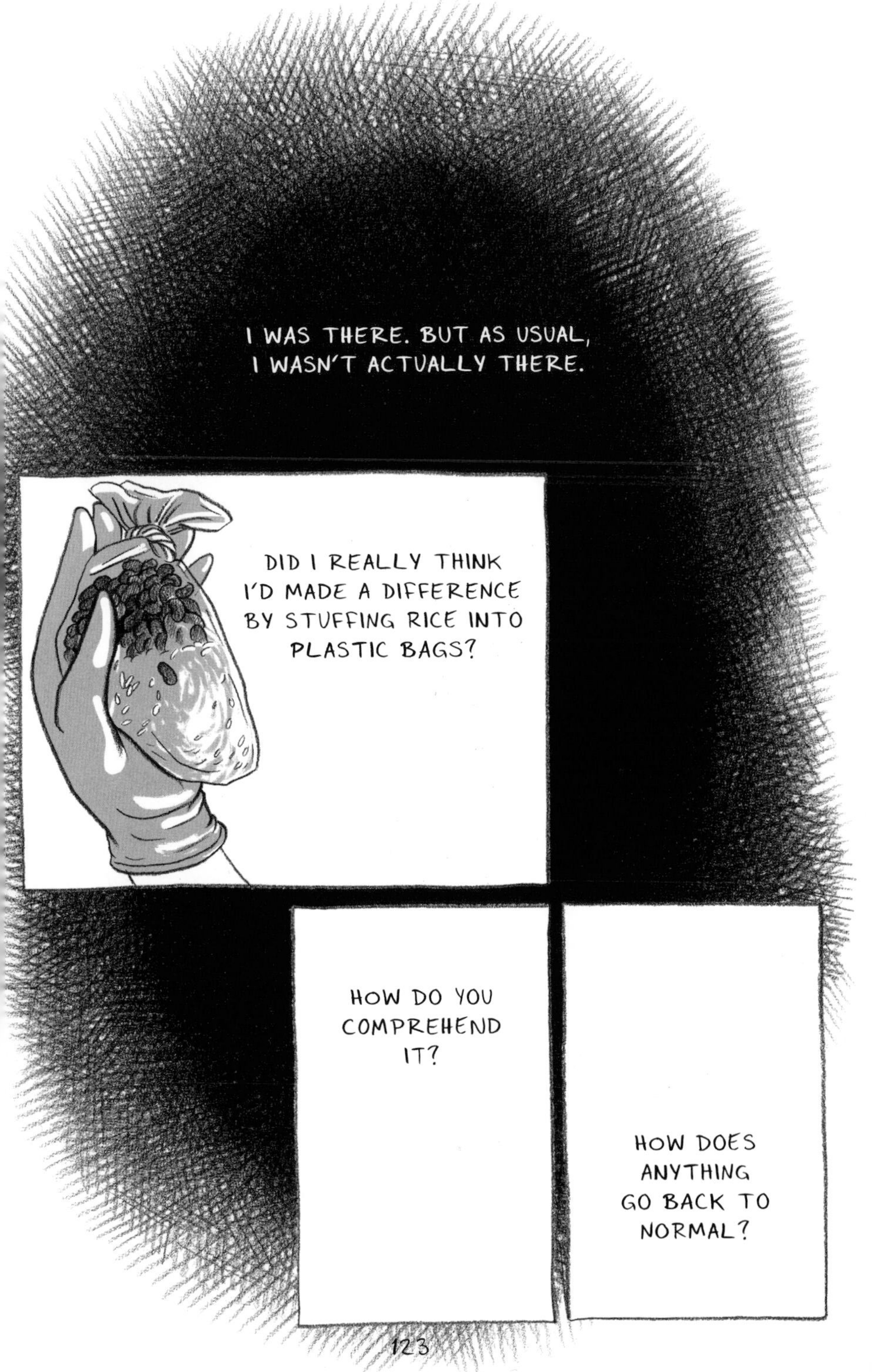
I WAS THERE. BUT AS USUAL, I WASN'T ACTUALLY THERE.
DID I REALLY THINK I'D MADE A DIFFERENCE BY STUFFING RICE INTO PLASTIC BAGS?
HOW DO YOU COMPREHEND IT?
HOW DOES ANYTHING GO BACK TO NORMAL?

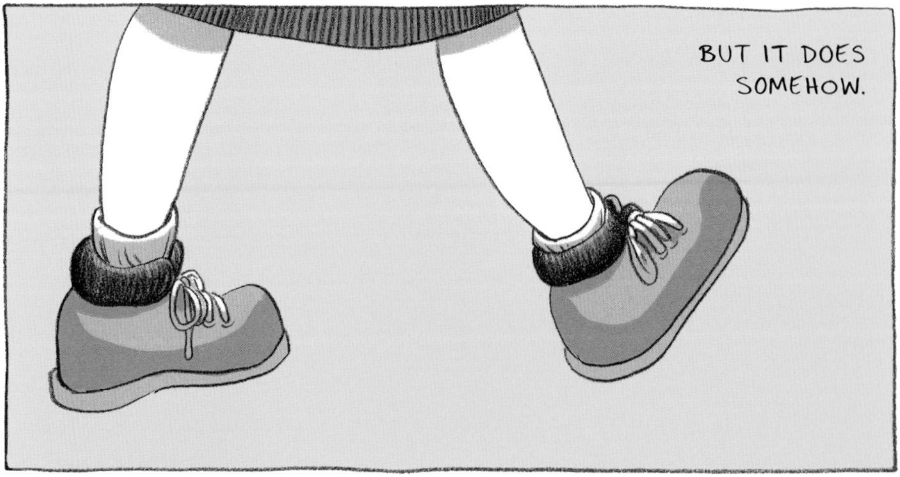
BUT IT DOES SOMEHOW.

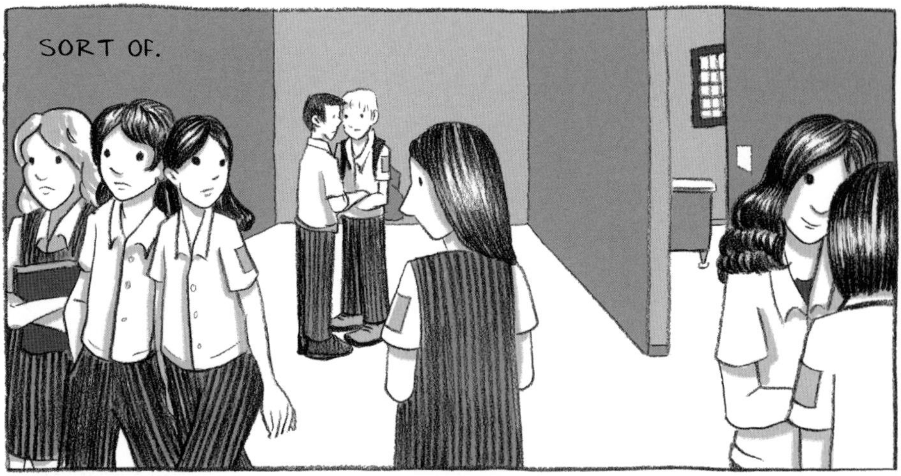
SORT OF.

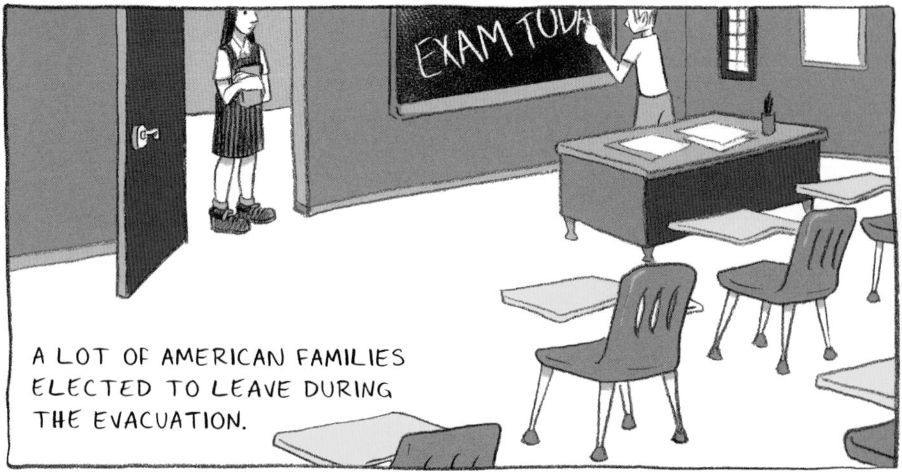
EXAM TODA
A LOT OF AMERICAN FAMILIES ELECTED TO LEAVE DURING THE EVACUATION.

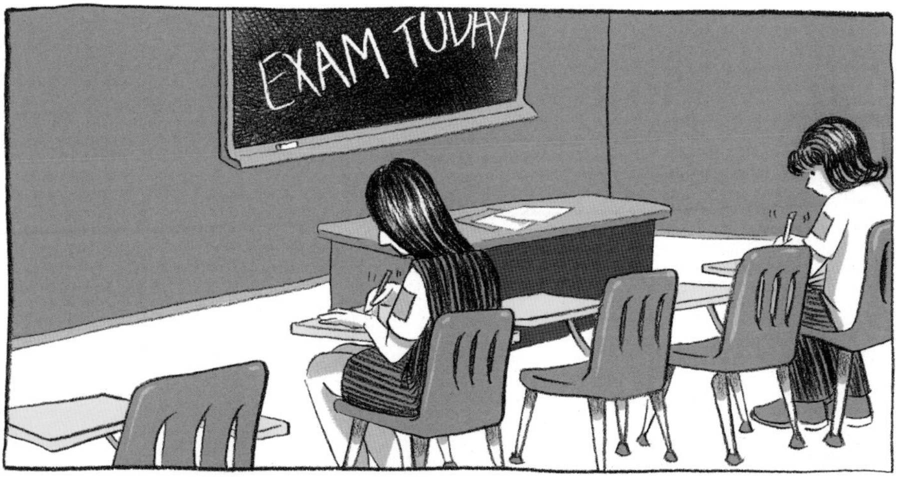
EXAM TODAY

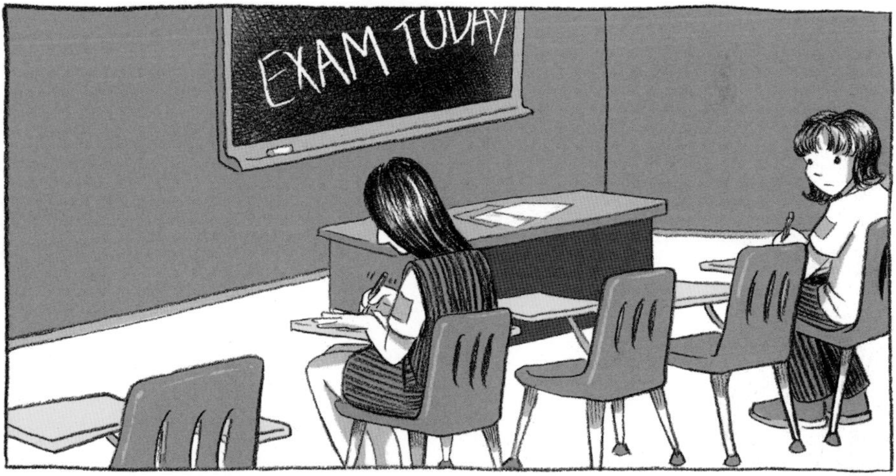
EXAM TODAY

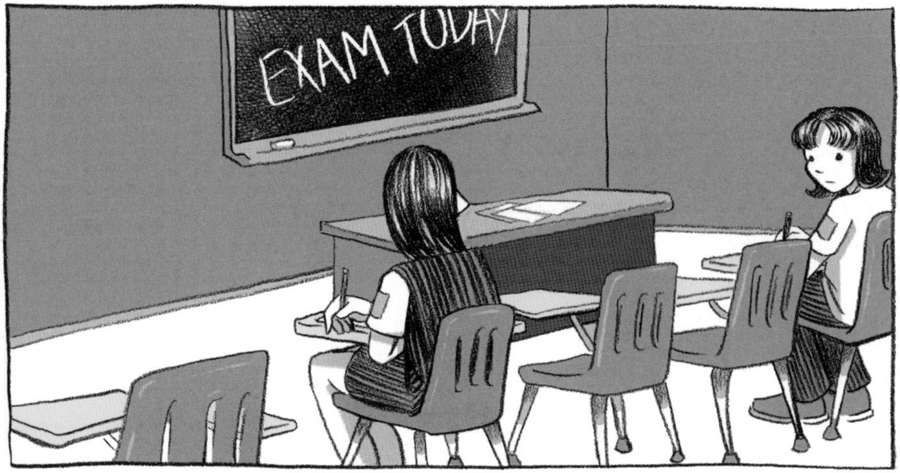
EXAM TODAY

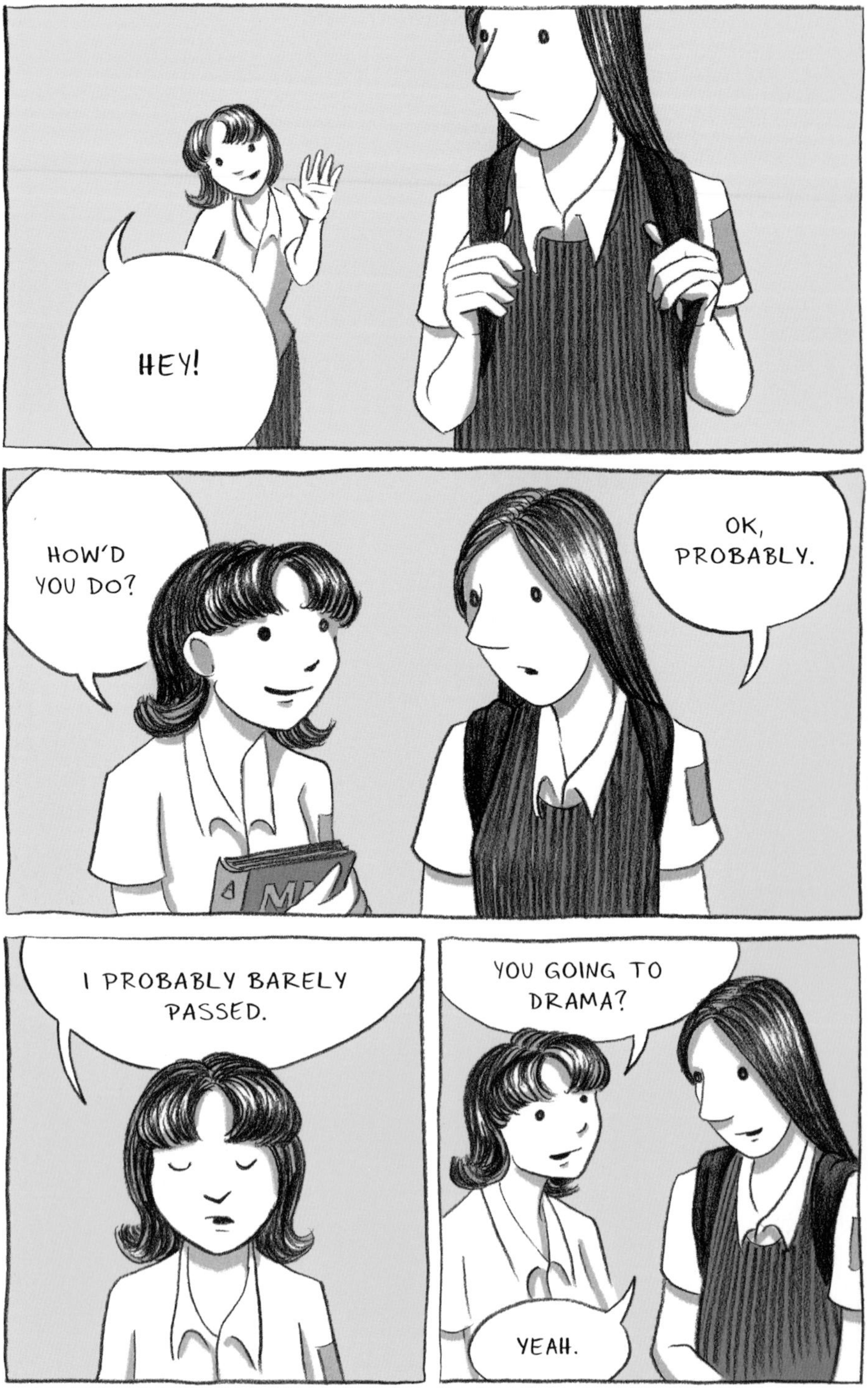
HEY!
HOW'D YOU DO?
OK, PROBABLY.
I PROBABLY BARELY PASSED.
YOU GOING TO DRAMA?
YEAH.

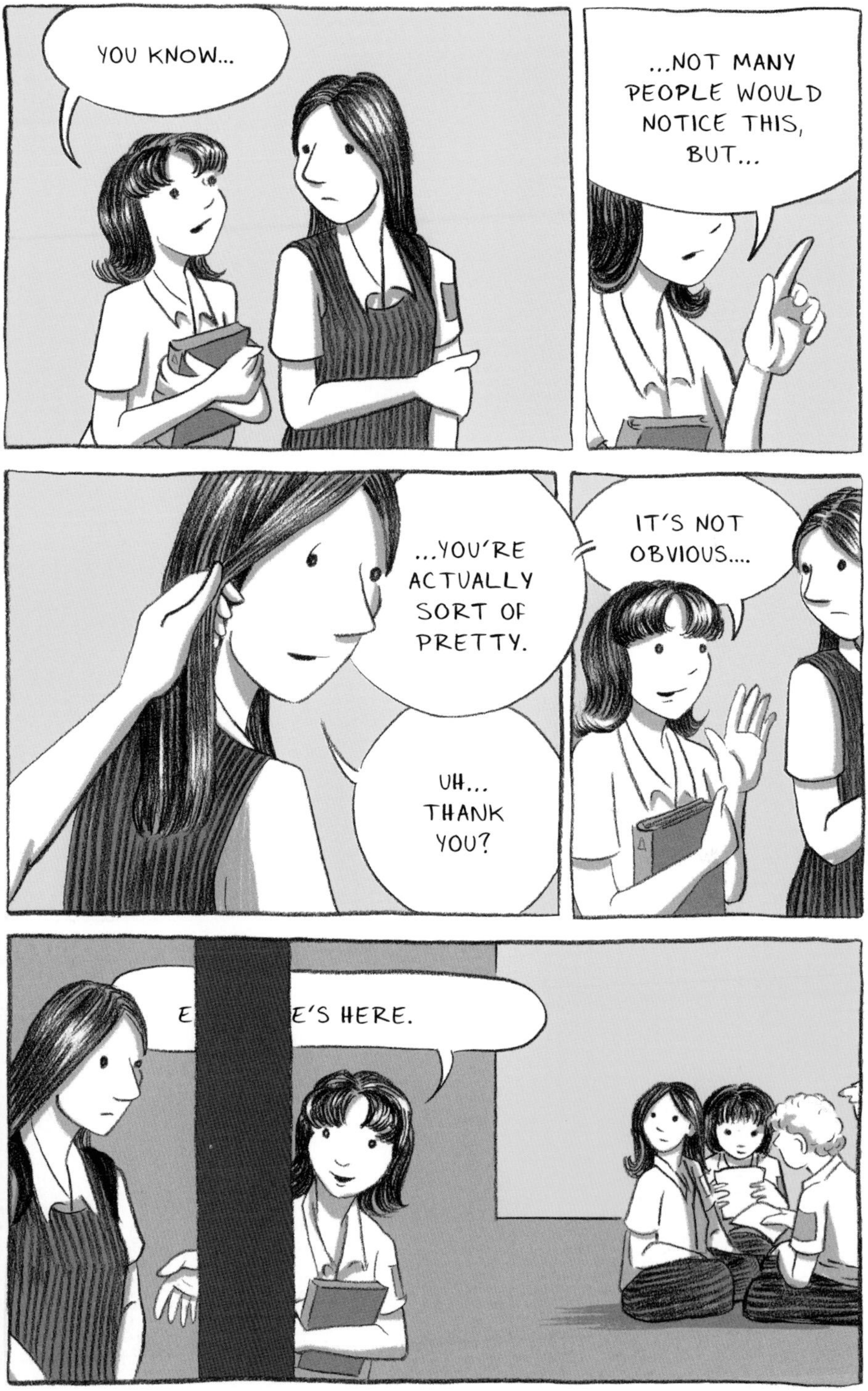
YOU KNOW...
...NOT MANY PEOPLE WOULD NOTICE THIS, BUT...
...YOU'RE ACTUALLY SORT OF PRETTY.
UH... THANK YOU?
IT'S NOT OBVIOUS....
E[redacted]E'S HERE.

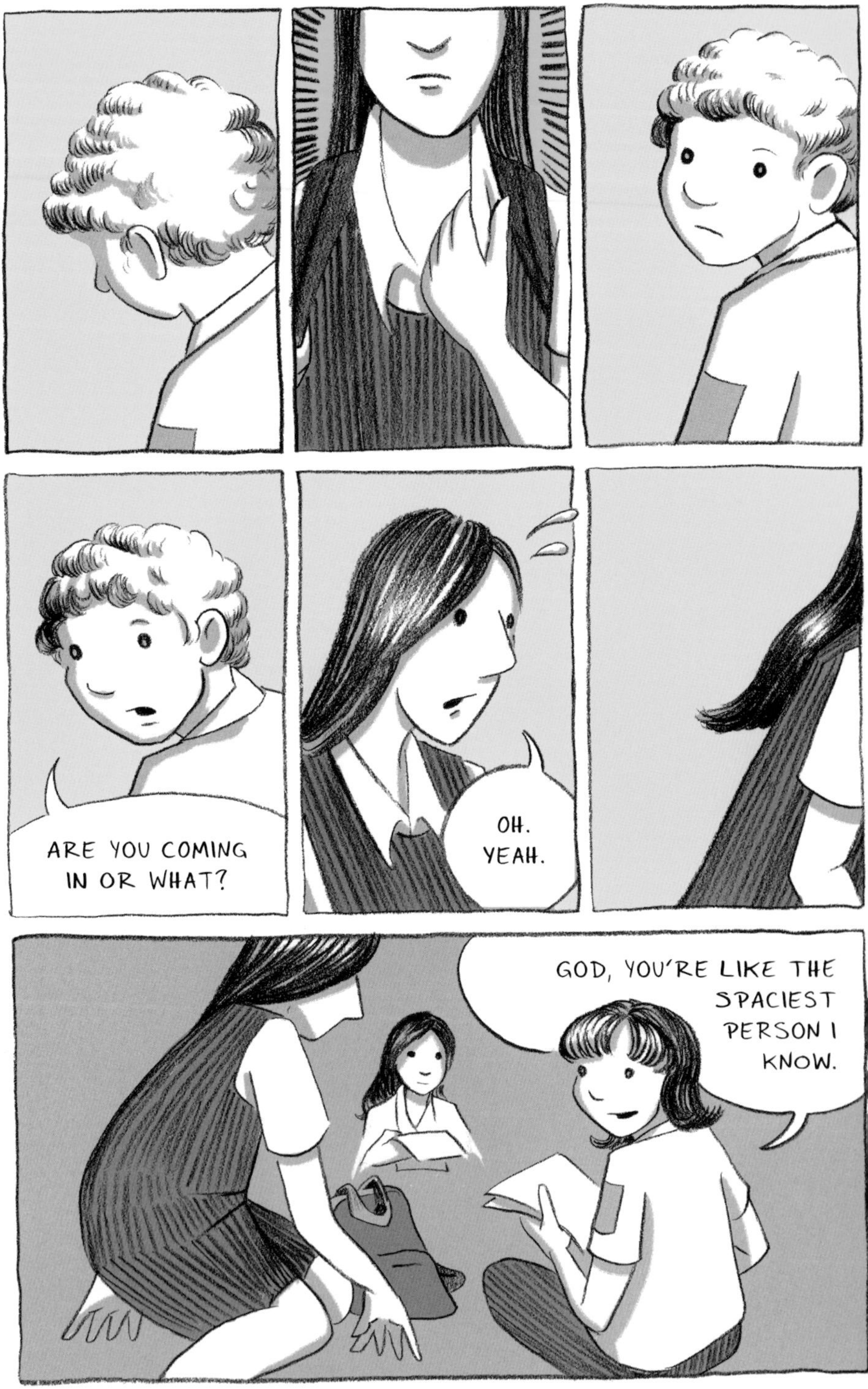
ARE YOU COMING IN OR WHAT?
OH. YEAH.
GOD, YOU'RE LIKE THE SPACIEST PERSON I KNOW.

REALLY?

SO ARE YOU GOING TO THIS PARTY ON SATURDAY?

I HADN'T REALLY—

I CAN NEVER GO TO THESE THINGS BECAUSE I LIVE SO FAR AWAY...

RIGHT. BECAUSE YOUR MOM TEACHES OUT AT THE COLLEGE.

...UNLESS I HAVE A PLACE TO STAY.

HEY! I COULD STAY WITH YOU!

UM...

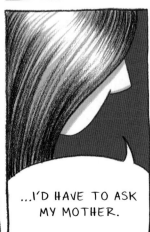

...I'D HAVE TO ASK MY MOTHER.

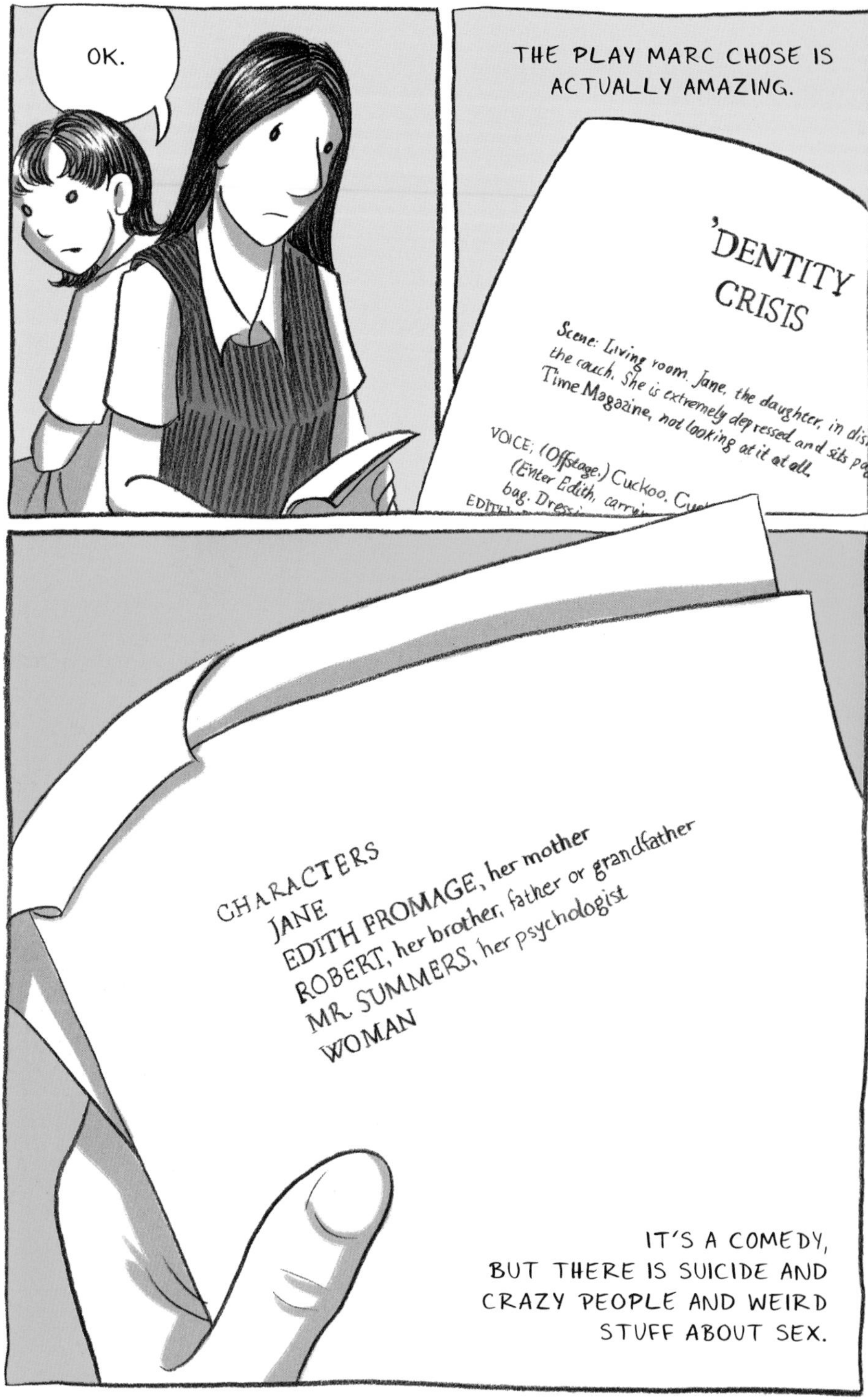
OK.
THE PLAY MARC CHOSE IS ACTUALLY AMAZING.
'DENTITY CRISIS
Scene: Living room. Jane, the daughter, in dis
the couch. She is extremely depressed and sits p
Time Magazine, not looking at it at all.
VOICE: (Offstage.) Cuckoo. Cu
(Enter Edith, carry
bag. Dress
CHARACTERS
JANE
EDITH FROMAGE, her mother
ROBERT, her brother, father or grandfather
MR. SUMMERS, her psychologist
WOMAN
IT'S A COMEDY, BUT THERE IS SUICIDE AND CRAZY PEOPLE AND WEIRD STUFF ABOUT SEX.

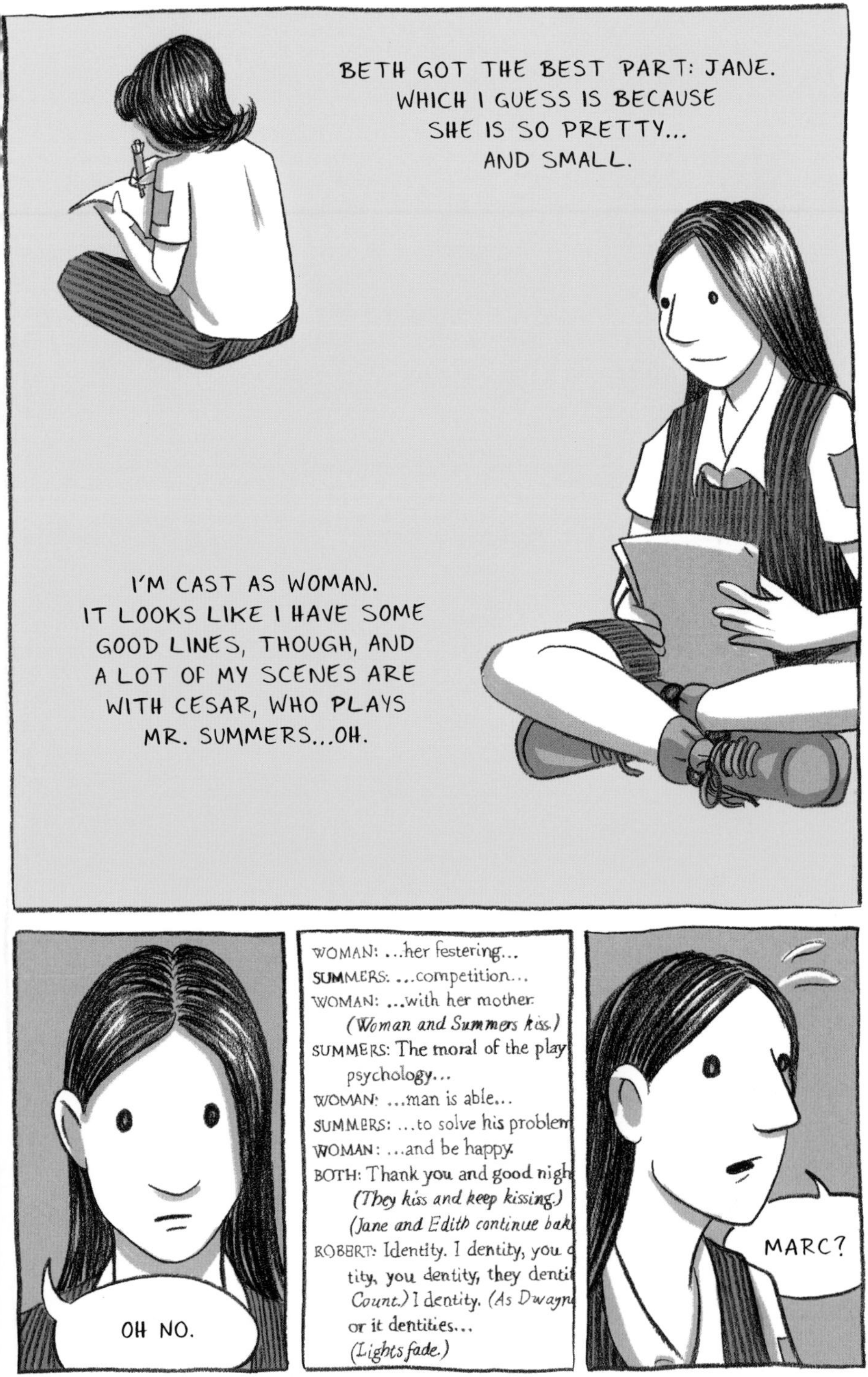
BETH GOT THE BEST PART: JANE. WHICH I GUESS IS BECAUSE SHE IS SO PRETTY... AND SMALL.
I'M CAST AS WOMAN. IT LOOKS LIKE I HAVE SOME GOOD LINES, THOUGH, AND A LOT OF MY SCENES ARE WITH CESAR, WHO PLAYS MR. SUMMERS...OH.
OH NO.
WOMAN: ...her festering...
SUMMERS: ...competition...
WOMAN: ...with her mother.
(Woman and Summers kiss.)
SUMMERS: The moral of the play
psychology...
WOMAN: ...man is able...
SUMMERS: ...to solve his problem
WOMAN: ...and be happy.
BOTH: Thank you and good nigh
(They kiss and keep kissing.)
(Jane and Edith continue bak
ROBERT: Identity. I dentity, you
tity, you dentity, they denti
Count.) I dentity. (As Dwayn
or it dentities...
(Lights fade.)
MARC?

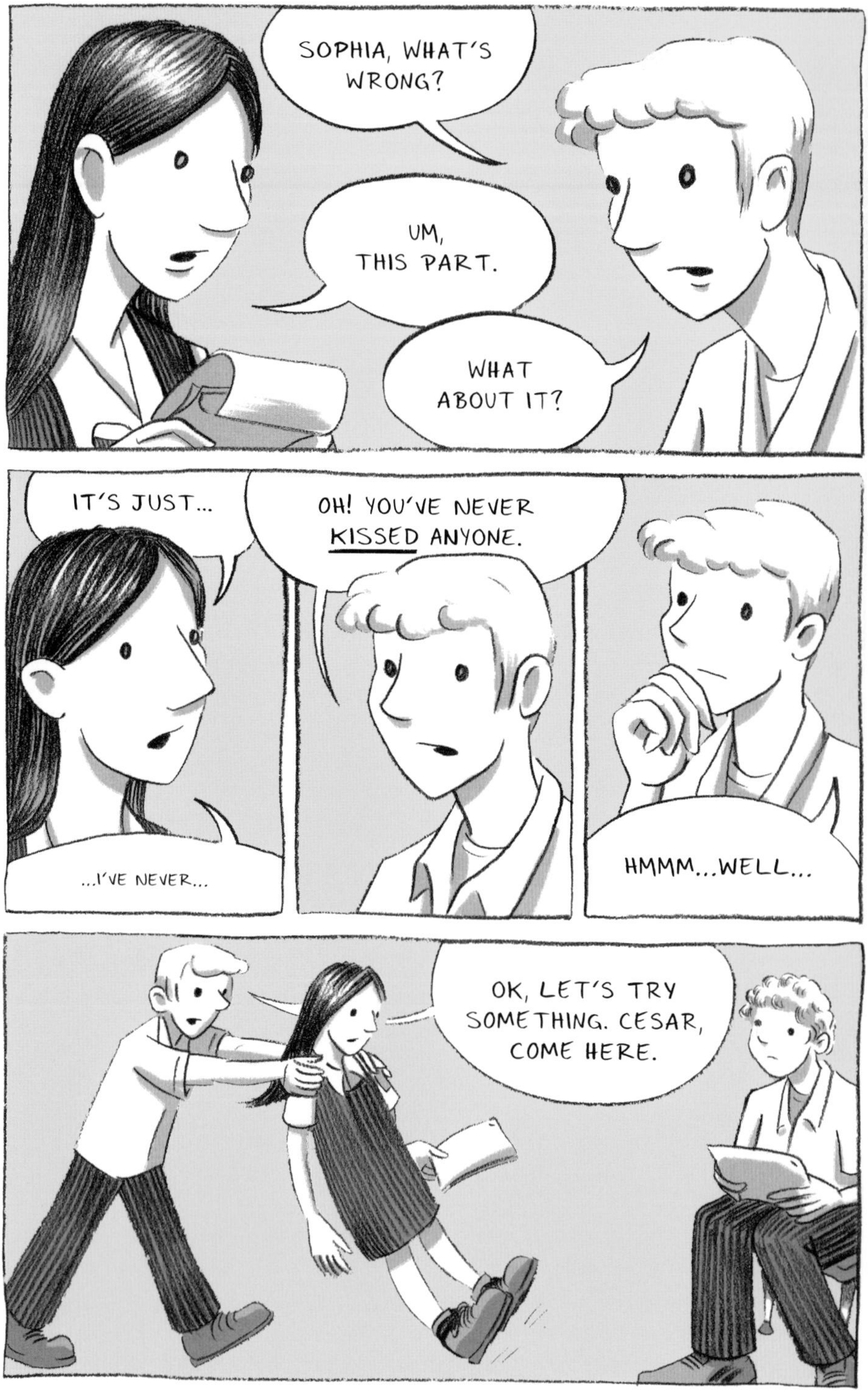
SOPHIA, WHAT'S WRONG?
UM, THIS PART.
WHAT ABOUT IT?
IT'S JUST...
...I'VE NEVER...
OH! YOU'VE NEVER KISSED ANYONE.
HMMM...WELL...
OK, LET'S TRY SOMETHING. CESAR, COME HERE.

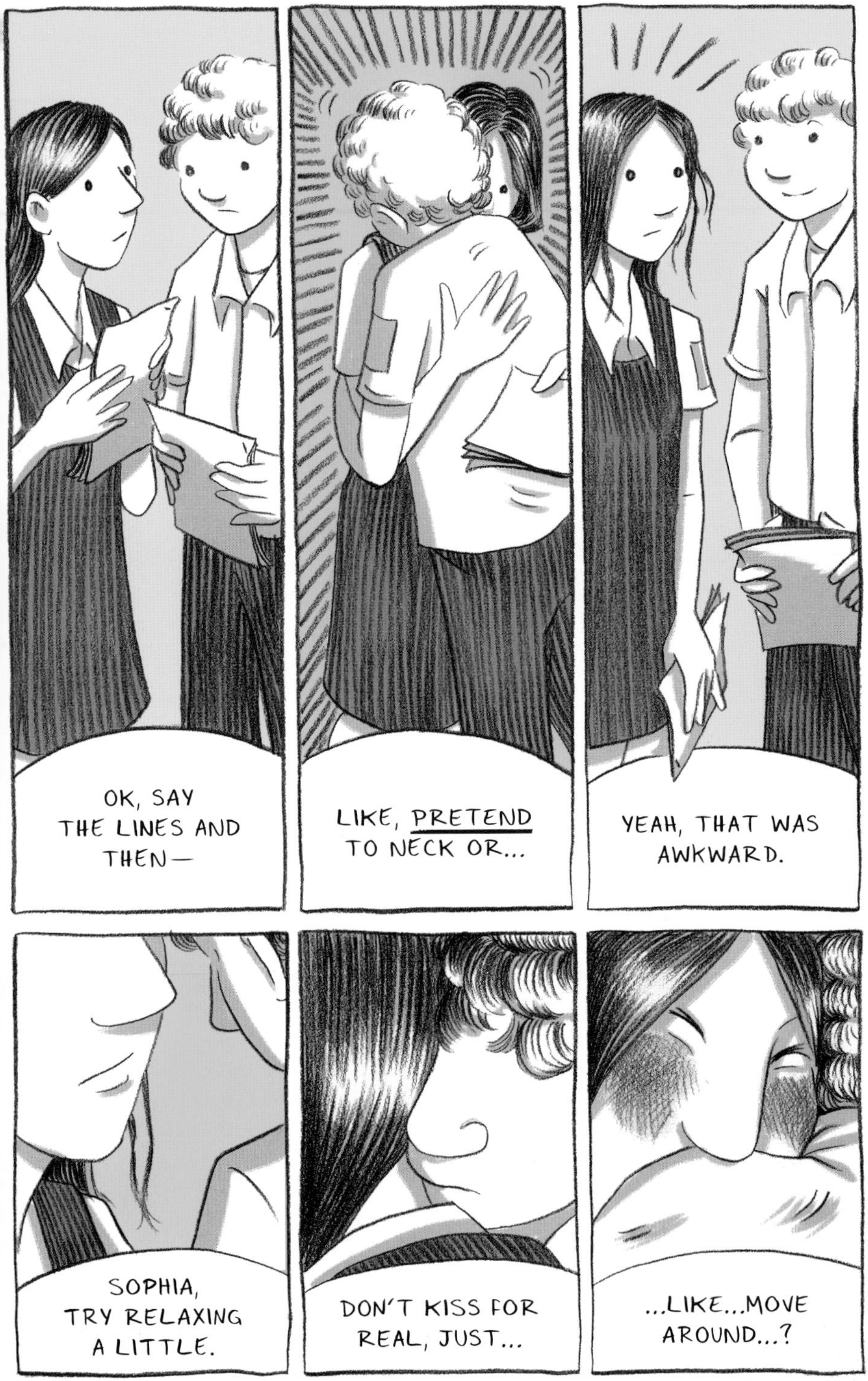
OK, SAY THE LINES AND THEN—
LIKE, PRETEND TO NECK OR...
YEAH, THAT WAS AWKWARD.
SOPHIA, TRY RELAXING A LITTLE.
DON'T KISS FOR REAL, JUST...
...LIKE...MOVE AROUND...?

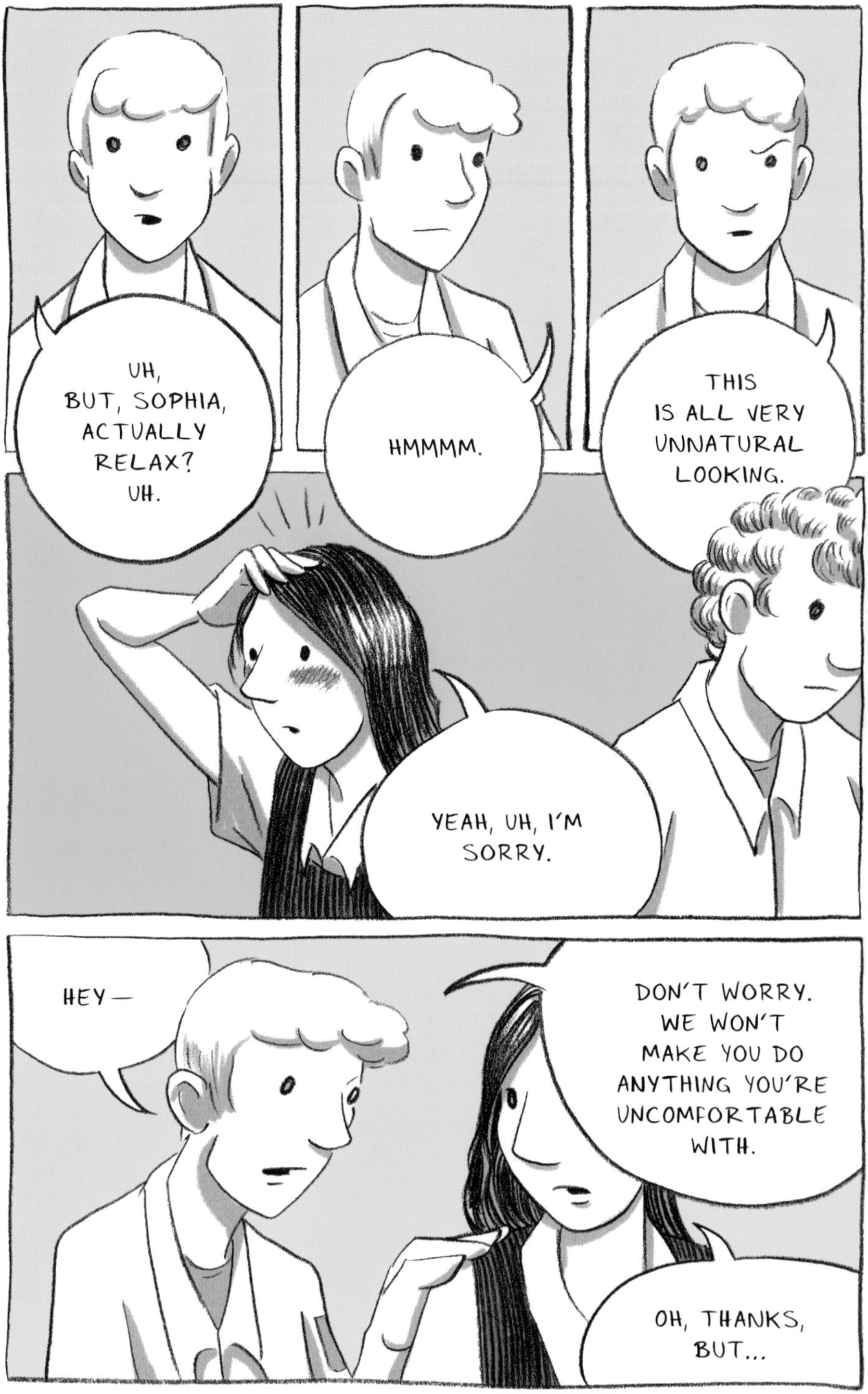
UH, BUT, SOPHIA, ACTUALLY RELAX? UH.
HMMMM.
THIS IS ALL VERY UNNATURAL LOOKING.
YEAH, UH, I'M SORRY.
HEY—
DON'T WORRY. WE WON'T MAKE YOU DO ANYTHING YOU'RE UNCOMFORTABLE WITH.
OH, THANKS, BUT...

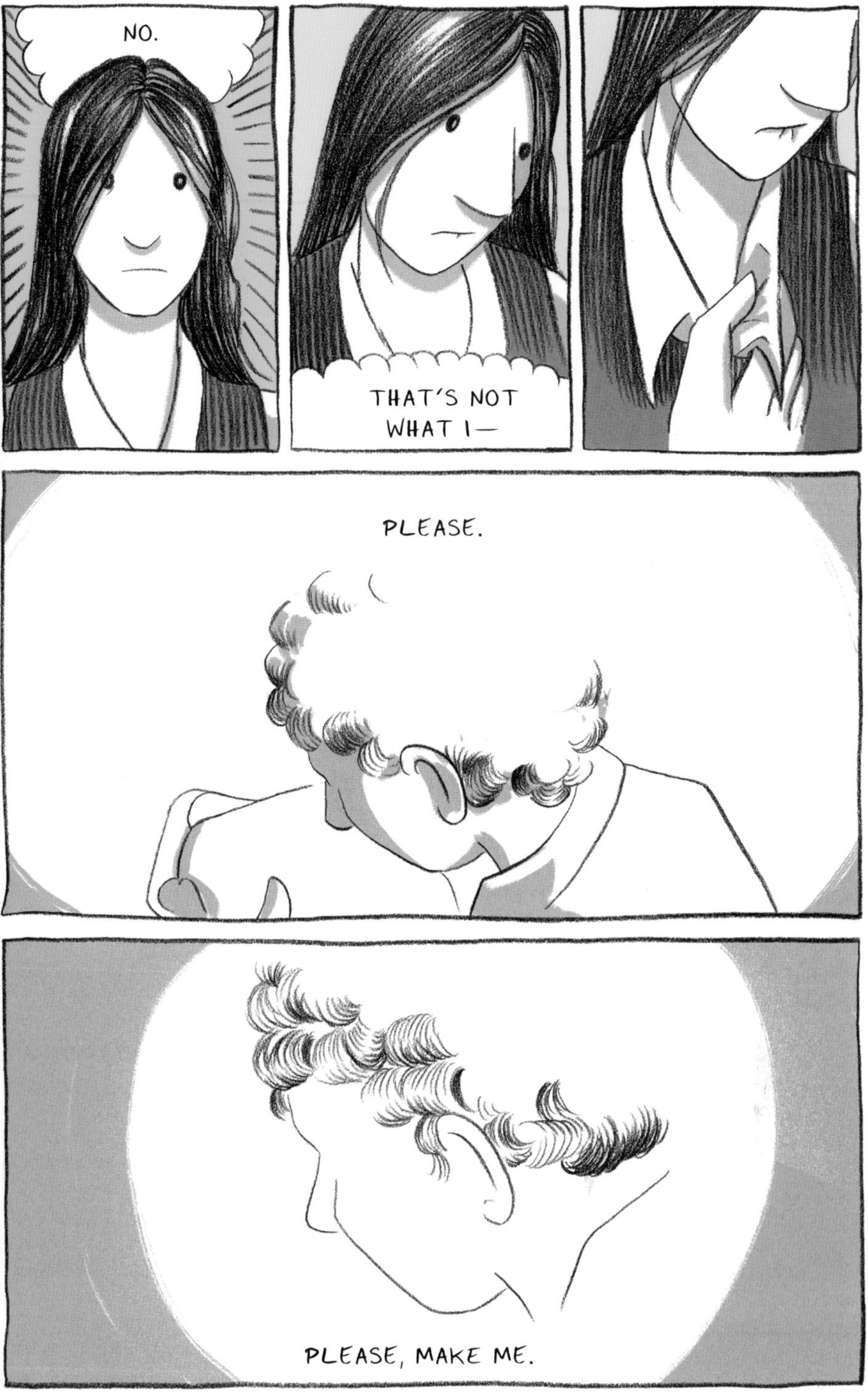
NO.
THAT'S NOT WHAT I—
PLEASE.
PLEASE, MAKE ME.

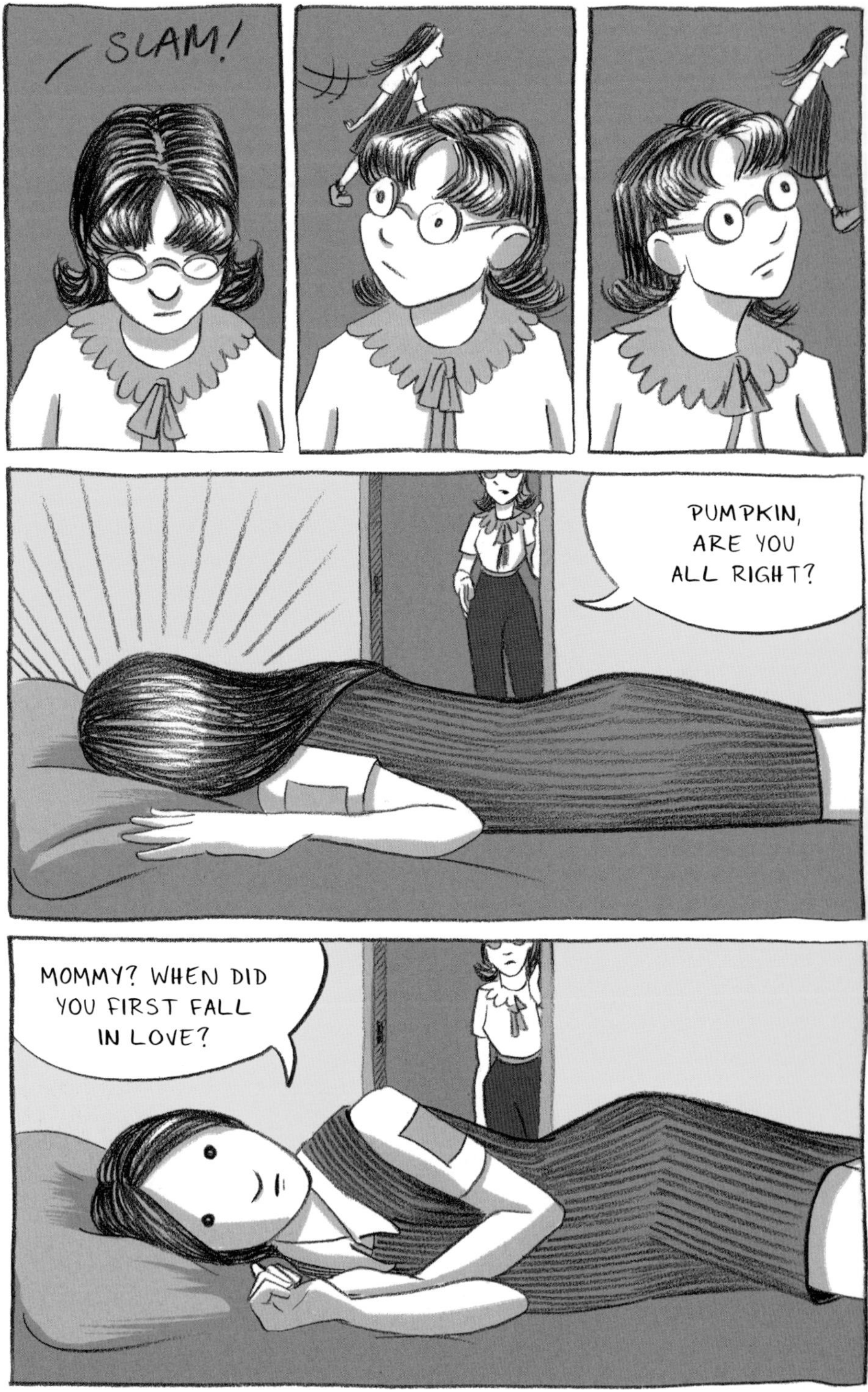
SLAM!
PUMPKIN, ARE YOU ALL RIGHT?
MOMMY? WHEN DID YOU FIRST FALL IN LOVE?

SOPHIA, YOU'RE TOO YOUNG TO FALL IN LOVE.
THAT'S WHAT I THOUGHT.
MOM?

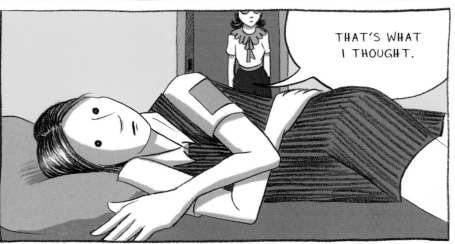

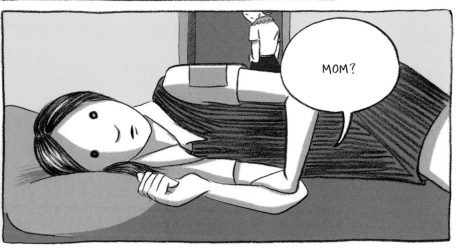

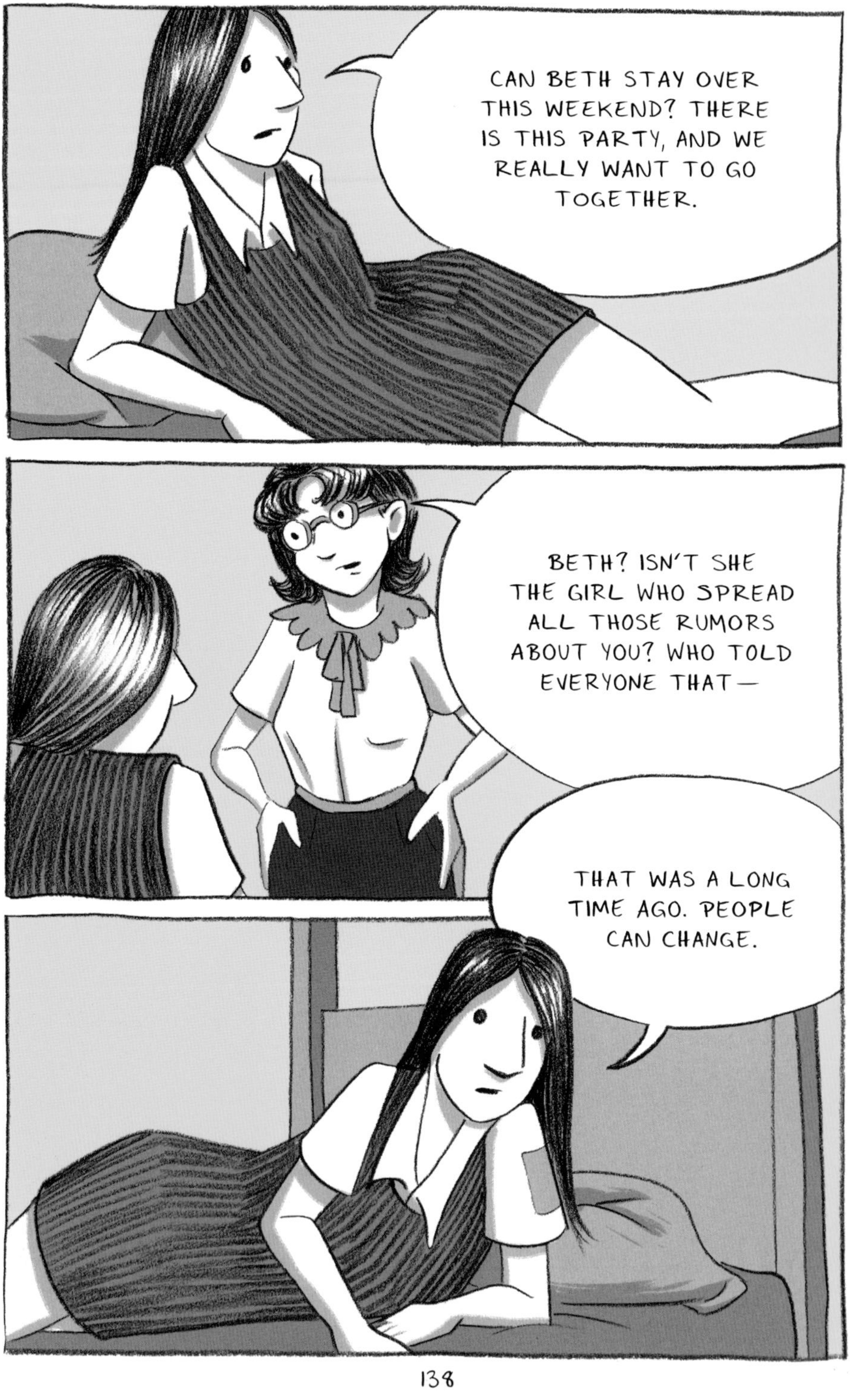
CAN BETH STAY OVER THIS WEEKEND? THERE IS THIS PARTY, AND WE REALLY WANT TO GO TOGETHER.
BETH? ISN'T SHE THE GIRL WHO SPREAD ALL THOSE RUMORS ABOUT YOU? WHO TOLD EVERYONE THAT—
THAT WAS A LONG TIME AGO. PEOPLE CAN CHANGE.

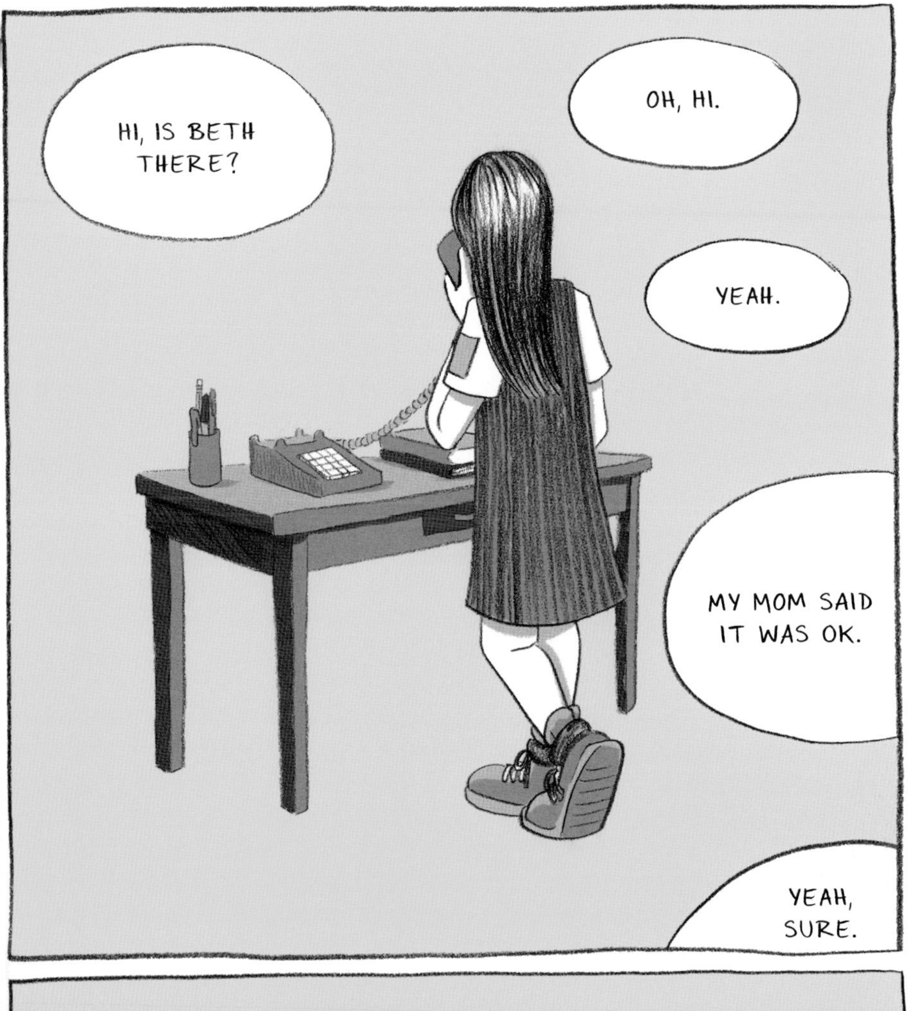
HI, IS BETH THERE?
OH, HI.
YEAH.
MY MOM SAID IT WAS OK.
YEAH, SURE.

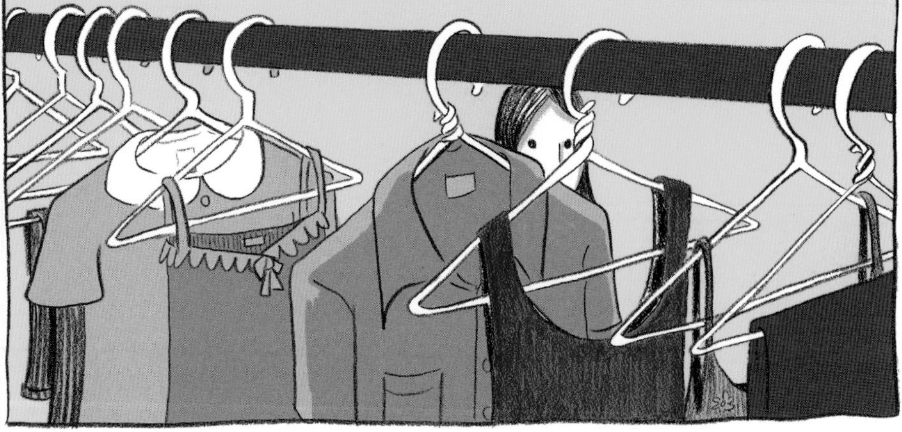

WHEN WE WERE LITTLE, MY SISTER WAS
THE CHAMPION OF SAVING HALLOWEEN CANDY.

I COULDN'T MAKE
MINE LAST MORE
THAN A WEEK, BUT
JULIA COULD SAVE
HERS FOR MONTHS.
ALMOST UNTIL IT
WENT STALE.

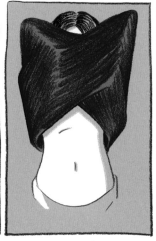

I USED TO THINK I WANTED TO BE MORE LIKE THAT.

BUT WHAT'S THE POINT?

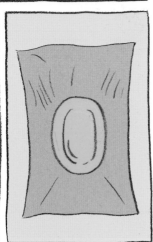

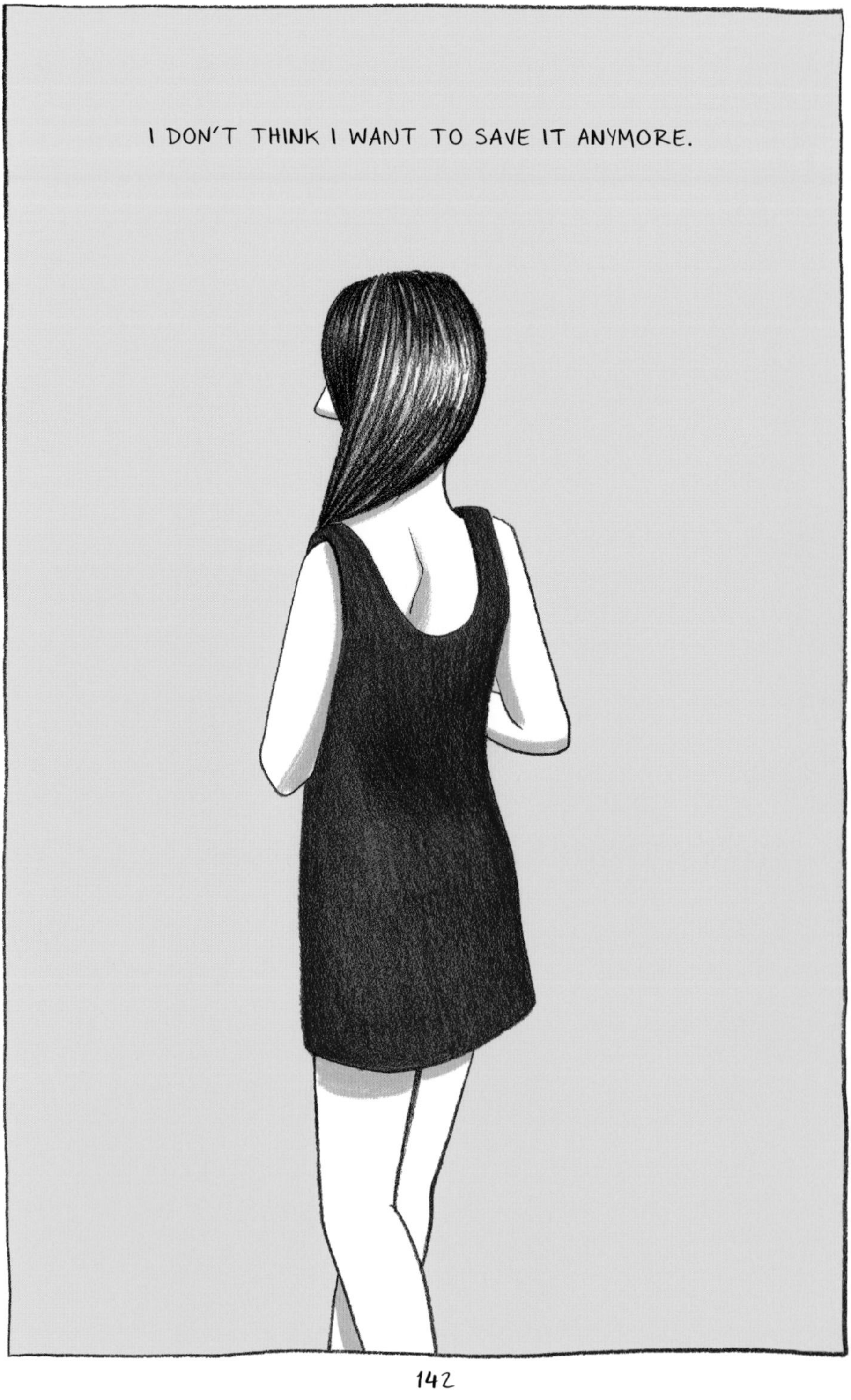
I DON'T THINK I WANT TO SAVE IT ANYMORE.

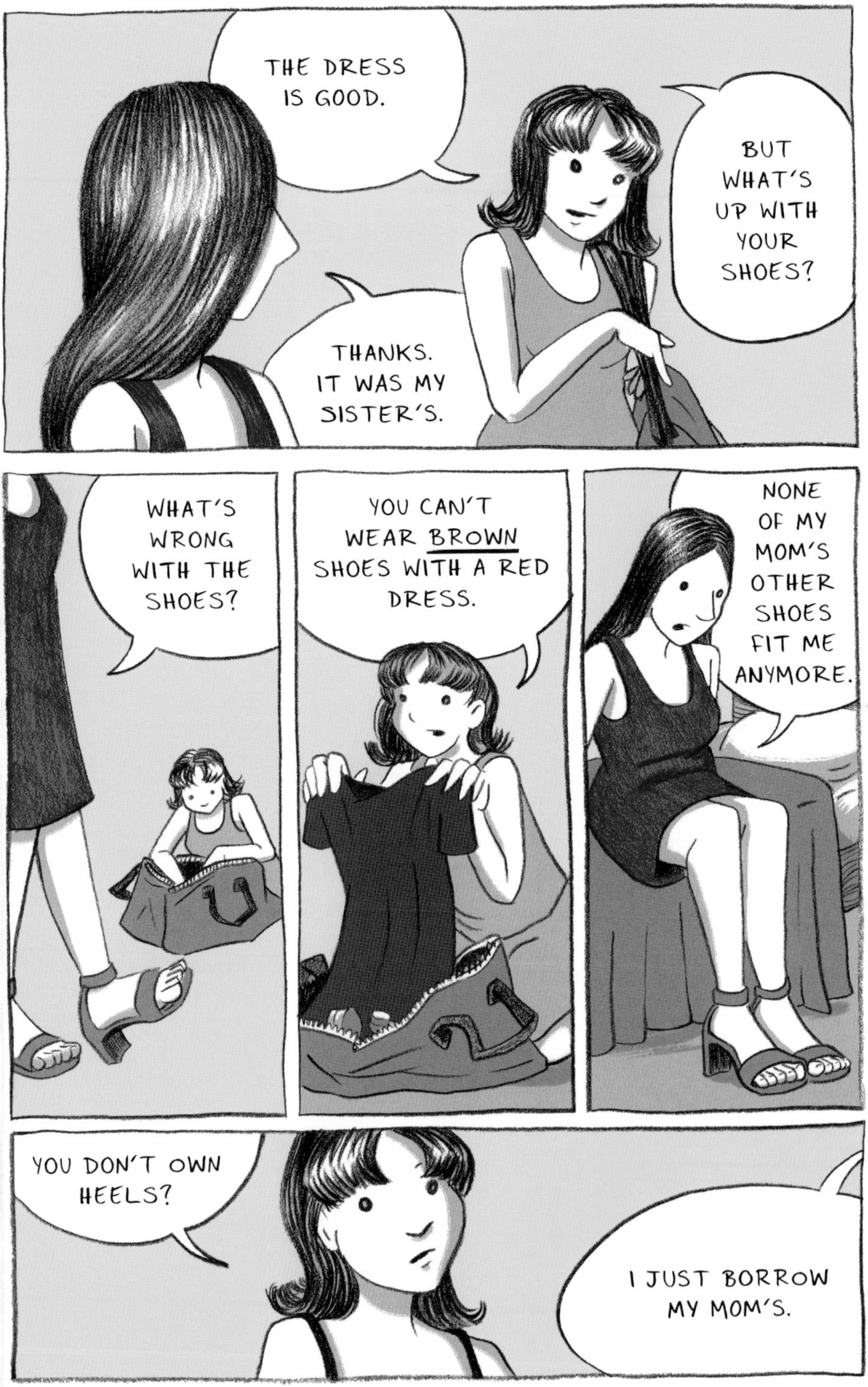
THE DRESS IS GOOD.
BUT WHAT'S UP WITH YOUR SHOES?
THANKS. IT WAS MY SISTER'S.
WHAT'S WRONG WITH THE SHOES?
YOU CAN'T WEAR BROWN SHOES WITH A RED DRESS.
NONE OF MY MOM'S OTHER SHOES FIT ME ANYMORE.
YOU DON'T OWN HEELS?
I JUST BORROW MY MOM'S.

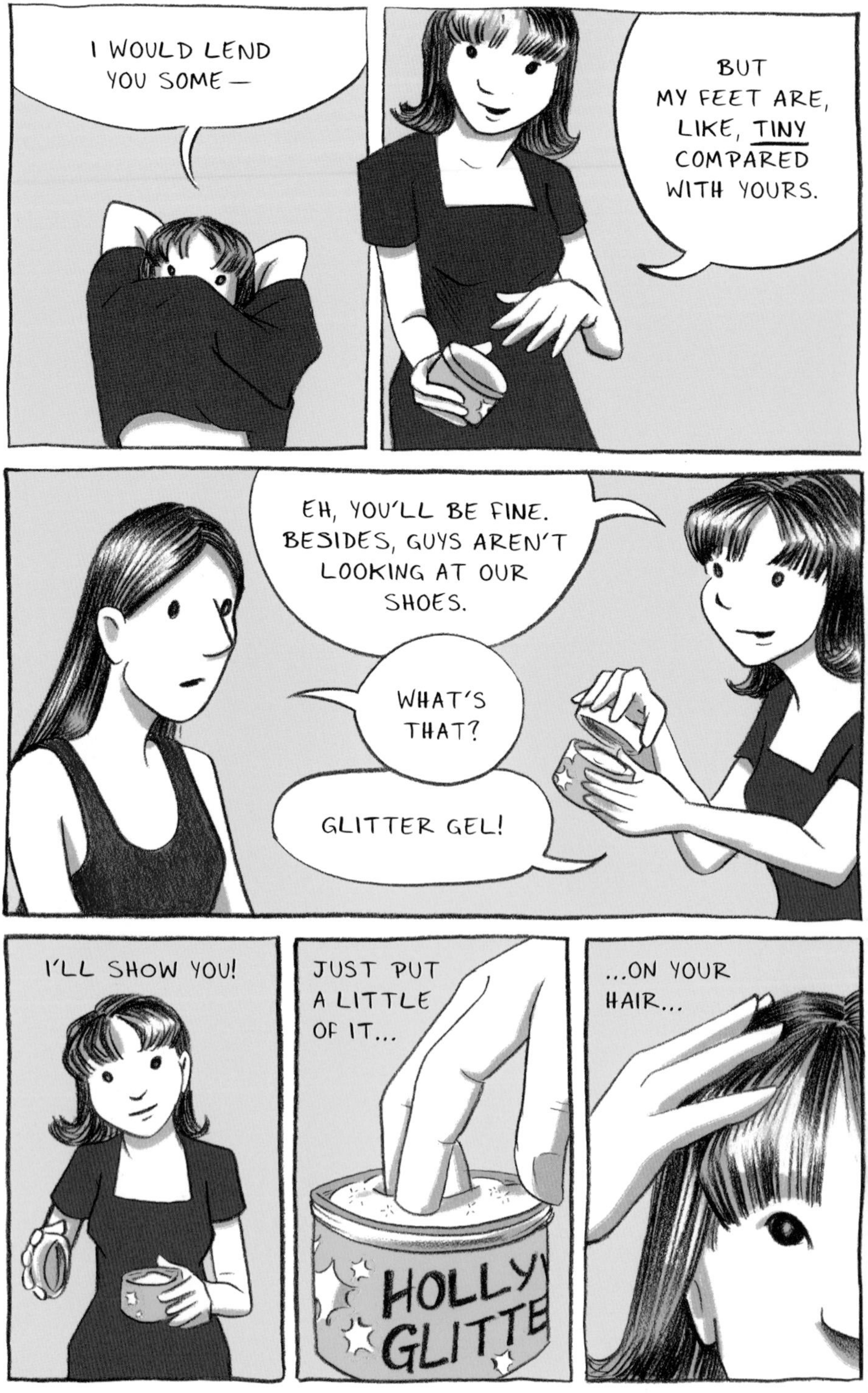
I WOULD LEND YOU SOME—
BUT MY FEET ARE, LIKE, TINY COMPARED WITH YOURS.
EH, YOU'LL BE FINE. BESIDES, GUYS AREN'T LOOKING AT OUR SHOES.
WHAT'S THAT?
GLITTER GEL!
I'LL SHOW YOU!
JUST PUT A LITTLE OF IT...
...ON YOUR HAIR...

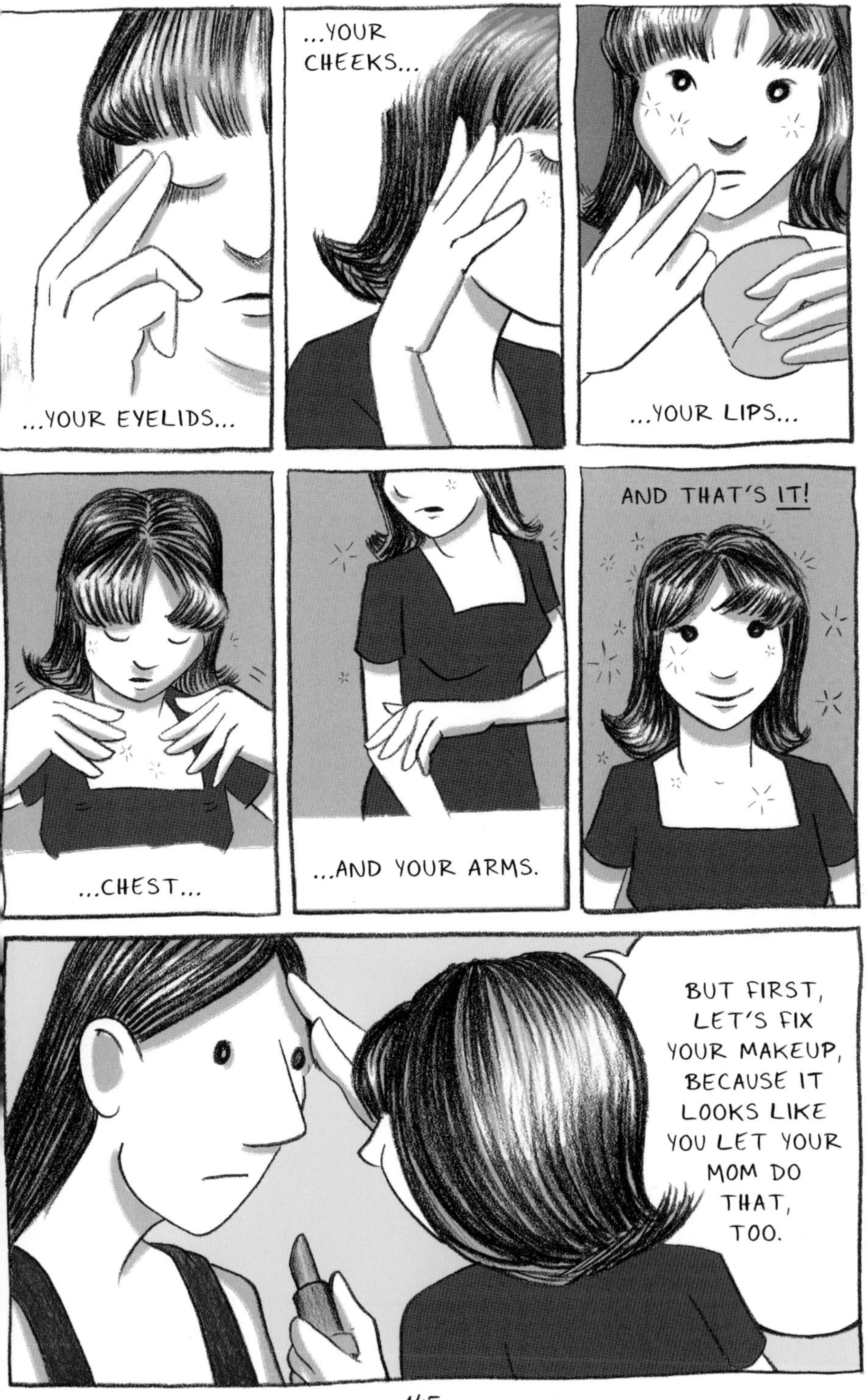
...YOUR EYELIDS...
...YOUR CHEEKS...
...YOUR LIPS...
...CHEST...
...AND YOUR ARMS.
AND THAT'S IT!
BUT FIRST, LET'S FIX YOUR MAKEUP, BECAUSE IT LOOKS LIKE YOU LET YOUR MOM DO THAT, TOO.

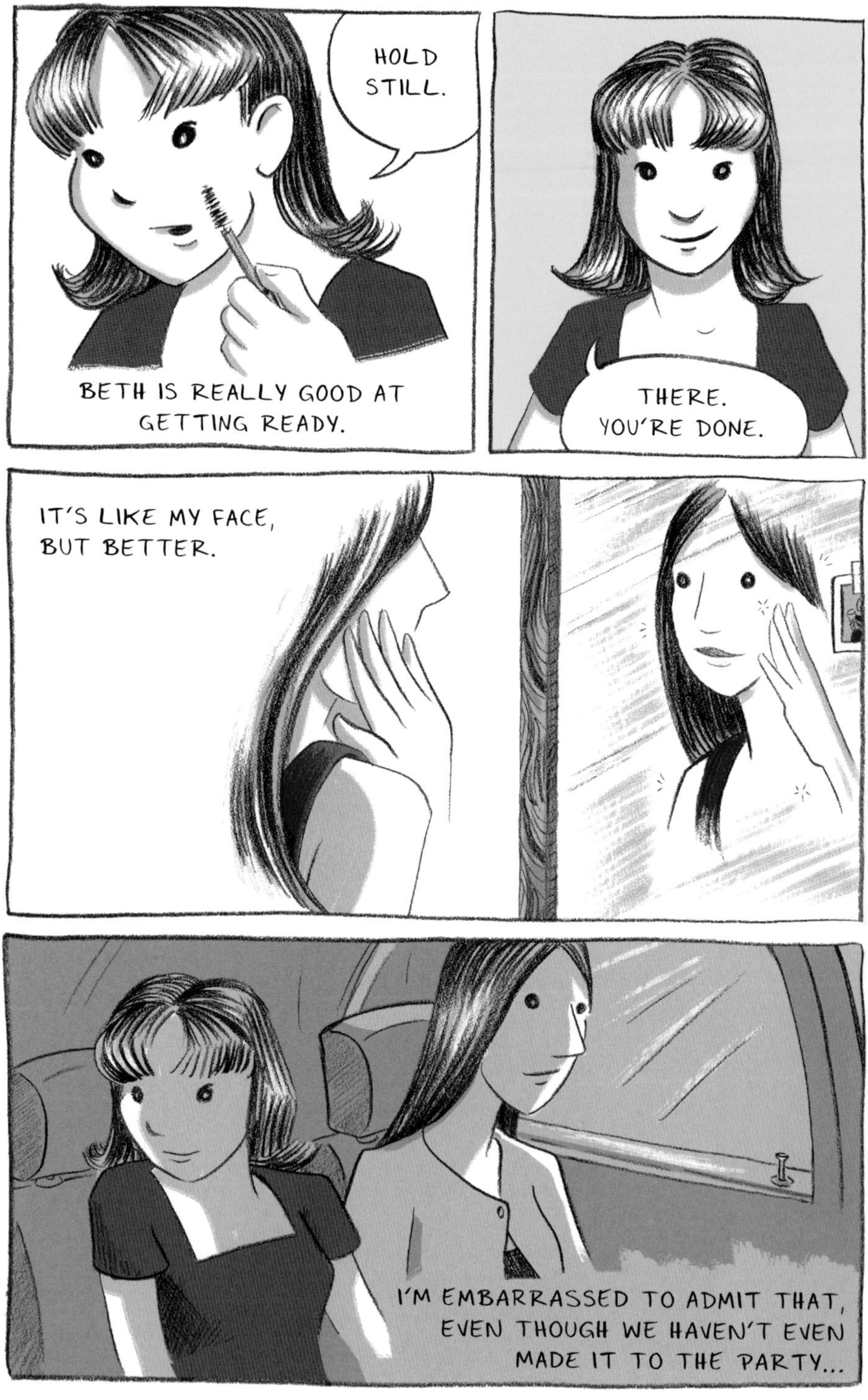
HOLD STILL.
BETH IS REALLY GOOD AT GETTING READY.
THERE. YOU'RE DONE.
IT'S LIKE MY FACE, BUT BETTER.
I'M EMBARRASSED TO ADMIT THAT, EVEN THOUGH WE HAVEN'T EVEN MADE IT TO THE PARTY...

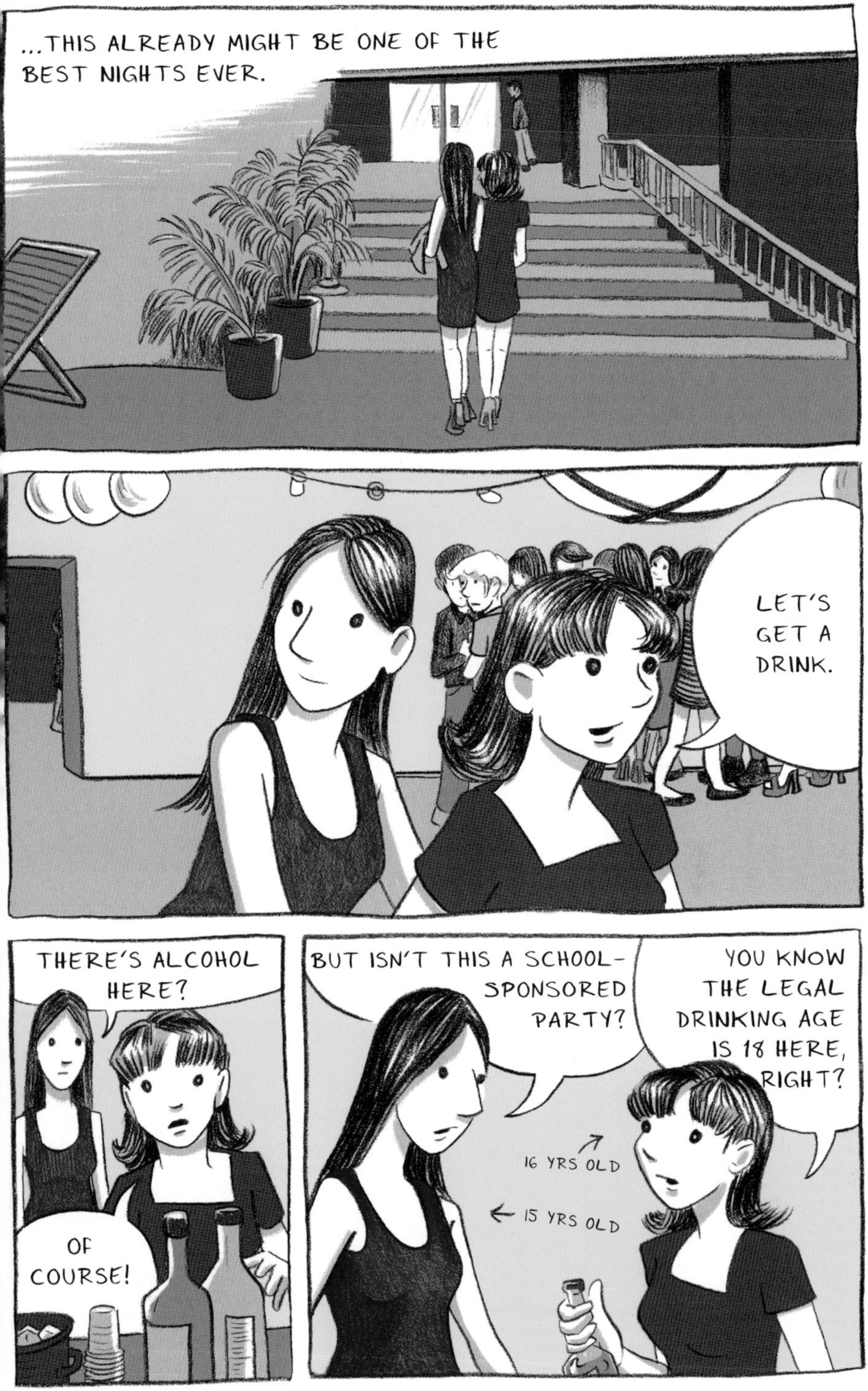
...THIS ALREADY MIGHT BE ONE OF THE BEST NIGHTS EVER.
LET'S GET A DRINK.
THERE'S ALCOHOL HERE?
OF COURSE!
BUT ISN'T THIS A SCHOOL-SPONSORED PARTY?
YOU KNOW THE LEGAL DRINKING AGE IS 18 HERE, RIGHT?
16 YRS OLD
15 YRS OLD

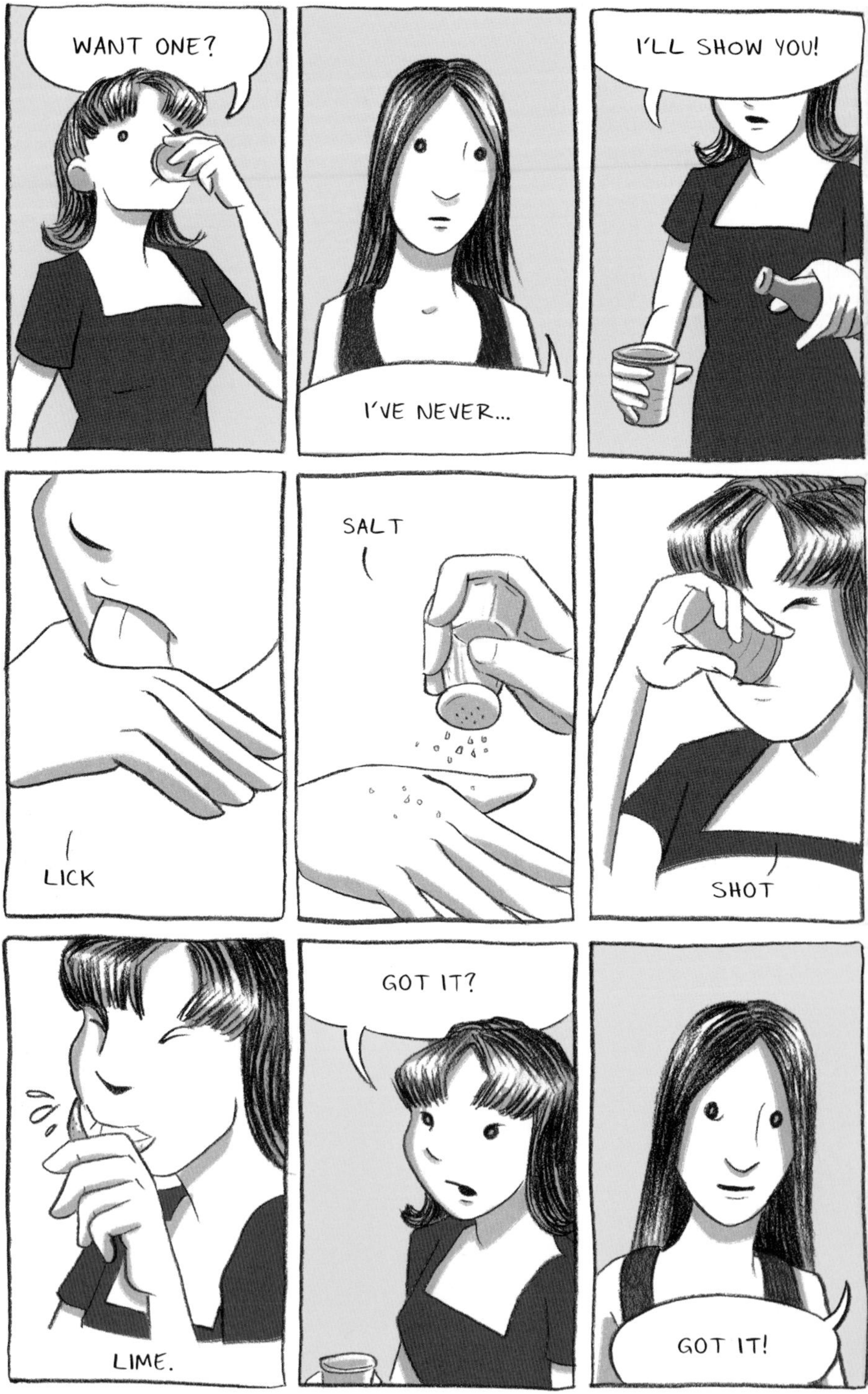

WANT ONE?
I'VE NEVER...
I'LL SHOW YOU!
LICK
SALT
SHOT
LIME.
GOT IT?
GOT IT!

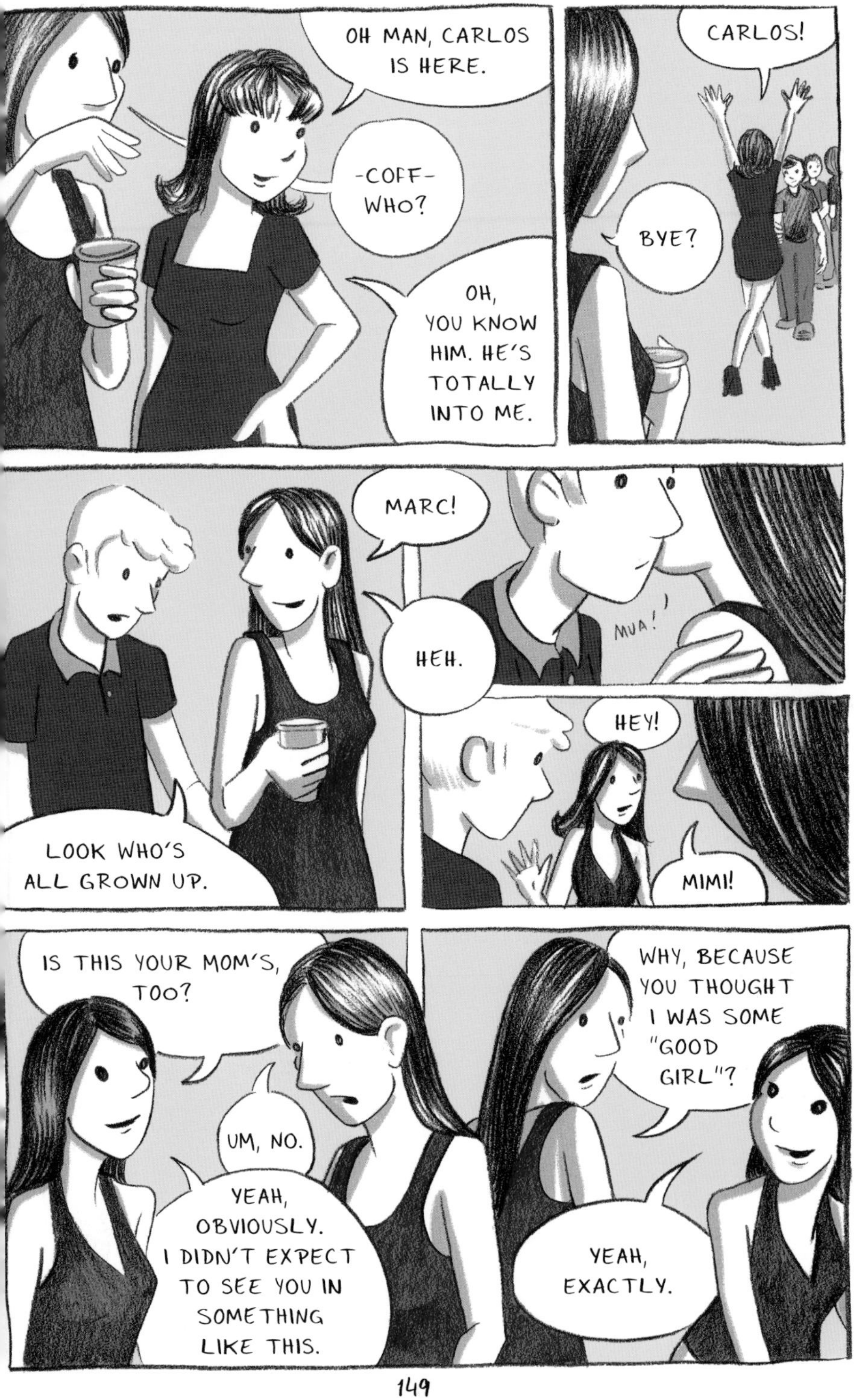
OH MAN, CARLOS IS HERE.
-COFF- WHO?
OH, YOU KNOW HIM. HE'S TOTALLY INTO ME.
CARLOS!
BYE?
MARC!
HEH.
LOOK WHO'S ALL GROWN UP.
MUA!
HEY!
MIMI!
IS THIS YOUR MOM'S, TOO?
UM, NO.
YEAH, OBVIOUSLY. I DIDN'T EXPECT TO SEE YOU IN SOMETHING LIKE THIS.
WHY, BECAUSE YOU THOUGHT I WAS SOME "GOOD GIRL"?
YEAH, EXACTLY.

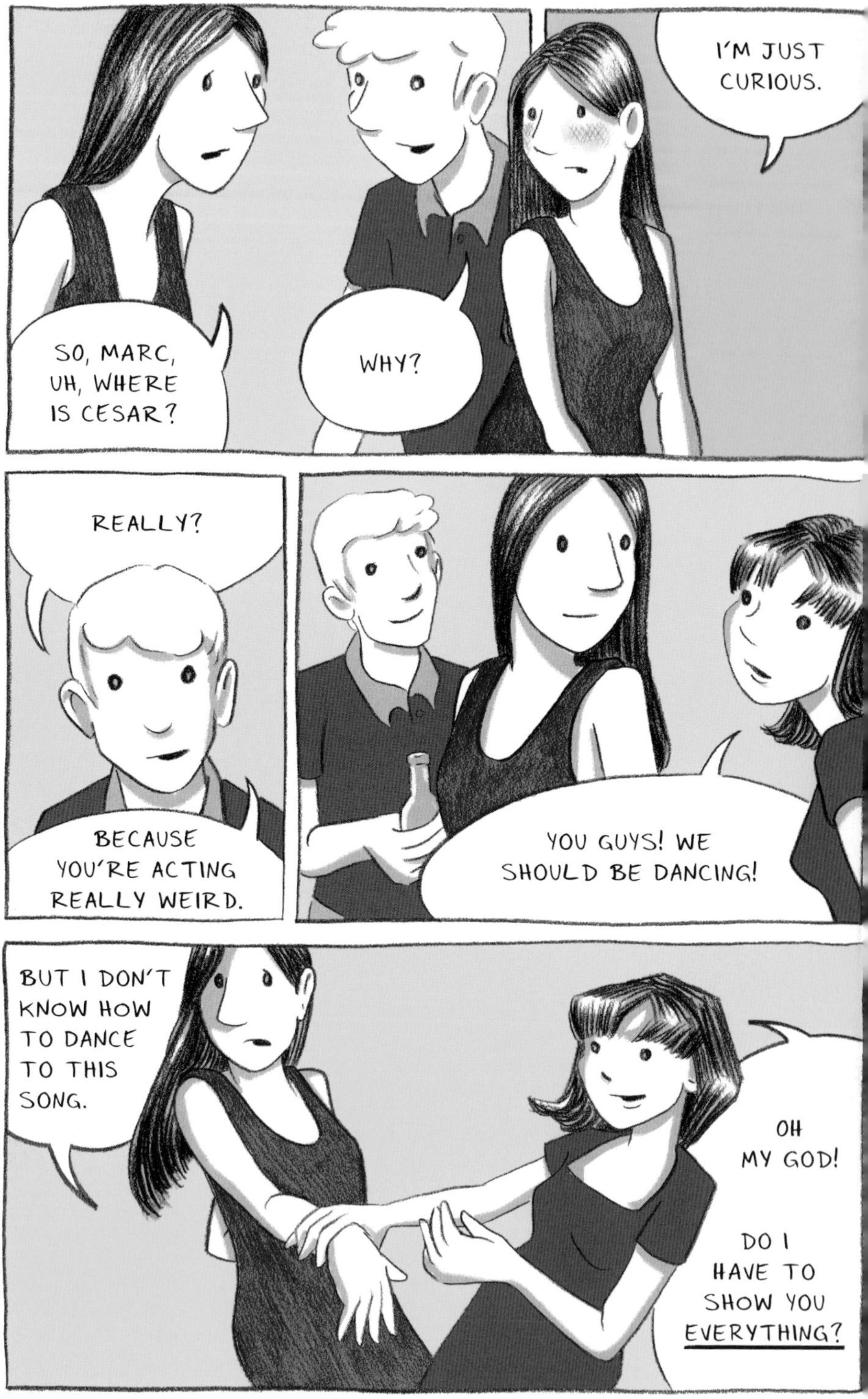
SO, MARC, UH, WHERE IS CESAR?
WHY?
I'M JUST CURIOUS.
REALLY?
BECAUSE YOU'RE ACTING REALLY WEIRD.
YOU GUYS! WE SHOULD BE DANCING!
BUT I DON'T KNOW HOW TO DANCE TO THIS SONG.
OH MY GOD!
DO I HAVE TO SHOW YOU EVERYTHING?

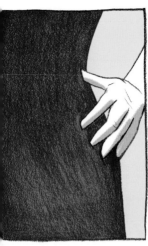

BETH IS RIGHT.

WE SHOULD ALWAYS BE DANCING.

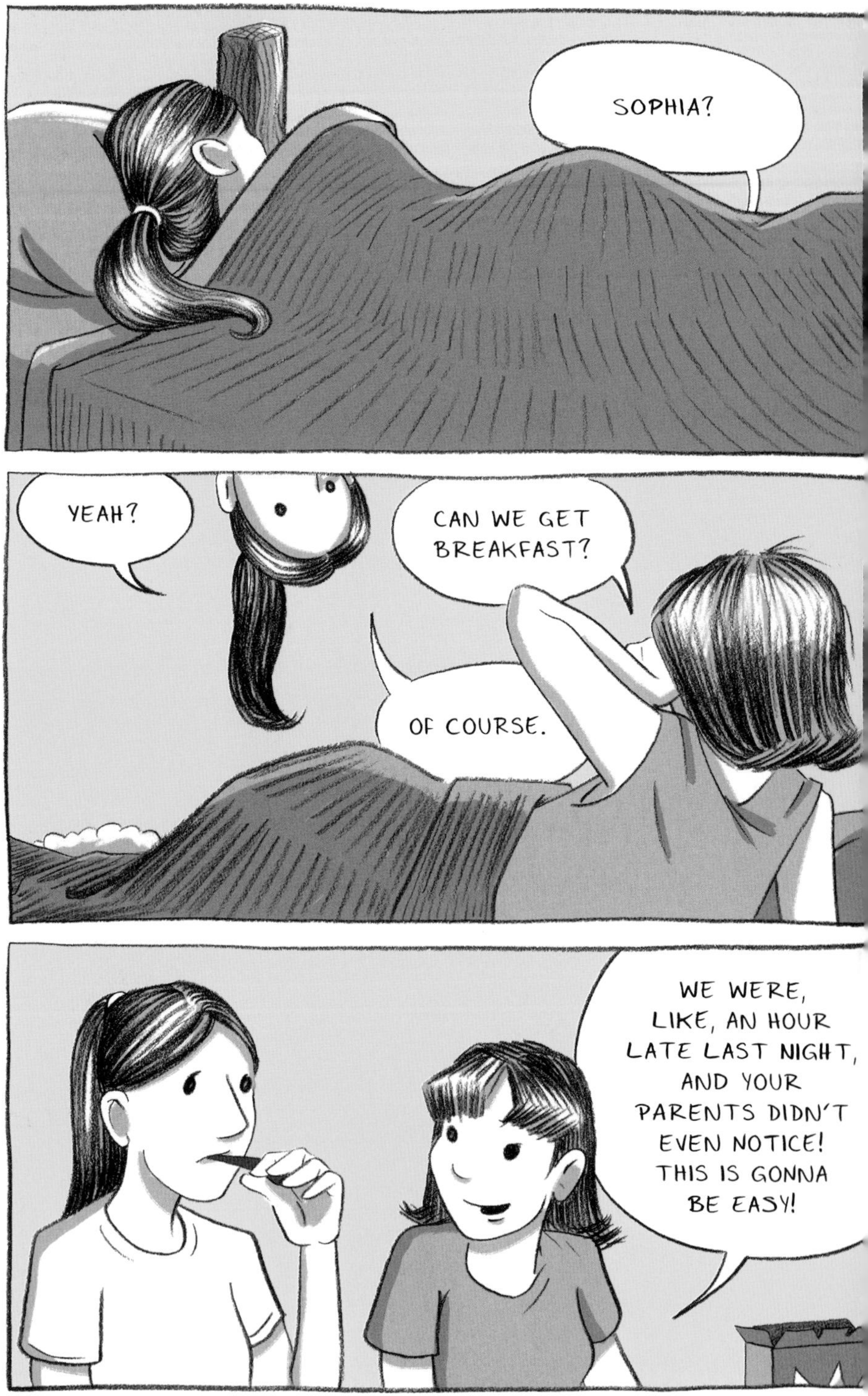
SOPHIA?
YEAH?
CAN WE GET BREAKFAST?
OF COURSE.
WE WERE, LIKE, AN HOUR LATE LAST NIGHT, AND YOUR PARENTS DIDN'T EVEN NOTICE! THIS IS GONNA BE EASY!

HI!

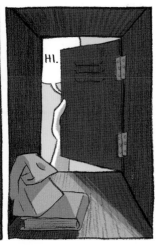

HI.

DID YOU DO THE CHEM HOMEWORK?

OH. YEAH.

GREAT!

YOU'RE A LIFESAVER. THANKS.

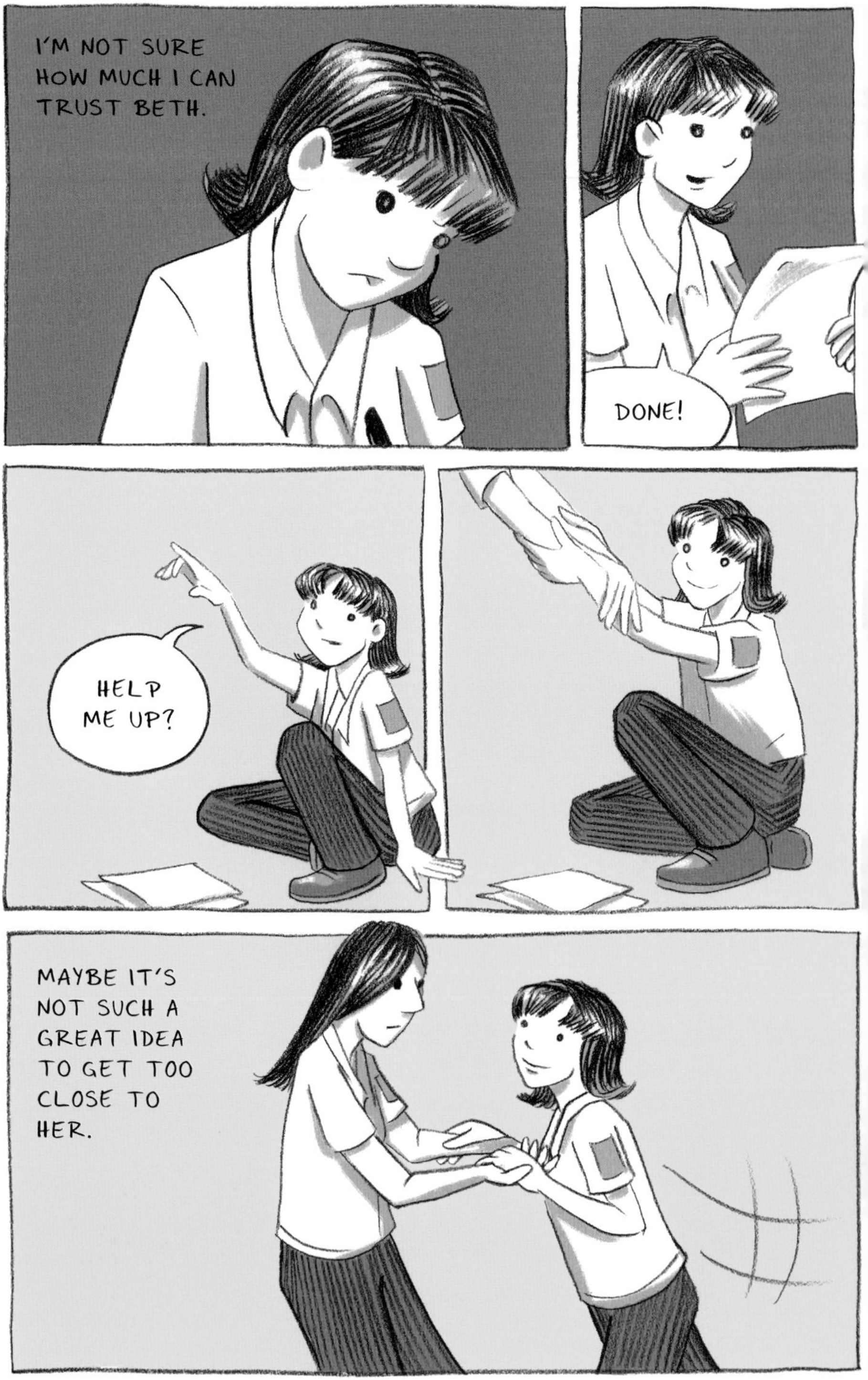
I'M NOT SURE HOW MUCH I CAN TRUST BETH.
DONE!
HELP ME UP?
MAYBE IT'S NOT SUCH A GREAT IDEA TO GET TOO CLOSE TO HER.

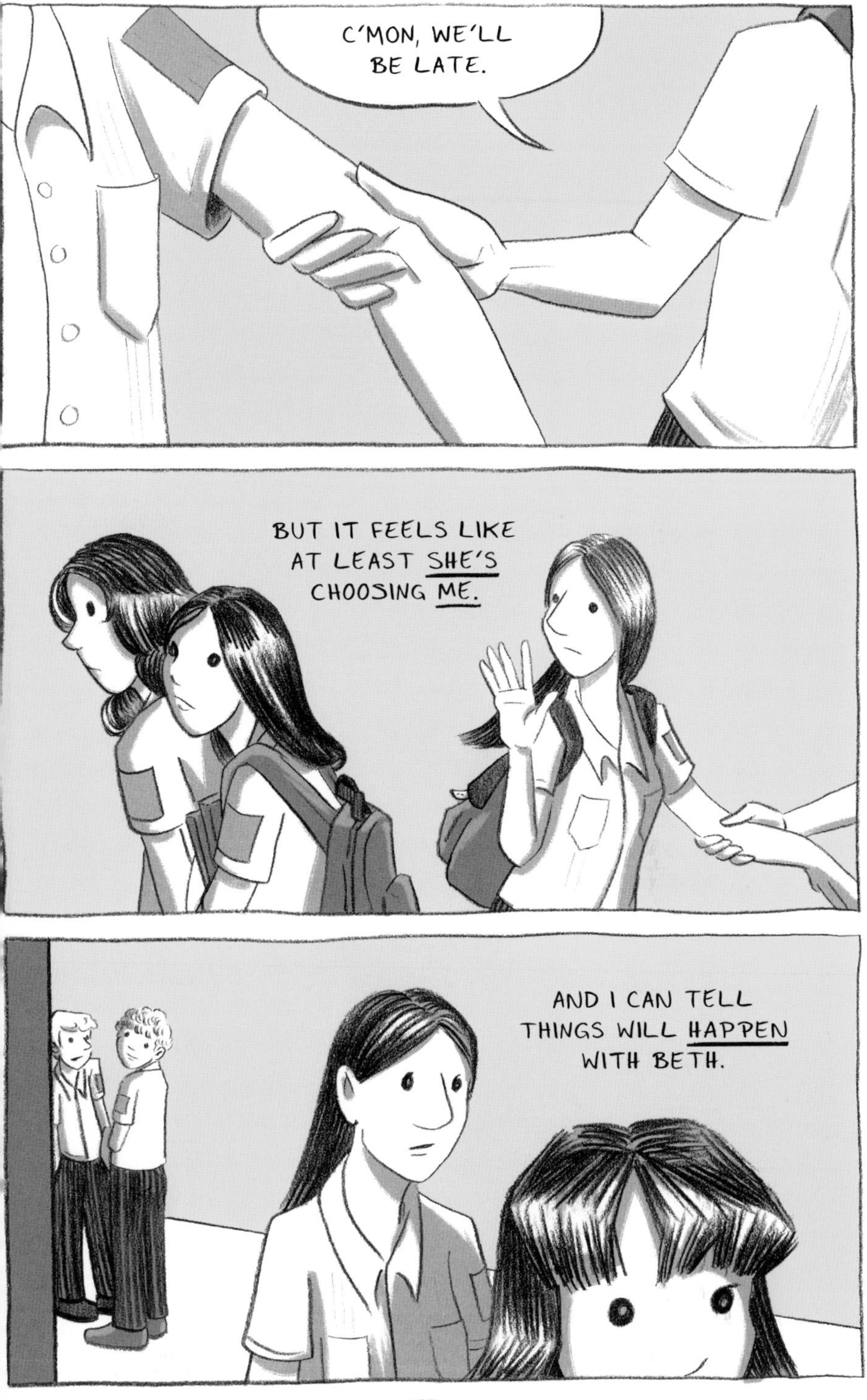
C'MON, WE'LL BE LATE.
BUT IT FEELS LIKE AT LEAST SHE'S CHOOSING ME.
AND I CAN TELL THINGS WILL HAPPEN WITH BETH.

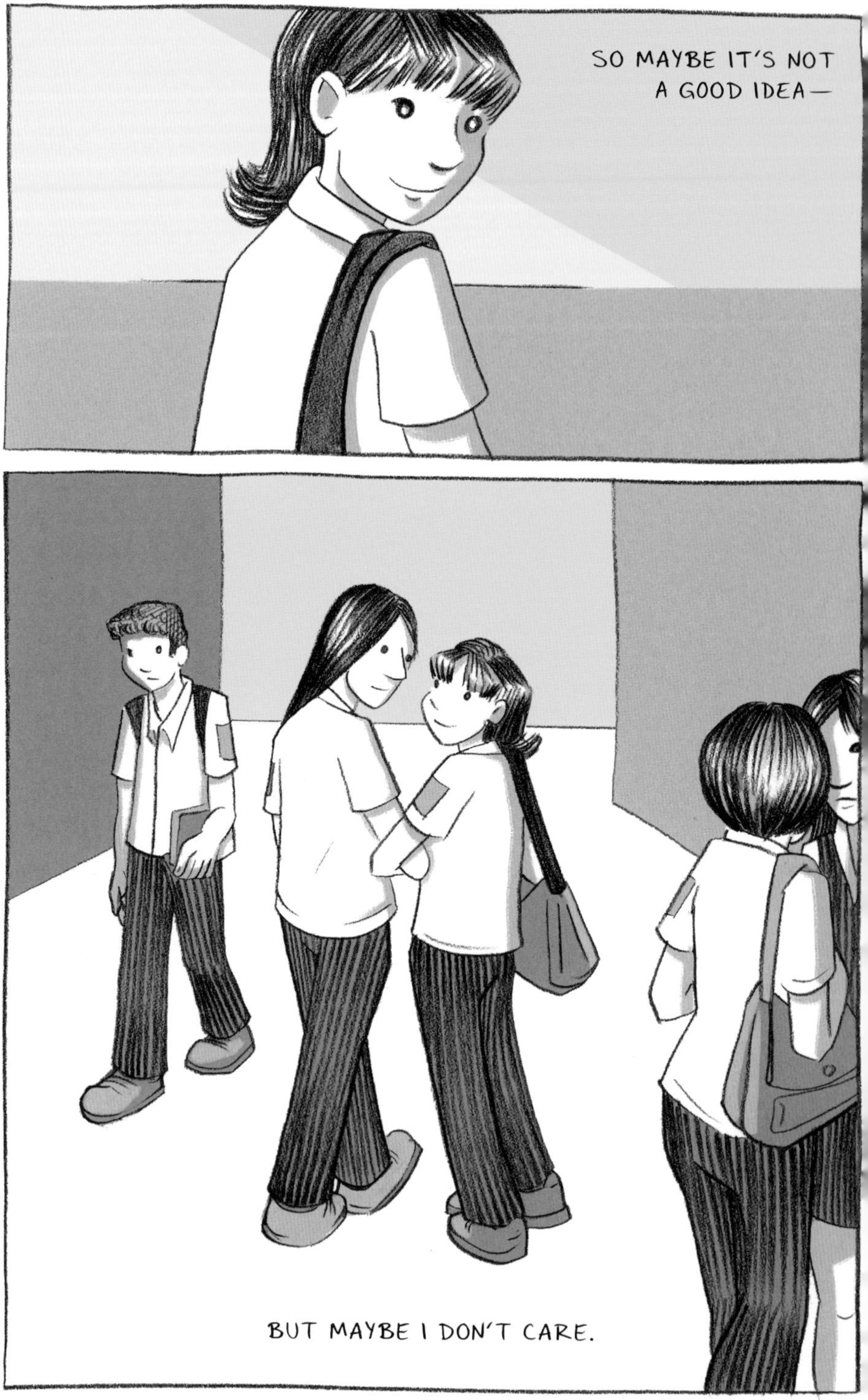
SO MAYBE IT'S NOT
A GOOD IDEA—
BUT MAYBE I DON'T CARE.

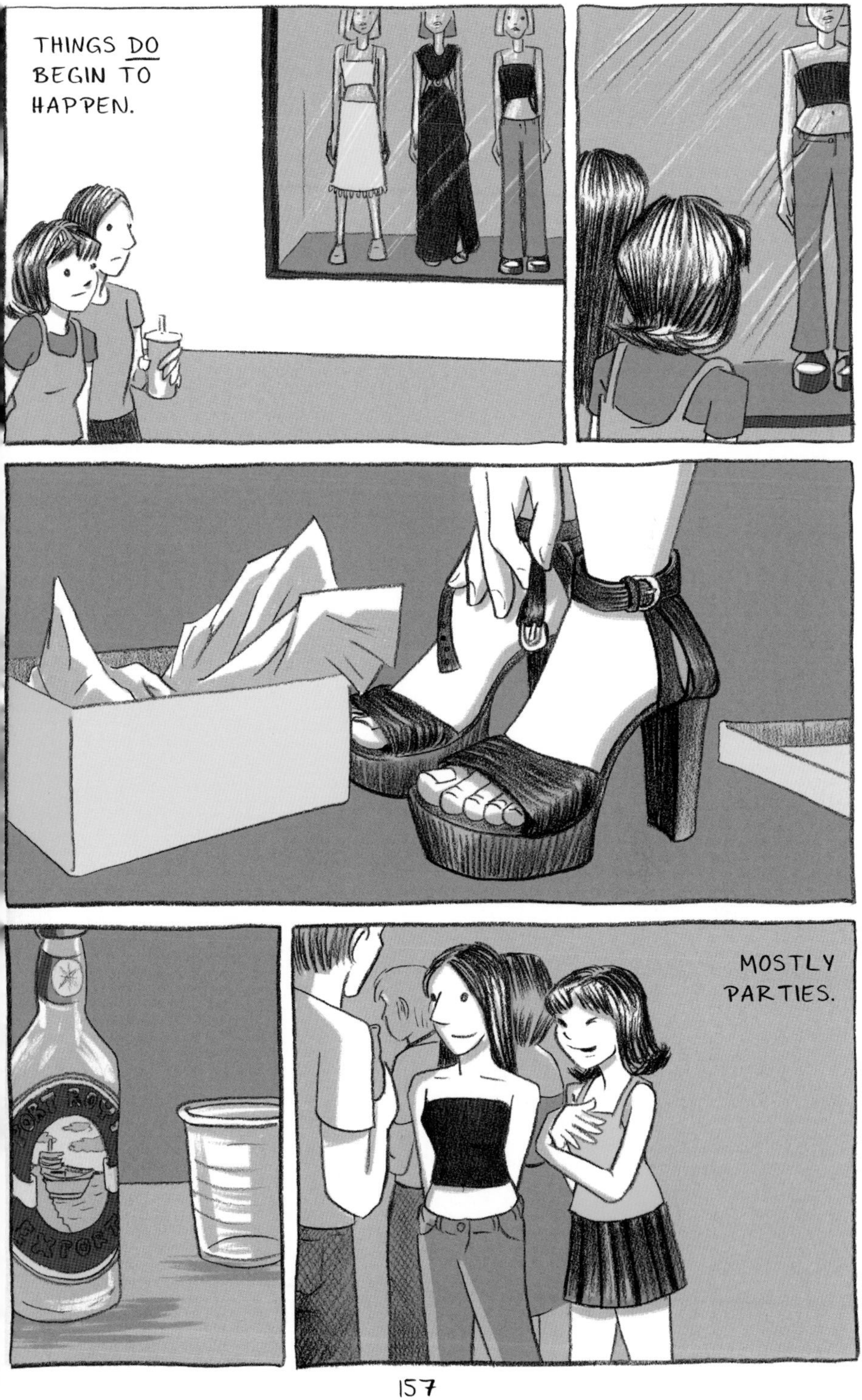
THINGS DO BEGIN TO HAPPEN.
PORT ROYAL EXPORT
MOSTLY PARTIES.

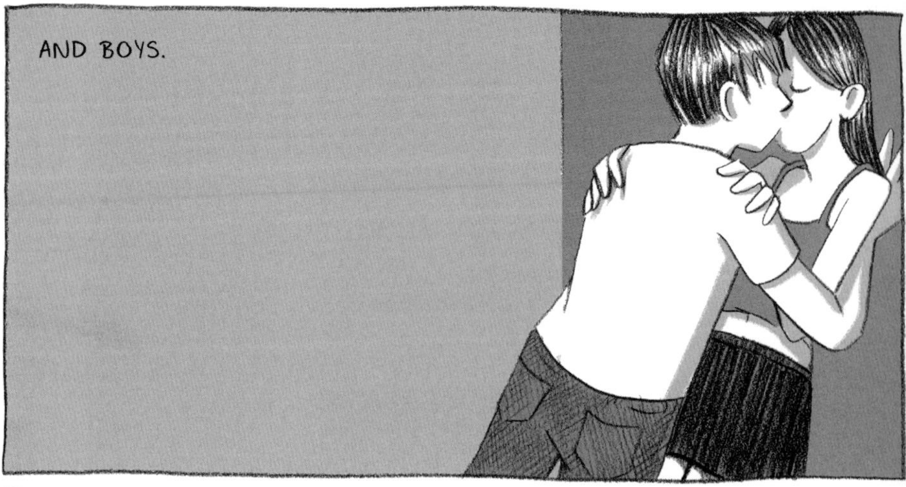
AND BOYS.

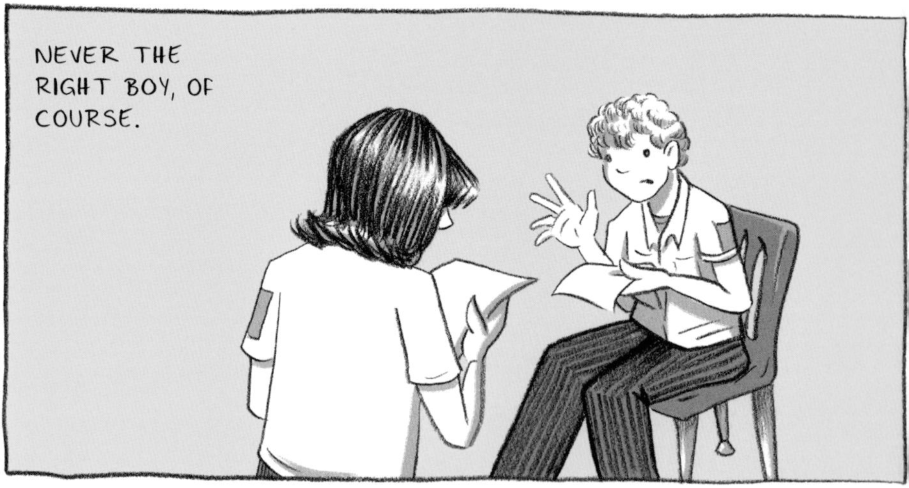
NEVER THE RIGHT BOY, OF COURSE.

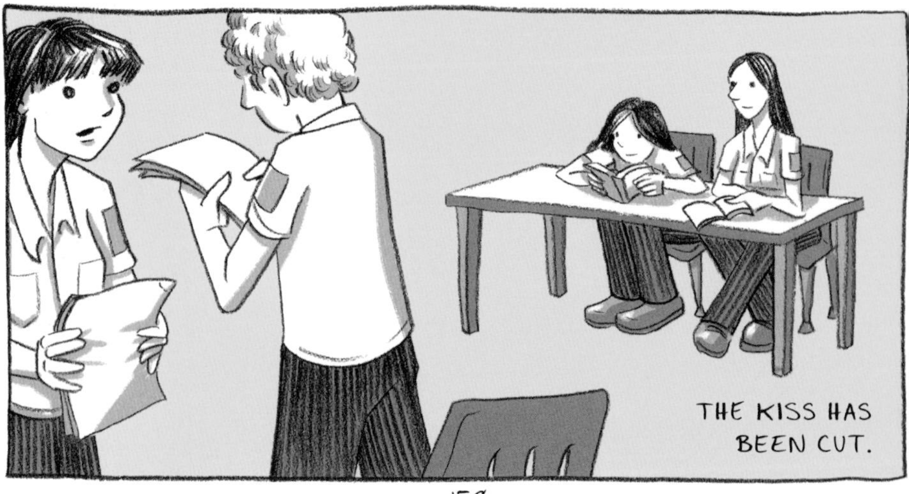
THE KISS HAS BEEN CUT.

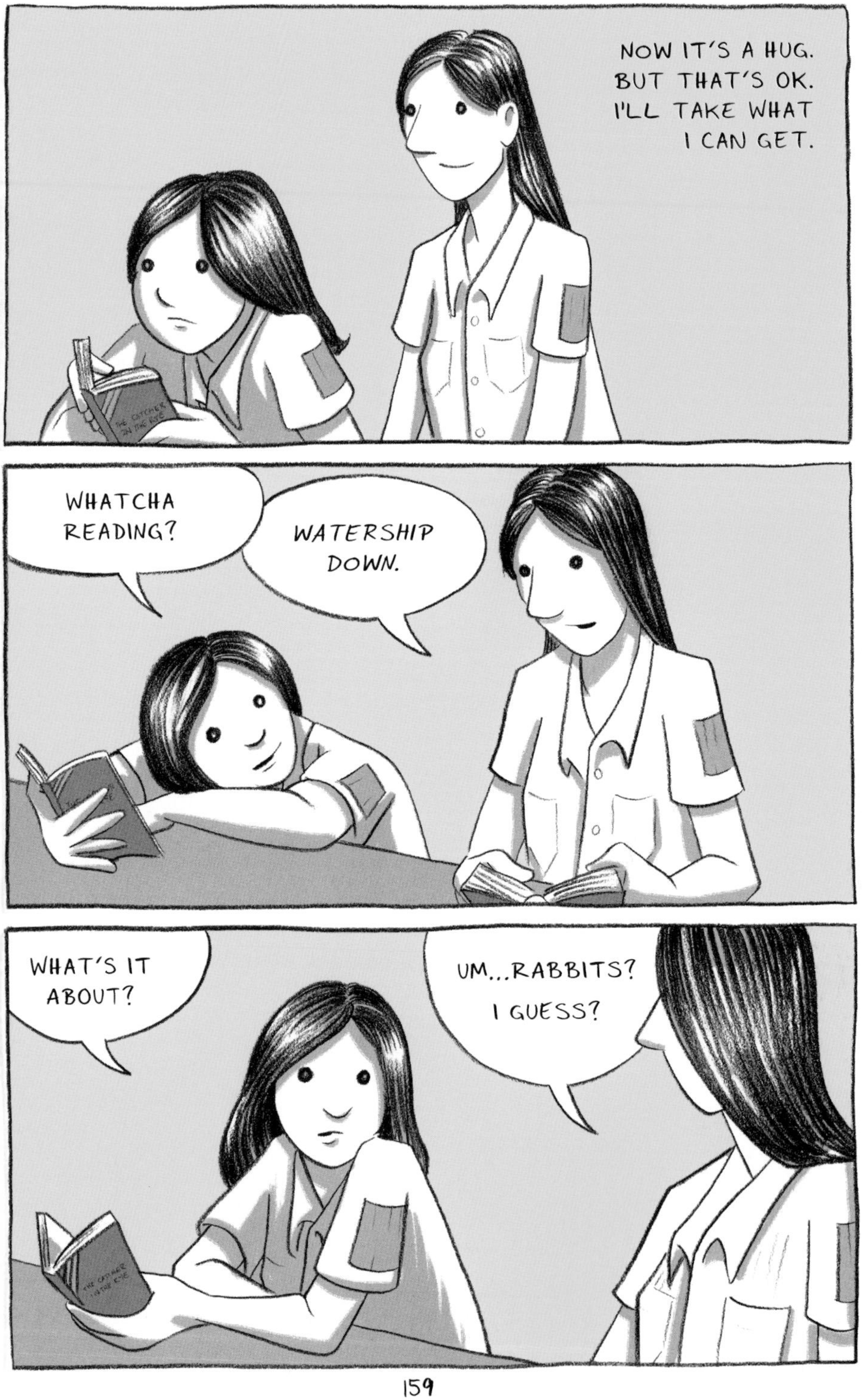
NOW IT'S A HUG. BUT THAT'S OK. I'LL TAKE WHAT I CAN GET.
WHATCHA READING?
WATERSHIP DOWN.
WHAT'S IT ABOUT?
UM...RABBITS? I GUESS?

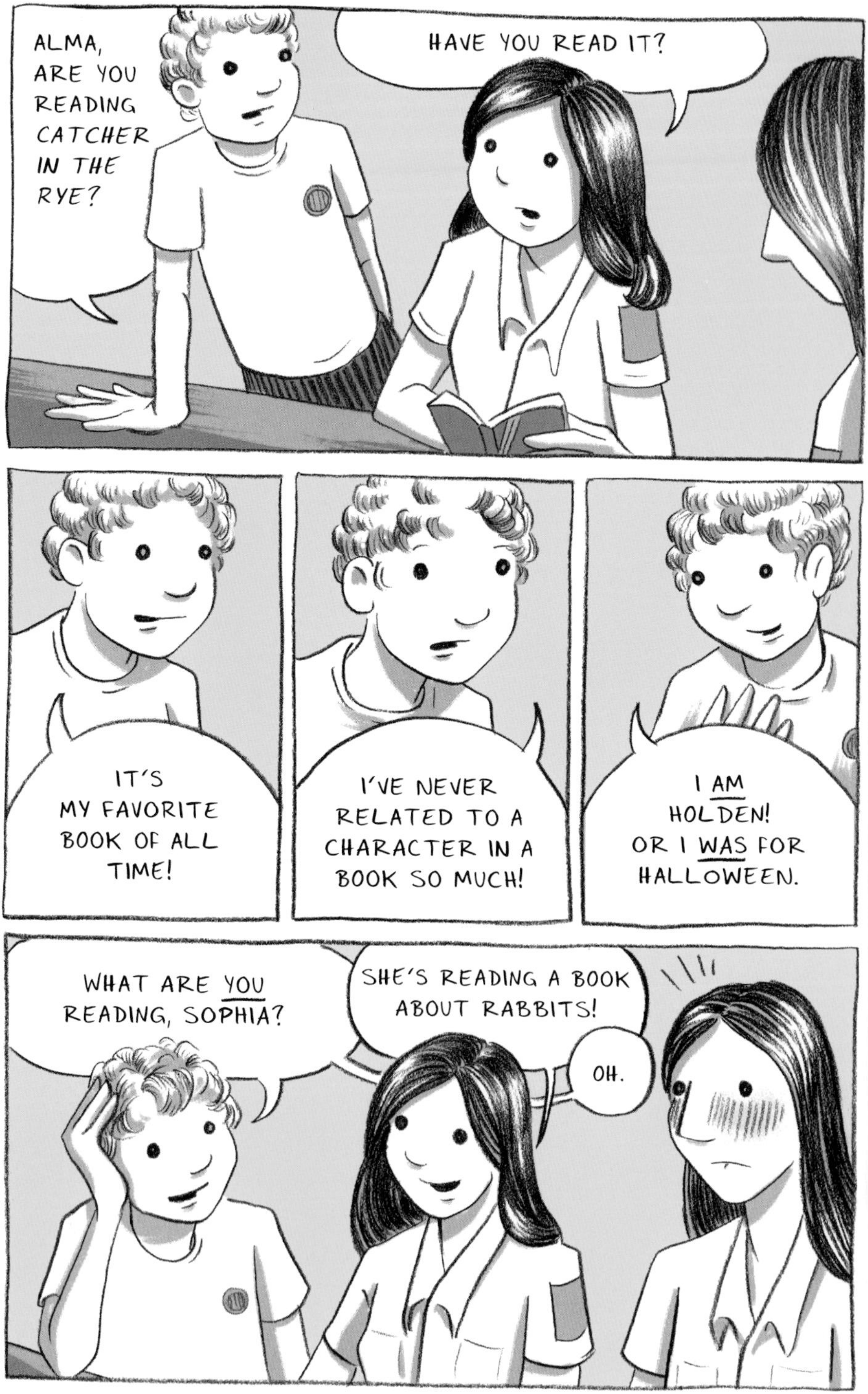
ALMA, ARE YOU READING CATCHER IN THE RYE?
HAVE YOU READ IT?
IT'S MY FAVORITE BOOK OF ALL TIME!
I'VE NEVER RELATED TO A CHARACTER IN A BOOK SO MUCH!
I AM HOLDEN! OR I WAS FOR HALLOWEEN.
WHAT ARE YOU READING, SOPHIA?
SHE'S READING A BOOK ABOUT RABBITS!
OH.

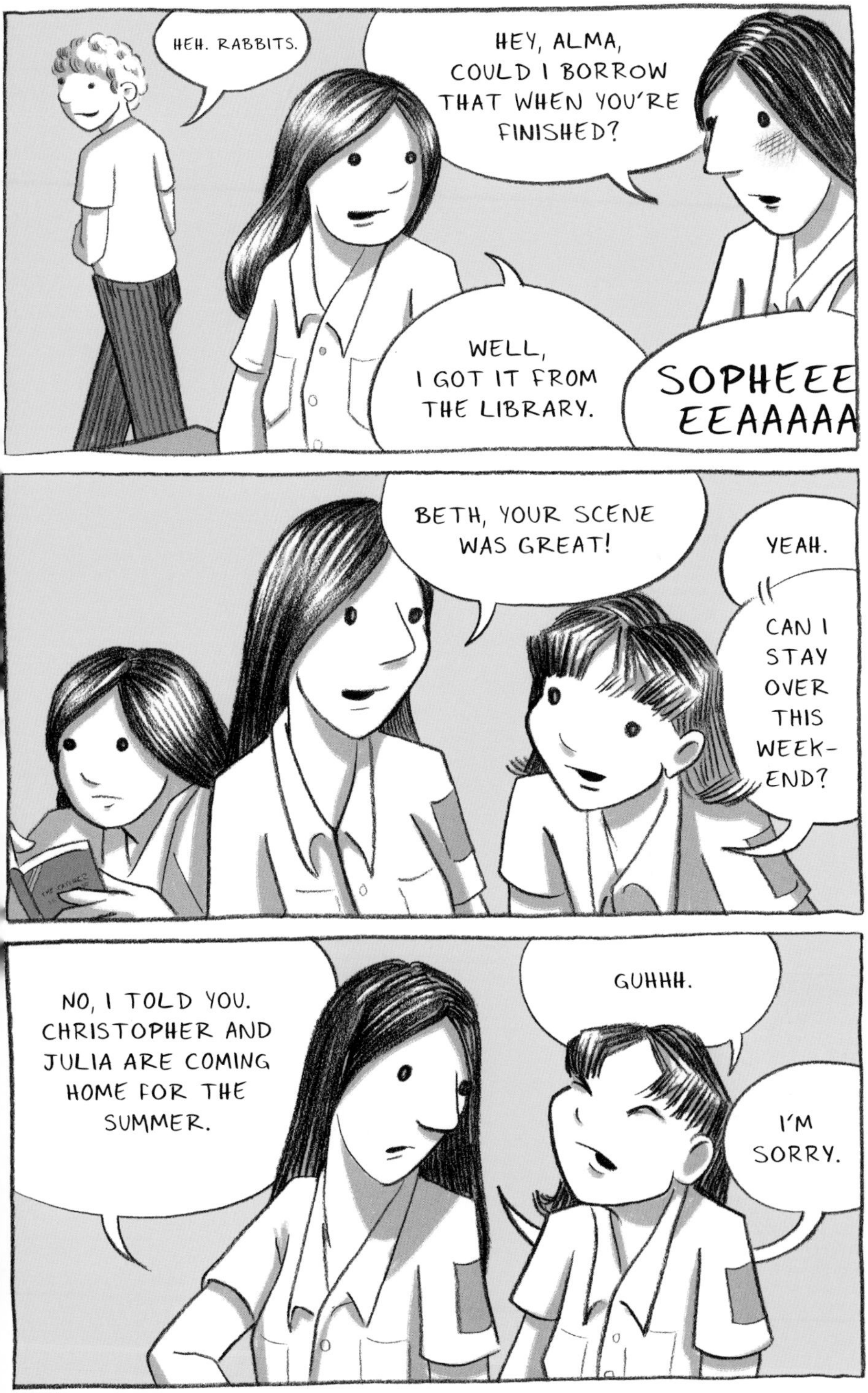
HEH. RABBITS.
HEY, ALMA, COULD I BORROW THAT WHEN YOU'RE FINISHED?
WELL, I GOT IT FROM THE LIBRARY.
SOPHEEEEEAAAAAA
BETH, YOUR SCENE WAS GREAT!
YEAH.
CAN I STAY OVER THIS WEEK-END?
NO, I TOLD YOU. CHRISTOPHER AND JULIA ARE COMING HOME FOR THE SUMMER.
GUHHH.
I'M SORRY.

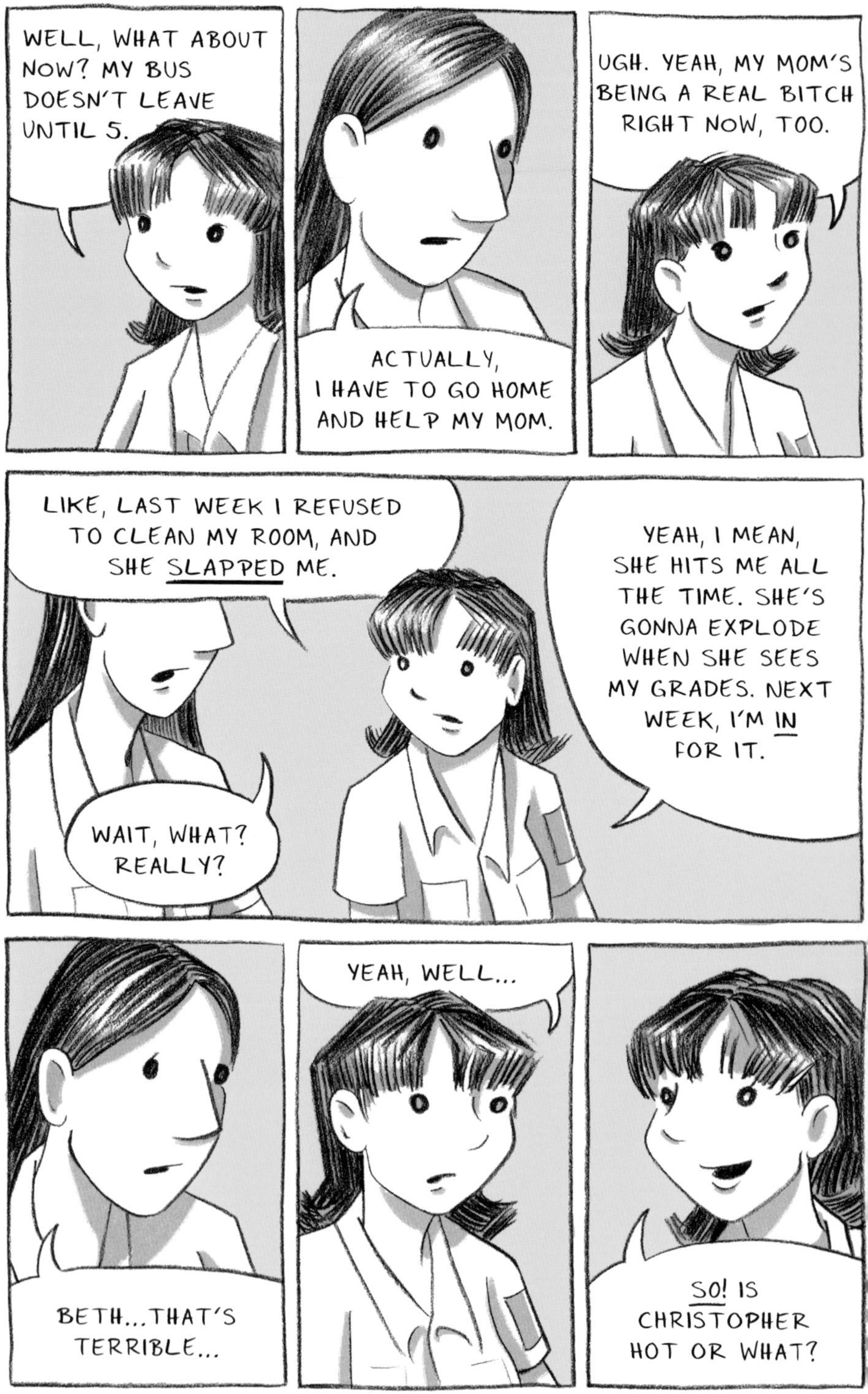
WELL, WHAT ABOUT NOW? MY BUS DOESN'T LEAVE UNTIL 5.
ACTUALLY, I HAVE TO GO HOME AND HELP MY MOM.
UGH. YEAH, MY MOM'S BEING A REAL BITCH RIGHT NOW, TOO.
LIKE, LAST WEEK I REFUSED TO CLEAN MY ROOM, AND SHE SLAPPED ME.
WAIT, WHAT? REALLY?
YEAH, I MEAN, SHE HITS ME ALL THE TIME. SHE'S GONNA EXPLODE WHEN SHE SEES MY GRADES. NEXT WEEK, I'M IN FOR IT.
BETH...THAT'S TERRIBLE...
YEAH, WELL...
SO! IS CHRISTOPHER HOT OR WHAT?

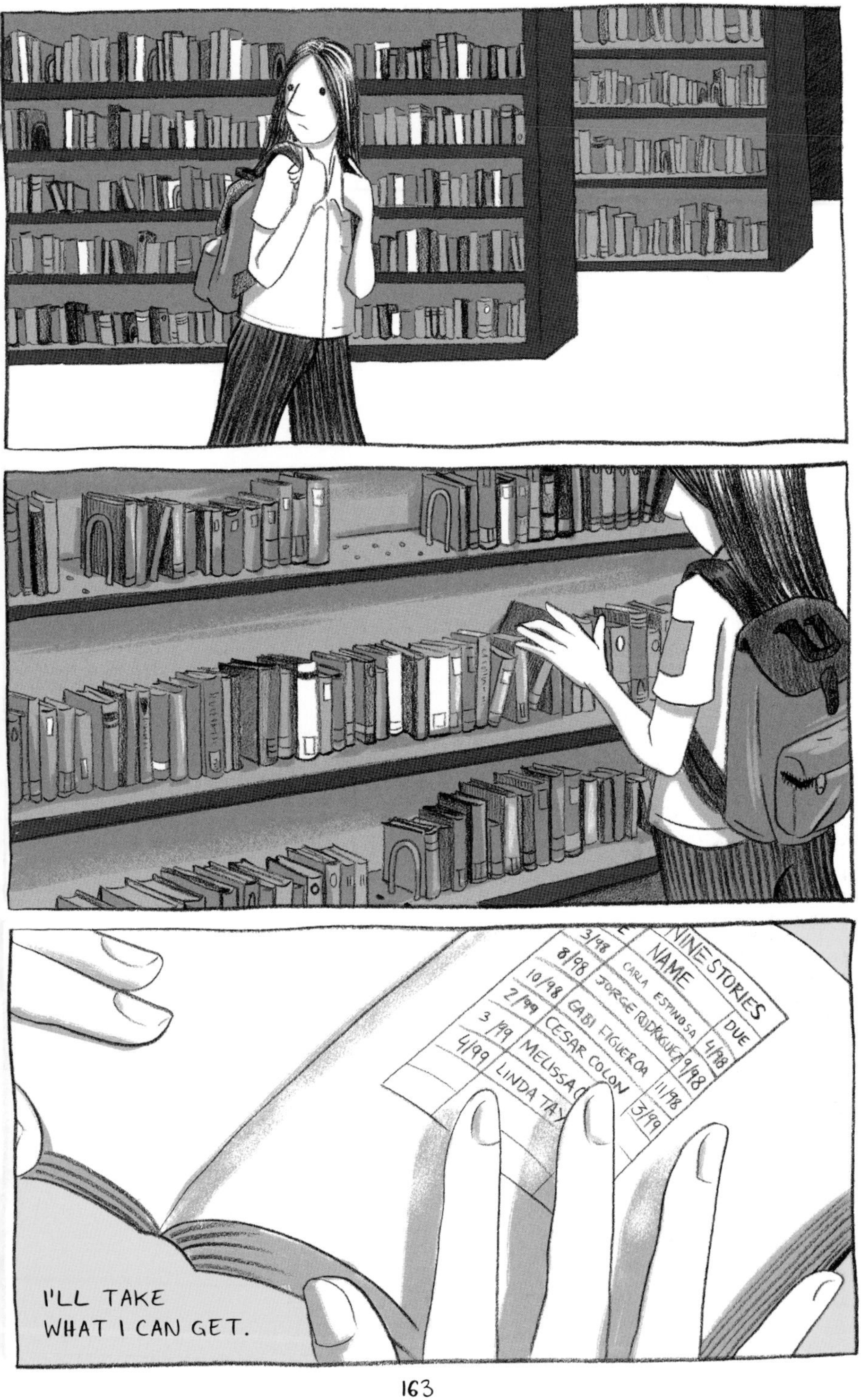
NINE STORIES
NAME
DUE
3/98
8/98 CARLA ESPINOSA 4/98
10/98 JORGE RODRIGUEZ 9/98
2/99 GABI FIGUEROA 11/98
3/99 CESAR COLON 3/99
4/99 MELISSA
LINDA TAY
I'LL TAKE
WHAT I CAN GET.

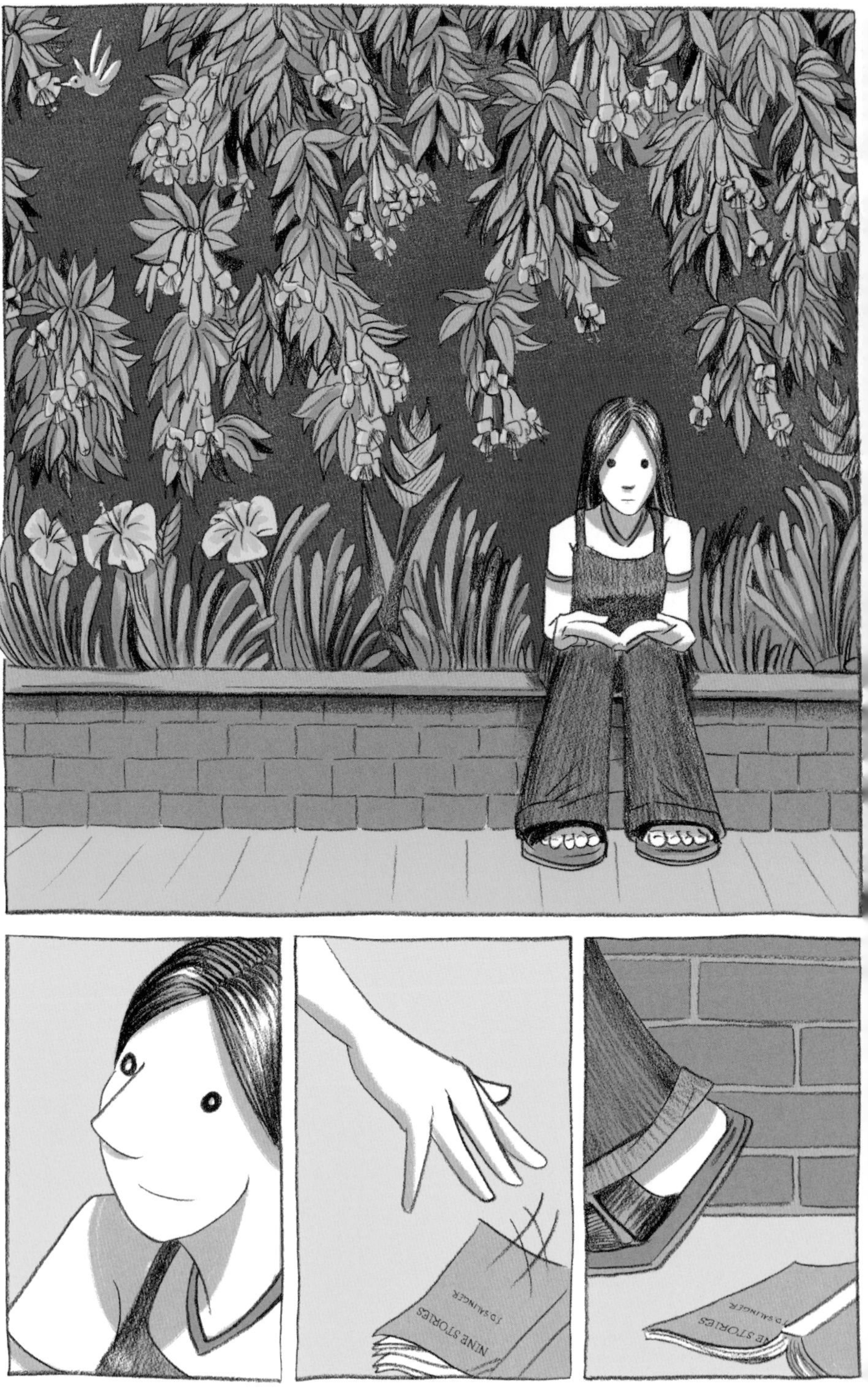
NINE STORIES
J.D. SALINGER

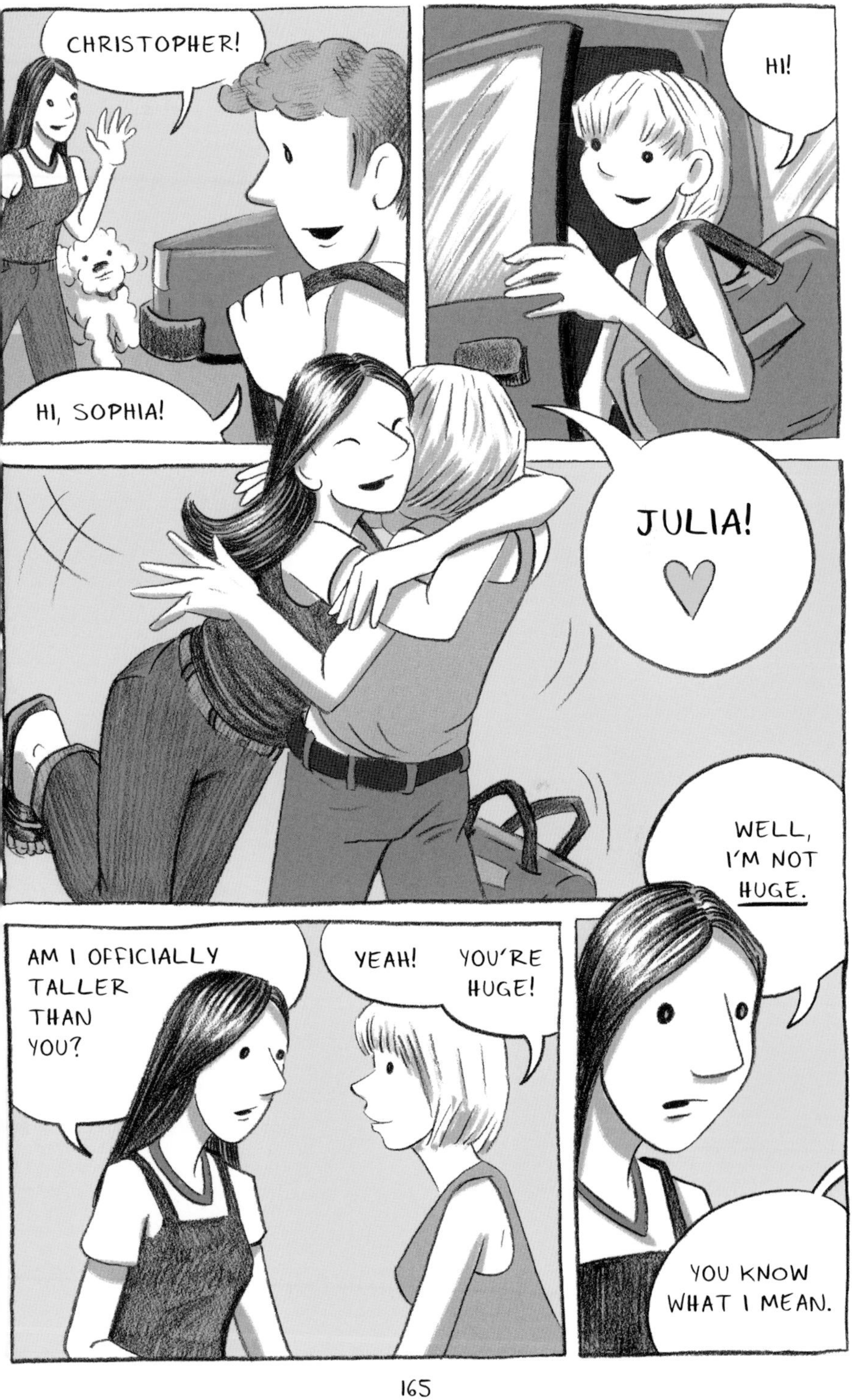
CHRISTOPHER!
HI, SOPHIA!
HI!
JULIA!
WELL, I'M NOT HUGE.
AM I OFFICIALLY TALLER THAN YOU?
YEAH! YOU'RE HUGE!
YOU KNOW WHAT I MEAN.

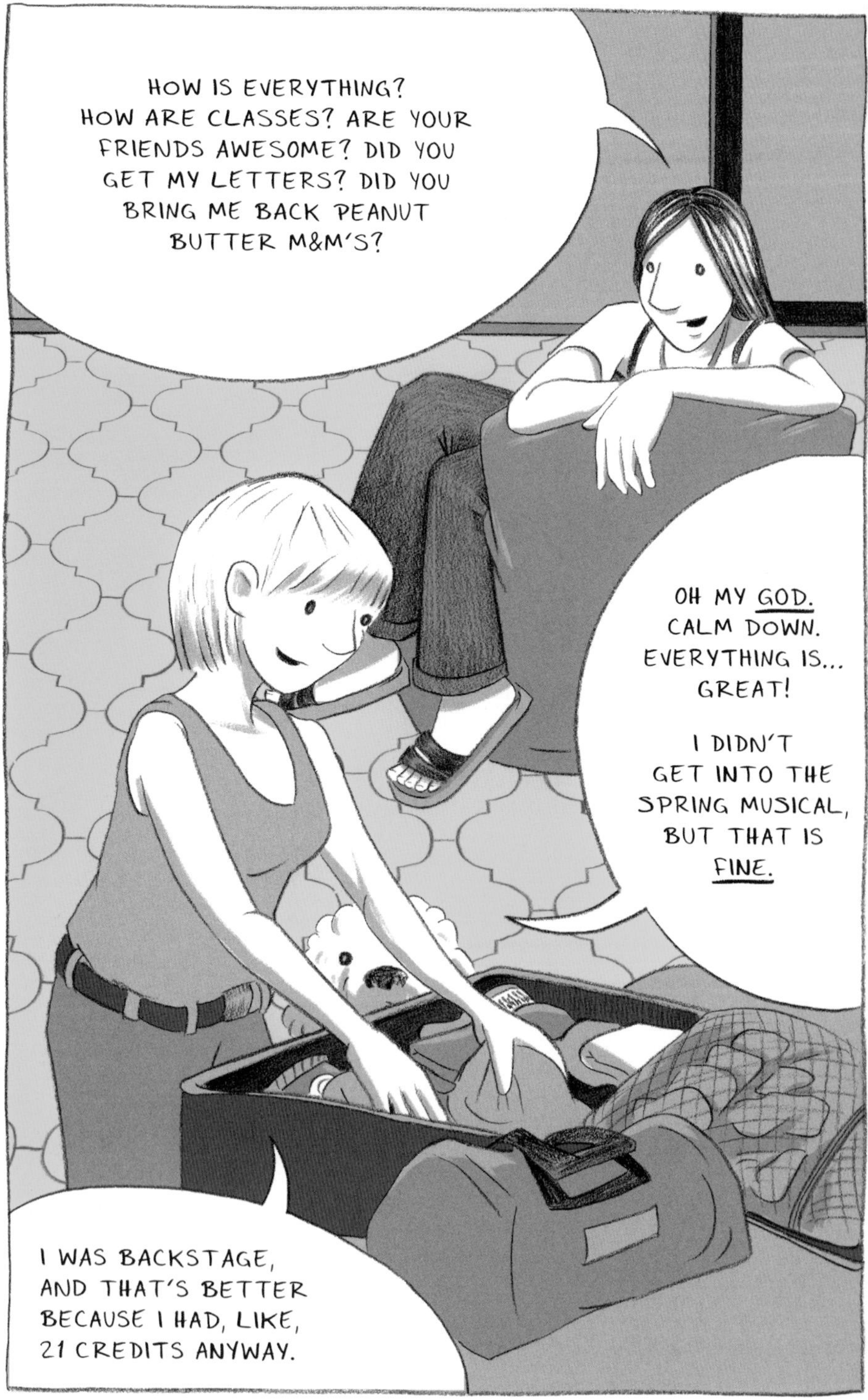
HOW IS EVERYTHING? HOW ARE CLASSES? ARE YOUR FRIENDS AWESOME? DID YOU GET MY LETTERS? DID YOU BRING ME BACK PEANUT BUTTER M&M'S?
OH MY GOD. CALM DOWN. EVERYTHING IS... GREAT!
I DIDN'T GET INTO THE SPRING MUSICAL, BUT THAT IS FINE.
I WAS BACKSTAGE, AND THAT'S BETTER BECAUSE I HAD, LIKE, 21 CREDITS ANYWAY.

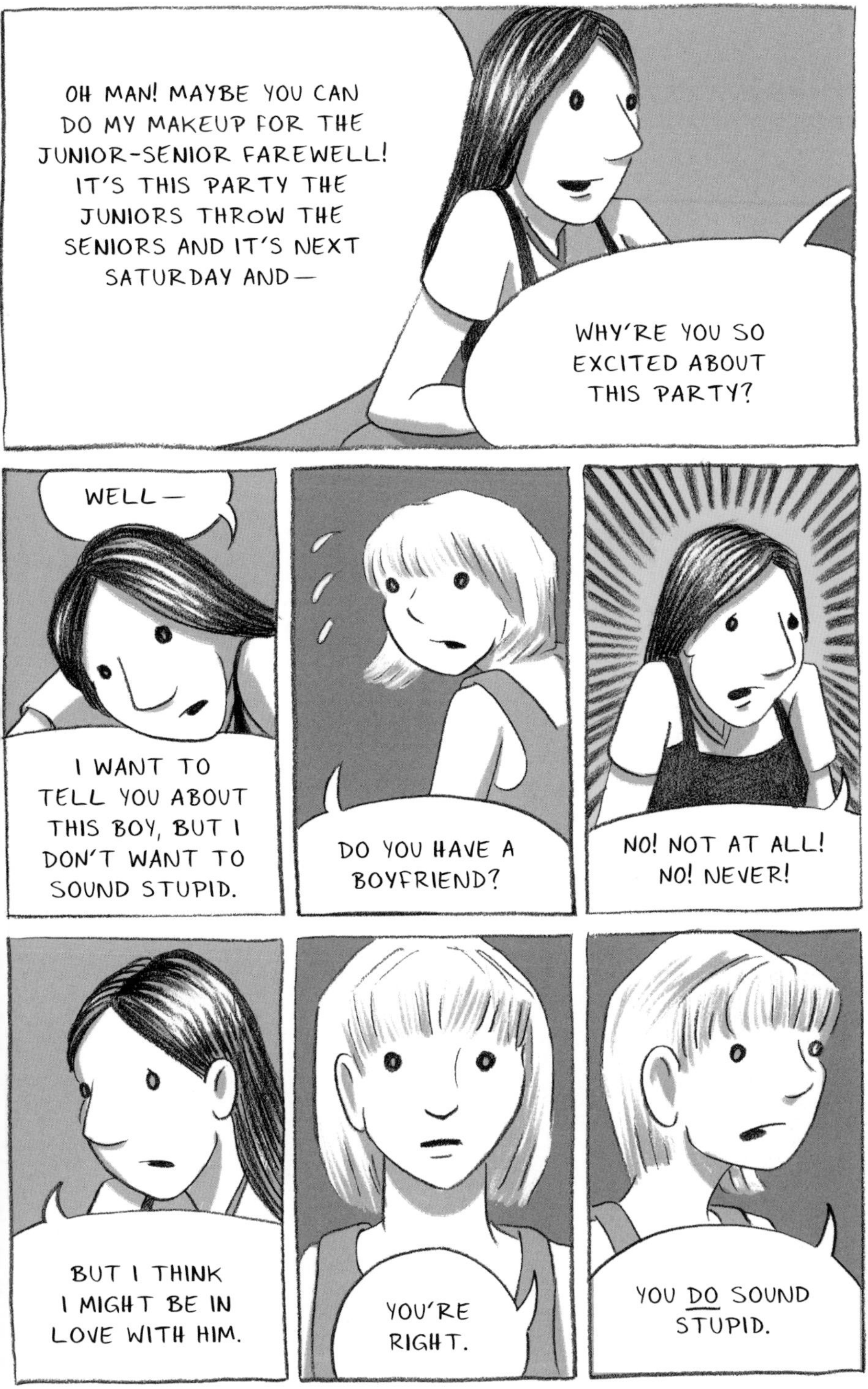
OH MAN! MAYBE YOU CAN DO MY MAKEUP FOR THE JUNIOR-SENIOR FAREWELL! IT'S THIS PARTY THE JUNIORS THROW THE SENIORS AND IT'S NEXT SATURDAY AND—
WHY'RE YOU SO EXCITED ABOUT THIS PARTY?
WELL—
I WANT TO TELL YOU ABOUT THIS BOY, BUT I DON'T WANT TO SOUND STUPID.
DO YOU HAVE A BOYFRIEND?
NO! NOT AT ALL! NO! NEVER!
BUT I THINK I MIGHT BE IN LOVE WITH HIM.
YOU'RE RIGHT.
YOU DO SOUND STUPID.

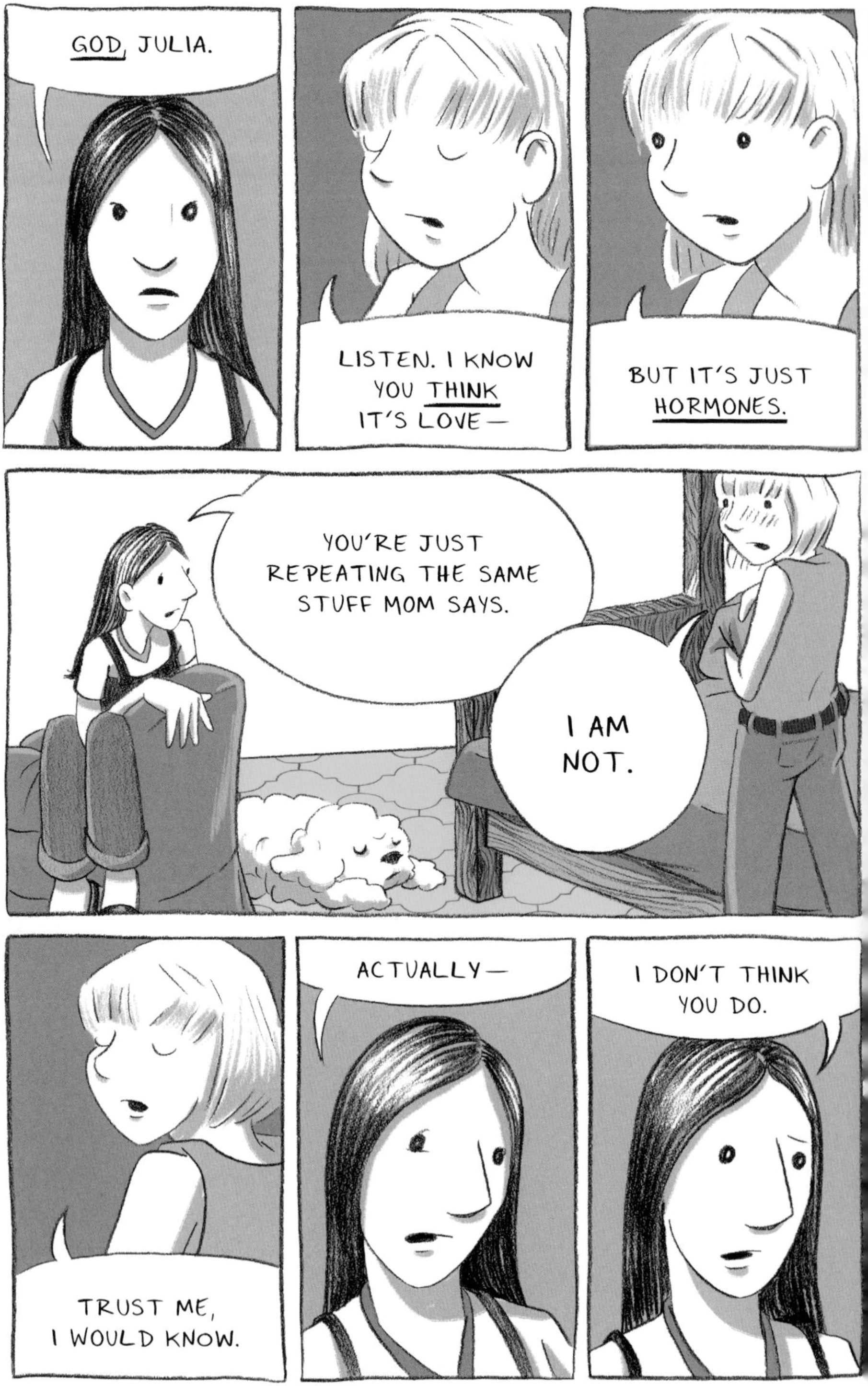
GOD, JULIA.
LISTEN. I KNOW YOU THINK IT'S LOVE—
BUT IT'S JUST HORMONES.
YOU'RE JUST REPEATING THE SAME STUFF MOM SAYS.
I AM NOT.
TRUST ME, I WOULD KNOW.
ACTUALLY—
I DON'T THINK YOU DO.

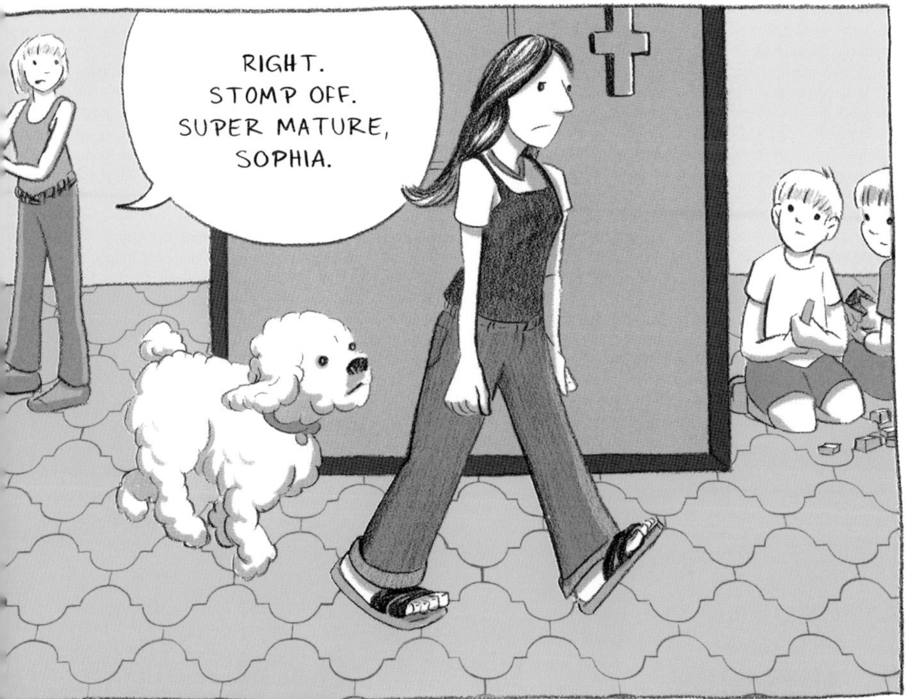
RIGHT. STOMP OFF. SUPER MATURE, SOPHIA.

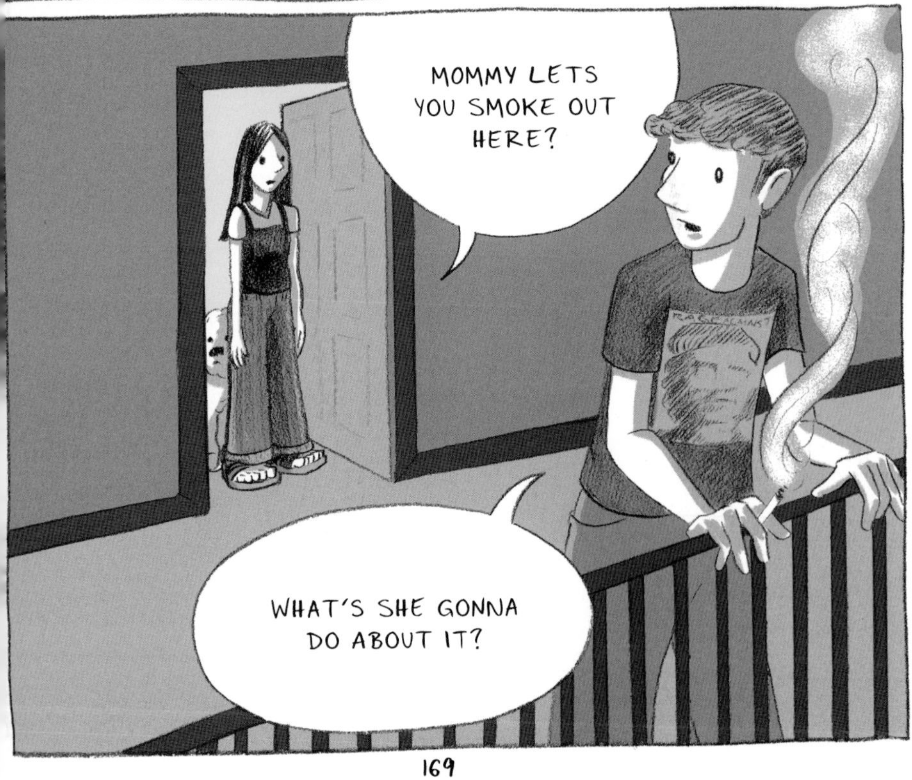
MOMMY LETS YOU SMOKE OUT HERE?
WHAT'S SHE GONNA DO ABOUT IT?

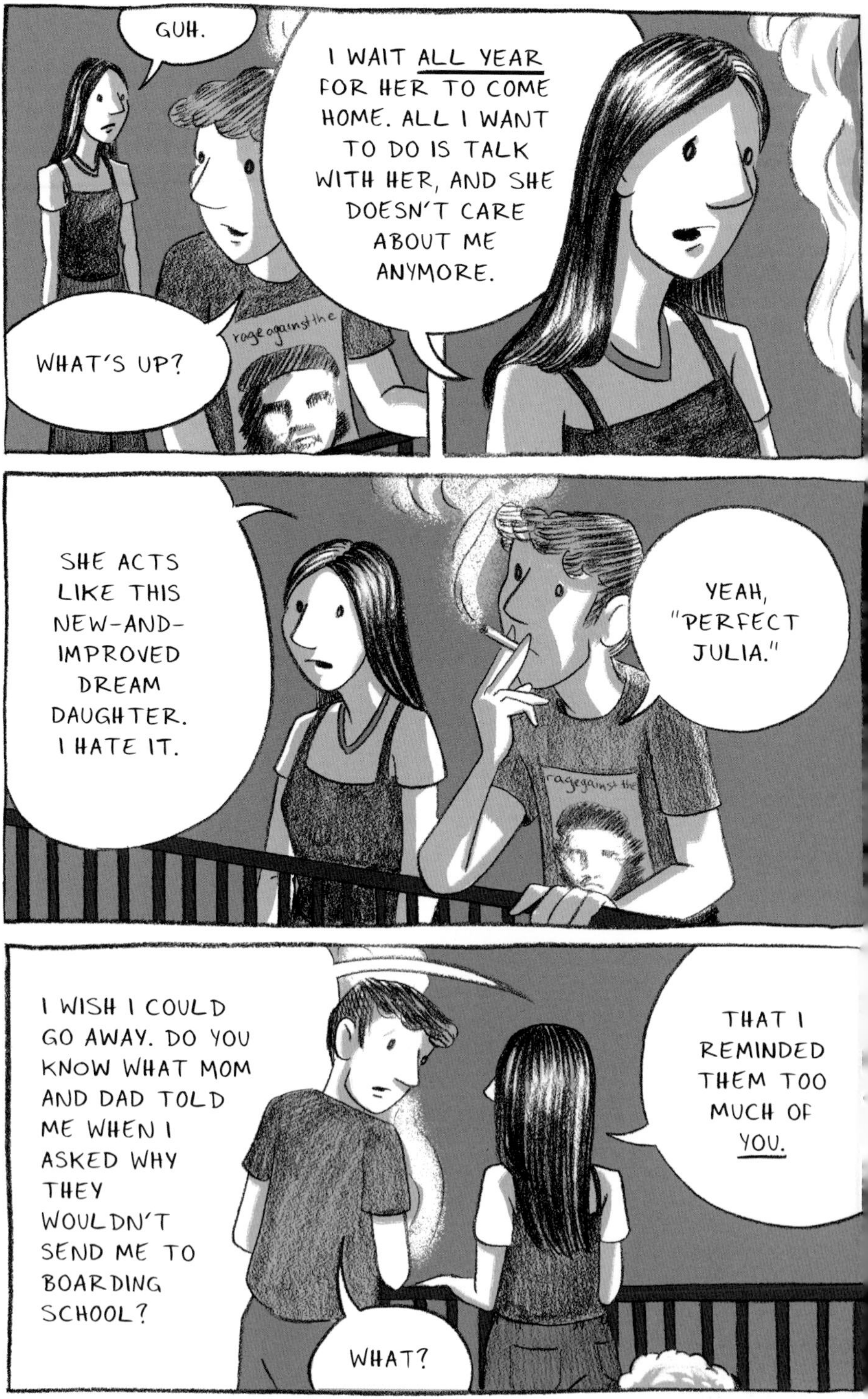
GUH.
I WAIT ALL YEAR FOR HER TO COME HOME. ALL I WANT TO DO IS TALK WITH HER, AND SHE DOESN'T CARE ABOUT ME ANYMORE.
WHAT'S UP?
rage against the
SHE ACTS LIKE THIS NEW-AND-IMPROVED DREAM DAUGHTER. I HATE IT.
YEAH, "PERFECT JULIA."
rage against the
I WISH I COULD GO AWAY. DO YOU KNOW WHAT MOM AND DAD TOLD ME WHEN I ASKED WHY THEY WOULDN'T SEND ME TO BOARDING SCHOOL?
WHAT?
THAT I REMINDED THEM TOO MUCH OF YOU.

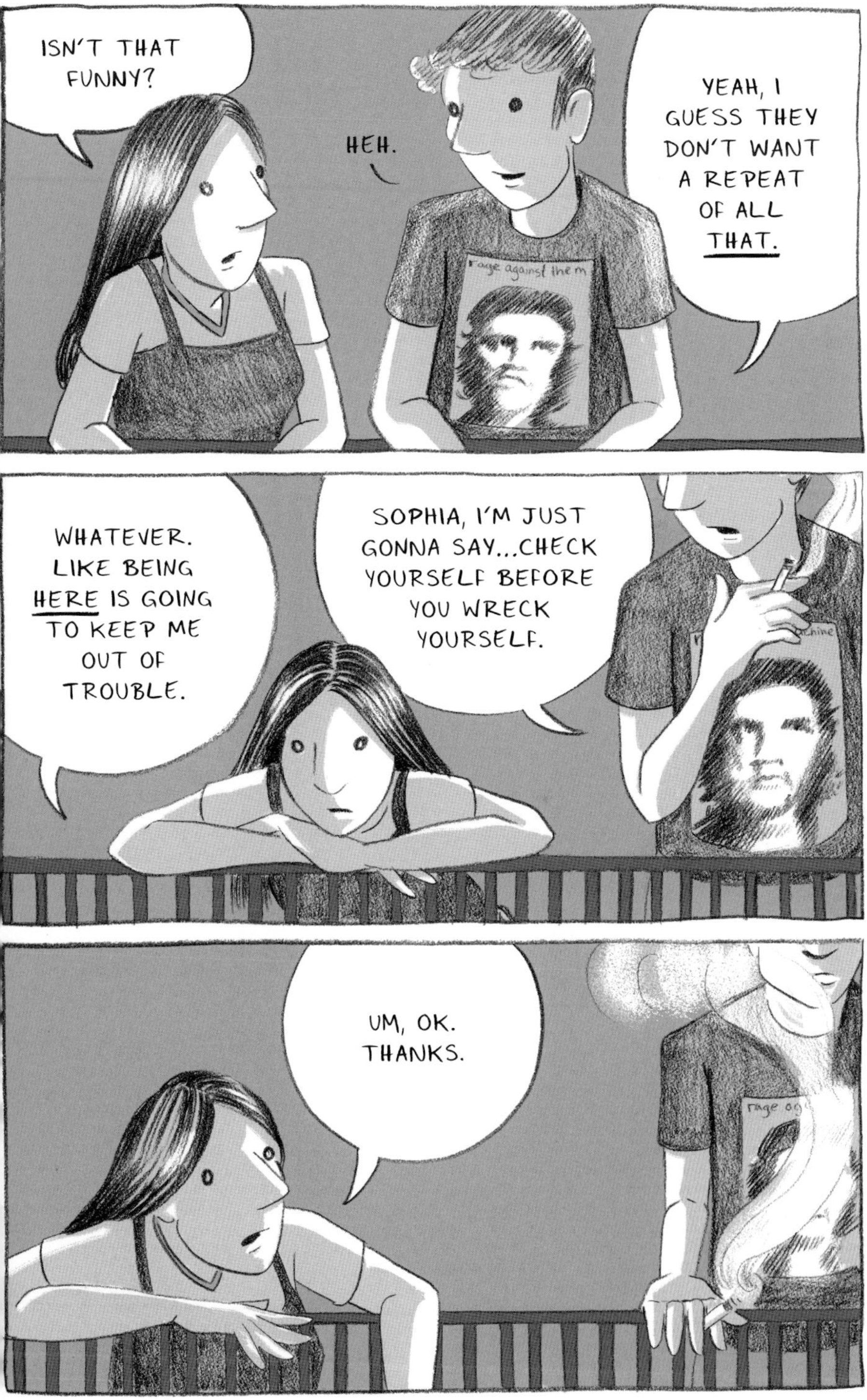

ISN'T THAT FUNNY?
HEH.
YEAH, I GUESS THEY DON'T WANT A REPEAT OF ALL THAT.
rage against the m
WHATEVER. LIKE BEING HERE IS GOING TO KEEP ME OUT OF TROUBLE.
SOPHIA, I'M JUST GONNA SAY...CHECK YOURSELF BEFORE YOU WRECK YOURSELF.
UM, OK. THANKS.

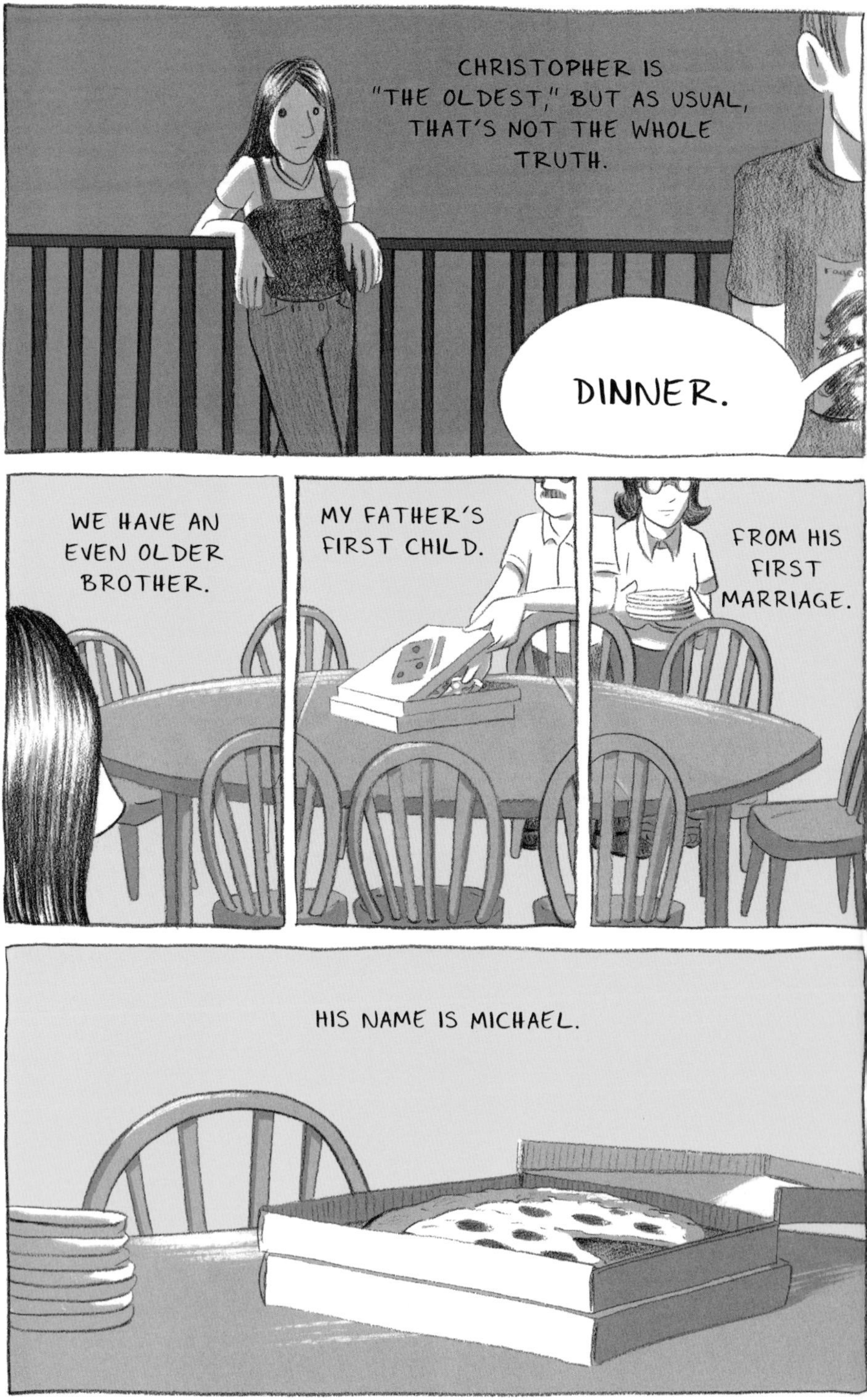
CHRISTOPHER IS "THE OLDEST," BUT AS USUAL, THAT'S NOT THE WHOLE TRUTH.
DINNER.
WE HAVE AN EVEN OLDER BROTHER.
MY FATHER'S FIRST CHILD.
FROM HIS FIRST MARRIAGE.
HIS NAME IS MICHAEL.

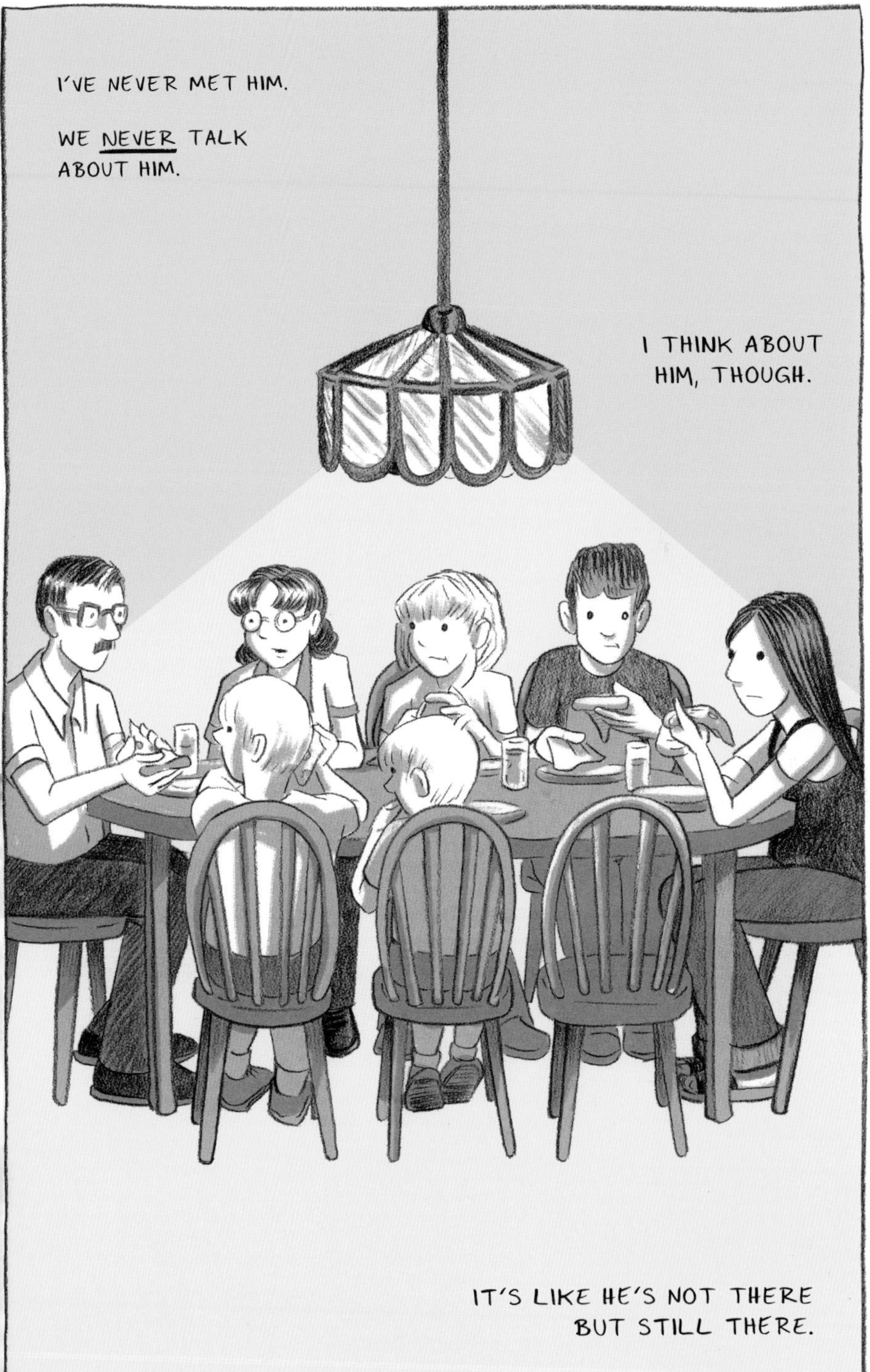
I'VE NEVER MET HIM.
WE NEVER TALK ABOUT HIM.
I THINK ABOUT HIM, THOUGH.
IT'S LIKE HE'S NOT THERE BUT STILL THERE.

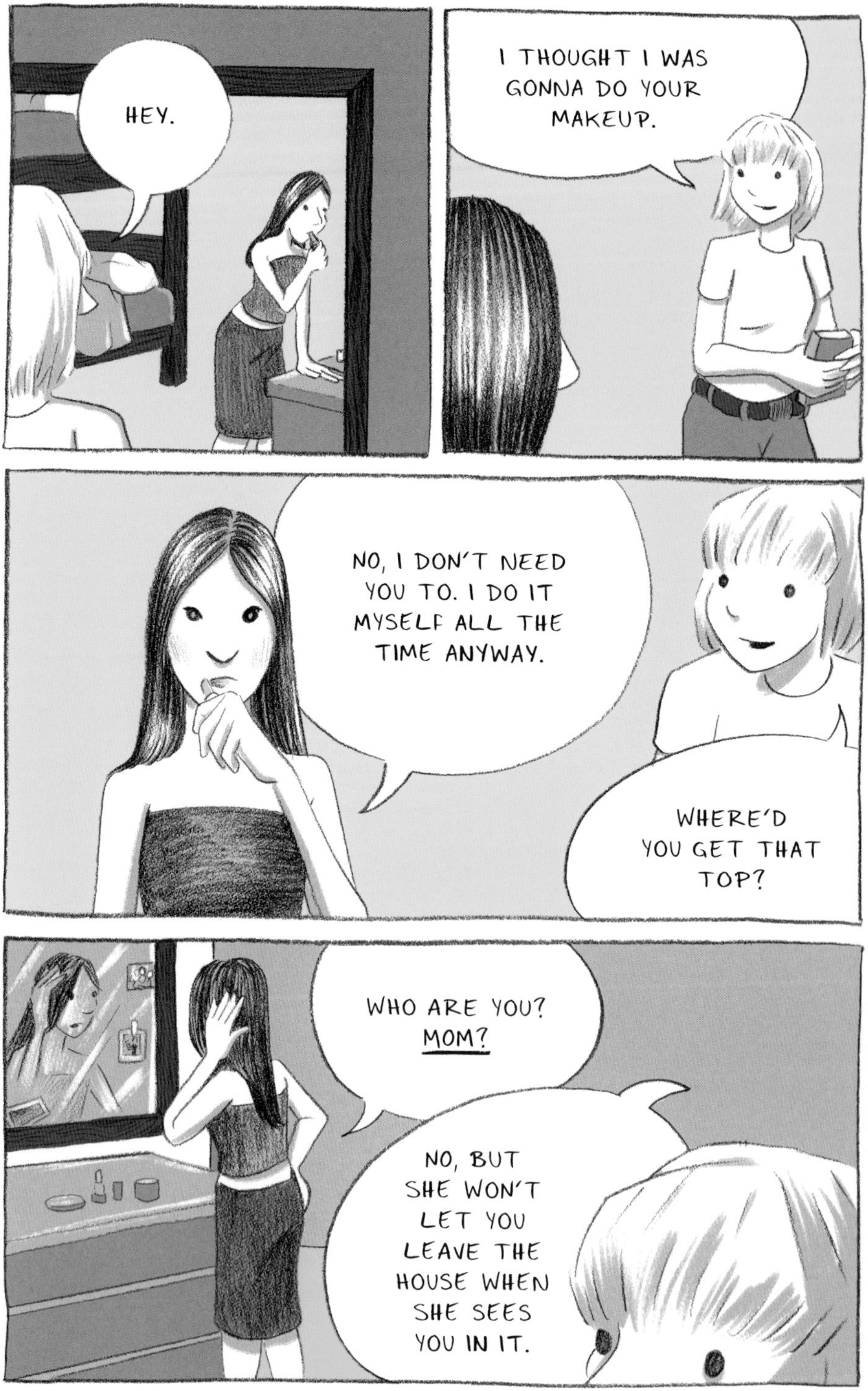
HEY.
I THOUGHT I WAS GONNA DO YOUR MAKEUP.
NO, I DON'T NEED YOU TO. I DO IT MYSELF ALL THE TIME ANYWAY.
WHERE'D YOU GET THAT TOP?
WHO ARE YOU? MOM?
NO, BUT SHE WON'T LET YOU LEAVE THE HOUSE WHEN SHE SEES YOU IN IT.

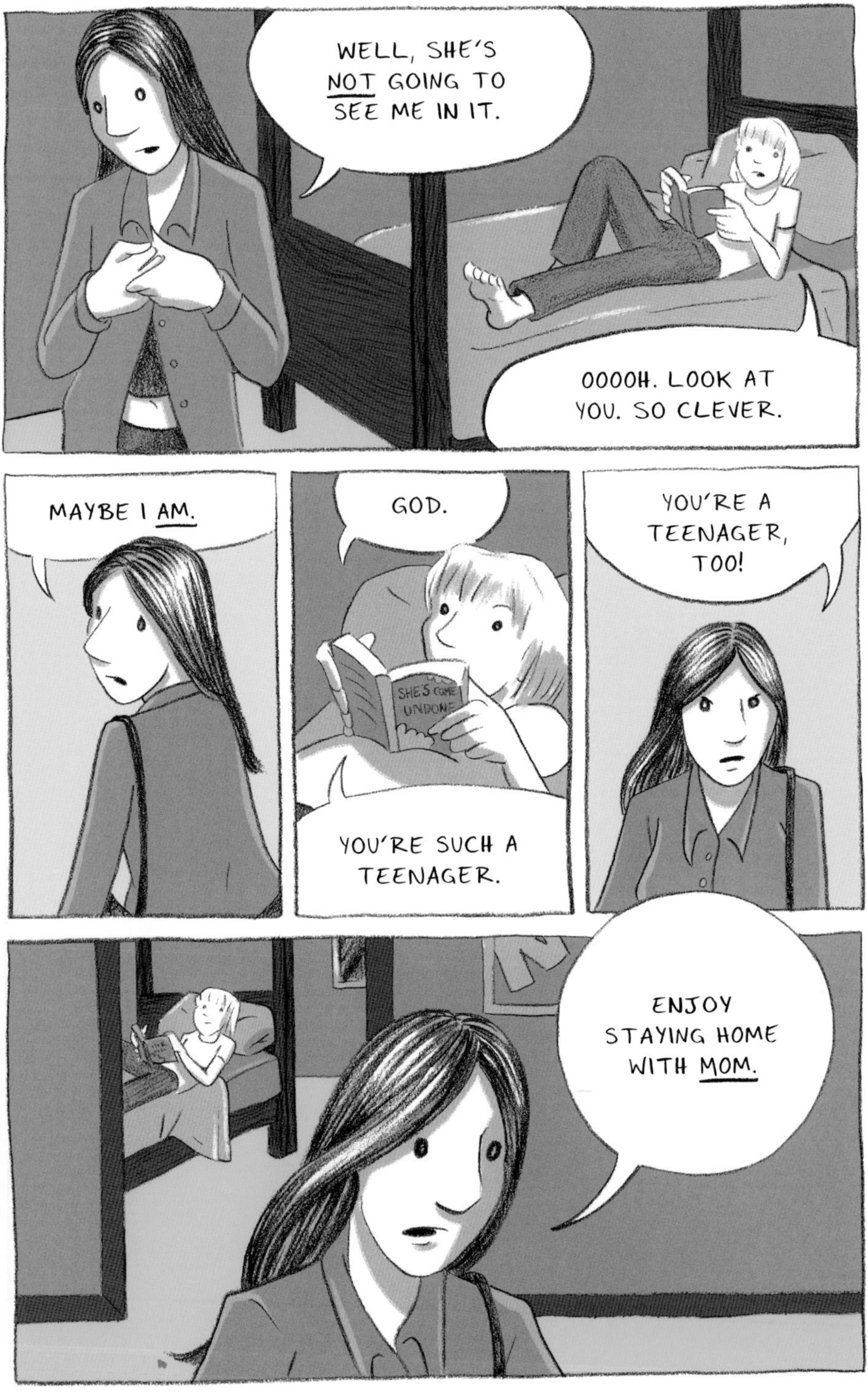
WELL, SHE'S NOT GOING TO SEE ME IN IT.
OOOOH. LOOK AT YOU. SO CLEVER.
MAYBE I AM.
GOD.
SHE'S COME UNDONE
YOU'RE SUCH A TEENAGER.
YOU'RE A TEENAGER, TOO!
ENJOY STAYING HOME WITH MOM.

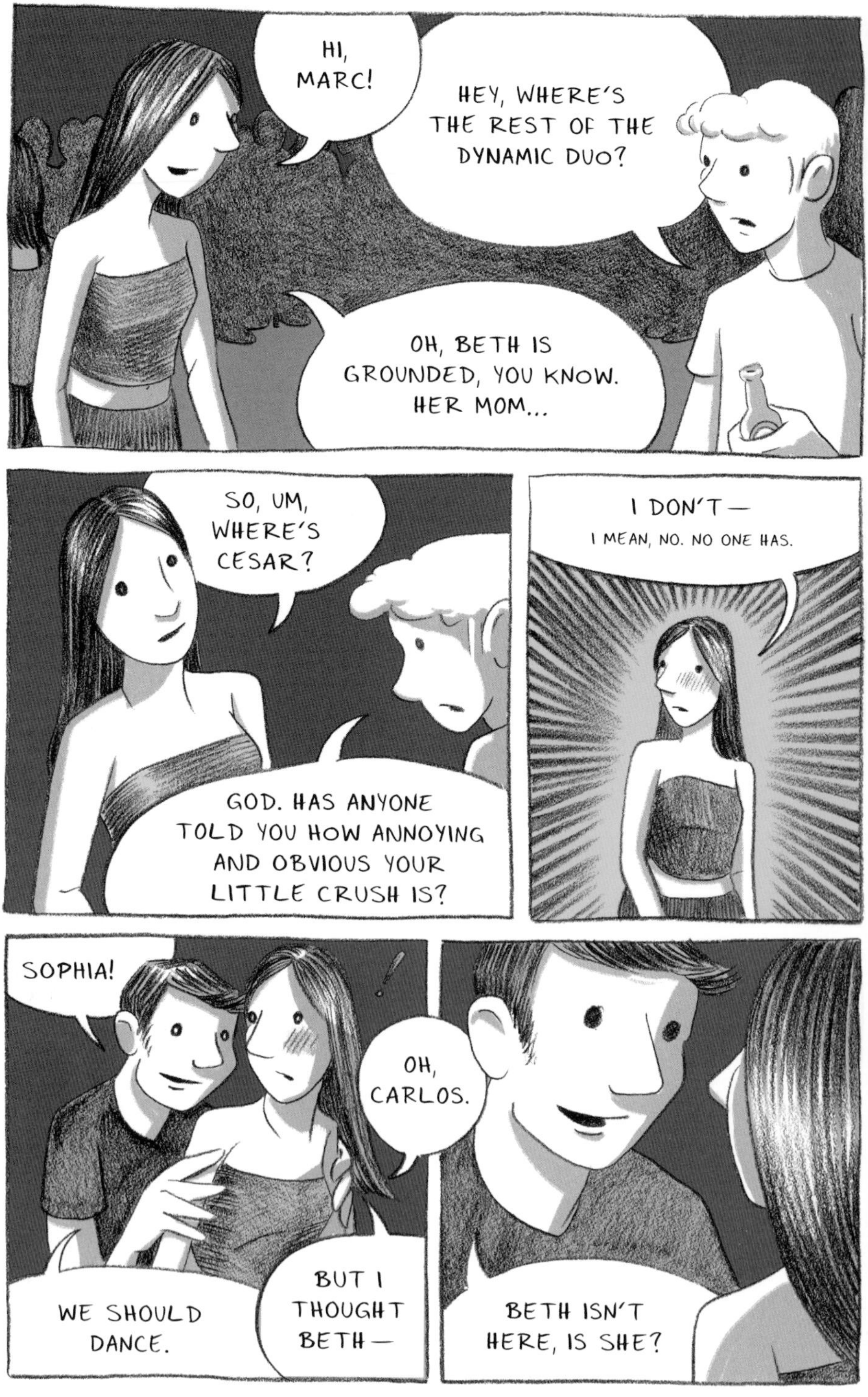
HI, MARC!
HEY, WHERE'S THE REST OF THE DYNAMIC DUO?
OH, BETH IS GROUNDED, YOU KNOW. HER MOM...
SO, UM, WHERE'S CESAR?
GOD. HAS ANYONE TOLD YOU HOW ANNOYING AND OBVIOUS YOUR LITTLE CRUSH IS?
I DON'T—
I MEAN, NO. NO ONE HAS.
SOPHIA!
!
OH, CARLOS.
WE SHOULD DANCE.
BUT I THOUGHT BETH—
BETH ISN'T HERE, IS SHE?

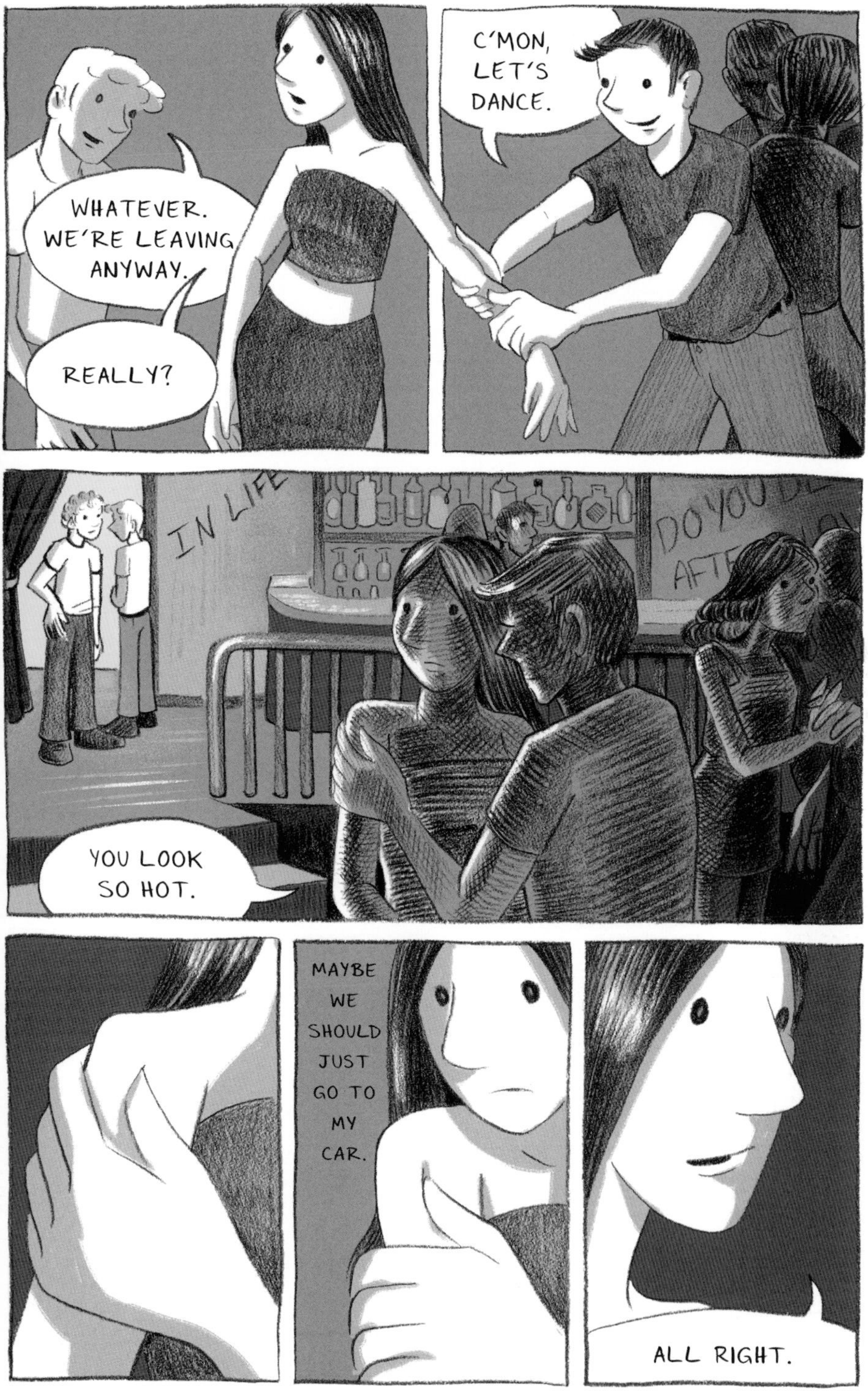
WHATEVER. WE'RE LEAVING ANYWAY.
REALLY?
C'MON, LET'S DANCE.
IN LIFE
DO YOU
YOU LOOK SO HOT.
MAYBE WE SHOULD JUST GO TO MY CAR.
ALL RIGHT.

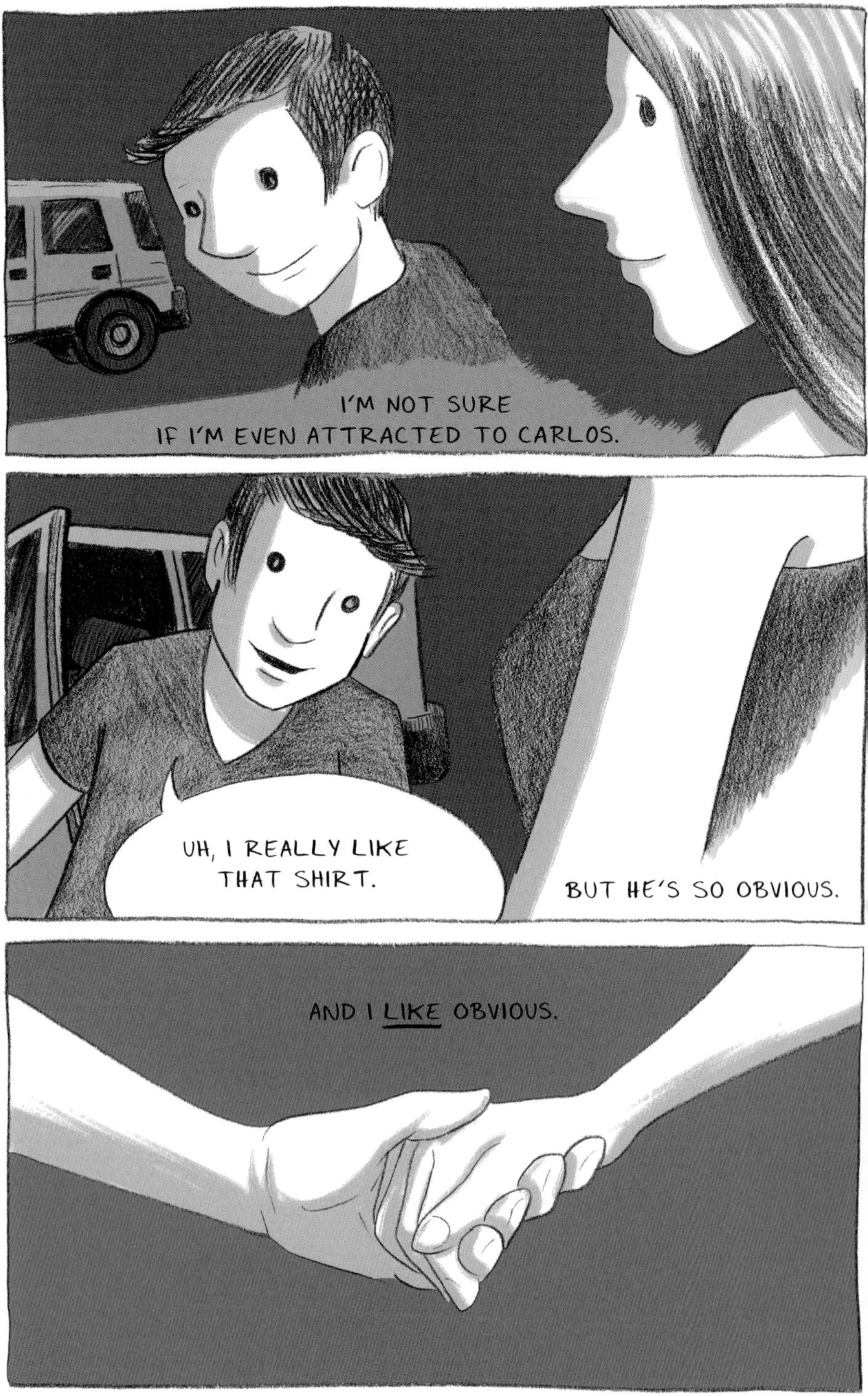
I'M NOT SURE
IF I'M EVEN ATTRACTED TO CARLOS.
UH, I REALLY LIKE THAT SHIRT.
BUT HE'S SO OBVIOUS.
AND I LIKE OBVIOUS.

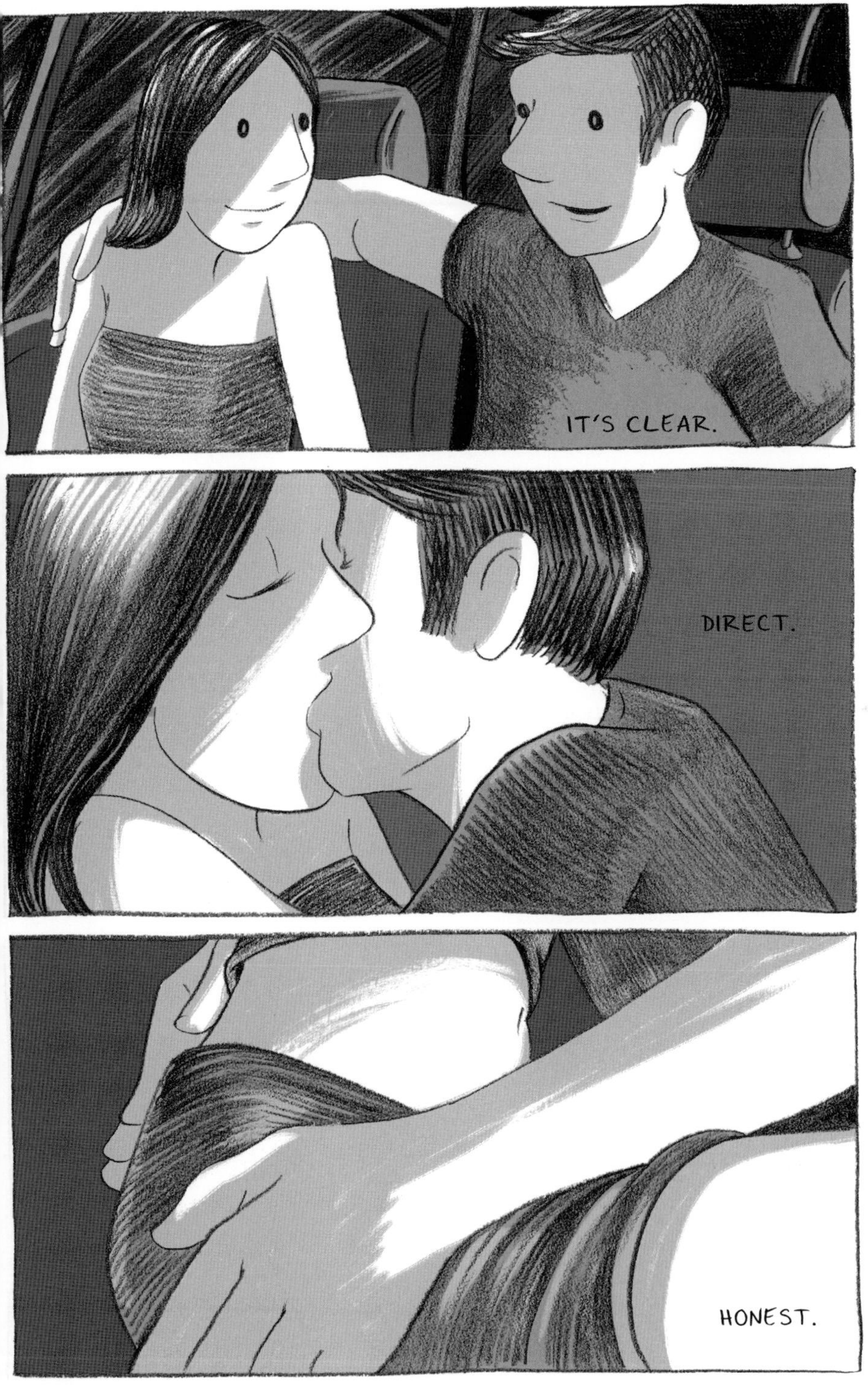
IT'S CLEAR.
DIRECT.
HONEST.

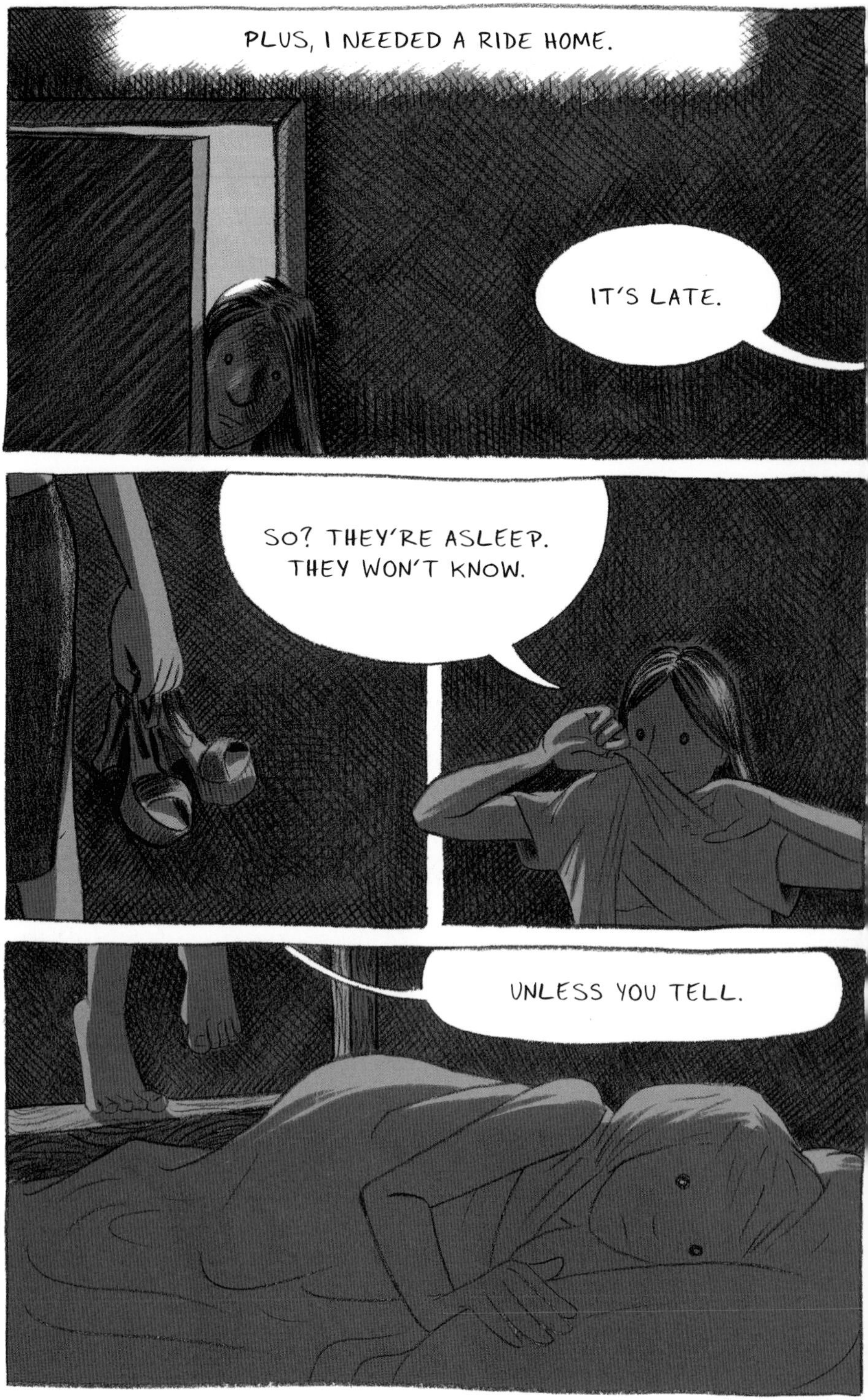
PLUS, I NEEDED A RIDE HOME.
IT'S LATE.
SO? THEY'RE ASLEEP. THEY WON'T KNOW.
UNLESS YOU TELL.

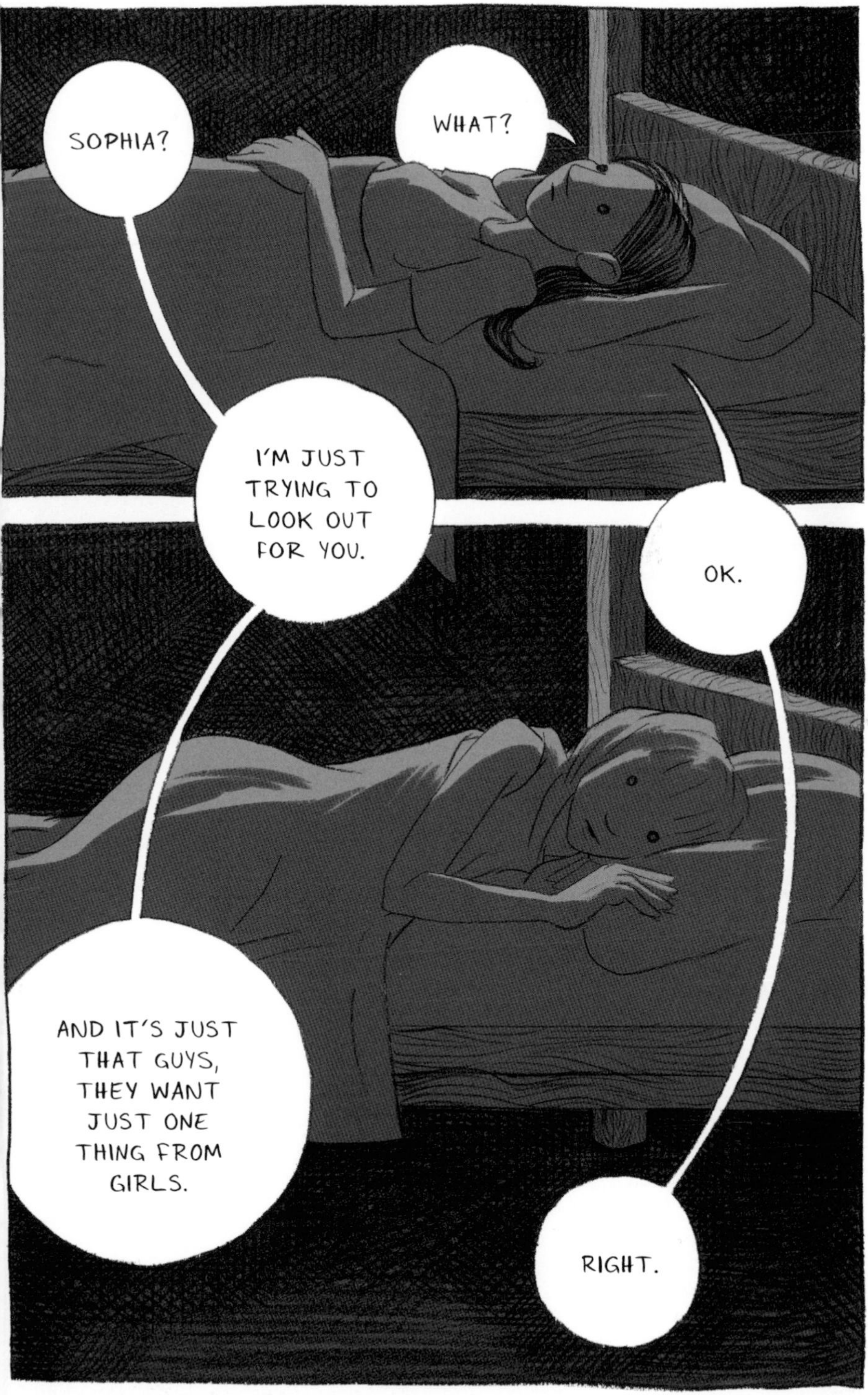
SOPHIA?
WHAT?
I'M JUST TRYING TO LOOK OUT FOR YOU.
OK.
AND IT'S JUST THAT GUYS, THEY WANT JUST ONE THING FROM GIRLS.
RIGHT.

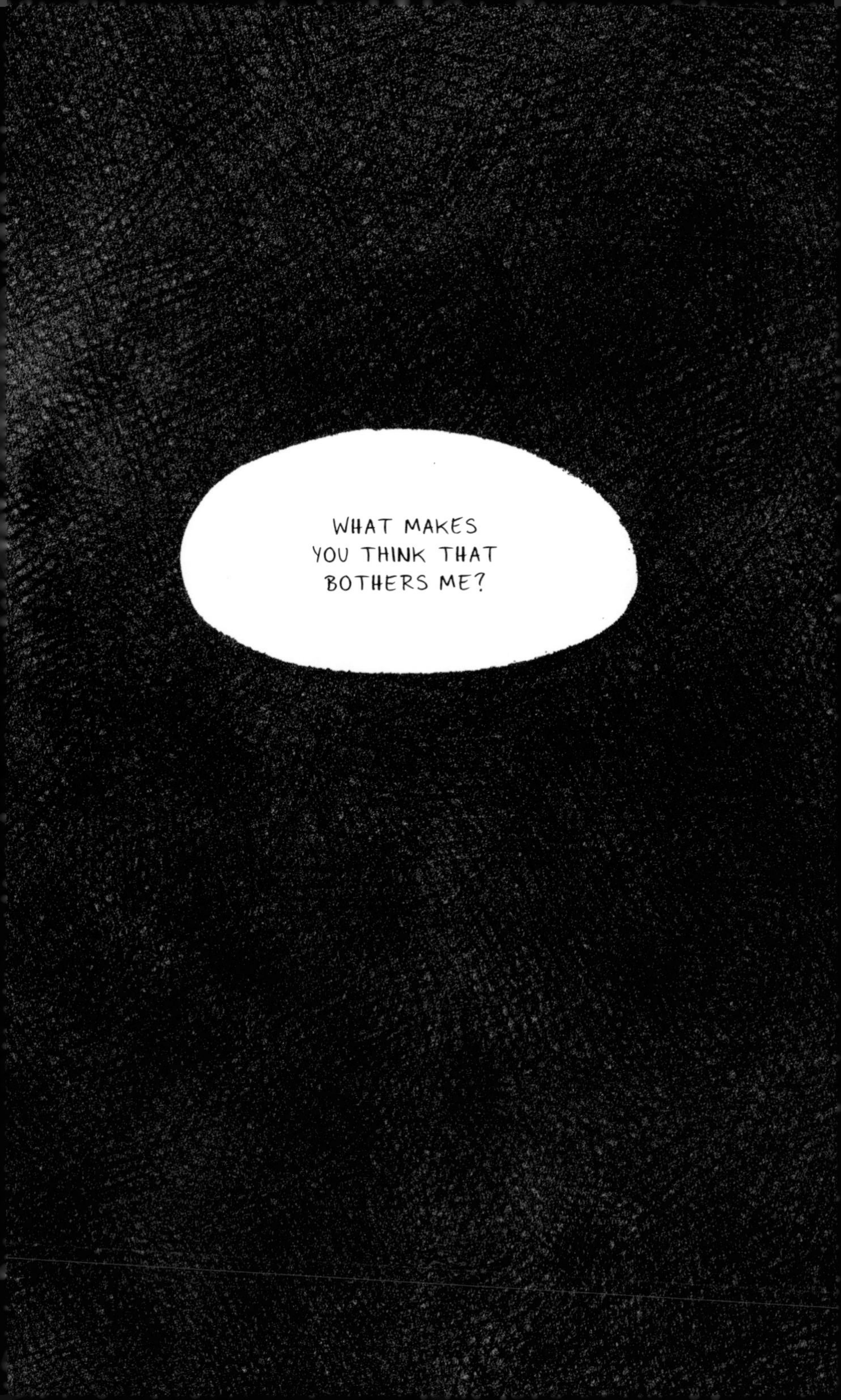
WHAT MAKES YOU THINK THAT BOTHERS ME?

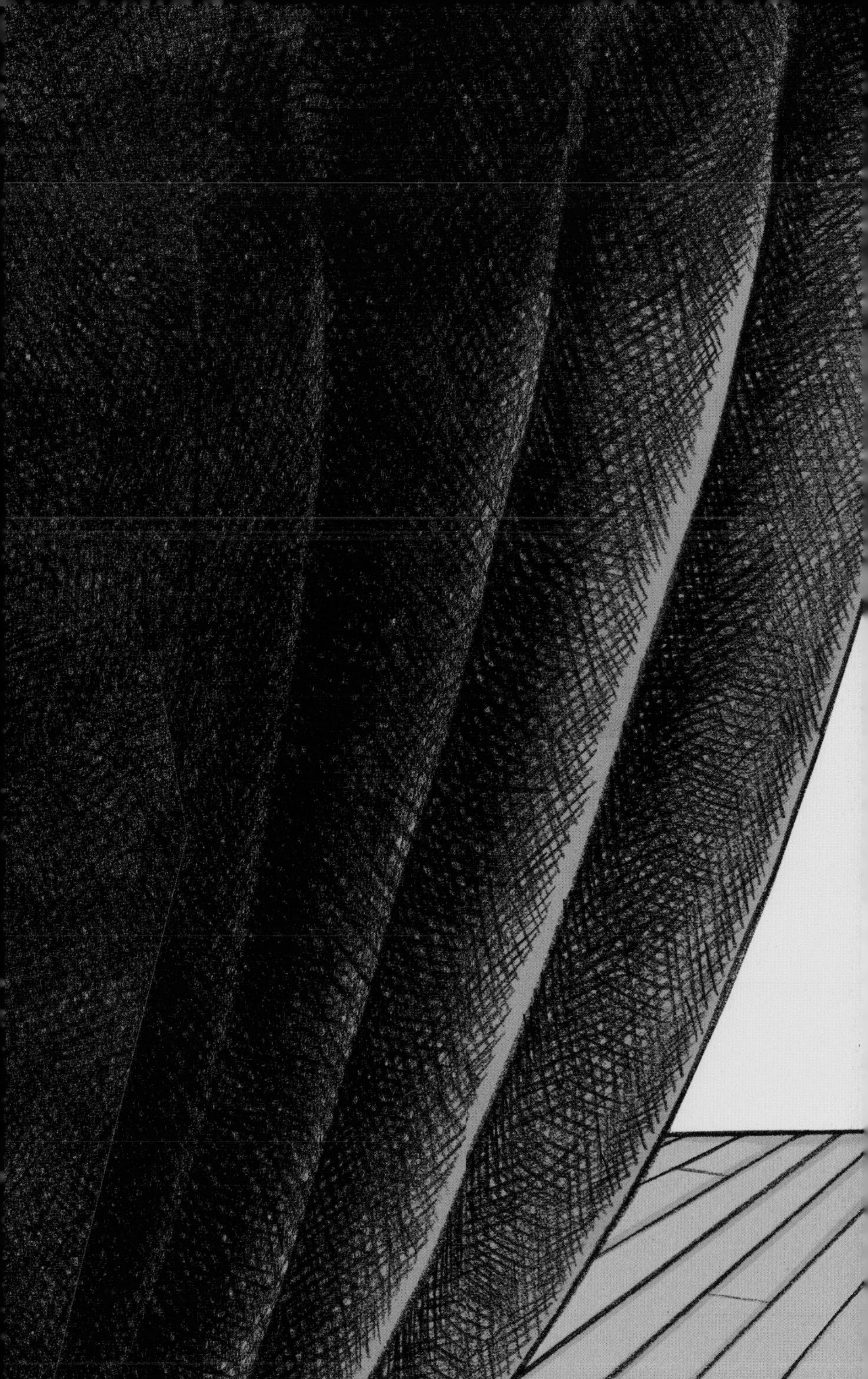

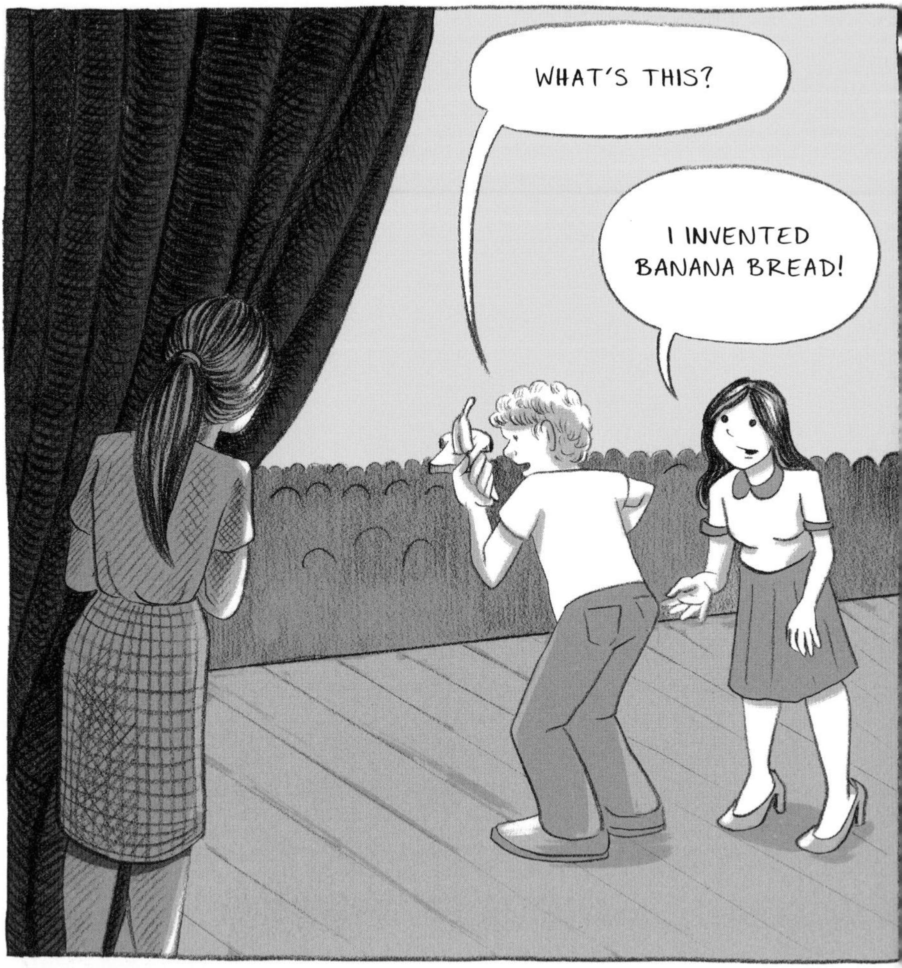
WHAT'S THIS?
I INVENTED BANANA BREAD!

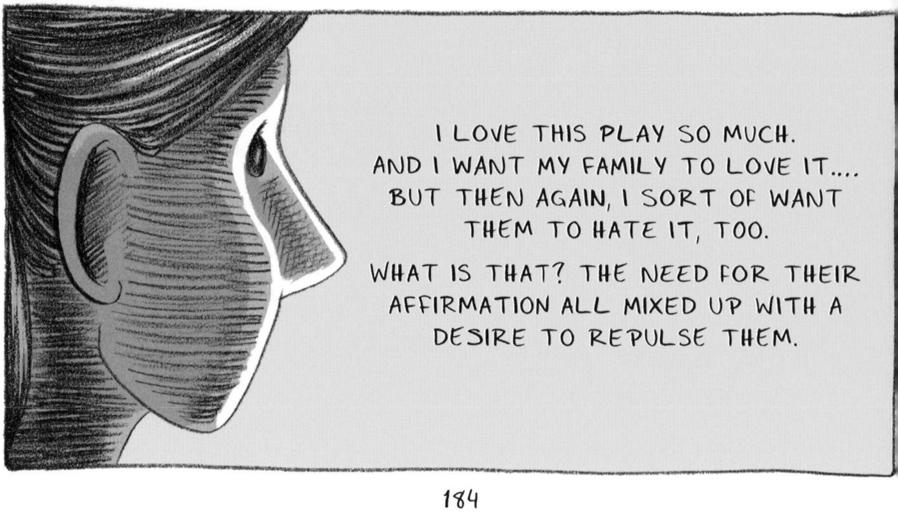
I LOVE THIS PLAY SO MUCH. AND I WANT MY FAMILY TO LOVE IT.... BUT THEN AGAIN, I SORT OF WANT THEM TO HATE IT, TOO.
WHAT IS THAT? THE NEED FOR THEIR AFFIRMATION ALL MIXED UP WITH A DESIRE TO REPULSE THEM.

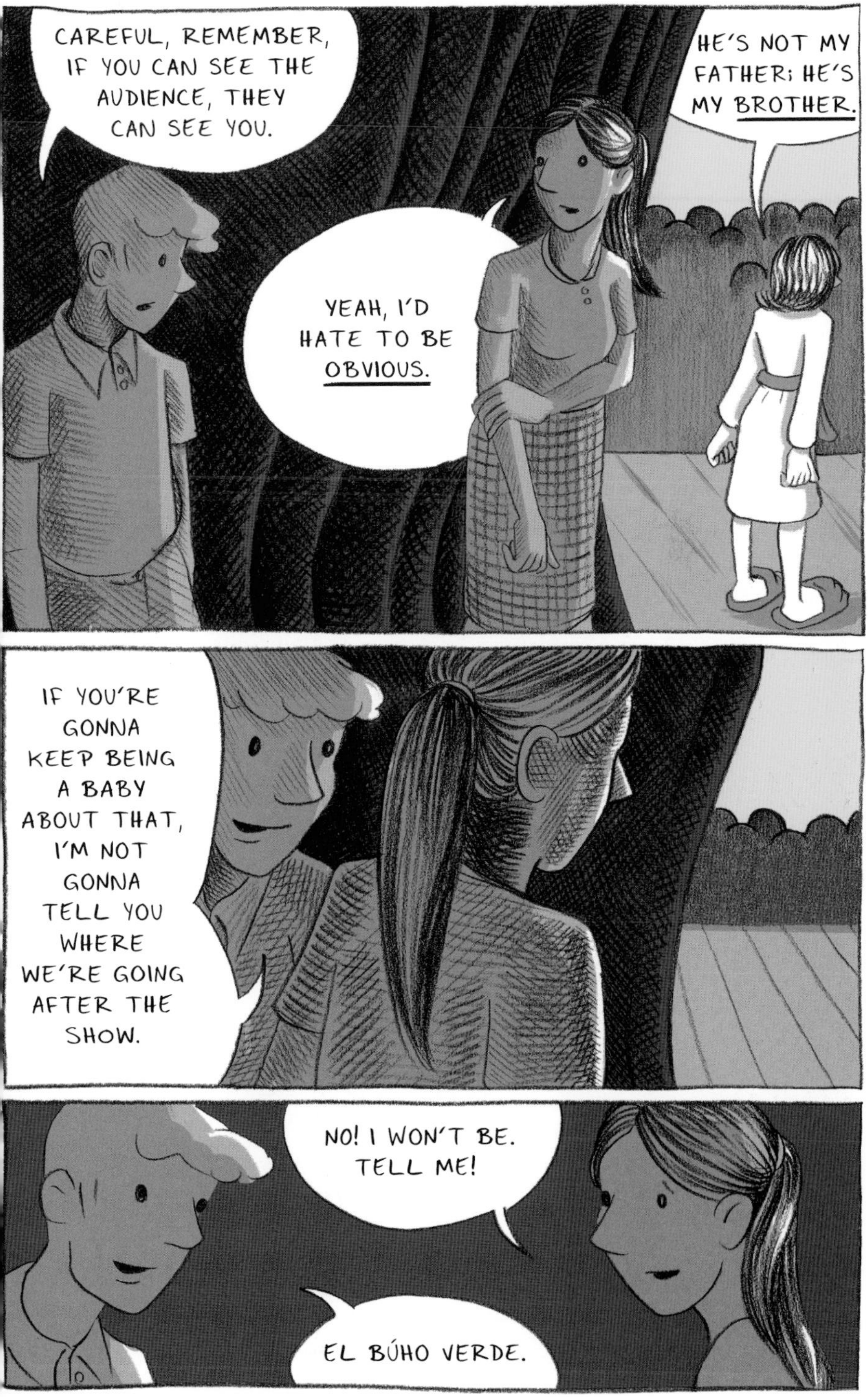
CAREFUL, REMEMBER, IF YOU CAN SEE THE AUDIENCE, THEY CAN SEE YOU.
HE'S NOT MY FATHER; HE'S MY BROTHER.
YEAH, I'D HATE TO BE OBVIOUS.
IF YOU'RE GONNA KEEP BEING A BABY ABOUT THAT, I'M NOT GONNA TELL YOU WHERE WE'RE GOING AFTER THE SHOW.
NO! I WON'T BE. TELL ME!
EL BÚHO VERDE.

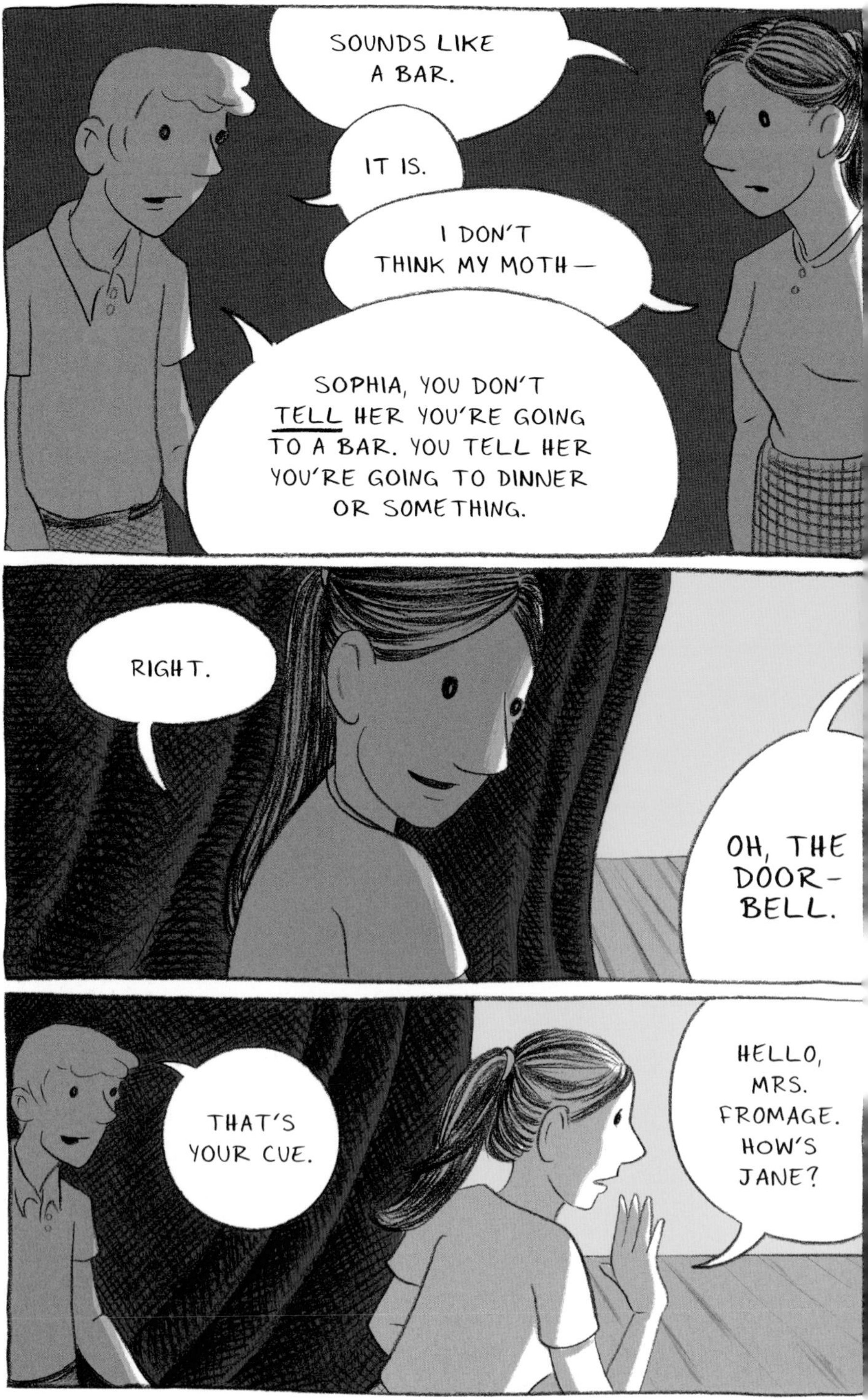
SOUNDS LIKE A BAR.
IT IS.
I DON'T THINK MY MOTH—
SOPHIA, YOU DON'T TELL HER YOU'RE GOING TO A BAR. YOU TELL HER YOU'RE GOING TO DINNER OR SOMETHING.
RIGHT.
OH, THE DOOR-BELL.
THAT'S YOUR CUE.
HELLO, MRS. FROMAGE. HOW'S JANE?

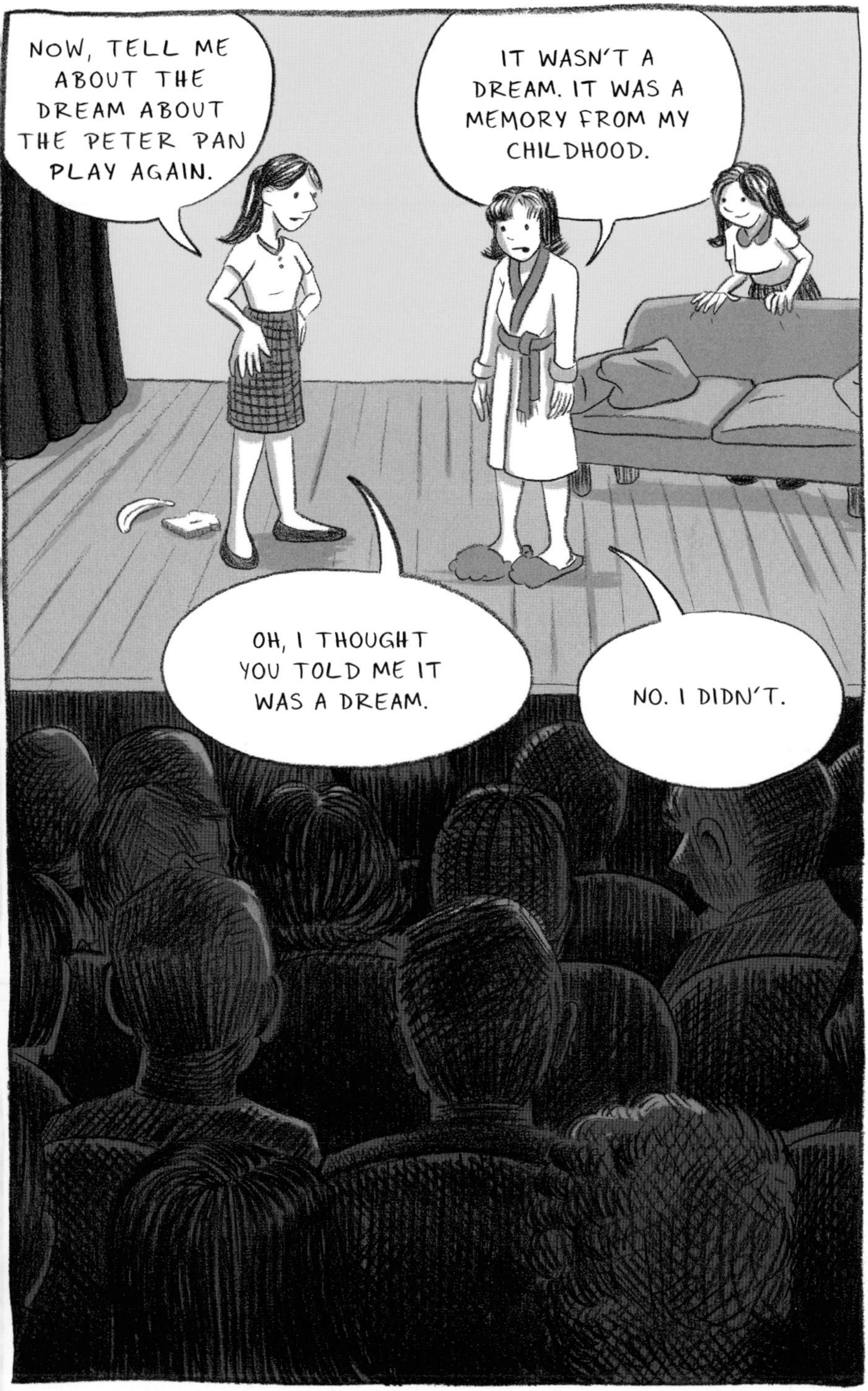
NOW, TELL ME ABOUT THE DREAM ABOUT THE PETER PAN PLAY AGAIN.
IT WASN'T A DREAM. IT WAS A MEMORY FROM MY CHILDHOOD.
OH, I THOUGHT YOU TOLD ME IT WAS A DREAM.
NO. I DIDN'T.

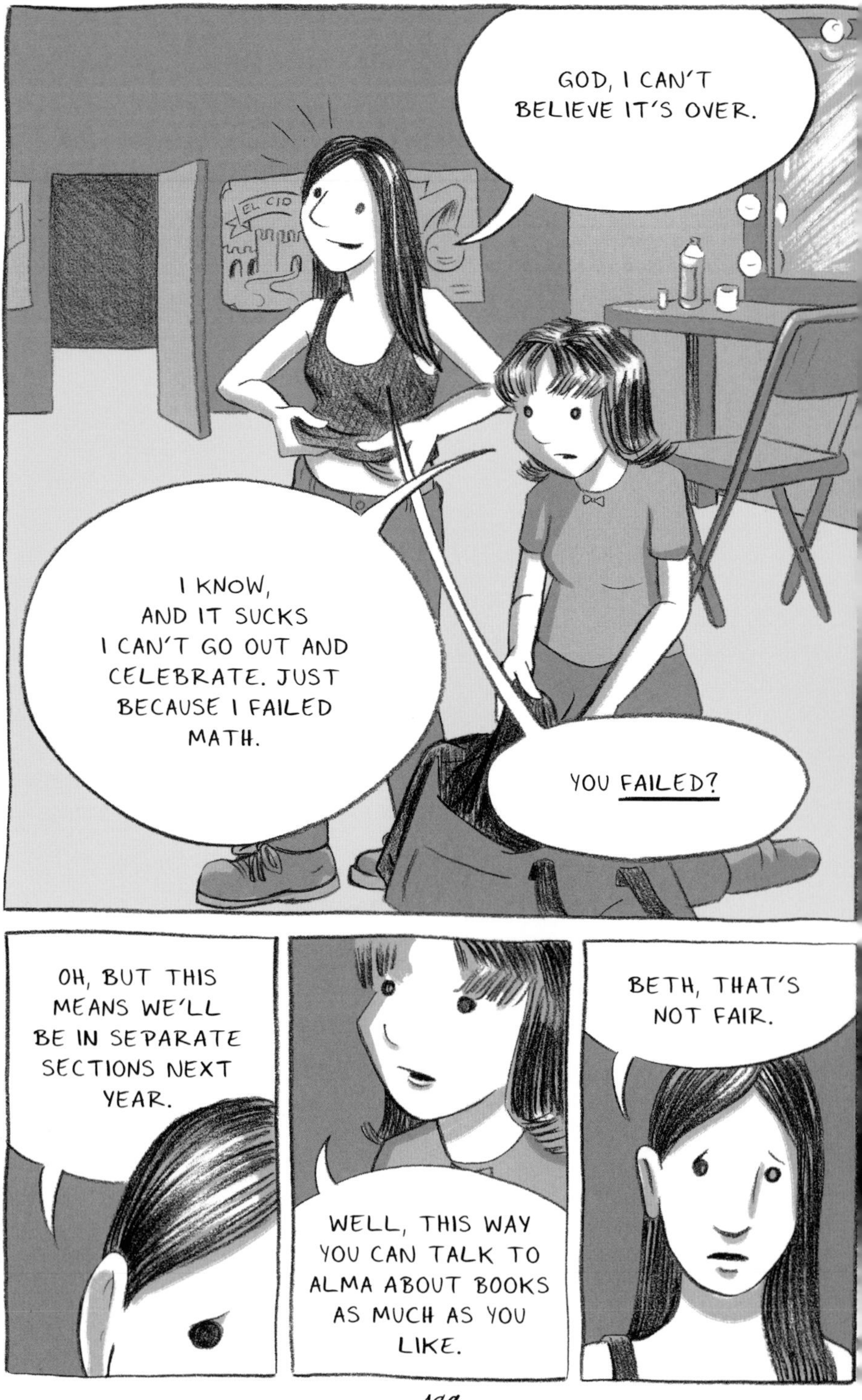
GOD, I CAN'T BELIEVE IT'S OVER.
I KNOW, AND IT SUCKS I CAN'T GO OUT AND CELEBRATE. JUST BECAUSE I FAILED MATH.
YOU FAILED?
OH, BUT THIS MEANS WE'LL BE IN SEPARATE SECTIONS NEXT YEAR.
WELL, THIS WAY YOU CAN TALK TO ALMA ABOUT BOOKS AS MUCH AS YOU LIKE.
BETH, THAT'S NOT FAIR.

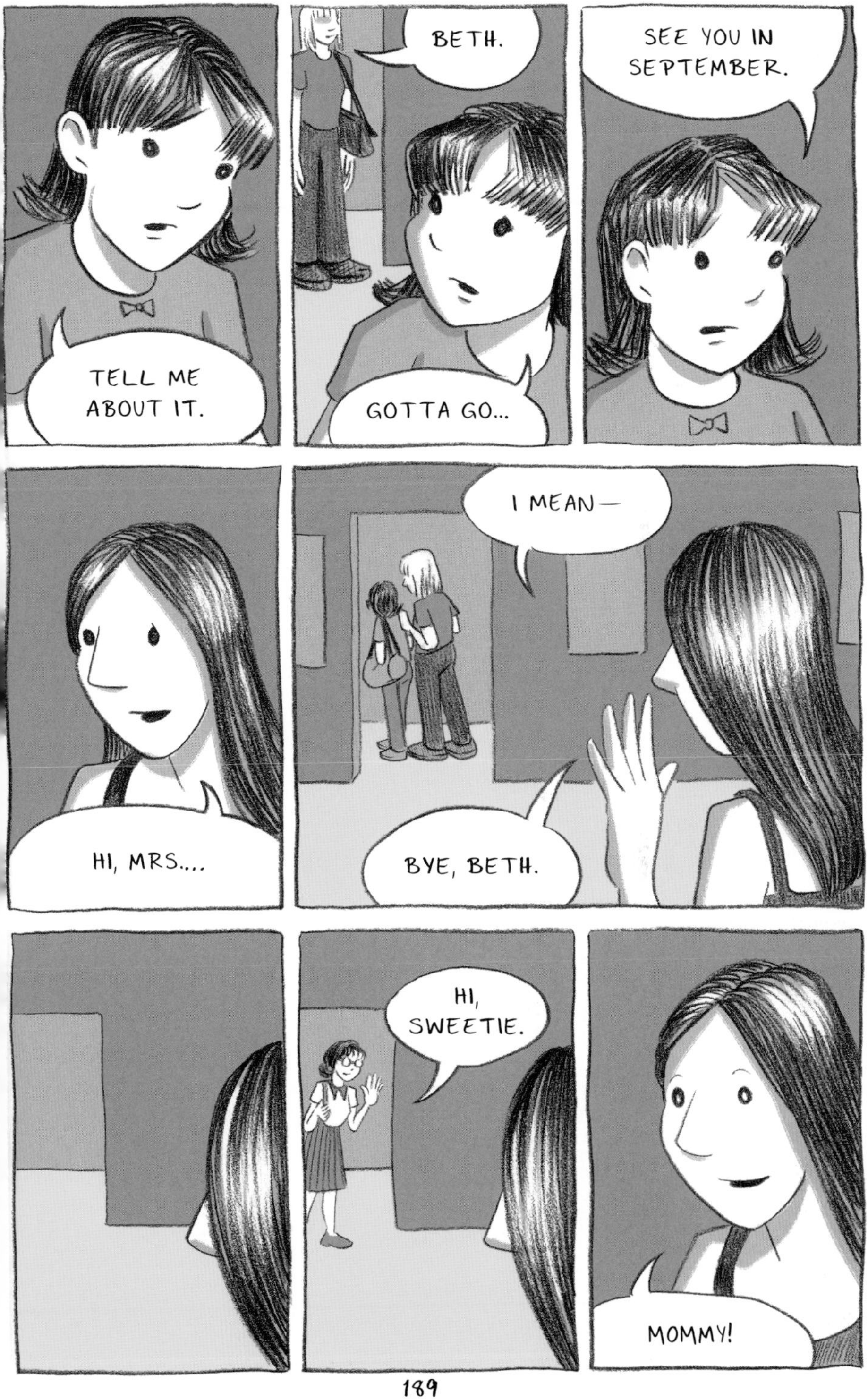
TELL ME
ABOUT IT.
BETH.
GOTTA GO...
SEE YOU IN
SEPTEMBER.
HI, MRS....
I MEAN—
BYE, BETH.
HI,
SWEETIE.
MOMMY!

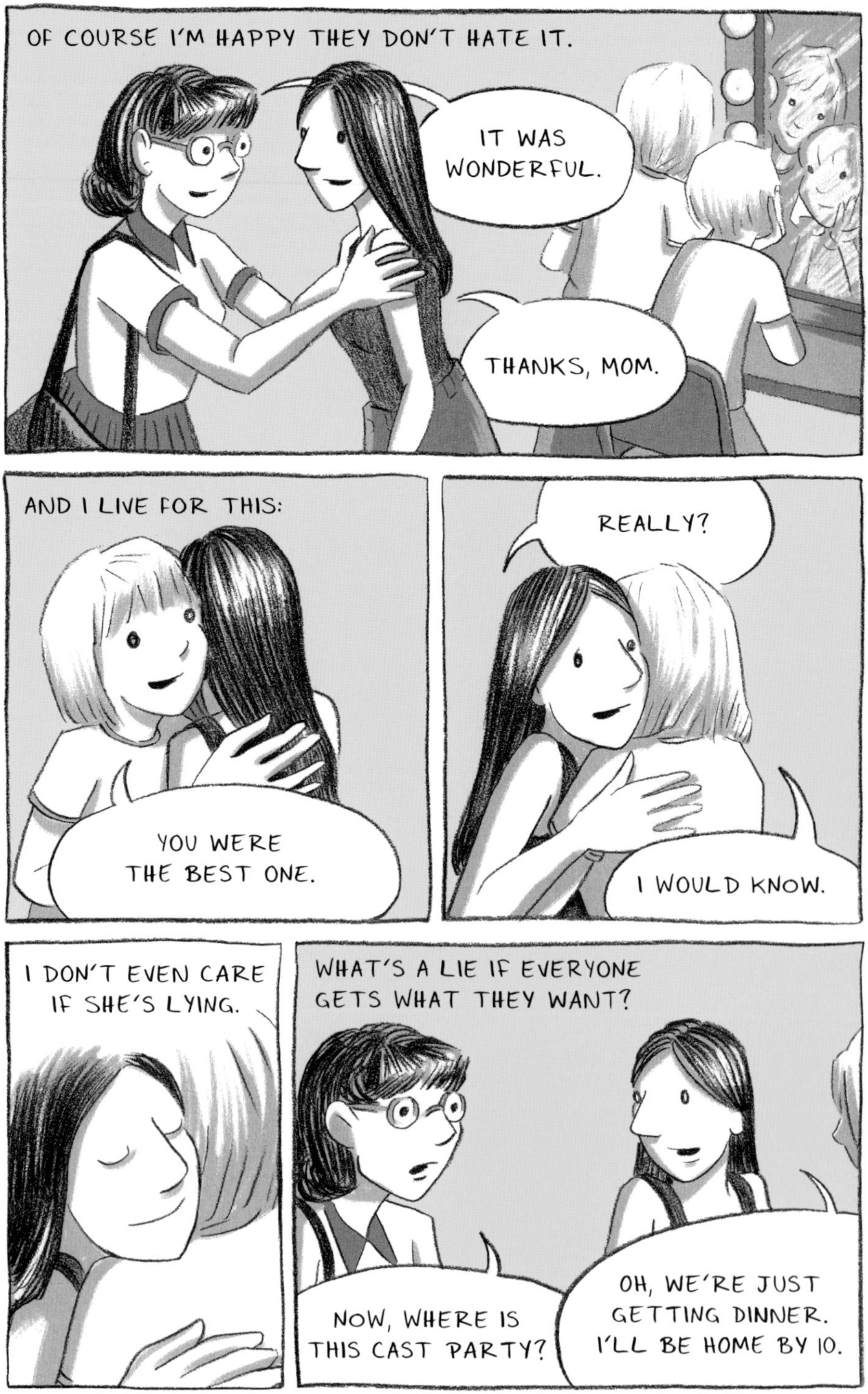
OF COURSE I'M HAPPY THEY DON'T HATE IT.
IT WAS WONDERFUL.
THANKS, MOM.
AND I LIVE FOR THIS:
YOU WERE THE BEST ONE.
REALLY?
I WOULD KNOW.
I DON'T EVEN CARE IF SHE'S LYING.
WHAT'S A LIE IF EVERYONE GETS WHAT THEY WANT?
NOW, WHERE IS THIS CAST PARTY?
OH, WE'RE JUST GETTING DINNER. I'LL BE HOME BY 10.

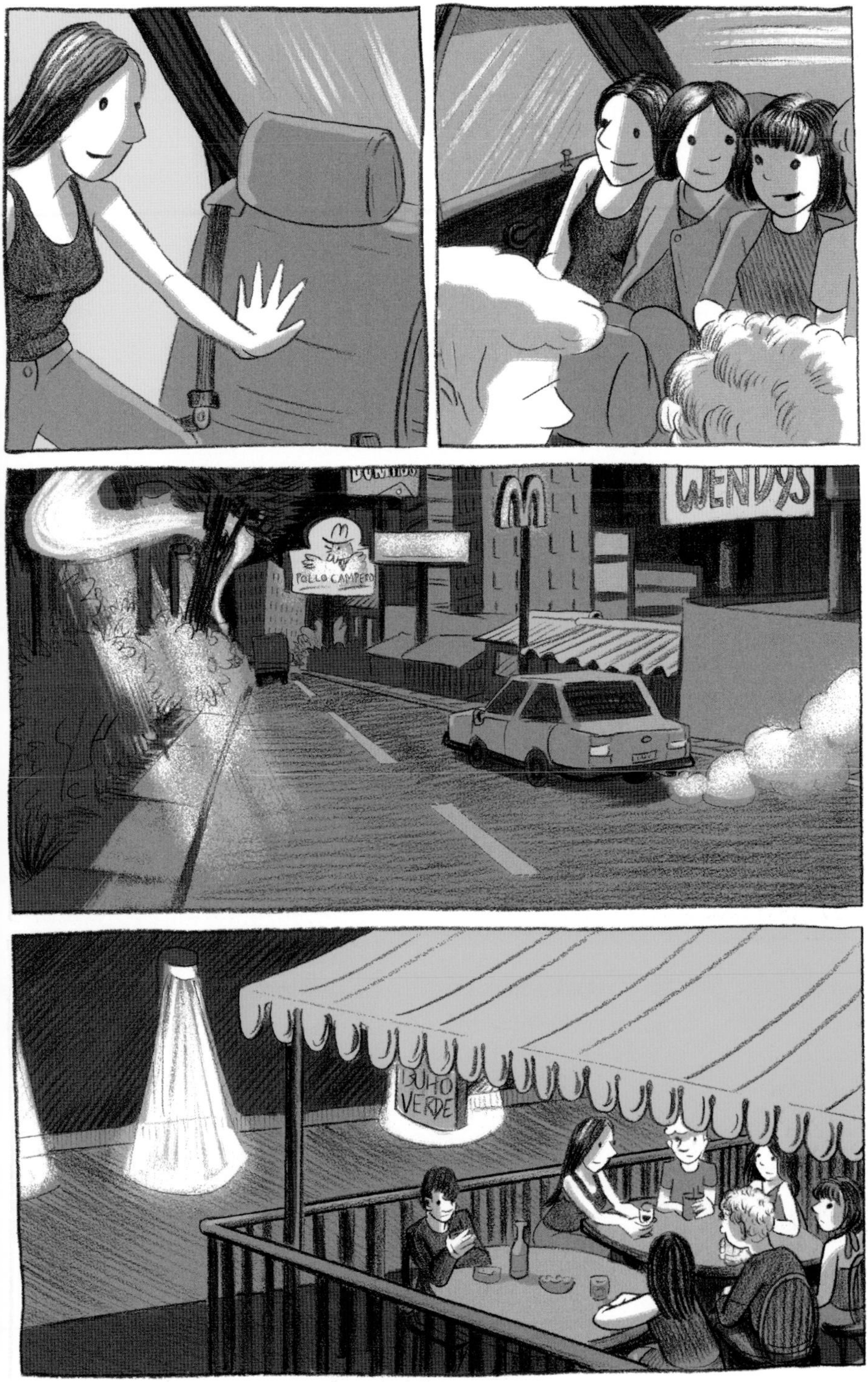
WENDYS
POLLO CAMPERO
BUHO VERDE

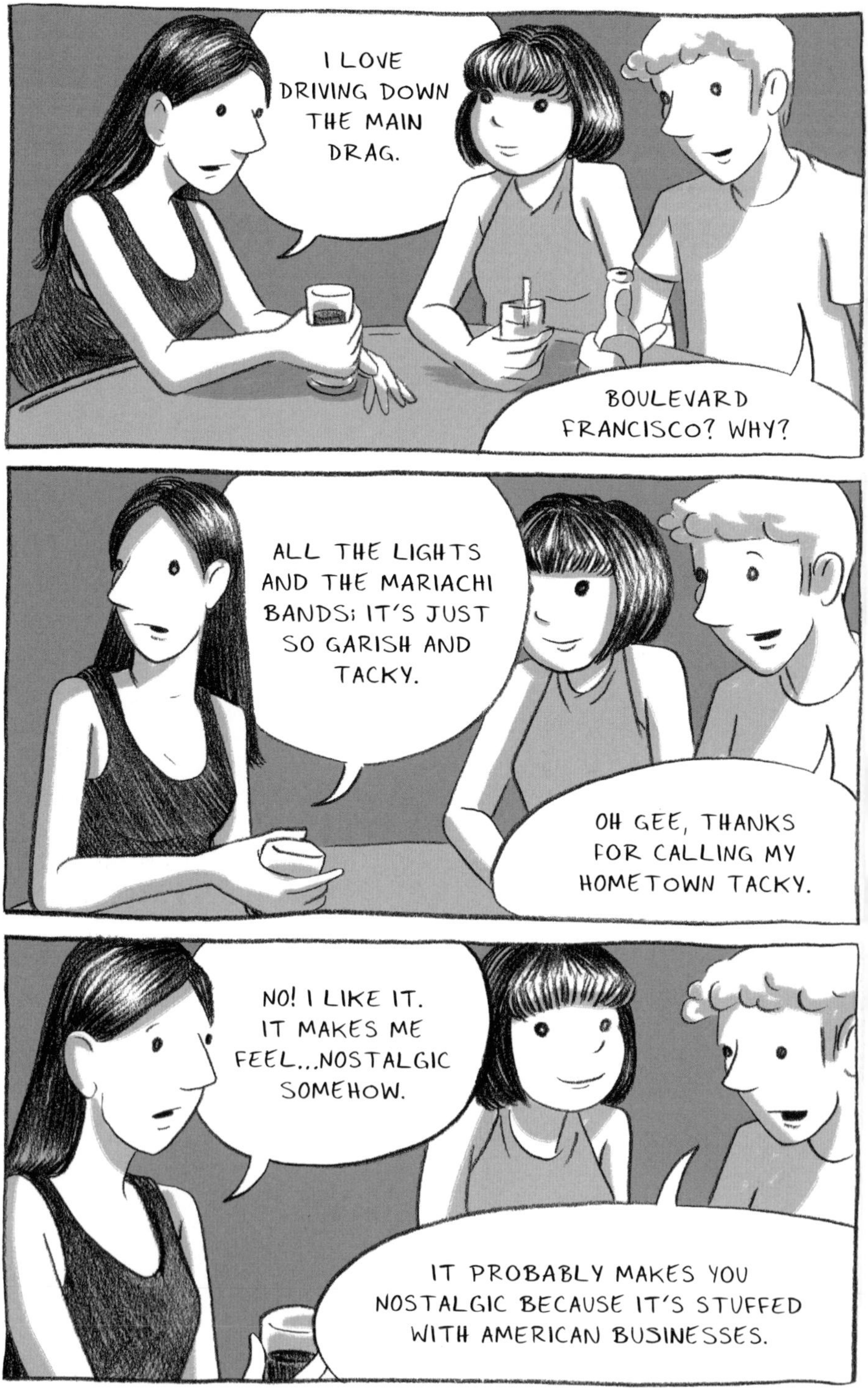
I LOVE DRIVING DOWN THE MAIN DRAG.
BOULEVARD FRANCISCO? WHY?
ALL THE LIGHTS AND THE MARIACHI BANDS; IT'S JUST SO GARISH AND TACKY.
OH GEE, THANKS FOR CALLING MY HOMETOWN TACKY.
NO! I LIKE IT. IT MAKES ME FEEL...NOSTALGIC SOMEHOW.
IT PROBABLY MAKES YOU NOSTALGIC BECAUSE IT'S STUFFED WITH AMERICAN BUSINESSES.

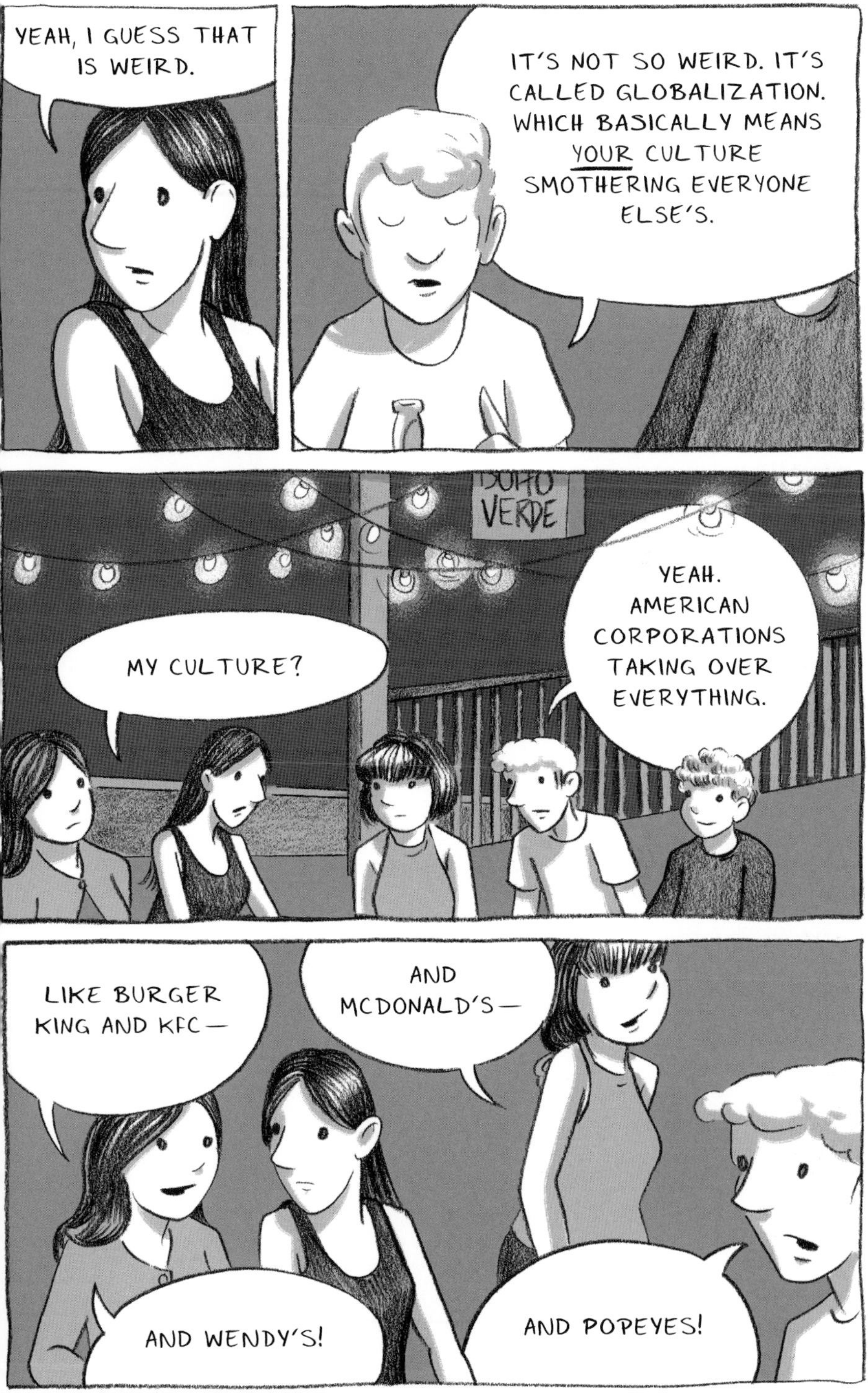
YEAH, I GUESS THAT IS WEIRD.
IT'S NOT SO WEIRD. IT'S CALLED GLOBALIZATION. WHICH BASICALLY MEANS YOUR CULTURE SMOTHERING EVERYONE ELSE'S.
VERDE
MY CULTURE?
YEAH. AMERICAN CORPORATIONS TAKING OVER EVERYTHING.
LIKE BURGER KING AND KFC—
AND MCDONALD'S—
AND WENDY'S!
AND POPEYES!

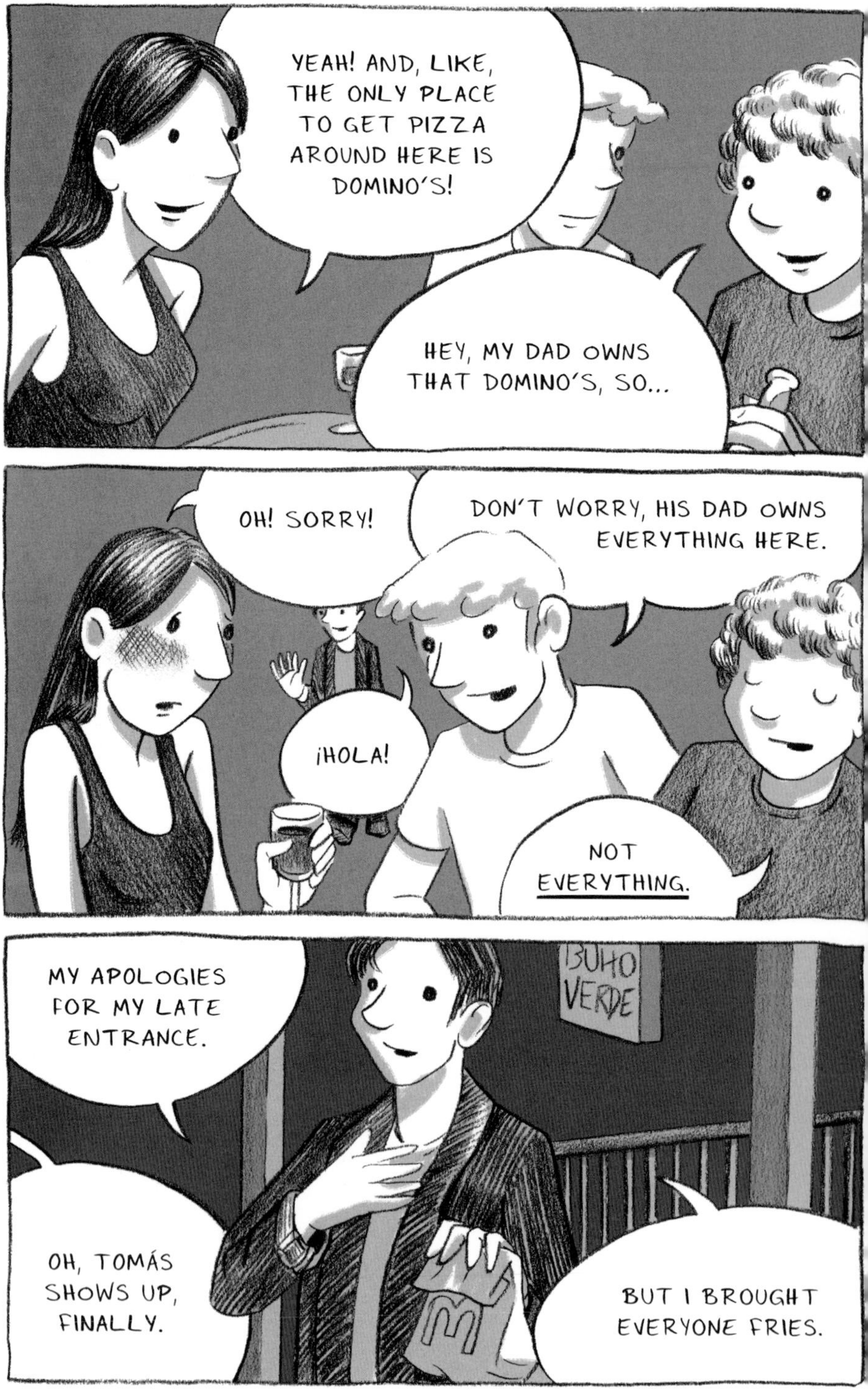
YEAH! AND, LIKE, THE ONLY PLACE TO GET PIZZA AROUND HERE IS DOMINO'S!
HEY, MY DAD OWNS THAT DOMINO'S, SO...
OH! SORRY!
DON'T WORRY, HIS DAD OWNS EVERYTHING HERE.
¡HOLA!
NOT EVERYTHING.
MY APOLOGIES FOR MY LATE ENTRANCE.
BUHO VERDE
OH, TOMÁS SHOWS UP, FINALLY.
BUT I BROUGHT EVERYONE FRIES.

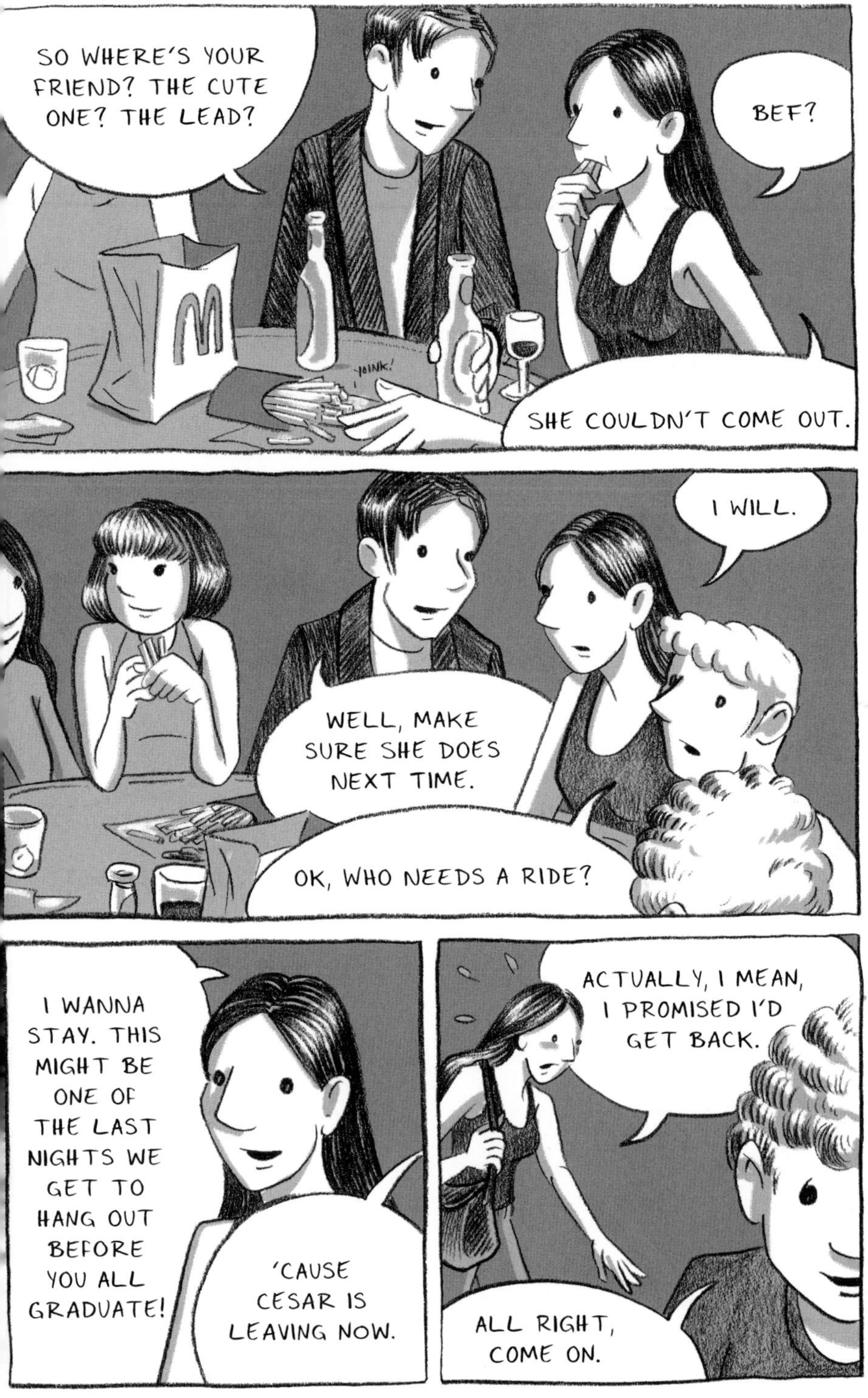
SO WHERE'S YOUR FRIEND? THE CUTE ONE? THE LEAD?
BEF?
YOINK!
SHE COULDN'T COME OUT.
WELL, MAKE SURE SHE DOES NEXT TIME.
I WILL.
OK, WHO NEEDS A RIDE?
I WANNA STAY. THIS MIGHT BE ONE OF THE LAST NIGHTS WE GET TO HANG OUT BEFORE YOU ALL GRADUATE!
'CAUSE CESAR IS LEAVING NOW.
ACTUALLY, I MEAN, I PROMISED I'D GET BACK.
ALL RIGHT, COME ON.

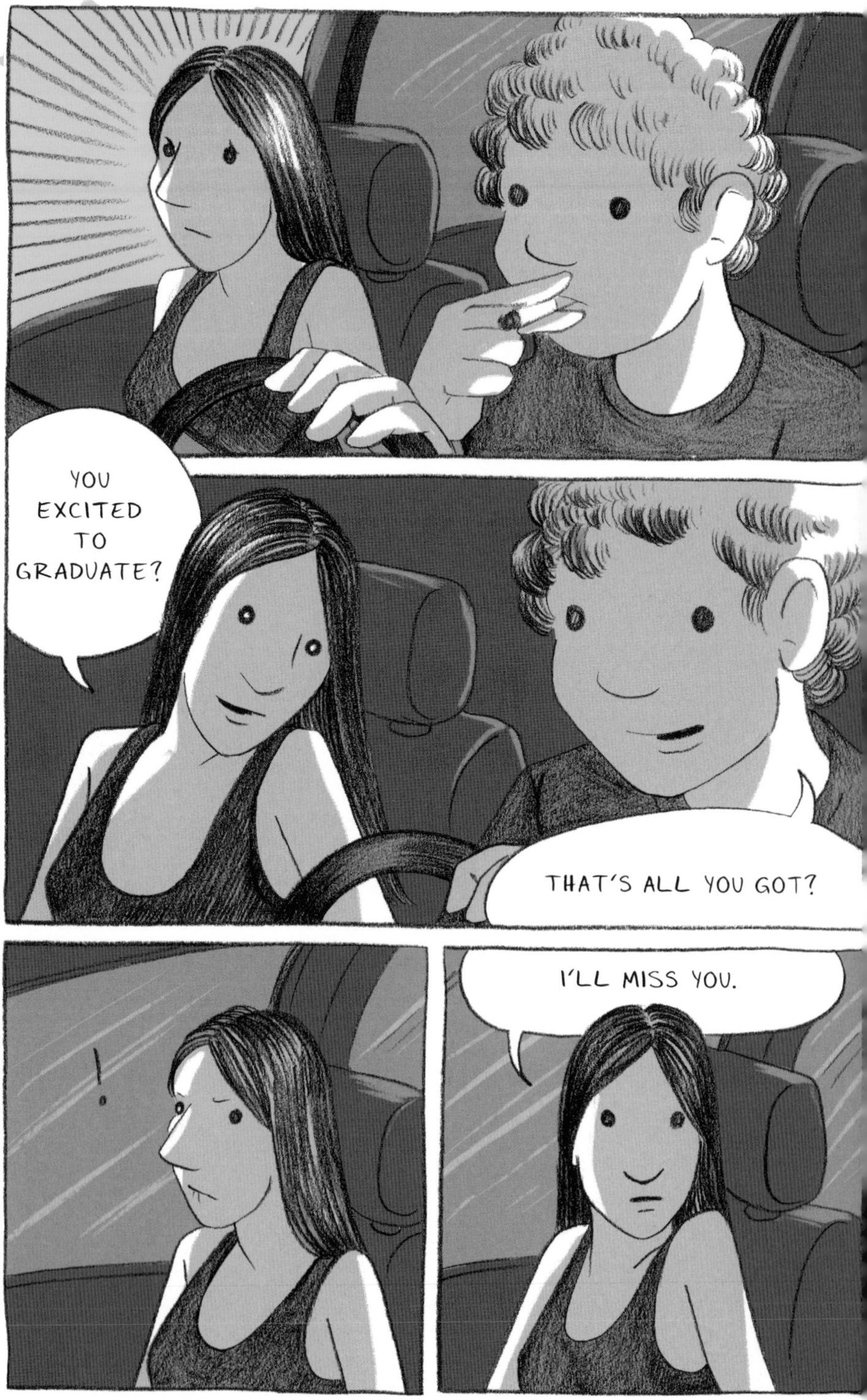
YOU EXCITED TO GRADUATE?
THAT'S ALL YOU GOT?
!
I'LL MISS YOU.

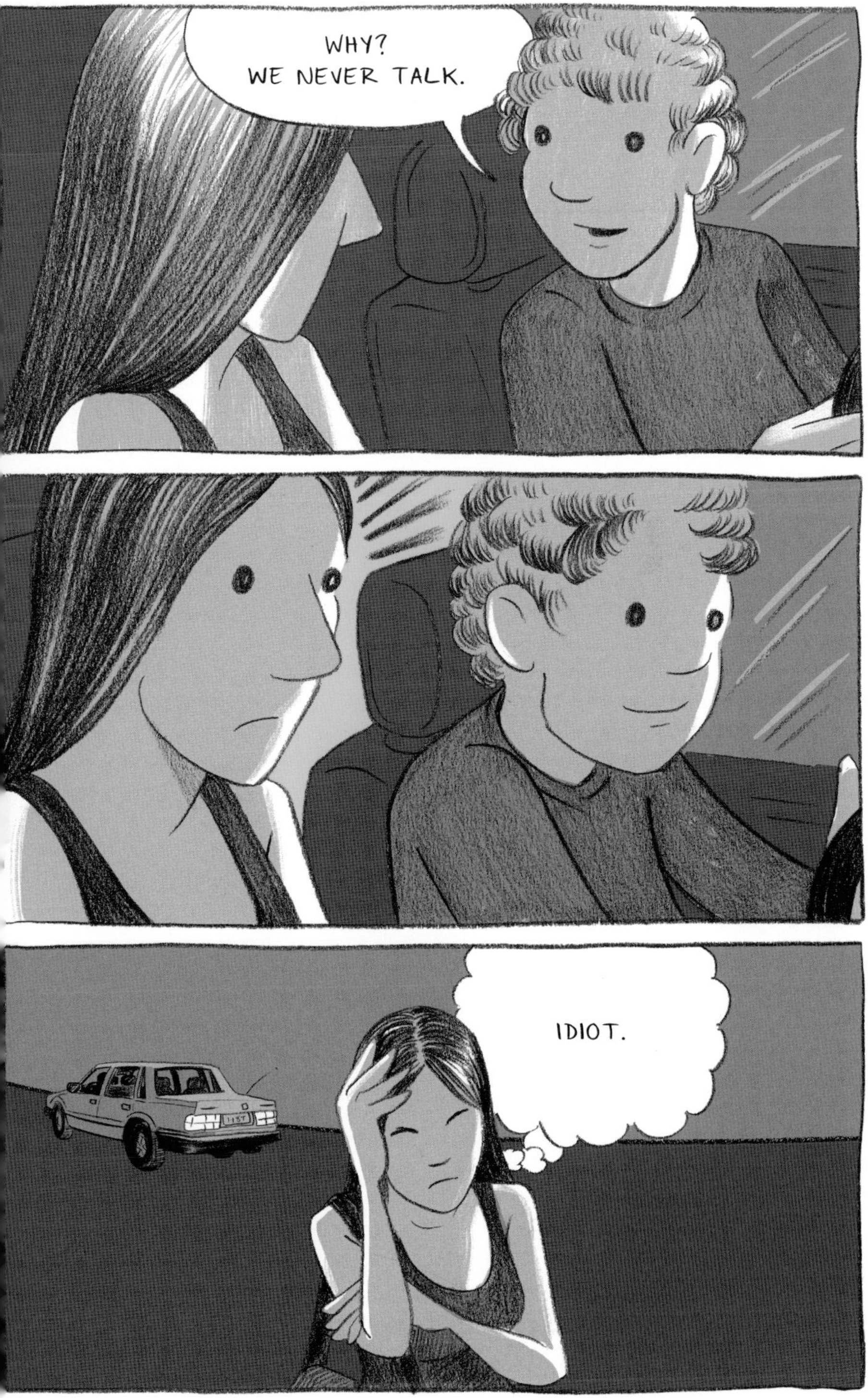
WHY?
WE NEVER TALK.
IDIOT.

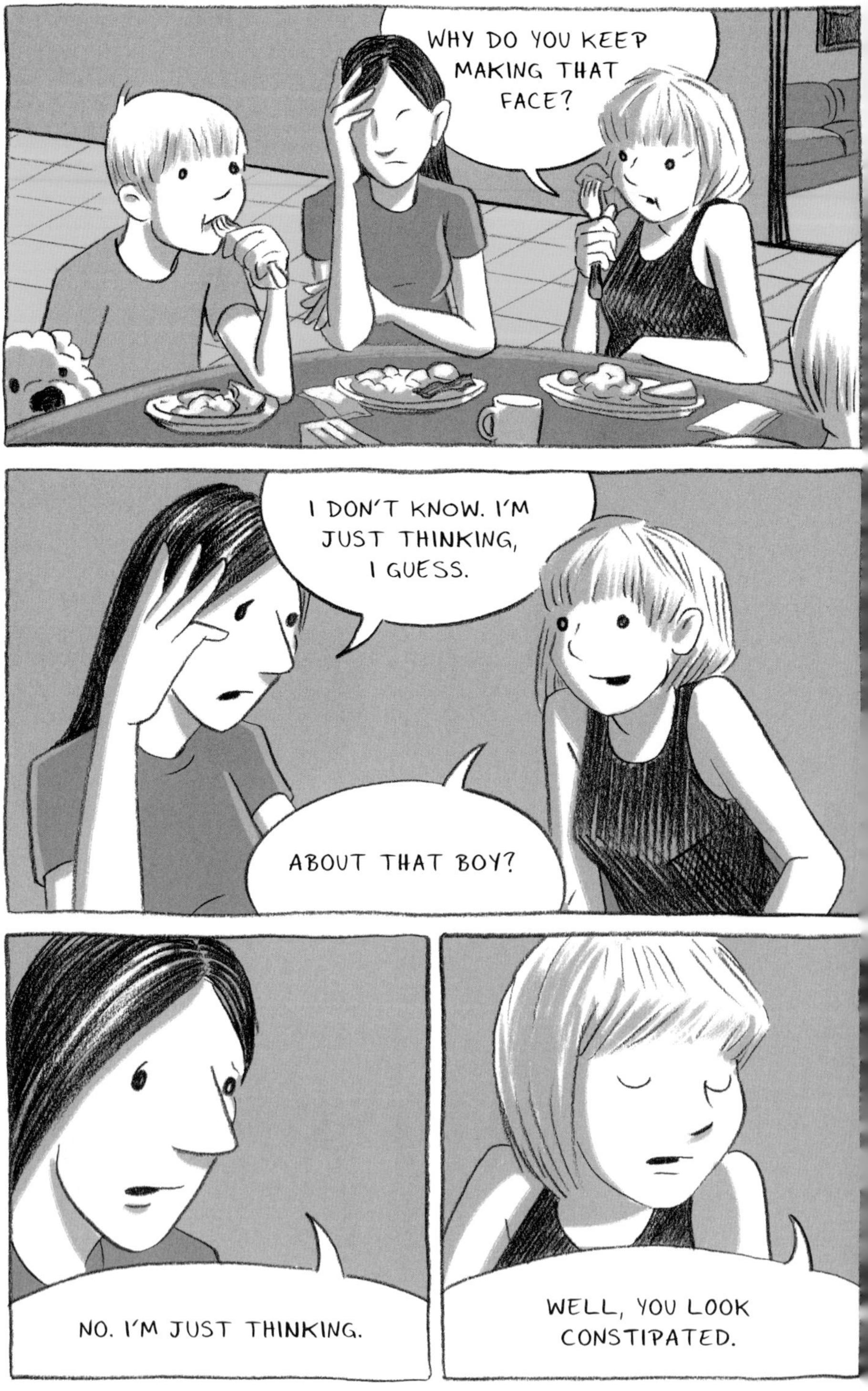
WHY DO YOU KEEP MAKING THAT FACE?
I DON'T KNOW. I'M JUST THINKING, I GUESS.
ABOUT THAT BOY?
NO. I'M JUST THINKING.
WELL, YOU LOOK CONSTIPATED.

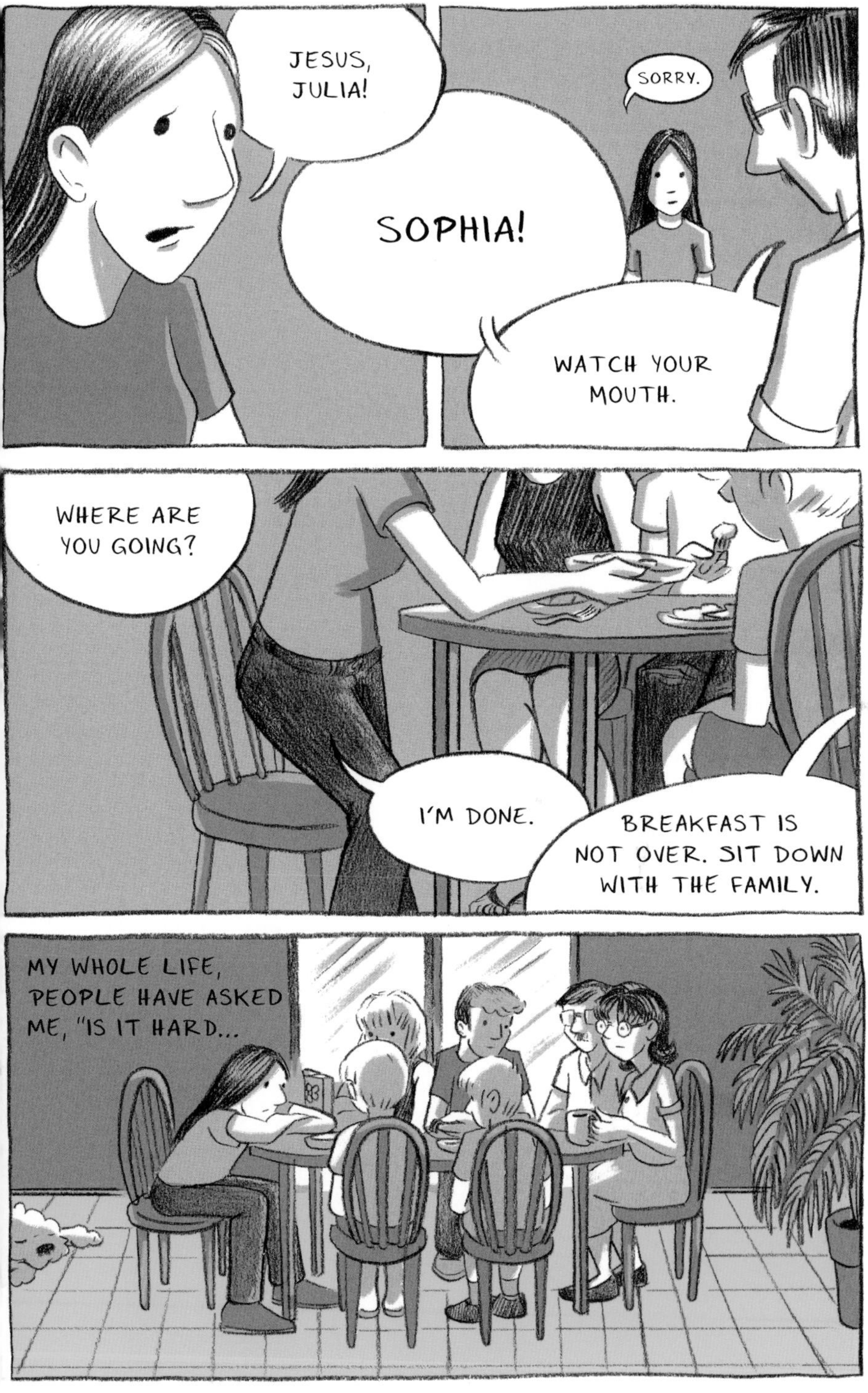
JESUS, JULIA!
SORRY.
SOPHIA!
WATCH YOUR MOUTH.
WHERE ARE YOU GOING?
I'M DONE.
BREAKFAST IS NOT OVER. SIT DOWN WITH THE FAMILY.
MY WHOLE LIFE, PEOPLE HAVE ASKED ME, "IS IT HARD...

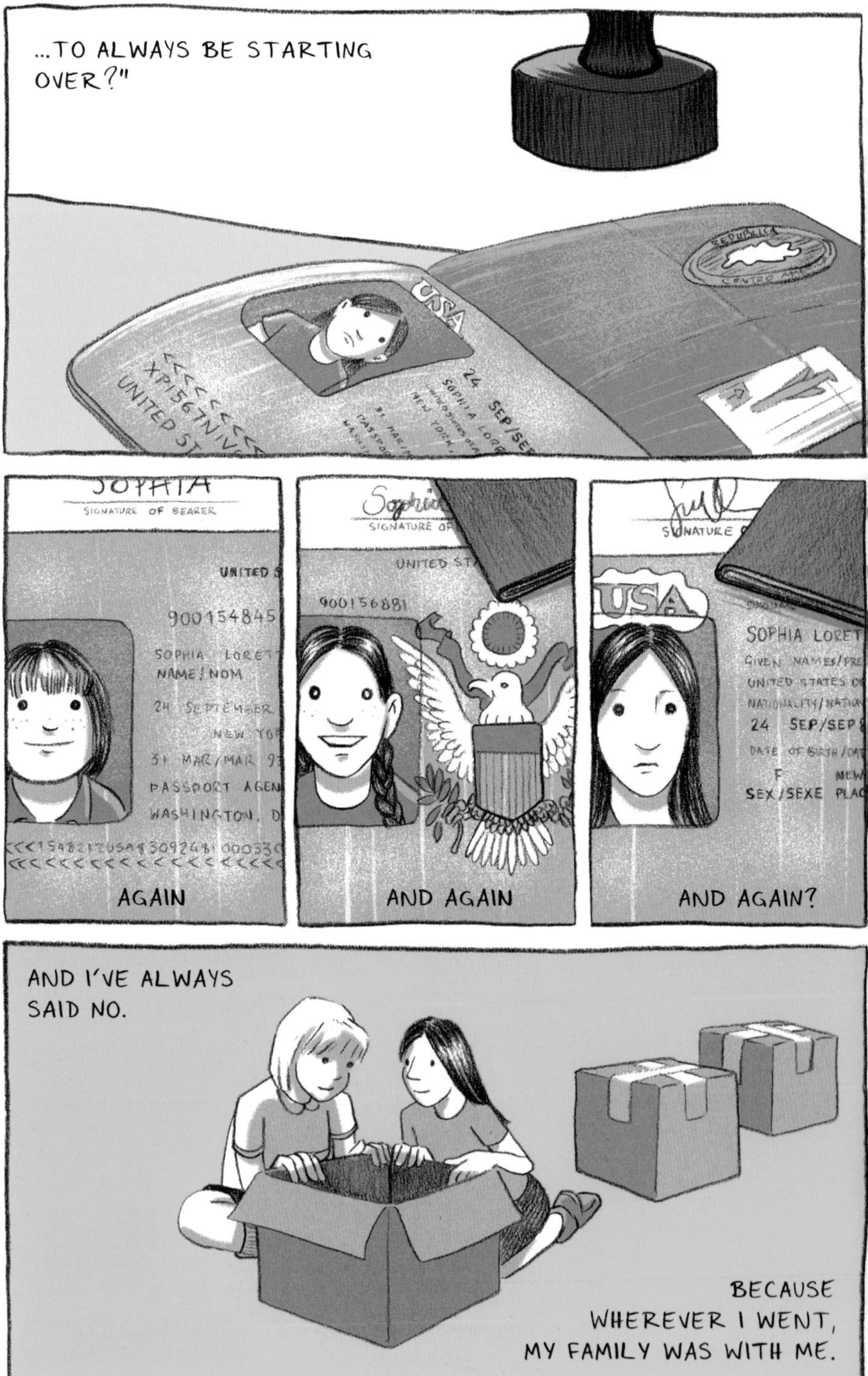
...TO ALWAYS BE STARTING OVER?"
USA
SIGNATURE OF BEARER
AGAIN
AND AGAIN
AND AGAIN?
AND I'VE ALWAYS SAID NO.
BECAUSE WHEREVER I WENT, MY FAMILY WAS WITH ME.

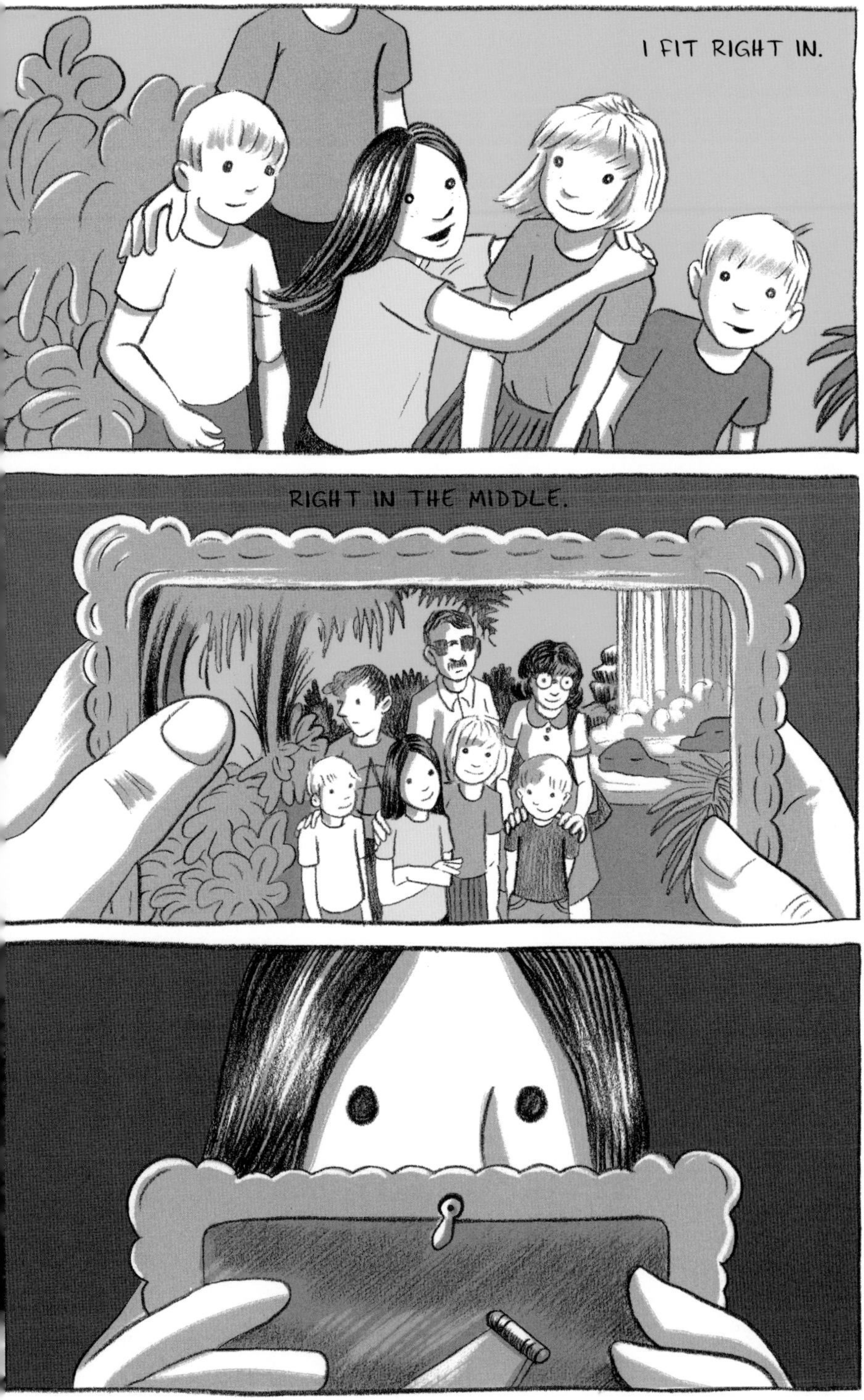
I FIT RIGHT IN.
RIGHT IN THE MIDDLE.

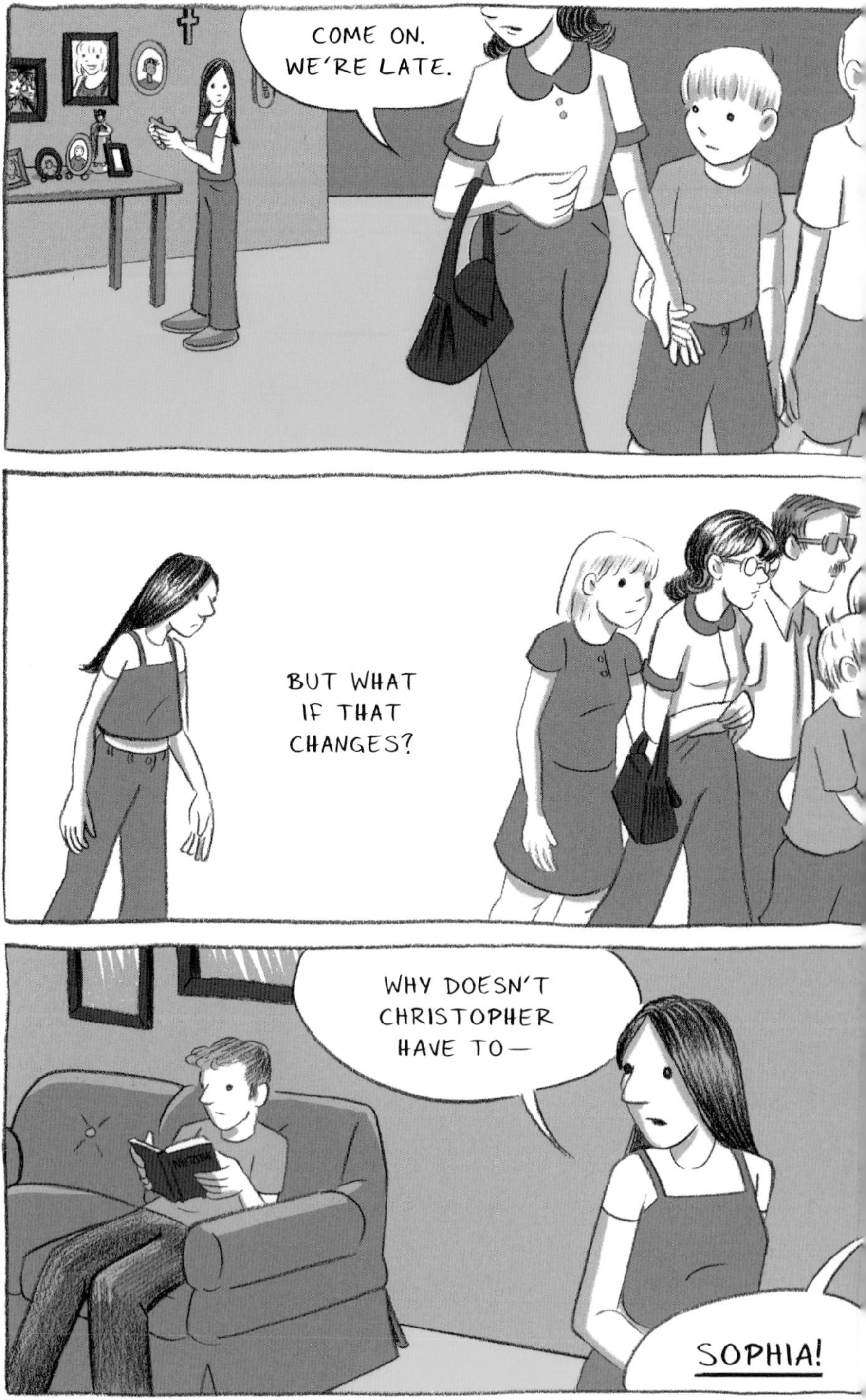
COME ON. WE'RE LATE.
BUT WHAT IF THAT CHANGES?
WHY DOESN'T CHRISTOPHER HAVE TO—
SOPHIA!

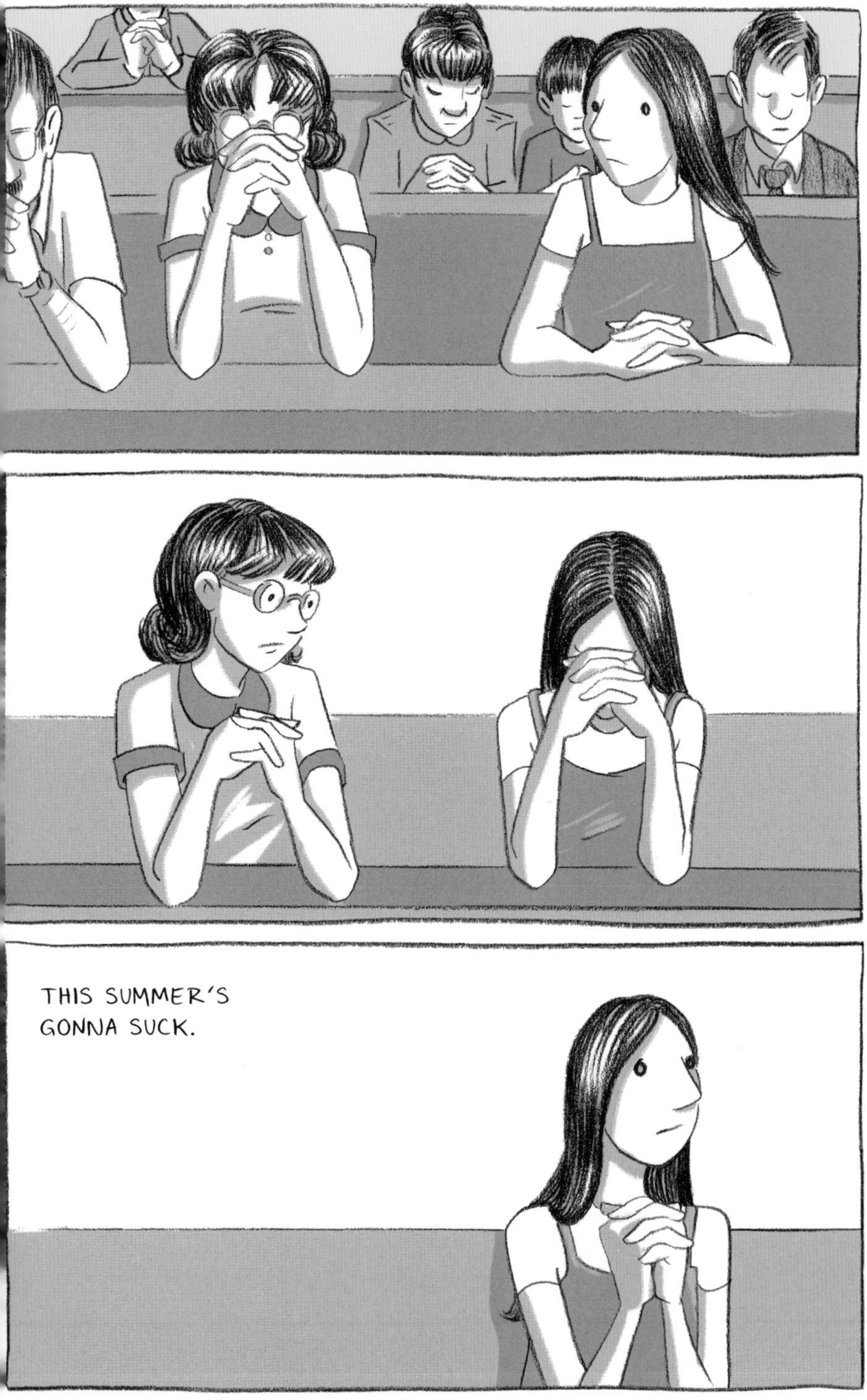
THIS SUMMER'S
GONNA SUCK.

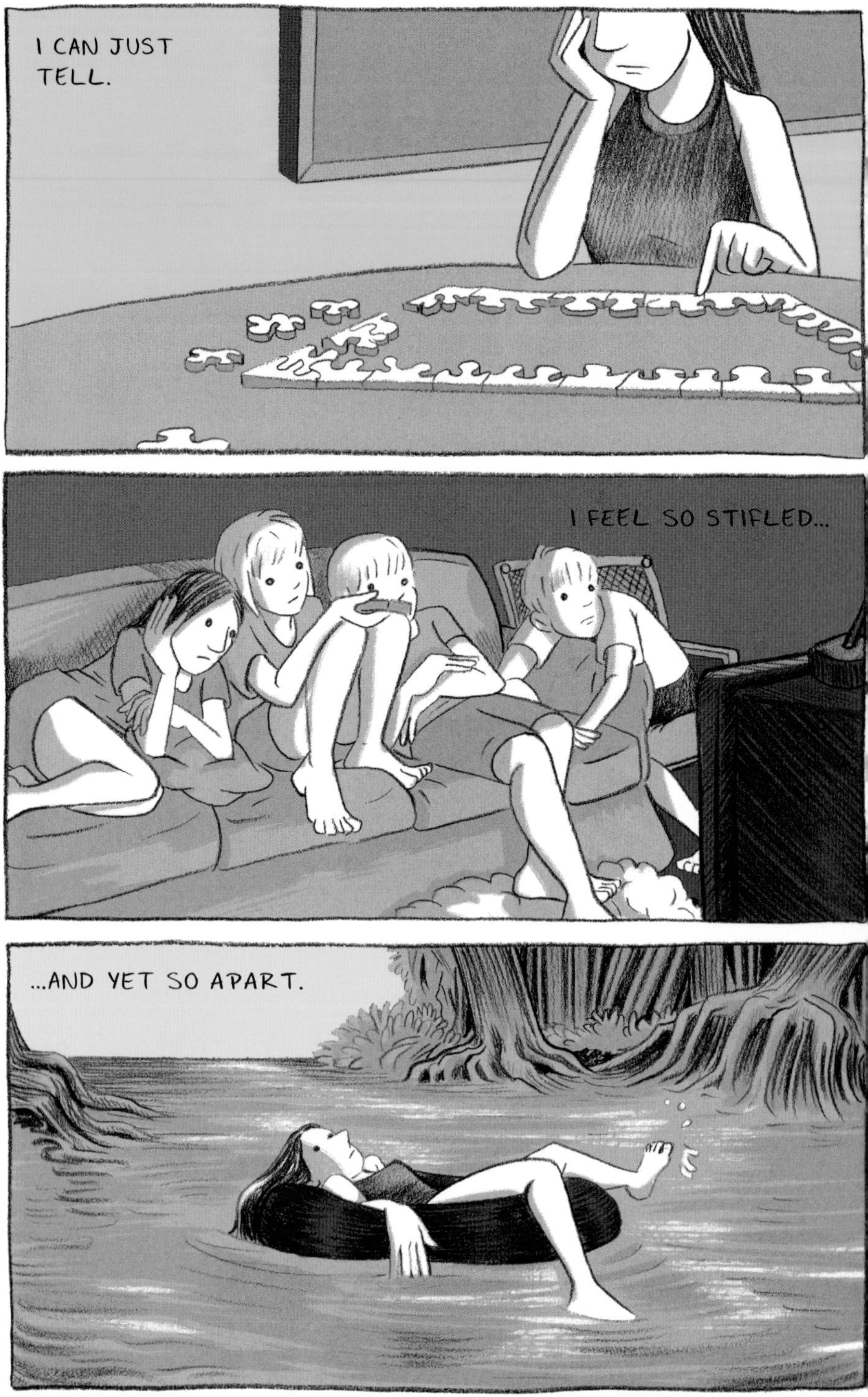
I CAN JUST TELL.
I FEEL SO STIFLED...
...AND YET SO APART.

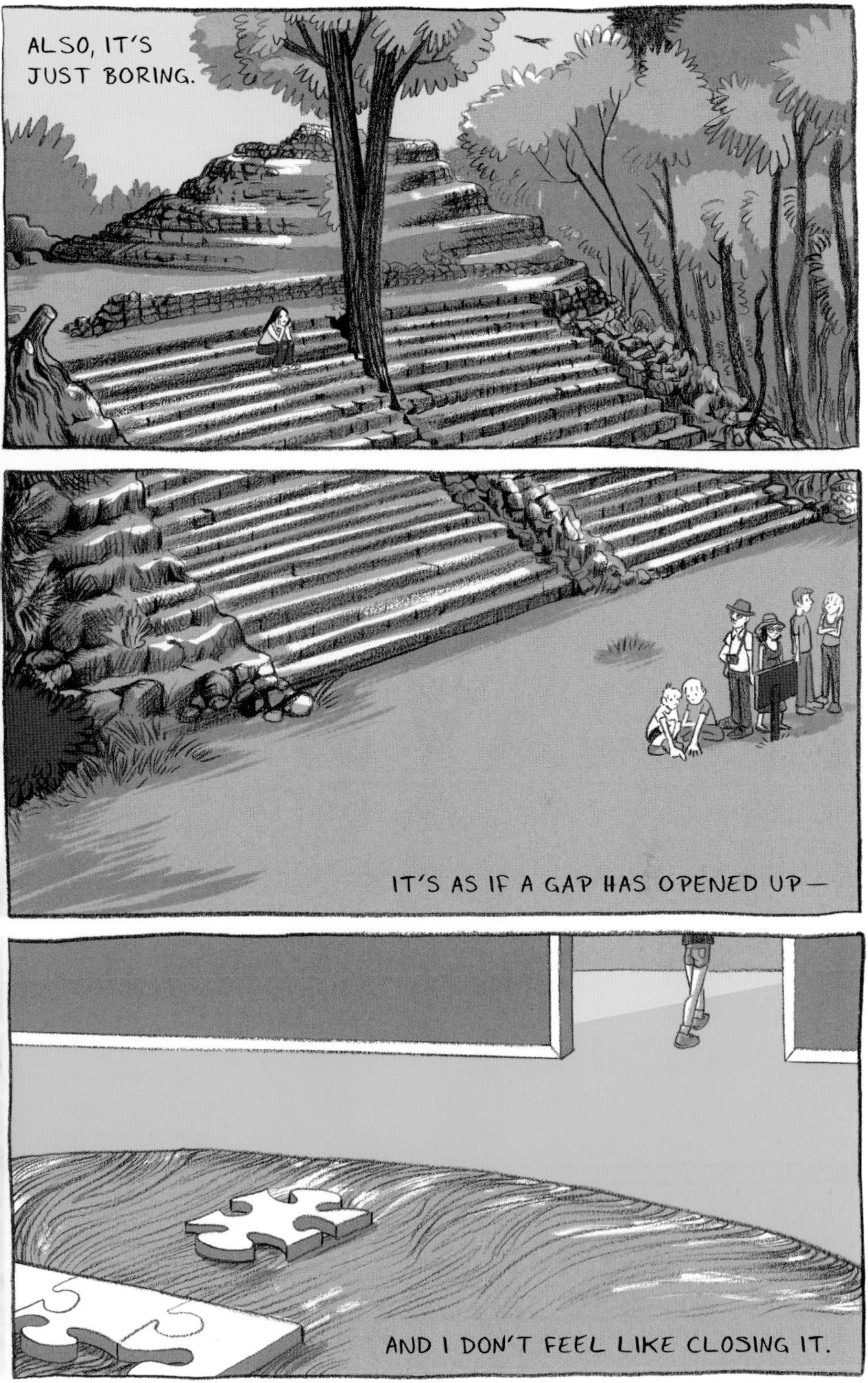
ALSO, IT'S JUST BORING.
IT'S AS IF A GAP HAS OPENED UP—
AND I DON'T FEEL LIKE CLOSING IT.

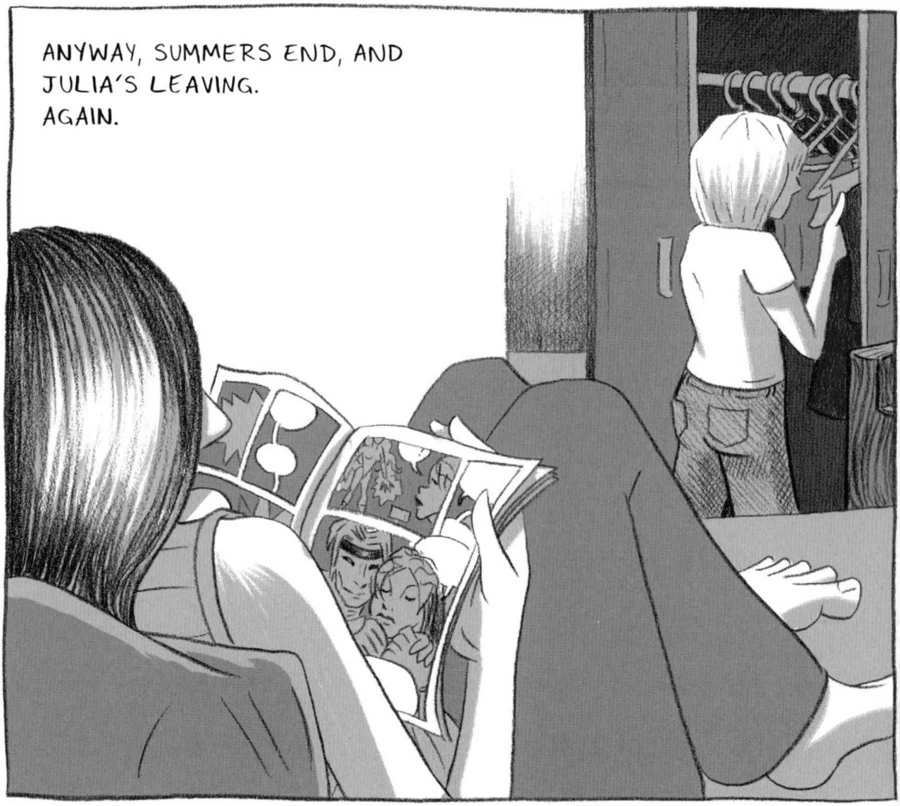
ANYWAY, SUMMERS END, AND
JULIA'S LEAVING.
AGAIN.

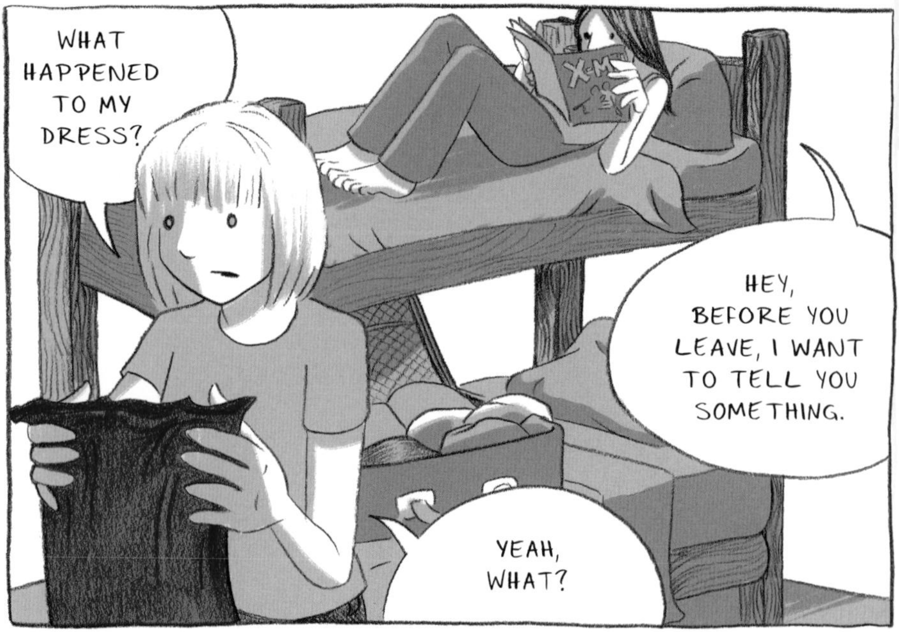
WHAT HAPPENED TO MY DRESS?
HEY, BEFORE YOU LEAVE, I WANT TO TELL YOU SOMETHING.
YEAH, WHAT?

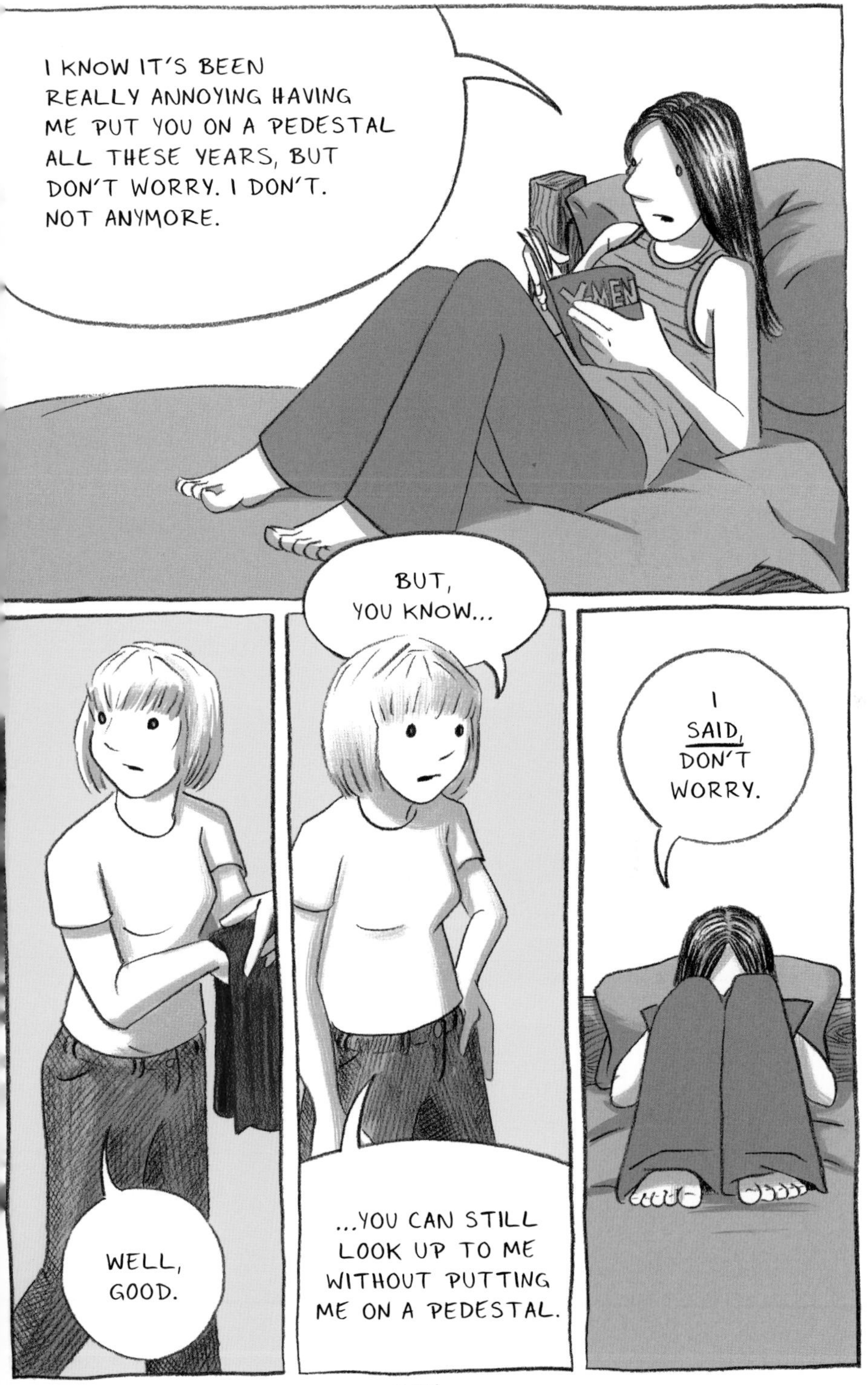
I KNOW IT'S BEEN REALLY ANNOYING HAVING ME PUT YOU ON A PEDESTAL ALL THESE YEARS, BUT DON'T WORRY. I DON'T. NOT ANYMORE.
X-MEN
WELL, GOOD.
BUT, YOU KNOW...
...YOU CAN STILL LOOK UP TO ME WITHOUT PUTTING ME ON A PEDESTAL.
I SAID, DON'T WORRY.

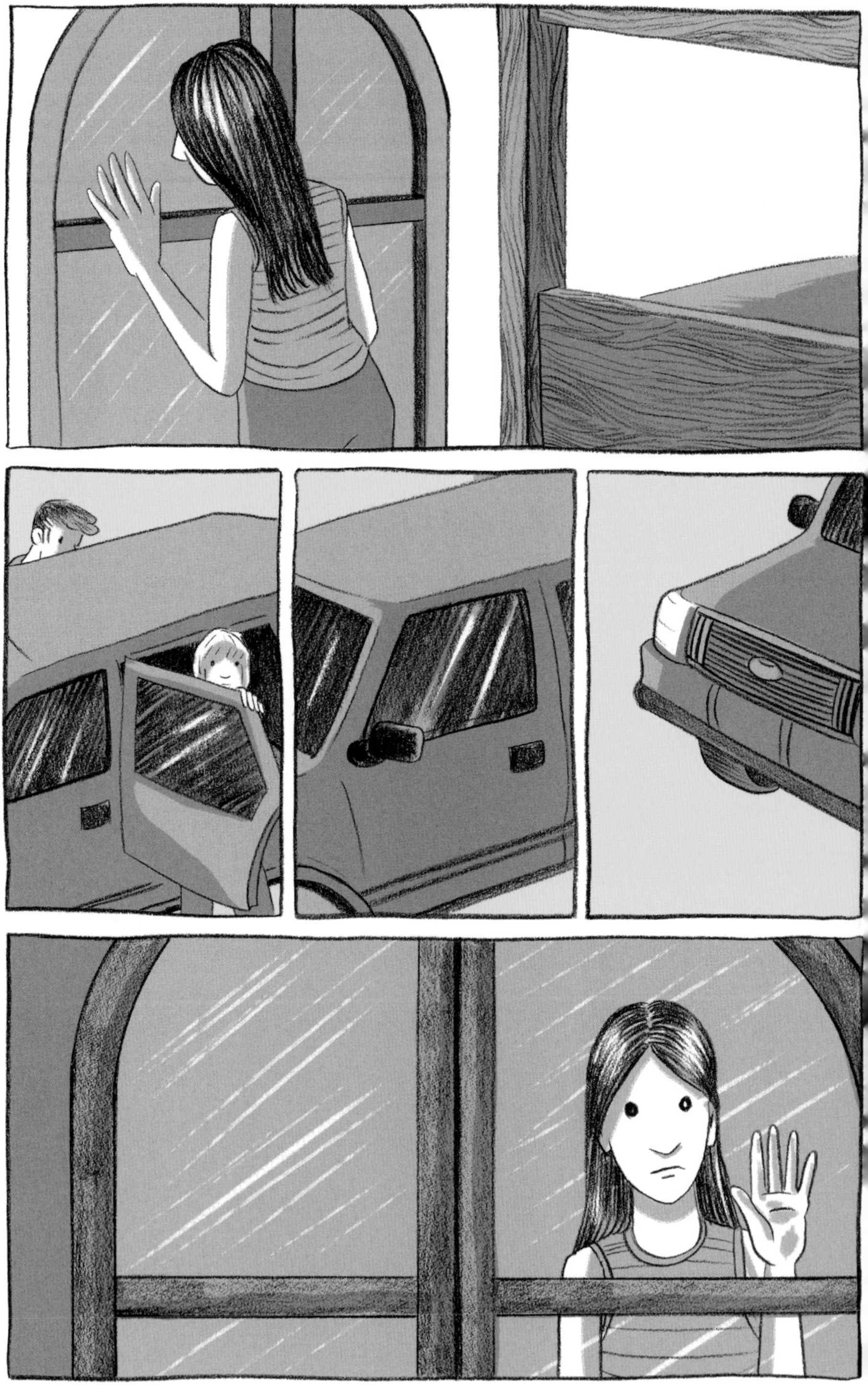

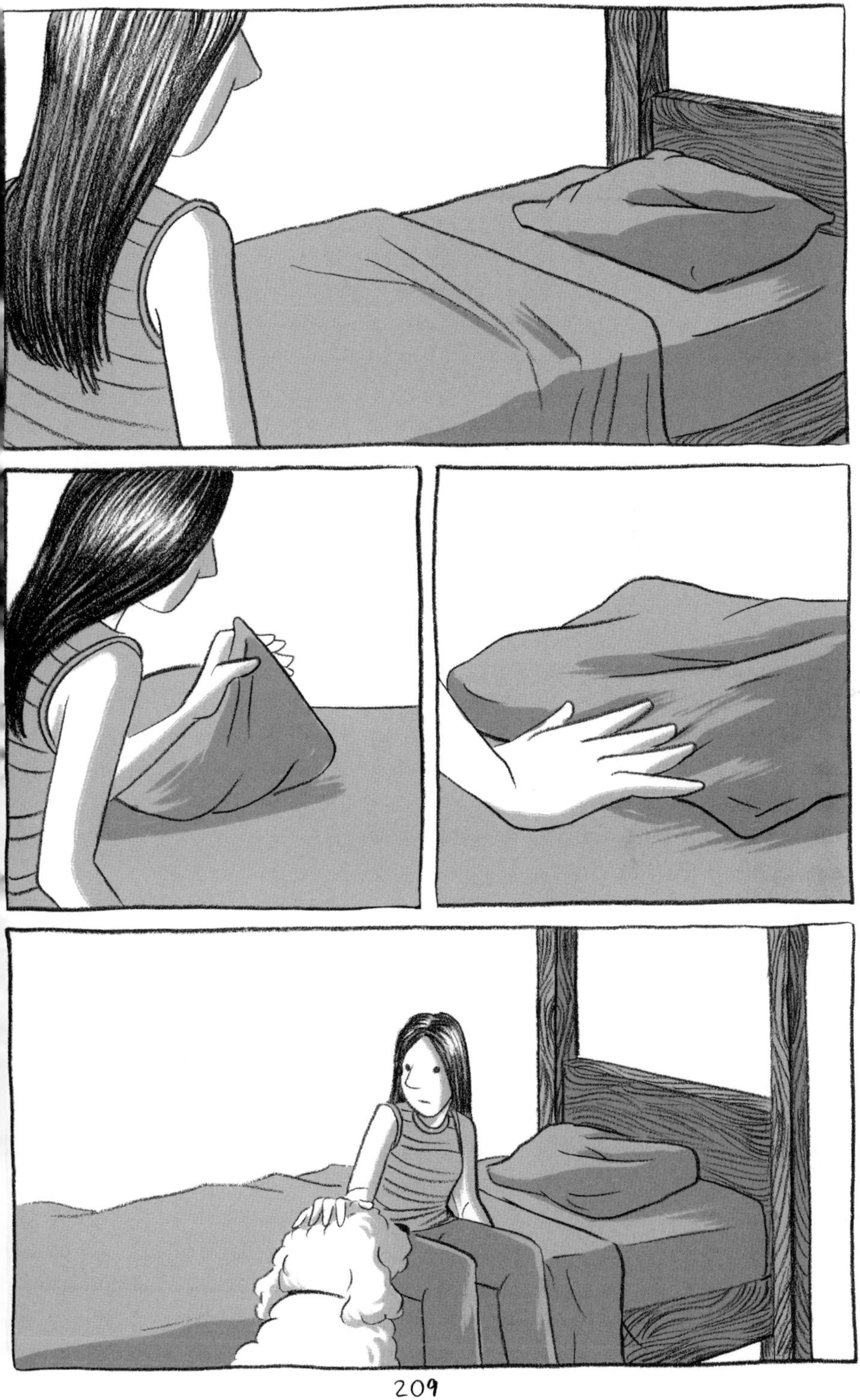

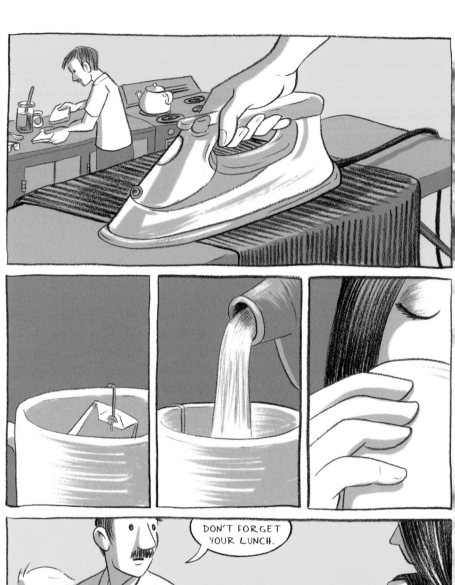

DON'T FORGET YOUR LUNCH.

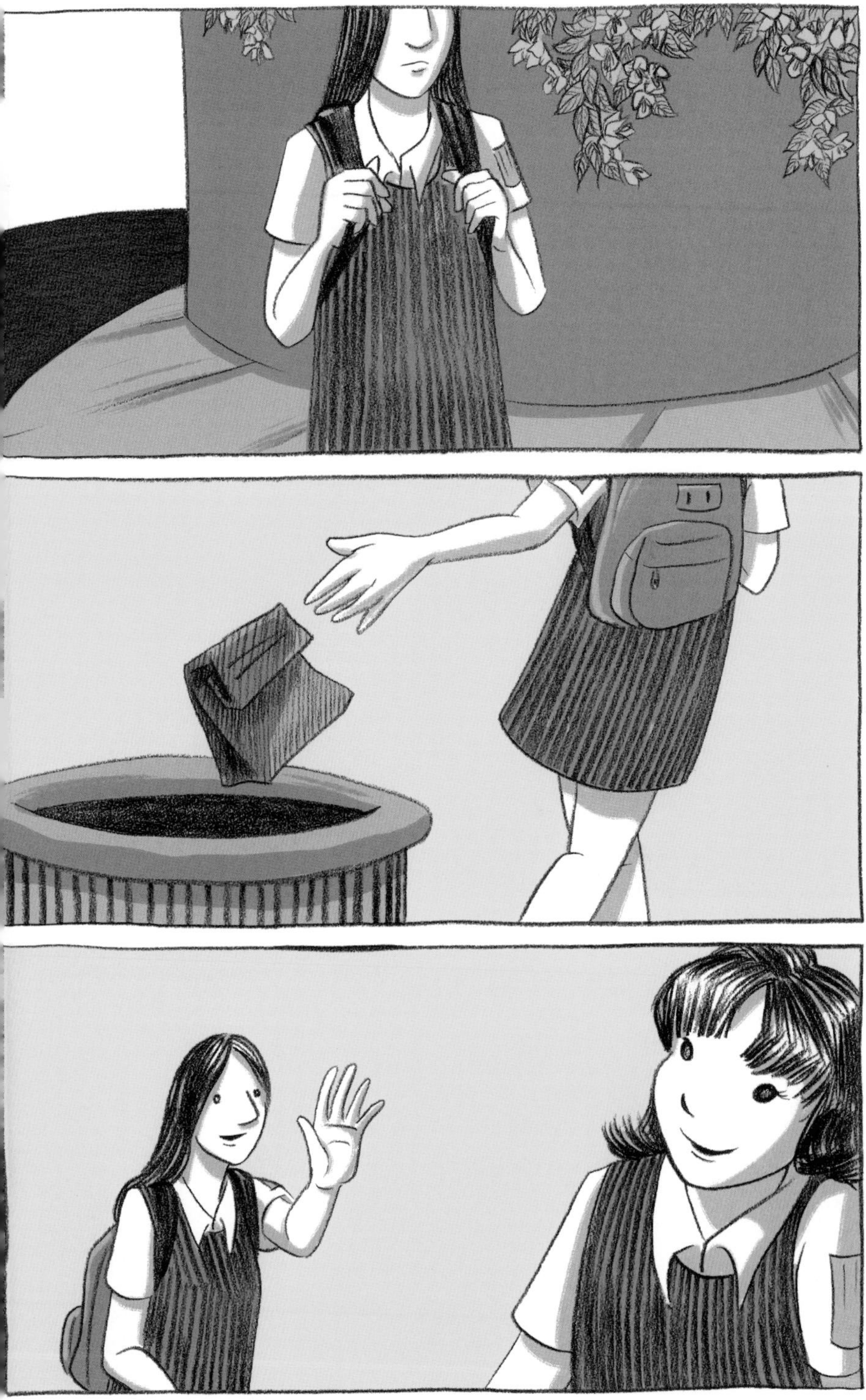

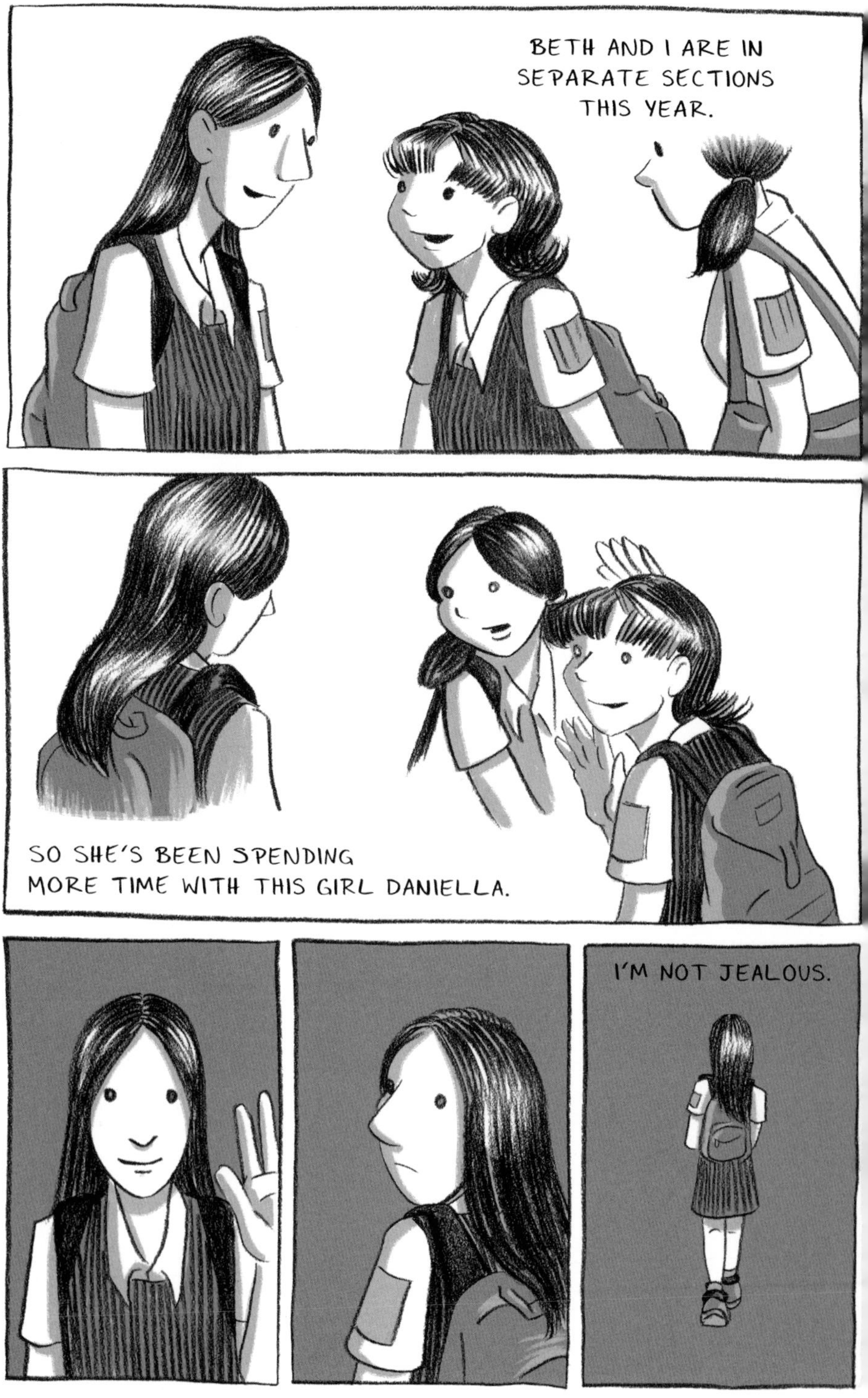
BETH AND I ARE IN SEPARATE SECTIONS THIS YEAR.
SO SHE'S BEEN SPENDING MORE TIME WITH THIS GIRL DANIELLA.
I'M NOT JEALOUS.

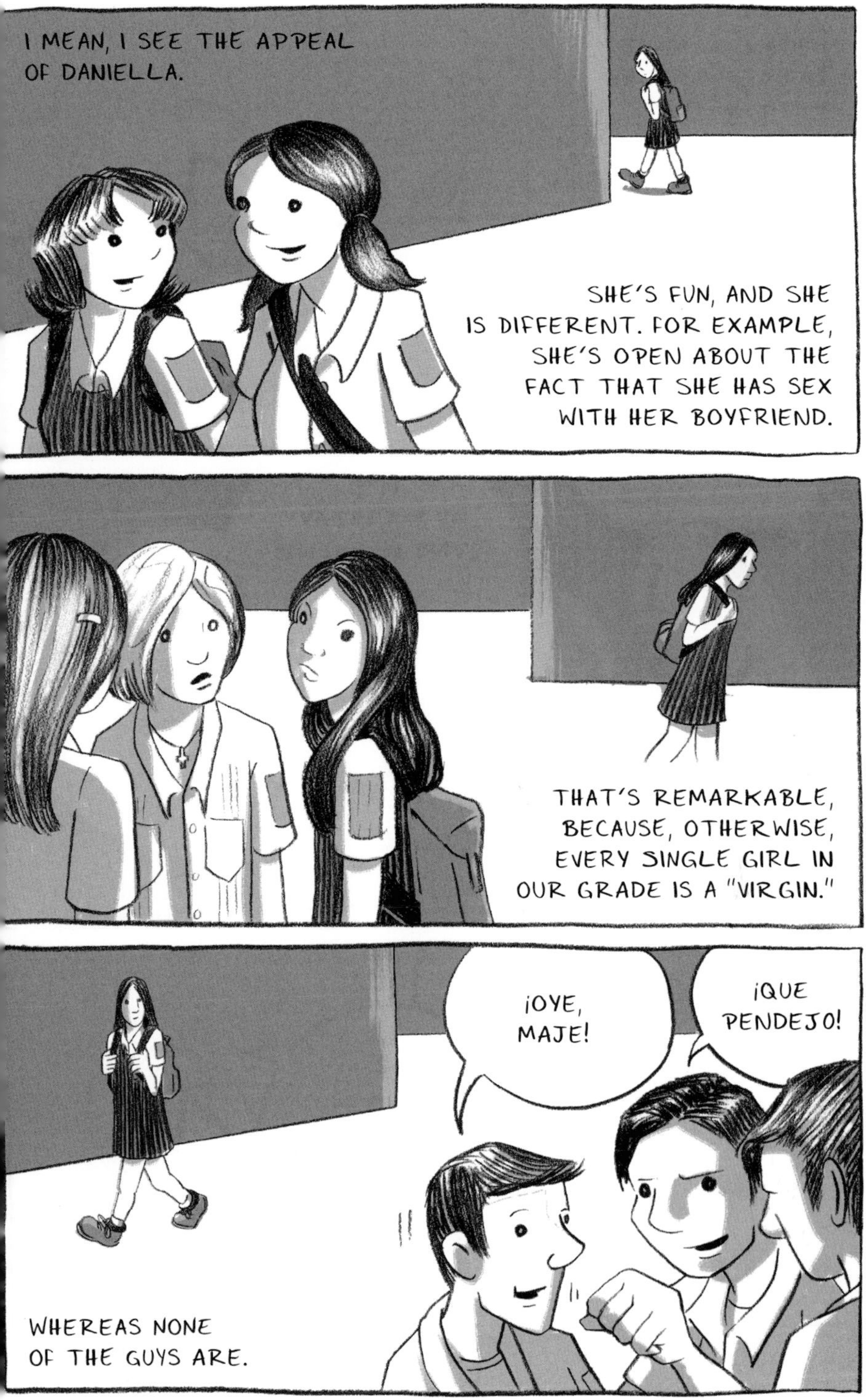
I MEAN, I SEE THE APPEAL OF DANIELLA.
SHE'S FUN, AND SHE IS DIFFERENT. FOR EXAMPLE, SHE'S OPEN ABOUT THE FACT THAT SHE HAS SEX WITH HER BOYFRIEND.
THAT'S REMARKABLE, BECAUSE, OTHERWISE, EVERY SINGLE GIRL IN OUR GRADE IS A "VIRGIN."
¡OYE, MAJE!
¡QUE PENDEJO!
WHEREAS NONE OF THE GUYS ARE.

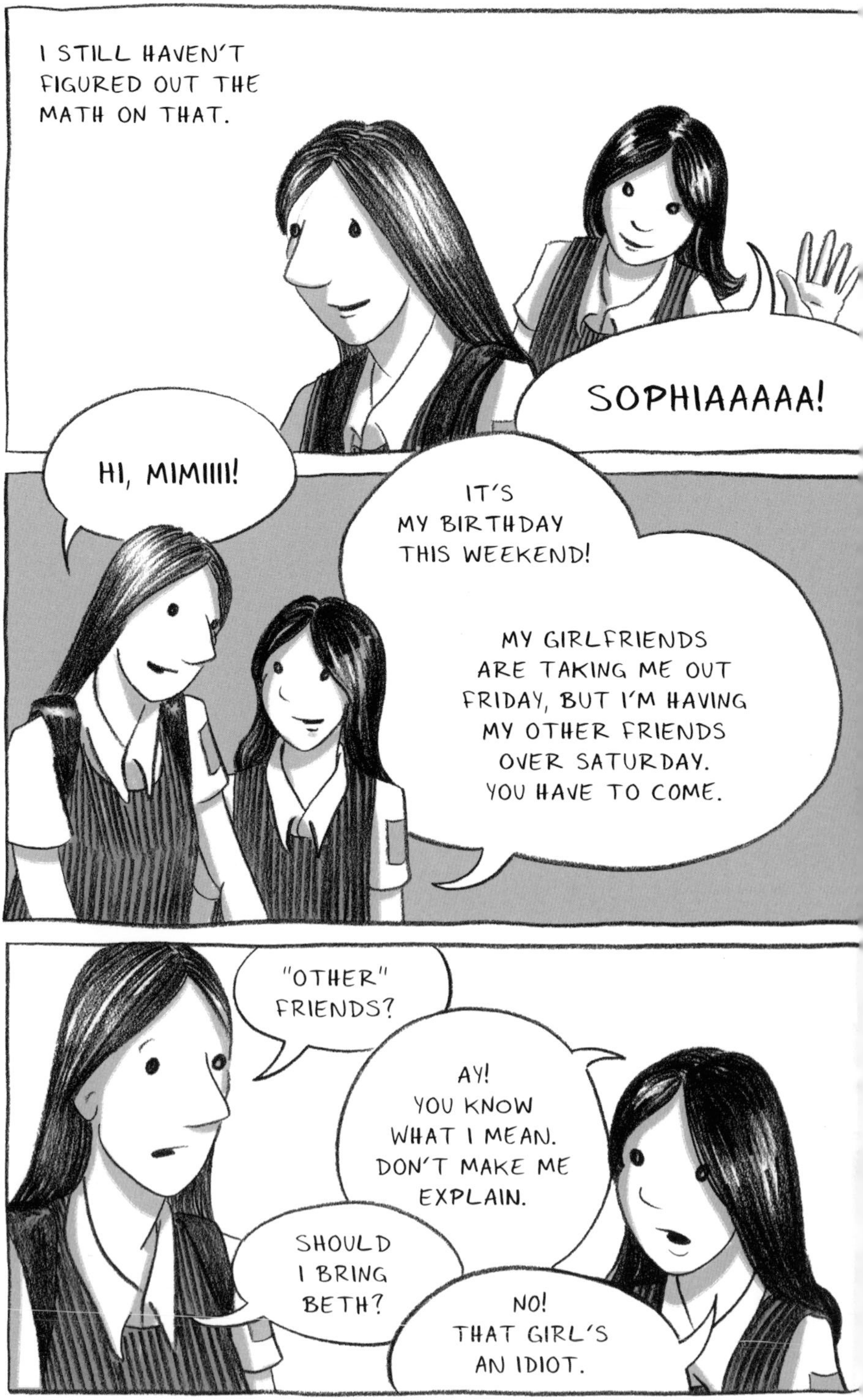
I STILL HAVEN'T FIGURED OUT THE MATH ON THAT.
SOPHIAAAAA!
HI, MIMIIII!
IT'S MY BIRTHDAY THIS WEEKEND!
MY GIRLFRIENDS ARE TAKING ME OUT FRIDAY, BUT I'M HAVING MY OTHER FRIENDS OVER SATURDAY. YOU HAVE TO COME.
"OTHER" FRIENDS?
AY! YOU KNOW WHAT I MEAN. DON'T MAKE ME EXPLAIN.
SHOULD I BRING BETH?
NO! THAT GIRL'S AN IDIOT.

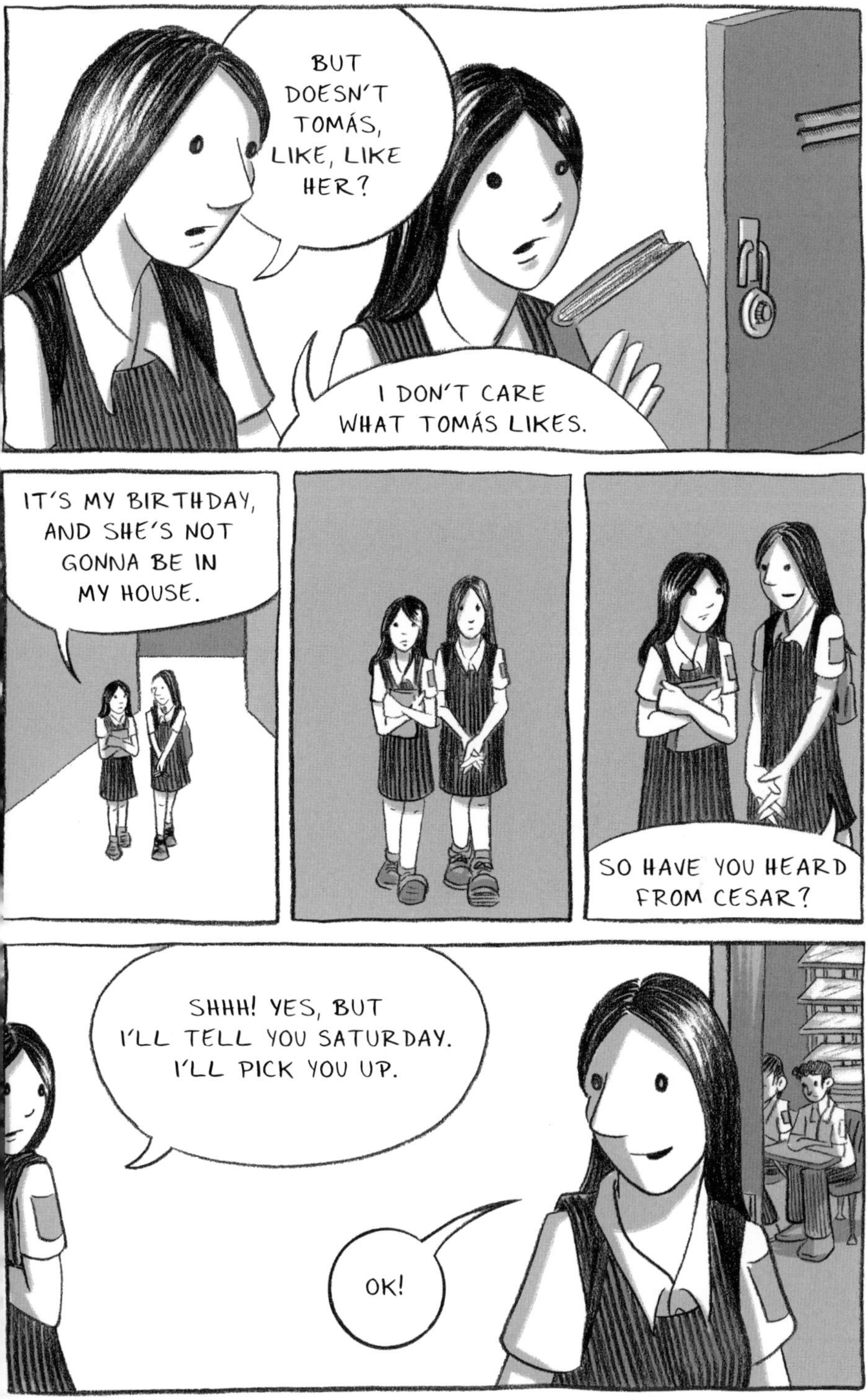
BUT DOESN'T TOMÁS, LIKE, LIKE HER?
I DON'T CARE WHAT TOMÁS LIKES.
IT'S MY BIRTHDAY, AND SHE'S NOT GONNA BE IN MY HOUSE.
SO HAVE YOU HEARD FROM CESAR?
SHHH! YES, BUT I'LL TELL YOU SATURDAY. I'LL PICK YOU UP.
OK!

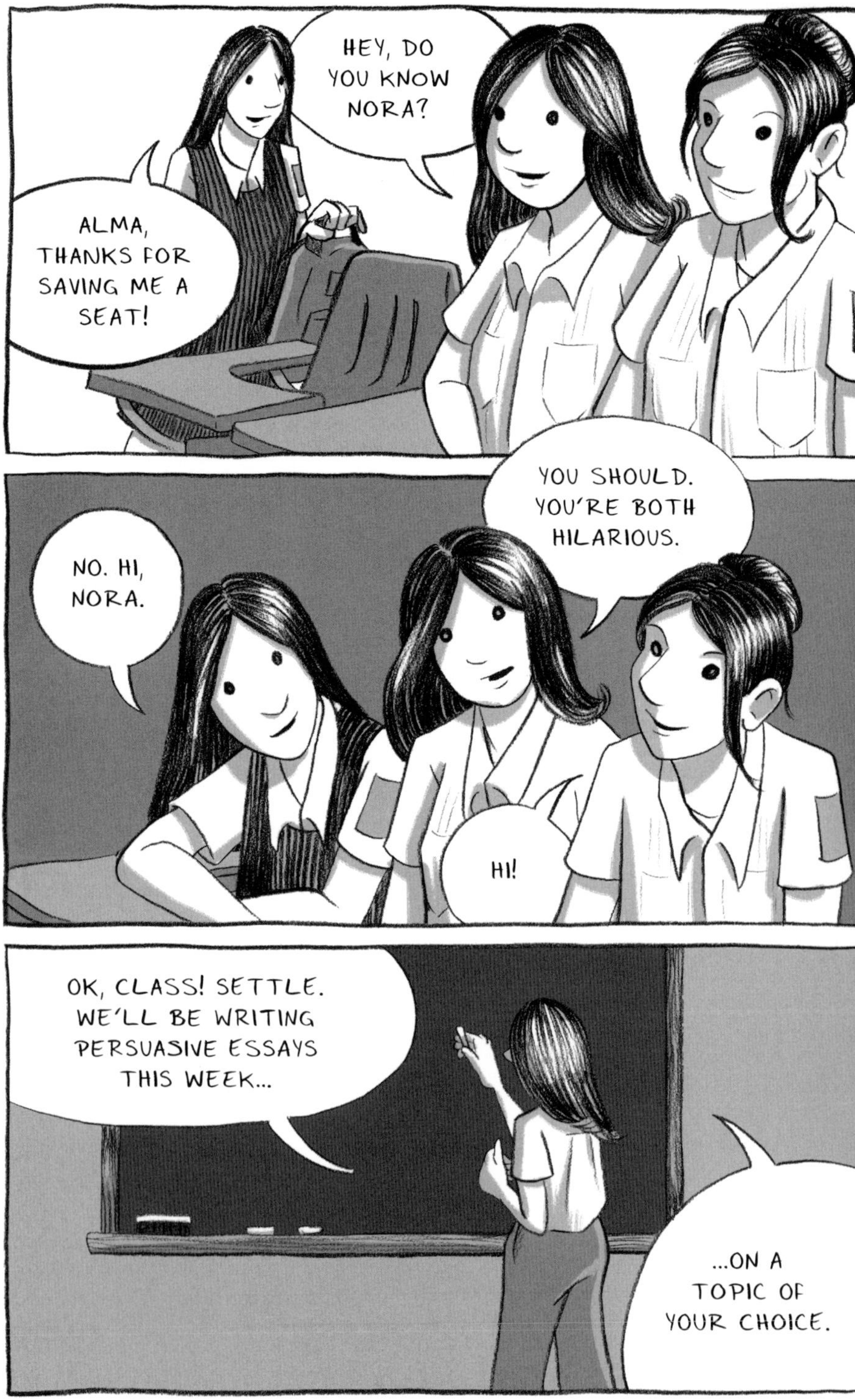
ALMA, THANKS FOR SAVING ME A SEAT!
HEY, DO YOU KNOW NORA?
NO. HI, NORA.
YOU SHOULD. YOU'RE BOTH HILARIOUS.
HI!
OK, CLASS! SETTLE. WE'LL BE WRITING PERSUASIVE ESSAYS THIS WEEK...
...ON A TOPIC OF YOUR CHOICE.

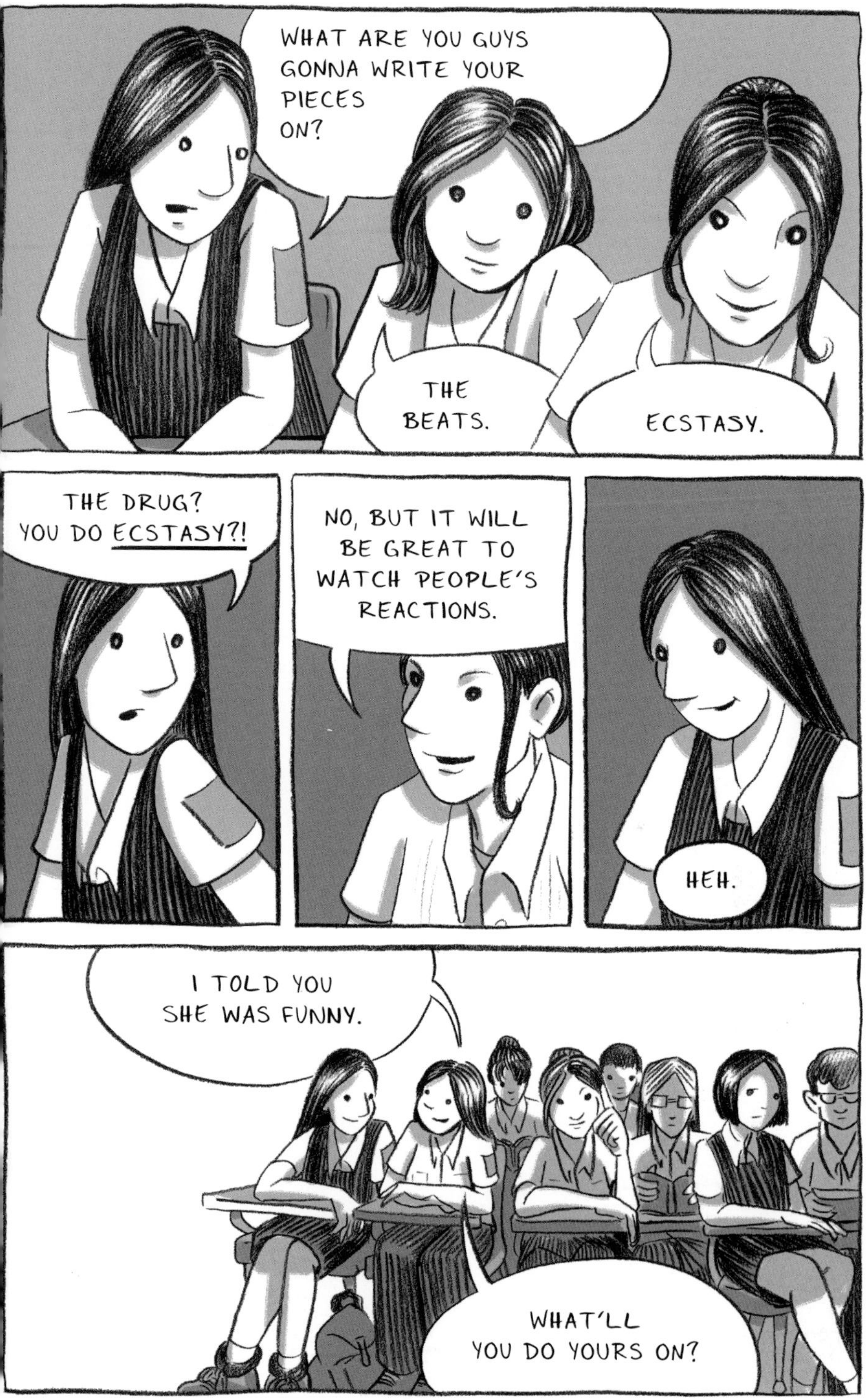
WHAT ARE YOU GUYS GONNA WRITE YOUR PIECES ON?
THE BEATS.
ECSTASY.
THE DRUG? YOU DO ECSTASY?!
NO, BUT IT WILL BE GREAT TO WATCH PEOPLE'S REACTIONS.
HEH.
I TOLD YOU SHE WAS FUNNY.
WHAT'LL YOU DO YOURS ON?

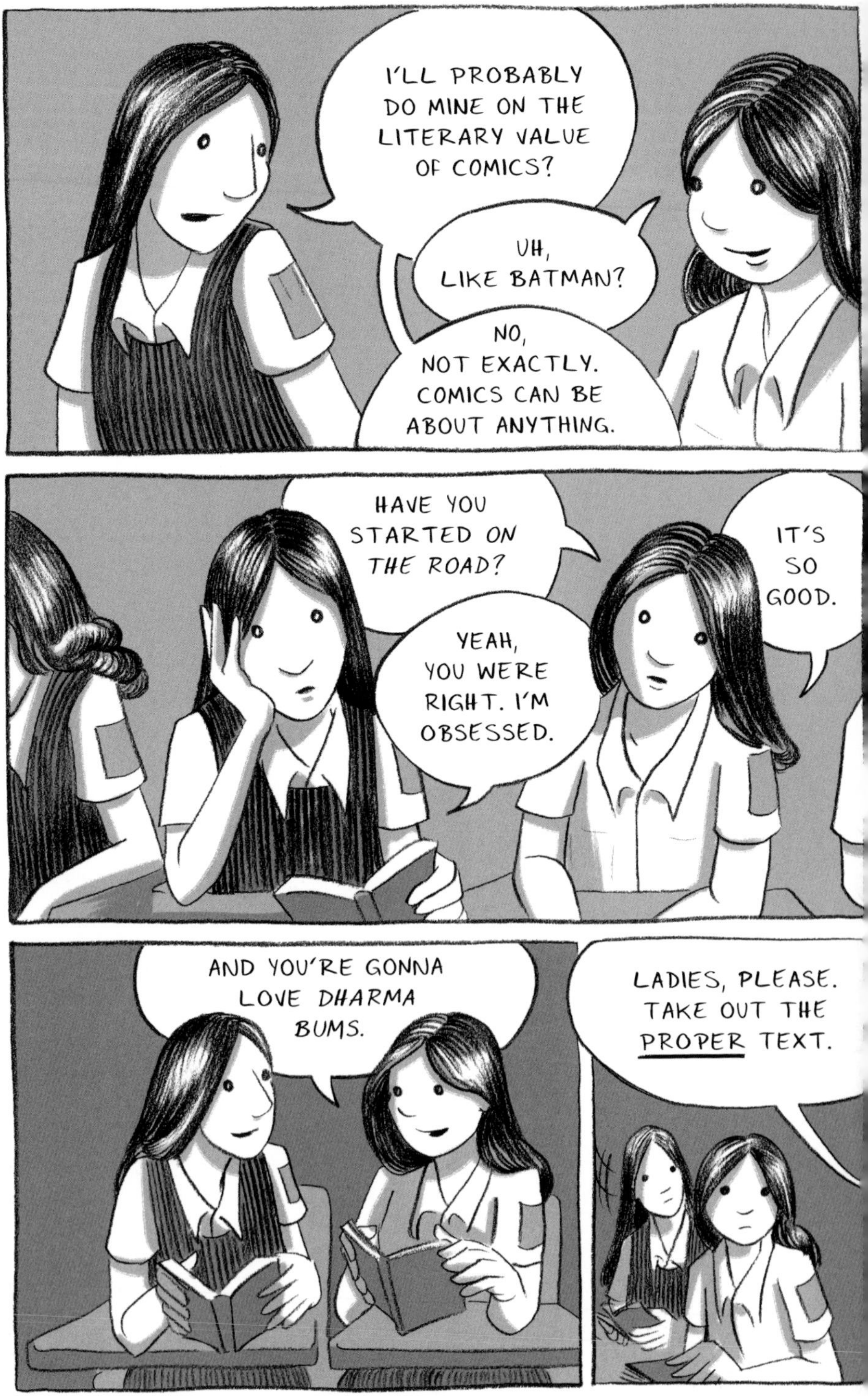
I'LL PROBABLY DO MINE ON THE LITERARY VALUE OF COMICS?
UH, LIKE BATMAN?
NO, NOT EXACTLY. COMICS CAN BE ABOUT ANYTHING.
HAVE YOU STARTED *ON THE ROAD*?
IT'S SO GOOD.
YEAH, YOU WERE RIGHT. I'M OBSESSED.
AND YOU'RE GONNA LOVE *DHARMA BUMS*.
LADIES, PLEASE. TAKE OUT THE PROPER TEXT.

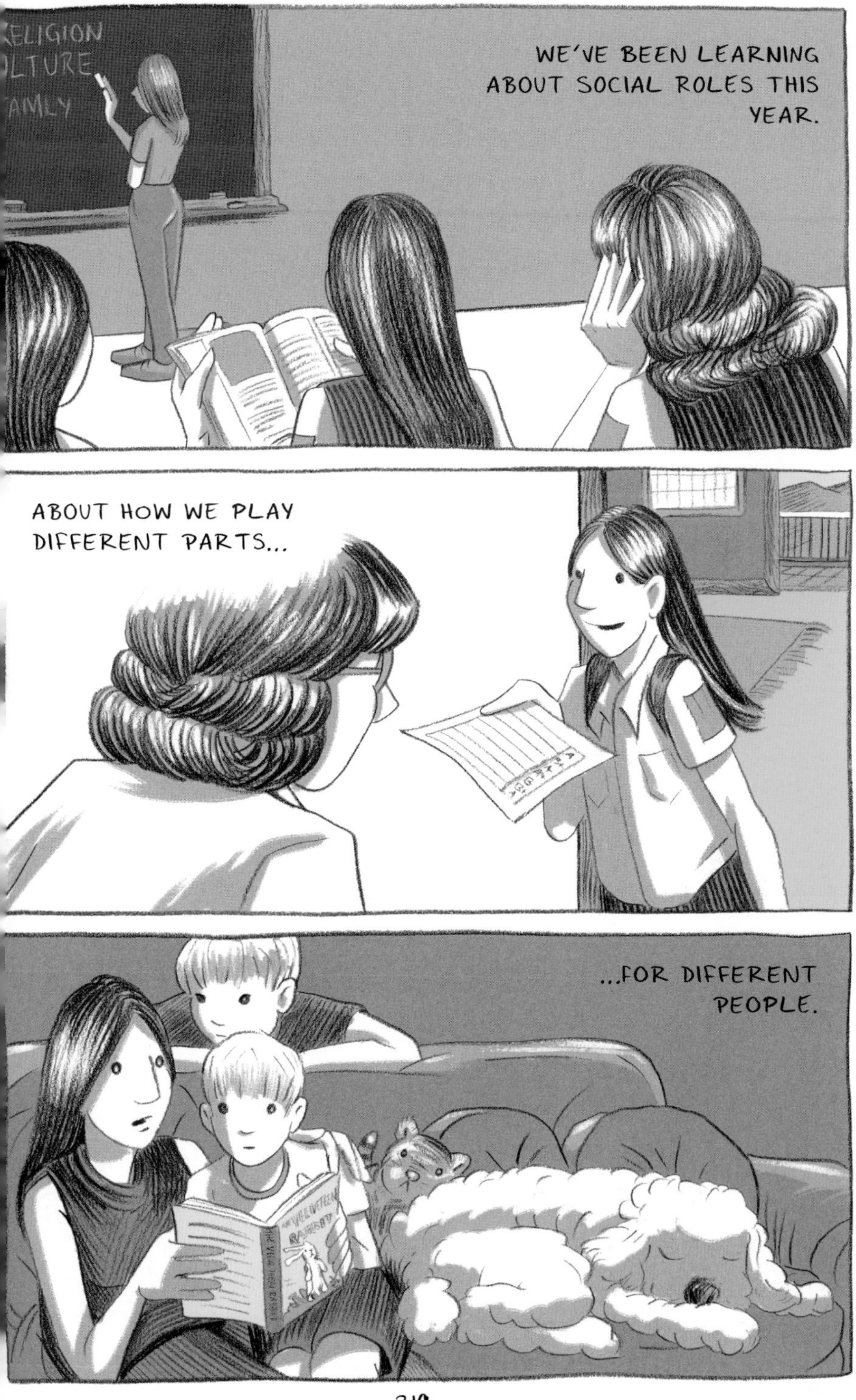
WE'VE BEEN LEARNING ABOUT SOCIAL ROLES THIS YEAR.
ABOUT HOW WE PLAY DIFFERENT PARTS...
...FOR DIFFERENT PEOPLE.

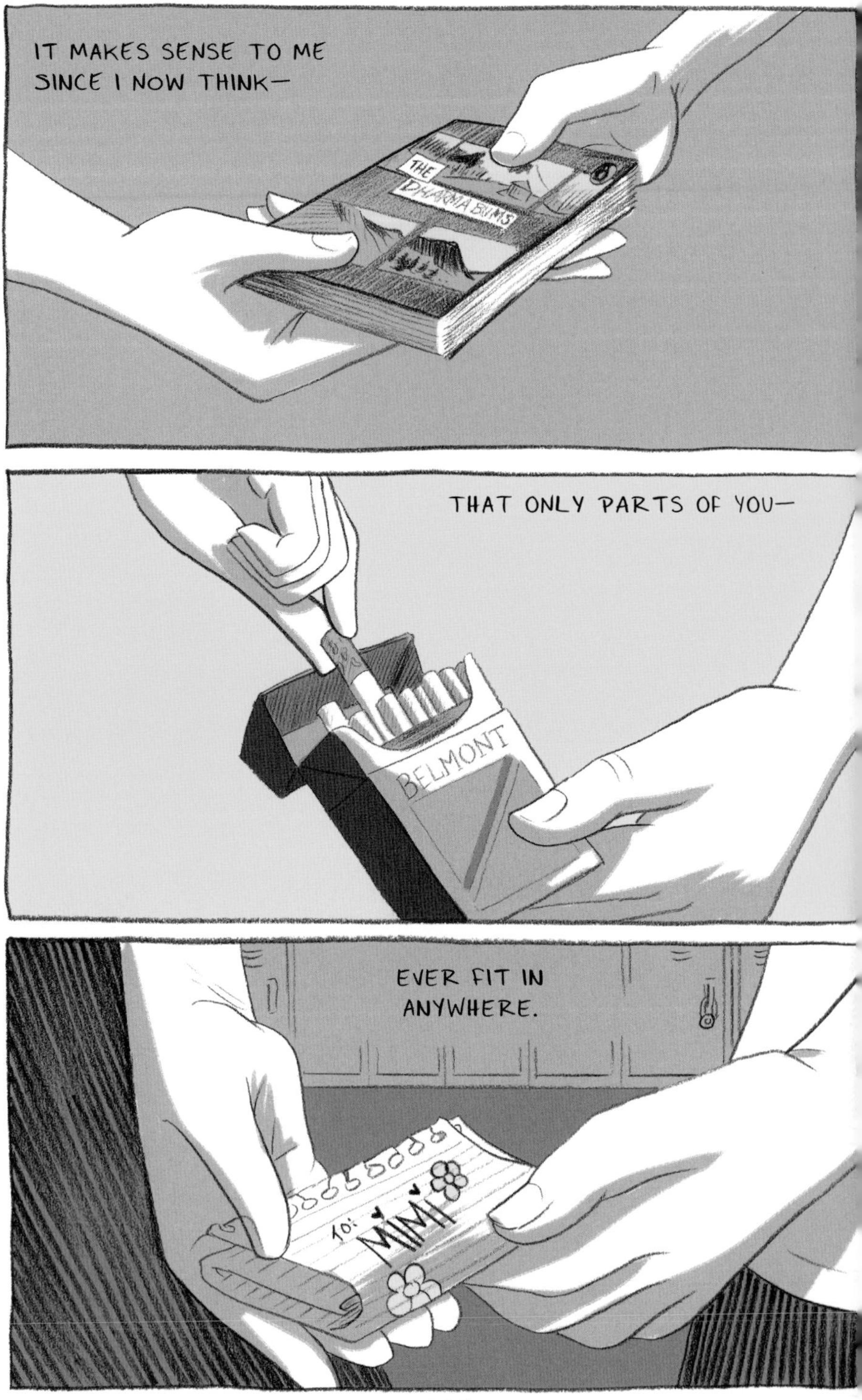
IT MAKES SENSE TO ME SINCE I NOW THINK—
THE DHARMA BUMS
THAT ONLY PARTS OF YOU—
BELMONT
EVER FIT IN ANYWHERE.
TO: MIMI

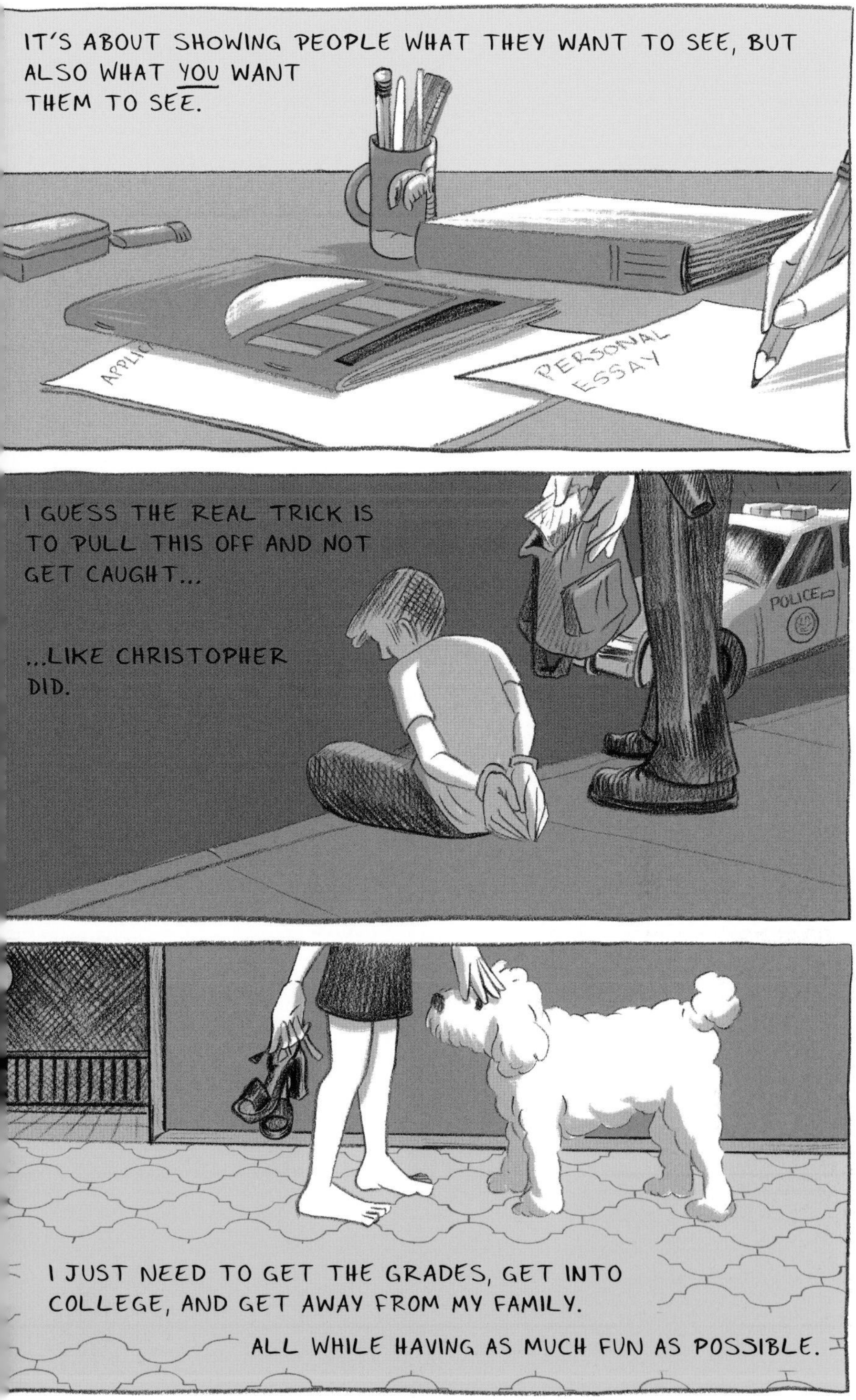
IT'S ABOUT SHOWING PEOPLE WHAT THEY WANT TO SEE, BUT ALSO WHAT YOU WANT THEM TO SEE.
APPLIC
PERSONAL ESSAY
I GUESS THE REAL TRICK IS TO PULL THIS OFF AND NOT GET CAUGHT...
...LIKE CHRISTOPHER DID.
POLICE
I JUST NEED TO GET THE GRADES, GET INTO COLLEGE, AND GET AWAY FROM MY FAMILY.
ALL WHILE HAVING AS MUCH FUN AS POSSIBLE.

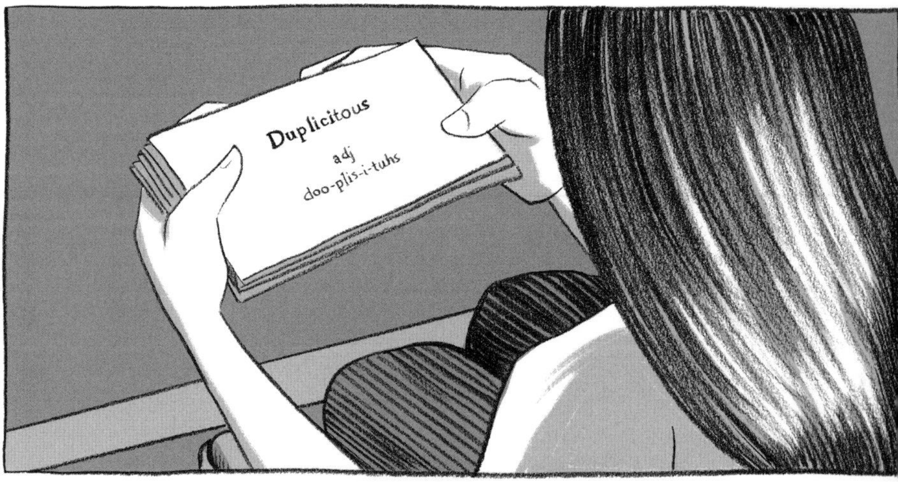
Duplicitous
adj
doo-plis-i-tuhs

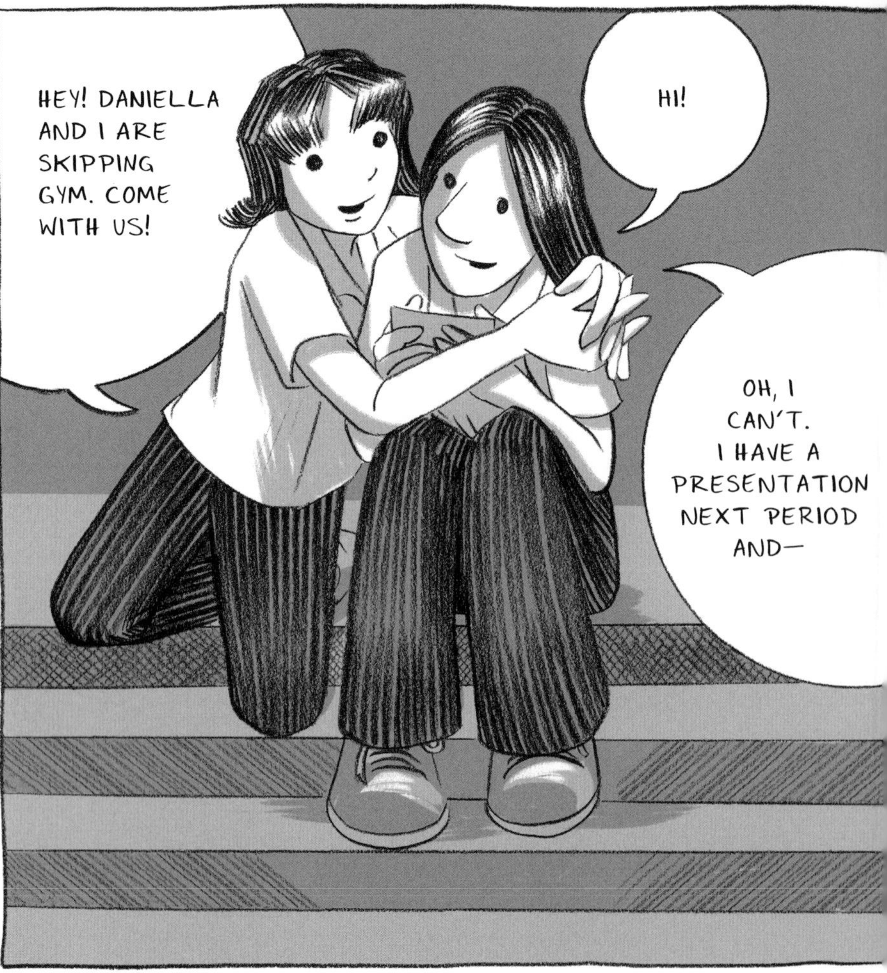
HEY! DANIELLA AND I ARE SKIPPING GYM. COME WITH US!
HI!
OH, I CAN'T. I HAVE A PRESENTATION NEXT PERIOD AND—

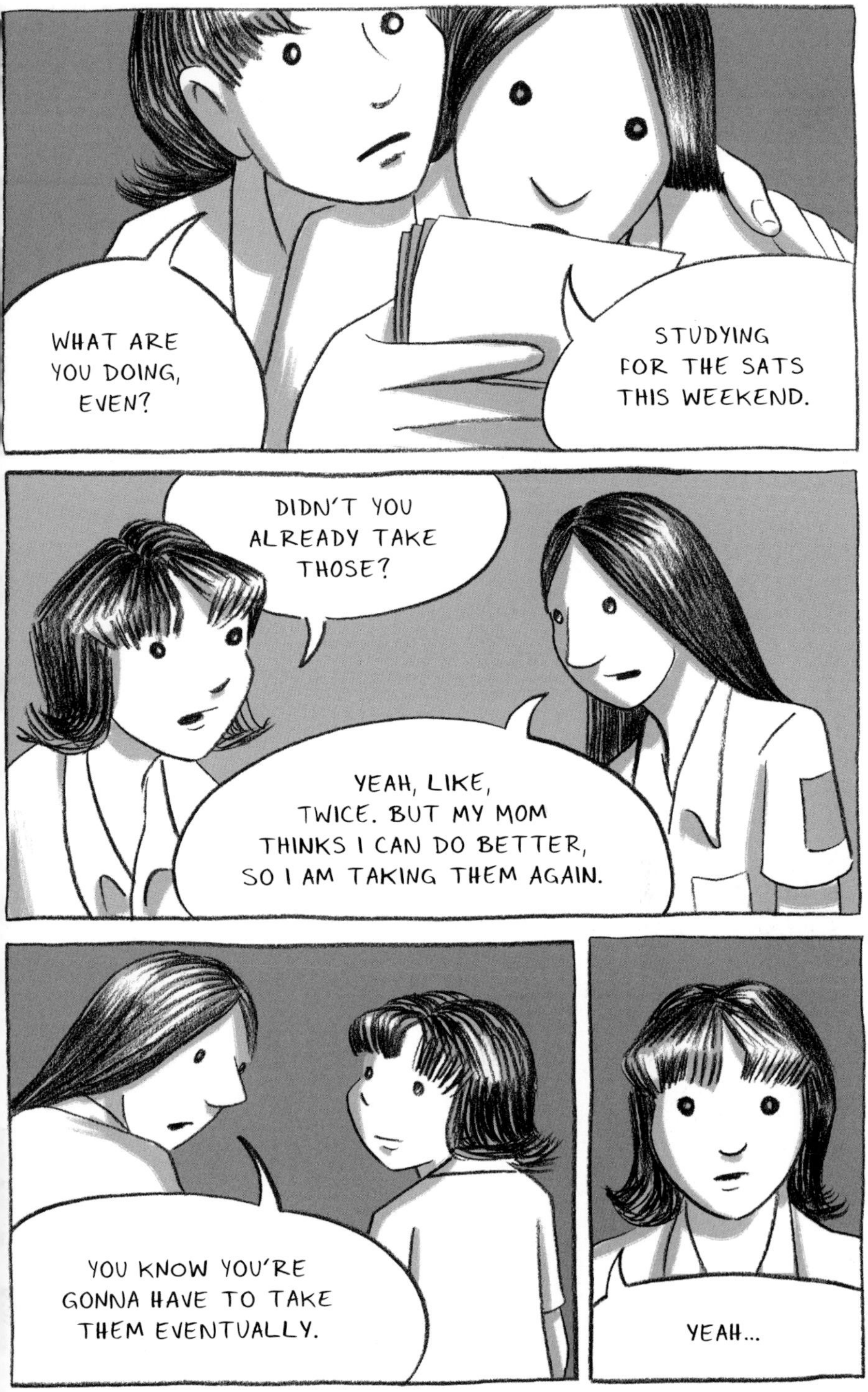
WHAT ARE YOU DOING, EVEN?
STUDYING FOR THE SATS THIS WEEKEND.
DIDN'T YOU ALREADY TAKE THOSE?
YEAH, LIKE, TWICE. BUT MY MOM THINKS I CAN DO BETTER, SO I AM TAKING THEM AGAIN.
YOU KNOW YOU'RE GONNA HAVE TO TAKE THEM EVENTUALLY.
YEAH...

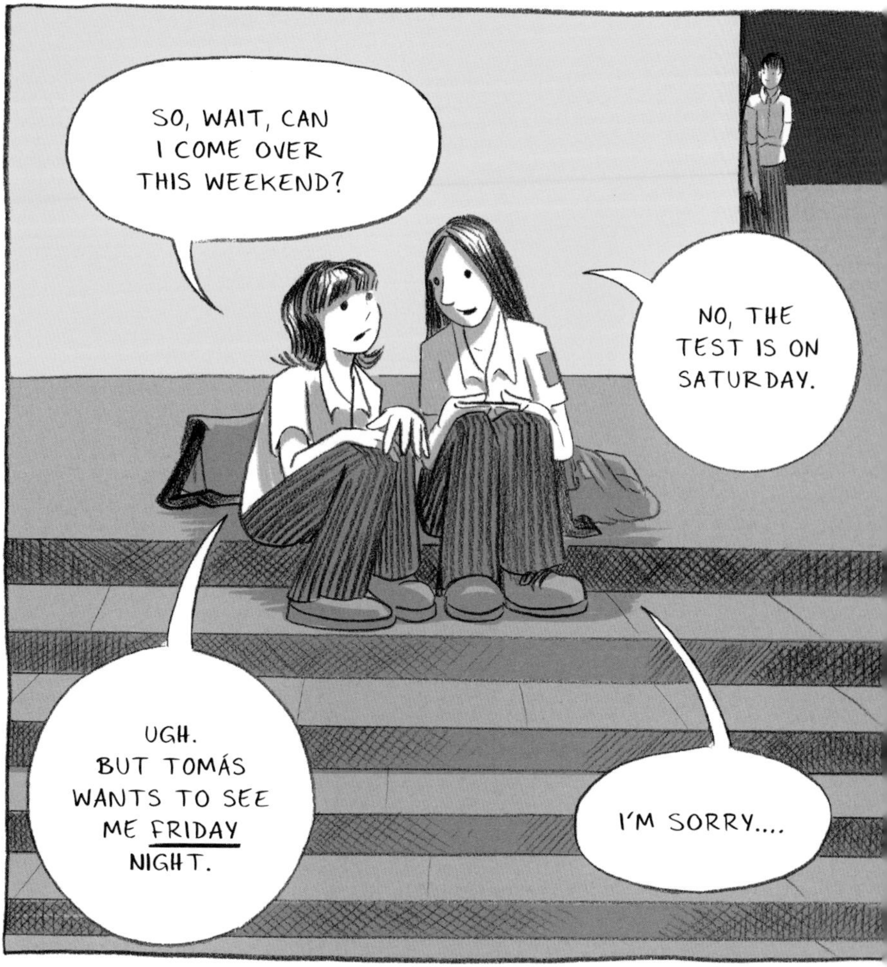
SO, WAIT, CAN I COME OVER THIS WEEKEND?
NO, THE TEST IS ON SATURDAY.
UGH. BUT TOMÁS WANTS TO SEE ME FRIDAY NIGHT.
I'M SORRY....

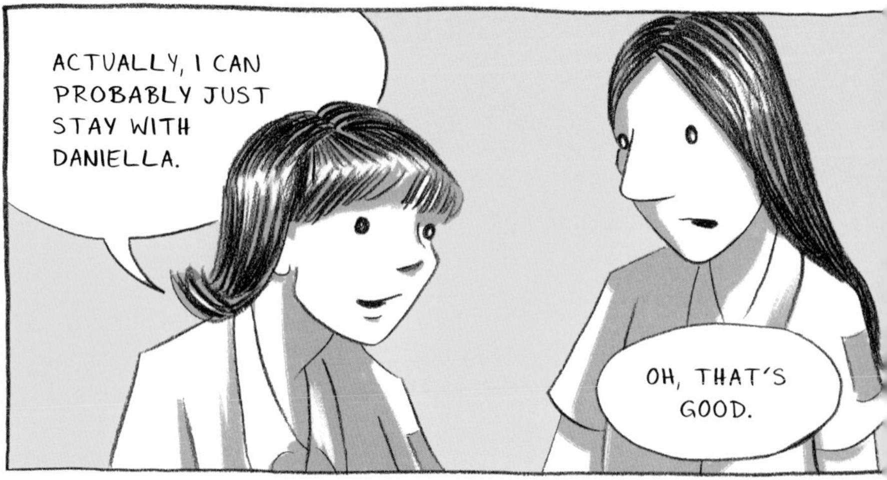
ACTUALLY, I CAN PROBABLY JUST STAY WITH DANIELLA.
OH, THAT'S GOOD.

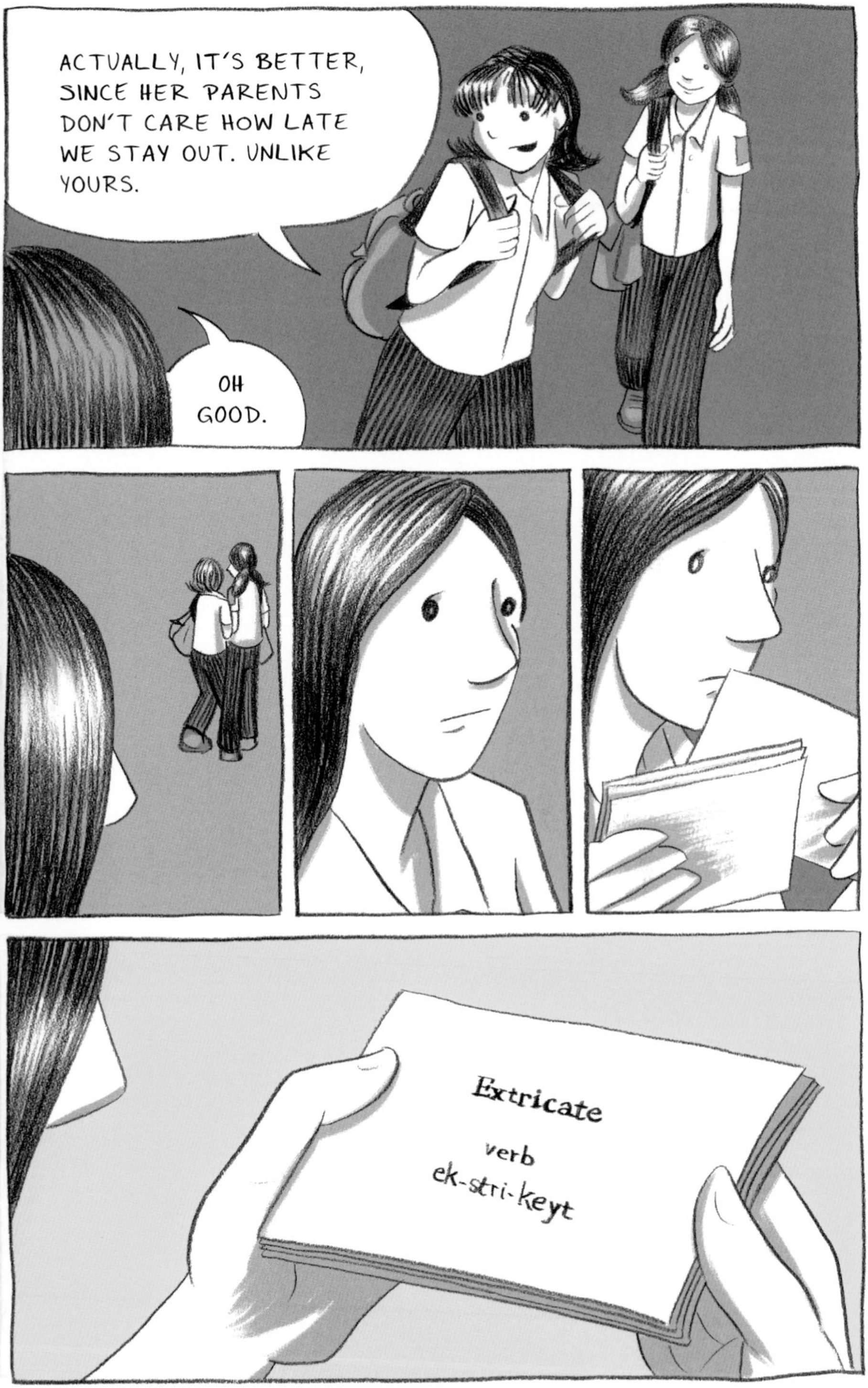
ACTUALLY, IT'S BETTER, SINCE HER PARENTS DON'T CARE HOW LATE WE STAY OUT. UNLIKE YOURS.
OH GOOD.
Extricate
verb
ek-stri-keyt

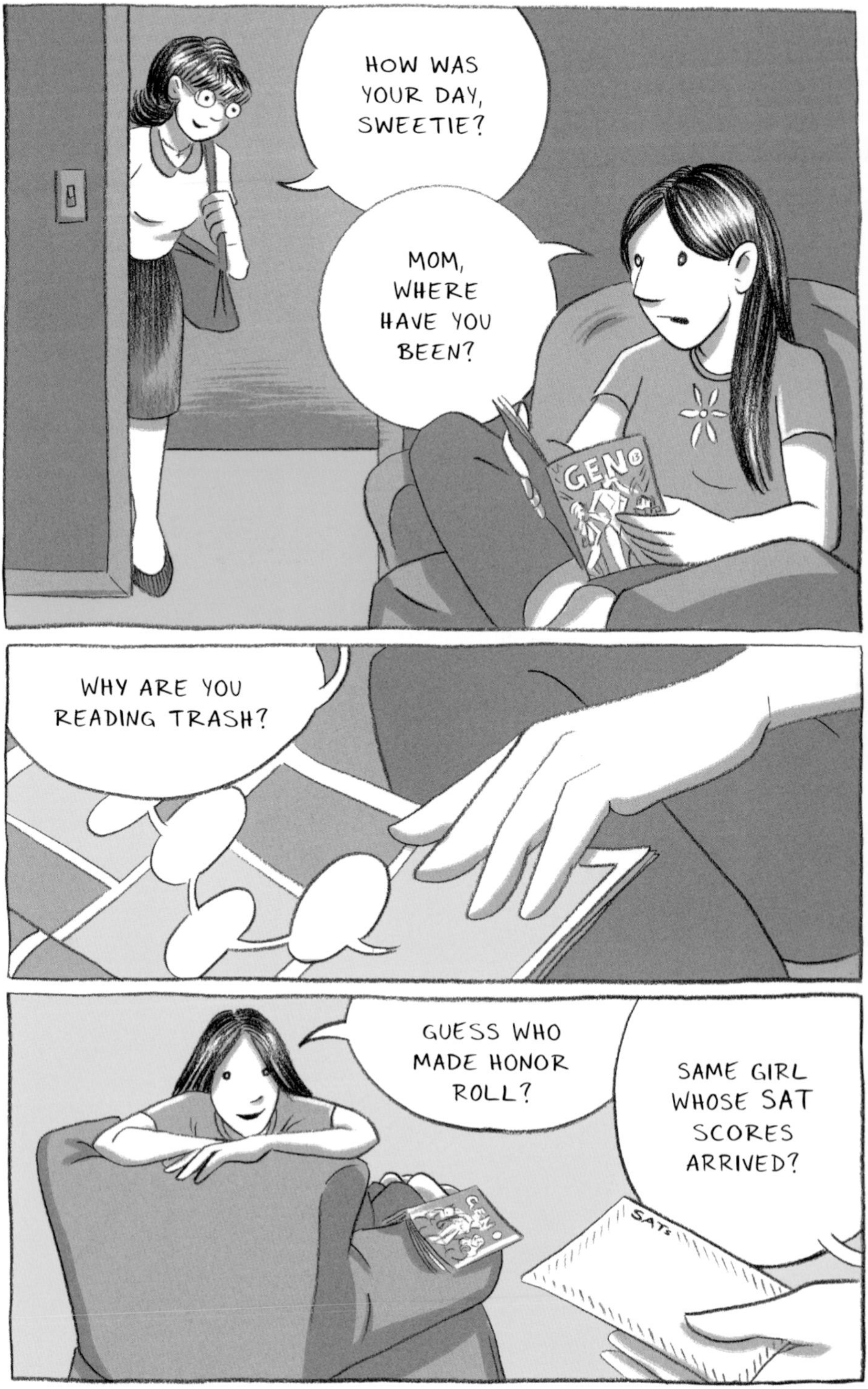
HOW WAS YOUR DAY, SWEETIE?
MOM, WHERE HAVE YOU BEEN?
GEN 13
WHY ARE YOU READING TRASH?
GUESS WHO MADE HONOR ROLL?
SAME GIRL WHOSE SAT SCORES ARRIVED?
SATs

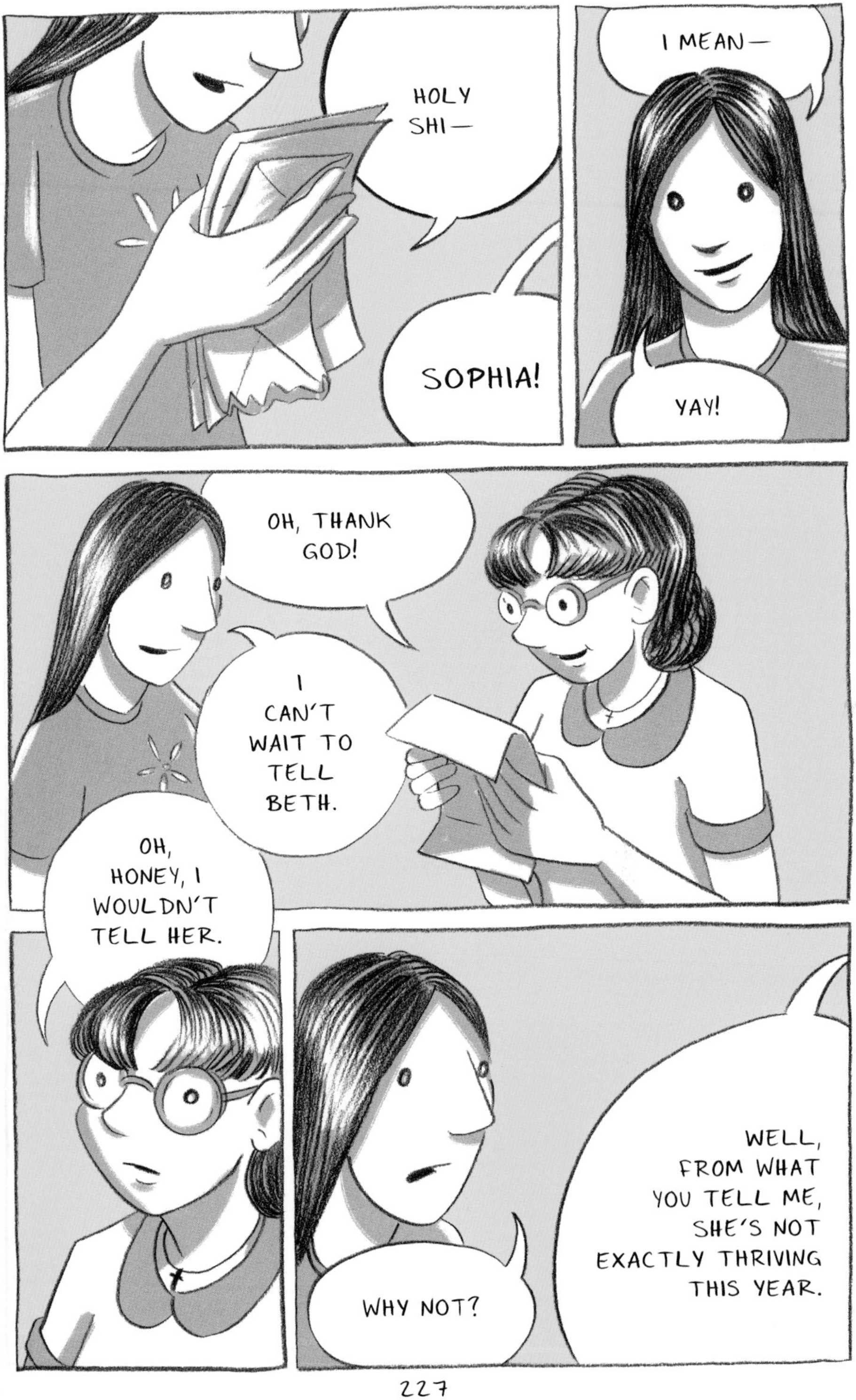
HOLY SHI—
SOPHIA!
I MEAN—
YAY!
OH, THANK GOD!
I CAN'T WAIT TO TELL BETH.
OH, HONEY, I WOULDN'T TELL HER.
WHY NOT?
WELL, FROM WHAT YOU TELL ME, SHE'S NOT EXACTLY THRIVING THIS YEAR.

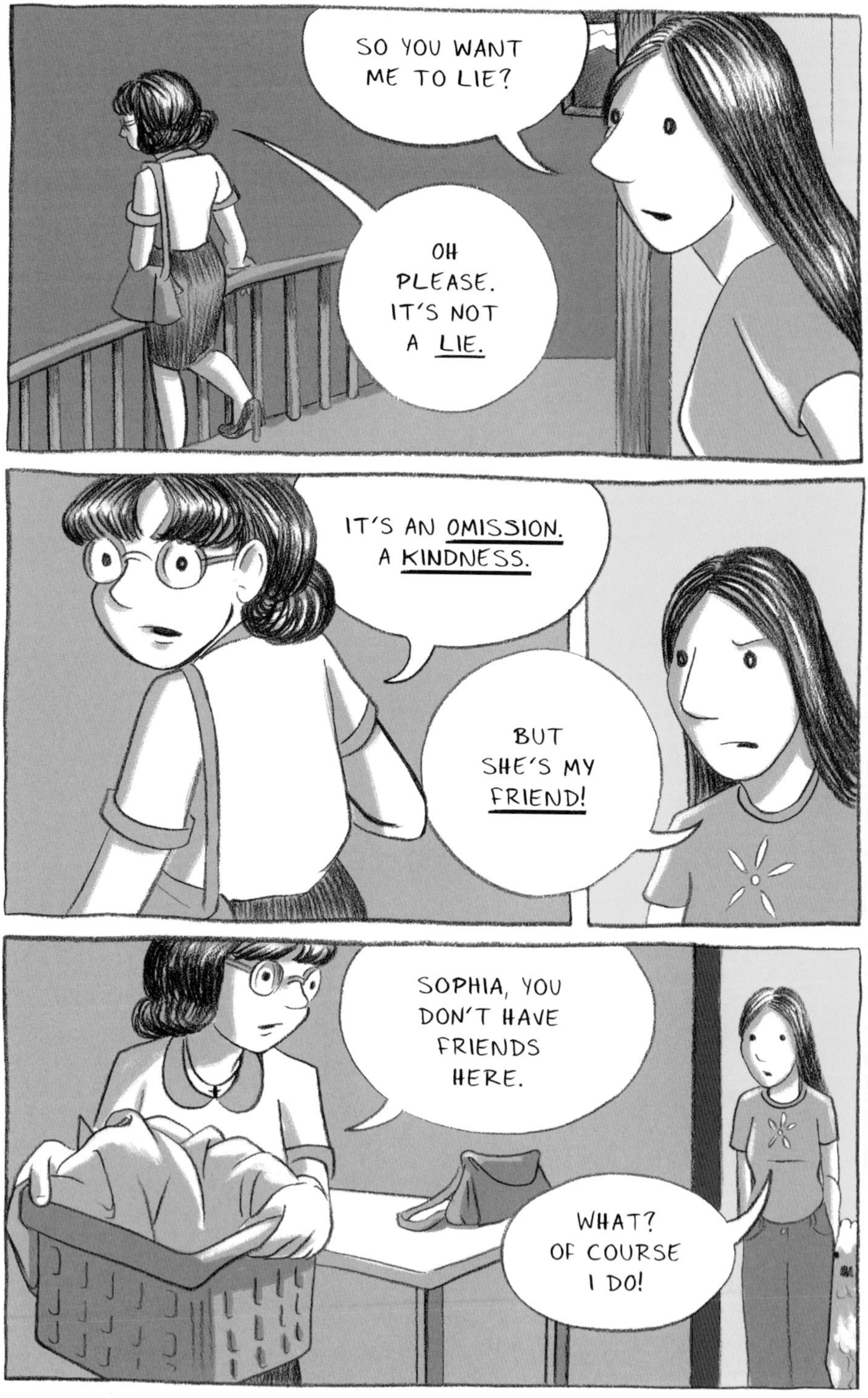
SO YOU WANT ME TO LIE?
OH PLEASE. IT'S NOT A LIE.
IT'S AN OMISSION. A KINDNESS.
BUT SHE'S MY FRIEND!
SOPHIA, YOU DON'T HAVE FRIENDS HERE.
WHAT? OF COURSE I DO!

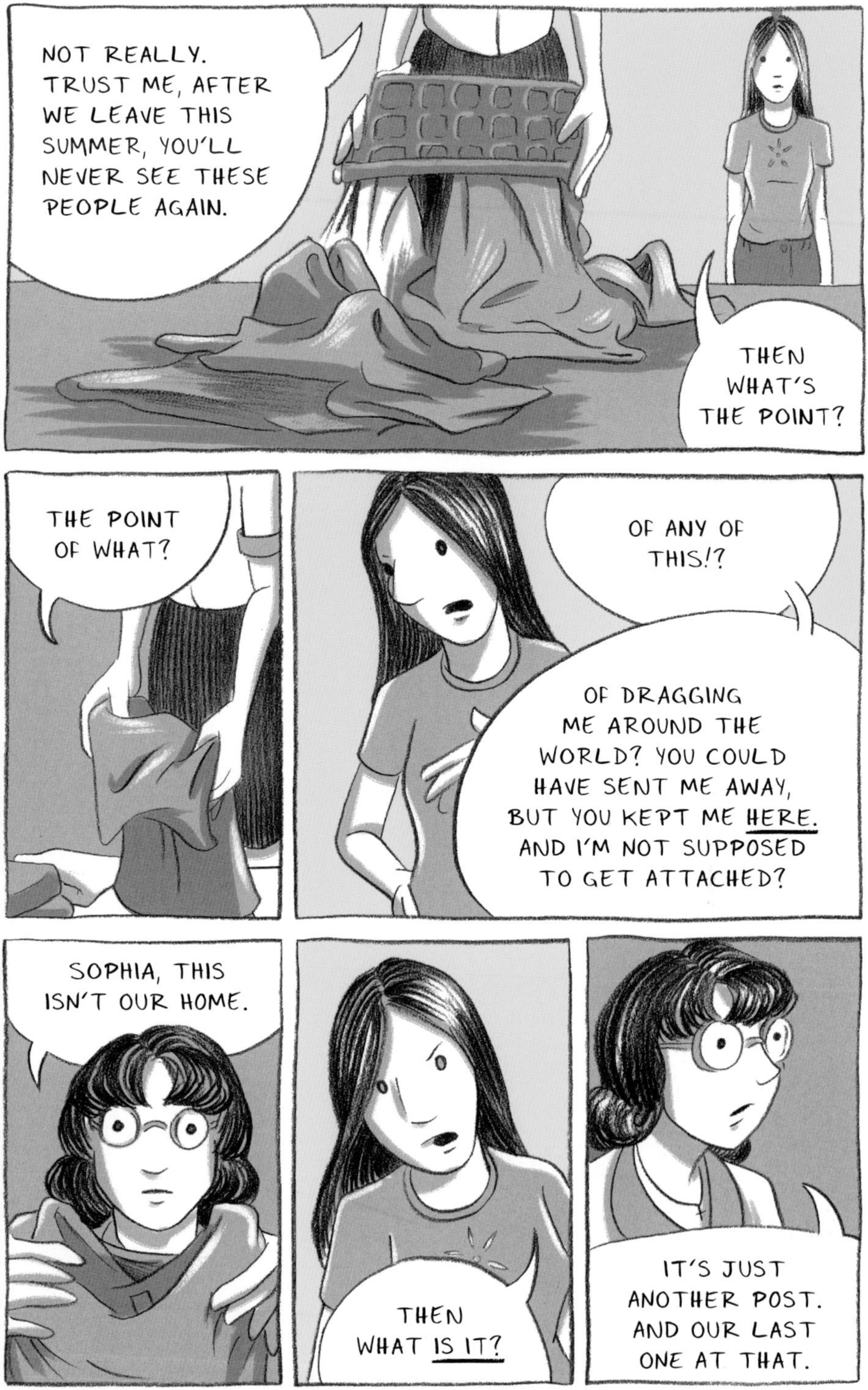
NOT REALLY. TRUST ME, AFTER WE LEAVE THIS SUMMER, YOU'LL NEVER SEE THESE PEOPLE AGAIN.
THEN WHAT'S THE POINT?
THE POINT OF WHAT?
OF ANY OF THIS!?
OF DRAGGING ME AROUND THE WORLD? YOU COULD HAVE SENT ME AWAY, BUT YOU KEPT ME HERE. AND I'M NOT SUPPOSED TO GET ATTACHED?
SOPHIA, THIS ISN'T OUR HOME.
THEN WHAT IS IT?
IT'S JUST ANOTHER POST. AND OUR LAST ONE AT THAT.

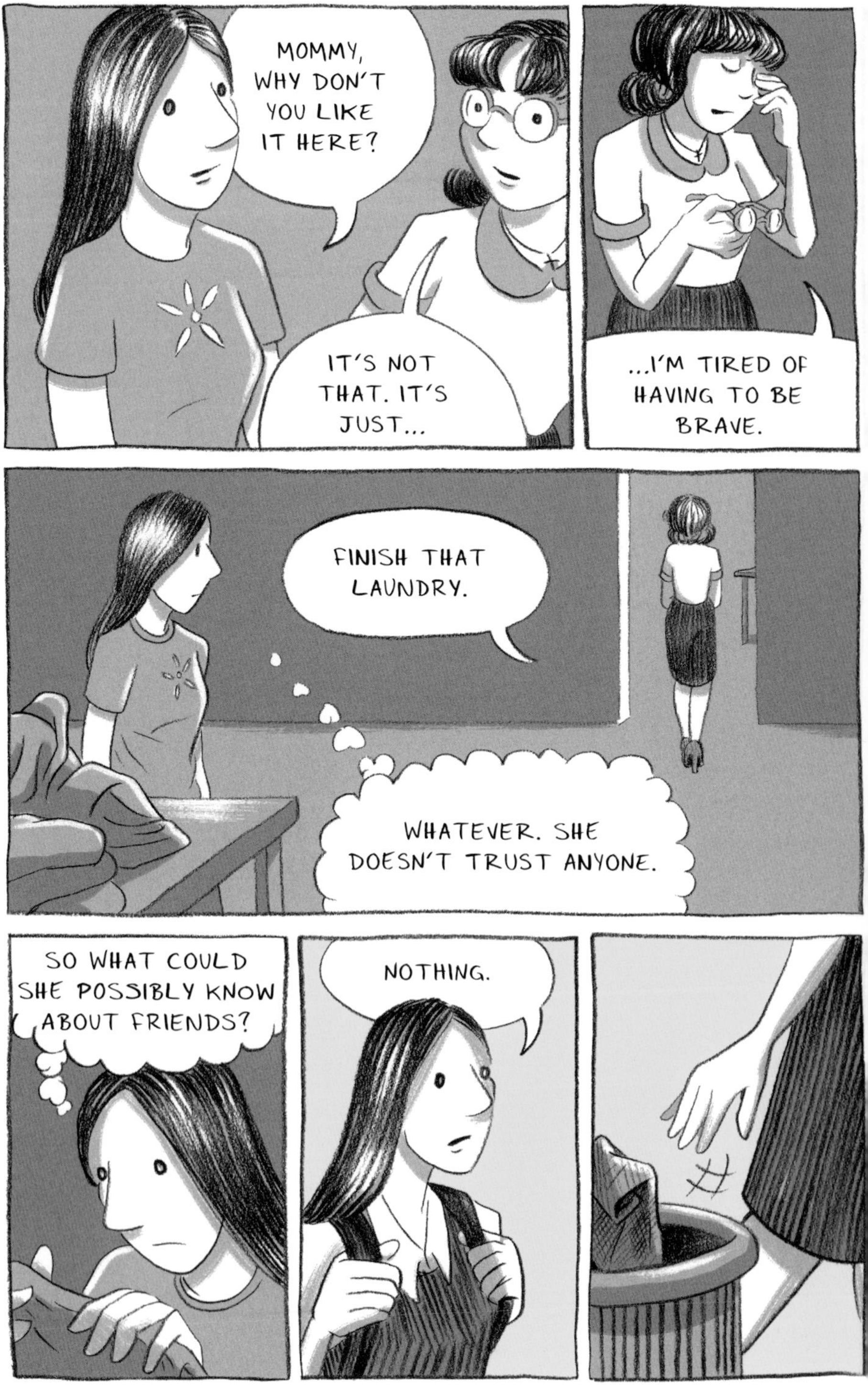
MOMMY, WHY DON'T YOU LIKE IT HERE?
IT'S NOT THAT. IT'S JUST...
...I'M TIRED OF HAVING TO BE BRAVE.
FINISH THAT LAUNDRY.
WHATEVER. SHE DOESN'T TRUST ANYONE.
SO WHAT COULD SHE POSSIBLY KNOW ABOUT FRIENDS?
NOTHING.

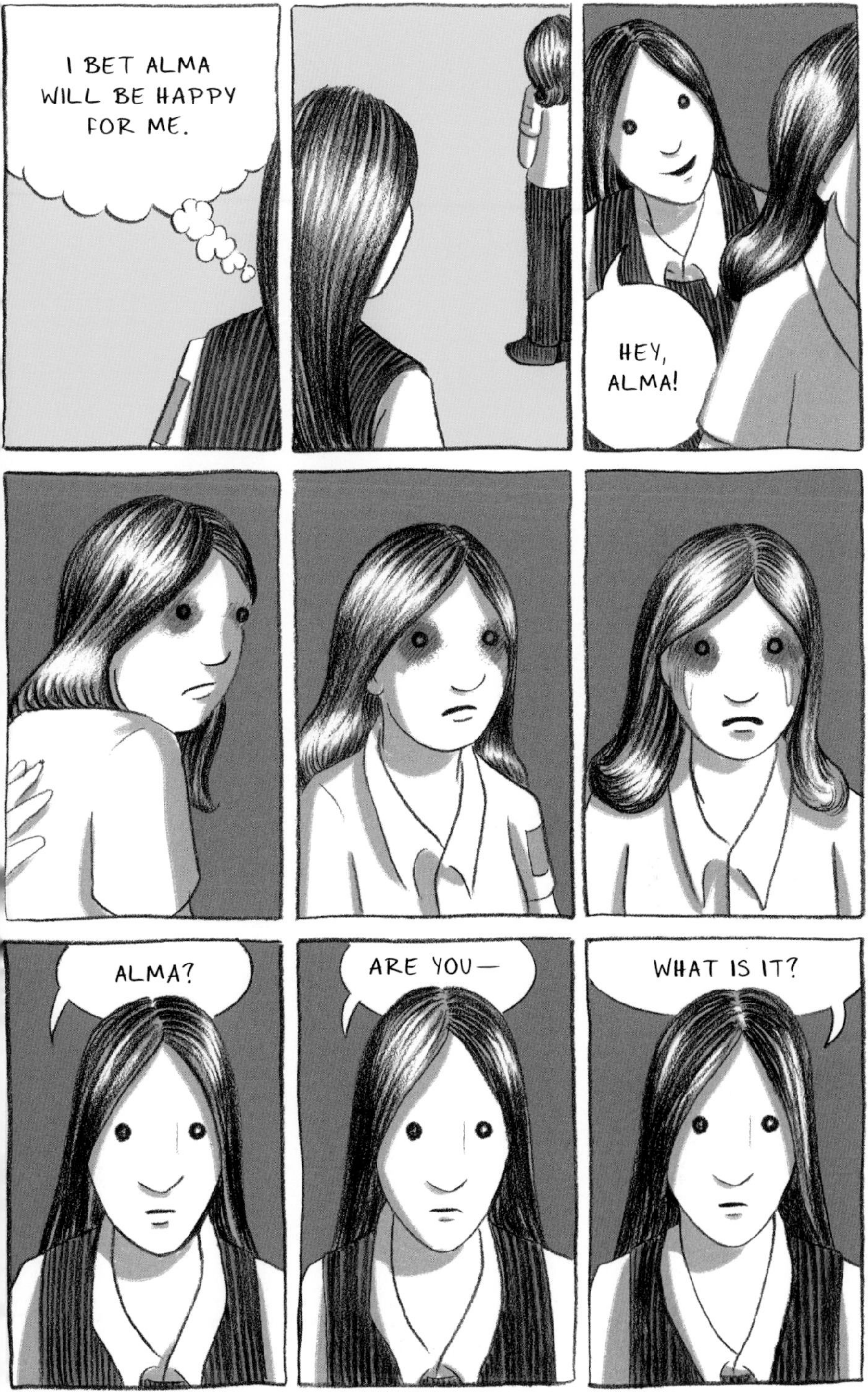
I BET ALMA WILL BE HAPPY FOR ME.
HEY, ALMA!
ALMA?
ARE YOU—
WHAT IS IT?

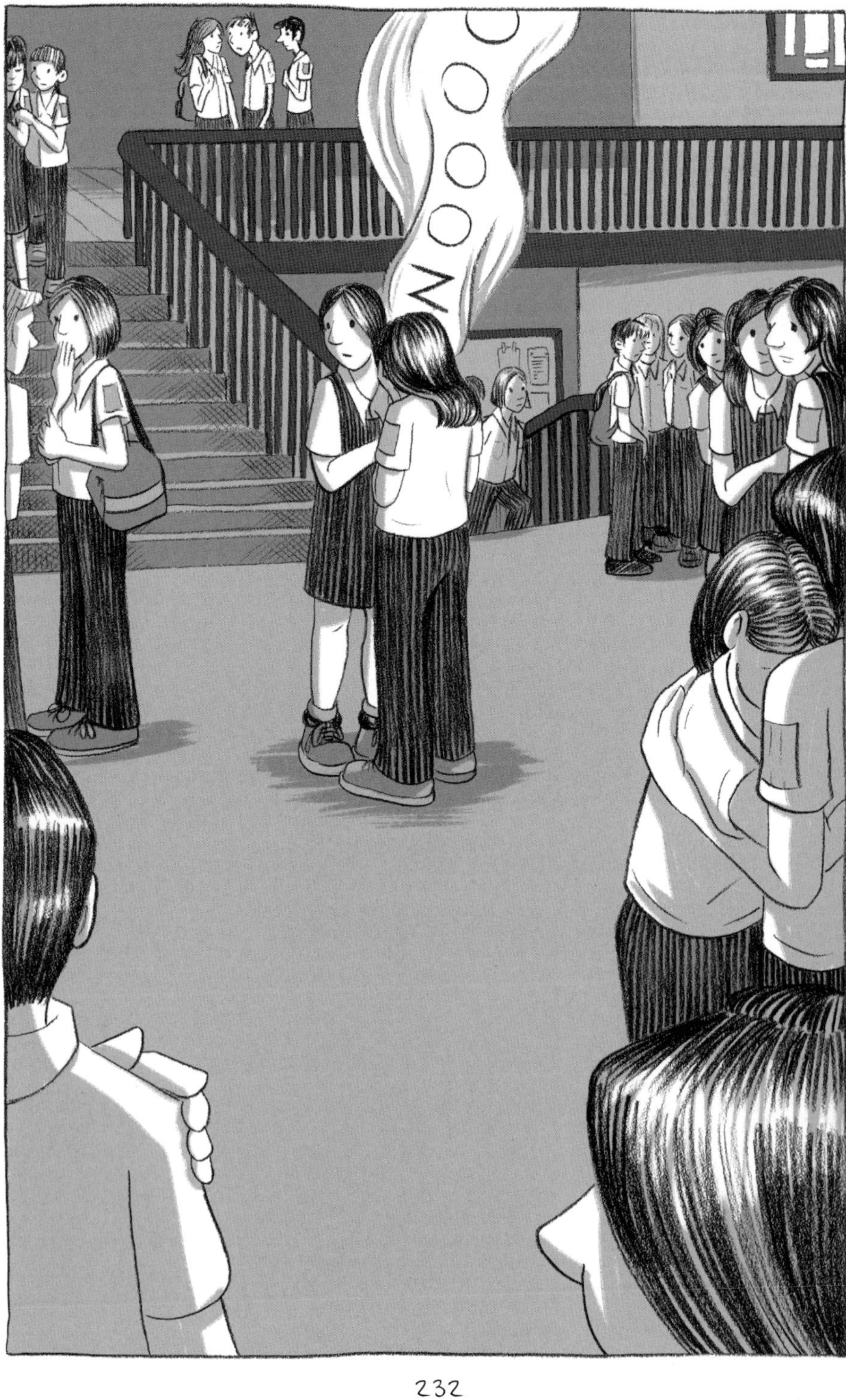
NOOOOO

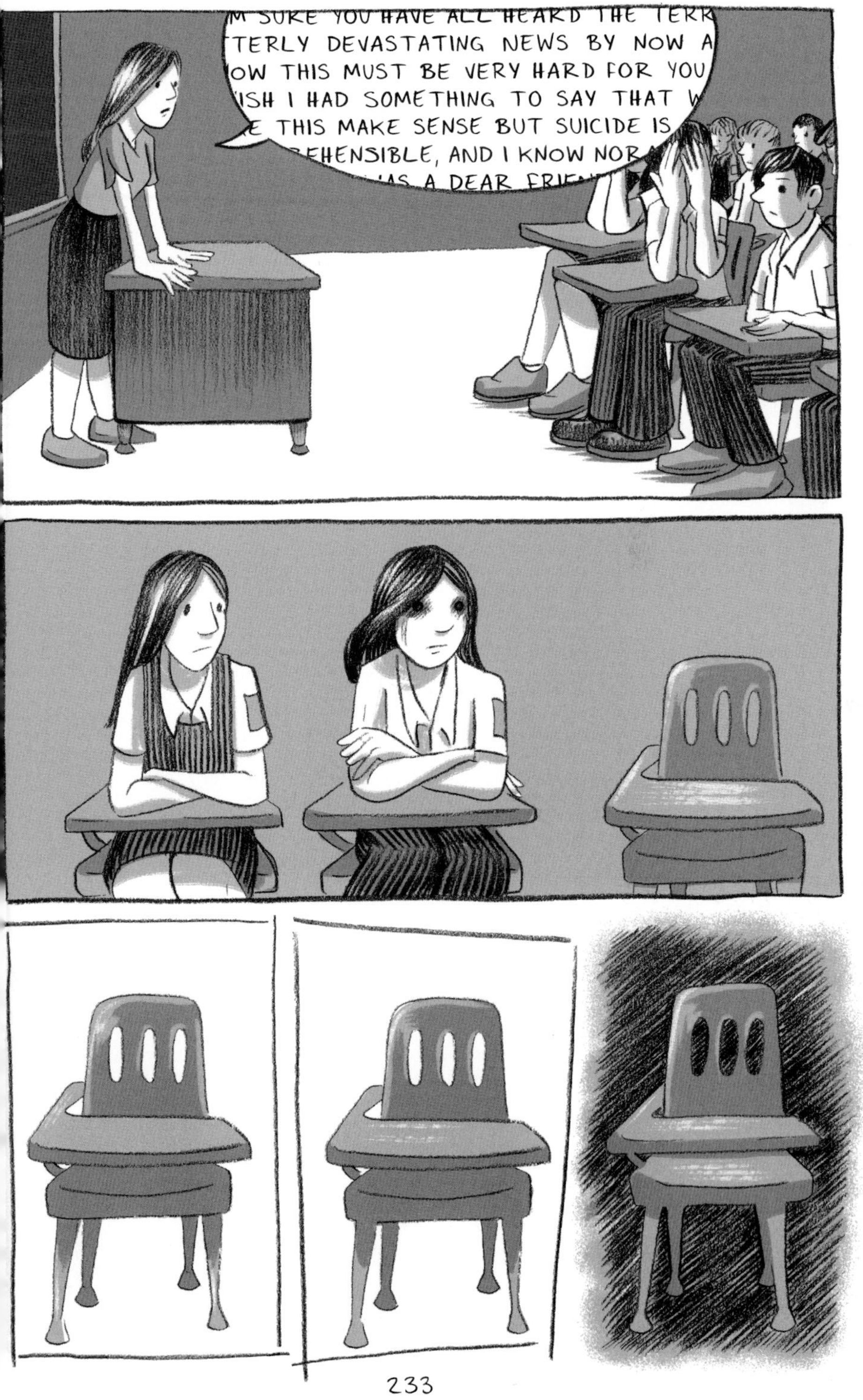
M SURE YOU HAVE ALL HEARD THE TERR
TTERLY DEVASTATING NEWS BY NOW A
OW THIS MUST BE VERY HARD FOR YOU
ISH I HAD SOMETHING TO SAY THAT W
E THIS MAKE SENSE BUT SUICIDE IS
REHENSIBLE, AND I KNOW NOR
AS A DEAR FRIEN

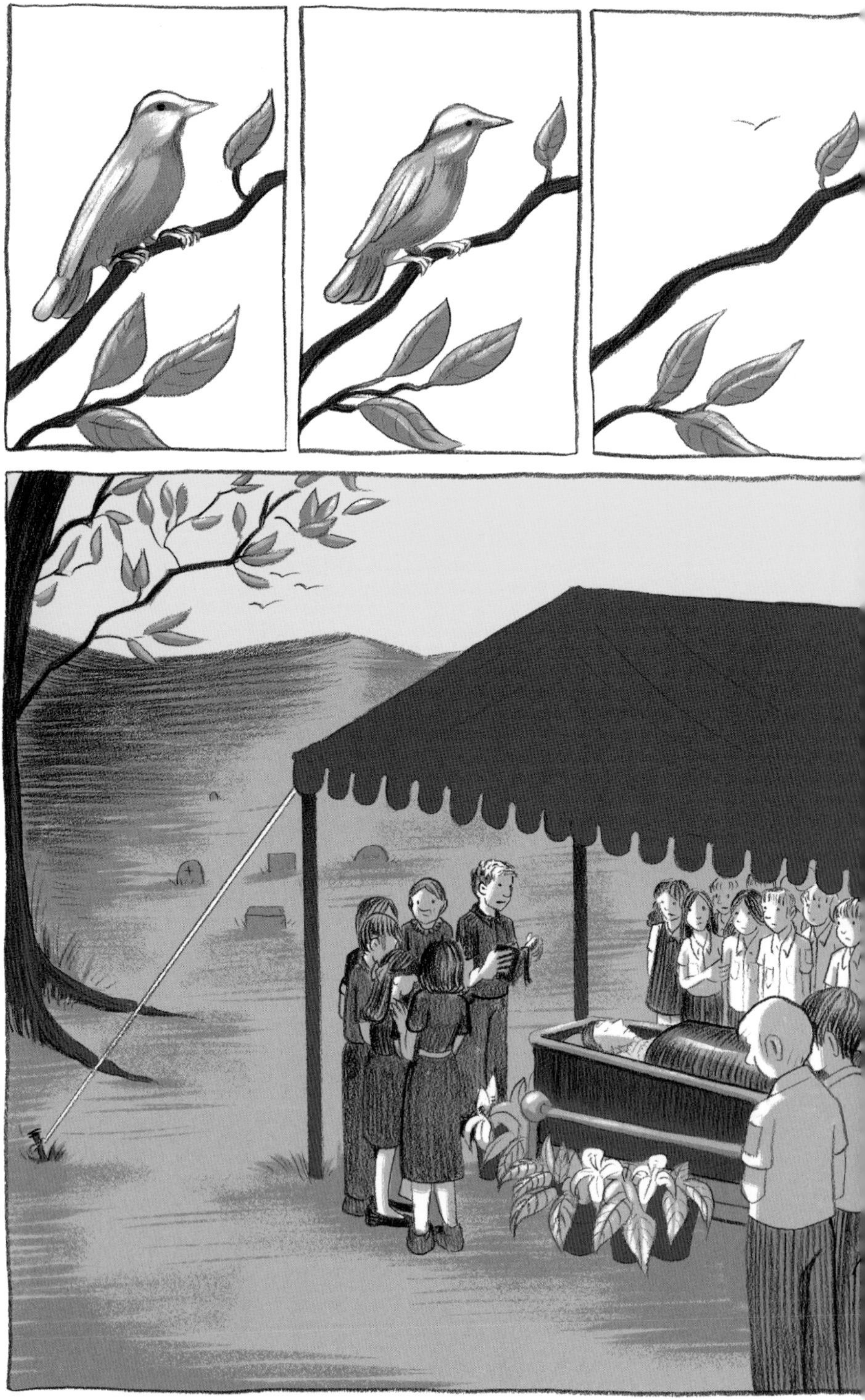

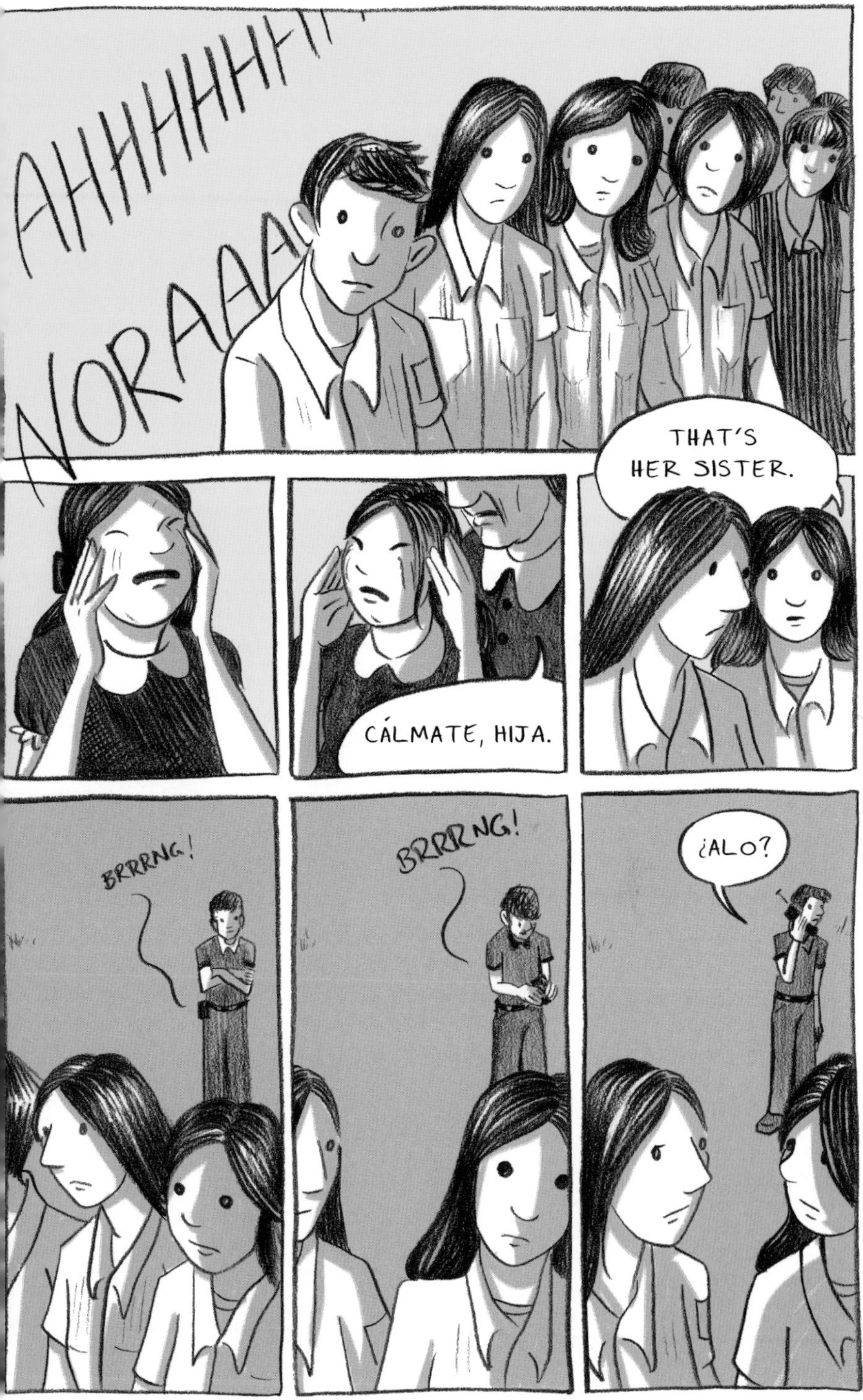
AHHHHHH!
NORAAA
THAT'S HER SISTER.
CÁLMATE, HIJA.
BRRRNG!
BRRRNG!
¿ALO?

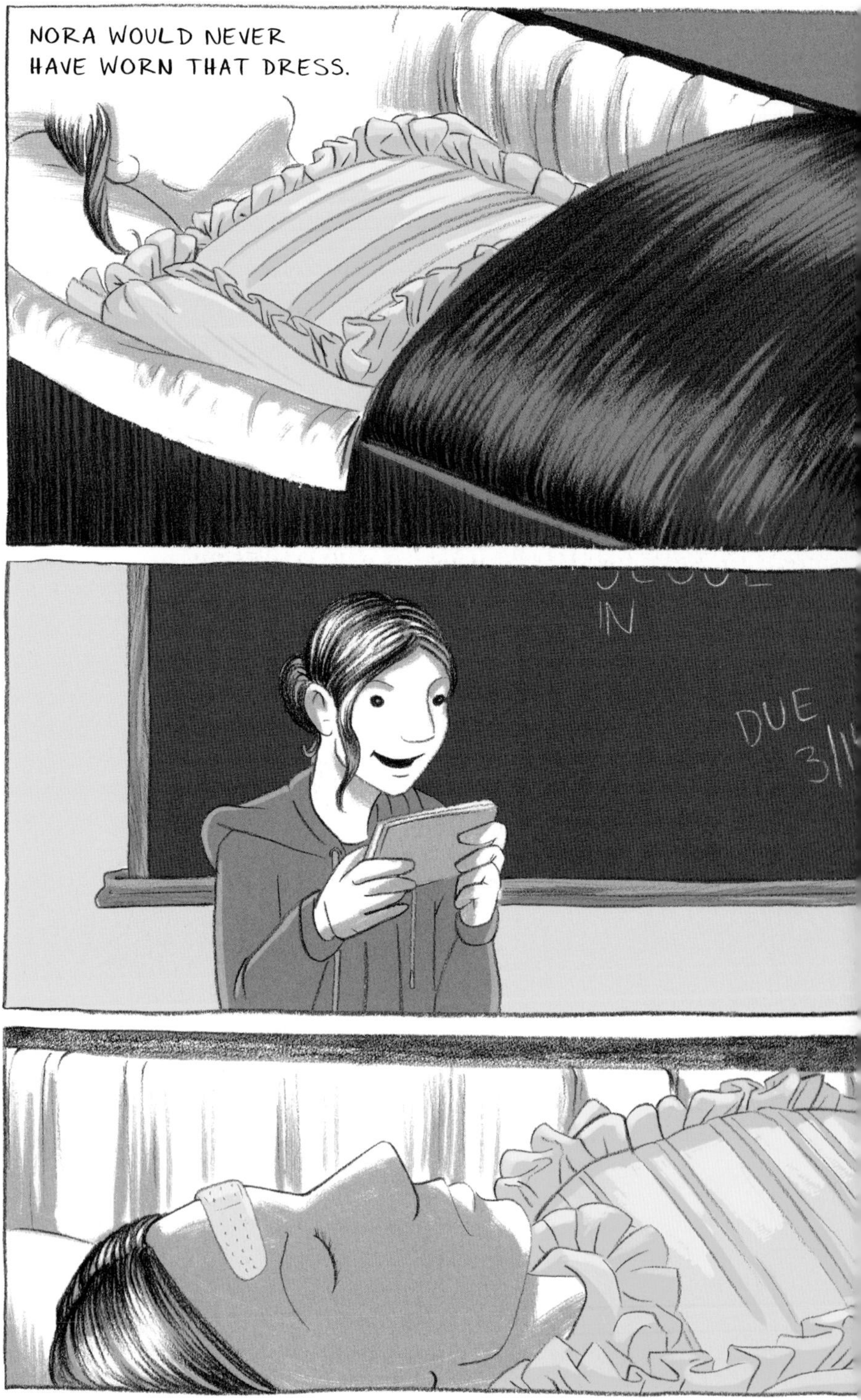
NORA WOULD NEVER
HAVE WORN THAT DRESS.
IN
DUE

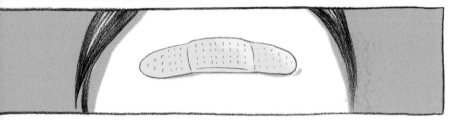

ALMA...

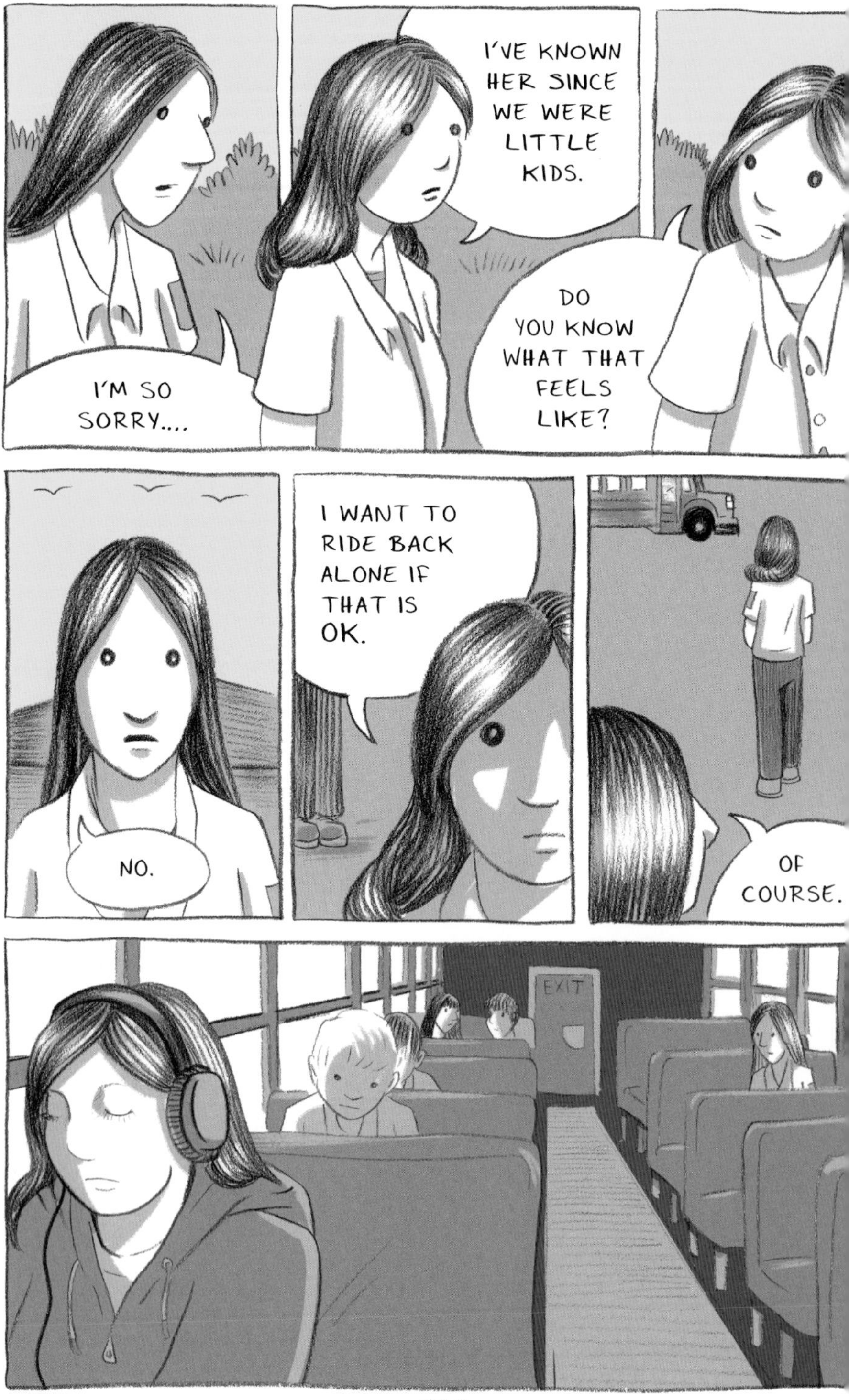
I'M SO SORRY....
I'VE KNOWN HER SINCE WE WERE LITTLE KIDS.
DO YOU KNOW WHAT THAT FEELS LIKE?
NO.
I WANT TO RIDE BACK ALONE IF THAT IS OK.
OF COURSE.
EXIT

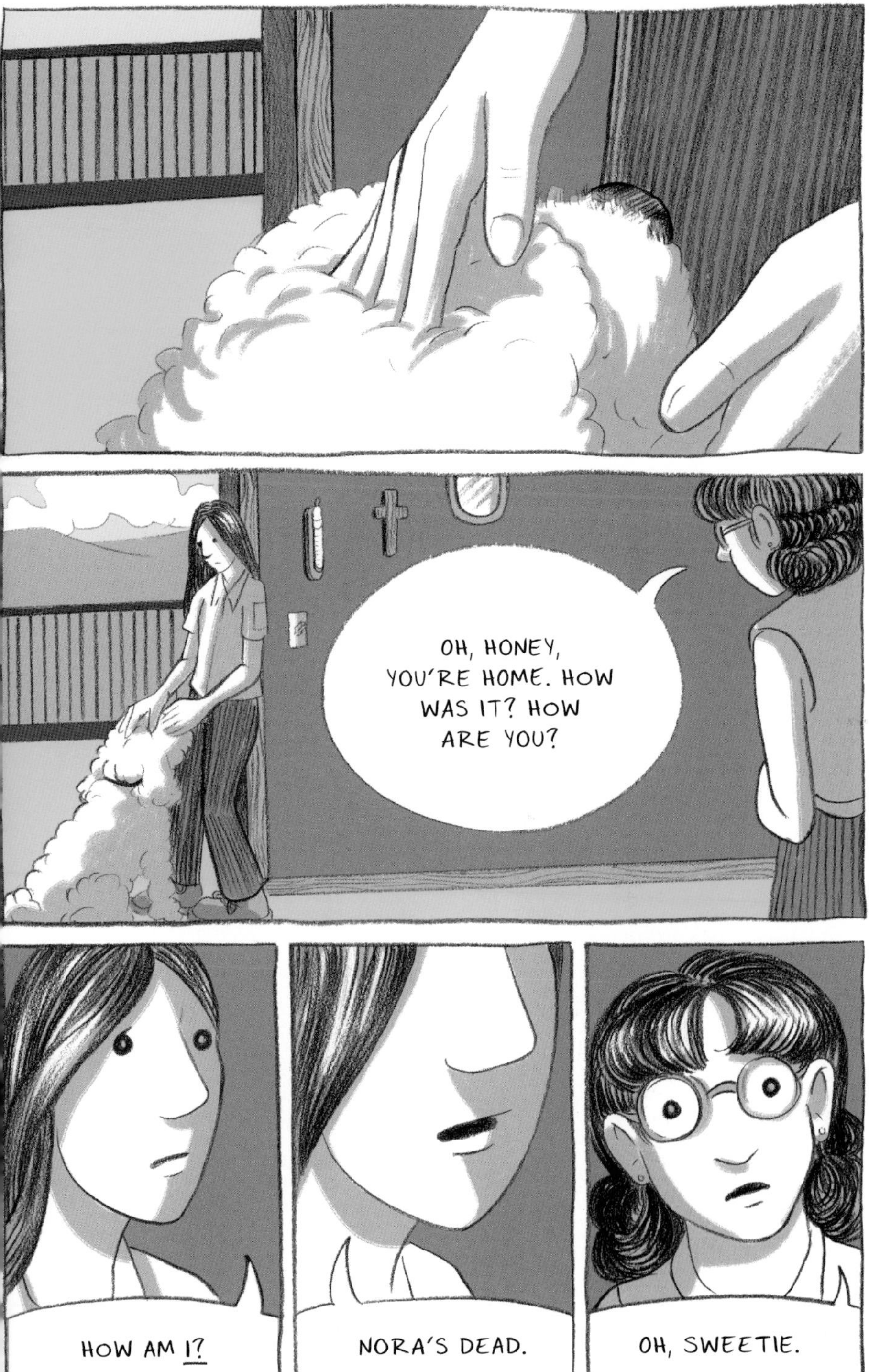
OH, HONEY, YOU'RE HOME. HOW WAS IT? HOW ARE YOU?
HOW AM I?
NORA'S DEAD.
OH, SWEETIE.

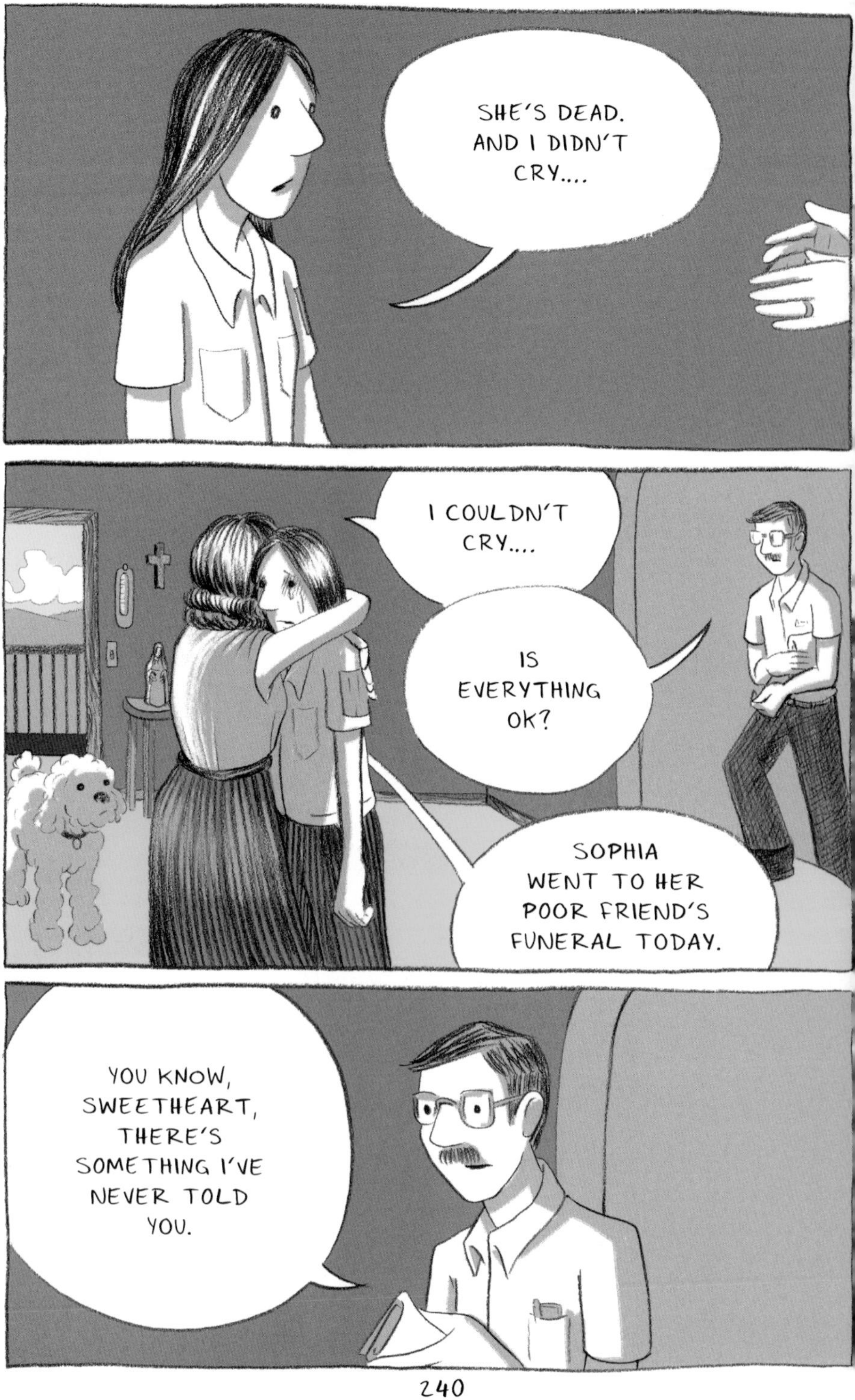
SHE'S DEAD. AND I DIDN'T CRY....
I COULDN'T CRY....
IS EVERYTHING OK?
SOPHIA WENT TO HER POOR FRIEND'S FUNERAL TODAY.
YOU KNOW, SWEETHEART, THERE'S SOMETHING I'VE NEVER TOLD YOU.

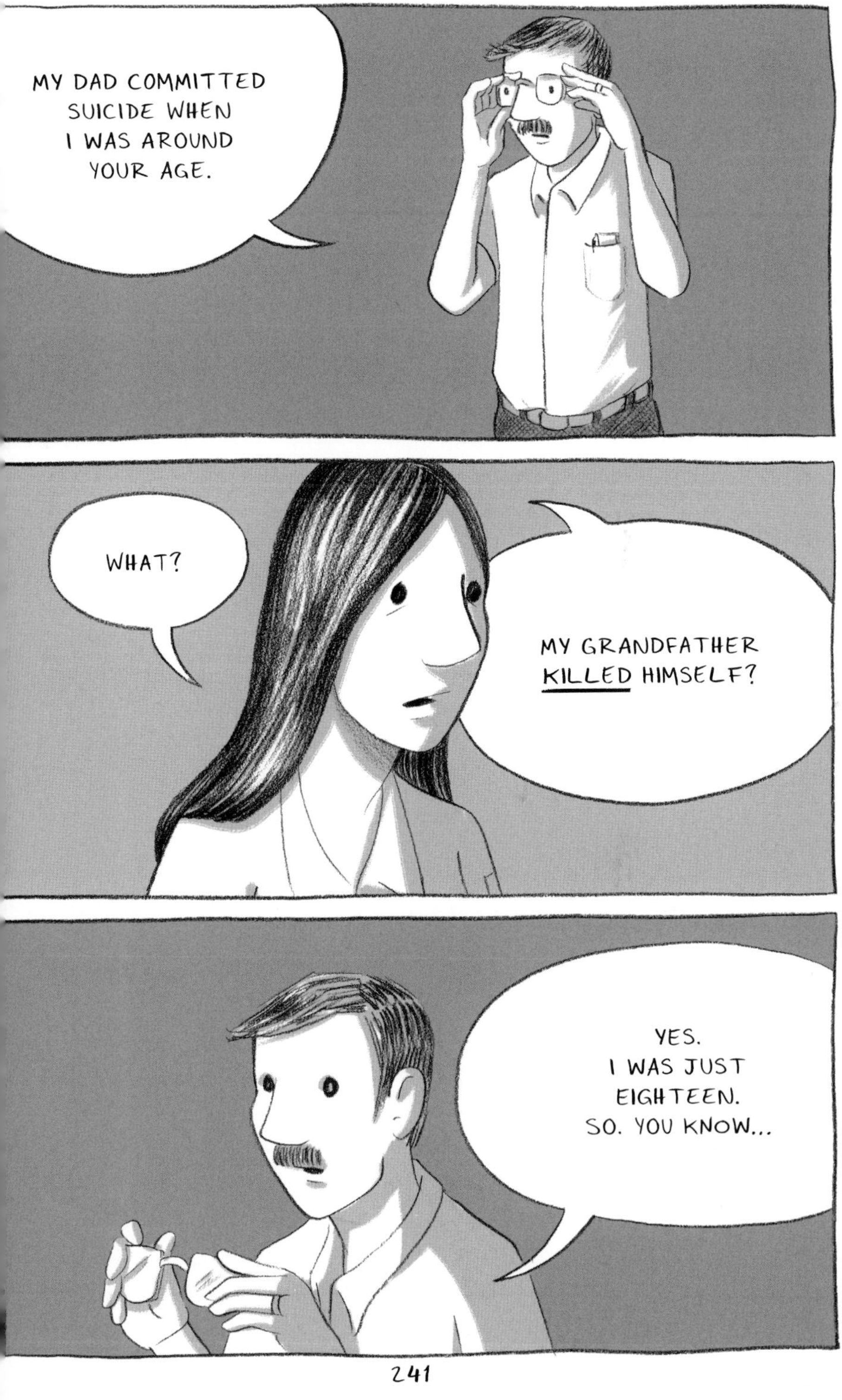
MY DAD COMMITTED SUICIDE WHEN I WAS AROUND YOUR AGE.
WHAT?
MY GRANDFATHER KILLED HIMSELF?
YES. I WAS JUST EIGHTEEN. SO. YOU KNOW...

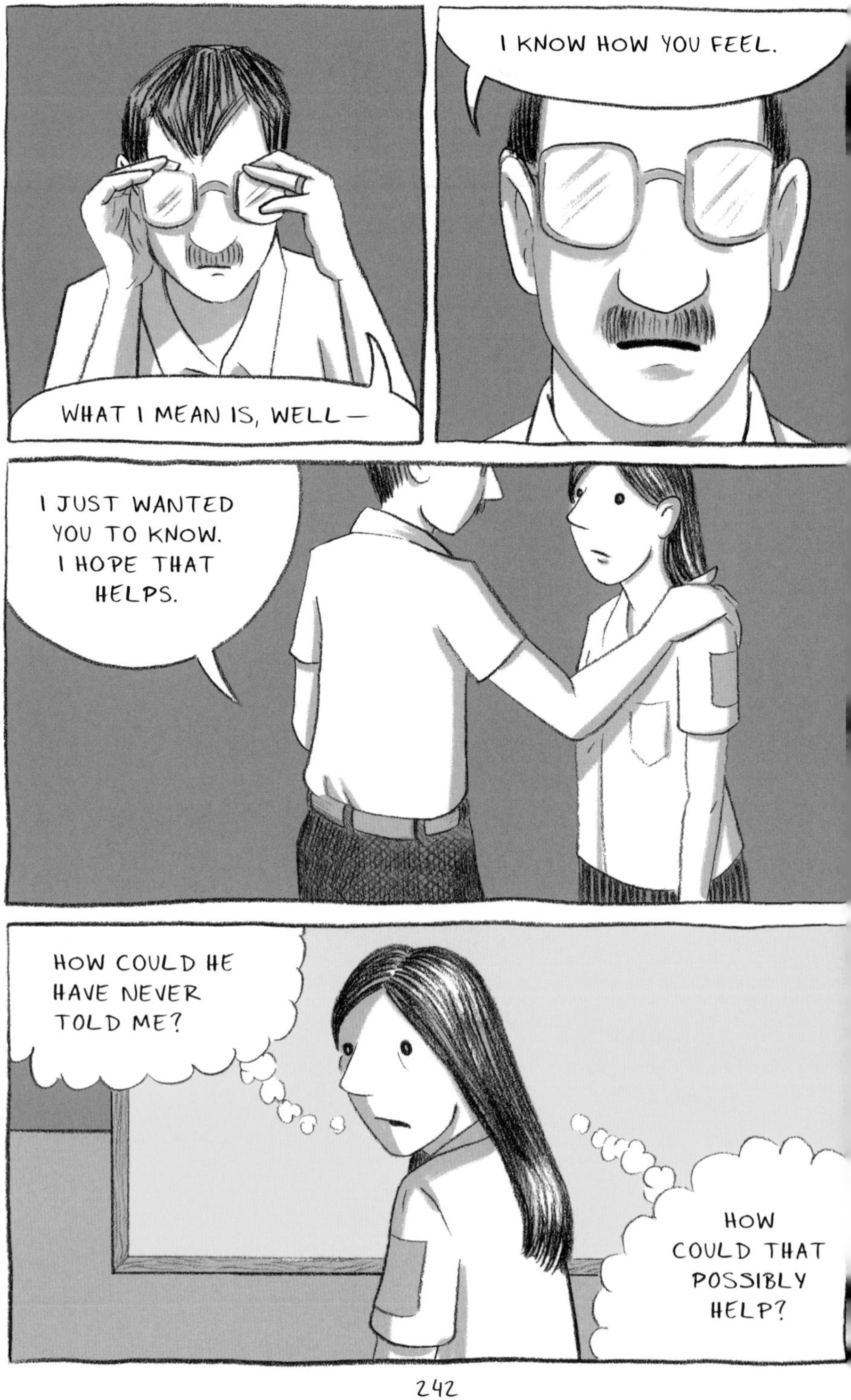
WHAT I MEAN IS, WELL—
I KNOW HOW YOU FEEL.
I JUST WANTED YOU TO KNOW. I HOPE THAT HELPS.
HOW COULD HE HAVE NEVER TOLD ME?
HOW COULD THAT POSSIBLY HELP?

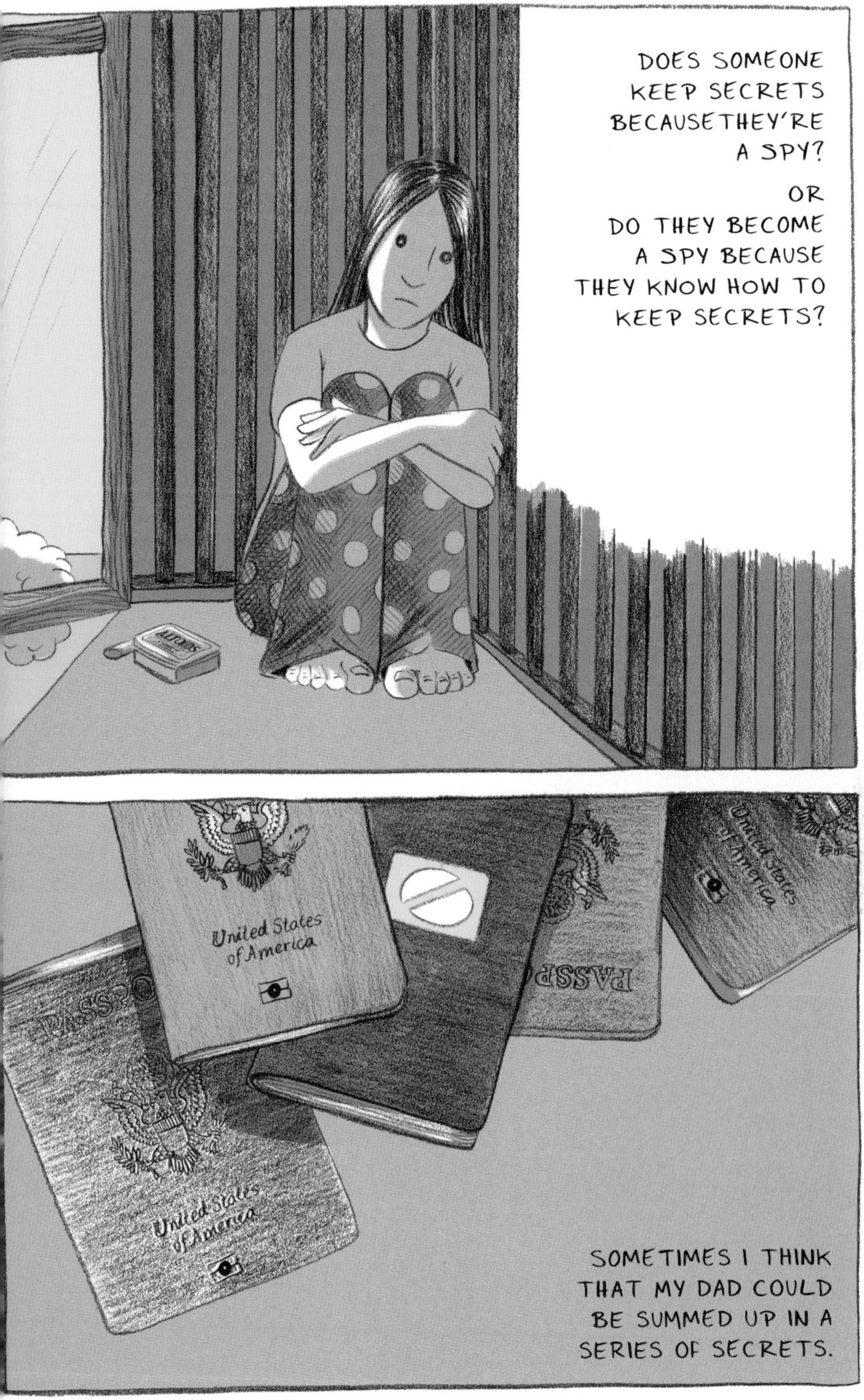
DOES SOMEONE KEEP SECRETS BECAUSE THEY'RE A SPY?
OR DO THEY BECOME A SPY BECAUSE THEY KNOW HOW TO KEEP SECRETS?
ALTOIDS
United States of America
United States of America
United States of America
SOMETIMES I THINK THAT MY DAD COULD BE SUMMED UP IN A SERIES OF SECRETS.

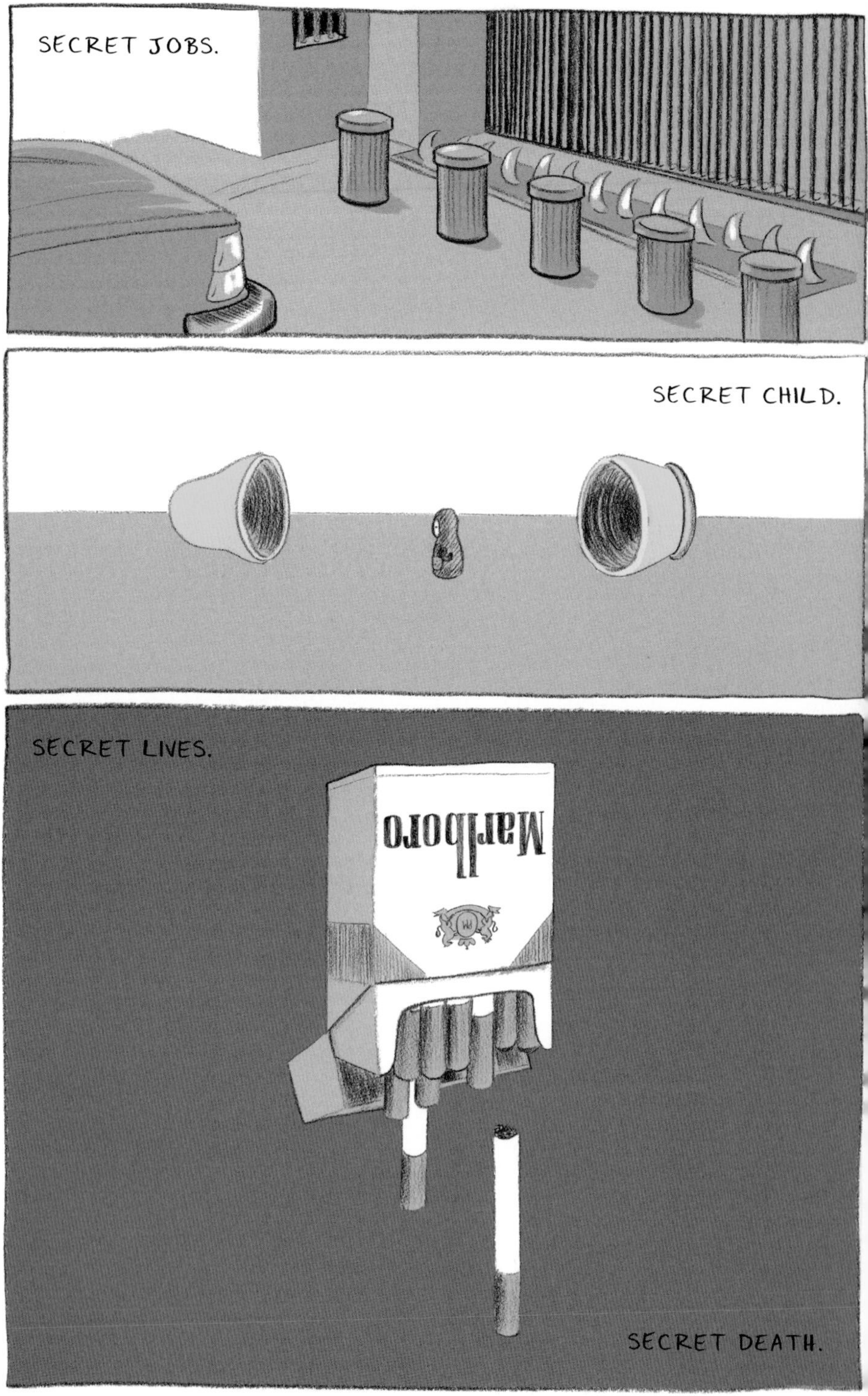
SECRET JOBS.
SECRET CHILD.
SECRET LIVES.
Marlboro
SECRET DEATH.

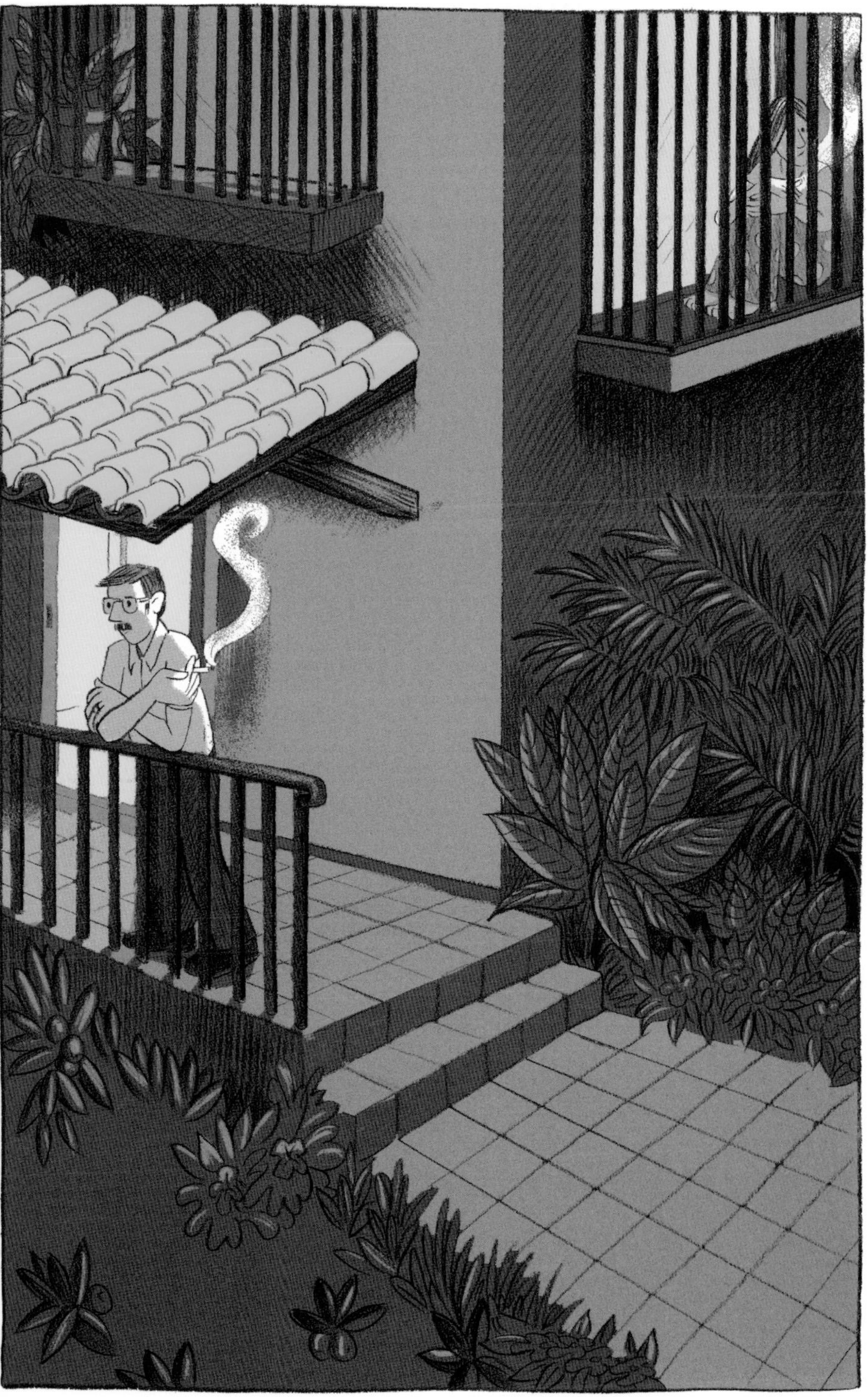

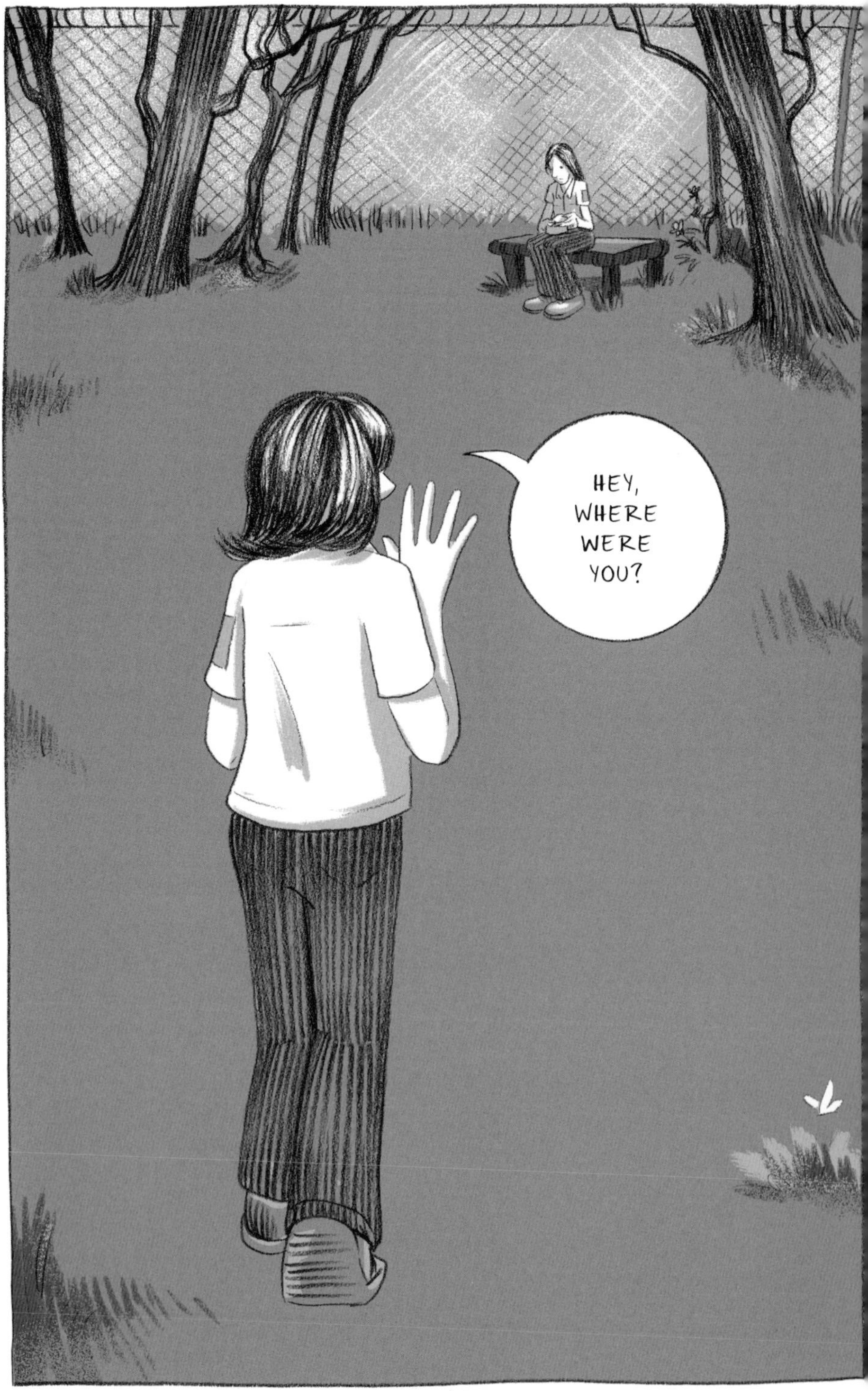
HEY, WHERE WERE YOU?

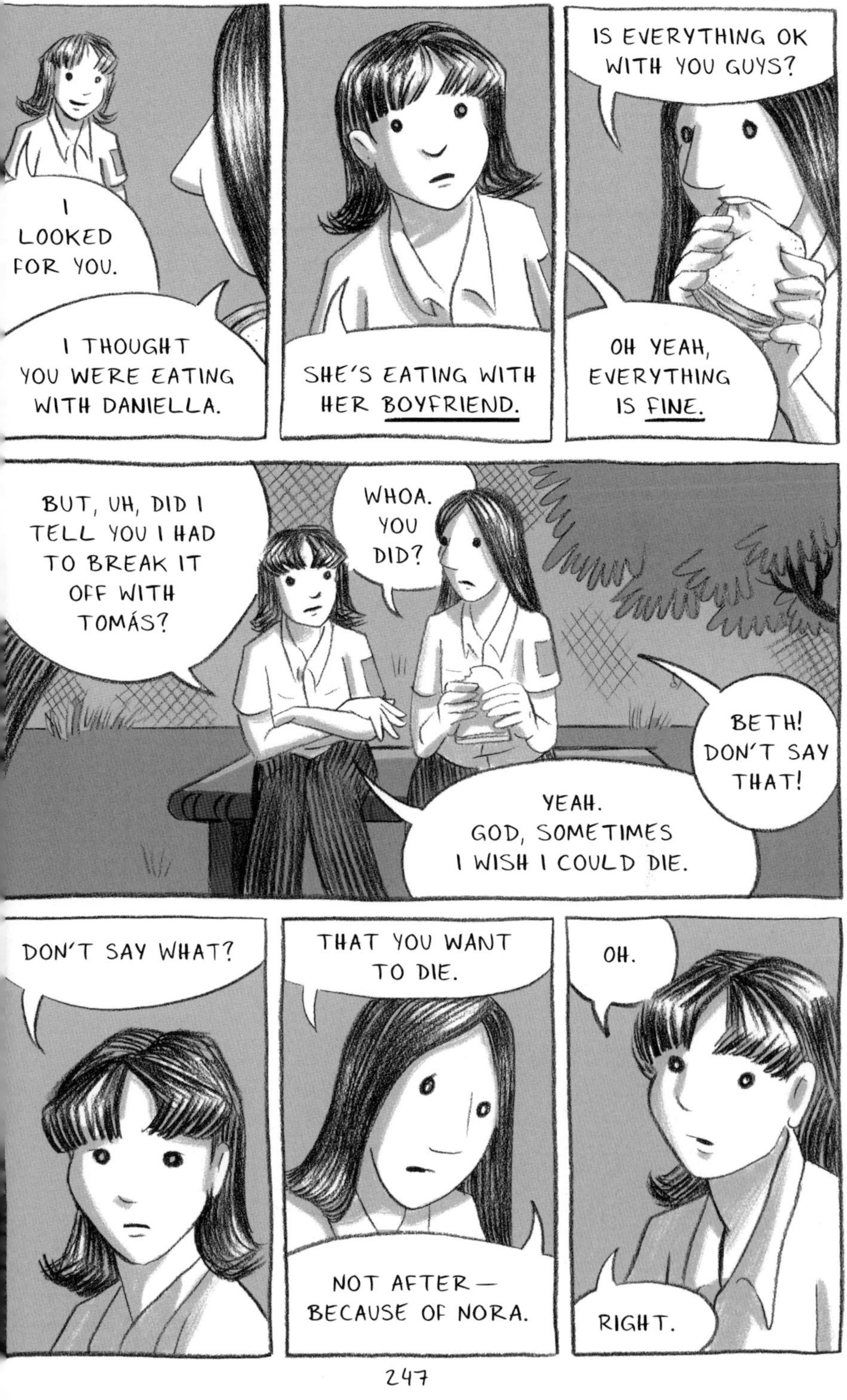
I LOOKED FOR YOU.
I THOUGHT YOU WERE EATING WITH DANIELLA.
SHE'S EATING WITH HER BOYFRIEND.
IS EVERYTHING OK WITH YOU GUYS?
OH YEAH, EVERYTHING IS FINE.
BUT, UH, DID I TELL YOU I HAD TO BREAK IT OFF WITH TOMÁS?
WHOA. YOU DID?
YEAH. GOD, SOMETIMES I WISH I COULD DIE.
BETH! DON'T SAY THAT!
DON'T SAY WHAT?
THAT YOU WANT TO DIE.
NOT AFTER— BECAUSE OF NORA.
OH.
RIGHT.

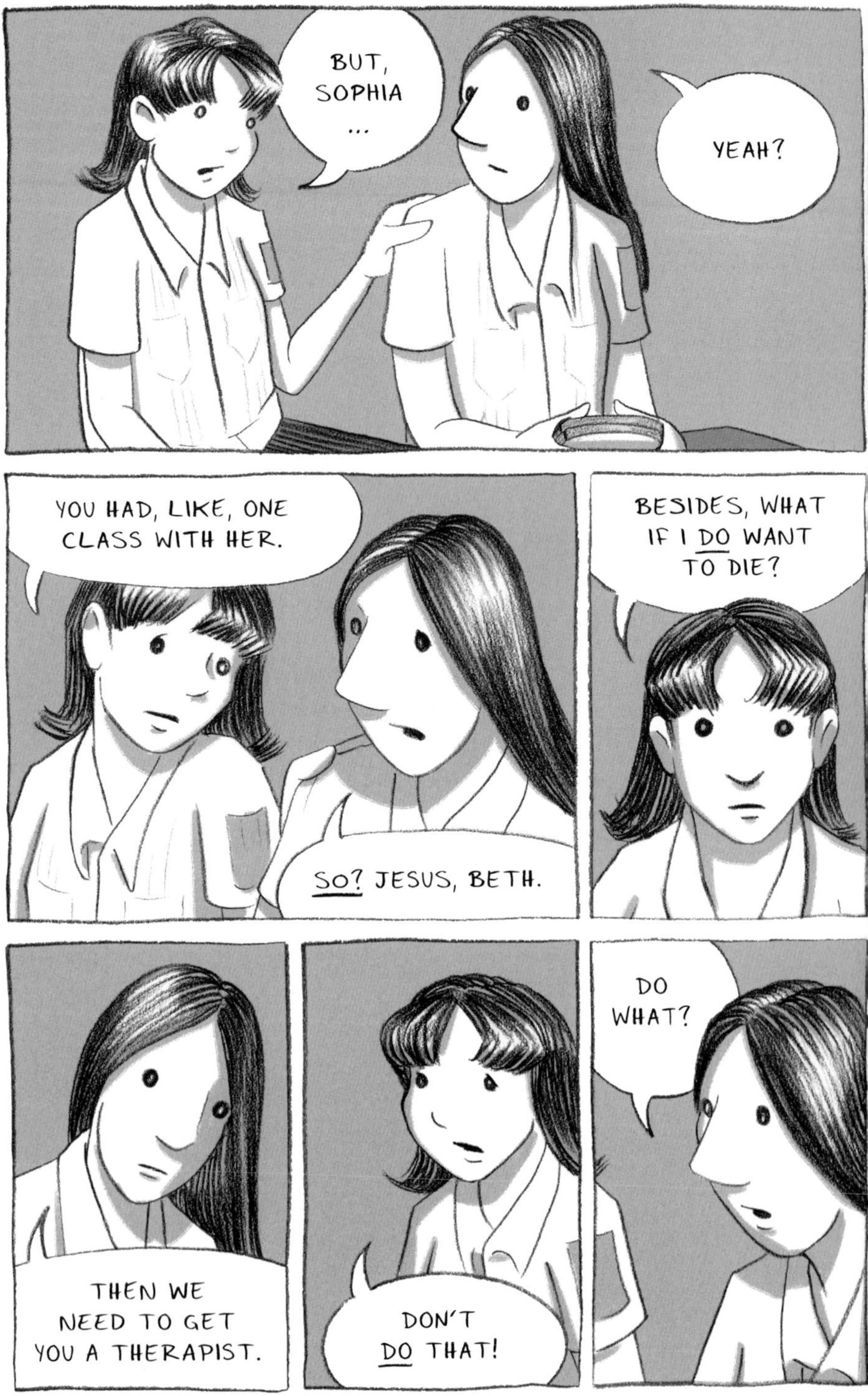
BUT, SOPHIA ...
YEAH?
YOU HAD, LIKE, ONE CLASS WITH HER.
SO? JESUS, BETH.
BESIDES, WHAT IF I DO WANT TO DIE?
THEN WE NEED TO GET YOU A THERAPIST.
DON'T DO THAT!
DO WHAT?

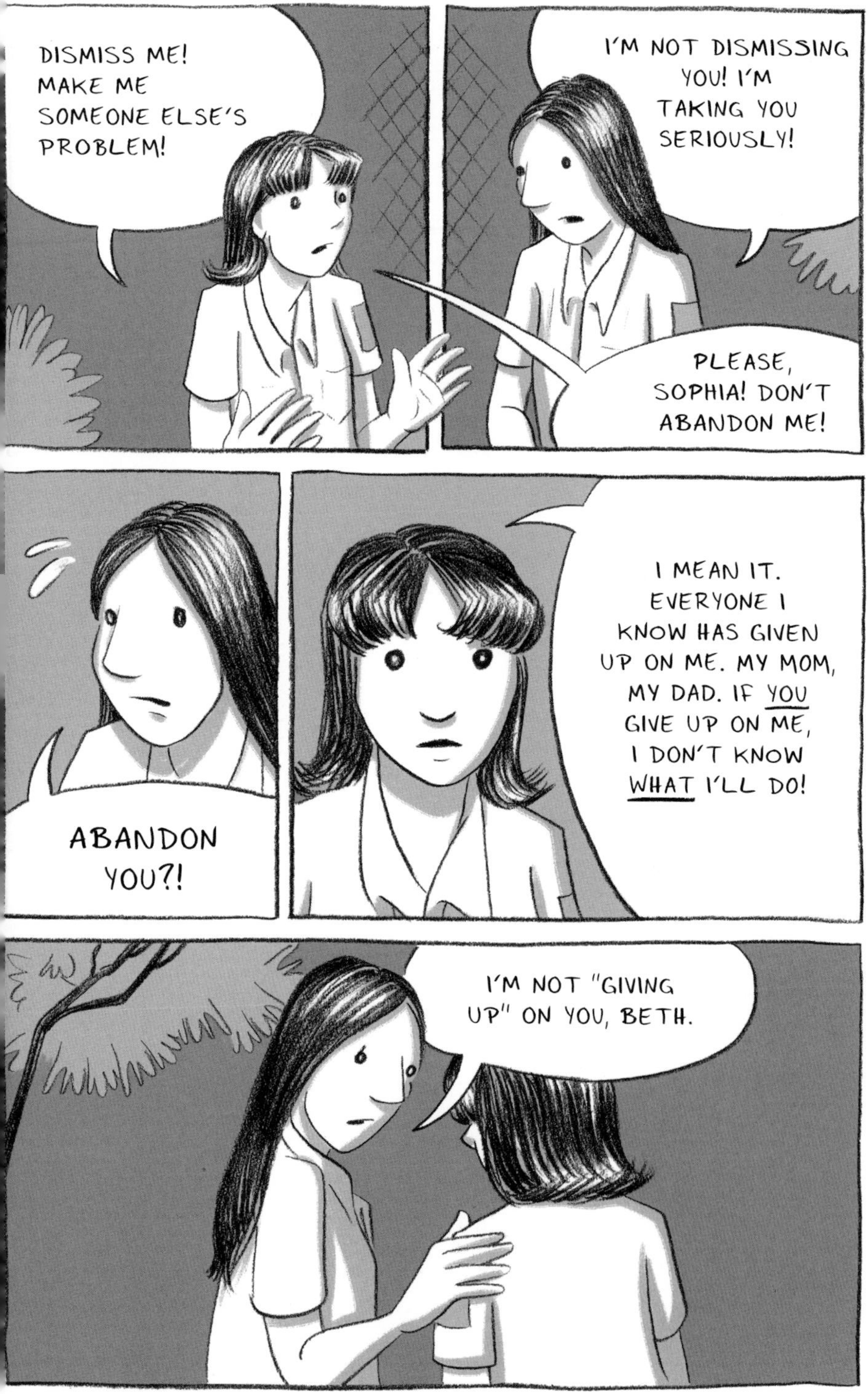
DISMISS ME! MAKE ME SOMEONE ELSE'S PROBLEM!
I'M NOT DISMISSING YOU! I'M TAKING YOU SERIOUSLY!
PLEASE, SOPHIA! DON'T ABANDON ME!
ABANDON YOU?!
I MEAN IT. EVERYONE I KNOW HAS GIVEN UP ON ME. MY MOM, MY DAD. IF YOU GIVE UP ON ME, I DON'T KNOW WHAT I'LL DO!
I'M NOT "GIVING UP" ON YOU, BETH.

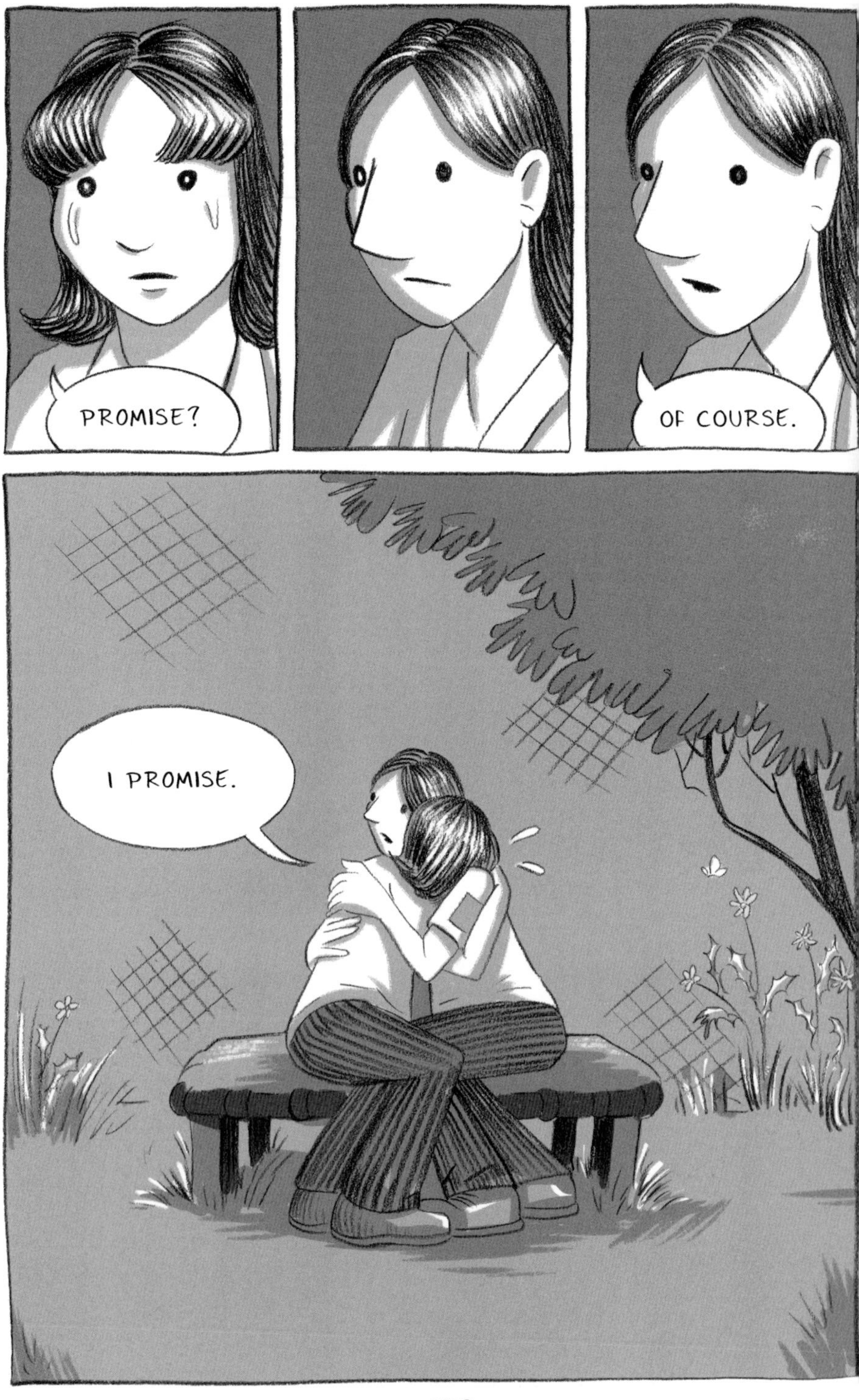
PROMISE?
OF COURSE.
I PROMISE.

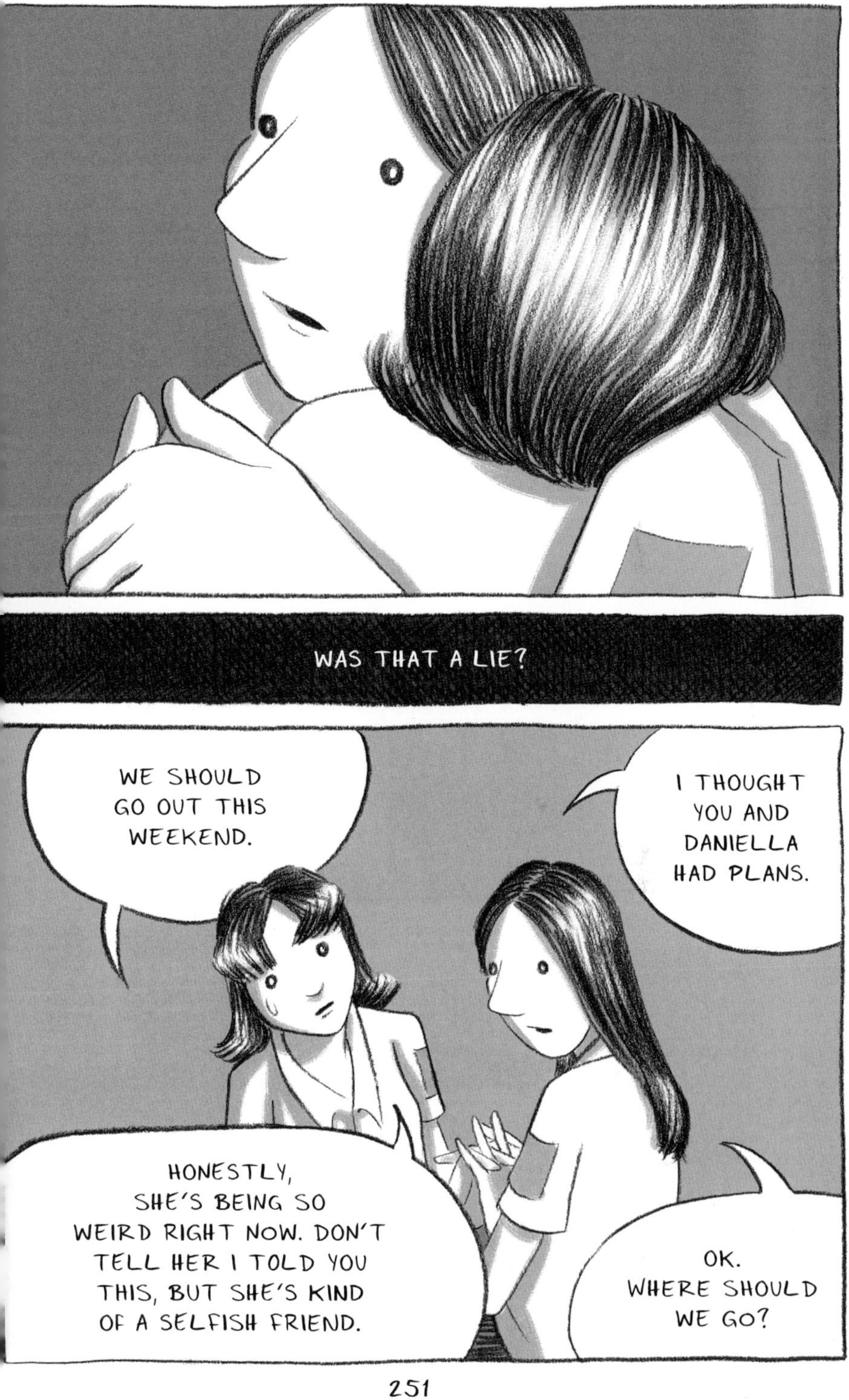
WAS THAT A LIE?
WE SHOULD GO OUT THIS WEEKEND.
I THOUGHT YOU AND DANIELLA HAD PLANS.
HONESTLY, SHE'S BEING SO WEIRD RIGHT NOW. DON'T TELL HER I TOLD YOU THIS, BUT SHE'S KIND OF A SELFISH FRIEND.
OK. WHERE SHOULD WE GO?

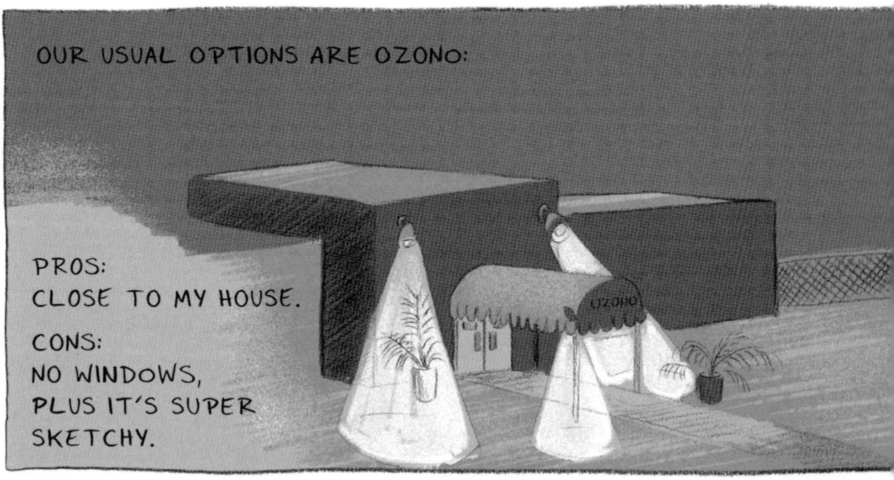
OUR USUAL OPTIONS ARE OZONO:
PROS:
CLOSE TO MY HOUSE.
CONS:
NO WINDOWS,
PLUS IT'S SUPER
SKETCHY.

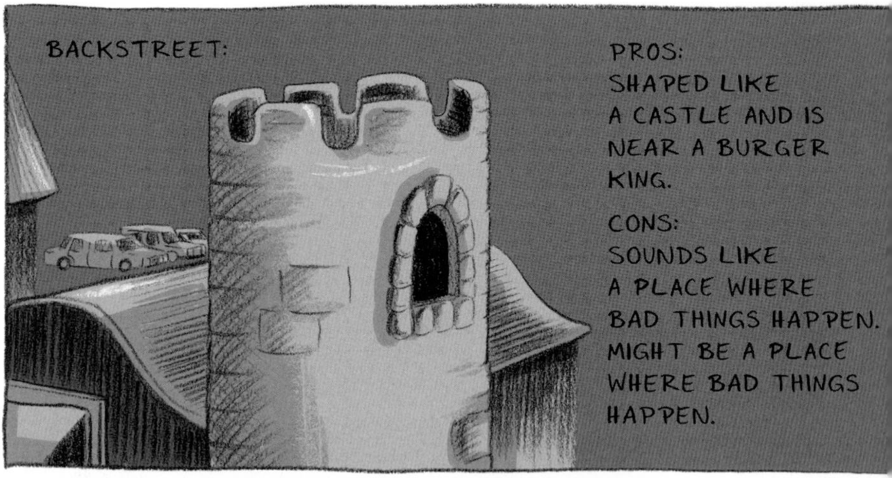
BACKSTREET:
PROS:
SHAPED LIKE
A CASTLE AND IS
NEAR A BURGER
KING.
CONS:
SOUNDS LIKE
A PLACE WHERE
BAD THINGS HAPPEN.
MIGHT BE A PLACE
WHERE BAD THINGS
HAPPEN.

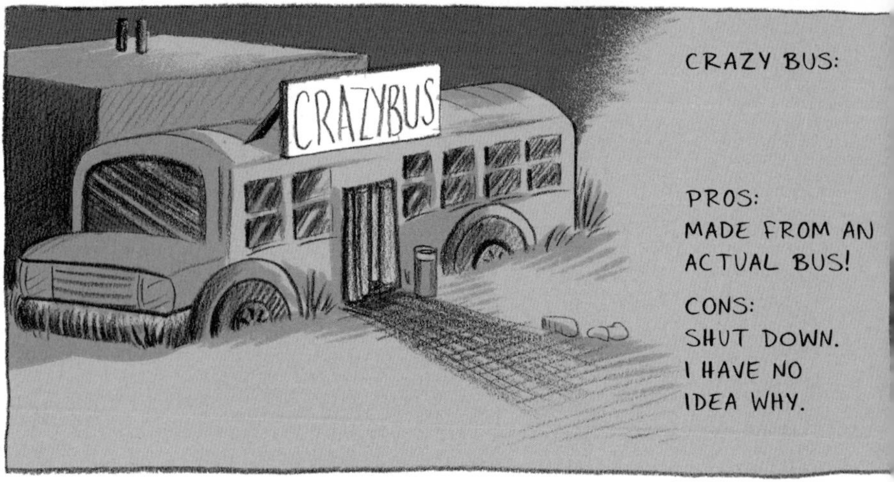
CRAZYBUS
CRAZY BUS:
PROS:
MADE FROM AN
ACTUAL BUS!
CONS:
SHUT DOWN.
I HAVE NO
IDEA WHY.

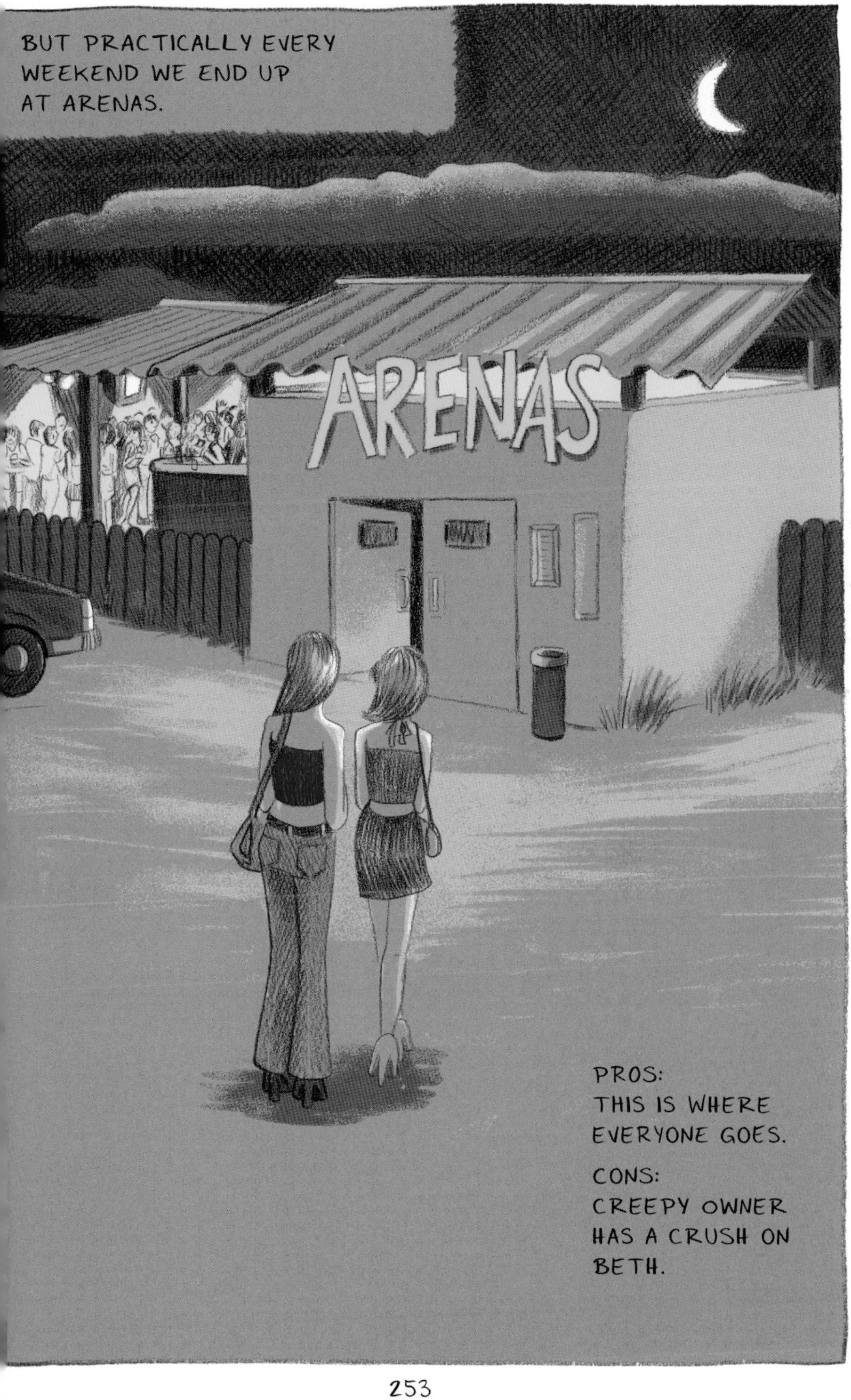
BUT PRACTICALLY EVERY WEEKEND WE END UP AT ARENAS.
ARENAS
PROS:
THIS IS WHERE EVERYONE GOES.
CONS:
CREEPY OWNER HAS A CRUSH ON BETH.

BETH WOULD CALL THAT A "PRO," SINCE HE USUALLY INSISTS THAT WE HANG OUT IN THE VIP SECTION.

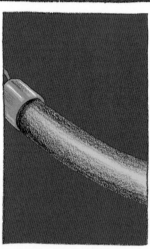

HMMMM.

ISN'T THIS COOL?

IT'S EXACTLY THE SAME. THERE'S JUST THAT STUPID ROPE.

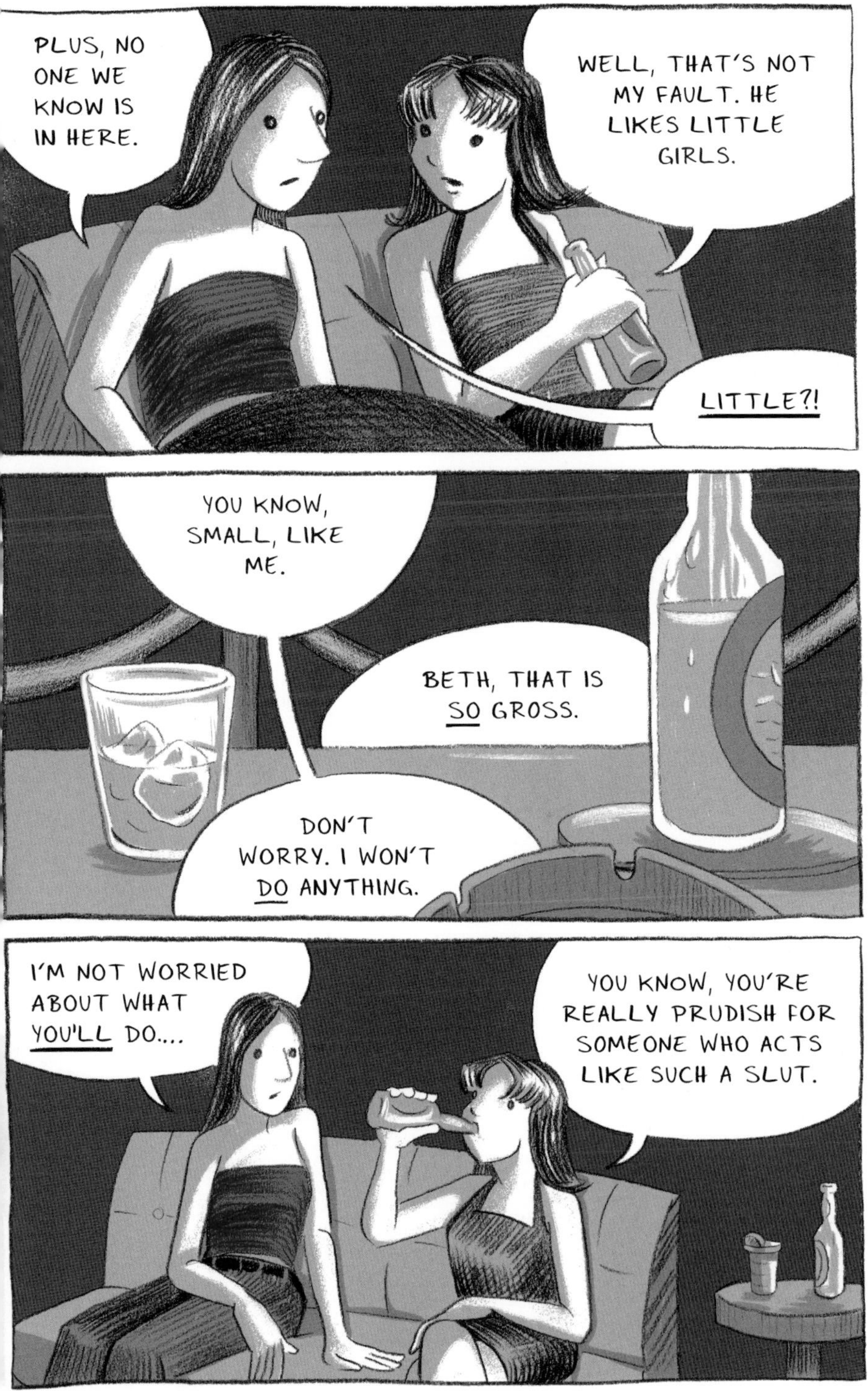
PLUS, NO ONE WE KNOW IS IN HERE.
WELL, THAT'S NOT MY FAULT. HE LIKES LITTLE GIRLS.
LITTLE?!
YOU KNOW, SMALL, LIKE ME.
BETH, THAT IS SO GROSS.
DON'T WORRY. I WON'T DO ANYTHING.
I'M NOT WORRIED ABOUT WHAT YOU'LL DO....
YOU KNOW, YOU'RE REALLY PRUDISH FOR SOMEONE WHO ACTS LIKE SUCH A SLUT.

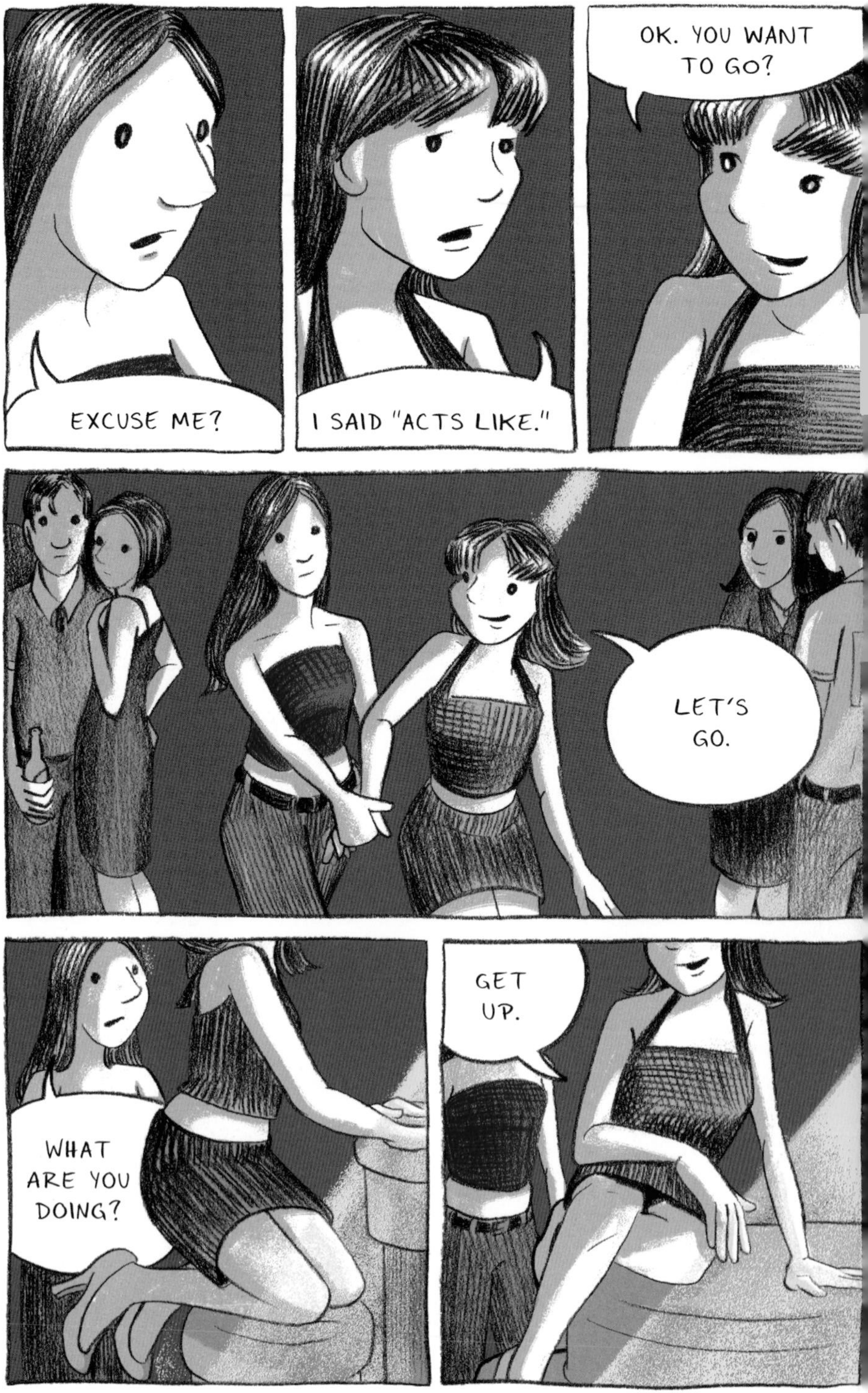
EXCUSE ME?
I SAID "ACTS LIKE."
OK. YOU WANT TO GO?
LET'S GO.
WHAT ARE YOU DOING?
GET UP.

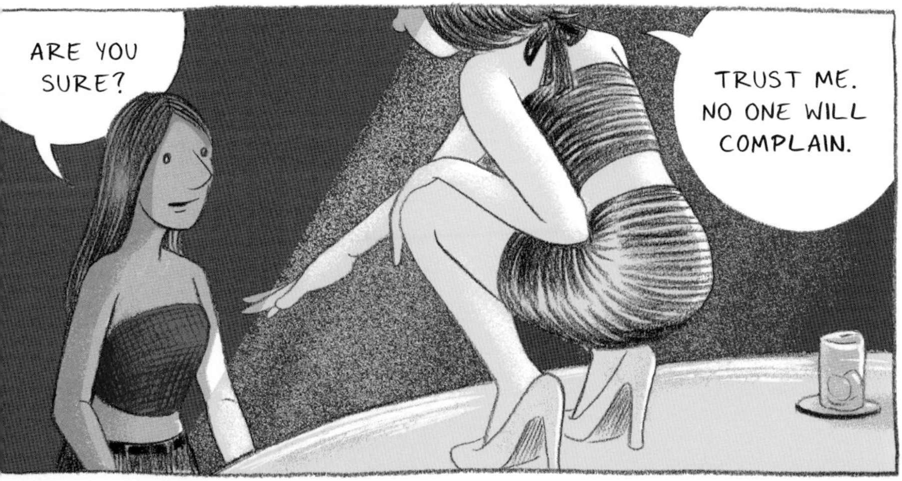
ARE YOU SURE?
TRUST ME. NO ONE WILL COMPLAIN.

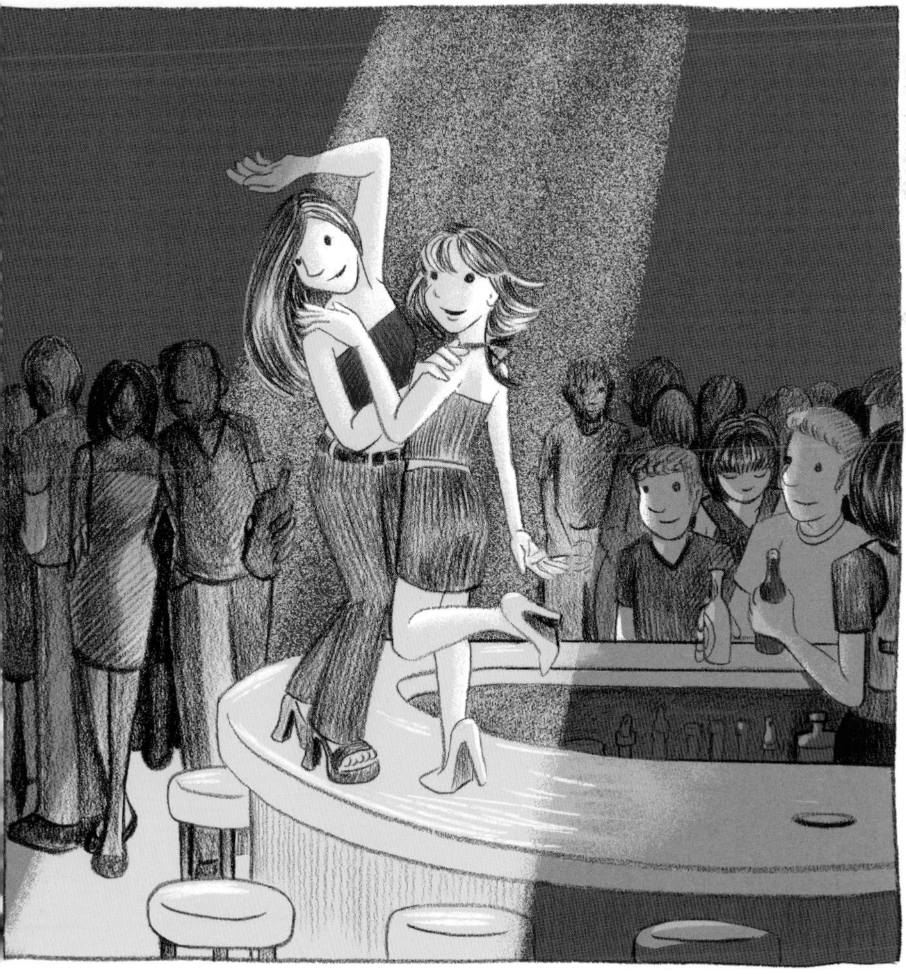

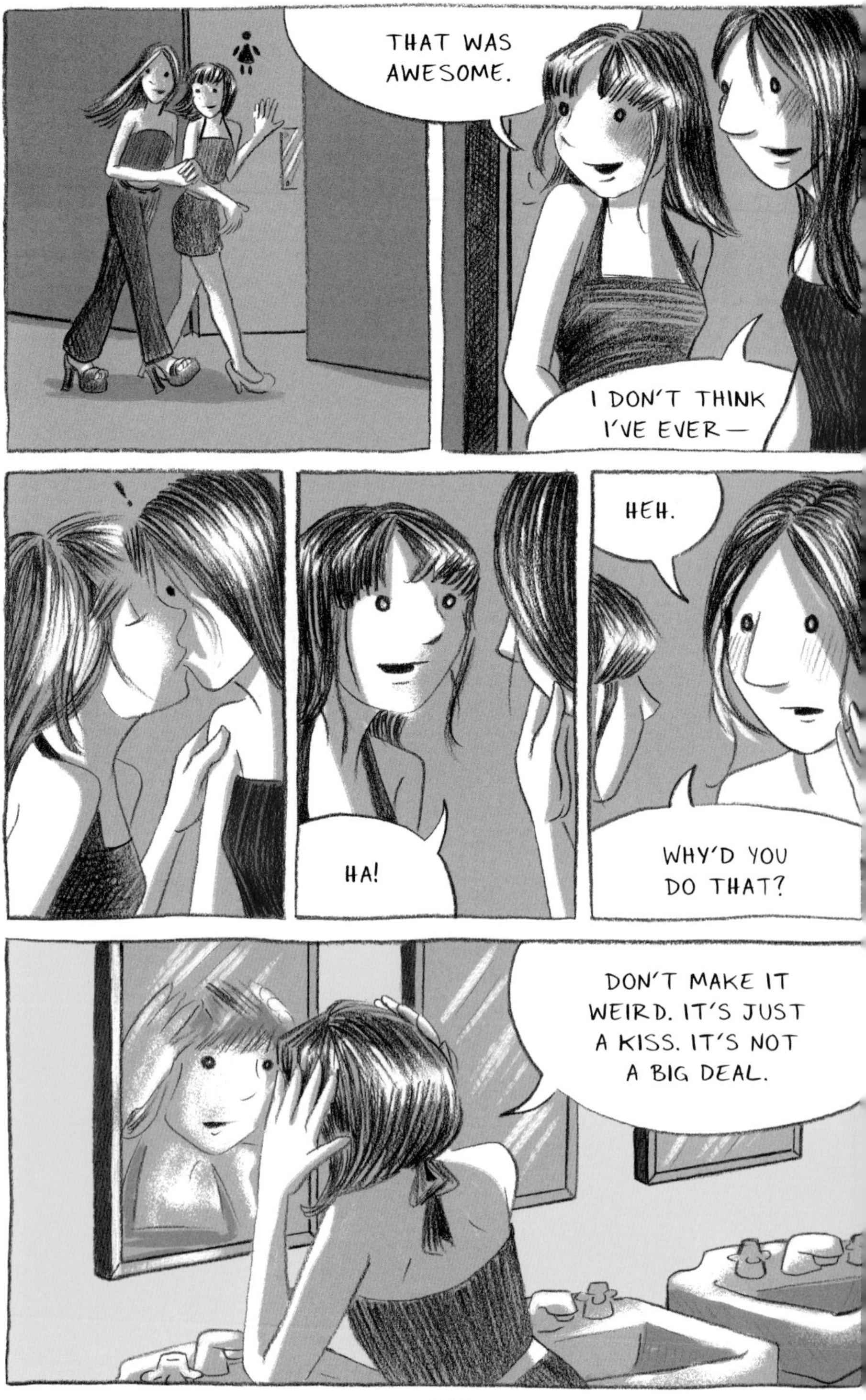
THAT WAS AWESOME.
I DON'T THINK I'VE EVER—
!
HEH.
HA!
WHY'D YOU DO THAT?
DON'T MAKE IT WEIRD. IT'S JUST A KISS. IT'S NOT A BIG DEAL.

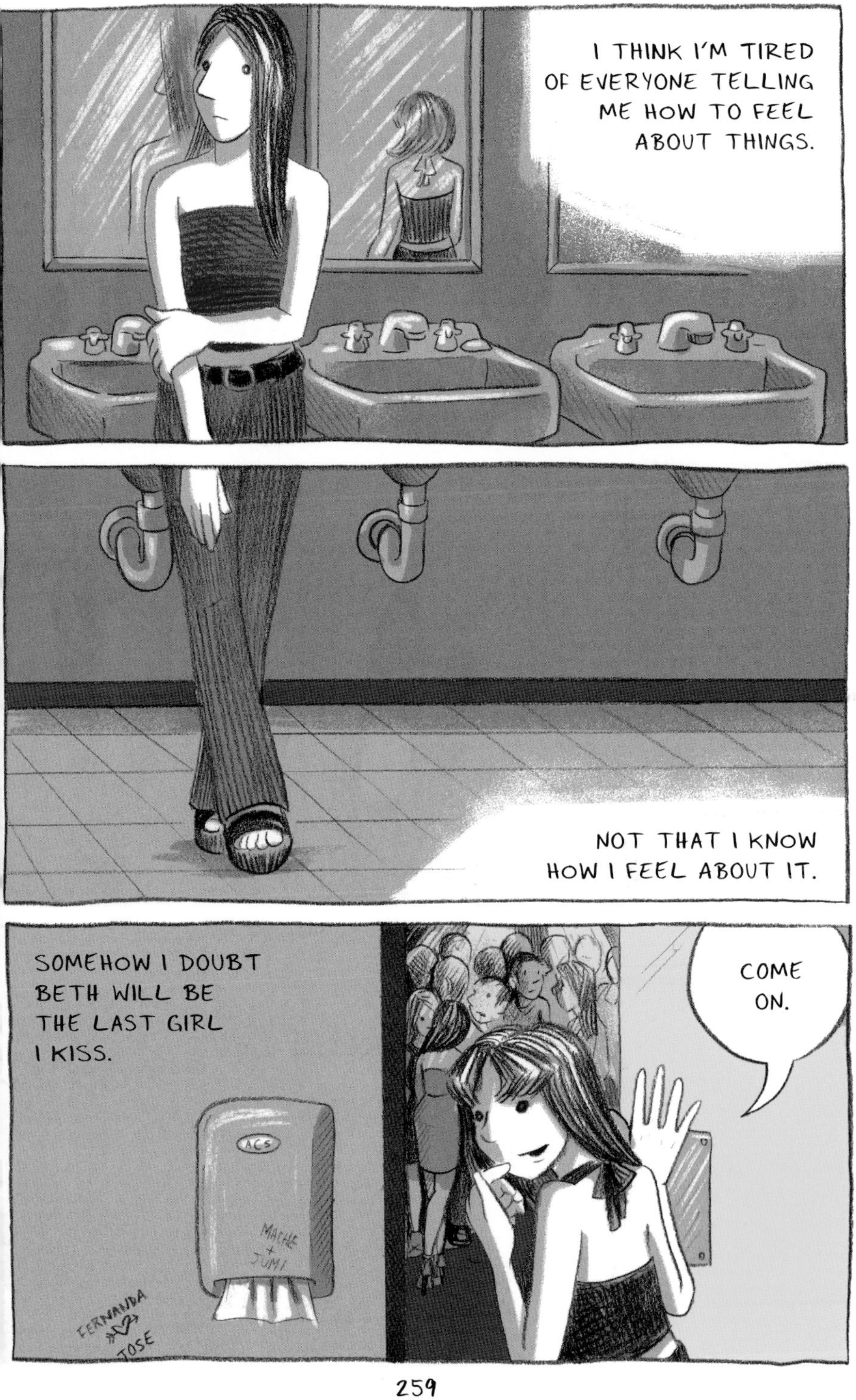
I THINK I'M TIRED OF EVERYONE TELLING ME HOW TO FEEL ABOUT THINGS.
NOT THAT I KNOW HOW I FEEL ABOUT IT.
SOMEHOW I DOUBT BETH WILL BE THE LAST GIRL I KISS.
COME ON.
ACS
MACHE + JUMI
FERNANDA JOSE

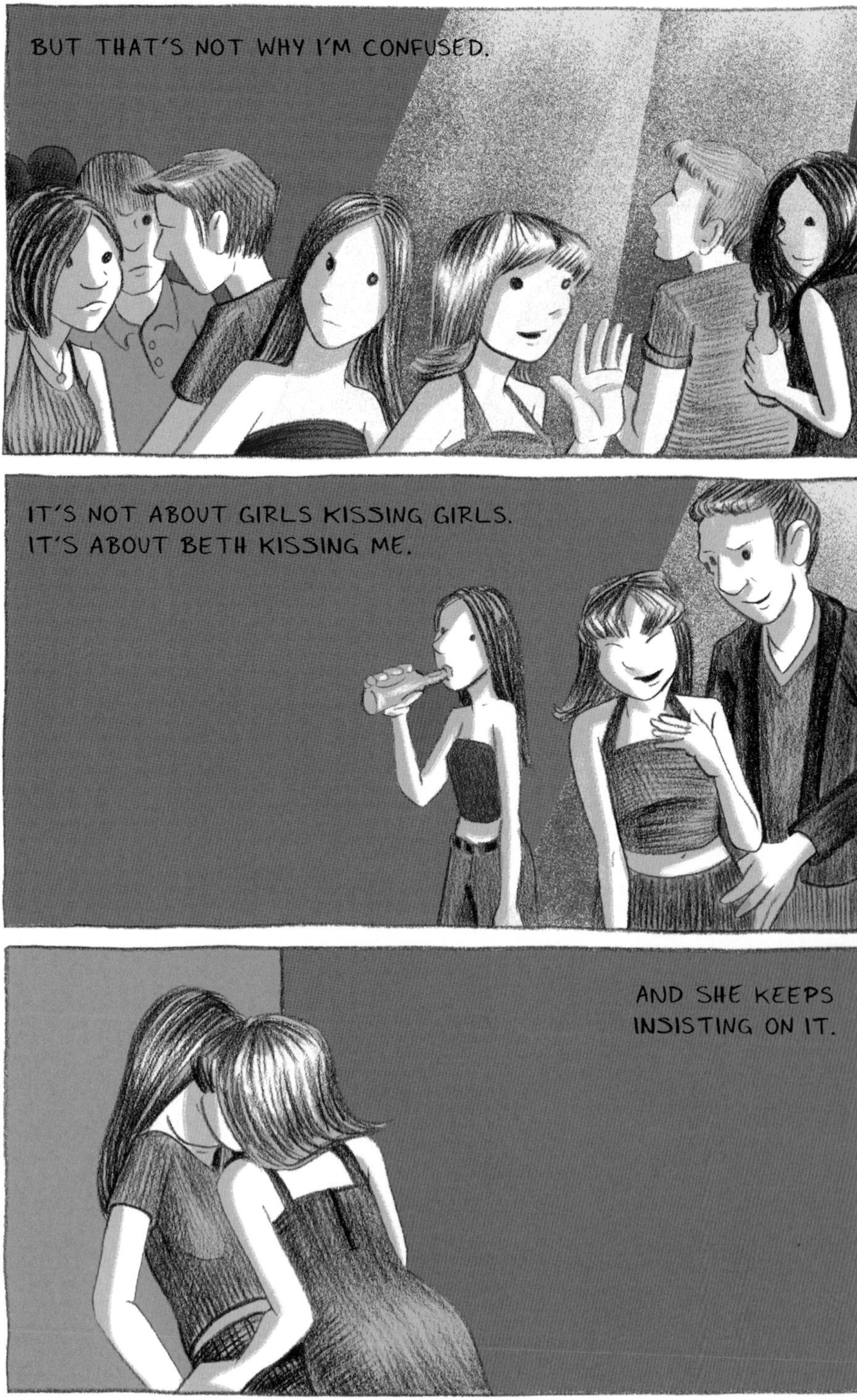
BUT THAT'S NOT WHY I'M CONFUSED.
IT'S NOT ABOUT GIRLS KISSING GIRLS.
IT'S ABOUT BETH KISSING ME.
AND SHE KEEPS INSISTING ON IT.

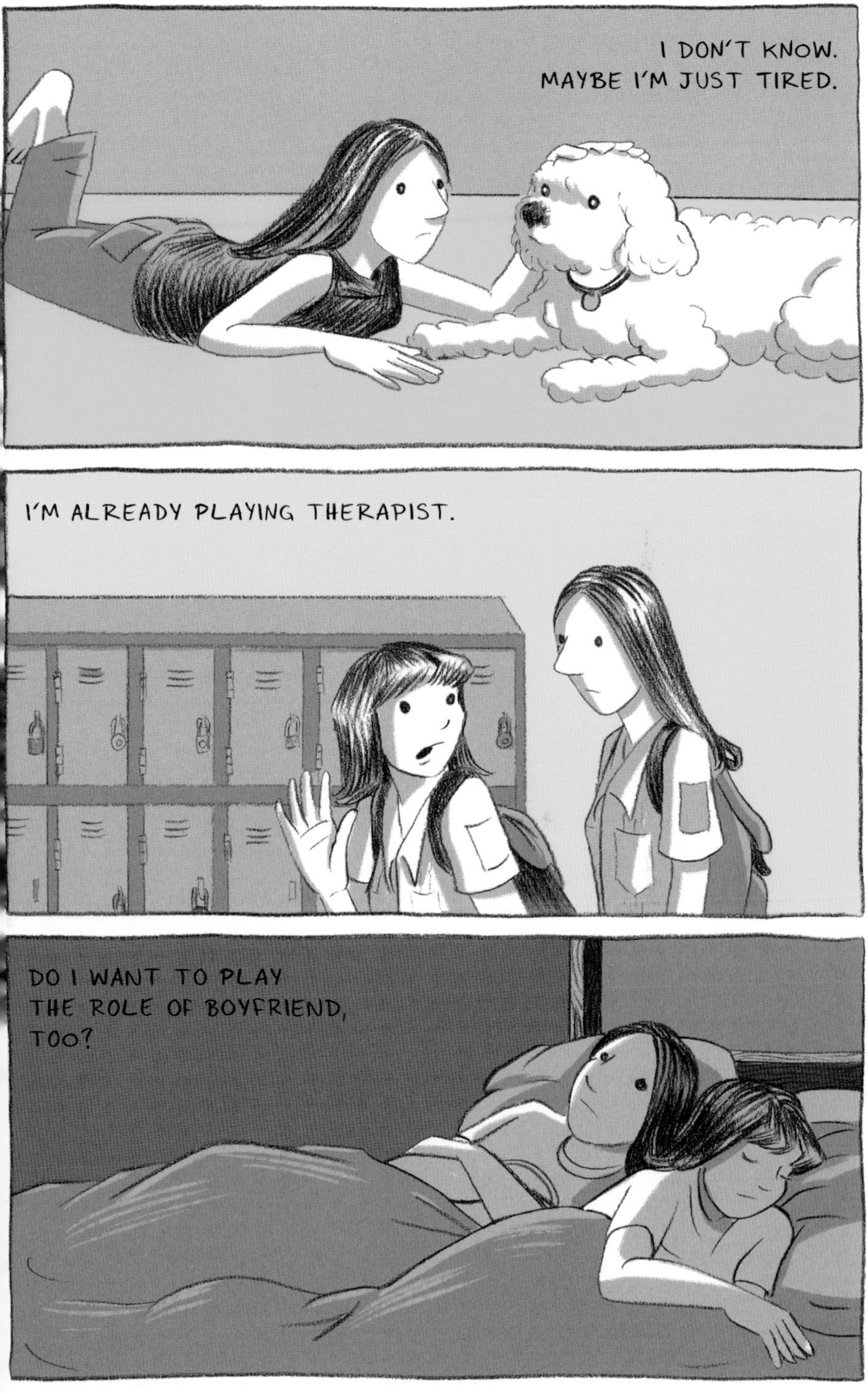
I DON'T KNOW.
MAYBE I'M JUST TIRED.
I'M ALREADY PLAYING THERAPIST.
DO I WANT TO PLAY
THE ROLE OF BOYFRIEND,
TOO?

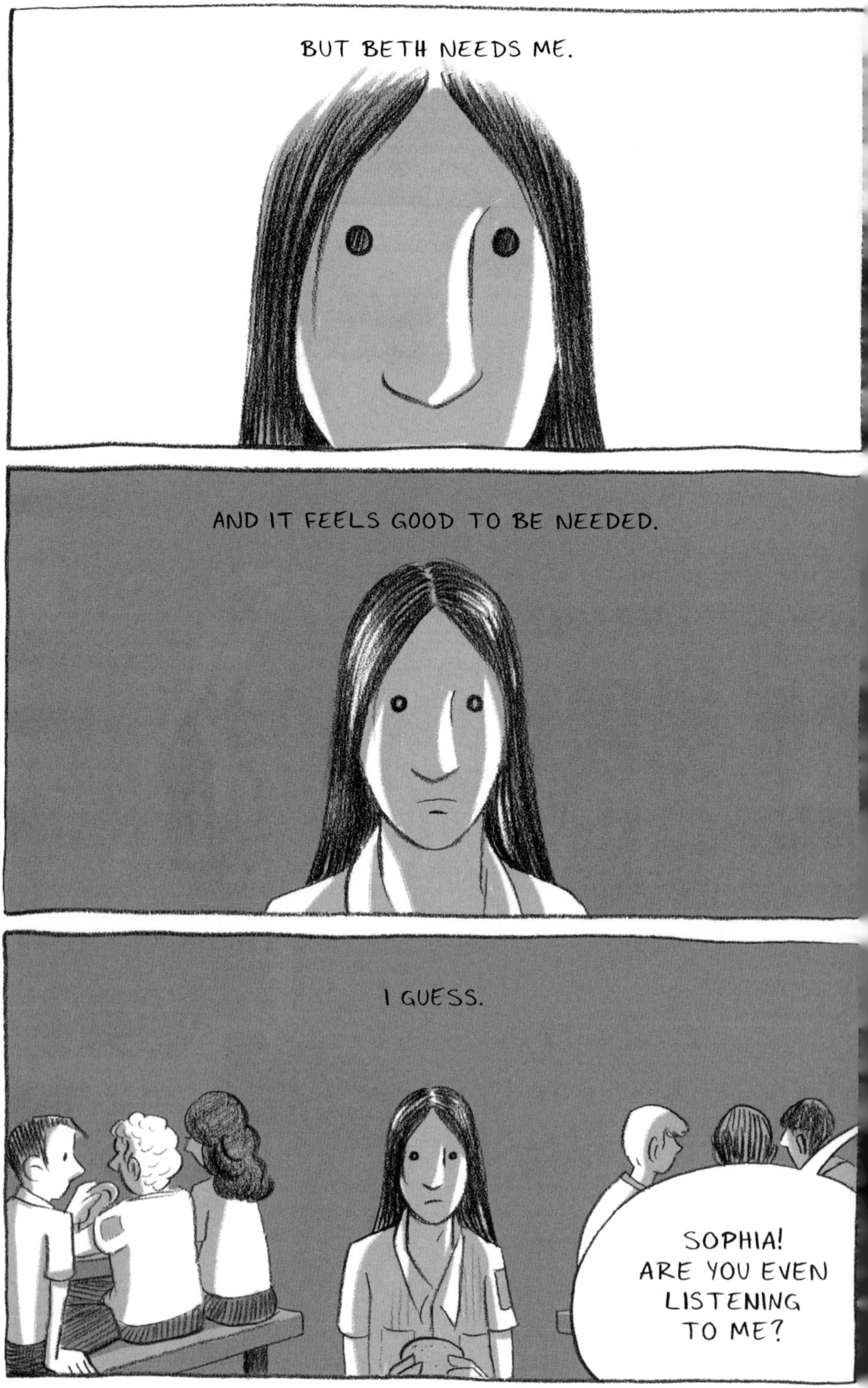
BUT BETH NEEDS ME.
AND IT FEELS GOOD TO BE NEEDED.
I GUESS.
SOPHIA! ARE YOU EVEN LISTENING TO ME?

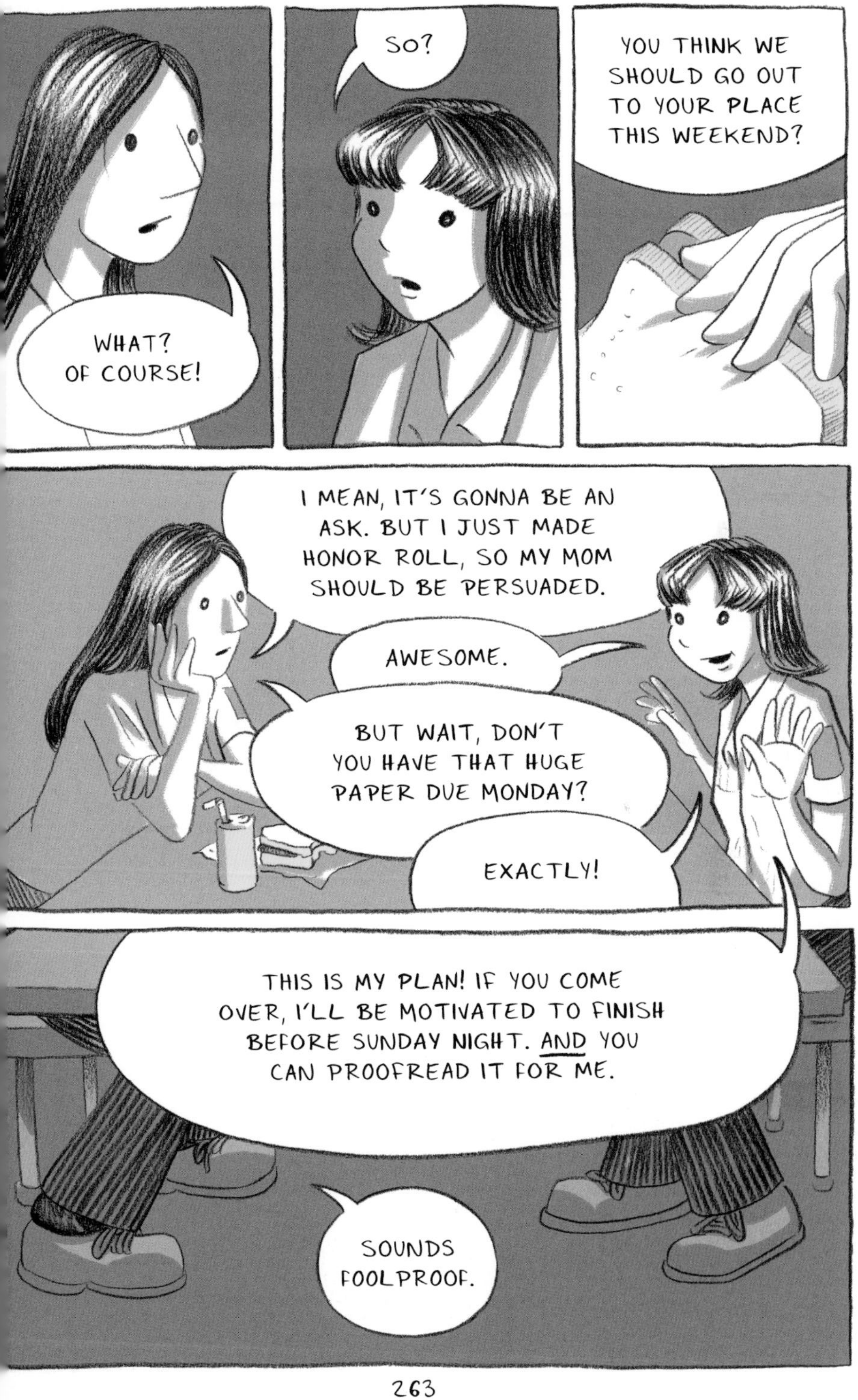
WHAT? OF COURSE!
SO?
YOU THINK WE SHOULD GO OUT TO YOUR PLACE THIS WEEKEND?
I MEAN, IT'S GONNA BE AN ASK. BUT I JUST MADE HONOR ROLL, SO MY MOM SHOULD BE PERSUADED.
AWESOME.
BUT WAIT, DON'T YOU HAVE THAT HUGE PAPER DUE MONDAY?
EXACTLY!
THIS IS MY PLAN! IF YOU COME OVER, I'LL BE MOTIVATED TO FINISH BEFORE SUNDAY NIGHT. AND YOU CAN PROOFREAD IT FOR ME.
SOUNDS FOOLPROOF.

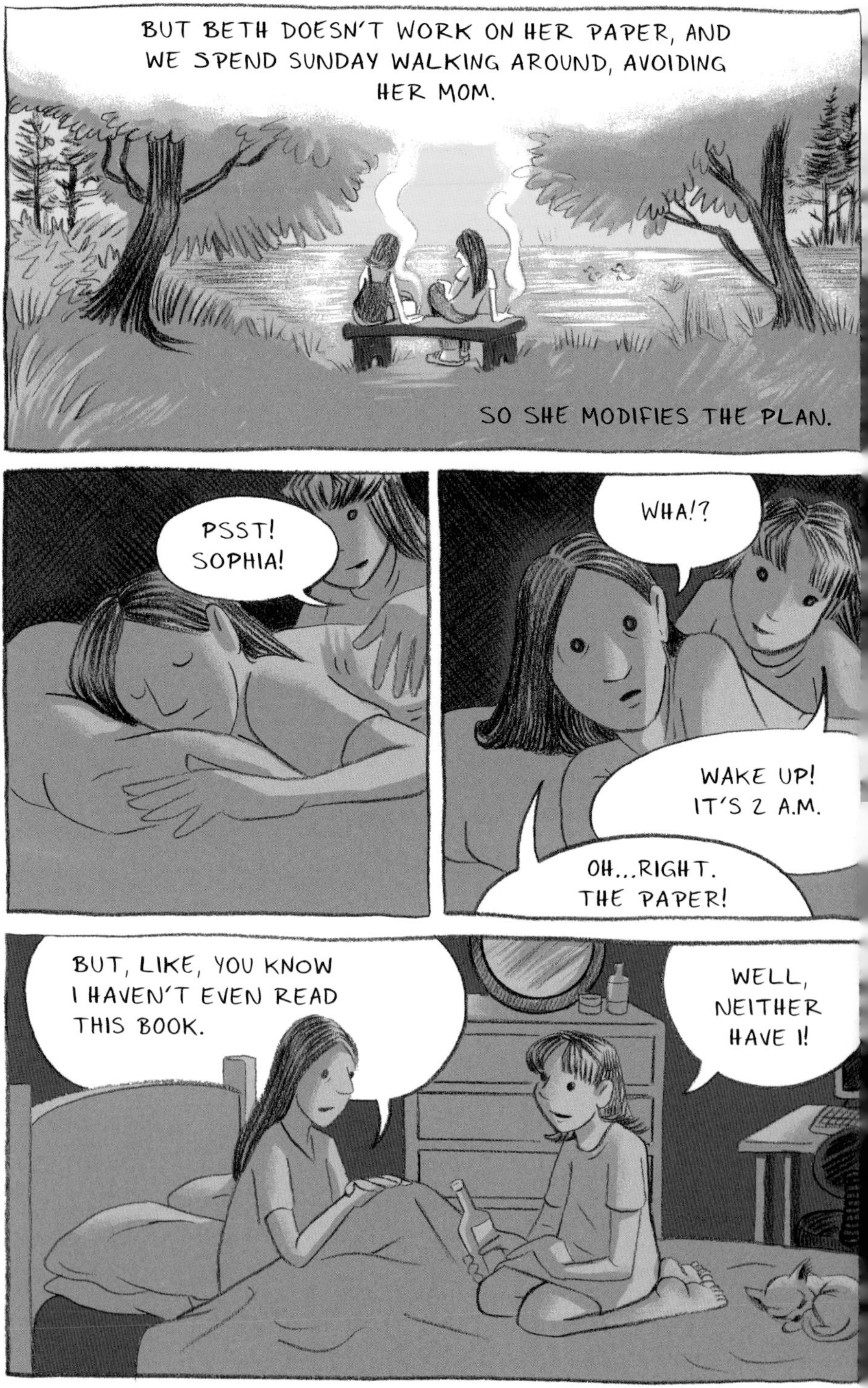

BUT BETH DOESN'T WORK ON HER PAPER, AND WE SPEND SUNDAY WALKING AROUND, AVOIDING HER MOM.
SO SHE MODIFIES THE PLAN.
PSST! SOPHIA!
WHA!?
WAKE UP! IT'S 2 A.M.
OH...RIGHT. THE PAPER!
BUT, LIKE, YOU KNOW I HAVEN'T EVEN READ THIS BOOK.
WELL, NEITHER HAVE I!

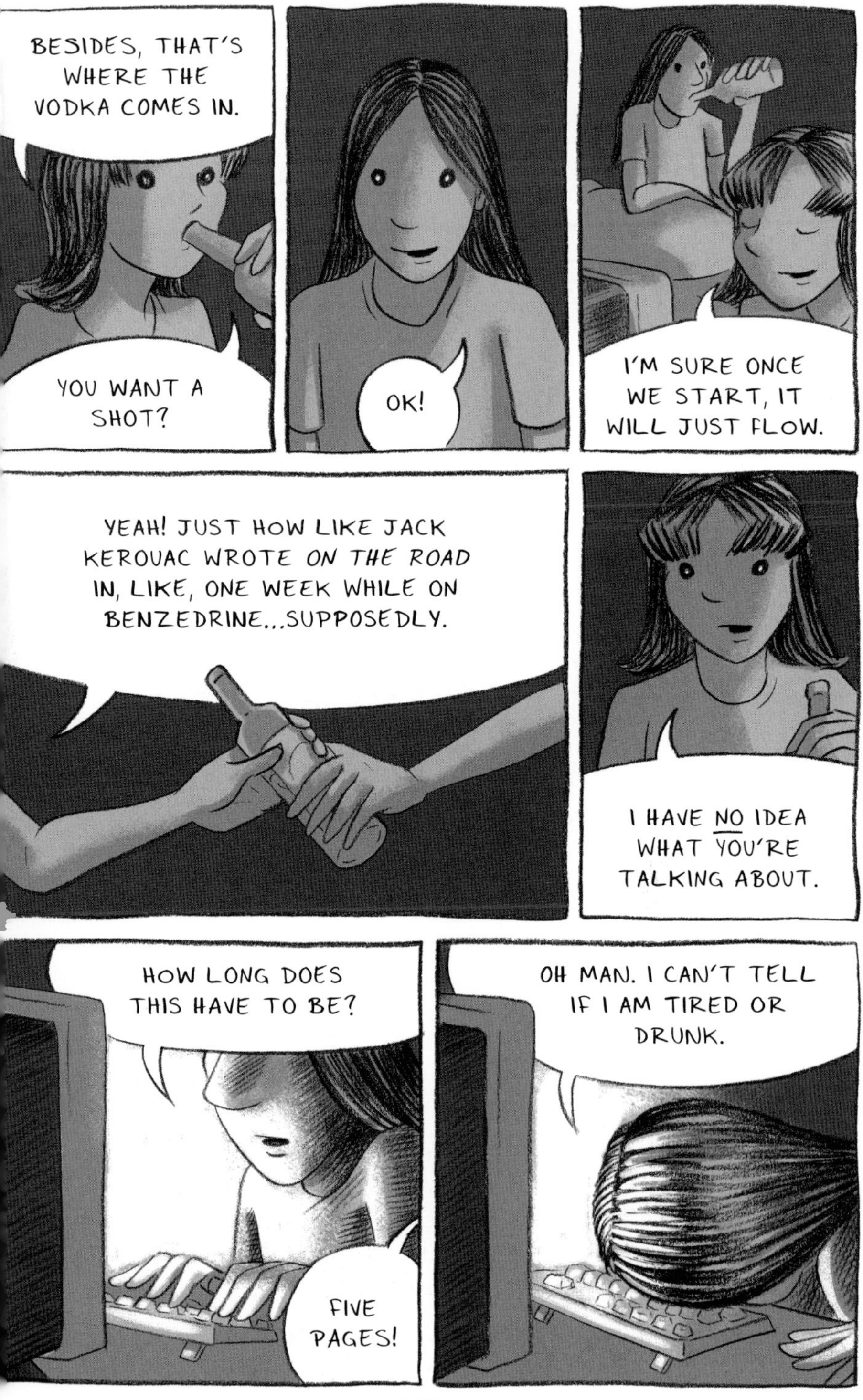

BESIDES, THAT'S WHERE THE VODKA COMES IN.
YOU WANT A SHOT?
OK!
I'M SURE ONCE WE START, IT WILL JUST FLOW.
YEAH! JUST HOW LIKE JACK KEROUAC WROTE *ON THE ROAD* IN, LIKE, ONE WEEK WHILE ON BENZEDRINE...SUPPOSEDLY.
I HAVE NO IDEA WHAT YOU'RE TALKING ABOUT.
HOW LONG DOES THIS HAVE TO BE?
FIVE PAGES!
OH MAN. I CAN'T TELL IF I AM TIRED OR DRUNK.

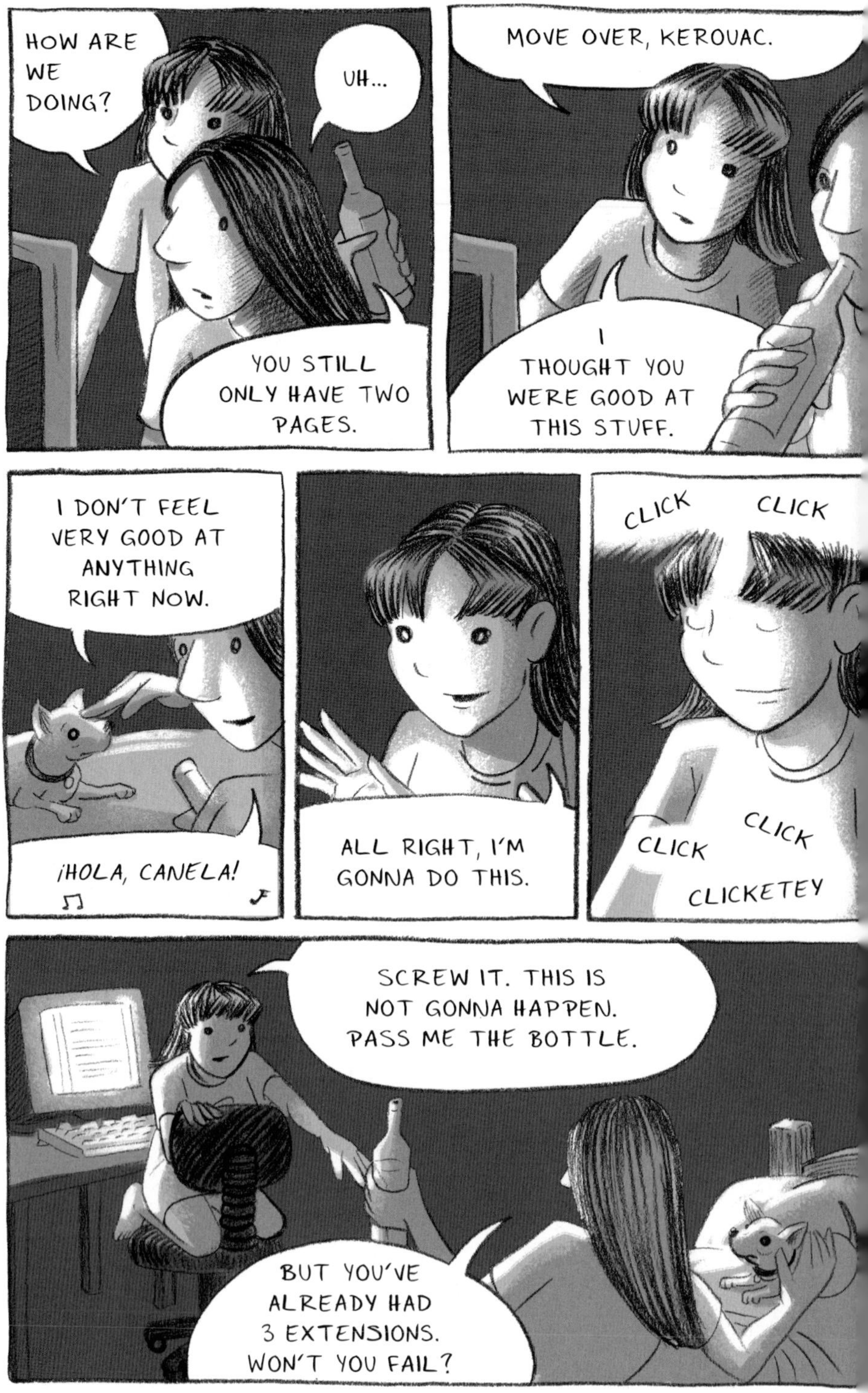
HOW ARE WE DOING?
UH...
YOU STILL ONLY HAVE TWO PAGES.
MOVE OVER, KEROUAC.
I THOUGHT YOU WERE GOOD AT THIS STUFF.
I DON'T FEEL VERY GOOD AT ANYTHING RIGHT NOW.
¡HOLA, CANELA!
ALL RIGHT, I'M GONNA DO THIS.
CLICK
CLICK
CLICK
CLICK
CLICKETEY
SCREW IT. THIS IS NOT GONNA HAPPEN. PASS ME THE BOTTLE.
BUT YOU'VE ALREADY HAD 3 EXTENSIONS. WON'T YOU FAIL?

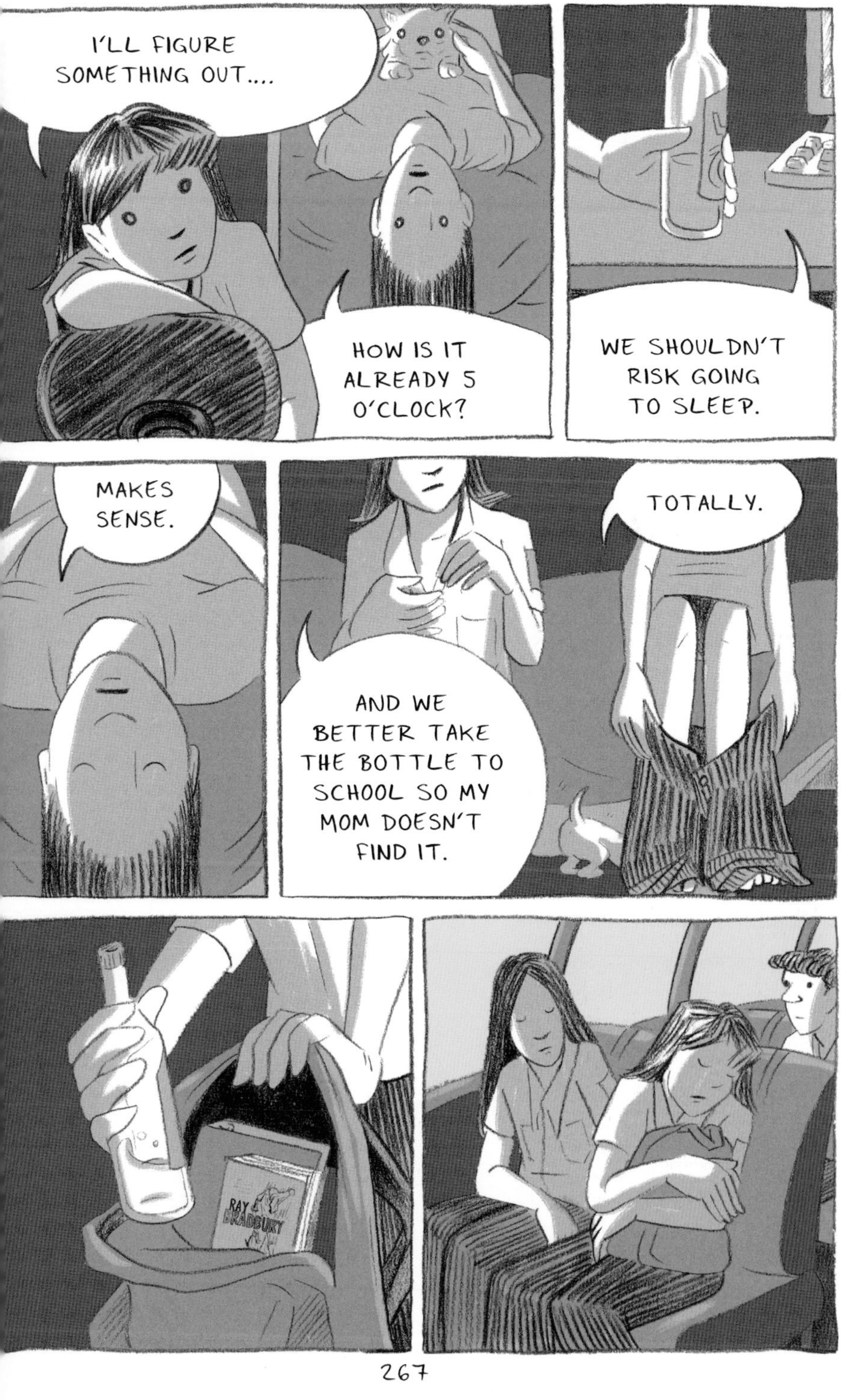
I'LL FIGURE SOMETHING OUT....
HOW IS IT ALREADY 5 O'CLOCK?
WE SHOULDN'T RISK GOING TO SLEEP.
MAKES SENSE.
AND WE BETTER TAKE THE BOTTLE TO SCHOOL SO MY MOM DOESN'T FIND IT.
TOTALLY.
RAY BRADBURY

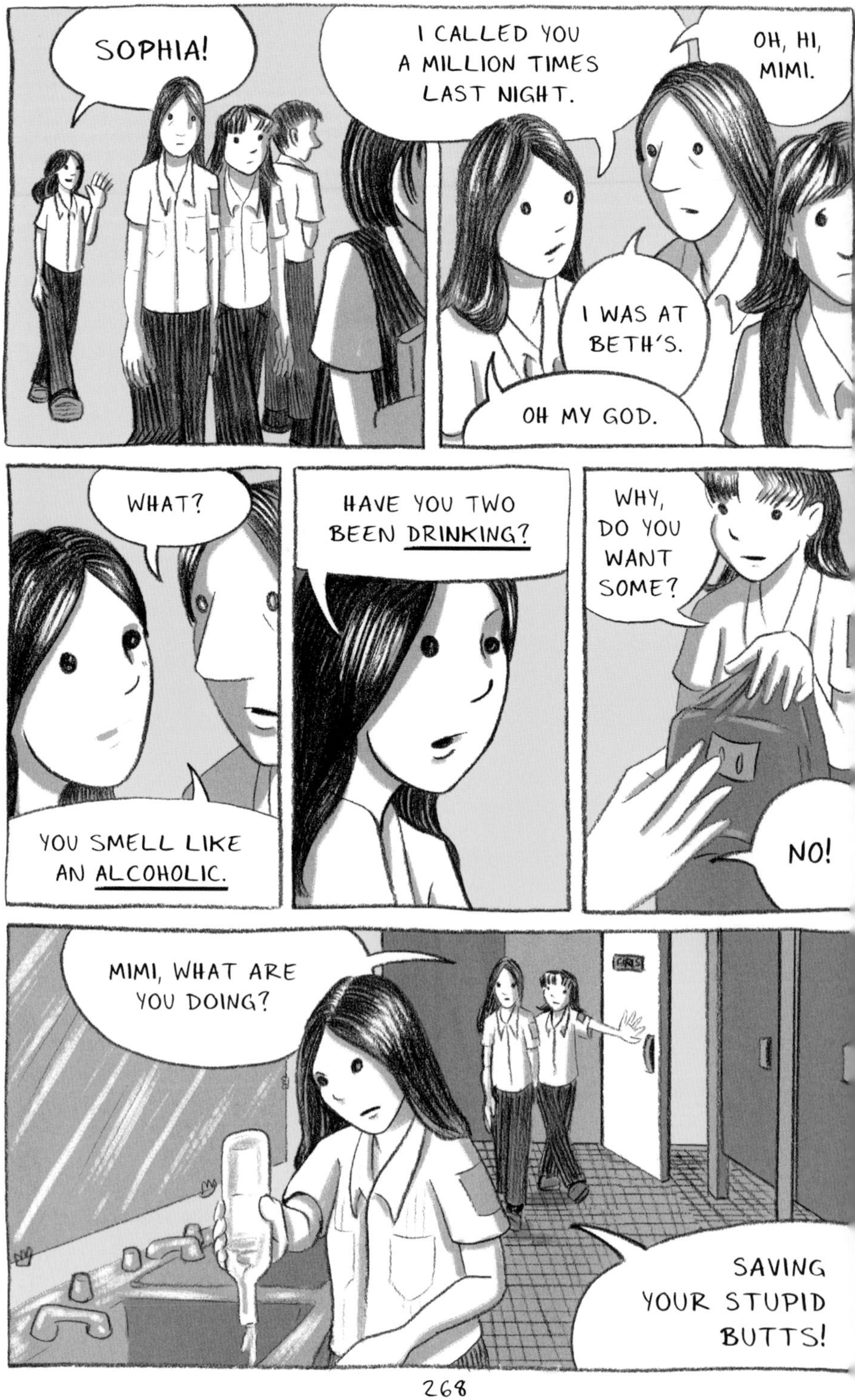

SOPHIA!
I CALLED YOU A MILLION TIMES LAST NIGHT.
OH, HI, MIMI.
I WAS AT BETH'S.
OH MY GOD.
WHAT?
YOU SMELL LIKE AN ALCOHOLIC.
HAVE YOU TWO BEEN DRINKING?
WHY, DO YOU WANT SOME?
NO!
MIMI, WHAT ARE YOU DOING?
SAVING YOUR STUPID BUTTS!

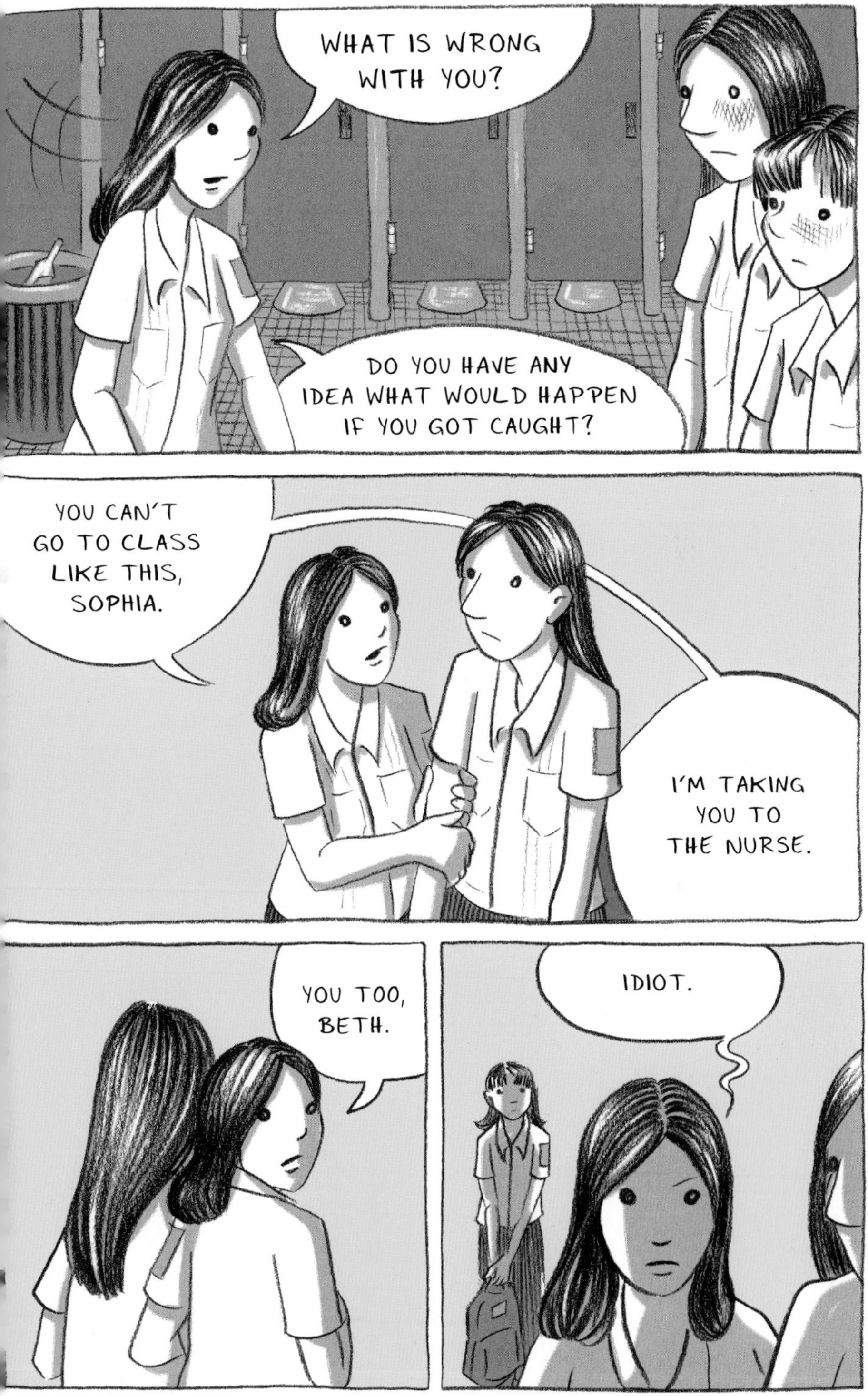

WHAT IS WRONG WITH YOU?
DO YOU HAVE ANY IDEA WHAT WOULD HAPPEN IF YOU GOT CAUGHT?
YOU CAN'T GO TO CLASS LIKE THIS, SOPHIA.
I'M TAKING YOU TO THE NURSE.
YOU TOO, BETH.
IDIOT.

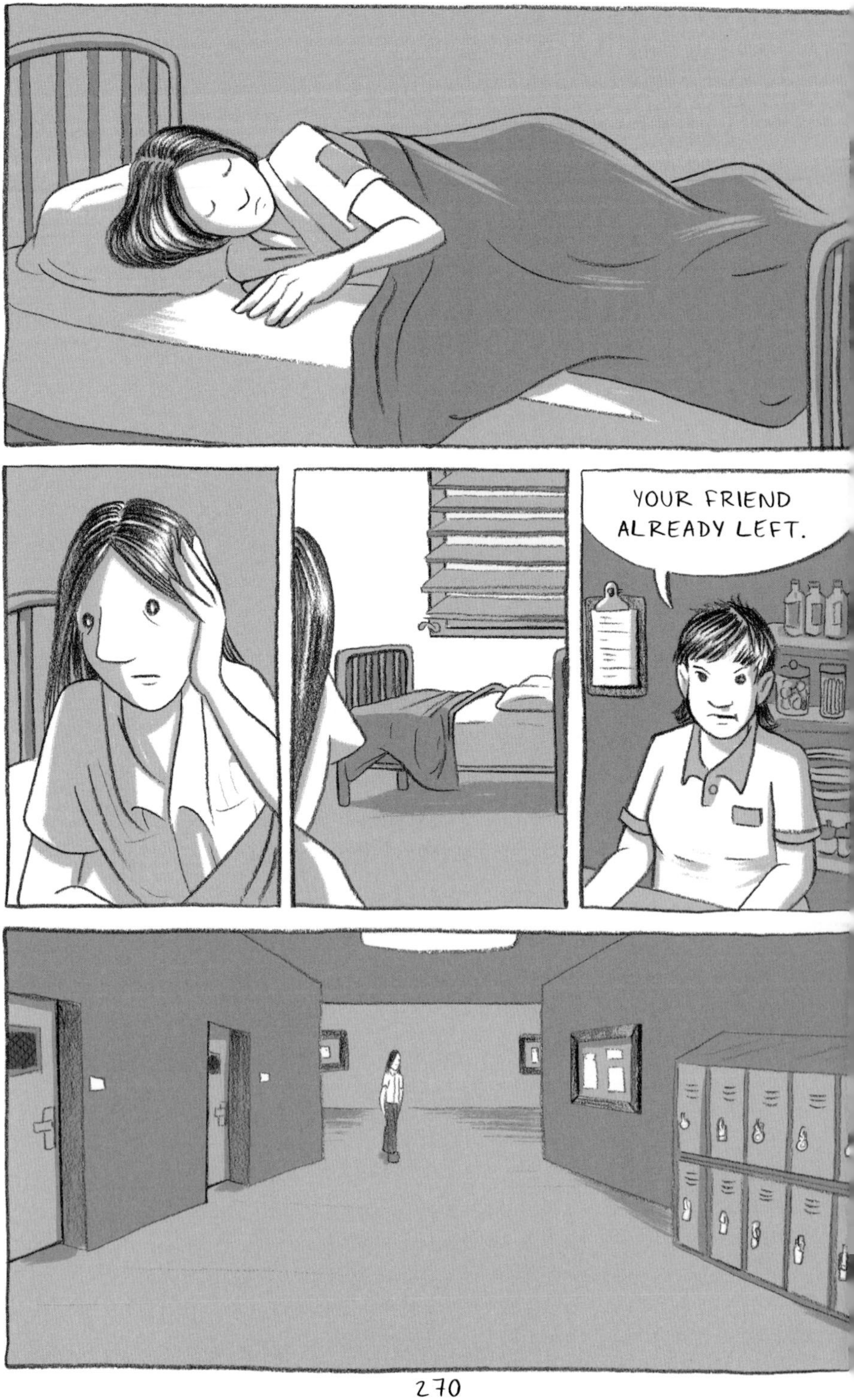
YOUR FRIEND ALREADY LEFT.

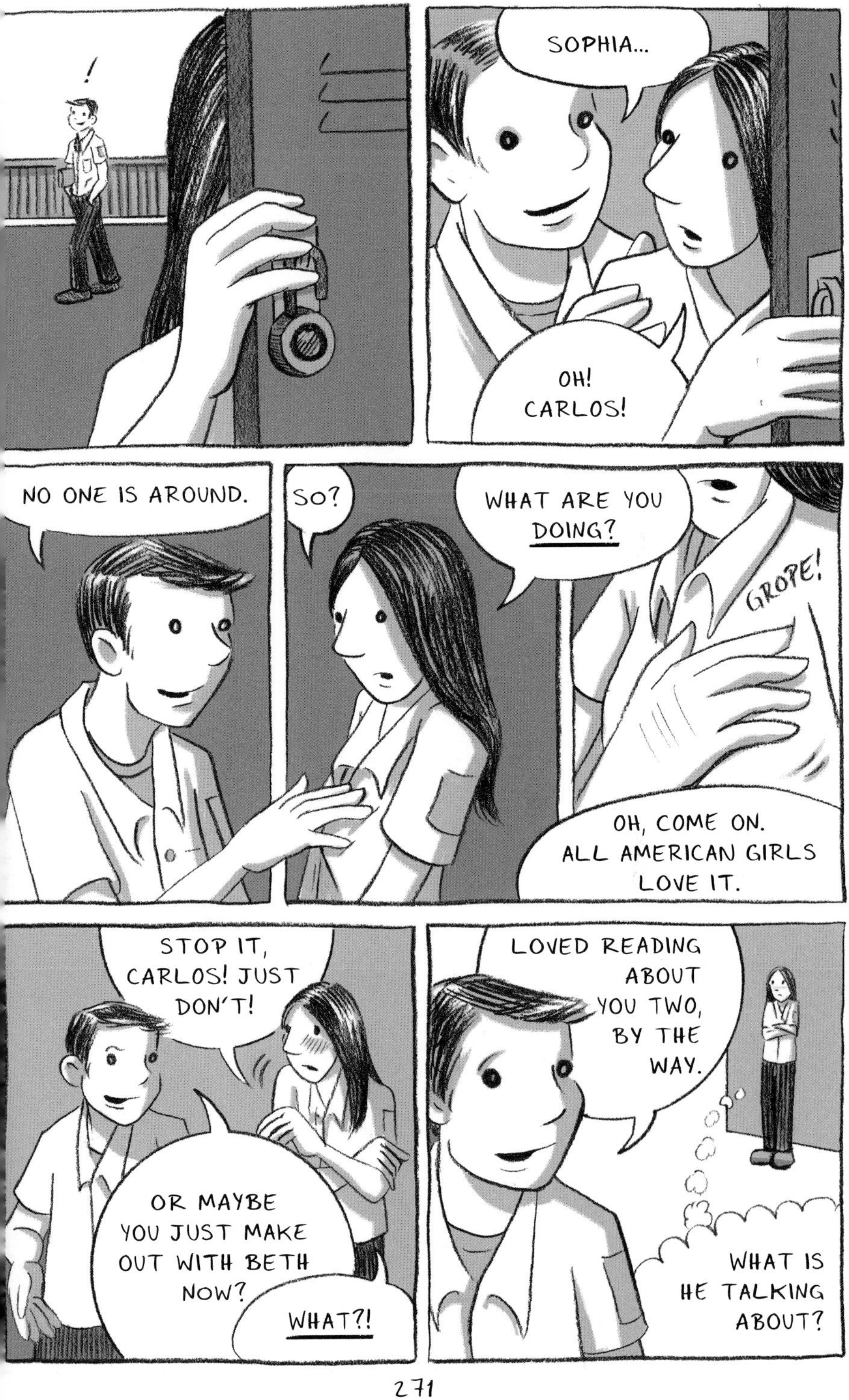
!
SOPHIA...
OH! CARLOS!
NO ONE IS AROUND.
SO?
WHAT ARE YOU DOING?
GROPE!
OH, COME ON. ALL AMERICAN GIRLS LOVE IT.
STOP IT, CARLOS! JUST DON'T!
OR MAYBE YOU JUST MAKE OUT WITH BETH NOW?
WHAT?!
LOVED READING ABOUT YOU TWO, BY THE WAY.
WHAT IS HE TALKING ABOUT?

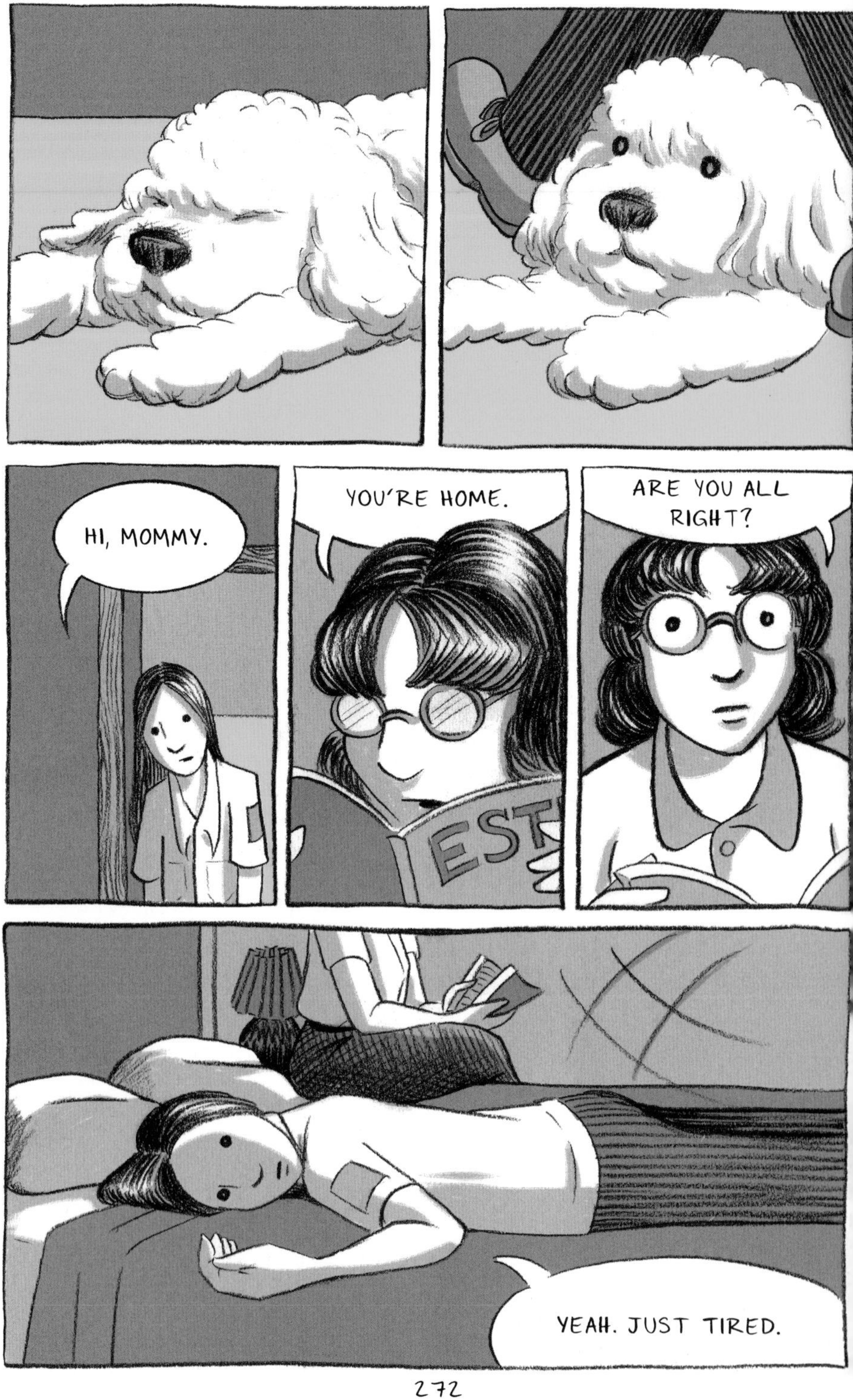
HI, MOMMY.
YOU'RE HOME.
ESTI
ARE YOU ALL RIGHT?
YEAH. JUST TIRED.

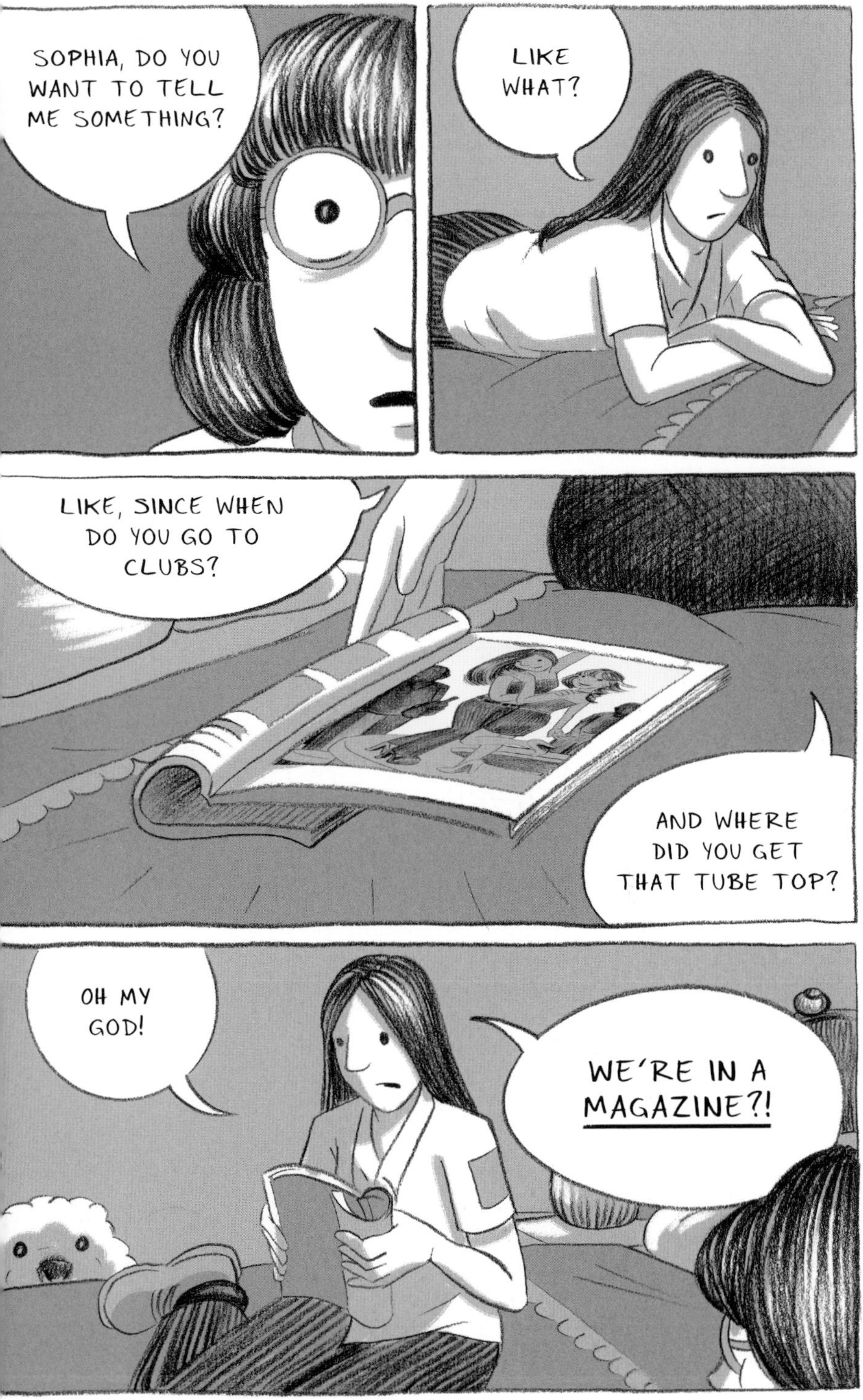
SOPHIA, DO YOU WANT TO TELL ME SOMETHING?
LIKE WHAT?
LIKE, SINCE WHEN DO YOU GO TO CLUBS?
AND WHERE DID YOU GET THAT TUBE TOP?
OH MY GOD!
WE'RE IN A MAGAZINE?!

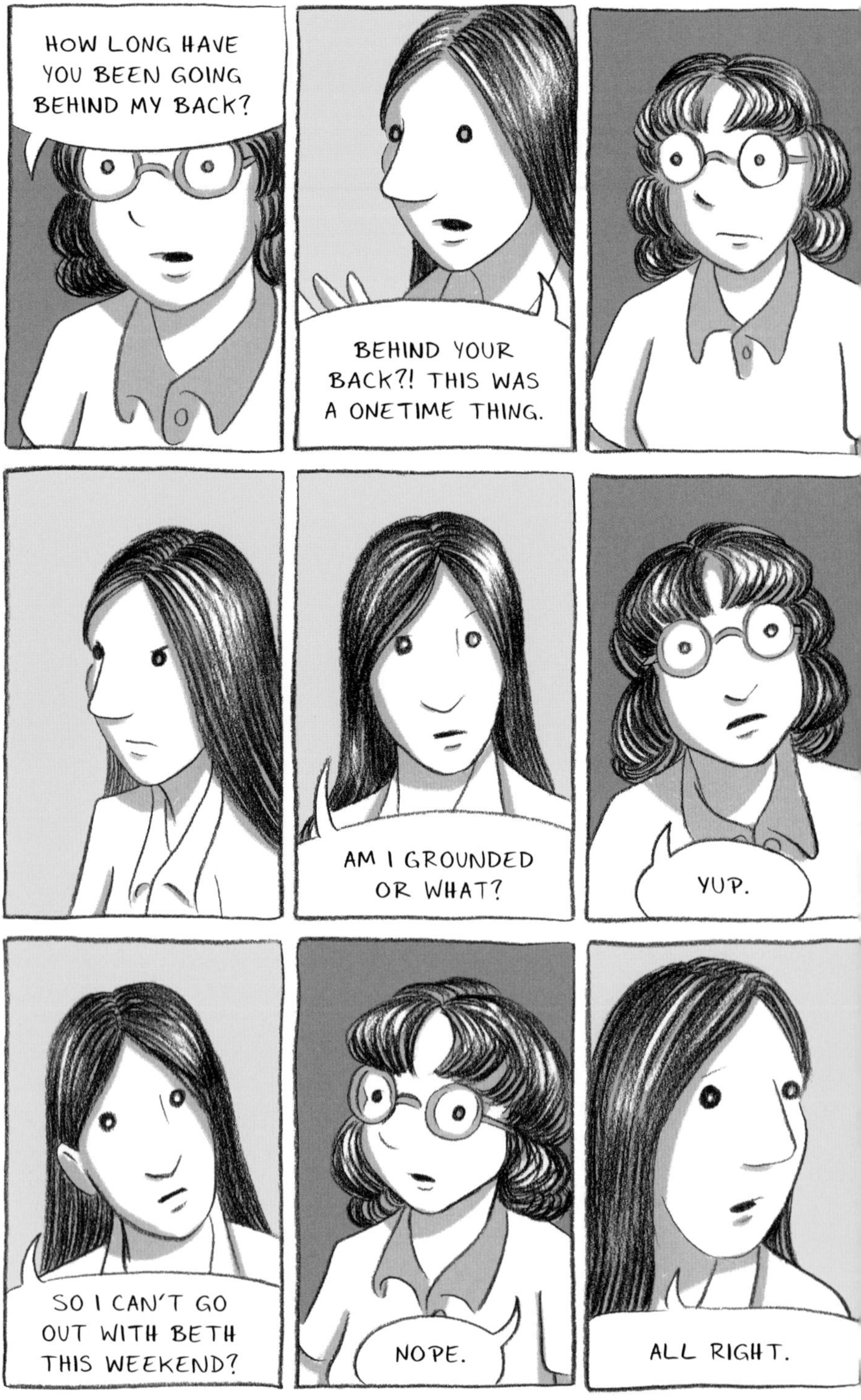
HOW LONG HAVE YOU BEEN GOING BEHIND MY BACK?
BEHIND YOUR BACK?! THIS WAS A ONETIME THING.
AM I GROUNDED OR WHAT?
YUP.
SO I CAN'T GO OUT WITH BETH THIS WEEKEND?
NOPE.
ALL RIGHT.

IN EVERY HOME WE'VE EVER LIVED IN, THERE HAS BEEN A DESIGNATED "SAFE ROOM" IN CASE OF EMERGENCY. IN THIS HOUSE, IT'S MY ROOM.

THE DOOR IS STEEL-PLATED. NO JOKE.

THERE IS A DEAD BOLT.

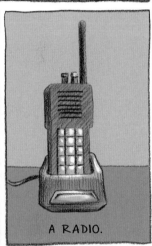

A RADIO.

AND A CHAIN LADDER IN MY CLOSET.

FOR MONTHS, I'VE HAD AN ELABORATE PLAN IN PLACE IN CASE MY PARENTS DIDN'T GIVE ME PERMISSION TO GO OUT.

THE ENTIRE HOUSE IS ALARMED AT NIGHT, AND IF ANY DOOR OR WINDOW IS OPENED, A SEAL IS BROKEN AND TRIGGERS AN ALARM.

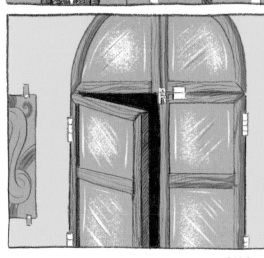

BUT ONLY ONE HALF MY FRENCH WINDOWS ARE SET UP FOR THIS, SO I ALWAYS KEEP ONE AJAR AT NIGHT.

THE GATE OUTSIDE THE
WINDOW HAS A PADLOCKED DOOR.

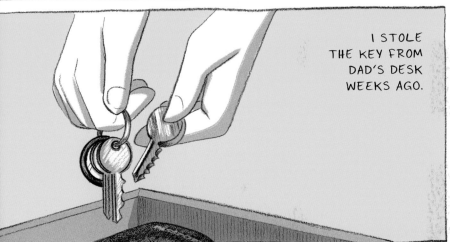

I STOLE
THE KEY FROM
DAD'S DESK
WEEKS AGO.

THIS IS WHERE THE
CHAIN LADDER COMES IN.

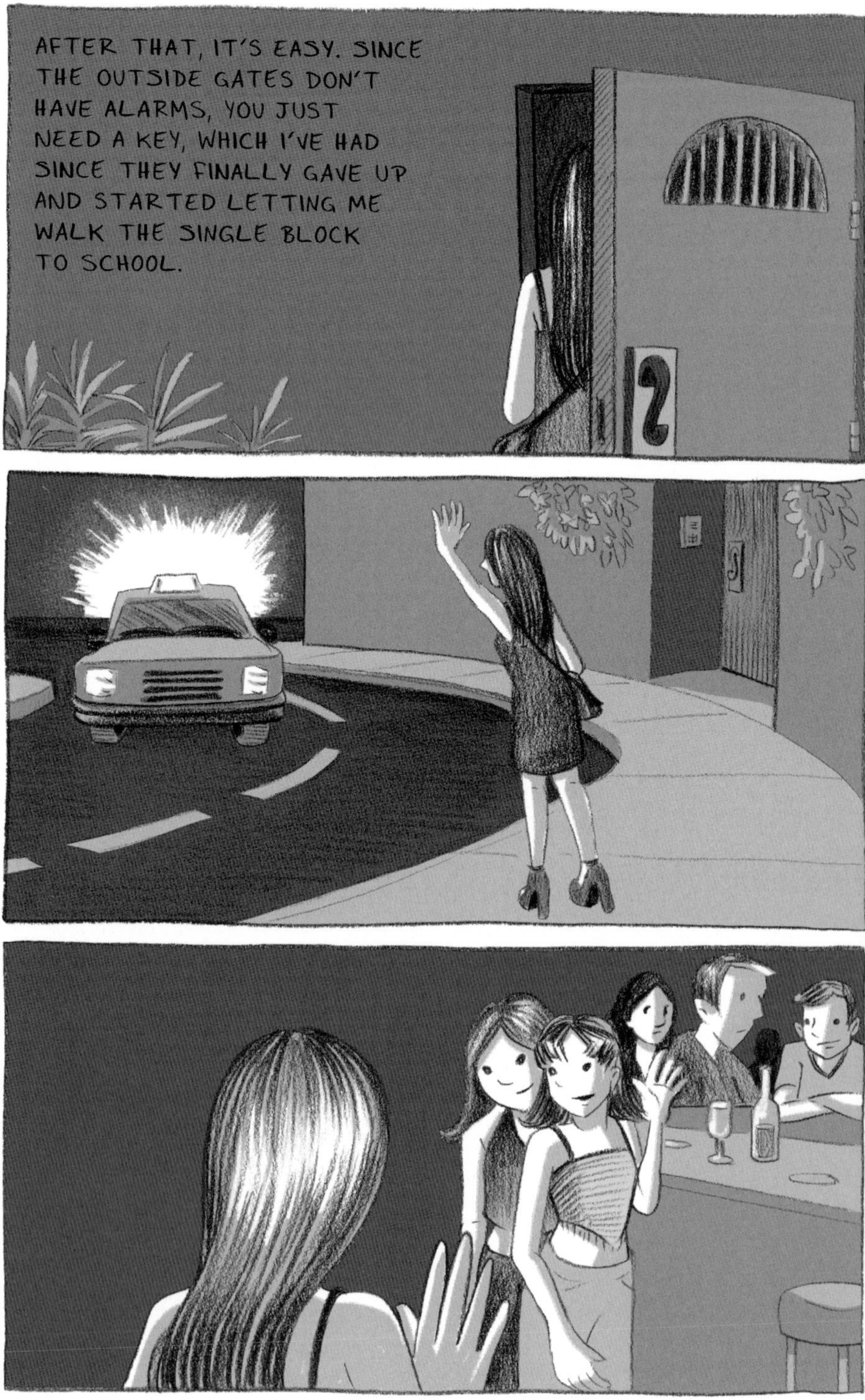
AFTER THAT, IT'S EASY. SINCE THE OUTSIDE GATES DON'T HAVE ALARMS, YOU JUST NEED A KEY, WHICH I'VE HAD SINCE THEY FINALLY GAVE UP AND STARTED LETTING ME WALK THE SINGLE BLOCK TO SCHOOL.
2

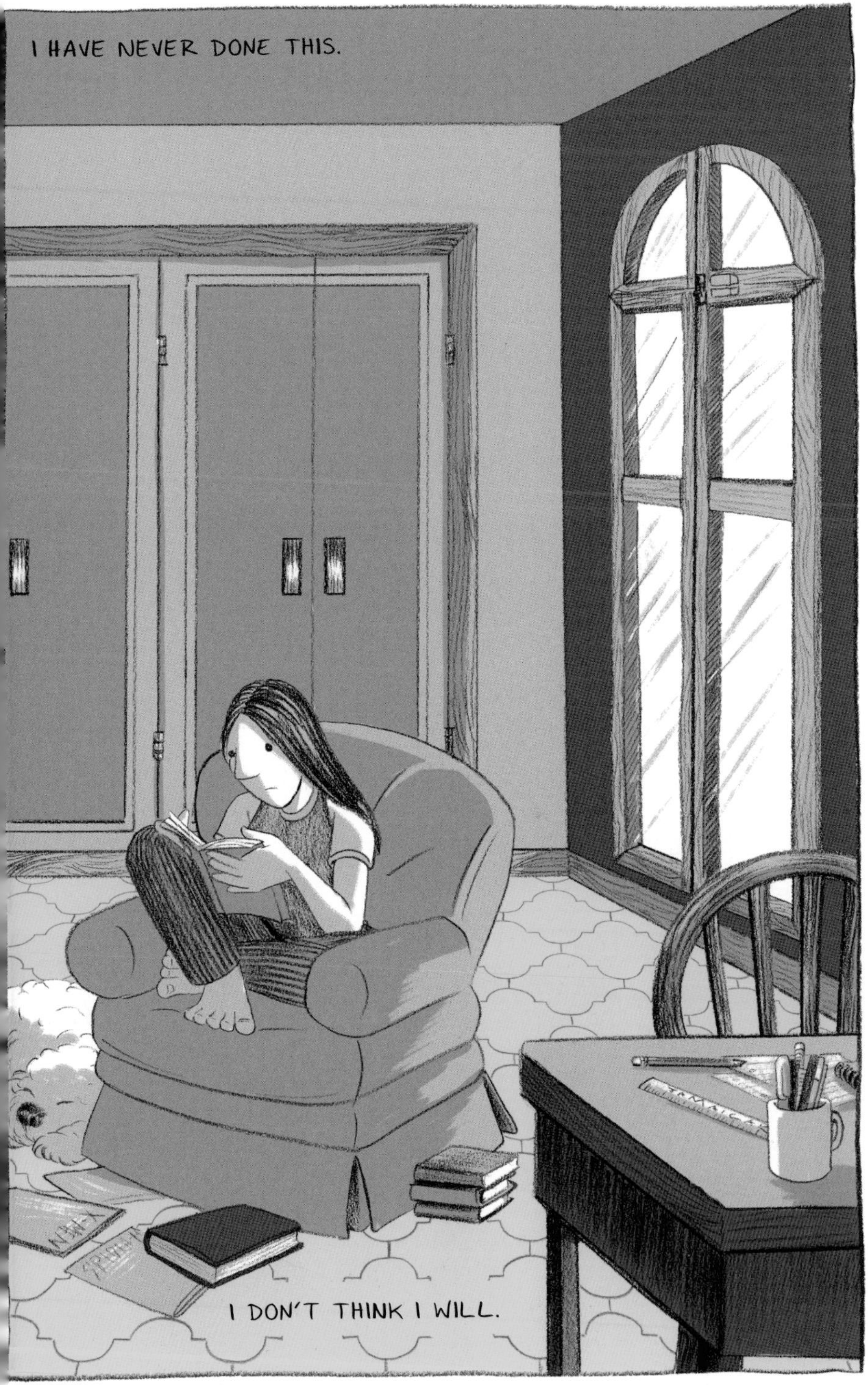

I HAVE NEVER DONE THIS.
I DON'T THINK I WILL.

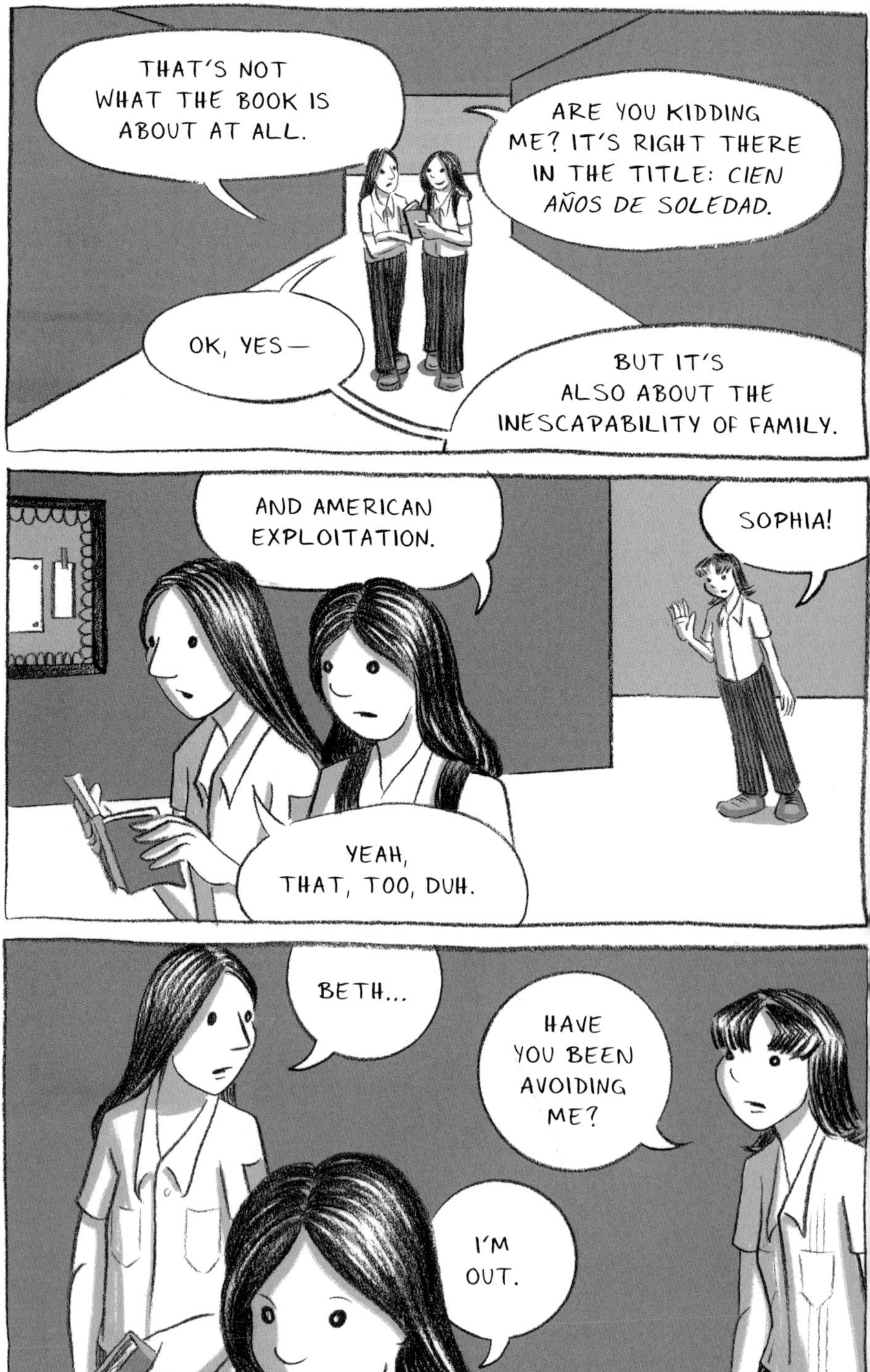

THAT'S NOT WHAT THE BOOK IS ABOUT AT ALL.
ARE YOU KIDDING ME? IT'S RIGHT THERE IN THE TITLE: *CIEN AÑOS DE SOLEDAD.*
OK, YES—
BUT IT'S ALSO ABOUT THE INESCAPABILITY OF FAMILY.
AND AMERICAN EXPLOITATION.
SOPHIA!
YEAH, THAT, TOO, DUH.
BETH...
HAVE YOU BEEN AVOIDING ME?
I'M OUT.

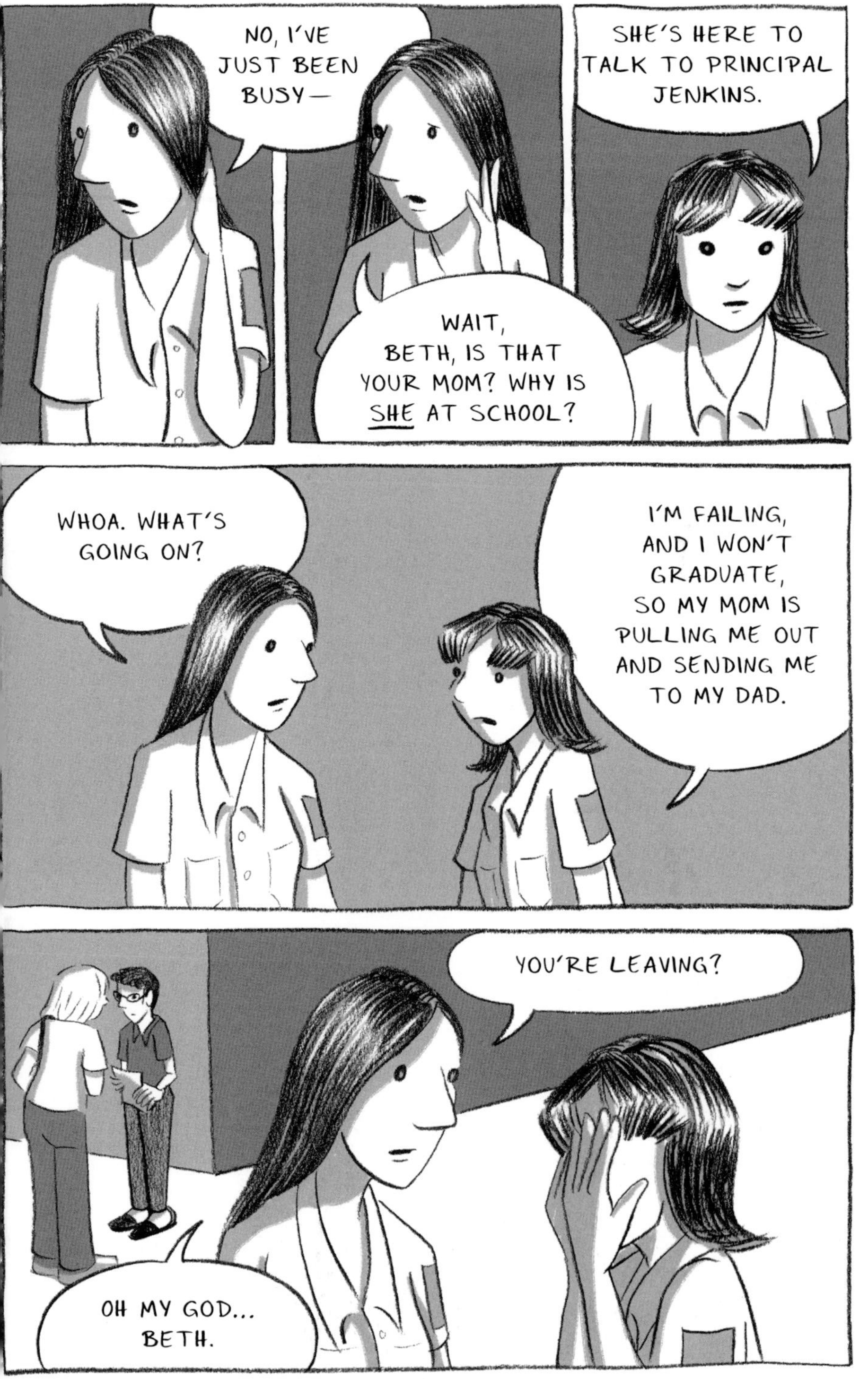
NO, I'VE JUST BEEN BUSY—
WAIT, BETH, IS THAT YOUR MOM? WHY IS SHE AT SCHOOL?
SHE'S HERE TO TALK TO PRINCIPAL JENKINS.
WHOA. WHAT'S GOING ON?
I'M FAILING, AND I WON'T GRADUATE, SO MY MOM IS PULLING ME OUT AND SENDING ME TO MY DAD.
YOU'RE LEAVING?
OH MY GOD... BETH.

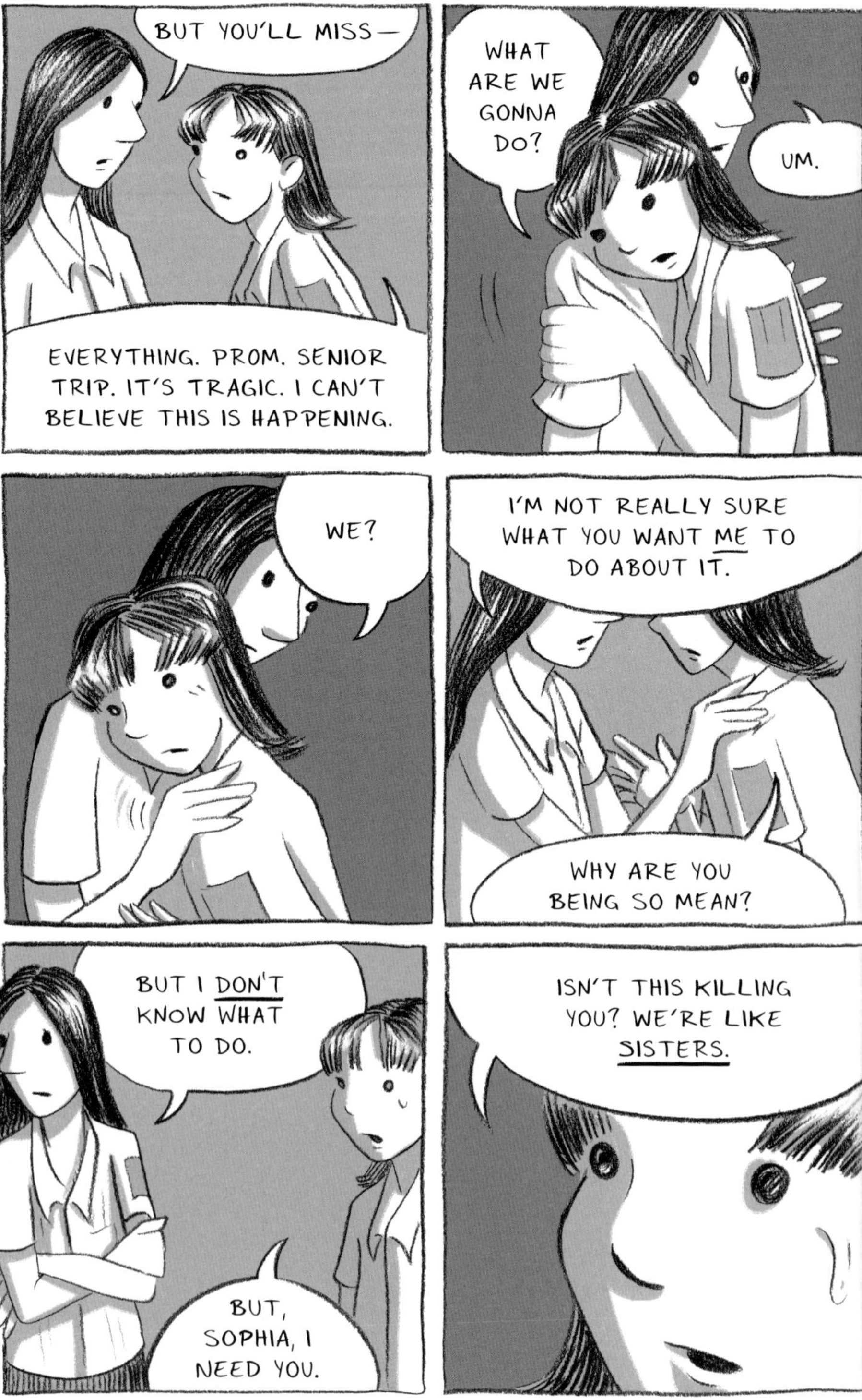
BUT YOU'LL MISS—
EVERYTHING. PROM. SENIOR TRIP. IT'S TRAGIC. I CAN'T BELIEVE THIS IS HAPPENING.
WHAT ARE WE GONNA DO?
UM.
WE?
I'M NOT REALLY SURE WHAT YOU WANT ME TO DO ABOUT IT.
WHY ARE YOU BEING SO MEAN?
BUT I DON'T KNOW WHAT TO DO.
BUT, SOPHIA, I NEED YOU.
ISN'T THIS KILLING YOU? WE'RE LIKE SISTERS.

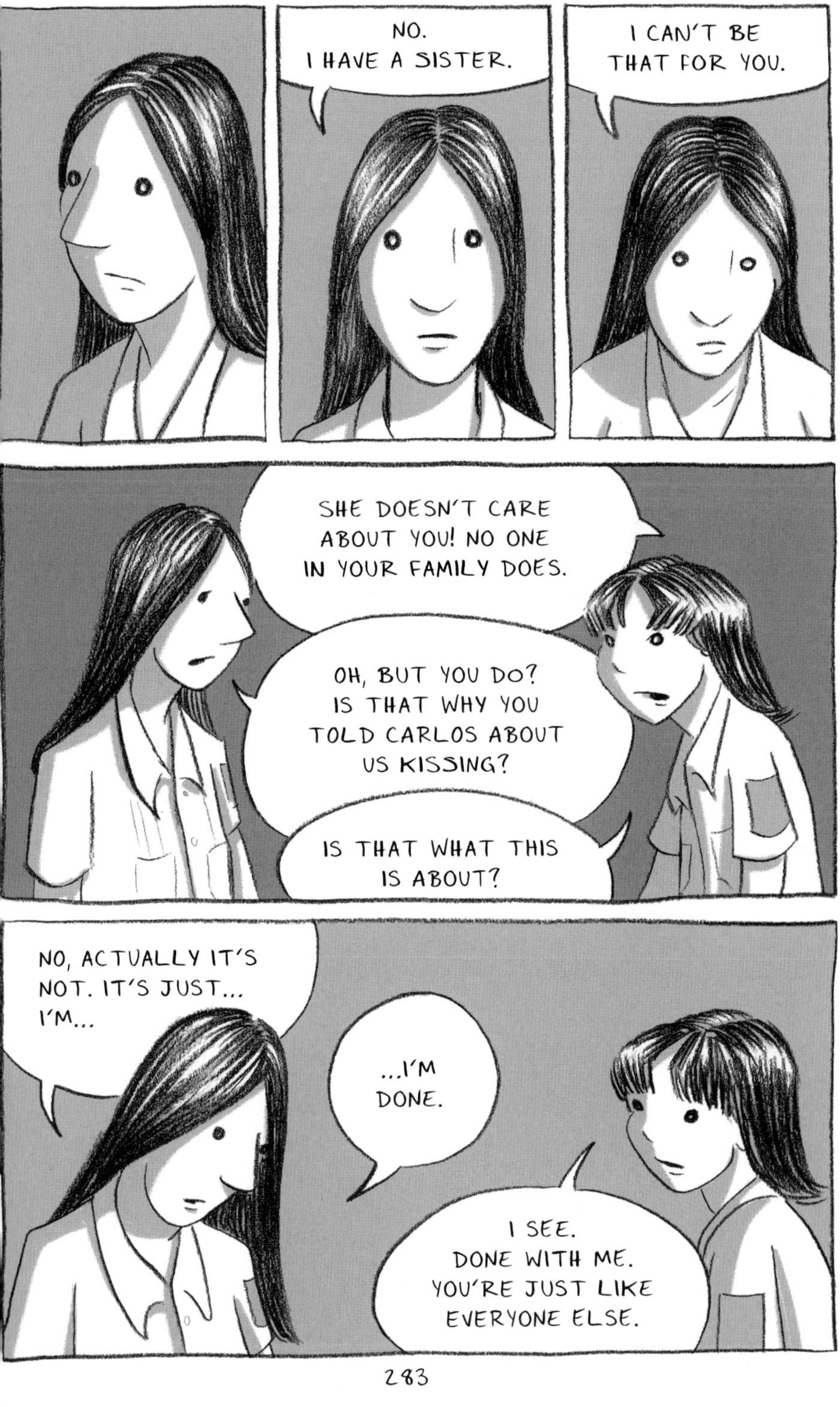
NO.
I HAVE A SISTER.
I CAN'T BE THAT FOR YOU.
SHE DOESN'T CARE ABOUT YOU! NO ONE IN YOUR FAMILY DOES.
OH, BUT YOU DO? IS THAT WHY YOU TOLD CARLOS ABOUT US KISSING?
IS THAT WHAT THIS IS ABOUT?
NO, ACTUALLY IT'S NOT. IT'S JUST... I'M...
...I'M DONE.
I SEE.
DONE WITH ME. YOU'RE JUST LIKE EVERYONE ELSE.

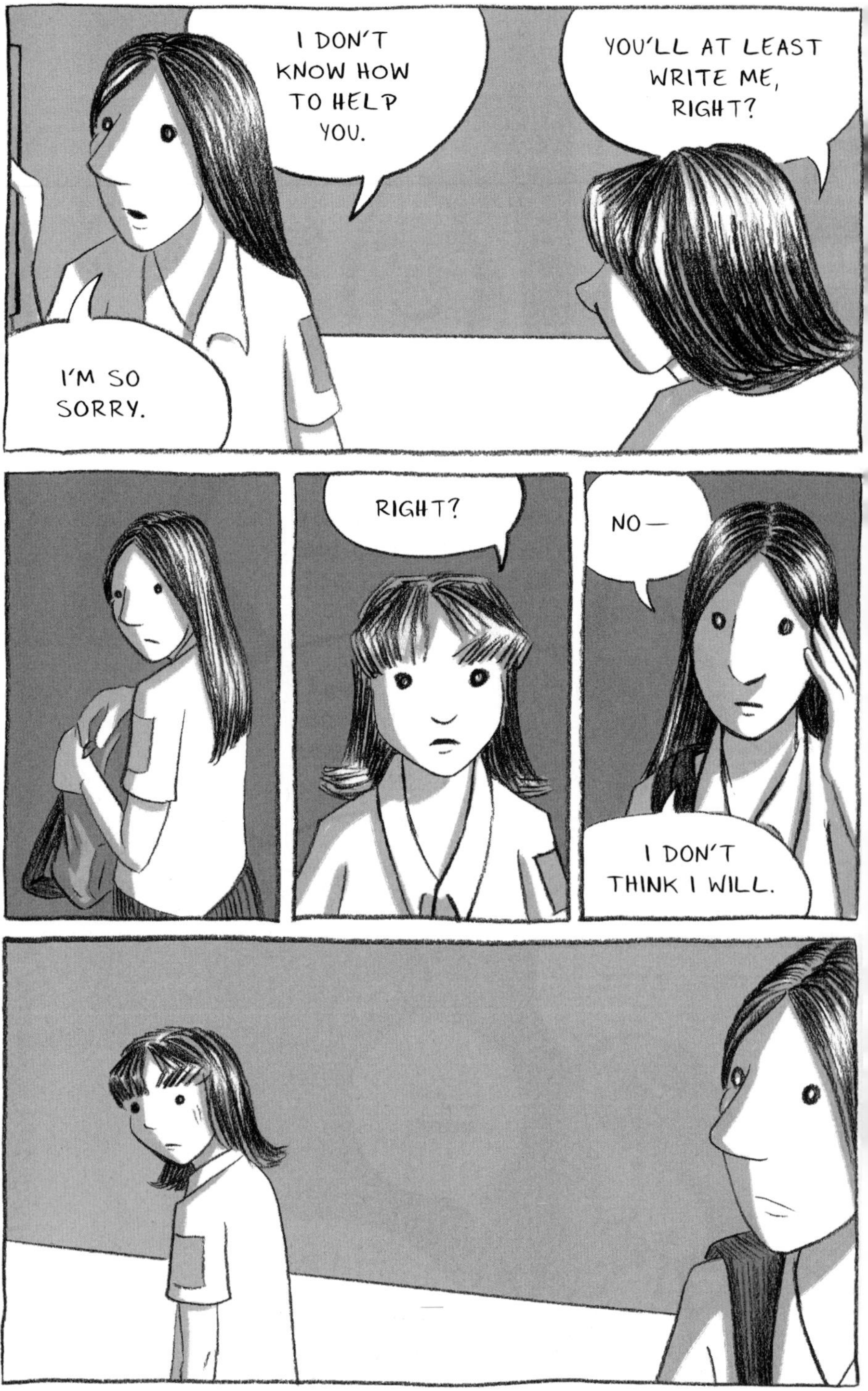
I DON'T KNOW HOW TO HELP YOU.
I'M SO SORRY.
YOU'LL AT LEAST WRITE ME, RIGHT?
RIGHT?
NO—
I DON'T THINK I WILL.

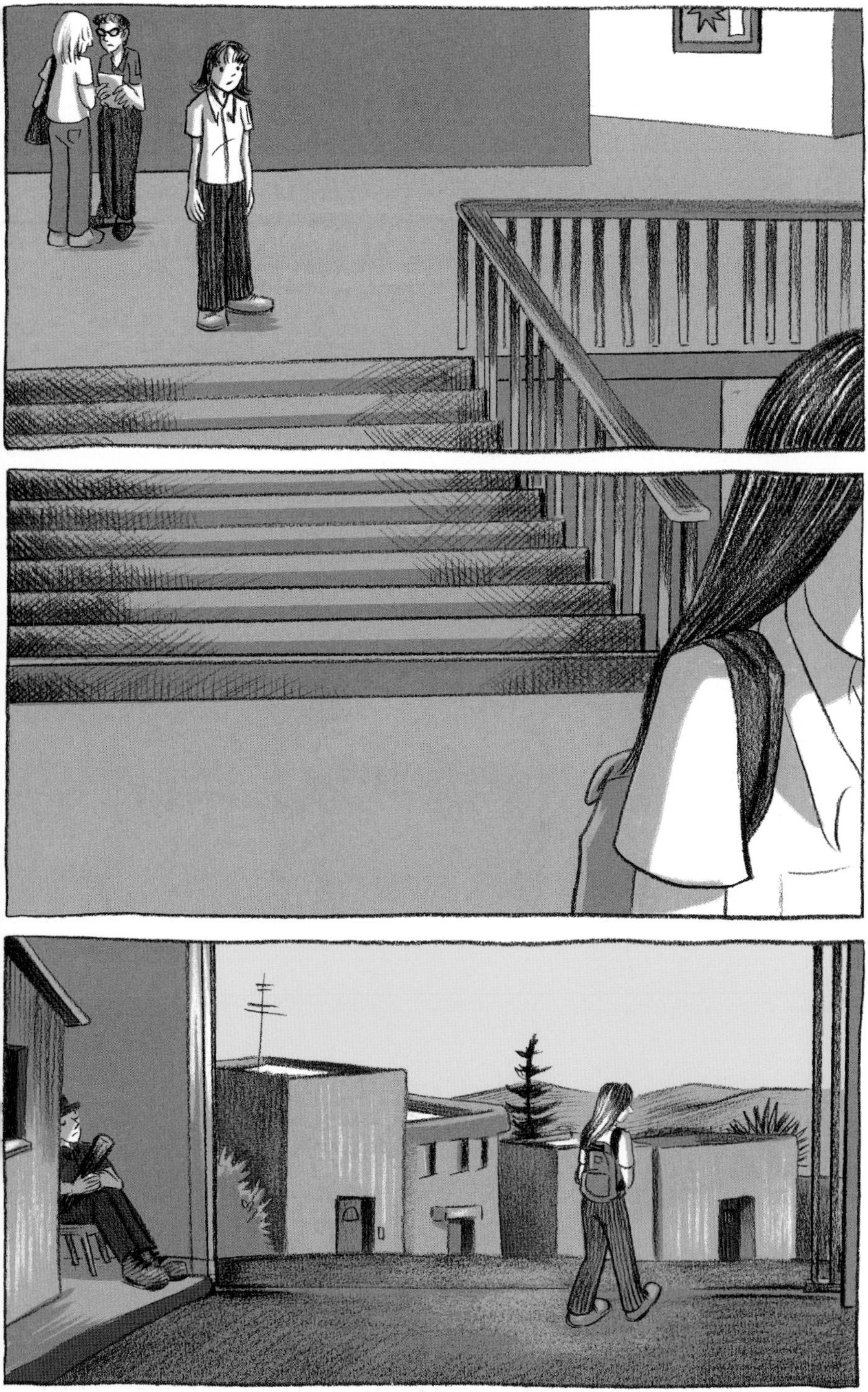

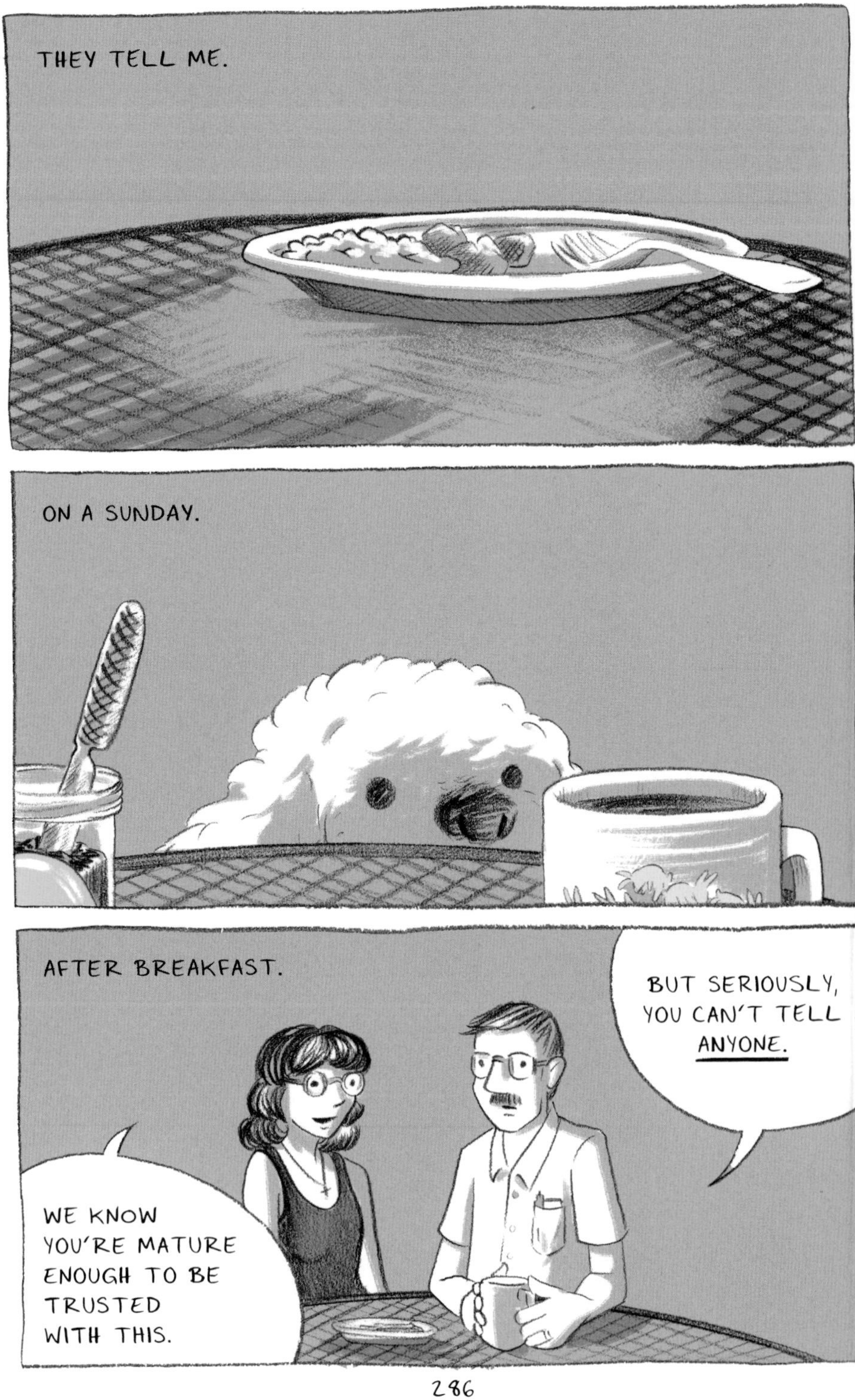
THEY TELL ME.
ON A SUNDAY.
AFTER BREAKFAST.
BUT SERIOUSLY, YOU CAN'T TELL ANYONE.
WE KNOW YOU'RE MATURE ENOUGH TO BE TRUSTED WITH THIS.

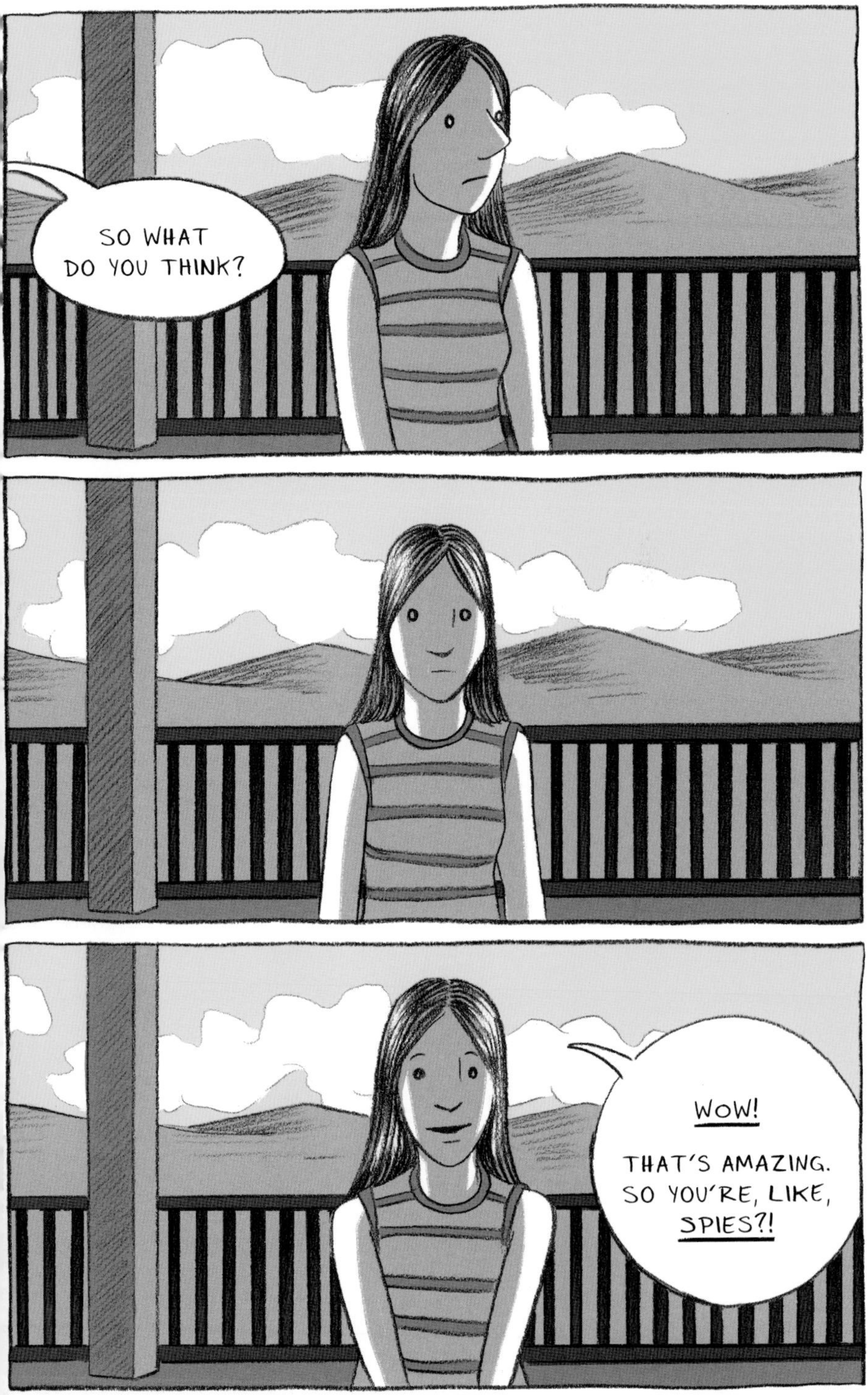
SO WHAT DO YOU THINK?
WOW!
THAT'S AMAZING. SO YOU'RE, LIKE, SPIES?!

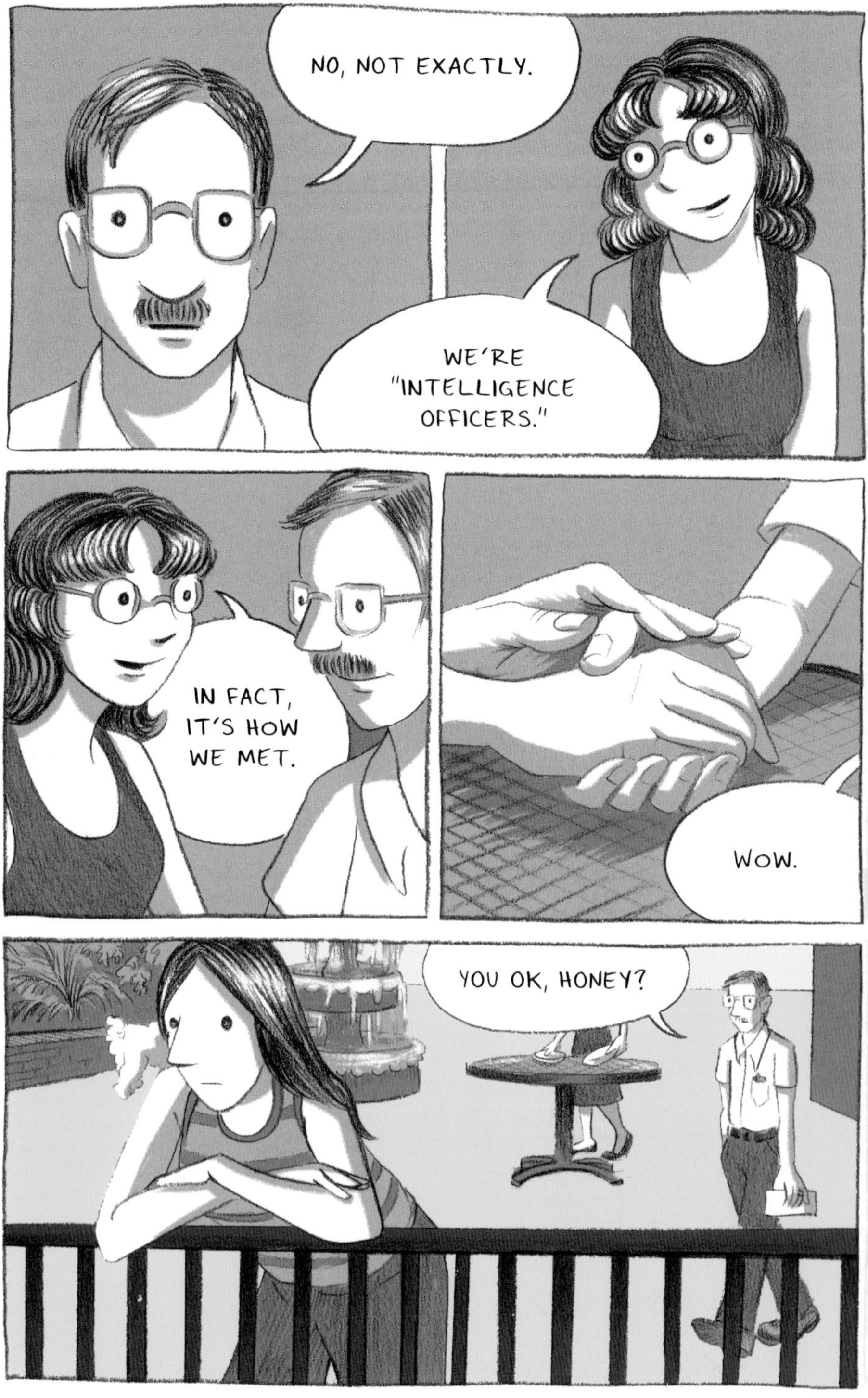
NO, NOT EXACTLY.
WE'RE "INTELLIGENCE OFFICERS."
IN FACT, IT'S HOW WE MET.
WOW.
YOU OK, HONEY?

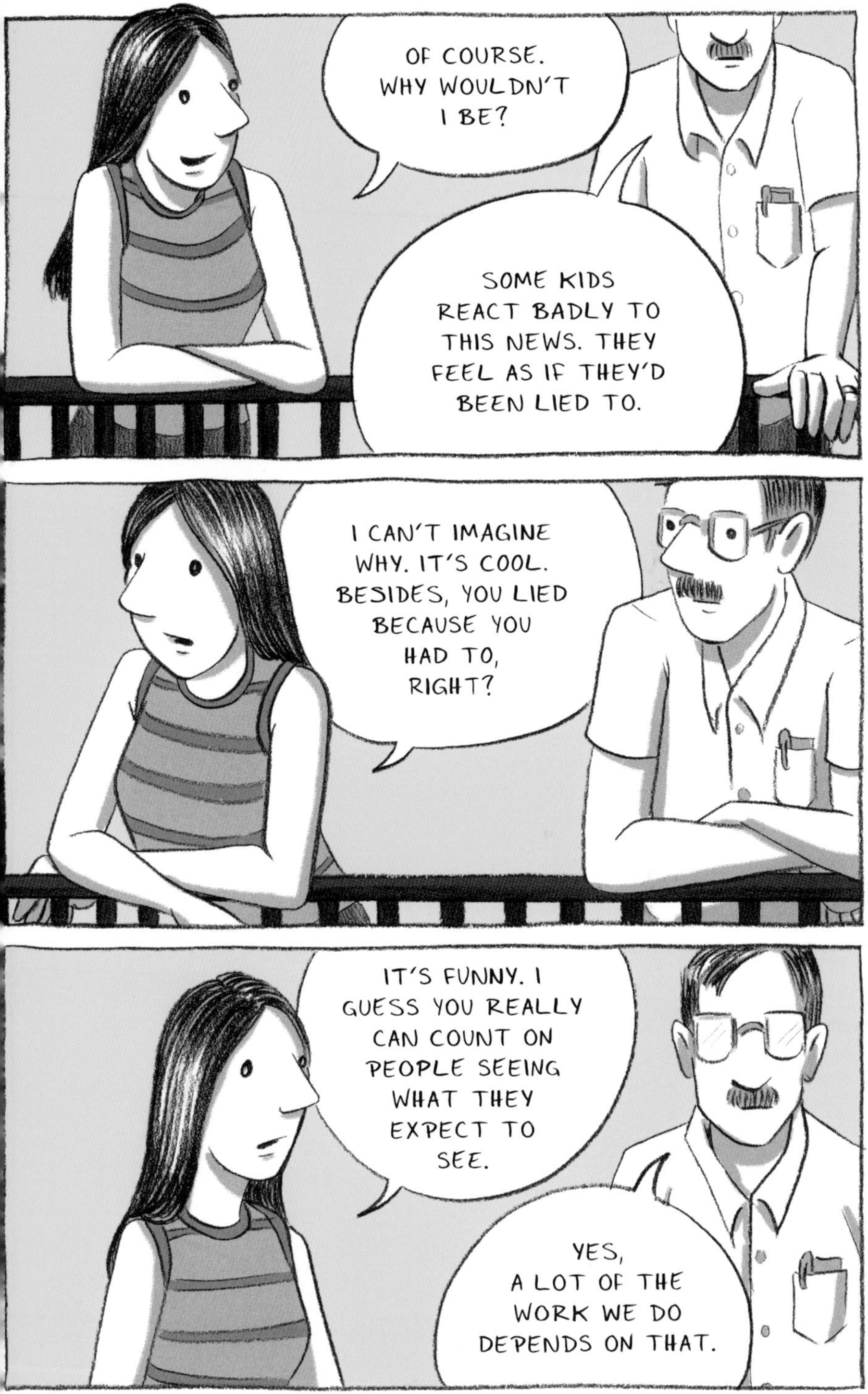

OF COURSE. WHY WOULDN'T I BE?
SOME KIDS REACT BADLY TO THIS NEWS. THEY FEEL AS IF THEY'D BEEN LIED TO.
I CAN'T IMAGINE WHY. IT'S COOL. BESIDES, YOU LIED BECAUSE YOU HAD TO, RIGHT?
IT'S FUNNY. I GUESS YOU REALLY CAN COUNT ON PEOPLE SEEING WHAT THEY EXPECT TO SEE.
YES, A LOT OF THE WORK WE DO DEPENDS ON THAT.

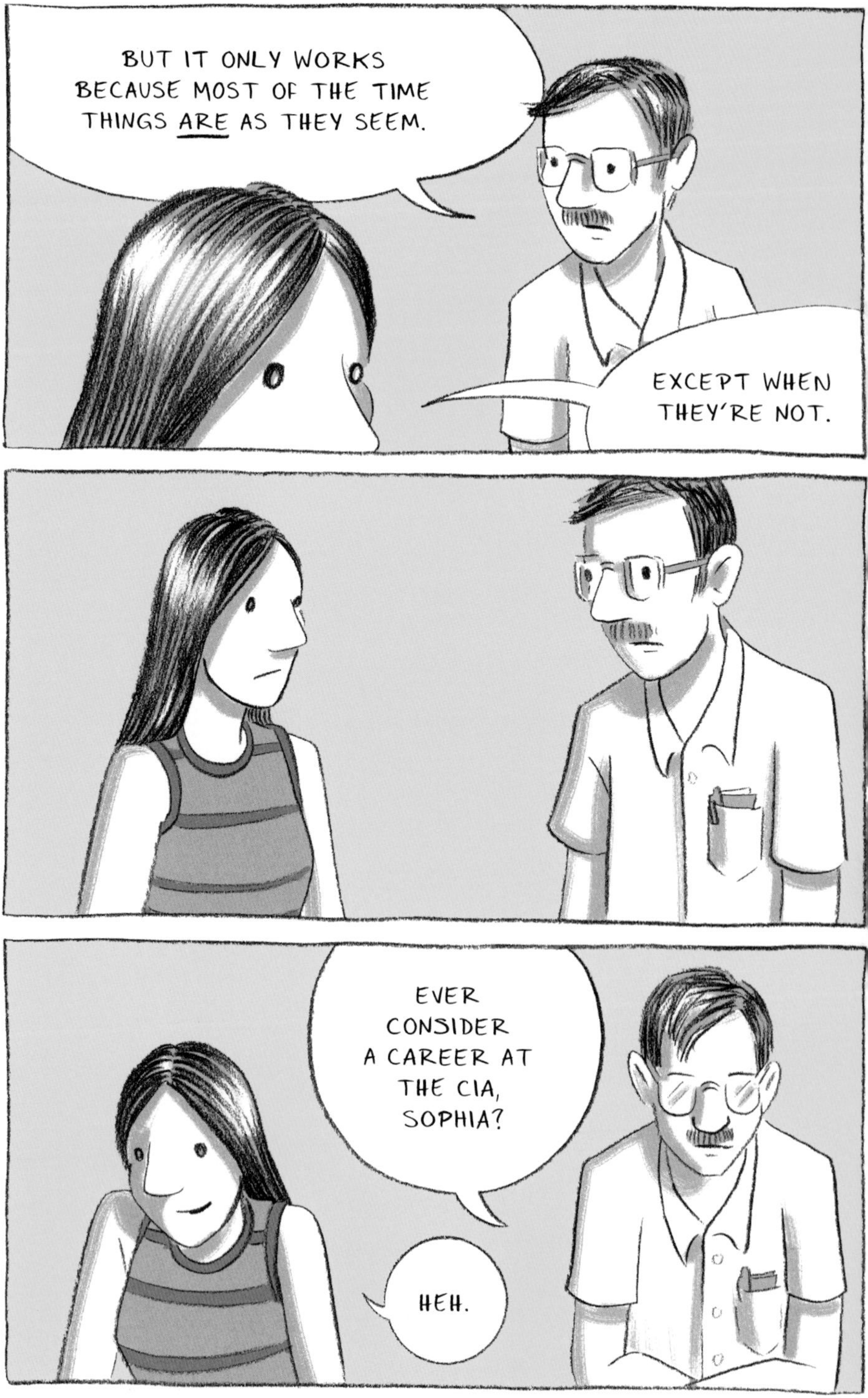
BUT IT ONLY WORKS BECAUSE MOST OF THE TIME THINGS ARE AS THEY SEEM.
EXCEPT WHEN THEY'RE NOT.
EVER CONSIDER A CAREER AT THE CIA, SOPHIA?
HEH.

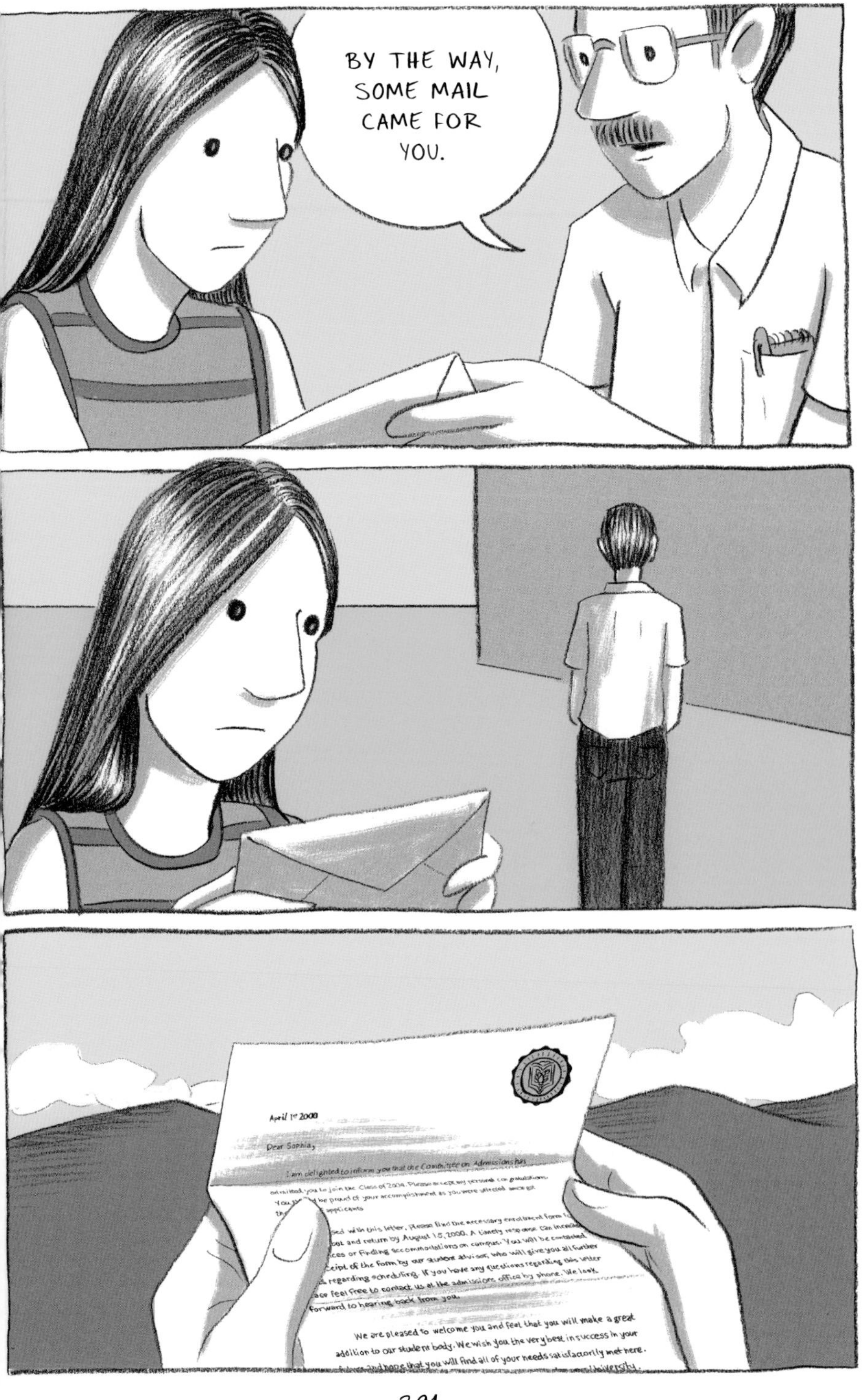

BY THE WAY, SOME MAIL CAME FOR YOU.
April 1st 2000
Dear Sophia,
I am delighted to inform you that the Committee on Admissions has
forward to hearing back from you.
We are pleased to welcome you and feel that you will make a great
addition to our student body. We wish you the very best in success in your

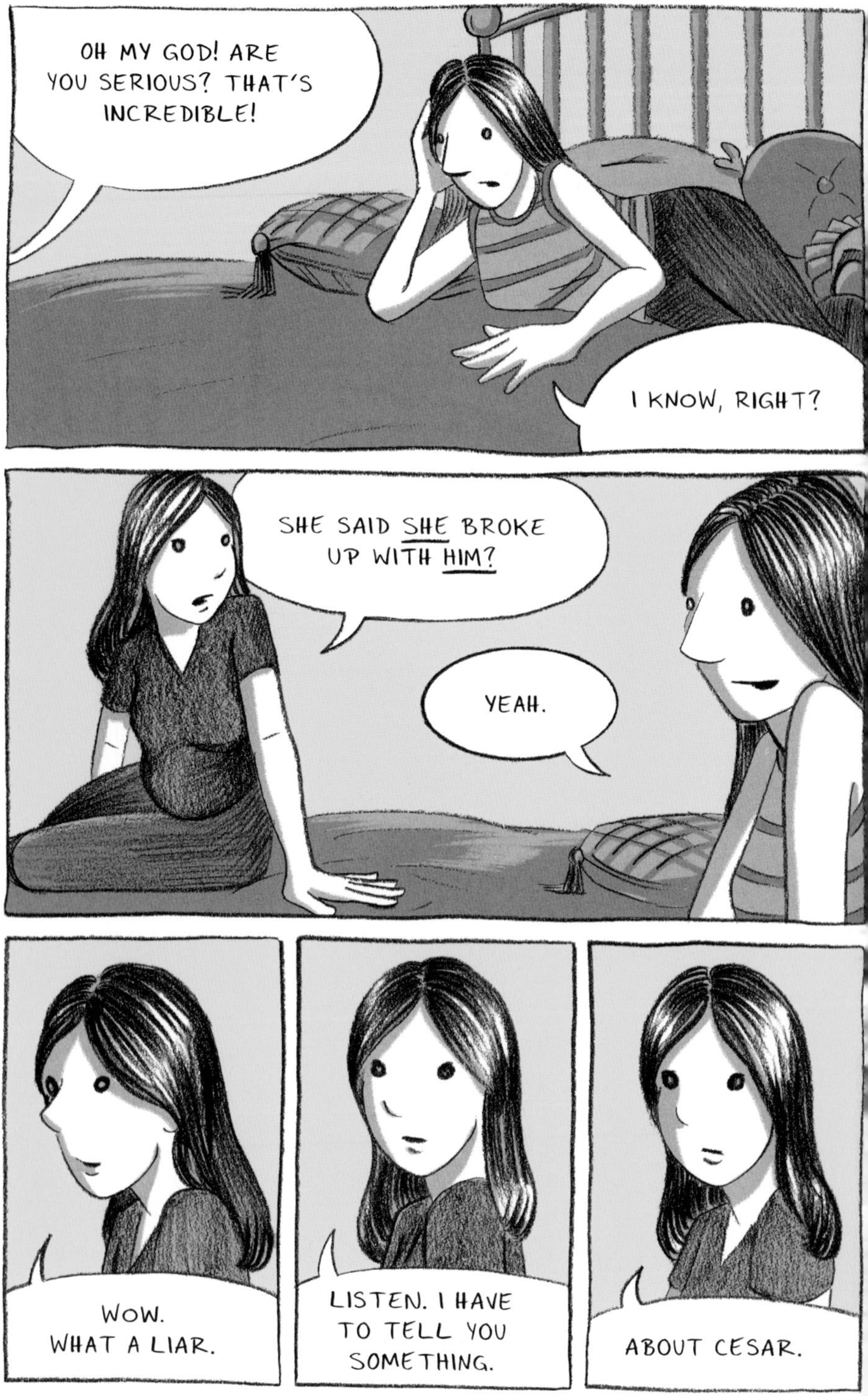
OH MY GOD! ARE YOU SERIOUS? THAT'S INCREDIBLE!
I KNOW, RIGHT?
SHE SAID SHE BROKE UP WITH HIM?
YEAH.
WOW. WHAT A LIAR.
LISTEN. I HAVE TO TELL YOU SOMETHING.
ABOUT CESAR.

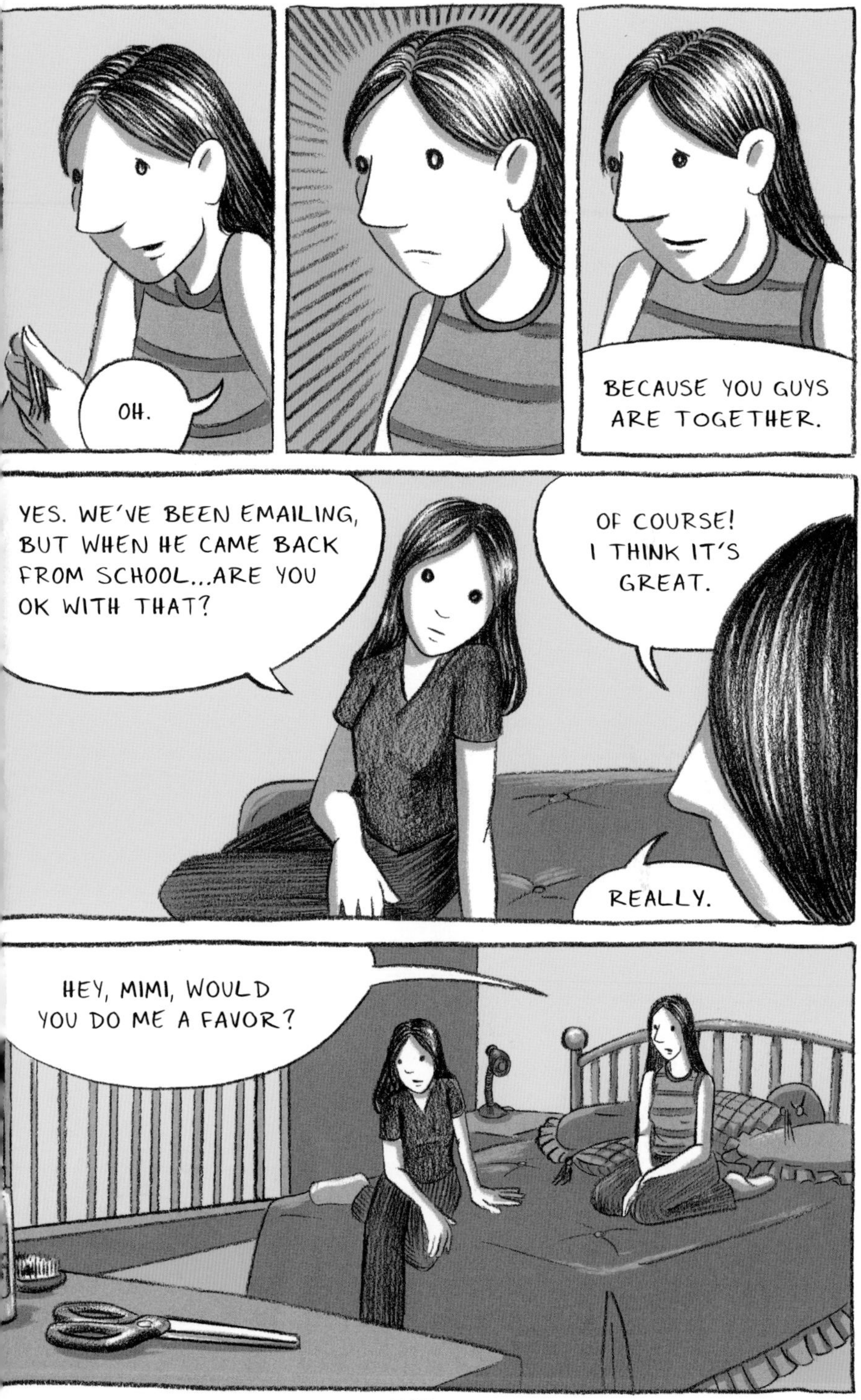
OH.
BECAUSE YOU GUYS ARE TOGETHER.
YES. WE'VE BEEN EMAILING, BUT WHEN HE CAME BACK FROM SCHOOL...ARE YOU OK WITH THAT?
OF COURSE! I THINK IT'S GREAT.
REALLY.
HEY, MIMI, WOULD YOU DO ME A FAVOR?

ARE YOU SURE ABOUT THIS?

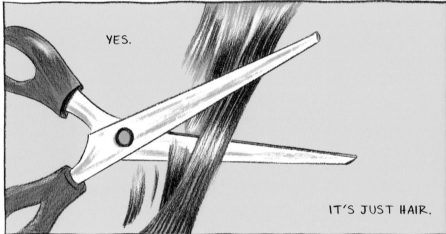

YES.

IT'S JUST HAIR.

YOUR MOM IS GOING TO KILL ME.

NO. SHE'S GOING TO KILL _ME_.

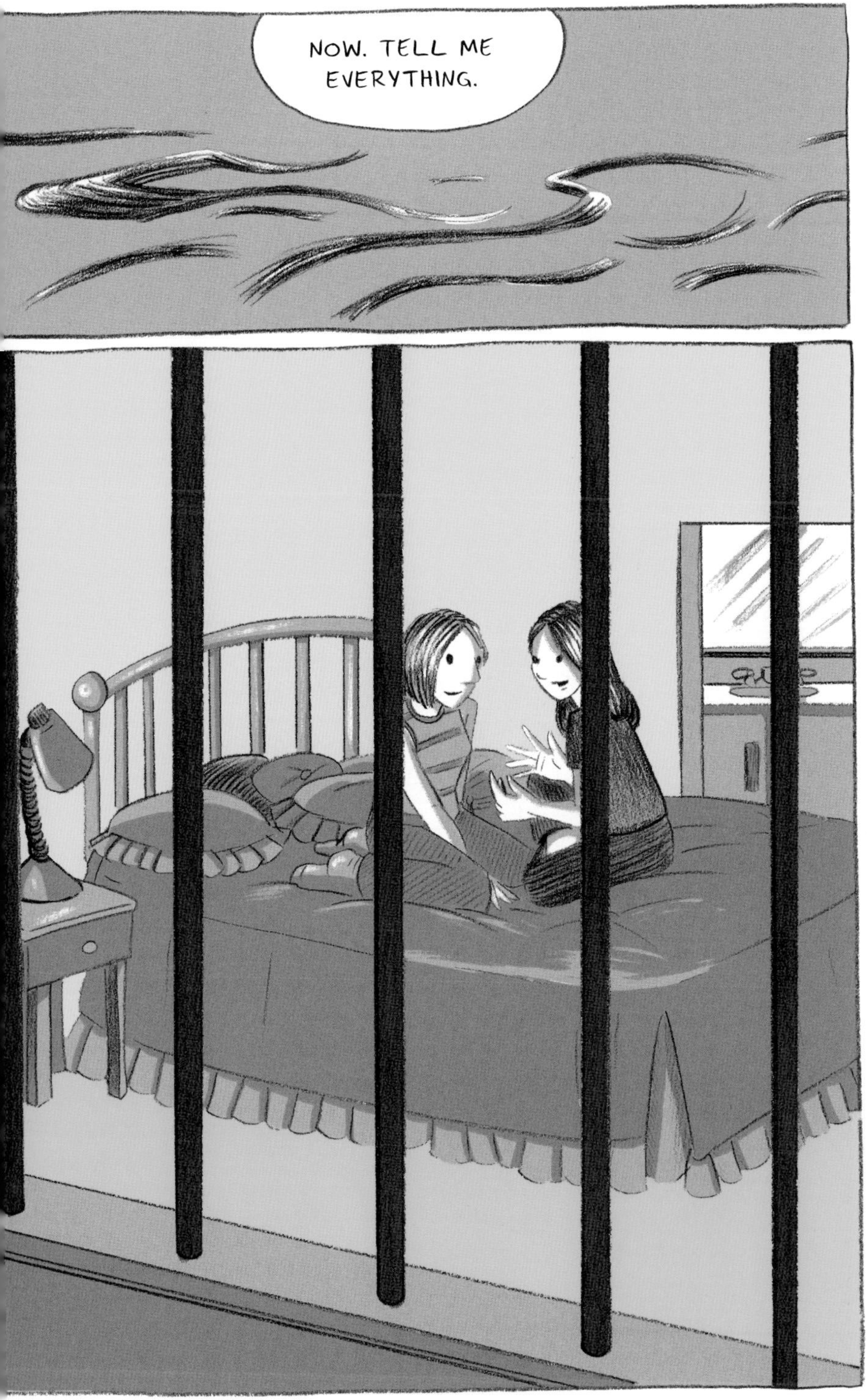
NOW. TELL ME EVERYTHING.

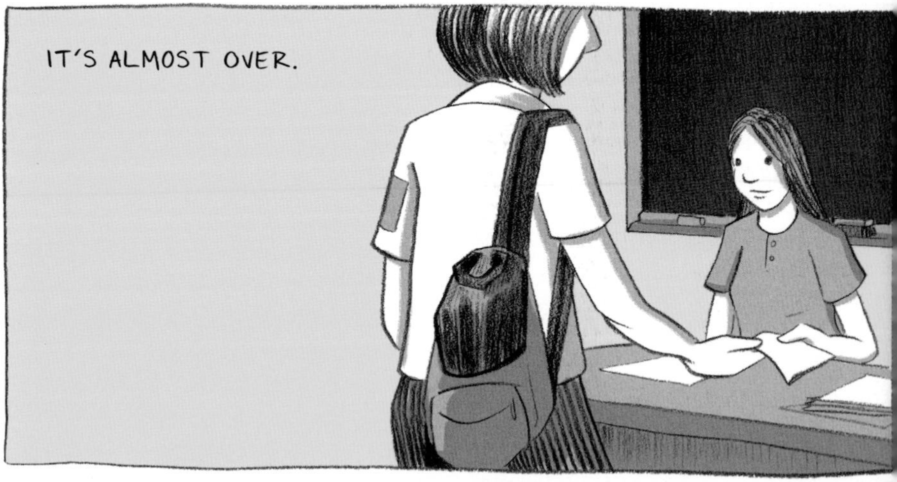
IT'S ALMOST OVER.

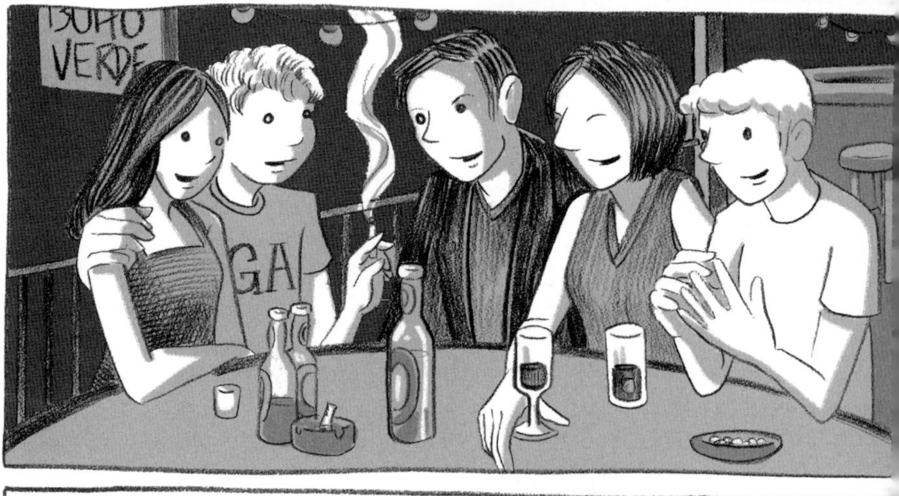
BUHO
VERDE

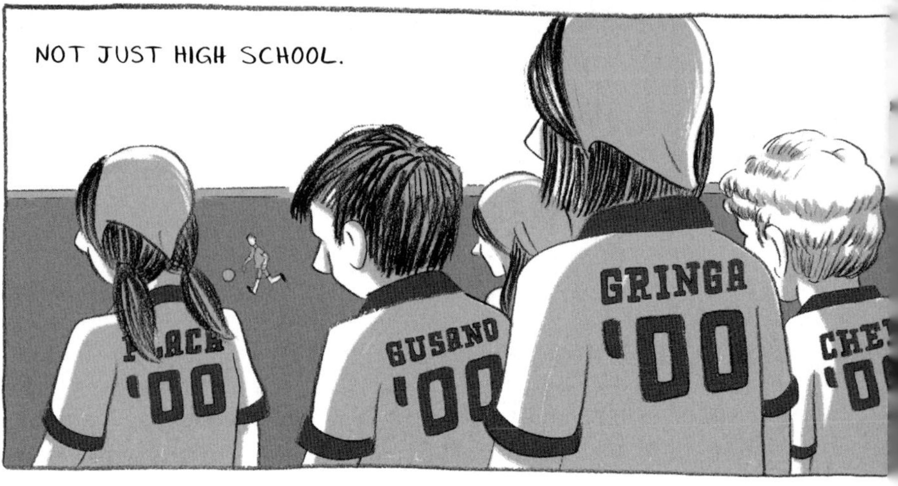
NOT JUST HIGH SCHOOL.
GUSANO
'00
GRINGA
'00

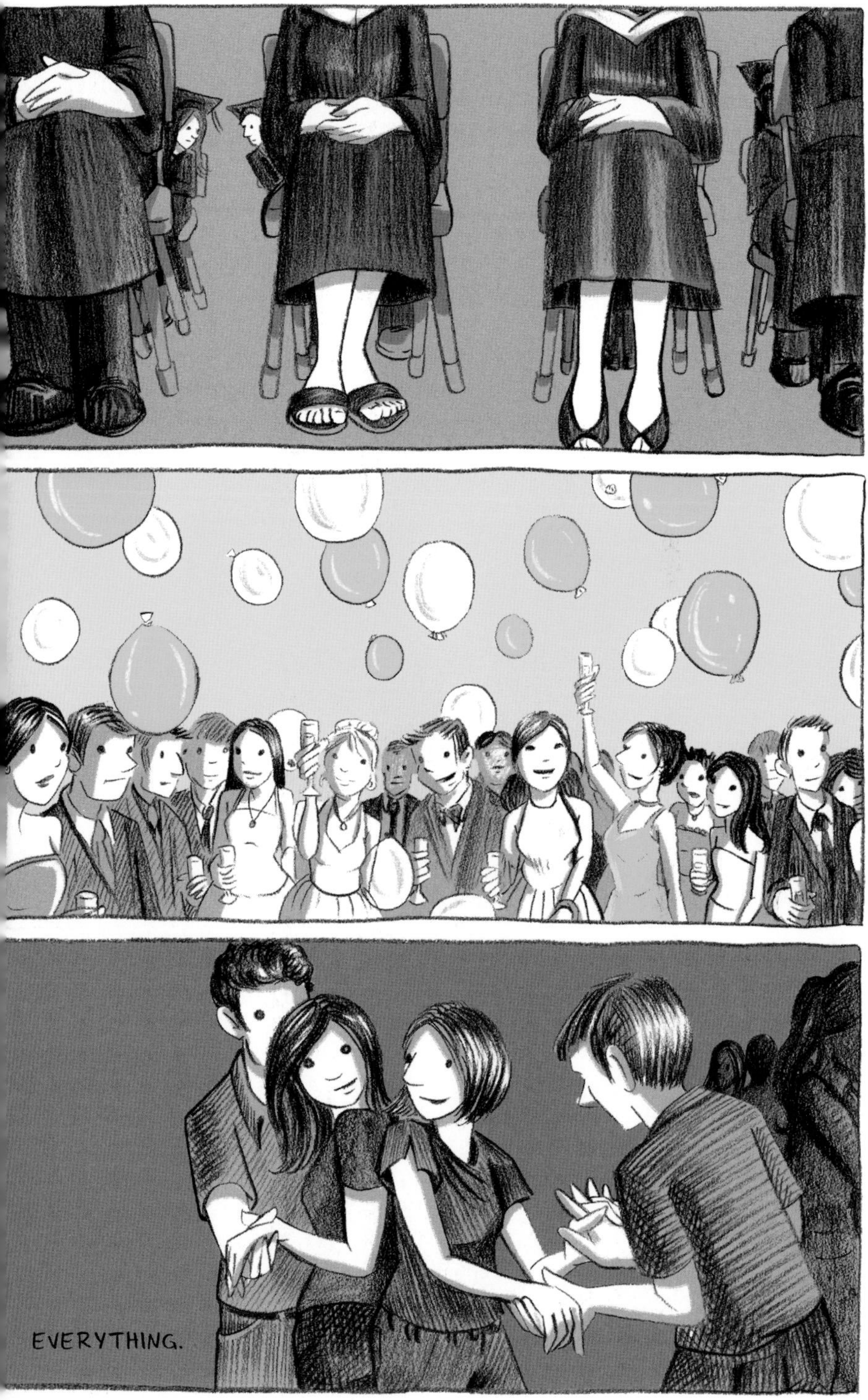
EVERYTHING.

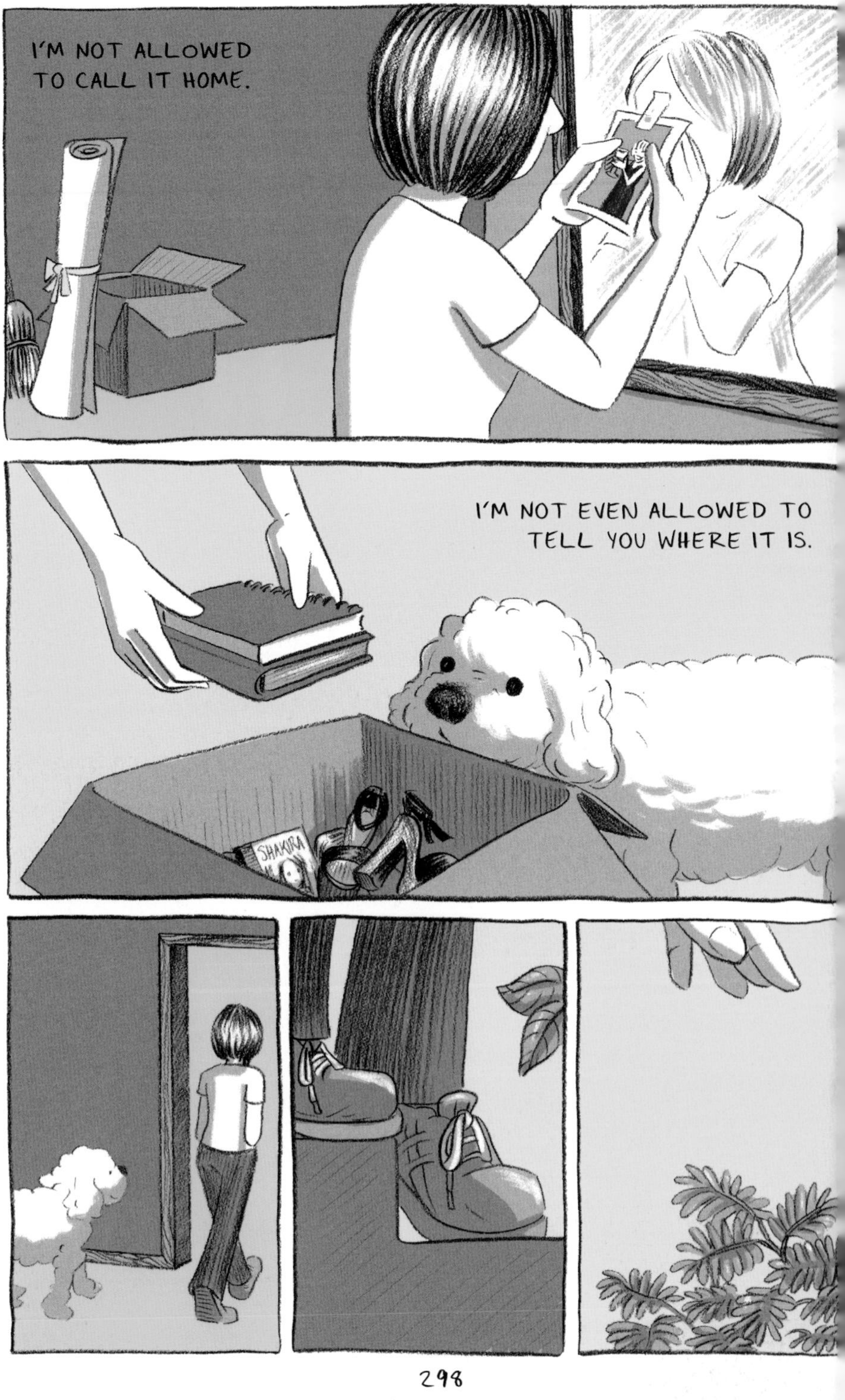
I'M NOT ALLOWED TO CALL IT HOME.
I'M NOT EVEN ALLOWED TO TELL YOU WHERE IT IS.
SHAKIRA

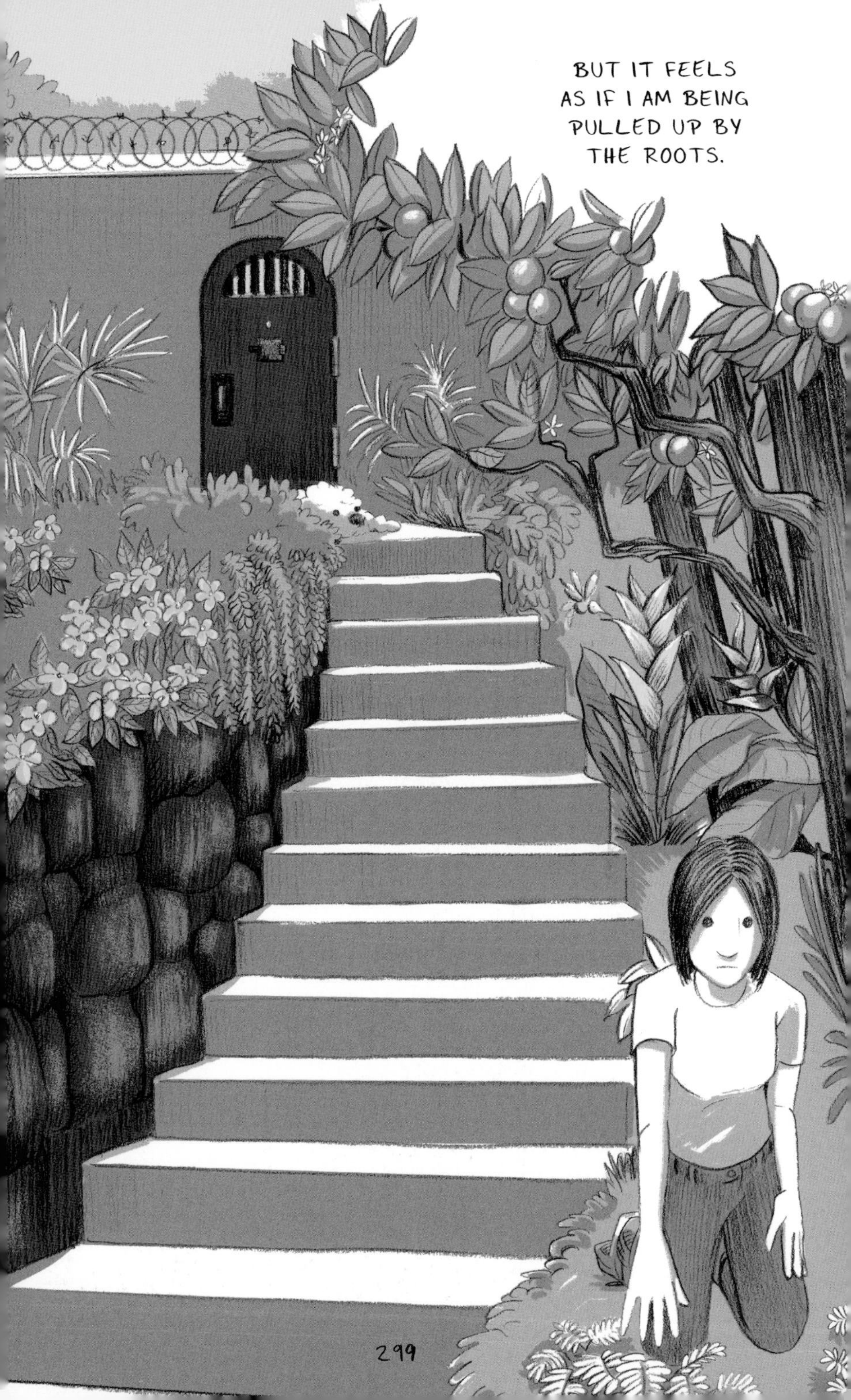
BUT IT FEELS
AS IF I AM BEING
PULLED UP BY
THE ROOTS.

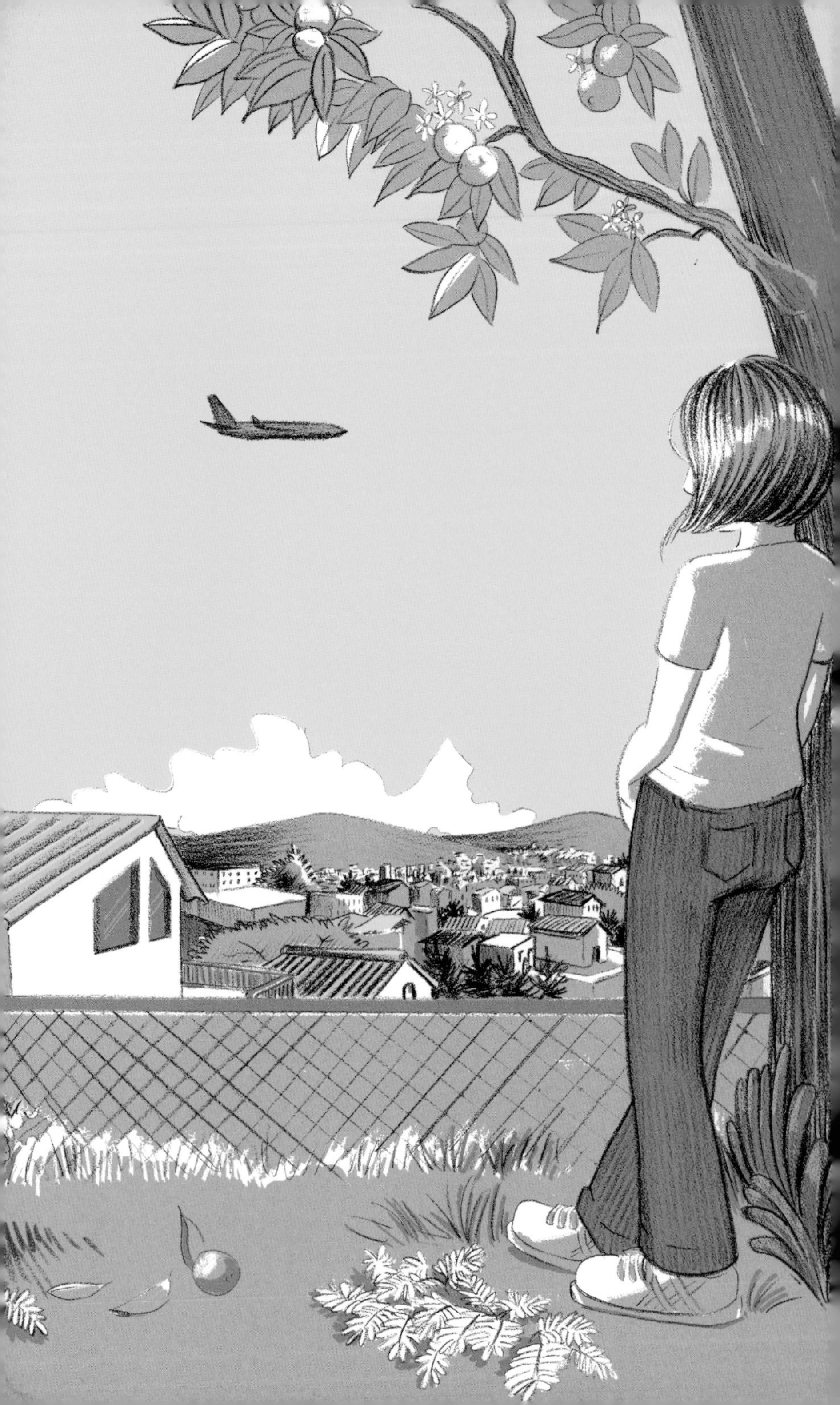

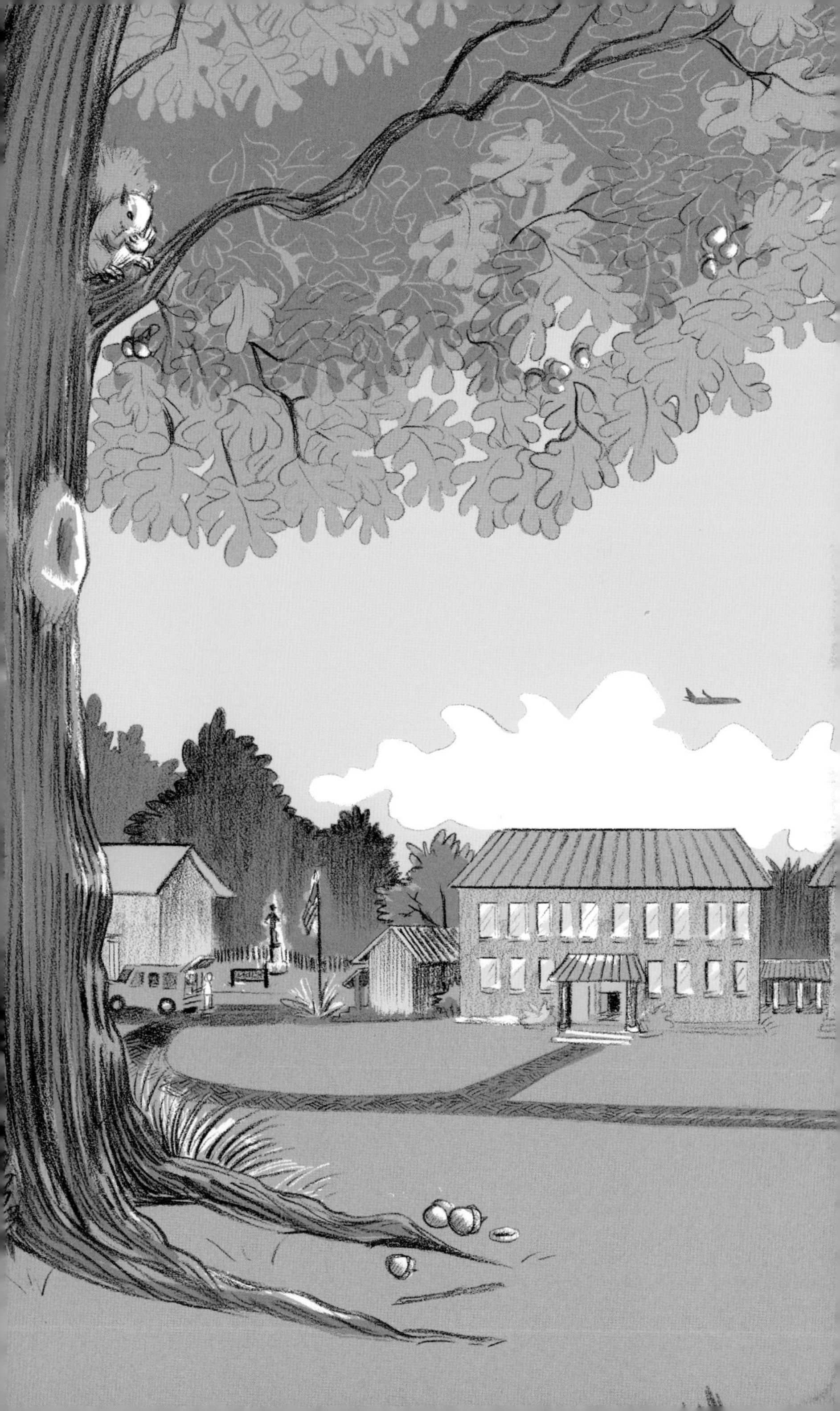

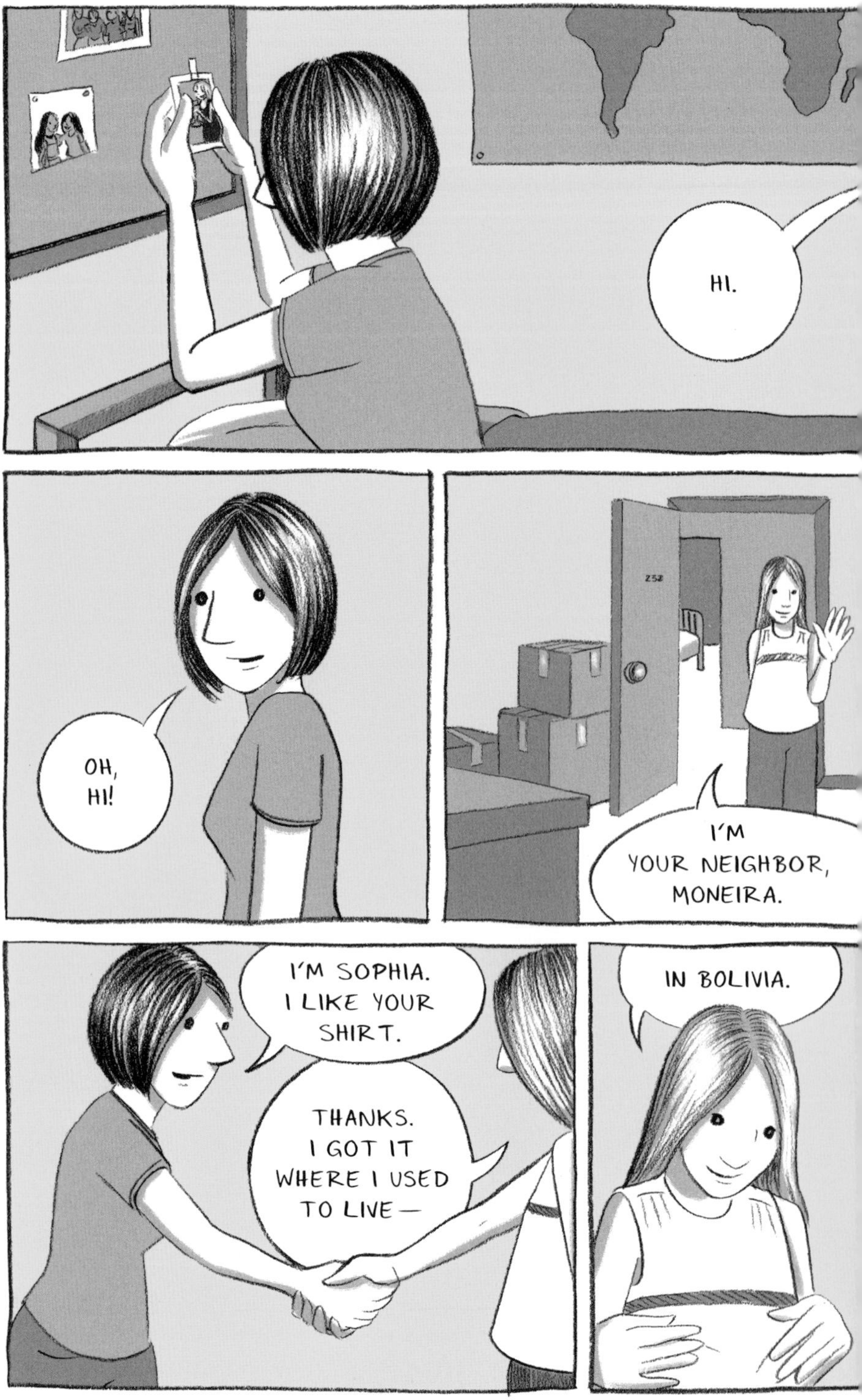
HI.
OH, HI!
I'M YOUR NEIGHBOR, MONEIRA.
252
I'M SOPHIA. I LIKE YOUR SHIRT.
THANKS. I GOT IT WHERE I USED TO LIVE—
IN BOLIVIA.

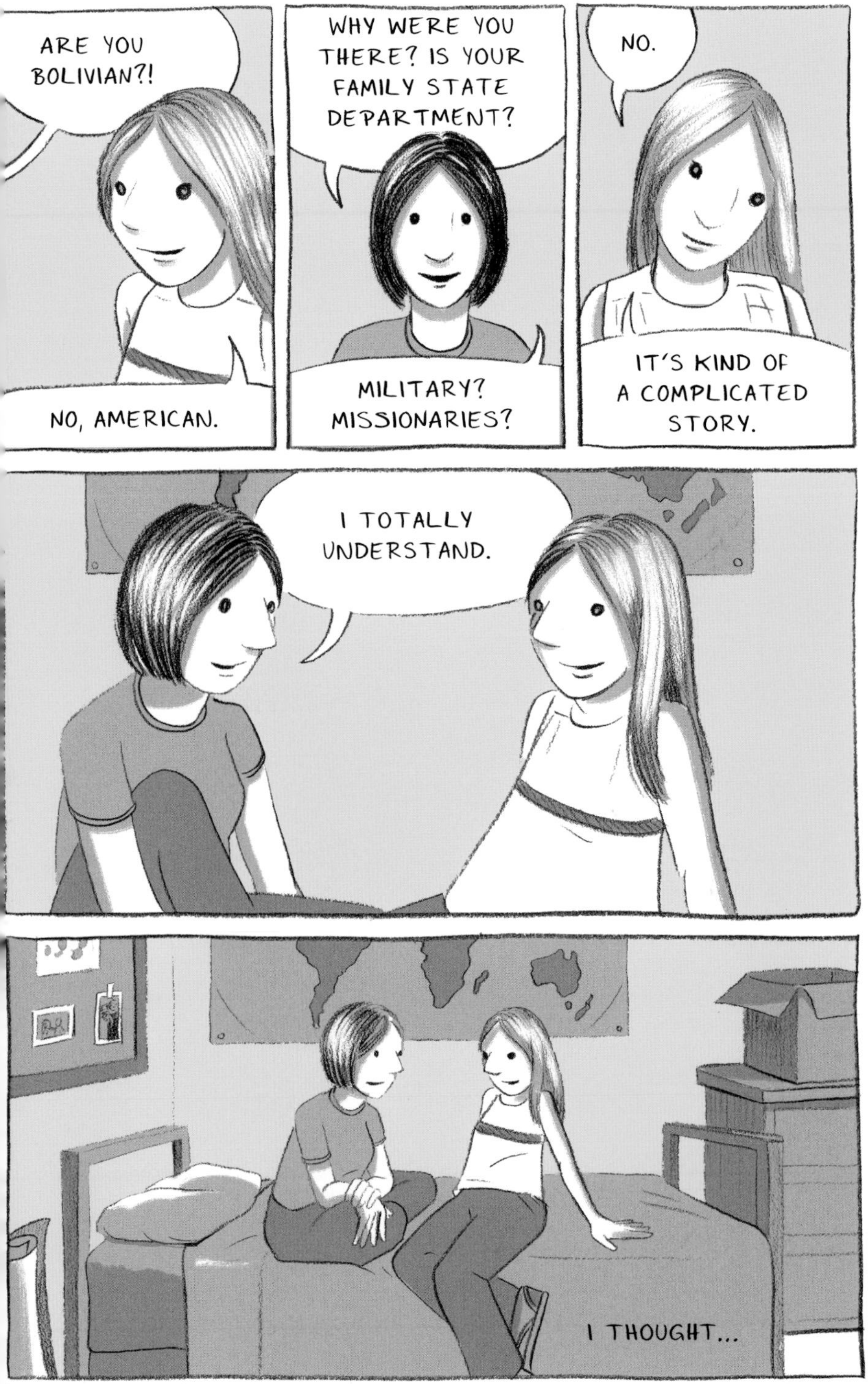
ARE YOU BOLIVIAN?!
NO, AMERICAN.
WHY WERE YOU THERE? IS YOUR FAMILY STATE DEPARTMENT?
MILITARY? MISSIONARIES?
NO.
IT'S KIND OF A COMPLICATED STORY.
I TOTALLY UNDERSTAND.
I THOUGHT...

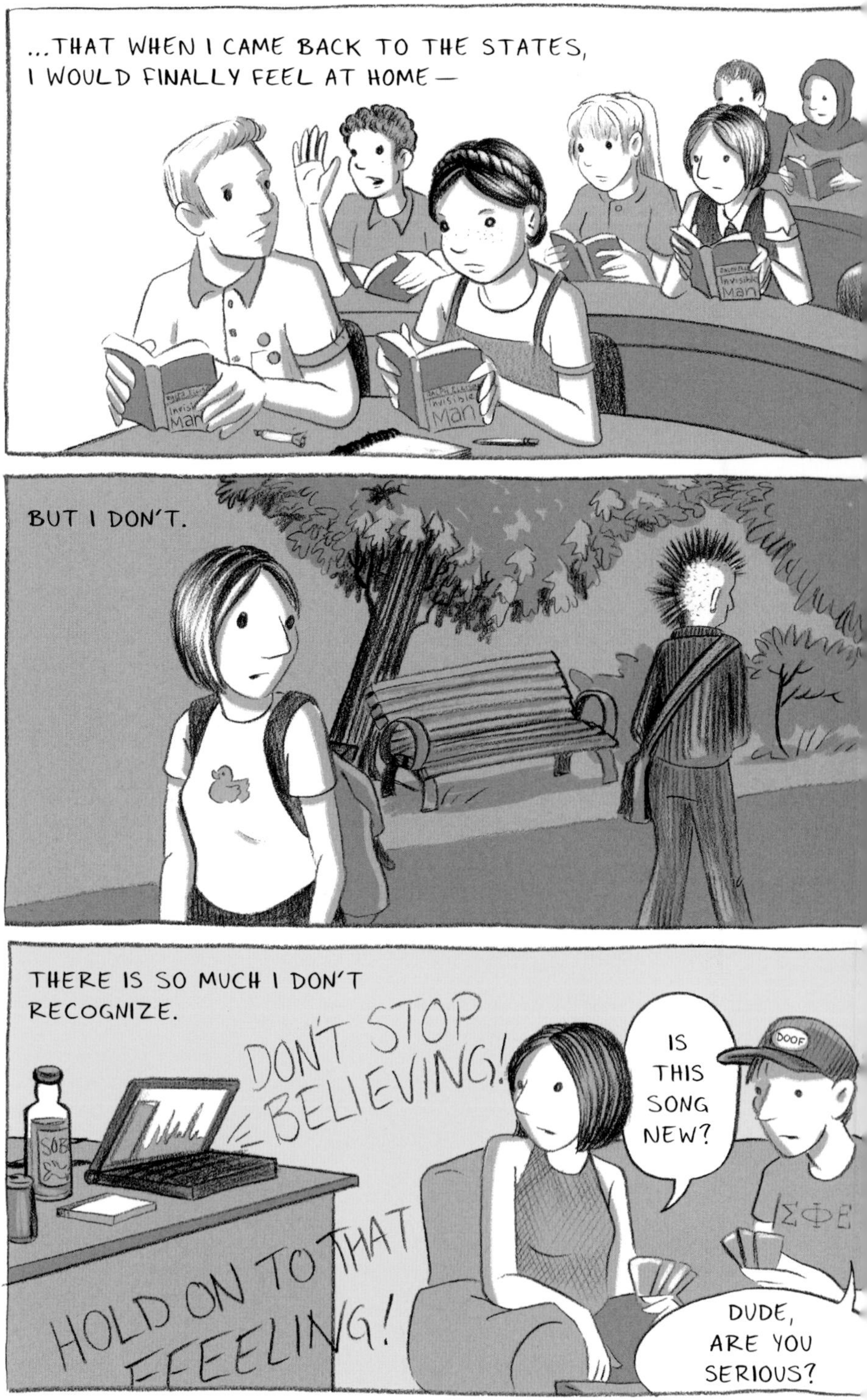
...THAT WHEN I CAME BACK TO THE STATES, I WOULD FINALLY FEEL AT HOME—
Invisible Man
BUT I DON'T.
THERE IS SO MUCH I DON'T RECOGNIZE.
DON'T STOP BELIEVING!
HOLD ON TO THAT FEEELING!
DOOF
IS THIS SONG NEW?
ΣΦΕ
DUDE, ARE YOU SERIOUS?

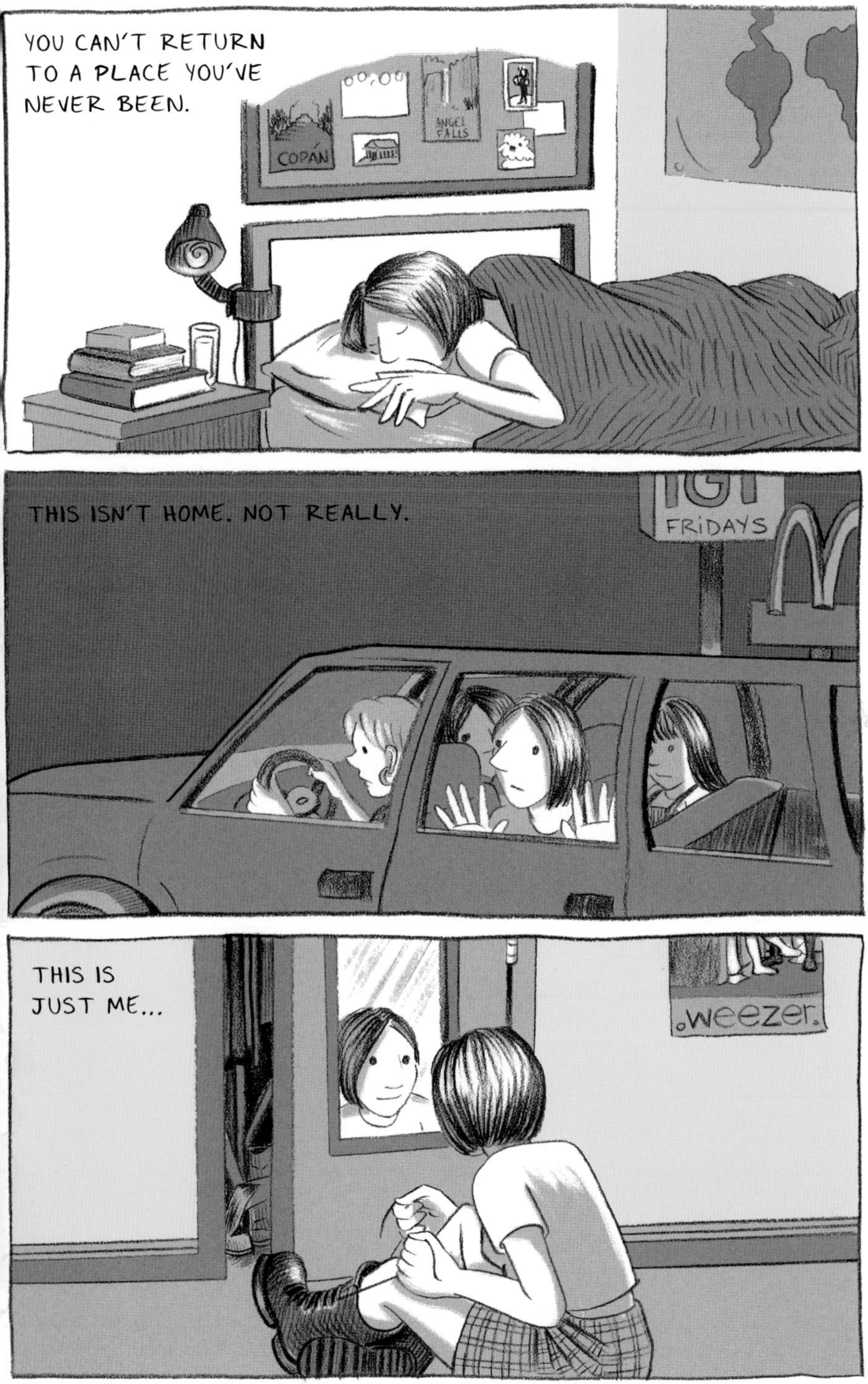
YOU CAN'T RETURN TO A PLACE YOU'VE NEVER BEEN.
COPÁN
ANGEL FALLS
THIS ISN'T HOME. NOT REALLY.
FRIDAYS
THIS IS JUST ME...
.weezer.

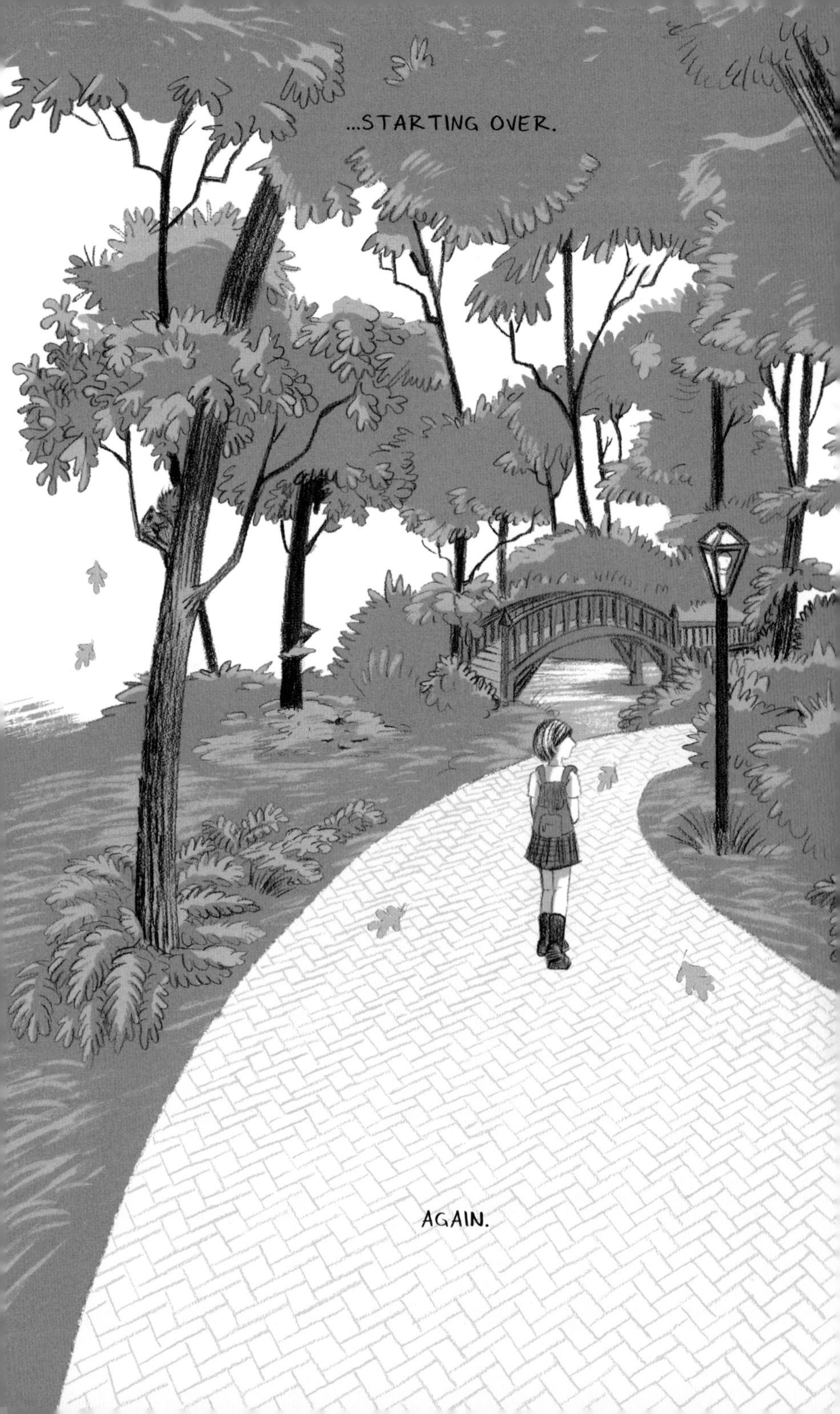
...STARTING OVER.
AGAIN.

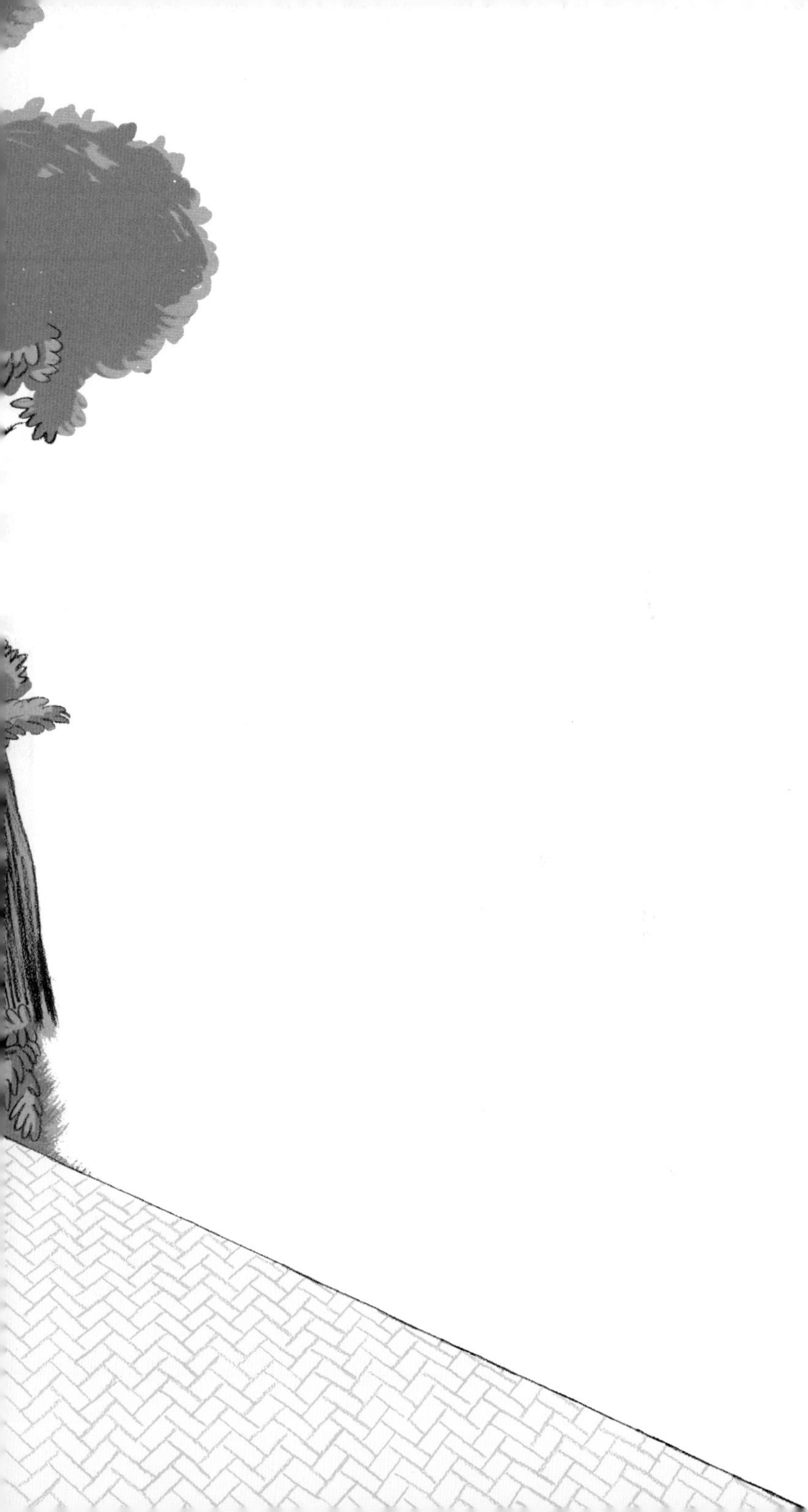

AUTHOR'S NOTE

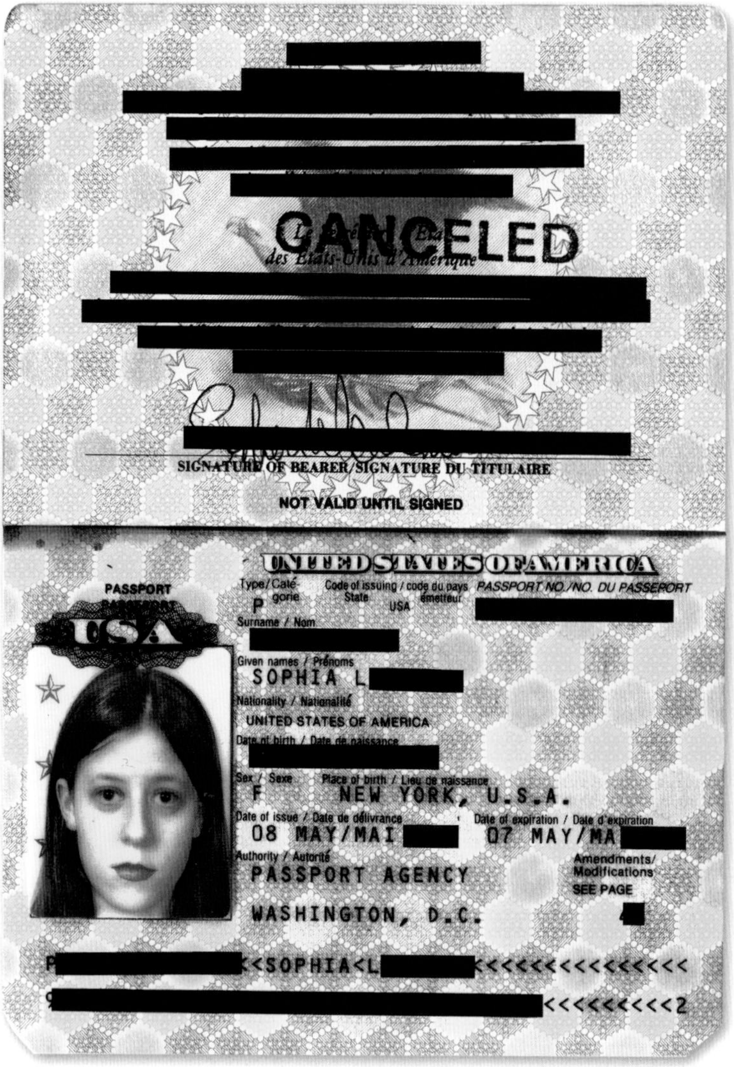

[redacted]
CANCELED
[redacted]
SIGNATURE OF BEARER/SIGNATURE DU TITULAIRE
NOT VALID UNTIL SIGNED
UNITED STATES OF AMERICA
PASSPORT
USA
Type/Catégorie P
Code of issuing State / code du pays émetteur USA
PASSPORT NO./NO. DU PASSEPORT [redacted]
Surname / Nom [redacted]
Given names / Prénoms SOPHIA L[redacted]
Nationality / Nationalité UNITED STATES OF AMERICA
Date of birth / Date de naissance [redacted]
Sex / Sexe F
Place of birth / Lieu de naissance NEW YORK, U.S.A.
Date of issue / Date de délivrance 08 MAY/MAI [redacted]
Date of expiration / Date d'expiration 07 MAY/MA[redacted]
Authority / Autorité PASSPORT AGENCY WASHINGTON, D.C.
Amendments/ Modifications SEE PAGE [redacted]
P[redacted]<<SOPHIA<L[redacted]<<<<<<<<<<<<<<<<<<
[redacted]<<<<<<<<<<2

I never thought I would tell this story. For years I deflected and demurred when people asked me questions about where I grew up and what my parents did. Guarding certain secrets was so ingrained in me that I could not imagine a world where I actually discussed them, let alone put them down on paper. But as my comics have become more personal, there has been a small and persistent voice growing within me that has insisted this is my life, my story to tell.

But these stories and secrets also belong to all the other people who share my history, some of whom have devoted their lives to protecting such secrets. At the early stages of this project, I would tie myself up in knots over what to say and how to say it. Would my parents approve? Would I embarrass my family? Would I hurt someone's feelings? But sometimes the trick to writing is giving up the pretense of pleasing anyone at all. So I began to write. When I showed my parents an early draft of my story I was surprised and relieved when they did not hesitate to give me their blessing. Obtaining the permission of the Publication Review Board at the Central Intelligence Agency was a far more daunting and complicated task and is the reason many details have been removed from the book. I stand by my right to tell the truth as I lived it, but in doing so, I have also been extremely careful to protect those who still have secrets to keep and who risk their lives in dedication to their work.

I still flinch around explaining my past. Secrets are sticky. I cling to mine out of habit and in no small part because I sort of love my secrets, having held them close for so long. But here I strove to be as honest as possible. I have a vivid memory, but I am sure I've gotten some of it wrong. There will be people in my family and among my friends who will read this and think, *That's not how it happened*, and I apologize for any discrepancies. I wrote about our experiences from a place of love, and I hope that comes through.

These stories are true as I remember them; however, this is a work of creative nonfiction. I have taken artistic liberties when it was necessary to create a cohesive story. If you ever want to learn how crowded your life is and how deep and myriad the connections you make in this world are, try writing a memoir. The most painful process of this book was not reliving the humiliations of unrequited love but streamlining complicated social relationships into a comprehensible narrative. In short, some events have been rearranged or combined but never invented. Many characters here are composites to protect their privacy as well as maintain narrative clarity. Some conversations are verbatim as I recall them or as I recorded them in my diaries at the time, while others are approximations, meant to illustrate several different events and relationships. As challenging as it felt writing the story, I did find immense pleasure in resurrecting certain parts of my past: the exact pattern of the terra-cotta tiles on my bedroom floor, the unkempt woolly head of my dog, and the friendships that sustained me.

ACKNOWLEDGMENTS

To my classmates who were there at those parties and in the hallways, I may have changed your names, but squint and you will see yourself in these pages. Specifically, I want to thank Carla, Linda, Melissa, and Naa for their assistance in fact-checking my memories and tracking down reference photos. I also want to thank Jorge, Chema, Ana Maria, Ethling, Andrea, Virgilio, Biki, Damien, Carmen, Vivi, Dianne, and Dessiré.

And Cecilia. I wish our story had a different ending, but we had fun, didn't we?

Thank you to Carly, Amie, and Stephanie. I could not imagine a more supportive and inspiring writer's group or group of humans.

Thank you to my ridiculously talented agent, Molly O'Neill, who saw something that I could not yet see. I offer my boundless gratitude to my formidable editor, Susan Rich, who saw what I saw and elevated it. And to the supportive production team at Little, Brown Books for Young Readers, especially Sasha Illingworth and Angelie Yap. And to my adroit and thoughtful colorist, Mike Freiheit.

To my brave and dedicated parents, who gave me the world. Thank you for your unyielding support. To my brother Christopher, who taught me that art is serious business and took mine seriously before anyone else did. Perhaps before even I did. To my sister and second brain, Julia. I could not do this without you. To Byron and Patrick, who remember with me.

And to my first reader and last love, Judge, who encouraged me to tell this story in the first place.

SOPHIA GLOCK

is a cartoonist who lives and draws in Austin, Texas. She attended the College of William & Mary and the School of Visual Arts. Her work has been featured in the *New Yorker*, Buzzfeed, and *Time Out New York*. She talks to her sister every day.